FOUR

SPIRITS

WILLIAM MORROW

An Imprint of HarperCollins*Publishers*

FOUR SPIRITS

a novel

Sena Jeter Naslund

HarperCollins books may be purchased for educational, business, or sales promotional use. For information please write: Special Markets Department, HarperCollins Publishers Inc., 10 East 53rd Street, New York, NY 10022.

FIRST EDITION

Designed by Shubhani Sarkar

Printed on acid-free paper

Library of Congress Cataloging-in-Publication Data
Naslund, Sena Jeter.
    Four spirits: a novel / Sena Jeter Naslund.
        p. cm.
    ISBN 0-06-621238-3
    1. Birmingham (Ala.)—Fiction. I. Title.

PS3564.A827F68 2003
813'.54—dc21   2003051170

03 04 05 06 07 WBC/RRD 10 9 8 7 6 5 4 3 2 1

IN MEMORIAM

Addie Mae Collins
Denise McNair
Carole Robertson
Cynthia Wesley

Killed Sunday, September 15, 1963, in the racist bombing of
Sixteenth Street Baptist Church, Birmingham, Alabama,
as they prepared to participate in a Youth Worship Service.

Jesus loves the little children,
All the children of the world;
Red and yellow, black and white,
They are precious in his sight;
Jesus loves the little children of the world.

The past isn't dead; it's not even past.

WILLIAM FAULKNER

We were spirit people, seed people;
no matter how bleak the terrain looked out there,
we were planted for a rich harvest.

VICTORIA GRAY

CONTENTS

CONTENTS

CONTENTS

OLD TIMES THERE, 1948

HELICON, ALABAMA

IN THE WOODS, A CHILD IS FIRING A PISTOL.

"Aim at the trees," her father tells her because she is five years old.

She must shoot the trees, but it doesn't make sense, because her father is the one who says he will die, and soon. Maybe death is hiding in the trees, the little girl thinks, and what if she kills death? Then it can't get her father. *Aim at the trees,* yes, he surely said to do that, and she would do anything for him, and never be disobedient again.

Since her parents and two brothers are standing behind, Stella sees nothing but trees, their slender pine bodies upright and endless as the soldiers marching down Twentieth Street in the Birmingham Armistice Day parade.

In the piney forest, Stella holds the heavy, grown-up gun in her hand; she must lift the barrel to aim, and that tiny blade, like a fragment of razor blade on the end of the barrel, is called the *sight.* But will she become a soldier, if she fires a gun? And what if someone fires back at her? *What if?*

During the parade, her mother pointed up to the balcony of the Tutwiler Hotel. "The reviewing stand"—Mama said—"General Omar Bradley."

"Now fire," Stella's father murmurs to his five-year-old daughter in his liquid-kind doctor voice. She knows the instruction is for her finger. Just her finger should ever so slightly pull the trigger toward her, toward them, but what if *if if if if if if if* the pistol has its own will and the barrel looks up above the green woods, up toward the sky that has turned pale, hardly blue at all anymore, and if the pistol continues to rear up like a stallion but instead of the must-be return of hoofs to the earth, what if the stallion rears past return, arcs backward till the horse is going to land on its own back, and then the stallion-gun fires, and it's *us* all soft in our skin bags with hair on our heads and *us* limber jointed (with blood inside!), *us* in the gun's sights and we are the target when the bullet races down the barrel?

Because of death, Daddy reminds, "Aim at the trees!"

Because Stella is hesitating in pulling the trigger, his voice comes booming now from the bedrock bottom beneath the sand beneath the sea: command: "Fire!"

Her father's voice roars like a cannon. Stella remembers the cannon roar and recoil not from the parade but from the movies of World War II, and she remembers Carlotta Shirley's father and her mother's explanation of shell-shocked Mr. Shirley: *the toll of war.*

In the woods, her mother is wearing bright red lipstick, fresh, but Stella wears her faded overalls with the bib over her chest that always makes her feel safe. Perhaps (Stella imagines) the bullet she has fired dodges all the tree trunks in the woods before her; perhaps the bullet takes no toll but slips harmlessly like a snake between slender trunks, forever. Or, perhaps the bullet has hit a young pine, entering the bark lovingly like a ghost leaving not so much as a kiss-mark of lipstick on the flinty brown scales encircling a trunk just the size of your wrist. What happens to a bullet fired?

And how could the repercussion of that shot be in the woods, when it rings in Stella's own head? The sound of pistol fire big as apocalypse has entered Stella's brain.

(She has kept the barrel from rearing back.) "That's right," her father says. It's his kind, lapping-waves doctor voice again. His face is pale and scrubbed so clean she can see the delicate red veins beside the flange of his nose.

His blood is inside those vessels, and he is fully and completely alive. Is it possible that today while he was driving the car, he said, "I have lung cancer. That's why I spit all the time," and the car just kept going south? "You've seen me spitting. And I'll die of it." But his hair is still thick and gray, beautifully brushed. She loves his big nose and thinks him handsome as a hawk.

ON THE DRIVE DOWN Highway 31, which links Birmingham to Montgomery and beyond to the even deeper rural South of virtually forgotten places like Helicon, Dr. Silver had spoken solemnly to his family. When he was a boy at Helicon, he loved Sunday school and squirrel hunting equally, he told his two sons and daughter as they drove south, back toward his old home—he'd never lost touch—where he had picked cotton alongside the colored folks. And then while he drove the car toward Helicon, he sang his children his favorite Methodist Sunday school song: "Jesus loves the little children, / all the children of the world; / red and yellow, black and white, / they are precious in his sight. / Jesus loves the little children of the world." Because she is Jewish, Stella's mother never sang a word about Jesus.

Before he dies, Mama had explained to the children in the car, but the children are not to tell anybody at Helicon, *he wants to visit.* He wants to see again the woman he always called Old Aunt Charlotte, but Mama said only "Charlotte" and she explained that Daddy meant "honor" not "kin" when he said "Aunt" and that when he said "Old," he meant respect for her years.

When they first piled out of the car, they stopped at the little hut-house at Helicon, but Daddy had said, "Let her sleep. We'll go fire the pistol."

But Stella and her brothers peeked and saw her sleeping—Old Aunt Charlotte, the one Who-Was-Born-into-Slavery. Not her son Christopher Columbus Jones, whose hair was cotton-boll white on his dark head, not her gaunt-cheeked daughter Queen Victoria Jones, whose head was crowned not by precious metal studded with gems but by a faded bandanna. Though ancient, Christopher Columbus Jones and Queen Victoria Jones are too young to have been slaves. It is their mother, Old Aunt Charlotte, who survived both before and after the time when the world convulsed in civil war to set her free. And Daddy wants his three children to know her. "It's important to Daddy. He grew up at Helicon," Mama, who grew up in Chicago, said in her special deep voice while they were in the car. Mama's voice meant *you have got to understand, or act as if you understand, and obey.*

Stella, of course, has always understood that Helicon was the place where the true South was. To her country-bred father, industrial Birmingham was an impostor place, not the real South at all, and so—is Stella herself real? Probably not. If her father denies the reality of Birmingham (or is it the importance of the place that he refuses to embrace?) and if, to Stella, no place is so real as the neighborhood of Norwood, or their red clay driveway, then are her feet real? And if not her feet, what of her legs? Bit by bit, when she tries to understand, she dissolves into unreality. She has come into a world that may never be real, and she and it are always going to be almost as nothing as ghosts or maybe, at best, spirits.

NOW THEY'VE ALL SHOT the trees, except Mama who says, "Oh, I don't want to do that," and dismisses the whole issue. It seems to Stella that Mama has no use for guns.

But during the parade, Stella had heard her murmur, "Blessed guns, blessed boys."

Stella had gotten bored; there were so many soldiers, all dressed in brown; one block after another, then a few tanks, more blocks of soldiers, all their legs waving forward together. "Stand up straight, children," Mama had murmured in a voice that sounded like crying. And Stella and her brothers had lifted and squared their shoulders. Just like a flatiron, Mama's hand had pressed right up Stella's spine to straighten it.

Now while the pistol bullets wander forever in the wilderness of woods, Stella and her family must go back to the small old Helicon house, two rooms and a dogtrot between. Shooting trees in the woods was just to pass the time till Old Aunt Charlotte, the spirit of the house, awakens.

Shooting, down in the woods, Charlotte thinks. *Yes, that was the real world Charlotte was waking to, not heaven, just like—was it almost a hundred years ago, the musket fire—when Charlotte heard it first? The shooting?*

Stella raises her arms in a wide V and shakes her hands at the ends of her arms and yells, "Whooooo!" just like a ghost as she runs ahead of all of them, out of the woods.

Five-year-old Stella believes the house reappearing through the trunks of the trees is a ghost, something like a hallucination, something at least more real in her father's memory than *that*—a feeble shack—standing now among the little sharp-edged stones, existing really not just in *his* but also in *their* memories. When she looks at these people, the Negroes of rural south Alabama, this world, she sees it through the lens of memory, not sharp and clear, but with a blurry uncertainty, as though she has been made to wear her daddy's spectacles. Stella stops running; she wishes to loiter at the edge of the clearing and to think.

Charlotte raises herself on her elbows on her bed and hunches toward the headboard to be sitting up when Doctor comes in.

Stella has no doubt Old Aunt Charlotte, dark as wet coffee grounds in the percolator basket, is awake now because those four explosions in the woods were a mighty alarm clock not to be denied, though Daddy seems to think it is simply time for an old person's nap to end, and time is something he knows all about. He keeps it in his pocket. He winds it up on the mantel.

Slowly Stella crosses the raked yard to check the dreamy structure—weak, it leans—a dwelling envisioned but possibly insubstantial. The house should stand up straight, square its shoulders. She reaches out and touches the corner of the two-room dwelling while she waits for her family to catch up.

Stella believes she could shake this house right off the stacks of rocks that hold it up at each corner. Perhaps she could pick up the little house, with them inside, and carry it to Birmingham.

But Stella does not want to stop at Birmingham where, they say, in a few months, after she starts first grade, Daddy will die; she thinks *I will go to Chicago.* Already she plays the cello, and in Chicago her mother learned to play the violin and the piano. Stella could ride her pint-size cello, like a horsey, all the way to Chicago. *Back to Chicago,* she thinks, though she has never been there. But her bones know, if Chicago was the origin of her mother's music, then Chicago is hers as well. She can ride almost straight north—Huntsville, Nashville, Louisville, Indianapolis: Chicago.

At home, in Birmingham, if the piano part is ever pitched too high to sing, then down, down, down, Mama skillfully makes the piano go as low as she likes but it is always the same tune. *Transposition,* her mother says when her two sons and her daughter stand around the piano in the living room, and she smiles because she does it so easily. Her fingers touch the black keys as readily as the white ones, but Stella plays the piano only in the key of C and Stella uses only the level white notes.

Touching the corner of the old house, Stella's fingertips learn that this house is surely not made of wood but cloth, soft as worn denim with a nap. *First you shoot a tree,* Stella decides, *then the sawing across the fibers and the piercing by nails don't hurt.* It's Time that transforms boards into cloth. When Daddy approaches the tall mantel clock, he holds a brass key: one end of the long key is crenellated like a bit of castle wall, the other end is two stiff lobes, wings from a brass butterfly. Daddy's clock contains time, but Mama's music always floats free. Wisps of her mother's music, like clouds, often float through Stella's mind and the air around her.

One glass window, swung open like a gate by hinges on its side, exposes a square hole leading to the inside of the Helicon house. No window screen bars the entrance to flying insects or the meandering of air. In the backyard in Birmingham, Stella has a playhouse with just such a window attached only to its frame by hinges on one side. Inside the playhouse, Stella and Nancy, her beautiful best friend, pretend that dirt is flour and mix their mud pies. Stella wonders if she has remembered to hook the eye to lock the window to secure the playhouse. Do people eat mud pies here in Helicon? Once, when Nancy wasn't looking, Stella tasted a crumb of Birmingham mud.

Now her brothers and parents have caught up with her, and the little Silver family clomps into the shanty. A faint ambiance of pride moves along with them, above their noisy feet, because her father's people had been small landowners, not tenants, after the war (which still means, in 1948, to many southern people the Civil War, not the recent one of Dwight Eisenhower and Omar Bradley).

Doctor and Mrs., two boys and the little girl, Stella, hear the voice born into slavery quavering like the rattle of oak leaves refusing to let go even in winter, the voice rattling inchoate till Old Aunt Charlotte's eyes focus on Dr. Silver-come-home, and Charlotte forces the throe of nature into words: "These hands, these were the ones, these were the first to touch him when he came into this world."

Stella sees the hands are two-toned, like the latest cars, the palms held up, as though a young woman, not an ancient, were presenting a ghost baby, as though in her upturned palms the young woman could feel the weight of him who would become Doctor and Daddy.

Those pale palms (Stella imagines) have caught the light streaming through the little window she had noticed while she stood outside stroking the corner of the house, its colorless wood transmogrified into colorless denim. Without benefit or hindrance of wire screen or venetian blind and definitely not double-hung window frames, the open square in the wall admits light, and the light replaces the ghost baby in the palms of the old slave's hands.

"This your wife? Lord, so pretty and stout. These children! Lord, let me touch these babies."

Say your names. Having already instructed the children while they traveled south inside the car like a blue egg, her mother doesn't need to repeat instructions now. Though youngest, Stella steps forward. Curious, she wants to examine Old Aunt Charlotte more closely. This woman could be the one who will die, not Daddy.

"I'm Stella. Did we wake you up with the shooting?"

From the small carved wooden woman comes a cackle that is almost strangling; a bit of drool wets the lower lip, which is not wood after all but moving flesh. "Lord, honey, can't no shooting wake up your old great-great-great (How great Thou art!) grannie." Old Aunt Charlotte raises her eyes to their father. "Would I got any rest these years if shooting wake me up?"

"Are you dead then?" Ruben asks.

The eyes of Old Aunt—or is it Grannie?—widen. "I don't think so. Lord, are we all dead, Doctor?"

"I don't believe you'll ever die," Queen Victoria speaks up. Everybody grown-up snickers, even Christopher Columbus over in the corner, looking down. Even Daddy, who will die (so he said privately), and soon (it's a secret), but his laugh sounds wounded.

While she laughs, Charlotte scans the ceiling to check for large dusty wings, but she sees nothing waiting for her that resembles the Angel of Death. Because she won't ever die, Charlotte's glee is greatest of all, and the joke is on all of them.

"I been tried," Charlotte says.

She sees a moth up there above her bed, but its wings are caught in a cobweb.

"Tried many a time."

Then her father reaches out his hand to the woman on the bed whose body doesn't even reach halfway to the footboard. When the two-toned hand and the white hand meet, she snatches his to her mouth, quick as a dog taking a bone. She kisses the back of Daddy's hand and murmurs, "Best baby in the world. Best baby, white or black."

Chris's neck ratchets his chin another notch closer to his chest and Victoria's straight-ahead stare hardens into a stone beam.

The old eyelids slide down like a window shade, then raise up. "Let me touch them—the next gen-er-a-ti-on." The doctor's children are nudged closer by both their parents into the reality of family-but-not-family that Dr. Silver not only thinks to be right but holds as being sacred.

The hands of Who-Was-Born-into-Slavery rest on Stella's head.

"Blessed girl!" Old Aunt Charlotte squeaks in high-pitched surprise. Both her hands spring away from Stella's head as though the child's head has burned her old fingers.

Those words shock Stella, zing from her ears down the neck bones, through her body to her smallest toe bone. *Blessed, blessed.* Stella knows that she has been waiting to hear those words. What did it matter that they were spoken in the voice of a mouse? She feels like Samuel in the Bible, as though she should say, "Here am I; send me." But she steps back and gives her bedside place to her brothers.

No words at all are uttered over the boys, when the brown fingers slowly muss their hair. The boys have been neglected, and she, the girl, has been selected.

Blessed girl! and the world is illumined as never before, as though sheet lightning has shimmered the dead air. In exchange for her special blessing, her scalp still tingling, though she is ignored in the little sepia room crowded with family and nonfamily, Stella intones aloud in her deepest voice: "Live forever, live forever!"

Though the whole room vibrates with laughter, Charlotte's laughter the highest of all, a descant, Stella knows that she and the woman sitting up in bed have exchanged gifts better than birthday presents. And she knows Charlotte knows, too.

Finally Charlotte asks feebly, "Did you fire the pistol, Mrs. Doctor?"

Stella watches her mother shaking her head from side to side.

"I didn't think so," Charlotte says.

Mrs. Doctor would never shoot the pistol, and the world was the same as always. Charlotte closes her eyes, exhausted by her foray back into the realm of the living who could never be real. Except for Doctor. Oh, he was real from the moment he came out of the woman place, covered with white cheese.

Charlotte asks politely, "How Miss Krit and Miss Pratt?" While Doctor tells her his sisters in Birmingham are fine, Charlotte wonders, *And where did Mrs. Doctor come from?* She looks like a gypsy. Dark, but not colored-folks dark. *Swarthy*—that is the word Charlotte wants. It comes drifting up through the decades in her mind, comes to her from fifty, no sixty, maybe seventy years ago. *Swarthy-complected.* But all these children, fair as Doctor.

"*Fairest Lord Jeeee-sus.*" *Once Charlotte had stood outside the Methodist church whose Sunday school and service were faithfully attended by the Silver family, and Charlotte heard the church organ swell up like the blooming of a gigantic flower, and that was what the white folks sang.* "Fair are the mead-ows, Fair-er still the woodlands. . . . Je-sus is fair-er, Je-sus is pur-er."

Fair-er? young Charlotte had wondered, fair-er than the li-ly? And Charlotte had pictured not a lily, or Jesus, but a giant magnolia blossom, purest of whites with its overpowering fragrance, growing up from the boards of the country church, swelling bigger and bigger like organ music in their midst, suffocating their hearts.

Nostrils flare, lips clamp shut, the old woman sucks in a tremendous breath as though she would take in all the air of the room for herself. Stella hears a hound, out on the breezeway, thump its tail against the boards as though now it is satisfied. Magnolia perfumes the air.

In the distance the crack of a gun splits through the trees, the sound reverberating from the low hills again and again till Stella almost wishes it would not die but last forever in its loneliness.

"Rifle," her father says.

Dreaming now, Charlotte sees a whole battalion of ghost soldiers step out of the trunks of trees. The boys in gray have been hiding there, and now, transparent, they march forever through the woods; facing them, other soldiers emerge from trees on other hillsides, march to close, to aim, and finally, always, to fire at one another.

Mama is humming a lullaby for Charlotte, as though they were all at home in Birmingham. All throat, she is singing a song that breaks Stella's heart, that always breaks Stella's heart in the same place. Just Mama's voice in a language that sounds like Stella's cello—Yiddish, which only Mama knows. *Aye, yi, yi, yi, yih . . . Ah, yi, yi, yi, yih . . .* Mama's song becomes a violin whispering sorrow, without a syllable from any language.

ON THE WAY HOME, the blue car with the Silver family inside—a car not so much like an egg as like a nest equipped with seats—runs into bad weather. Wind and rain lash the car, and Stella's mother sings "La Cucaracha" and "Frère Jacques" to keep their spirits up, but Stella wishes they were home sitting on the worn red rug singing while Mama played the piano—or even just played her own music—Chopin and Mozart. Instead, lightning jitters before their wide eyes, and the terrifying wind bends the trees beside the road. Like a long finger, the cyclone reaches down to tip the car and make it roll over and over, down the bank, till all those inside are broken and blood is everywhere before the car comes to rest.

After the storm passes and the highway patrolman frantically circling the crushed car calls out, "Anybody alive?" only Stella shrieks, "I am! I am!"

In the hospital, all of Stella's desire is to go back to her own time of shooting trees.

Daddy's arm is around her. One, two, three, four—she hears the shots they fired, all except Mama, in the woods at Helicon. And the past is real again.

one

UNLEASHING THE DOGS, May 1963

STELLA

FROM MANY PLACES IN THE VALLEY THAT CRADLED BIR-
mingham, you could lift up your eyes, in 1963, to see the gigantic cast-iron
statue of Vulcan, the Roman god of the forge, atop his stone pedestal. Silhouetted against the pale blue skyline, atop Red Mountain, Vulcan held up a torch
in one outstretched, soaring arm. In other mountain ridges surrounding the
city, the ore lay hidden, but the city had honored this outcropping of iron ore
named Red Mountain, as a reminder of the source of its prosperity (such as it
was—most of the wealth of the steel industry was exported to magnates living
in the great cities of the Northeast), by raising Vulcan high above the popu-
lace, south of the city.

Fanciful and well-educated children liked to pretend that Vulcan, who
looked north, had a romance with the Statue of Liberty, also made of metal.
But *she* was the largest such statue in the world, and he was second to her, and
that violated the children's sense of romance, for they understood hierarchy in
romance to be as natural as hierarchy among whites and blacks.

Looking down from Vulcan—his pedestal housed stairs, and around the
top of the tower ran an observation platform—you could see the entire city of
Birmingham filling the valley between the last ridges of the Appalachian
mountain chain as it stretched from high in the northeast to southwest.

In early May 1963, Stella's freckle-faced boyfriend, a scant half inch taller
(but therefore presentable as a boyfriend, if she wore flats), had persuaded
her to drive from their college, across the city, avoiding the areas where
Negroes were congregating for demonstrations, to Red Mountain. From the

observation balcony just below Vulcan's feet, Stella and Darl hoped for a safe overview.

I believe if outsiders would just stay out . . . Darl had told her. *Let Birmingham solve . . . Don't you?*

But Stella hadn't answered. Instead, she'd said, *I'd like to see. I'm afraid to go close.*

We can go up on Vulcan, Darl had offered, for he was a man who wanted to accommodate women; a man who loved his mother. Stella had met her.

He'd brought along his bird-watching binoculars. Darl could recognize birds by their songs alone; he could imitate each sound; he kept a life list of all the birds he had ever seen. His actual name was Darling, his mother's maiden name, and though Stella dared not call him *Darling,* she longed to do so.

"Do you know the average altitude for the flight of robins?" he asked.

A spurt of laughter flew from between Stella's lips. She imagined the giggle as though it had heft and was falling rapidly down from the pedestal, down the mountain, into the valley.

"I don't have the foggiest idea," she said.

"About thirty inches."

"What a waste!" she said. "To have the gift of flight and to fly so low."

She thought Darl might laugh at her sentence—half serious, half comic—but he didn't.

Stella glanced up the massive, shining body of Vulcan, past his classical and bare heinie, up his lifted arm to his unilluminated torch. At a distance, she had often observed that the nighttime neon "flame" made the torch resemble a Popsicle. Cherry red, if someone had died in an auto accident; lime green, otherwise. Even this close and looking up his skirt, Vulcan's frontal parts were completely covered by his short blacksmith's apron.

Though it was May and the police were already into short sleeves, on the open observation balcony, Darl and Stella were lifted above the heat into a layer of air with cool breezes. Stella wished she'd worn a sweater. Darl put his arm around her—*just for warmth,* she told herself with determined naïveté, but she thrilled at his encircling arm diagonally crossing her back. His fingers fitted the spaces between her curving ribs. They were alone up in the air; they weren't some trashy couple smooching in public. *Yes, this was what she had been wanting. Perhaps for years. Someone's arm around her, making her safe.*

Stella knew her breasts were terribly small. If they had been plumper, Darl's fingertips might have found the beginnings of roundness. *Sex, sex, sex,* she thought. His hand slid down to her waist; her mind careened. *Do I feel slender enough there? Inviting?* With his other hand, Darl trained the binoculars on the city. With one finger, he adjusted the ridged wheel between the twin eyepieces. The black leather strap looped gracefully around the back of his neck.

Darl was the complete darling: a lover of nature, a lover of music, a lover of God, considerate, a gentleman—if only he loved her. And best of all he was an organist, a master of the king of instruments. When Darl played Bach's "O Sacred Head, Now Wounded," creating his own improvisations, Stella felt understood. It was she who had been wounded, and the music was what she missed and needed. The way Darl played promised wholeness, profundity. Almost it seemed that the spirit of her father was hovering around Darl and her on this high place.

She placed her hand just below Darl's waist; she shivered as though to say "I only seek closeness for warmth, against the chill." Her palm loved the unfamiliar grain of the cloth of his trousers, and underneath, the firm flesh of his buttock just beginning to flare. How tantalized her hand felt, the hand itself wishing it dare move down to know the curve of his butt. She glanced again at the side of his cheek, the binoculars trained on the city. His hair was a rich brown, and his freckles almost matched his hair.

She wanted to brush the field glasses aside, to stand in front of him, for his eyes to look into hers and see in her more than a city's worth of complex feeling, then she would tilt her face up a bare half inch and kiss his lips, her whole front against his whole front. They would lose their bodies, become a shared streak of warmth.

Darl pointed to the rectangular finger of the Comer Building, twenty-one stories tall, Birmingham's lonely skyscraper. Down in the valley, the sweep of buildings was scarved with a haze from the steel mills. After finding the Comer Building, they looked west and north, searching for the parks—Woodrow Wilson Park adjacent to the beautiful library (only for whites) and a few blocks away, Kelly Ingram Park, for Negroes (no library). The demonstrations were launched toward city hall from the Negro park. But trees, already in full leaf, blocked their view, even with binoculars, of the violent attack of Bull Connor's police on the freedom demonstrators. Birmingham appeared as peaceful, from this distance, as when, long ago, Stella had stood here with her mother and brothers—one of their day trips.

Suddenly Stella felt like a coward. If she wanted to see, she should have the nerve to go downtown. *If she wanted to participate . . .* but the idea frightened her too much.

Darl said quietly, "May the Lord bless you and keep you . . ." He was saying it over the whole city, the Methodist benediction. "May the Lord lift up his countenance upon you . . ." Darl was trying, with words, to soothe the hidden unrest and violence of his city. It was one of the things she loved about Darl, his sincere belief. Her own belief was in chaos. Down below, the confrontation was hidden completely from their view, but Darl was addressing both sides someplace in the distance, under the greenery.

"We should go down," Darl said quietly. "You're cold."

"Amen," she answered, and she let herself smile. She imagined somebody with a tape measure, holding it, impossibly, from a flying robin down to the ground. She loved the idea—so unexpected, silly but fascinating, to juxtapose a flying robin and a floppy yellow tape measure.

What was humor? one of their professors had posed, and he had answered, *nondangerous, unexpectedly inappropriate juxtaposition.*

But as they began to descend the spiral stairs inside Vulcan's tower, Stella grew sober. She thought of the force of the powerful fire hoses turned on the Negroes peacefully congregating and marching for equality. She thought of the police dogs, standing on their hind legs, mouths open, snarling and barking.

In Birmingham, there was no romance between Vulcan and Lady Liberty.

CHRISTINE

IN EARLY MAY 1963, THE BLAST FROM THE FIRE HOSE caught Christine Taylor on the left shoulder, spun her counterclockwise, hit her on the back of her right shoulder. For the third day, the white firemen had been ordered to blast the demonstrators with their fire hoses. The force of water from the fire hose could rip the bark off a tree. As her front turned toward the fire hose, Christine brought up her forearms quickly to shield her breasts, was spun to face first the white mob, then the knot of firemen in red slickers. When the water blast crossed her upper chest, despite her shielding forearms and clenched fists, the force of the water knocked her breath away. Her body spun round the scream of her mind. Her legs tangled while she twirled. She fell to the pavement, and the pounding blast stomped hard on her back—one, two, three, four seconds, she counted through clenched teeth—then the high-pressure water moved on to punish another black person.

After the attack passed over, Christine panted into the pavement, counted four breaths of air smelling of wet asphalt, and opened her eyes. The water blast was sweeping toward Charles Powers, one of her students in the night school. She exhorted Charles to fall, now, before the white men got him, and he did, but the water pounded him anyway. *Stay on your belly! Don't let it roll you over!* she silently exhorted.

The water struck Charles's rump, lifting him, *Sweet Jesus!* abusing him through his trousers. Christine could see Charles screaming into the surface of the street, trying to get a fingerhold in the large cracks in the pavement. His lips inched over the asphalt while a policeman ran toward him, his nightstick raised. Releasing the pavement, Charles crossed his arms around the back of his head; the stick thudded his knuckles, but he protected his head, his hands crossed like pigeon wings over the skinny back of his neck.

("Got my trousers soaked with spray," LeRoy Jones, the policeman, would later tell his buddies and his brother Ryder, "but I whacked that nigger till he yelled uncle.")

Christine watched the blast moving away from Charles, chasing the running feet of children dressed in Sunday school clothes.

The fire-hose water hadn't rolled him over; Charles was safe in front. Christine wondered, *Would it have torn him up? Ripped his prick off?* She wanted to press herself into the pavement she lay on.

Charles, soaked, slowly rose to his feet. He was tall and lanky, had the broad shoulders and sinewy arms of a man. He moved slowly and cautiously.

You're not beat. You're not beat, Christine thought as loudly as she could.

With her cheek lying against the street, she watched him brush the street dirt off his lower lip. Christine knew she should get up, too, but she felt safer lying on the street, its grayness fanning away from her eye. She tugged down the skirt of her navy suit, her best suit, drenched now. Close to her cheek, a sparrow landed on the asphalt. When Christine glanced at Charles again, she noticed a little blood on his fingertips, which were next to his mouth (*Must have scraped his lip on the asphalt*). He was standing still, slumped, watching. She ought to speak to him. Encourage him.

There was the Reverend Fred Shuttlesworth reciting loudly, "I will fear no evil." Water rocketed against his ribs, spun him once, twice, and he was down, his hands pressed against his side.

Rising to her knees, Christine watched the running children and heard their high-pitched yelps. Like little dogs yelping. The torrential water splashed just at their heels, then traveled to their ankles and up the backs of their legs. The power of the fire hose pushed a little girl forward, drenched the back of her yellow organdy dress. The girl in sodden yellow lifted her hands and spread her fingers to push the children in front of her. All the children were soaked. The water cannon was moving the schoolchildren like kites in a wind against a brick wall; Christine fixed her gaze on a wet white shirt (*Dressed up for nonviolence, poor boy*) plastered against dark skin. When the blast moved on, the boy against the wall turned to face the firemen.

He raised an elbow to protect his face, if need be, but he didn't avert his attentive eyes. It was Edmund, Charles's little brother. Eyes wide with disbelief, Edmund wanted to see what was happening to them. Christine felt proud of him, glad that he wanted to see, to know. Edmund stepped forward from the wall and ran to kneel beside Reverend Shuttlesworth. The boy surely wasn't more than seven.

If not my generation, yours, she thought.

EDMUND

"WHY DON'T THEY COME TO VISIT ME, HERE IN THE HOS-pital?" Reverend Shuttlesworth asked the boy. "You come."

Nobody could smile like Edmund's minister—all teeth, all sunshine. Smiling now, smiling up from his hospital bed. Same as the pulpit smile, but Reverend Shuttlesworth was lying in white sheets, not standing, not weaving left and right before his people, his narrow tie leaping like a dancing snake.

"Who?" the boy asked.

"King," his minister answered. "King and Abernathy. You here. Where they?"

The boy shrugged. He retreated back into the ignorance of youth; he was little, he could shrug and say "I don't know," but he smiled when he said it, like sunshine, he hoped. (He knew nobody was admitted here to the bedside of Reverend Shuttlesworth—doctor and wife orders—but he had slipped in. So if he slipped in, why couldn't the Reverend Martin Luther King Jr.?)

"I just got to come see you 'cause you my hero," Edmund soothed.

"I thought Lone Ranger was your hero?" Minister was pleased, teasing him.

"Not anymore. I gonna be you."

"Martin Luther King Jr. is a man of God, and I love him. But we ain't the same. We ain't no identical twins."

"Yes, sir."

"Pray with me!" He reached out his hand from under the white sheet to Edmund, and then Reverend Shuttlesworth closed his eyes. "Jesus, take this youngun. Be at Edmund's side as you ever have by mine. When the house fall, lead him out. When the bomb burst, be his shield; put a helmet on his head and be his protection. Put love in his heart. Teach him. 'Love your enemies; bless them that persecutes you.' In the jail cell, tell Edmund—you with him, you with him even to the end of the world. In Christ's holy name, Amen."

They opened their eyes, and Edmund said, "I didn't let them put me in jail. I just ran off."

"Did you?" Minister wrinkled his forehead. He stared hard but loving. "Then I got to tell you. Don't be afraid of the jail. They can't jail a soul. Your spirit—it remain free, body behind bars."

"Yessir."

"Next time, you go on to jail like a good boy."

DARL

AS THEY STARTED THEIR DESCENT DOWN THE NARROW SPI-
ral steps inside Vulcan's pedestal, Darl apologized to Stella. "I'm sorry we
couldn't see anything."

"The trees blocked the view," she answered. She was descending the stairs
behind him. This way Darl could catch her if she stumbled, break her fall. It
was like walking on the street side; his mother had taught him manners: a gentleman should be killed first, if a car jumped the curb. Going up the stairs, he
should walk behind, in case she (any she) should slip.

From their high perch, Darl had admired the vast volume of air filling the
space over the city in the valley. God's love was suggested by a tension between
immensity and insignificance—sparrows plying the ocean of air. From left to
right, all the way to a vague horizon, the city had lain resolved into white, gray,
and tan buildings, a monochromatic mosaic of little squares and rectangles.
The tops of the bubbling green trees had resembled broccoli heads.

At the head of Twentieth Street stood a green carpet, landscaped with fish-
ponds; Darl knew the big trees of the park provided a canopy to the children's
entrance of the library, though the main library was too far away to serve children from his part of town, the West End. That other concentration of green
he had seen from the balcony would have been Kelly Ingram Park, where the
colored children gathered, the pawns of their leaders. If only people could be
patient, God had his plan.

The air over the city had not been invisible but perceptible as a gray haze
hovering over the tiny buildings and trees. When Darl had looked up higher,

he had seen some real blue, pale and tender. He felt that God had a tender attitude toward Birmingham, despite her shortcomings.

Darl took his time descending the metal steps in the dim light. He needed to decide if he should arrange to see Stella again in the evening.

"Did your folks take you to the library when you were little?" Stella asked, her voice floating down over his shoulder. Sometimes she seemed to follow his unarticulated thoughts.

"We had a branch in West End. Not so grand." He glanced out a narrow window set in the curve of the stone tower. He wished he had grown up nearer the center of things. Not that he didn't love his own blue-collar people. He did, and fiercely.

"When I was ten," Stella said, "my aunt allowed me to take the bus alone to the library."

He could hear her steps slowing. She lived in Norwood, once the residence of the well-to-do, with its wide boulevard, but now an area that had headed steadily downhill for many decades. Still, he liked its quiet decay, the remnants of elegance.

"It was my first visit to the library," she went on, "after I lost my family. I turned ten. Aunt Krit said double digits meant I could take the 15 Norwood to town, on my own."

He paused and turned to look up at her.

"They had been gone five years." Her upturned face looked peaked and scared.

"I'm sorry, Stella."

"The library had a revolving brass door." She had stopped, stood as though suspended in the dim tower, one hand on the metal handrail. "You entered the door from the outside world, pushed, then emerged in another world. A quiet, interior world." She seemed imprisoned in her sadness. Slowly she took another step down, closer to him; he continued their descent. "That's how it was," she said in a little voice. "They died and the world changed. Like passing through a revolving door from one world to another." She paused again, as though she wanted this spiraling down to last and last. "Actually, it was like crossing a river from one state to another. The driveway passes between my original home with my brothers and parents and where I live now with my father's sisters, Aunt Pratt and Aunt Krit. I crossed the driveway into another world."

At the bottom of the tower, they stepped out into the bright May sunshine. Though it had been chilly up on the pedestal, it was pleasantly warm at its base, with a slight breeze. How sad Stella had sounded. Darl took her hand, and they walked forward.

"I need to go on to Fielding's," she said, referring to her evening work on the switchboard at one of Birmingham's large department stores.

He turned to face her. "I'll pick you up after. On the Vespa."

"All right," she said.

BOBBY JONES

"LET'S GO FISHING, DAD. PLEASE, DAD," LITTLE BOBBY Jones begged his father.

"I promised your mom I'd stake up them tomatoes."

Bobby saw the twelve plants sprawled over the backyard. But this afternoon provided Bobby with a rare opportunity for fishing. His dad's service station was close to town, and they'd shut down because of the demonstrations. His little brother and sister—Tommy and Shirley—were playing in the sandbox. It was just an old truck tire that held sand. Bobby had seen cats nasty in it, and he didn't want to have anything to do with the sandbox. His mom was pinning a sheet on the clothesline. It was the kind of clothespin he liked, not the two sticks with a spring that could snap your fingers hard as a mousetrap.

"Please, Mom?" he whined.

"Oh, Ryder, y'all go on," she said. "It won't hurt the tomatoes none to wait."

"Where you want to go, son?"

"Village Creek! Village Creek! And I'll take my galoshes and wade."

"What'll we use for a pole?"

"Cut a pole!"

"Son, if we was to catch anything we couldn't eat it. That creek's too dirty. Nobody but niggers eats out of Village Creek."

Bobby had no reply. He'd only heard about Village Creek. He'd never seen it. He'd heard a white boy went over the Village Creek Falls in a barrel and it made him a half-wit. He asked his father about it.

"Them falls ain't but two feet high," Ryder answered. "And the water ain't more than a yard deep anyplace. It's an open sewer."

Bobby tried to hold back his tears. He had imagined the water of the creek to be a bright blue with a fish hopping out of it, smiling, like in Shirley's coloring book. Village Creek was the only body of water he'd ever heard of.

"Tell you what," his father said. "We'll go explore."

Bobby watched his father take off his black cowboy hat and smooth back his hair. He watched his parents squint their eyes in the sunshine and smile at each other. Bobby put his hands on his hips, grinned, triumphant. He felt as though he were holding a Brownie camera and taking their picture.

"We need a emergency plan," his father said, "case the house catches fire."

Bobby glanced anxiously at his house. Gray-white, it sat securely on the dirt.

"You carry out the kids and the TV," his father said to Bobby's mother, "and I'll get the guns and my recliner."

She just cracked her gum and smiled. "All right, hon."

The house was safe and square: four rooms not counting the bathroom. It was perfect.

Bobby reached down to pick up his child-size football—a lumpy, waddy thing, stuffed with rags. His mother had made the football for his last Christmas, stitched it up on her machine out of brown oilcloth.

Bobby threw a sure, spiraling pass toward his father, who snagged the ball with one hand.

TJ

WHEN TJ LOOKED OVER KELLY INGRAM PARK, FULL AND pulsing with demonstrators—his people—he thought *This is the heart of it* and then he thought of a real heart, how it pulsed and surged. *How many days can it go on?*

He wasn't a part of it. But today he would take its pulse.

When he was a boy, Kelly Ingram Park had no importance—a place where a few bums sat on the few benches under the big shade trees, a place more hopeless than a cemetery, a dull place for the exhausted. Now it was the beating heart of the protest movement in Birmingham, and Birmingham was the heated-up heart of Alabama, and Alabama was the Heart of Dixie.

The streets that lead from Kelly Ingram Park into the city, only short blocks away, became blood vessels: black people, black children flowing down the streets till they met the blockage of police, of fire hoses. So far, it was just city firemen and police, but TJ wondered how long till Governor Wallace sent the state troopers, men who thought of themselves as soldiers, who wanted to fire on people with something more deadly than fire hoses—how long?

A man who has a job at night, a man such as himself, he can use a spring day for his own. He can go down to Kelly Ingram Park, witness the scene in person instead of reading the paper, or watching the TV. He can stand on the high steps of Sixteenth Street Baptist Church right across from the park. He can get his *own* overview. So thought TJ, a steady man, night porter at the Bankhead Hotel.

He'd gotten work at the hotel just after he came back from World War II, still hardly more than a boy. During the war, he'd seen Europe like a tourist and never fired a shot. He'd worked steady once back in Birmingham, and they held the job for him when he went to Korea. Still a stupid boy then who thought he wanted to see Asia.

What TJ saw from the high church steps was a park full of children, faces shining, small, sharp voices twittering like a vast flock of starlings. And here came another covey, streaming down the steps of the church, boys and girls, all eagerness. Eager as water babbling down the steps. Been trained inside—he gathered that—been trained in the ways of nonviolence. In limpness, in silence. Just schoolchildren. His wife, Agnes, went to night school, a special school for people who'd dropped out, never finished high school.

Your body speak for you, he heard one boy say to another, pulling on his friend's arm. *No cussing.* The friend squawked out his own version of their instructions like a startled jay: *Your body on the line.* And they were gone—down the steps—crossing the street to the park. Remembering Korea, TJ wondered with dread about the new fighting in Vietnam. Yesterday another lone picture in the back of the newspaper. Yes, he'd noticed it, being a vet himself: another black boy killed 'cross the Pacific Ocean. All his family got left, a photo of a handsome boy, dead forever, in a uniform.

Yes, there the blue uniforms, the Birmingham police, forming up. Warm enough already in May to be in their uniform shirtsleeves. Wearing ties. Hadn't worn any *ties* in Korea.

During the first attacks of the Chinese against his company, he remembered, a red flare soared high over the ridge to the west, and he said to his buddies, "That flare is telling us. Our bodies are on the line." He could see the dark shadows of the Communist Chinese coming silently over the ridge. Bent over with packs on their backs, they moved close to the frozen grass. Many were cut down by his company's fire, but others leapt forward and scrambled into the outlying foxholes. He heard screams and the occasional blast of a grenade. Later, after more than forty-eight hours of fighting, he had fallen down exhausted near the top of a low hill, near frozen in the bitter cold. With the members of his company scattered around him in clumps on the hill, he had looked up into the rolling clouds and felt a strange sense of peace.

The Chinese Communists moved past his company in the dark, pushing south to cut off the route of escape. Chinks, he thought. We called them chinks. TJ wondered what their lives were like now. Looking down on Kelly Ingram Park, he thought, *It looks tough in the park today. I've seen worse.*

Moving down the church steps, he began weaving himself into the riffraff bystanders, trained in nothing. He bargained with himself—well, okay, he'd stand in with the unemployed, for a moment. Dirty men, ragged. They had nothing better to do. The unemployed. Even as a boy, he'd shunned them. Curiosity, that was all they had left of their minds. Probably couldn't half read even the newspaper. Idle curiosity. He had to admit, he was curious, too. Wanted to see for himself.

Why had children flowed into the jails, filling them up, when the adults were too afraid to demonstrate? TJ had heard that children filled not only the Birmingham jail, but the Jefferson County jail, some held in the Bessemer jail, some kept penned up in dormitories at the fairgrounds—904 juveniles. Children! He'd seen a little Korean girl lying in a ditch, turned into a crisp of flesh by a flamethrower. He remembered the weight of the bazooka on his shoulder as he aimed at other almost brown faces.

He saw the Birmingham police lower their clear visors over their white faces.

He thought he recognized some of the policemen and firemen in the park. More than a thousand men and women from Birmingham had fought in the Korean War. Returning home, many white men chose to be policemen or firemen. Blacks were excluded. TJ looked at a middle-aged policeman lowering the visor over his thin face. Doug Carter, Fox Company, 9th Infantry. They had ridden out of Birmingham together on the same bus at the start of the Korean War. TJ remembered how his company fought to protect the flank of Fox company in the desperate firefight at Ch'ongch'on River. Looking at Doug now, TJ felt anger rising in his arms and shoulders. *We were men enough to cover their asses in the war, but we're not men enough now to drink from the same water fountain.*

If his side won, would he want to become a black policeman? Maybe they'd want him. His war experience—he knew weapons, discipline. Had his Honorable. Could show his medal. That had been one of Shuttlesworth's demands of the early demonstrations: we want, we need, we demand some black police.

King said Birmingham was the most segregated city in the South. Only city over 50,000 with no black men on the police force. Shuttlesworth had petitioned years ago. *Not gonna arrest white folks. Just let us have black officers in our own neighborhood. We need police who won't wink at crime in our communities.* But TJ knew he'd arrest a white man quick as a black man, quick as he'd shot yellow men. He wasn't a racist.

He shouldered his way through the riffraff surrounding the demonstrators. The fringe. Maybe Agnes would work in ladies' shoes at Loveman's, maybe Pizitz. He could see her, dressed so neat, soft but not fat—no babies for them—kneeling with her eyes down, helping some well-dressed white lady try on a shoe. He'd always liked that gadget for measuring feet, that metal plate with a slide to measure length, and especially the slide for taking the width snugged up against the big toe joint inside a clean sock.

TJ didn't like these riffraff men brushing up against him. He could smell beer breath, saw a fellow tilt up his bottle wrapped in a greasy sack, the paper all twisted up around the long neck of the bottle. *Vagrant!* But TJ appreciated the colors of the schoolchildren's clothes. All colors, bright red and blue and yellow, pretty as a painting, a giant, dangerous picnic. TV couldn't catch all this pretty color. He noticed the nice white shirts on some of the boys, some patent leather shoes on girls' feet with white socks and a ring of lace on the sock cuff. *Upgrade employment for blacks in the stores*—that was a demand. Agnes, his own wife, was as neat and clean and more pleasant than any white woman.

Never mind Loveman's. Fielding's Department Store—that was where a black woman might hope to work. Not just be the bathroom maid, run the elevator. The Fielding brothers were Methodists, supported the Salvation Army. They had an annual Christmas party, and last year, Agnes phoned the Fielding's switchboard and asked if black people could come, and she said the telephone operator girl just sang it out: "Everybody welcome, black and white"—she had a white voice for sure—"come on down. We got cheese and crackers and cider and Santa Claus."

When she hung up the receiver, Agnes just sang it out again, in an imitation white voice right at the decorated tree: "We got cheese and crackers and cider and Santa Claus," but she was happy, not making fun. "That what the girl said."

And something else about Fielding's. No COLORED and WHITE signs on the drinking fountains. Just one fountain, and a plastic tube of paper cups beside it. You could pull down a cup, step on the foot treadle, and when the water arced up, catch your drink in the little white cup. Pretty little cup, sides all folded into pleats and a rolled rim around the top. Kind you could put mints in, or nuts, for a child's birthday party. Agnes could work in Accessories, not be back in Shoes in the corner. Accessories right there in the front of the store soon as you walked in.

TJ watched the back door opening on a police wagon and a German shepherd dog stepped out—Lord, God!—on a chain, then the dark blue leg and the whole of a policeman. And another pair—dog and man, linked by a leash. And another dog and man. Dogs always panting, muscles straining against the harness. The sun glinted from the metal snap that connected harness to leash. Several more pairs of dogs and handlers coming out of the truck, leaping down to the ground.

Over on the south side of Kelly Ingram Park the fire trucks began to pull up, and the kids drifted that way, wanted to see the trucks the way kids always love a red truck. He'd seen kids in the neighborhood, so excited to see a fire engine. Suddenly, like a flock of pretty birds, the children all veered away from the fire truck—a jumble of bright clothing—and started for the street to downtown. Somebody had given a signal.

It was early, TJ checked his watch, only around one o'clock, and the papers said the demonstrations usually started at three. Already on the city schedule—demonstrations at three. Acted like black folks was weather. Something mindless in nature they could observe. Predict like nature. (But he was surprised, he'd thought the demonstrations wouldn't start till three.) Police weren't ready at one o'clock. Now the bystanders were laughing at the police and ridiculing them. Five girls in a line played "Strut Miss Lizzie" in front of them, shaking their shoulders, noses in the air. Then a policeman shoved the big girl, last in the line. Big girl, might be fourteen, playing like a child, but shaking her new tits like a woman. She scowled at the police like any woman might scowl at a man who pushed her, then put her hand over her mouth and giggled like a child. The first gush of water scattered a patch of adults.

TJ marveled at how the flat fire hose went plump, how water leapt powerfully from the hose. Took two firemen to hold the brass nozzle between them. In a flash of sunlit water, a little girl in her Sunday best—pale blue—was drenched and smacked onto the pavement. TJ saw the riffraff man next to him change his grip on the neck of his bottle: now he had a short club.

Over there an explosion of rocks rained down on the helmets of the police, and the police raised nightsticks above their heads. Pulling their handlers behind them, the dogs lunged barking toward a human wall of retreating demonstrators. Black folks were commencing to run, and TJ found himself running toward what was becoming a riot. He saw a Negro man exhorting the children to nonviolence, and they waited or moved at the commands of the adults, their hands empty, their faces stunned, as though they were dreaming.

The children were wary but not afraid. Some excited. Some closed their eyes, held hands, and sang the freedom songs with all their might. At the end of a blasting fire hose, a woman went skittering down the street, swept over the pavement by the water, her face bleeding. The dogs leapt at a boy, trapped against a wall, surrounded by popping flashbulbs, a TV camera, and TJ found himself picking up a rock. Five policemen held a fat woman down in the gutter. Every pound of her was piety and innocence.

"God! God!"

Was that her shrieking? Some other voice gone high as a woman's?

Like an avenging angel, TJ hurled his rock toward a police face.

TJ was a trained soldier. No dogs on children! He'd show riffraff how to charge. He stooped for a broken brick as he ran. Heard the curses and scuffling feet of his platoon behind him. Way too many fighting folks to arrest 'em all. *Not gonna blast no chile! No sweet fat woman in the gutter. Get 'em! Get 'em! No snarling dogs leaping for a boy, just a boy.*

TJ wanted to sink his own teeth in their necks.

AT THE ATHENS

AS CHRISTINE STIRRED HER MARTINI THAT EVENING, SHE thought *angular momentum*—a term from her physics class, and she had thought it while the fire hose spun her body. Who was she? Physics student by day; teacher by night. Miles College—same place, both roles, different station.

In the bar, her bar, the Athens Cafe and Bar, Christine felt pampered as a queen. Grateful for the puffs of air-conditioning soothing her body, she stirred the liquid —slightly viscous, she noted—her own drink, specially made for her, Christine Taylor. Maybe she hadn't thought *angular momentum* when they blasted her round and round like a top; she just thought it now, watching the magic liquid twirl in her glass.

Better than in her own basement apartment, here in her bar, she could claim safety and peace. This was only a beer joint, with a pink neon STERLING sign in the window, but Christine loved the sign. The jukebox belted out Ray Charles, and a large jar of pickled pigs' feet sat on the counter.

Weeks before, Christine had marched into the Athens Cafe and Bar and had taken out her Martini and Rossi from an innocuous paper sack. When she presented the booze as being just for her own personal use, Mr. Constantine had accepted the bottle and put it under the counter. Here white waited on colored. Mr. Constantine kept a skinny jar of green olives for her, too.

Angular—she liked the word; her own face could be described as angular. She liked it that she had strong facial bones, that her whole body was strong and wiry. Leaning against the back of the booth, Christine's sore body made her feel again the hard street when she had fallen and rolled. She was bruised all across her back from the water pressure.

By dint of nothing but her angry, imperial manner, Christine felt she had brought *class* to the Athens Cafe. Christine stirred her martini. Like a goddess, she ruled the transparent liquid world inside the glass, made it swirl and sway to the music. She dominated here, relaxing with the drink and a new friend sitting across the table.

"Whose ribs?" Gloria Callahan, her classmate at Miles, asked Christine.

Gloria was so shy, she could scarcely look at any listener while she uttered a whole sentence, even one two words long. *Shy Bird,* Christine thought of her that way. Gloria was a shy bird but she had classy, high-toned habits. She brought in all her papers typed on thick paper and without any ink corrections. Gloria couldn't even look her professors in the eye, let alone a white, but Christine had taken Gloria under her wing. Already, Christine had convinced her to teach in the night school to help the dropouts, but when it came time to demonstrate, Gloria said she had to practice her cello.

"Yeah, Gloria," Christine said slowly. "Reverend Shuttlesworth got broke ribs today. He in the hospital. I witnessed when the hose water struck him down. Me laying on the street."

"Sure am sorry to hear that." Through her whole utterance, Gloria stared down at Christine's swirling of her drink.

"You ever heard Reverend Shuttlesworth preach?" Christine asked sharply.

"No, ma'am."

"Don't you *ma'am* me. I not but five, six years older than you." Christine's speech had shifted into the vernacular. They all had seesaw speech; sometimes they talked home talk, sometimes school talk. Up and down, first one then the other.

"All right," Gloria said.

Christine knew Gloria was forcing her eyes to glance into Christine's irritation. "I saw the hose get you," Gloria said to Christine, but she whispered the statement toward the floor. "On TV."

"Yeah? What you think when you see that, you safe at home watching TV?"

Christine knew Gloria wanted to join the protests.

"Pryne, pryne in a gyre!"

"Girl! What you talking about?"

"It's from William Butler Yeats. 'Sailing to Byzantium.' And he wrote that all will be 'changed, changed utterly: / A terrible beauty is born.' " Gloria said all this with her rare green eyes fastened on the dirty concrete floor. "That's from 'Easter 1916.' " She was tracing the cracks, running like tributaries toward some river.

Sometimes Christine thought Gloria's complexion had a reddish cast to it like maybe she had Indian blood. Gloria sat still as a sculpture, as though she had no right to move. She sat like a brooding dove, full-breasted, soft, with a short body.

"Where is Byzantium?" Christine demanded. "Girl, look at me when you answer!"

"It not but half real." Gloria studied the floor again, whispered, "Mythological. Constantinople."

"Mr. Constantine," Christine called out boldly to the Greek bar owner, "you ever been to Constantinople?"

The man just shook his head while he dried the inside of a glass with a cloth towel.

Mr. Constantine tried to keep conversation to a minimum with his customers. After nearly thirty years, his English was still uncertain.

Constantinople! Uncle Theo had taken him across the water to Constantinople when he was a young boy, led him through the confusing city to Saint Sophia glittering and glowing with gold mosaic. "Now you've seen heaven," Uncle had said to him, in Greek. While they visited the sights of the marvelous city, Uncle Theo had been identified, mistakenly, for a spy. After the pleasure trip, Turks had followed him home, tracked him to his hilly slopes. They had murdered him while he peacefully herded his goats back in Greece.

"Ever been to Byzantium?" Christine insisted.

"Birmingham," Mr. Constantine answered, but the image of his kind uncle passed like mist through his mind. He saw Uncle Theo leaning on his staff on the hillside, daydreaming of the dome of Saint Sophia in Constantinople. "This Birmingham," Mr. Constantine repeated firmly.

"Birmingham's half mythological, too," Gloria said. Then she asked firmly, "What about tomorrow?"

Under her tutelage, Christine saw, Gloria would make progress. Even on the third word, *tomorrow,* Gloria managed to maintain her gaze, to look Christine full in the eyes. Suddenly Gloria was as striking as a Polynesian idol with her rich, red-brown skin and jade eyes. Fierce. Christine blinked.

GLORIA AT HOME

IT WAS CARD NIGHT IN THE BACKYARD IN THE GARAGE apartment where her father's four sisters lived. Gloria's mother never joined the maiden aunties for cards, but she sent Gloria over to wait on them. For five days a week, the four aunts cleaned for and waited on twenty rich families of Mountain Brook and Vestavia. They wore starched pearl gray uniforms and white aprons. But on Friday nights, they put on their tight, jewel-tone toreador pants and played bridge.

When each of them placed a jeweled clip in her hair, they became the Queen of Spades and the Queen of Clubs, the Queen of Diamonds and the Queen of Hearts. The older sisters were the black queens and the two younger ones were the red queens. Emerald, topaz, ruby, and rhinestone—the glass jewels twinkled in their hair.

" 'Cept your daddy, we got no use for menfolks," they said to Gloria, from time to time. Born right in the middle of the sisters, Gloria's father was the Exceptional One—a successful man who had brought his sisters in from the country and installed them all in his garage apartment behind the new house. While they played cards, Gloria made popcorn and fudge for them. As they slapped the cards down on the flimsy table, the aunts cracked their gum, threw back their heads so you could see the arch of their teeth, and laughed their big laughs.

Gloria loved the oldest one and the youngest one most—the Queen of Spades, Alice, with her ample hips stuffed into the cerise pants, and the Queen of Hearts, Lily Bit, who had green eyes like Gloria, but something of the color of Lily Bit's eyes was in her skin so she looked almost khaki in her skinny yellow, raw-silk pants.

Among them, Gloria felt as light and salty as a kernel of the popped corn she piled into big blue bowls. They wouldn't let her be shy. But she didn't tell them her new secret: I went to a beer joint. I, the silent sophomore, have a new friend, a senior. *You can't guess what I might do next.*

Two weeks ago, I went with Christine to Mr. Parrish's office. I'm teaching in the night school: H.O.P.E. I speak in a low, quiet tone, but the students pull up their desks close to mine. They listen to me. I teach them the facts of history, but I could teach poetry or music or almost anything you could name.

Gloria wouldn't tell any of that, but she would show off: she tossed a handful of popcorn up over her head and caught some of it in her mouth. The aunts hollered and clapped and tossed popcorn up over their heads till it was snowing popcorn. Gloria wouldn't let them clean it up; she got down on all fours and picked up every piece. Then she boiled up a pan of glossy fudge.

That night, under the influence of fudge, Gloria dreamed dreams of things no one could possibly see: a chart of the human skeleton came off the wall and danced and sang like Mr. Bones in a minstrel show. She had seen a skeleton poster in handsome Mr. Parrish's office for H.O.P.E. at the college. Mr. Parrish had introduced her to the poster: "Meet Mr. Bones."

In her dreams, a cloud whizzed by like a bus full of schoolchildren singing gospel music, their bright young faces framed by puffs of whipped-cream clouds, on their way to jail. The sun rose like a plate of fudge, scored crisscross, in a diamond pattern. Her four aunts, their colorful pants tight as tree bark, grew four stories tall, uprooted themselves, stalked the earth, and Gloria leapt high on her cello, which had turned into a pogo stick.

EDMUND AT HOME

WHEN EDMUND CAME HOME FROM VISITING HIS PASTOR IN the hospital, he said to his mother, "Mama, tomorrow I'm going to be arrested." (He didn't tell her that he'd seen his big brother lying on the pavement. Just about lifted off the pavement by the fire hose shooting him. Charles was grown, had quit school, and moved out long ago.)

"You make me shamed I do so little," his mother answered. She set down her cracked coffee cup.

"Mama, you'll come get me, won't you?"

CHRISTINE WALKING

EIGHT WHITE MINISTERS, CHRISTINE KNEW, HAD WRITTEN
King a letter (she thought about this as she walked home through the stifling
night from the Athens Cafe and Bar). Eight white ministers had told him his
coming to Birmingham was untimely, unwise. King was an outsider; he ought
to let Birmingham folks work out Birmingham problems, in the name of Our
Lord and Savior, so said eight white ministers in the spring of 1963. Christine's beautiful martini ran in her veins while she walked the night street
toward home.

Gloria? Green-eyed Gloria might amount to something. She was smart;
she was willing to try to teach in the night school. Gloria had sat in the bar for
an hour, asked for ice water, not even beer.

Christine enjoyed walking home. *This my neighborhood,* she'd explained
when she declined Gloria's offer of a lift. Christine didn't envy anybody anything, but she wouldn't be beholden.

Such a quiet, still night closing down the screaming day. *The sea-fight tomorrow:* it was a phrase from Greek philosophy. It meant you couldn't know the
outcome, who would win. Next to physics, Christine loved best to study philosophy. From physics to metaphysics—she aimed to know it all. She aimed to
put her will to the wheel till it turned round to freedom.

Reverend Shuttlesworth, Reverend King, said love always wins. But Aris-
totle—or was it Plato?—pointed at the ships in the Aegean and asked mysteriously, philosophically, about how you couldn't know who would win the
sea-fight tomorrow. Christine pictured the white sails against Aegean blue,

wished she lived close to the sea or at least a big river. She wished away the dark street with a picture of sunlight on sparkling water.

But the small Greek ships in the offing disappeared because a black man down the street was unzipping his trousers. Christine watched the man aim his piss into the storm sewer. Once she had squeezed down that same dark rectangular sewer opening, squeezed her little-girl body underneath the heavy steel cover because her playmates had dared her to. She had known there was a kind of shelf to stand on down there. Nine years old, she had gone down. Had hoped no rat would dash out of the pipe to bite her ankle.

Christine walked on toward home, past the grown man pissing under cover of darkness, pissing into the same sewer where once she had stood. She imagined her little-girl head peeping out through the rectangular slot, eyes just above the level of the pavement, triumphant. How, after she climbed out, she had held out her hand to receive the nickel into her palm.

In the wake of the memory, for all its bravado, came anger.

King had written back to the white ministers, written to anybody who would read his letter from the jail, that his people could no longer wait. It was wrong to wait. The smooth sheen of martini evaporated. The heat of the sultry May night pressed against her. She felt anger in the way her feet came down on the sidewalk.

While she walked home through the night, it was as though she had decided to squat before an ember, to blow on it. Her heart flared big and red-hot, became a cauldron, a crucible of rage. As a child she'd seen a photo of a crucible conveying molten steel from the furnace, and the bright liquid seemed to be leaping at the sides of its container, as mobile as water in a gigantic bucket.

Touching the bone between her breasts, Christine wished as she walked that she could reach in, pluck out the cauldron with its seething contents. If only she could spill that anger out of her, onto the ground. Piss it away.

She would let the anger out, stamp it through the soles of her feet.

She tried to love the quiet of the hot, still night—her neighborhood—so far from the little yelps, the police shouting, the sirens and the scuttling feet. *We shall overcome.* She tried to think of King's letter, so strong and dignified. He refused to strut his stuff; with all his brilliance and all his knowledge, he refused to show off. Christine loved the tone of his writing—reasonable, sad, dedicated, brave. They couldn't make him mad. King had no use for her rage; he wanted her to love. His sentences were the cool breeze she needed in the smoldering of the night. *Let the night be sweet and kind,* but she could hear the day again, the movement of feet, the assault of firemen, police, the crowd of black people, a solid square block of people set on freedom.

With the dissipation of the alcohol, every step jolted her backbone, made it ache.

A block ahead, under the streetlight stood a group of teenage boys, colored boys smoking cigarettes. They stood in a mist of humidity, six of them, almost grown, passing a flask among them, the tips of their cigarettes burning red through the mist. In the light, the moisture hung in the air like dust motes in a shaft of sunlight.

The boys with their smooth brown faces, sixteen, nineteen years old, their flask, the burning cigarettes—all appeared fuzzy. Their noses emanated twin streams of smoke as though these teens were young dragons swaddled in a gauze of light from the streetlamp.

The sea-fight tomorrow.

Christine wished for a wooden sword. She would run the dragon boys through their worthless bodies. One by one she would slay their street booze, their cigarettes, them, if necessary. But why did she wish her sword was only wood? Like something from the funnies. Just two pieces of wood, like a cross.

"Onward, Christian Soldiers" hummed in her brain. "Onward, onward!"— the Reverend Shuttlesworth would break away from the song to exhort his people with plain words. The congregation kept singing straight ahead: "With the Cross of Je-sus going on before." Shuttlesworth was a man like an electric spark. Small, potent, a force of nature.

She thought of King, when he was first on TV; he had looked down—like Gloria; he had ducked the camera's eye. When he had spoken for the Montgomery bus boycott, King had been quiet and humble-seeming. Close to scared, she had thought. (But it was Rosa Parks who had sat down on the bus in the all-white section; it was a woman who had led King into history.) Now Martin Luther King Jr. was putting on weight—adding ballast—looking into the camera, his eyes full of sorrow. A Man of Sorrows, as much as Christ himself, Christine thought, but others didn't see him as she saw him, didn't see the deep sorrow.

She knew Shuttlesworth was the Survivor. It was Shuttlesworth in 1956 who had risen up from the bombing of his own house. The bomb had been tossed up under the house on Christmas Day, and it had exploded just under the floorboards beneath his bed. He had been in the bed. It was Shuttlesworth who was truly fearless. Shuttlesworth might have his church in Cincinnati—but so what?—he had toiled long in the vineyard of Birmingham. Shuttlesworth would always have one foot in this city. No, his heart.

Christine thought of the popular song "I Left My Heart in San Francisco." She wished she could see San Francisco. She imagined the bay full of sailboats. Of *the sea-fight tomorrow.* How would it turn out, their struggle for freedom? Like Susan B. Anthony had said long ago about women's rights, "Defeat is impossible."

Christine pictured the Reverend Fred Shuttlesworth as a mighty colossus; one foot in Birmingham, one in Cincinnati, he straddled the Ohio River. His stature was a matter of his spirit. The paddle wheel boats and the barges passed between his legs.

In the flesh, Reverend Shuttlesworth was little and wiry. Not as tall as the shortest of the six boys who stood under the streetlight, smoking and drinking, but he would have no fear of them. She was as tall as Shuttlesworth. Steadily, the sound of her feet on the sidewalk closed the distance between her and the tough boys.

How Shuttlesworth loved the children! Saw the future in them. Smiled at her three like they were important. He believed in them. His quick mind enlivened theirs.

And what about her boss, Lionel Parrish, organizer of the night school, handsome as Martin Luther King? (Those pretending to be dragons ought to take their minds to night school. But no, they wanted numb minds, lazy bodies.) Less important, sure, but Lionel Parrish was stamped from the same dough as Martin Luther King.

Christine pictured rolling out biscuit dough on her metal cook-top table, of taking the mouth of a glass and pressing it into the dough, cutting out biscuits. She liked to think of the ministers all over the South, how now they lifted up their heads, became little Kings, little Shuttlesworths. Ready to encourage if not to lead.

She imagined Lionel Parrish, part-time minister, full-time schoolteacher—Lionel Parrish—sitting at her own table, a cloth printed with faded fruit but clean and without stain, her tablecloth, on the table, Lionel Parrish eating breakfast, lifting a fragrant biscuit, butter visible at its sides, lifting the beautifully browned, hot, fresh biscuit to his lips. Lionel Parrish had never been in her house.

Lionel Parrish looked like Martin Luther King, with that smooth, benign face, and Lionel Parrish was fighting his own doubt and fear about something. It was something in himself he sorrowed about, as though he felt ashamed to be proud of his leadership. That sorrow might not have much to do with leadership, with freedom for the people. What did she see behind Lionel Parrish's handsome eyes? What kind of freedom did Lionel want for himself? Christine wondered. What did King want, for that matter, in his heart of hearts?

She knew what Shuttlesworth wanted. Victory! Unequivocal victory for her children, for herself, for all the people he knew. *In Birmingham*, let freedom ring! King might come and go from Birmingham, but Shuttlesworth would always be back.

One of the boys, the tallest one, detached himself from the group, held out his hand.

"Lady, can you let me have a quarter?" he said. He didn't smile.

She shook her head no, folded her lips tight in on themselves. *Don't you beg from me.*

Another one reached out and took her arm; he talked with his cigarette waggling in his lips. "Didn't you hear the man?"

"Get your hand off me."

They all shifted around her. She kept walking. They walked with her. She speeded up, and they snickered.

"This here some *fast*-moving woman."

"Run!" one of them roared in her ear, and she jerked and ran a few steps, them laughing around her, running, too.

Then she made herself stop. No, she wouldn't run. They stopped, surrounded her. She clasped her purse hard against her side. Her bruised side. She didn't know these boys. Not from her neighborhood. She was safe long as strangers stayed out.

From nowhere, she heard loud humming. She herself was humming "Onward Christian Soldiers." It came from deep in her like the low pedal of a pipe organ on TV church. A grainy, buzzing sound she didn't know she had.

Slowly, she started to walk forward. She hummed from the lowest pipes on the organ. Not one took a step after her. They snickered, but they let her go.

With the Cross of Jesus, she hummed loudly, knowing the knot of boys (now watching her go on without them) must have heard the song sometime in their past. They had to be remembering the words to that hummed music,

With the Cross of Jesus going on before. They knew her for a Christian, church-going woman just like their mamas.

As Christine walked toward the dark middle of the block, she projected herself toward the streetlamp at the next corner. Safe again. In the warm night air of May in Birmingham, her song and fear evaporated like a nightmare. But they'd scared her. She felt herself starting to fill with anger. She didn't want anger now.

She thought of home, her apartment in the basement. It was a big old house, and many years ago white people had lived there. Christine would step down into the kitchen. Her three kids would be there and her sister watching them. There'd be four empty Pabst Blue Ribbon bottles on the counter, but her sister would be there in her beer haze, keeping them safe. (Gloria wouldn't even drink beer in a beer joint.) Her sister ought to be in night school herself, but then how could she, Christine, teach in it? She was grateful to her sister, keeping her kids safe, free of charge.

Soon Christine would go down the steps, use her key, open the door, step into the kitchen light, and they'd all be there, safe. Her woozy sister with one straightened lock of hair sticking up from her head, the hair clamped at the bottom with a brown barrette.

Christine hurried on down the sidewalk; like heaps of dirty rags, last fall's leaves still lay on the ground in places. One yard had iris blooms, white and lavender, rising above the old leaves. *I am the Resurrection and the Life.* Christine felt her own life had been resurrected, by Reverend Shuttlesworth's preaching, by going to school.

Baptized! Yes, that was what had happened to her today. Baptism by hose water. *Let my heart be clean and fresh,* she prayed. *Free of hatred.* That's what she owed Jesus, who had saved her from the rough boys. She hated her anger sometimes, and yet to hate *it* was like hating herself.

So many schoolchildren in the demonstrations now. Not her kids, too young for school, too little for trouble. Yet. Demonstrating was for grown-ups. Shuttlesworth believed the children in the protests were as invulnerable as himself. He gloried in their numbers, their willingness. King was in agony—suppose a child was hurt? Although King was afraid for them every minute and every hour, just as she was, publicly King said the children had already suffered abuse because of the society they lived in.

In the Christian Crusades, in medieval times, there had been a Children's

Crusade. Did King know that? Of course. Did Shuttlesworth? The freedom struggle had never called on children before, and she wondered if calling out the children was a tactic out of desperation—if no more adults could be recruited.

(She could see the big old house, her home, up ahead.) How could a person such as herself, how could a woman, live like Shuttlesworth, like Rosa Parks—unafraid? Rosa Parks was the start of it all. Christine wanted to remember that. One brave, middle-aged Montgomery, Alabama, black woman.

Five hundred children arrested today, they said, ages six to sixteen. The principals tried to lock the children in the schools, and they jumped out the windows to join the demonstration.

Rosa Parks, King, Abernathy, Shuttlesworth—leaders, leaders.

Lionel Parrish, Christine Taylor. Leaders, leaders. *He is trampling out the vintage where the grapes of wrath are stored.* Her feet marched proudly on the sidewalk. She peered into shadows lest somebody be hiding there. Somebody ready to take her down.

The first man in her life had shoved her down to the carpet, bound her up with white clothesline. Did her. Somebody she knew. She hated him with a righteous hate. Coward, devil! She wanted somebody to do to him what he had done to her. Fuck him up his ass till he screamed. Terrify him. You don't forgive somebody who treats you that way. You put as much space between him and you as you can, as fast as you can. You don't ever forgive him because he'll do worse next time. A coward, a shit. She believed in nonviolence, but maybe she'd have him tortured to death one day.

Bound her with rope, turned her over, pissed on the back of her head, the scalding piss dripping round the curve of her skull toward her eyes and mouth. *She would not be humiliated.* She would not feel shame.

His was the shame! *He ain't me, babe. No, no, no, I ain't him, babe.* She survived that union; separated herself from him. She had the strength to make anything she wanted of her life. She walked toward home with determination in each step: to learn, to study, to make herself achieve. To find the work right for her. Yes, that was her resolve. From physics to metaphysics, with music and art in between.

He was gone from her life, now.

But he was human, just like her.

She had known him; he hadn't been a stranger coming up out of the dark.

She could wish him well.

Far from her life, let him live. (She began to hurry toward home.)

But he had come whining back around about how he had just wanted her to have his baby. She spat on him, wouldn't dignify him with any words. And her heart had said to her, You done right! Just spit on *that*. She'd had babies. Not his. She wouldn't have a crazy, cruel, cowardly shit as the father of her babies.

Even now, years later, she imagined herself turning away from his false love, and she felt strength well up in her and fill her soul and mind with purity. (Her feet scurried over the pavement toward home.) Didn't matter what all had happened to her. Didn't matter what mistakes she'd made. Now on, she loved herself. Loved her own independence. Loved the future.

FIELDING'S DEPARTMENT STORE

ALL EVENING AS STELLA ANSWERED THE DEPARTMENT store telephone, she thought of Darl, how when she came out the back door of the department store ("Good evening, Fielding's"), he would be there, straddling the seat of the Vespa, one foot out on the pavement for balance.

Between telephone ringings ("Good evening, Fielding's"), she tried to read *The Divine Comedy*. It was not assigned in any of her classes, but she had heard of it and wanted to know why it was supposed to be great. T. S. Eliot had referred to Dante in *The Waste Land*. When Stella tried to imagine the levels of hell spiraling down, all she could think of was Darl, the thrill of riding behind him on the motor scooter as he took the best curves down Red Mountain. Then she envisioned the brown freckles thrown like a net over all his classic handsome face.

From her perch on the mezzanine, she saw a boy she had known in high school. He had had a tiny hand, a birth defect. She had been a senior and Blake a freshman at Phillips High School, but they took drama and speech together. ("Good evening, Fielding's.") One day, their speech teacher, Miss White, from the North, had jabbed her own skin with her index finger and said, "Some people are so ignorant that they think the pigmentation of their skin means who's smart and who's dumb, who's superior and who's inferior." While others looked down at their desks in embarrassment, she and the freshman boy had exchanged an electric glance across the room, made a connection, she had thought.

("Fielding's Department Store. May I help you?") The school had buzzed about Blake, his weird hand, of course but also because he was a math whiz and had whole symphonies in his head. He was *different.* When Blake looked at other students, it was with contempt for their inadequacies.

High school hadn't been that way with Stella's friend Cat, who was in a wheelchair. ("Good evening, Fielding's.") Cat was as smart as Blake, but she was friendly. From the balcony, Stella watched Blake walk into the shoe department and throw himself down into a chair. He looked like a spoiled prince, his head topped by curls, his defective hand held up like a scepter. Maybe Stella would telephone Cat and gossip a bit. No, this was a night when Cat's brother was escorting her to a party given by one of her handicapped friends.

Nancy was doubtlessly on a date. Ellie would be at a rehearsal for *The Fantasticks.*

During her break from the switchboard, Stella wandered toward the dress department. The store was quiet, almost empty of customers. With the trouble going on, people didn't want to be out at night. She nodded to Sadie, the store maid, already running the vacuum in her neat gray and white uniform, and at two clerks chatting at a cash register. The store felt lonely.

Stella went to the dress rack and closed her eyes. She liked to feel the textures of the dresses first, before she looked at them. She always made sure no one was watching her. Touching the sleeve of a denim jacket made Stella feel young and tender about herself. She loved to touch corduroy, grooved like a plowed field. Some fabrics had a bright, glazed finish, and then there was the new no-iron shagbark fabric. She had bought a no-iron dress, its fabric covered with tiny knots. Aunt Krit had said she preferred a plain cloth. "I always tried the latest fashions," Aunt Pratt had called from her bed, "when I was young."

While she touched the fabrics of the dresses, Stella's hand remembered the reassuring twill of Darl's trousers, the curve of his buttock, and at their feet, the city down in the valley.

Stella wandered to the three-sided mirror and admired her dress, a smooth cotton broadcloth composed of tiny brown and black checks, edged with black rickrack at the collarless throat and short sleeves. When she had felt the dress on its hanger, the rickrack had pleased her fingertips. Small, bright black buttons ran down the front from the neck to the hem. That long line of little buttons somehow seemed brave.

With a part down the middle of her head, Stella thought she looked like the brave poet Emily Dickinson. Emily had not always worn white; she had not always been reclusive, but had become so, over time. Maybe Stella would be the reverse of Emily; maybe she was coming through the looking glass the other way. Coming out into the world, no longer in hiding.

Something in the air, or was it in the light reflected from the mirror, reminded her of her mother's voice. "You look nice, Stella." Emily Dickinson's hair had been dark and pulled smoothly back. Stella's blond hair ended in a flip just above her shoulders.

Both Emily's religious skepticism and her courage amazed Stella. Though the other girls in Emily's boarding school professed their faith in the divinity of Jesus, Emily had refused. From what starting point in yourself could you doubt what everyone you knew told you about Christ? Emily had believed in God, if not Jesus. Of course, if she wore a black-and-brown-checked dress such as Stella's, it would have come to the floor. Had a hoop under it and been the prettier for it.

What did Darl see in her? He seemed to know she was quiet, and he didn't care. What did she see in herself? Somebody who wanted to change. Somebody who wanted to live more fully. Someone whose scope was larger than the campus, broader than boring, part-time work, wider than a cloistered, borrowed home with two aunts, one a maiden teacher, the other an invalid (though she loved them and was grateful to them). Stella stepped out of the three-way mirror and returned to her station at the switchboard.

Though she opened *The Divine Comedy* again, she mostly daydreamed and gazed over the balcony at the business of the store, at the shoe department, men's clothing, jewelry and accessories, at hats left over from Easter. Sometimes she peered down into the glass cases of gloves and lipstick tubes, the minutiae of fashion. ("Good evening, Fielding's.") She sized up the customers passing in the aisles—who was attractive and who was not. A department store was like a city. She had loved looking out over Birmingham from Vulcan. Like looking from a castle wall, his arm around her, her fingers knowing the twill of his trousers. And where would they go tonight?

Someplace to hug and kiss. Some fine and private place. Since Darl had gotten the Vespa, they could explore the city. How important were congruent values to a happy relationship? Suppose he kept his religion (she hoped he did), but she lost hers?

MR. FIELDING

WHEN THE OWNER OF THE DEPARTMENT STORE CAME UP
the stairs to the mezzanine, on his way to his office behind the switchboard, he
gave the switchboard operator a terse little nod. He knew how she perceived
him: a short man, very erect, beautifully dressed in his well-pressed suit; his
white hair circled his head like frosting on the sides of a cake. His own daughter—who loved him—had described him that way.

"Pretty quiet, tonight, isn't it, Miss Silver?" he asked. He said it with grim
regret. The protests cut into everybody's business.

"Yes, sir," she answered.

"What do you think of these demonstrations. You all out at the college?"

"I just hope nobody gets hurt," Miss Silver said.

"Medieval universities were surrounded by high walls," he said. "The walls
were topped with broken glass to keep the world out and the students in."

Stella stared at him incredulously. How could she come to work for him if
she were cloistered in the college?

"You all are students," he went on, "and should bear in mind that now is
your opportunity. Your obligation is to devote yourselves to your education."

With a quick, definitive nod, he affirmed his own word and disappeared
into his office. He closed the door behind him. Inside his office, he hiked up a
leg of his expensive navy blue trousers. He placed one hand on his desk to
steady himself and knelt. Fielding was pushing sixty, but he had no trouble
kneeling. He'd kept in practice, in private, all his life.

Precious Lord Jesus, he prayed. *Let this cup of integration pass from us, if it be thy will. Still, thy will be done. And give us strength to face what we must face with a loving spirit. Give them patience, Lord, and give it also to us.* He pressed his chest with his spread hand. *Keep us safe from harm, on both sides. In Jesus' name, amen.*

He imagined a high stone wall studded with glass and crooked nails. Would something like that be enough? He imagined the university boys of Europe and England leaning ladders against the walls, padding the top with thick, coarse horse blankets. He had heard that the Negro children had jumped out windows, on the first floors, to join the demonstrations.

AT THE BANKHEAD HOTEL

THAT NIGHT, NOT A SCRATCH ON HIM, WHILE HE PUT ON his porter jacket, the noise of the protest still played in TJ's head. Screams, sirens, barking dogs, the thud of the billy clubs, the songs. You didn't go to war with songs. Over there in Korea it had been only the sounds of heavy weapons. Jeep motors. The clank of tank treads turning over. Cold and fierce snow like he'd never seen nor felt before. Men sobbing for their buddies. You didn't go to war singing. The flag of war was khaki stained with blood. This was better.

Not pretty, no, he wouldn't let himself say that when he pictured the fire-hose water blasts hitting the backs of huddled children. The blood on that woman's face, the hose scouring the pavement with her body. Children squatting on the ground, their heads tucked down. One girl, on her knees but straight up, tall, had pressed her hands together, praying. The water toppled her over, hurt, screaming, her hands spread to catch her fall. The savage barking of the dogs. The enthusiasm of the police cocking their clubs. Not pretty at all. All that colorful clothing. A giant freedom flag. *Noble*. That was the word he wanted.

Glory! Glorious on our part. All the colors of the rainbow.

ON THE VESPA

"WHERE ARE WE GOING?" ALREADY, THEY WERE ALMOST flying.

Pressing her hands tightly against his sides, Stella felt Darl's body contained between her palms. The wind of their speed rumpled her skirt, and she remembered the terrible wind buffeting the car on the way home from Helicon when the cyclone struck. She tried to stare over Darl's shoulder into the distance, but at the sides of her eyes the gray pavement slid by like an endless blade.

"To the cemetery," he answered, turning his mouth so the airstream could fly his words to her turned ear.

Darl steered the Vespa north, toward Oak Hill, a vast cemetery deployed over several hills. In the distance, a large water tower topped the highest elevation. When Darl found the gates closed to traffic, he parked the scooter. They climbed over a low brick wall and pushed through a tall, thick hedge of holly.

Once inside, they walked the narrow, deserted streets winding among the communities of the dead. Humidity veiled the trees and graves, the slopes of grass, homogenizing all the features of the cemetery. Hosts of gauzy monuments, like solid ghosts, rose solemnly from the graves toward the faint moonlight and fainter starlight. Behind them, the holly hedge held the ordinary world at bay. As Darl and Stella walked deeper into the cemetery, the darkness increased. To Stella, the quiet seemed holy, as though the slight noise of their walking was a sacrilege.

But Stella's people were not here; they were all buried at Helicon.

"You're not afraid, are you?" Darl asked, and lightly put his arm over her shoulders while they walked. "I drove through here earlier today," he went on. "I want to show you a special statue. It's deep in, over the next rise and down again."

Hardly speaking to each other, they passed a grove of specimen holly trees and then walked on a footpath through an expanse of cedars. "The older graves are ahead, among the magnolias beyond the oaks," Darl said.

Occasionally Stella saw a small grave marked with a lamb and assumed these were the graves of children. How quickly an aesthetic for monuments established itself. She disliked the heavy chunky monuments, especially if they were a dark, pretentious marble—the color of liver. She glanced up at the gibbous moon. The crowns of the elm trees spread like black lace against the deep blue satin sky. *Like fans,* she had said once to her cello teacher, Miss Ragrich, and the teacher had admired Stella's phrase.

But where were the right words to render what it is to be alive? To walk, to see? She wanted the words of Emily Dickinson and Virginia Woolf. She pitied the myriad dead who slept in their small houses underground. "Has death undone so many?" T. S. Eliot asked in a line from *The Waste Land.* She felt she shouldn't pass the graves so quickly.

When her foot crunched acorns underneath, the sound seemed wholesome. Occasionally she heard an unseen bird stirring on its night perch from within its shelter of thick oak leaves. Among the leaves, the bird made the sound of someone clearing his throat. While she walked, she closed her eyes and listened more intently. *What was an unseen world like? A world of the immaterial, of spirits?* Because they were walking rapidly, she could hear Darl's breathing and her own breathing like woodwinds sighing.

She imagined the feet of the birds sleeping in the trees, how the little hidden birds' feet were clasping their roosts, three toes curled in front, and from the back, one clamped over the twig. The birds were hot and restless.

"Let's slow down," she said, and Darl immediately responded to her request.

Quickly, he turned and kissed her cheek, like a reward, but a kiss such as a friend might give.

She opened her eyes.

"Listen," he said. "That's a horned owl."

NIGHT DUTY

WHILE HE ADJUSTED HIS MAROON BOW TIE, TJ LISTENED
to the radio in the porters' room. He kept the volume low; all night it was
something to come back to when he finished a porter duty. He stood still to
listen: twenty-five hundred protestors had stormed the downtown business
section. They replayed a recording of Shuttlesworth, on a different day: "We're
making history in that we've literally filled the Birmingham jails. Bull Connor
thought the jails were like hell to us, but you all have made a heaven out of the
jail. . . . You are fighting for what your country is and what it will be."

These were beautiful May days. All that colorful clothing on the children.
Like confetti at a parade. Yes, TJ had marched down Twentieth Street after
World War II. Hadn't seen much action in that war. But he'd never felt prouder
before or after than marching down the middle of the street, home from
France, paper bits drifting down from the open windows of the high-up floors
of the Tutwiler. He hadn't *looked* up, but with his face steady and straight
ahead, he'd *glanced* up, had seen the white hands tossing the paper out the
open rectangles of the high windows. Before the parade, they had told the soldiers a five-star general would be on the reviewing balcony. TJ could feel the
butt of his rifle cradled in his hand, the weight of the rifle, its stock and barrel
leaning against his body. Blue and pink confetti drifting right in front of his
nose and eyes.

Sitting in his porter's chair, TJ stooped down to polish the toes of his shoes
with an old gray piece of terry cloth.

He'd fought hard in Korea. Cried there. More than once. Cried for a white boy bleeding to death in his arms. Cried for himself, so cold and worn out. Not even after Korea, and he'd fought hard there, had he been so proud as when he came home from Europe, from World War II, marched Twentieth Street—a soldier-boy—no prouder day than that.

The all-night radio said Shuttlesworth had been injured in the demonstration today. Possibly his ribs were broken. Visitors to the hospital had been forbidden.

NIGHT PLEASURE

"THERE," DARL SAID. HE STOPPED AND POINTED TOWARD A crowd of tombstones.

Following the direction of his pale finger, Stella's gaze darted through a thicket of tall pointing columns, little Washington monuments, to the figure of an angel with flamboyant wings. As they walked along, Stella trailed her fingertips against the stones, some grainy, others smooth and cold. They were as different as the hands of strangers, but she must pay attention to Darl's angel.

With one knee down on a slab of marble, her wings stretched wide, as though she had landed only the moment before they arrived, the angel held a metal staff with a solid glass orb for its finial. The rusty rod passed through a neat hole in her marble hand. The figure's face was lifted upward and her eyes reviewed the night. A universe of energy and motion had come to a halt on the slab.

Darl said, "He's flown through a great distance, through a great darkness."

"Or straight from the Renaissance," she answered. "Traversed time instead of space?"

"Look at the eyes."

They were angry, furious. The marble eyebrows were arched accusingly. The hair looked wild, like another set of wings still held open from the force of the long journey through space. The chin was set at a defiant tilt.

"He blames God," Darl said. "He says, 'Why must we be so small?' "

"Who?"

"Angels and humans—why must we be so small?"

"Yes," Stella answered, and she was afraid. When God's finger flipped over the car and his fist crushed her family, she should have been defiant. She should have been angry instead of weak and afraid. When she came home from the hospital to the aunts' house next door, she had hidden her face in the lap of her frail and crippled Aunt Pratt. But she had only been five years old.

"They shouldn't have all this clutter around him," Darl said. "He ought to be in a public place so everybody could see him."

"Clutter?"

"These conventional monuments."

"These people have died, too."

"Not gloriously," he said, with contempt.

"How can you possibly tell?"

When Darl took her hand to lead her away, she felt annoyed with herself, letting him be so much in charge. The angel could have been deemed female as easily as male. She would think what she would think. She glanced back over her shoulder at the figure whose eyes were staring at the distant moon. That wild defiance—Darl had nothing in common with such a figure. Or had she misunderstood him?

"There's a pretty spot down this way," he said. "Not so crowded. It's more natural."

As soon as he said it, the night became peaceful. The unpleasant heat of her body dissipated. The air smelled good. Before her was the long graceful slope of the hill—just the natural earth, studded here and there with low rectangular monuments. These stones had the proportions of open books, wider than they were high, but their tops had a single graceful arch.

"This is more peaceful," she said quietly. This was the right place for her to be—where death and its peace were acknowledged. *Let us be true to one another,* Matthew Arnold had written in "Dover Beach" as he listened to the sobbing of the sea. So might she say to Darl into the silence of this place.

But there was no place on earth as peaceful as the cemetery at Helicon where her family lay: one headstone bearing the word *Silver,* with each of their four names incised lower down. When her time came, would she want to be laid down beside them?

Darl gestured at the gravestones on the slope. "Which one would you choose to have?" he asked, and suddenly the night went spooky. He became opaque as stone.

"None," she said angrily. "I choose to stay above ground for quite a while longer."

They walked on silently. She felt outraged by his comment. She thought but did not say, *You're not much acquainted with death. You'd fight it, if you were.*

" 'No man knoweth, the day or the hour,' " she quoted. *But had she embraced life?*

"I believe that's in reference to the Second Coming," he said quietly.

She knew he was right. The statement was about Jesus, but it might as well be about human life and when it would end. She didn't know what to say to him anymore. She felt as though her face had been rubbed in death.

Finally he said, "You can hear the city. Even in here."

And her attention focused on the sound of a car horn, then a sputtering motor baffled by acres of leafy trees and the prickly wall of evergreen holly leaves. Something gigantic settled in the night—a sound from the steel mills, muffled by the distance and the slopes of the cemetery but surely of deafening volume to anyone close by. She imagined men near the furnace; stripped to the waist, their bodies glistened with sweat in the red glow. They would mostly be black men, she knew. Then Stella noticed Darl and she were holding hands again, but she couldn't have said when he took her hand. She could love him; yes, she could.

Far away on the crest of a distant hill of the cemetery, she saw two people walking. They were dark figures silhouetted with clear edges, and they too were holding hands. It was a Negro couple, she could tell by the girl's hair, sticking up in pigtails. And she wore a much-too-large jacket, which ballooned around her body. His jacket probably. He was in short sleeves. She wouldn't have seen them except they were silhouetted by the backdrop of sky.

"Another couple," Darl said.

Couple. She loved the word, squeezed his hand, hoped he meant it. She craved the connection implicit in *couple.*

Darl stopped at the lip of a drop-off. They stood near the crown of a magnolia tree that had its base far below. The air was perfumed with the redolence of the large blossoms, big as two hands cupped together.

"It's gorgeous," she said.

"We can go down to it. Here's a dry creek bed."

He stepped down onto some rocks. The descent was steep at first. Then the stepping-stone rocks gave way to a rocky creek bed, a tilted, grooved surface.

"Does it ever flow?" she asked.

"I don't think so," he said. "But look at the sycamores. They may have their roots in underground moisture."

Over their heads, the sycamores from both sides laced their thick arms into an arch. The creek bed bent toward the magnolia and gave way to grass. They crossed a grassy place with no graves, a small meadow lying in the redolence of the beautifully symmetrical, huge magnolia. Covered with large white blossoms, the tree luxuriated in itself. Each blossom glowed, as though the tree were bedecked with lamps. Low-hanging branches hemmed in a profound darkness in the tree's interior. Stella certainly didn't want to go in there. She knew the bare-earth dankness under magnolia trees. Because the roots would be partially exposed, one could no more lounge there than on a bone heap.

Darl led her to the lush grass a short distance beyond the tree.

"It's a perfect specimen of a tree," Stella said.

"There's nothing big growing close enough to block its sun," Darl answered. "It faces south. The north side isn't so perfect because of the hill. Let's sit down."

Only then did Stella notice that he had brought a large, rolled-up towel along. Yes, she had seen him take it out of the side pocket of the Vespa. He spread the white towel on the grass.

"Do you want me to break you off a blossom?"

"I like them on the tree." She drew the aroma through her nostrils. So soapy. Decadent.

He flared his hand at the waiting towel, and they sat side by side on the rectangle. Little sticks pressed against her through the terry cloth and through the fabric of her checked dress, through her nylon slip, her cotton panties.

Darl moved close to her and positioned his arm diagonally for her to lean her back against. He quickly kissed her on the cheek again.

"Are you comfortable?" he asked.

"Yes."

CHRISTINE AT HOME

CHRISTINE CONTEMPLATED THE YELLOW BOWL OF COLD biscuits sitting on the table. Her three children regarded her mischievously. The oldest spoke: "Aunt Dee say she can't turn on the stove. The gas been shut off."

Christine looked at her sister, but she couldn't feel mad at Dee. Dee had stayed with her kids so she could go out. "Naw," Christine said fondly, "Dee just too lazy to get up. She got her beer to nurse."

"Her beer bottle like a baby bottle," Diane, her smart daughter, her oldest child, spoke up impertinently.

"Huh!" Christine and Dee chuffed the word together. No need to scold anybody.

Christine took a book of matches out of her purse. A waiter at Joy Young Chinese Restaurant had given her the matchbook. Christine had been impressed with him till he said, "How *could* I guess you had three—skinny woman like you?" She struck a match on the cover, opened the oven door, and held the flame to the pilot light. A swoosh of purple and red ran around the inert burner. "Get some foil out of the used, please, Diane."

Her little daughter slid from her place, opened the drawer in the cook table, and got out a foil sheet, crinkly with prior usage.

"Now put the biscuits on that, and I sprinkle in a little water before you close it up."

"I want to sprinkle," Diane answered.

"You might do too much. Make 'em soggy."

Christine glanced at her sister to try to invite her to talk, but Dee sipped her beer. Why didn't Dee manage to say something? Not even "Good evening." You didn't have to get off your fanny to *speak*.

Christine crossed to the sink, turned on the faucet, and wetted just the tips of her fingers; then she slung the water droplets into the foil nest of biscuits. "Close up the foil," she told Diane, "and you can put 'em in the oven." Her daughter moved purposefully, with confidence, to obey her mother.

Christine pulled a ladder-back chair out from the table and sat down across from her sister. "How you feeling, Dee?"

"I all right."

To make her sister speak again, Christine offered no reply.

Eventually Dee asked, "How you tonight, Eee?"

Something in her tone undermined the polite question, but she'd said Eee. Dee and Eee—that was their old language for each other. Eee for the last part of *Christine*.

"I drew a picture," Honey said. Her youngest, only three. His name was Henry, but he was the color of honey, and she called him that.

He showed her a tan paper sack marked with a patch of random black lines leading in all directions.

"That's good," Christine said. She put her arm around her little boy. "What you draw, Honey?"

"Blowed-up house."

Christine stared at the black lines. Planks. Lumber exploding.

"We heard it," Dee said. "Over on Dynamite Hill, I reckon."

Like a small adult, little Diane turned from the oven. "I told her, it was just the steel mill."

Christine reached out for her daughter. "That's right," she said. "Not every boom an explosion happening. Might of been a car, backfiring."

"Huh!" Dee said. She looked at Christine through half-closed eyes. Dee reached up and unclamped her barrette. Smoothed her hair straight up like a rooster tuft and clamped it again. "Reckon I'll go on, now you got home, Eee." Christine's own hair was straightened and oiled. Parted on one side, it fell in a beautiful stiff swoop, a pageboy just short of her chin. She tended it carefully.

"You don't have to go so soon," Christine said. "Stay and have a hot biscuit." Suddenly she didn't want to be alone with her children.

"Ain't hungry."

ENGAGED

THEIR FEET RESTING ON THE GRASS BEYOND THE EDGE OF their towel, Stella and Darl sat close together, kissing each other on the cheek, the neck, the lips, turning their bodies more and more inward with each address. She had forgotten the discomfort of sitting on sticks in the grass.

"Let's get up a minute," Darl said and started to stand. Stella got up but she was sorry that he had disrupted what she was enjoying so much. His voice was tight.

They stood, and he shook out the towel, repositioned it so that it lay lengthwise with the slope of the hill. "Now," he said, "let's lie down." When they were lying on their sides, their faces ten inches apart, he asked, "Do you like it here?"

"It's wonderful," she said and felt shaky, like froth, like a pink soda was inside her.

She reached out her hand toward his shoulder, and instantly their bodies clamped together. His hands were all over her back, holding her close, but he only kissed her, over and over, his clothed body straining against hers till they were panting as they kissed.

Suddenly he rolled away from her, onto his back, gazed up at the moon.

"Why is this kind of moon called *gibbous*," he asked in a low, intimate voice almost a whisper. Such intense trust in his voice, asking something he actually wanted to know, trusting her to be able to tell him. But who was he, and what did she know about him? How different were people who grew up in Norwood from those in the West End?

She replied softly, "Because its back is hunched, curved like a gibbon, an ape." She listened to her lips come together and part as she spoke. Sweet little sounds in the still, magnolia air. Like the extra sounds her fingers made on the fingerboard when she played the cello. She had ridden the cello through high school. In college, she'd wanted a new adventure.

She propped up on one elbow, looked down at Darl's beautiful moonlit face. His freckles were so close together, just a freckle-breadth of white skin between each dot. Then she saw a movement beyond him, on the other side of the dark magnolia. The sound of moving feet was so slight that she wouldn't have noticed had she not seen the movement.

Feet as quiet as fingers scurrying up the fingerboard, but human feet had moved. The sound of a slight scuffling. Someone crouched now under the skirt of dropping magnolia branches.

She reconstructed the sounds, retrospectively. Feet had brushed quickly over the tops of grass blades. A man had ducked under the skirt of the magnolia, had stopped still upon seeing them, was squatting there now. Waiting. Yes, that was what she must have seen—all of it so quick and quiet, barely lit by the moon, it seemed almost not to have happened. Now the dark man must be quieting his breathing, after running.

Stella leaned over Darl's face, as though to kiss him, but her lips went to his ear.

"There's somebody hiding under the magnolia tree behind you."

"What?" Darl said, quietly, and began to raise himself on his elbow. How she admired his poise, the forced languor of his movements.

Then she saw a group of colored men coming up the slope. "Yes," she said, and stood up. She spoke in a normal voice, "There they are." And Darl quickly stood up.

The group of four stopped still, surprised to see them.

"Good evening," Darl said formally, a formal dignity, neutrality, in his voice.

"Y'all taking a walk out here?" one of them asked, just an edge of assertiveness in his voice.

"Yes," Darl said. "We like to come here sometime." His voice was without emotion, flat, conveying information without affect or clue as to who they were. They might have been monuments, shrubs. Something just there. Like the blank towel, abandoned and silly on the grass.

"That your scooter parked out by the gate?" another asked.

They were big; young men really, not boys. Though she was fleet, if she ran they could probably catch her. She said nothing. Stood ready to try to outrun them.

"Did the cops get the bike?" Darl answered, and she knew he was trying to create a mutual enemy.

"Naw, it still there," one said.

The young men were constantly moving, restless. She and Darl stood very still. One of them nervously took a pack of cigarettes from his breast pocket.

Another said, "Hey, you got a quarter or something?"

Without speaking, Darl slowly reached in his trousers and then held out a coin at arm's length. He made no comment.

Better not to comment, Stella thought.

Then Darl took a pack of Camels from his pocket. Slowly he withdrew a cigarette for himself. "Got a light?" he asked evenly, his eyes fixed on the man who took the coin.

One of them, not that one, tossed him a lighter, which Darl snapped from the air with a quick downward pounce. He thumbed the wheel, looked down, and slowly leaned into the light. The little flame showed his brow pulled together, concentrating, dragging on the cigarette.

"Mind we have a smoke?" one asked.

He held out the lighter and his pack to them.

When they were all smoking, all but Stella, one of them asked, "Y'all see anybody come through here?"

Stella could still see the lone man crouching within the darkness of the tree.

"No," Darl answered.

"You ain't seen nobody run by?"

Darl just shook his head. He was handling everything just right. Calm, dignified. No bluster.

"We looking for somebody. Somebody who don't know how to share."

Darl said nothing for a moment. He drew on the cigarette again, kept it in his lips. Then he said, "I think we'll go on now," the cigarette tip wagging while he spoke. He reached down to pick up the towel. As he bent, his eyes no longer held theirs.

He was saving them. He was managing it. For the rest of her life, Stella knew she would remember and respect his savvy, his courage.

"She your fiancée?"

Stella was surprised to hear the black man use the French word so effortlessly.

"Yes," Darl said. Now his gaze into the other man's eyes was unflinching.

Stella knew he meant *"I'll fight."*

Darl reached out his hand for her, touched her bare arm. "Let's go on," he said quietly and initiated their steps away from the group.

It was hard for Stella to make her foot reach out the first time. She had tried to become a tree. It was as though she were stuck in the moment, and it was hard to step out of the definition of danger.

Her foot and leg *must* step forward, this second.

That was her part.

She had to move.

And the second step was easier. Then another, and she'd learned to walk again.

Darl steered them down the hill, toward the perimeter. He didn't look back, but they walked quickly.

After a distance, Stella's throat opened and she said, "I did see a man go up under the tree."

"That's who they wanted," he said. "Some sort of vendetta."

"Why didn't you tell?"

"It wouldn't be lucky," he said. "You don't betray somebody else in trouble to try to save yourself."

Now she knew she did love him. Admiration and gratitude collided in her heart and scattered throughout her body. From the soles of her feet to the crown of her hair, her nerves tingled with the fallout. But what was *luck*? And how had it played in her life? She'd never believed in luck of any sort.

They moved through the cemetery, past the plentitude of oaks—the cedars, the holly trees—every tree and monument seemed outlined with a special vividness. Stella's heartbeat echoed through the canals of her ears; all other sounds were faint and distant. "Everything looks so *distinct*," she said, but she couldn't hear herself well.

Her heart beat hard against all the edges she was seeing and made them pulse.

Darl said nothing, or was his voice muted by her heartbeats? Time between utterances was stretching. Finally she heard him say, as though his voice came through space from a great distance, "There's the wall up ahead. Then we'll be safe, when we reach the wall."

Then it was, Stella knew their lives could have ended. Yet the gang—they weren't fully men—hadn't been hunting for them. They had been startled to find them on the grass, lying on the towel, beside the specimen magnolia. Vulnerable. And suppose they had decided to rape her?

Darl would have fought.

We'll be safe, he'd said, but now she imagined the violence that hadn't occurred: fighting—her running away, someone catching up, right behind her, reaching out for her arm, her own screams. Kicking. Forced down. Sobbing. Darl might have been killed. First. It hadn't happened. Then her. Afterward. Events that disappeared into a slit of potential time. Disappeared forever.

Maybe she had manufactured the threat. *Got a quarter?*

Not the same as rape.

She your fiancée?

Again, she pictured the group of four staring at her. Wondering about her. She wanted to run—now!—past the ghostly white monuments, past the dogwood trees, the monuments like obelisks; instead, she made herself listen for delayed pursuit as hard as she could. She tried to hear if there *was* pursuit, if the men were coming after her.

"Don't run," Darl instructed.

She heard herself gasp, no words. Now that she had imagined it, every instinct was to run. No, the bush ahead was a crape myrtle, not a man.

"There's the wall," he said. "See, just ahead. Beyond the holly trees."

Safety, safety. They closed the distance between themselves and the dark stone wall stretching far out on both sides, demarcating what was the forbidden world of the dead from the normality of living. *Home free!*

They pushed through the sharp leaves, sat on the wall, dank with humidity, and swung their legs over. Like that, they were outside, safe on the sidewalk. There was the Vespa. With a deft movement, Darl wadded up the towel and stuffed it into the metal side compartment. She mounted her place on the passenger cushion. The key was turning, the motor was beginning to respond with its soft series of putts. He switched on the headlight, lifted his feet, released the clutch, and they began to glide away. She clamped her hands against his sides, could feel the precious warmth of his body coming through his shirt.

Darl turned his face to speak to her. "So we're engaged," he said cheerfully.

She leaned an inch forward and kissed the back of his neck. Very chastely. Maybe he was joking. Maybe he meant it.

FRED SHUTTLESWORTH

AT HOLY FAMILY HOSPITAL, AS THE REVEREND MR. SHUT-
tlesworth woke up to the midmorning sunshine, not just his ribs but his
whole body screamed pain. He remembered the flash of brass knuckles, the
swing of a big-link, rusty chain—no, that was in front of Phillips High School,
1957. Six years ago. He'd survived that, survived this. Water hose pounding like
a hammer. Now was now. Phillips was the seed, Kelly Ingram Park was the
blossom.

It wasn't his body. It was his brain burning. He knew what was happening
over at the Gaston Motel right now. Without him. He knew what was happening: King was negotiating without him.

King's inner group would be gathered around the magic one, advising him.
The disciples anxious, insistent. King calm in the middle, listening. Synthesiz-
ing. Yes, surely King was becoming anxious about his sojourn in Birmingham.
Rock throwing would give nonviolence a bad name.

Although Shuttlesworth groaned in bed, he knew he needed to be in King's
group. He needed to help. He needed to explain: it wasn't his nonviolence-
trained people picking up bricks, throwing bottles. Fred Shuttlesworth knew
that. Wasn't them. Wasn't kids he or James Bevel had trained. It was bystanders.
Folks who never went to church. Folks who had no concept of how to win.
Folks who needed nonviolence explained to them.

Shuttlesworth tried to sit up in his hospital bed. He knew the way it was
going over at the motel without him being there: King wouldn't risk more violence, which might be perceived by the national press as emanating from

demonstrators. Wouldn't want his name besmirched in history. No, King would negotiate. And nothing accomplished.

Not for Birmingham.

"No need for rocks and sticks." That's what Shuttlesworth would preach next to the people. " 'Put on the full armor of God!' " His own body was living proof. He was alive. They tried to kill him on Christmas, 1956, bomb thrown under his own house, under the spot where his bed was, him in pajamas, and he walked out, a song of praise on his lips. Surely King remembered that. It was a part of history.

King was a great man but he had a bad habit. He ought to consult with people before he made his reconciliation statements. What had they got for Birmingham?

King might be General Eisenhower, removed at his high post, but Fred Shuttlesworth was an action man, like General Patton. Fred Shuttlesworth was the one among the troops.

He had to get out of this hospital. His ribs wasn't broke. No more hypo sedatives for him. King over there at the Gaston Motel talking long-distance on the phone with the president of the United States or his brother. While him fuming in the hospital. Had he been yelling? There were the doctors, the nurses.

The doctor told his wife he might calm down better if he was closer to the action. *Course King wanted to back out—Mr. Nonviolent Leader. Yes, that would be his name in history. Mustn't besmirch himself with violence. Those folks on the sidelines, they didn't know nonviolence nor King.* "They know Fred Shuttlesworth," he tried to explain.

Hadn't any water hose been turned on King yesterday. Hadn't any chains or brass-knuckles mob beat King in front of Phillips High School. Well, in the past King had been beaten. They *had* blowed up King's home. But he, Fred Shuttlesworth, wouldn't *be* beat. Not in the long run. Couldn't nothing keep him down. *Victory through love,* he'd tell those violent types: *Call on the Lord. Call on the right hand of God Almighty, and he will not desert you.*

"Ruby! Ruby!" He held out his hand to his wife. "Roll the stone from the door. I'm coming out."

WANTING BACH

FROM OAK HILL CEMETERY TO STELLA'S HOME ON THE EDGE
of Norwood with her aging aunts, Darl thanked God. He thanked him for
sparing them, for sparing him a fight with four men who doubtlessly carried
knives.

As his grateful hands steered the Vespa, Stella's hands pressed hard against
his sides. *Press harder,* he wanted to say. *We're real.* He wished he didn't have to
take her home. He wanted to hug her close, sweet Stella. Horrible thrills swept
over him again and again, even as he prayed. Had the astonishing appearance
of the four men been a warning from God?

He wanted to be married; that was the proper refuge from lust and danger:
an apartment, just an apartment, with privacy and a welcoming bed. He knew
what his parents had—the way his father touched his mother's red hair, her
answering glance. He wanted that gratification for himself. At his age, his parents had been married several years, right out of high school. At his age, his
dad had already fathered a child: Darl himself had been born from their
teenage passion. But his dad had advised him to go to college, to get his education. Well, he would graduate soon.

He steered the Vespa up the rock and clay driveway that separated Stella's
aunts' home from the one next door, where Stella's family had lived before the
fatal wreck. From inside the aunts' house, a dog began to bark in hoarse
pulses. At the back gate—a tall wooden structure built by hand but
unpainted—he stopped the scooter to let her off.

"Wait," he said, "kiss me."

She turned back and kissed him chastely on the lips. Her lovely blond hair swung forward, and he gently pushed it back, like lifting back a shining curtain.

"You would have fought," she asked, "wouldn't you?"

"There were too many," he said. Really he didn't want to be anybody's hero.

"But you would have tried," she insisted.

He laughed. "I'd rather talk than fight."

"So would I," she said, and he felt glad.

"So we're engaged?" he said.

She kissed him again while he sat astride the scooter, its motor putting away, the dog barking intermittently from inside the house.

"Why not?" she said lightly and turned to take off the high rope loop that held the gate closed against the gatepost.

HE LET THE VESPA move down the driveway. *Wait! Take me to hear you play:* had she called that out to him? Too late, he was putting away, putting down the red clay trough of driveway between high banks. Quickly, he glanced back. The kitchen door was standing open, and in the spilled light, Stella bent to pet a white dog. In the wash of light, her blond hair hung over the dog's white fur. She might be an orphan, he thought, but Stella had a good home; she'd only had to move across the driveway to a house the mirror image of her own when her parents and brothers died in the wreck.

Into one bank, on the left, someone had cut a tiny Pueblo settlement, with square houses smaller than his hand perched at different levels. He wondered if Stella had constructed the mud village in the bank. Had she called out for him to wait? *Take me. . . . Take me. To hear you play.* Again he glanced back, then intuitively registered his driving position and centered the scooter to avoid the bank of iris foliage on his right. Perhaps Stella's mother had tended those irises, more than fifteen years ago.

Irises needed a slope for drainage. He sped the Vespa toward the street. When he got home, he'd say to his father, "Let's build a hill for Mom's irises." Mom would stand between them, an appreciative hand on each of their shoulders, her red hair bubbling wildly.

But Darl could not drive home now. He was too tense; he would pace around, and his mother would ask him what was wrong.

73

He needed to practice. The demon to make music was upon him. He would go to the church—he always had a key in his pocket—to practice on the grand old organ. It was Bach he wanted. When his hands and his feet were both engaged in their multiple keyboards, the music swallowed him. It let him in. The earth convulsed—he thought of Persephone's descent—and he seemed to fall through the deep pedal notes into a dark sensuality with all the contradictory glory of heaven.

Merely anticipating his time at the organ shook him.

He wished that Stella had not abandoned the cello. It would have been an anchor for her. She wanted to float free—he could tell that about her. On Vulcan, he could tell how the volumes of air tempted her, and he had put his arm around her. Not to restrain her but for warmth, he had pretended. It had made him nervous to stand on that height with her. There was something extravagant about Stella—all or nothing.

He drove along the narrow asphalt beside Norwood Boulevard where sometimes they strolled innocently in the dark. Once he had taken another girl walking on the boulevard to see if it had felt different. Was it Stella he wanted, or just somebody? A block wide, the grassy boulevard ran the crest of a hill, high above the streets on each side. Still, the median lacked the privacy for more than kissing.

His mother had told him, in a confidential manner, that chaste girls wanted a long courtship. In opposition to her words, his father's body, when he was near his mother, advised bold possession. It embarrassed Darl that his parents—only nineteen years older than himself—tried to school him about his love life. They would be surprised he was engaged.

Once he had taken Stella to attend church with his parents. After church, they'd gone out to Britling's cafeteria for Sunday dinner. All of them had driven her home and had an awkward introduction to the aunts. He saw right away that Stella's bond was more to her crippled aunt, Aunt Pratt, than to Aunt Krit, who taught high school math. Afterward, his mother had said of Stella, "They're awful skinny in that house," and his father had said, "Aw, you can fatten her up. She's sweet," and his mother had added, "She eats like a bird."

From the backseat of the car, Darl had explained to his mother that the expression wasn't apt. In proportion to their own sizes, birds actually ate a great deal. He thought his mother was afraid of Stella because she was a serious student and would soon be a college graduate.

His mother replied, "Reach up and massage my neck, Darling. I've got a crick in it." To Darl's relief, his father had taken his hand off the steering wheel to rub her neck. Darl felt like a child riding in the backseat, with no woman of his own.

The Vespa motor clucked as he rode through the city streets. Downtown was mostly deserted, but well patrolled by police cars. They paid no attention to him on the scooter; he was white.

A soft light was glowing through the stained glass of the church. Very faintly, he heard organ music, but it was so soft and spotty that he couldn't tell who the composer was. Buxtehude? Pachelbel? Something pre-Bach, with echoes of the medieval.

Several of Mrs. Carr's trusted students had keys to her church, but few came late at night.

Mrs. Carr. Beloved and elderly. Sometimes he felt like her spiritual son, or grandson. Years ago, she had gotten married and her new husband had drowned on their honeymoon. She had never remarried. How straight and tall she stood, whenever she was introduced. "Yes," she would say, "I'm Mrs. Carr."

Darl felt sure he would not drown on his honeymoon. He imagined Stella's head on a white pillowcase, looking up at him trustingly.

The mellow light inside the church beckoned him. He loved the mystery of this large stone church and its gorgeous stained glass. He would have become a member, but that would have hurt his parents, who were loyal to their own plain church of another denomination.

Since he was a small boy, Darl had believed the safest place in the world was standing between his parents, the hymnal held low, one of their hands on each side spreading the pages. After his mother noticed his confident soprano, even as a child, he had been sent to sing in the adult choir. All his music was rooted in his love for his parents and in the sacred. When he stood with the choir, he sang straight to his parents, imagined himself still standing between them. He resigned from the choir when he graduated from high school and became the youth director.

On their church date, Darl and Stella had shared a hymnal; she stood between him and his father. Darl knew his mother had resented being on the end of their configuration instead of between her men.

Several times, when he came late at night to practice, Darl had heard someone else at the organ. When he went inside, the lights would be burning dimly, but the musician had always fled. Though no girl should be in the sanctuary alone at night, he always assumed the elusive visitor was a young woman, someone as ethereal as Stella. He thought of her as even thinner, with a transparency about her. He sometimes fantasized it was the spirit of the girl he would marry.

But now he was engaged to Stella. He parked the scooter in the vacant parking lot. How did the other organist come and go? Maybe the invisible musician was his genie, his anima.

To his surprise, the basement door was unlocked. When Darl stepped quietly inside, he heard the progress of someone practicing footwork. A Bach toccata and fugue. The low pedal notes sounded fuzzy and muted. His own feet longed to engage the big pedals, to step down hard and then make the music swell like an enormous earthly mushroom under his shoe sole. She must have heard him enter; the pedal work ceased. He fancied he heard footfalls retreating down the aisle, barely audible in the plushy, wine-colored carpet. Someone shod in velvet.

KING

WHEN FRED SHUTTLESWORTH ARRIVED, KING AND ABER-
nathy weren't at the Gaston Motel, and Shuttlesworth had to admit to himself
how exhausted he was. His sedated body could barely walk. It was only eleven
o'clock in the morning, but he had to climb into the Gaston Motel *bed* for a
moment, rest a bit. He hardly had the strength to draw up his legs onto the
bed, and as soon as he lay down, Andy Young was saying they wanted *him* to go
over to John Drew's house.

They ought to come to him.

But King was the magnet, pulling him off the bed.

TRAVELING IN THE CAR wore him out more. When Shuttlesworth
arrived, he had to lean on his wife to get into the room. They looked at him as
though he was a ghost rose from the dead.

(Why hadn't they come to the hospital to visit him? Jesus had said, "I was
sick and ye visited me." Even Jesus knew how humans longed for human comfort. Not to be *all* alone.)

There was Burke Marshall, white man sent down from Washington. Assis-
tant attorney general, next in power to RFK.

From the time when he, Shuttlesworth, first invited King to come to Birmingham, Fred Shuttlesworth had known what King wanted—to regain his
leadership after Albany, Georgia. Too few folks willing to protest in Albany.

Too reasonable a police chief. No Bull Connor in Albany foaming at the mouth like a mad dog.

Surely it was farther away than just across the room that Fred saw his friends now. Felt like he was only creeping toward them, way over there 'cross the room. Felt like his bones were trying to explain it all to them, but really he was just concentrating to make his bones move. Focusing on covering the distance. There was King, looking defeated.

Maybe King was finally realizing, now when it was too late, that Albany *couldn't have* worked for him. Trial and error. Wasn't any blueprint to tell how to do what they were trying to do in the South. *For the South.* You had to learn what made the time ripe for victory. *For the country.* In Albany, Georgia, nobody had done the groundwork good enough, as he, Shuttlesworth, had done in Birmingham, so that enough people would join in the protests.

Yes, now King had got Washington's attention, through Birmingham. King was standing on the ground Shuttlesworth had prepared for him. When Shuttlesworth made it across the room, he would tell him, quietly: *No need to be dejected.*

No need because your John the Baptist has prepared the way. Alabama is tilled soil. Seed been dropped and watered. Take the harvest! Take the harvest, man!

King might be national now, but while Shuttlesworth was walking slowly toward him, holding on to Ruby, King was staring out past the well-to-do antique silk curtains as though he, King, didn't want to look the local working-class leader in the eye.

King ought to work on that, Shuttlesworth thought, look any man white or black, anytime, square in the eye. And so what was it about King that was so compelling?

I got to make it to the chair 'fore I collapse.

One foot in front of the other. Oh, he knew. One foot in front . . . He might grumble about King's style, pick at him, but Fred Shuttlesworth knew there wasn't anything he wouldn't forgive the man. He loved the man—that was what he needed to tell him. Needed to give him love.

King was speaking to him, but what was Shuttlesworth hearing? What was King saying to him: "Fred, we got to call off the demonstrations."

No, Fred thought, *I must have heard wrong.* He felt woozy in the head, his ribs hurt, the medicine confused him. But Martin couldn't have said what he thought he heard.

"Say that again, Martin?"

And King said it again, that the white merchants couldn't negotiate in the middle of demonstrations. The leadership in the black community had to call off the demonstrations.

Now Shuttlesworth's heart leapt in him. Now fury rose like a volcano. "You can't call them off because you ain't called nothing *on*."

He wanted to sound more reasonable, but King was going to throw it all away, throw away all Shuttlesworth's years of work and pain. Shuttlesworth tried to slow down, just remind King who was the *invited* party here, but the words boiled out: "And you and I promised that we would not stop demonstrating until we *had* the victory." (But he knew King was the Man of the Hour. The way Burke Marshall looked at Martin Luther King Jr. was enough to say that.)

Bitter, Shuttlesworth tried to get up from his chair. Yes, now he was sitting in a chair. "If you want to go against our promise, Martin, you go ahead and do it." Now he'd got his control back in his voice. "But I will *not* call it off. And if you do call it off"—his battered, sedated, weary body pleaded with him, but he ignored it—"I'm gonna lead the last demonstration with what little last ounce of strength I got."

But Fred Shuttlesworth couldn't get up. He fell back in his chair. Here was Abernathy. Here was his old friend Ralph Abernathy, kneeling down to talk to him, voice so soothing. "Fred, we went to school together. We can talk. Can't I talk with you, Fred?"

"Ralph, get up off your damn knees."

But somebody was talking about a press conference, an imminent press conference, and *that* couldn't be right either: "Oh, you've called a press conference, did you?" Shuttlesworth accused, collapsed as he was in his chair. They'd have to say this about him: Shuttlesworth was plainspoken; he'd said all of it right to King's downcast face. History would say that.

But Martin was suffering.

Shuttlesworth could see the strain in Martin: Martin wanted to lead, still he also wanted to cooperate, be part of a democratic group. But leadership was more important than fellowship or cooperation, finally.

He, Shuttlesworth, had to corner King. The truth had to be said: "I thought we were always going to make joint statements." His voice was firm, penetrant as ever, accusing (they would have to remember that, Abernathy, Burke, Drew,

Young, wife Ruby—but he couldn't even lift a finger to point. The arm of the expensive chair would have to remember that; a chair belonging to John Drew would have to remember how the exhausted hand had lain on the upholstery, the finger outstretched to accuse, but unlifted.)

King's face went stoic. He had to endure what had to be said.

"You go ahead with your press conference," Shuttlesworth said. "Go ahead, Mr. Big. I'm going home, get in bed."

While he strove to get his feet under him, to push out of the chair, there was sudden telephone talk with Washington. They must have had a hot line, these national ones. They were telling Washington, "We hit a snag. . . . The frail one is hanging things up."

Frail? You can't be frail with the power of truth, bitter as gall, red-hot as molten iron, rolling through your body.

"Burke," King pleaded, "we just got to have unity." King said it because *he* knew it was true.

(Oh, King's voice, the tremor in it: no angel could speak more sincere. Not angry. King was accepting the pain. Knowing his flaws, but seeing the light. Leading the way. No doubt King was the most chosen of God, was given the soul and special moral character that made his voice vibrant with humility, made you *revere* his leadership, even if you thought he was buckling under. A great soul was in that voice.)

Burke Marshall, down from Washington, D.C., took the cue. He said, "Don't worry, Fred, they're going to agree to what you say."

Uh! Shuttlesworth struggled upright, walked through that nice house.

Ruby was beside him, helping him to the car. His own children, his wife, would stand with him. He knew national coverage wasn't enough. Might be enough for King, but not enough for him, or those who'd endured with him for seven years through beatings, arrests, bombings. His church bombed three times. He'd talk to the youth; he'd talk to the hard-core activists. Maybe he'd telephone that white girl, Marti Turnipseed. Minister's daughter. She wouldn't back down.

THE TELEPHONE, THE MICROPHONE

FOR TWO DAYS, SHUTTLESWORTH URGED PEOPLE NOT TO
quit, raised a lot of spirits, but King announced a moratorium on the protests.
The local folks heard it on national TV. King didn't say the demonstrations
were called off permanently. *Moratorium* was a compromise with the city *and,*
King added quietly in his national voice, a compromise with the more urgent
demands of some increasingly impatient Negroes.

WITH ALL THE TIME spent in jails, hospitals, and the Gaston Motel,
Shuttlesworth had three more places as familiar to him as home.

On Friday, while he was again at the Gaston Motel, Shuttlesworth learned
the value of compromising with the vast majority of white folks: next to nothing. He couldn't believe what he was seeing on motel TV: King and his inner
group surrounded by police, going off to jail.

After the compromise, after the moratorium compromise King had wanted
to give and had given the white merchants, after that, there was still Bull Connor, their henchman, running the police. Shuttlesworth found out for sure
what he'd already suspected: it didn't matter what King and the president's
man said about negotiation and signs of good faith. The locals had the power,
for better or for worse.

Why didn't the federal government help more? But of course that was part
of King's plan—draw in the federal government.

Bull Connor arresting King, Abernathy—it was there in black and white on

TV—and two dozen more were arrested and jailed for having "paraded" without a permit. Bull had a place for King in the Birmingham jail.

"I'm putting on my marching shoes," Shuttlesworth told Andrew Young, and Andy didn't know what to say and didn't have any time to say it in because Shuttlesworth was almost out the door of the motel owned and named for black Birmingham millionaire A. G. Gaston.

"Moratorium's over," Shuttlesworth said again.

So Andy grabbed him, resorted to physical restraint as best he could, and somebody else phoned up Washington, D.C., fast as he could.

It was words, not Andy Young, that stopped a renewed Shuttlesworth in his tracks: "The attorney general would like to speak with you, Reverend Shuttlesworth."

And yes, it was Bobby Kennedy. And yes, Kennedy did listen, and yes, Shuttlesworth listened, too. He could understand better now how it was when you talked to Washington. You pressed the telephone against your ear till it hurt. There was an awe to it all. Not one word of that listening could be lost.

RFK explained: *Bull Connor wanted there to be protests. He arrested King in order to provoke the Negroes. He wanted the blacks not to trust the whites. Connor wanted there to be riots. Then Bull would have an excuse for violence. Wallace would get in the act. Governor Wallace would send in Al Lingo and the state troopers.*

When RFK spoke, it was the federal government talking to you. You sat up straight. You held the ballpoint pen tight in your hand, if you needed to write.

The whites didn't have any unity. The Birmingham merchants and lawyers were truly trying to make progress. Bull wanted them to seem untrustworthy.

You looked for whatever fiber in your being you had that could tie to the thread of Bobby Kennedy's voice. And he listened. Your ideas, too, could be conveyed now, over the telephone, woven into the fabric of Washington. You wanted to be in accord with the voice that was a Kennedy voice. Reasonable, strangely accented, but understandable. Firm voice. Here were ideas that— yes!—you could go along with that! Yes, you held that same ideal.

Of course.

Fred Shuttlesworth agreed to help make history as bloodless as possible. Certainly.

Would try his best to cooperate.

Not a long conversation at all, but he felt different now.

THROUGHOUT THE DAY, Shuttlesworth reviewed what he'd learned, asked himself if it really made any difference: *The merchants didn't run the police. You had to think of the city government and the business community separately. Bull Connor embarrassed the rich merchants and white lawyers; they hadn't invited him to the christening or compromise of whatever it was they had had with Communist-led Negroes. Yes, most southern whites thought the protests were Communist-led. They thought Birmingham-Southern College and Miles College were hotbeds of Communist activity. Naturally, Bull wouldn't keep the promises the merchants made, wouldn't acknowledge the compromise the Negro leaders so cautiously embraced. "The man is a hatemonger, Reverend Shuttlesworth, he doesn't understand the power of love. Don't let him trick you."* Had Bobby Kennedy said that, or was that Fred's own voice, wiser, himself teaching himself, not words from the telephone?

It was an important question. Shuttlesworth knew he was dead if he quit listening to his own voice, the one God sent him so he'd know what to do.

IT WAS A. G. GASTON, local owner of the Gaston Motel, the Gaston funeral parlor, and enough other enterprises with a black clientele to make his million the equal of any white man's million, who stepped forward with bail money. That being done, it would be Shuttlesworth's obligation to be forthcoming on his front. After A. G. Gaston bailed King out of jail, Shuttlesworth would need to say at their joint press conference (he had his local following; King would address the Negroes of the nation) that he still had hope that justice would come, despite the many betrayals, the broken promises down through the years, despite his good friend King's having been jailed. (Shuttlesworth walked toward the table, the press conference table.) He ought to plan to say that sort of thing, but he wanted to point out that the arrests had occurred "even after King had stopped the protesting, as he'd said he would do." (He walked toward the TV cameras, their long, thick cables snaking behind them on the floor.)

But it was hard for the Reverend Shuttlesworth to feel that he was telling his own story anymore. (He wouldn't say that into the microphone when it was his turn.) He wondered if he were telling King's story. King was there beside him, already speaking in his strange, calm voice. Almost neutral at times, King's voice. As though all people could come to his impartial voice and listen as equals. A voice that was not meant to make people mad; one that only wanted to console, inspire, reassure the frightened—black and white.

Shuttlesworth felt as though he himself had lost the sense of "I" as leading off a sentence such as "I am about to speak into this bouquet of microphones." He could feel the sweat running down his skin inside his clothes. Whose body? Whose voice? It was as though "he," Fred Shuttlesworth, was learning to recite a life "he" was living.

Maybe he knew this much was true: because the president's brother, the attorney general of the United States, had called long-distance telephone to talk with him, the Reverend Fred Shuttlesworth, he wanted to respond once again with hope. *I want to respond with hope*, he would say.

Before he spoke on the radio and the TV (he would be next, soon), he must reach deep in his heart to find a trusting response. (He knew he was scraping the bottom of the mayonnaise jar to bring up some small amount of faith.) But he wanted to believe the national government of his country, truly he did.

But he'd forgotten to tell Bobby Kennedy about the FBI! How they couldn't be trusted, how sometimes they made bargains with the Bull's police to allow so many minutes of beating before breaking things up. He'd forgotten!

"If there are demonstrations," Shuttlesworth said into the microphones, his shoulder almost touching King's shoulder (Lord, those lights were hot!), "they will be limited. We do believe that honest efforts to negotiate in good faith are under way."

RYDER JONES

RYDER JONES HAD HOPED TO SEE HIS BROTHER ON TV.
He'd had Bobby, his little son, stay up late, in hopes of seeing Uncle LeRoy.
Bull Connor had sent LeRoy's division downtown, and LeRoy claimed he'd
whacked plenty of niggers, but the camera just showed a stupid press conference with nigger ministers, and then replays of the dog-handler police and
droves of niggers singing "We Shall Overcome." *Over my dead body,* Ryder muttered, his jaw muscles so rigid they hurt. He kissed his son on his cheek and
sent him to bed.

He heard the snip of his wife's sewing scissors in the kitchen. He didn't
want to talk to Lee; he wanted to be alone, to think about the world and what
it was coming to. His feet took him to stand before his bedroom closet. He
took down his Klan robe on its hanger and made the robe flutter in the air like
a ghost. The way it rippled was noble, like a flag. *Over their dead body.*

That first time he had stepped out from behind a tree wearing his white
robe, he had relished the man's terror. When Smith had stepped out, and then
another, and another, each from behind a tree, it must have looked as though
they were passing through tree trunks. And Ryder himself had said slowly,
"Time to teach you a lesson, nigger. Think you can learn a lesson?" Then the
black fella saw the whips, the belts dangling from their hands and started to
run. But they were on him, dragged him to the cemetery to do it.

Alone in his bedroom, Ryder lifted his robe high over his head. He wig-
gled the coat hanger so the air would swivel the cloth. He twirled around in
fast circles, bumped his leg against the side of the bed. He wished he really

could fly. While he played with his robe, he hummed, "An old cowpoke went riding out, one dark and windy night." Ryder sang softly—he really loved that song, this part of it: "Ghost riders in the sky." He sang the song twice before he flew his robe back into the closet and sauntered back to the living room. Then he felt foolish. That was the way Bobby played, using a towel for Superman's cape.

TV was showing some jungle place; he turned it off. Black soldiers under netted helmets.

He heard Lee's scissors opening and closing. From a bolt of white cotton cloth she'd gotten on sale, she was cutting out robes on the cook table. She made gowns nice and full and stitched them sturdy—double seams. Starched and ironed them so a man would be proud to wear his robe. They gave them away—Christmas, birthday presents. But this was a rush order. He told her she could stay up till eleven-thirty working on them. All the uppity nigger trouble meant new Klan members. He had told Lee she had to do her part, had to finish up those robes.

No need to check on her. Ryder was back in their bedroom. Wasn't much place to go in the house, a rectangle divided into four parts. *Quadrants,* he remembered his high school math; he'd been good at it. Their bedroom was on the front and opened into the living room. The kitchen also opened into the living room, the three kids shared the smaller back bedroom that opened into the short hall to the kitchen. The bathroom had a window on the back of the house, and its plumbing backed up against the kitchen plumbing of course, and its door opened into the short hall. The two bedrooms were divided by two closets, one opening their way, one opening toward the kids. It was a neat house plan.

Here he was back in their bedroom. He glanced at the bedside Big Ben, on top of his stack of comic books, and saw it was 10:00 P.M. He had to be ready to pump gas by 6:00 A.M. No, tomorrow was Sunday. Rest. He was already tired because they'd called him in early to the filling station; somebody sick on Ryder's off-day. He was afraid not to go, afraid he'd lose his job. Some gas stations in white neighborhoods were letting the black window-washer boys start to pump gas. They'd do it for fifty cents an hour instead of sixty-five.

When they pumped, the colored boys took the money right out of white customers' hands.

Ryder went to the kitchen calendar on the closet door to be sure the next

day was Sunday. The calendar had a fine picture of the Grand Teton Mountains, Jackson, Wyoming, with snow on top and green grass in front. Yes, on
the wall calendar Saturday had a big *X* through it. First thing he did every
morning was cross out the day. Made it seem like it was over, with the work
already done. His spirit leapt ahead every morning after he x-ed out the day.
Then he didn't have to think about what he had to do. He just had to make his
body go on and do the work.

Snip-snip, nice little sound, steady but careful. You could hear anything all
over the house. She had her work; he had his. He went to the kitchen to watch.
Hi, he said softly. *Hi there,* she answered, but she didn't look up. She was
absorbed—clipping the inside of a curved seam. Her forehead was frowned
up. She ought to have looked up, been glad to see him. The points of the scissors were perpendicular to the machine stitches. *Perpendicular.* He'd always
liked that word, so long but easy to say. Learned it from his high school math
teacher. *Math,* that was a high school word, not *Arithmetic.* On his report card,
all spelled out: *Mathematics.* And then a big capital letter *A.*

GLORIA'S THOUGHT BOOK

IT'S BEEN A WEEK NOW SINCE THE DEMONSTRATIONS
ceased. But I do not want to write about that. I didn't participate.

I'm thinking about change more generally.

My challenge is shyness. My mother says she used to be shy, still is, but it
gets better in time. She said she chose an occupation where she didn't have to
meet the public; she chose to be an accountant. We're both short and full-
breasted. I'm probably shy like her, too.

But when I play the cello, I'm never shy. It's like a great big voice for me.
And it's like a shield for me, between me and the audience. The bow is my
magic wand, and the fingers of my left hand are like the four legs of a pony let
out to pasture, running along the fence.

I want a teacher who is worthy of me!

My hand is trembling. I cannot believe my boldness. On the typewriter I
can't let my thoughts out, only in handwriting, and I wrote that sentence
boldly, but now the writing is quavering. I will pretend this pen is my wand. It
lets my feelings out.

Last year, 1962, James Meredith became a student at the University of
Mississippi. What I would like is to become a student at the University of
Alabama, and to study cello with Margaret Christy. She was a student of Pablo
Casals. Then I would be a grandchild of Pablo Casals. Or go north to study
cello. Two people were killed when James Meredith integrated Ole Miss.

Once I heard Miss Christy play with the Alabama String Quartet in the
auditorium of the Liberty National Life Insurance Building. I have never seen

such a pretty auditorium; it had oak wooden paneling, and the lights were against the walls and shone upward along the grain of the wood. I was disguised as a maid. My Aunt Lil' Bit lent me her uniform. My mother went with me in Clarise's maid clothes. We took a long-handled dustpan and a broom and messed around in the lobby with a dust cloth.

That broom was my magic wand. Open sesame! Just after the lights went out, I slipped in and stood at the back of the auditorium. I got a program. Nobody noticed.

They opened with the addition of a pianist and played the Schubert "Trout" Quintet. I had never heard such joyful, playful music. When the cello is the trout, the music is droll. Floppy and leaping, perfectly fishlike. Standing there in the back, I started to cry. Mama took my hand and squeezed. It was so beautiful I wanted to shriek for joy and beautifulness. Like at country church. I *knew* I could play that music.

I love chamber music so much more than orchestral music. Every part stands out; every part is important. The weaving of the four voices! It's like my aunts singing quartet gospel music but infinitely more complex. It's what I need.

When the time is ripe, my parents will help me go where I need to go. I don't feel the time is ripe yet. I owe something here. I owe Christine and her student Charles Powers something because they stood up to the blast of the fire hoses till they were knocked down. I owe them for lying on the pavement, wet and hurt. I owe Lionel Parrish some work in the night school. I owe Rosa Parks and Jo Ann Robinson. Professor Robinson organized and helped run off 35,000 handbills: she launched the Montgomery bus boycott. At least I could turn the crank on a mimeograph machine. There's a seed in me, and it's starting to grow. Make a contribution, it says. Here in my own town.

That phrase "the time is ripe" is very important to me and my family. When I was a little girl and we still lived in the country, my daddy used to drink a lot. We lived with my grandparents, and he helped work the farm, but he never had any money. He couldn't buy anything. When he did get money, he'd go to the shack they called the tavern and buy shots of moonshine. One night he came home and hit my mother. I don't remember it. They've told me the story. Both of them. Then he passed out. The next morning when he woke up, he said, "The time is ripe." He apologized to my mother, and she forgave him. "Just once," she said. "Just this once I'll accept your apology." Then they decided they would both work, take correspondence courses, save everything, and move to Birmingham.

When he said "the time is ripe," he meant the time was ripe for him to change and take charge of his life. I want to be an independent woman doing work that she loves.

"Education is the key to the future." I wonder if they've told me that a million times.

RYDER'S SECOND HOUSE

TIME NOW FOR RYDER TO GO TO THE VACANT HOUSE IN Fountain Heights. Dynamite Bob might be there, might show him something new about bomb making. Ryder had the basics down pat, but the house itself scared him. Like a haunted house. Creepy when you were in there by yourself with all that dynamite. Big old house with rooms stacked around all over the place. Ryder thought about mad-scientist comic books—a mad scientist connecting wires.

WHILE HE DROVE THROUGH the neighborhood at night, Ryder checked the skin color of the people on the sidewalks. Made sure no niggers were out. Had he seen a black man, he would have done nothing. He was alone. But he would have felt his hate surge, rise up from his very balls.

Just a dim light shone from the shrouded basement window. Ryder whistled three times to give the signal. No answer. He opened the door with his key and clomped down the basement steps. Nobody was there.

He hated a deserted house. In the silence, he imagined screaming coming from the walls. Stupid somebody had left the light on over the workbench. A roll of fine electric line bounced light off its curve. Two boxes of dynamite sat, very still it seemed, beside the big spool. Five plastic fishing bobbers, red and white, lay in a row. It was easy to picture how Dracula might come busting through the window, right through the shade, if you were alone.

Ryder dipped his fingers into a small box and fished out a blasting cap. He knew a boy years ago who blew his hand off with a blasting cap he'd found on a construction site. Good-looking boy. That was long ago. The walls of the secret house rose up still and steep to the high old ceiling. He'd wanted to take solid geometry but they put him in Shop.

Beside the workbench, a sealed carton of little bedside clocks sat on the floor. Just to use his nervous hands, Ryder picked up the X-Acto knife and slit the brown-tape seal. All the clocks were neatly packed inside, still in their individual boxes.

Hadn't he been supposed to meet somebody here?

Ryder took a beige clock out of its little box; the small round face read three o'clock. When he wound it up, he found the clock had a quiet tick, almost just a clucking. Just for something to do, he twisted the scored stem on the back of the clock to twirl the hands around. He watched time fly. He wondered before the factory workers packed them up, had they set all the clocks at three o'clock?

He wouldn't mind to have such a neat little clock.

After Ryder squeezed the little circular clock headfirst into his jeans pocket, he closed its empty box and put it back in the shipping carton with the others. Somebody else would think, down the line, *Hey, one box is a dud. Like at the plant they forgot to fill one box and just packed it empty.* Since he'd cut the tape sealing the big carton, the top flaps didn't want to lie down, but Ryder lifted the roll of electric wire and used it to weight the flaps shut.

Close to the dynamite boxes, he moved his hands very carefully. Suddenly, the silent walls screamed as though somebody were being attacked in the empty house. The screams sounded like a rabbit, he decided, a brown rabbit with a white cottontail he'd snared as a boy.

Well, he'd better drive on back home, with his little clock ticking in his pocket. What time was it, really? He hoped he hadn't got the time mixed up. Lord, that would be bad. *You're almost too stupid to do this,* Bob said to him once. *Can't you tell time?*

Just remembering Bob's snide voice make Ryder cringe. Bob didn't talk like that to Blanton or Cherry. Hidden deep in Ryder's chest, a tiny spot about the size of a dime glowed with anger.

WASN'T ANY DOUBT who was in charge, once he was behind the wheel. Ryder was glad to be back in his car. Ryder guessed a man had to be mean like

Bob Chambliss to stand up for right the way Bob did. What with the way the world was going.

Car radio said the niggers had gone back on some of their demands.

Radio said King said he was calling off the demonstrations.

They were *negotiating*, like King was some kind of foreign power.

Ryder wanted to hurt somebody. Well, niggers *always* needed straightening out. Always had and always would. Police wouldn't touch him or Chambliss or any of them. Never had and never would. While he drove the car toward home, Ryder checked the face of anyone he saw on the sidewalk. *Better not be too many colored. Niggers always trying to take over.*

Ryder felt scared, but it wasn't the blacks. He could imagine a huge, elongated dark shape flying just over the treetops. It was like the shadow of Dracula had passed over the roof of his car. Ryder stepped on the gas.

AS HE ENTERED his kitchen, Ryder thought how the police were the one good thing about Birmingham. He measured himself a shot of Gentry's whiskey and sat at the kitchen table. The metal tabletop was bare and clean, wiped down. Ryder liked the delicate way the tabletop was covered with little scratches.

In Birmingham, the police were on your side. Not just LeRoy, his brother—all the police. He'd heard that Atlanta had started importing police from Chicago and New York City.

Saturday night at the kitchen table. Awful quiet. Not a sound in the house. He contemplated the little scratches all over the metal tabletop. The way his whiskey bottle sat there like a king.

LeRoy knew Bull.

Here it was, Saturday night, his bottle, his shot glass, and him. Peace and quiet. Nobody telling him to do nothing.

Hell, Bull used to *speak* at rallies. Used to stand on the hood of a car so everybody could see him. Hosts of white sheets, pointed hoods moved all mysterious in the woods. Three crosses, the big ten-foot one in the middle, wrapped in cloth soaked with gasoline. Somebody tossed a lighted match, and *whoosh*. Then two small whooshes. Ryder pitched another shot of whiskey into the back of his throat. Better than church, three crosses burning in the woods. The big one for Jesus. *With the Cross of Jesus going on before:* he loved that song.

The Klan's little kids' faces glowed with awe, the burning crosses teaching them. They were white, and what this was about was White Supremacy, right here, tonight, and forever. The glowing on their little faces reflected the flames of the burning crosses.

Sometimes Ryder pictured Evil flying high above the dark woods where the Klan was meeting, but it couldn't come down no matter what his power because they had crosses. The folks were gathered around burning crosses.

He wished he'd had something like Klan meetings when he was a kid. He never saw his dad stand up for anything. His dad didn't love the Bible, he didn't love the flag. All he loved was moonshine, till it killed him. Niggers could hold a job better than his dad, and he let the whole family sink down. Ryder wished he could have gone on being a Cub Scout. He'd saved pennies and bought himself the neckerchief. They'd let him wear just that around his throat, for a while, and then they said he had to get the whole uniform or drop out. That was when he first felt the burning dime, like it was inside his upper chest under the tails of his Scout neckerchief. He had a red-hot dime in his chest. It was a button he could press and rage like an atom bomb would explode.

From the bedroom, Ryder heard the sudden rackety of his wife's sewing machine commence. She was just starting up! That was why the house was so goddamned quiet. That wasn't right! Him gone only half an hour, and her quitting on him, going to bed. She must have slipped off to bed 'bout as soon as he went out. She'd took the cloth off the kitchen table and just sneaked off to bed. Didn't work on the new robes like she was supposed to. While he gathered his thoughts, Ryder stared at how the little scratches in the metal tabletop made a pattern of circles.

He'd better teach her.

Bob Chambliss sure taught his woman when she needed it. He'd say that for old Bob.

Relentlessly, Ryder crept up behind his wife. Oh, she heard him coming, pedaled the machine harder, faster. But nobody can make up for lost time.

"Too late, Lee," he said softly. "You oughta been sewing when I come home." His hand closed around the back of her neck. "Reckon you thought I wouldn't come back till midnight, didn't you?"

He lifted her up by the neck with his left hand; she rose partly on her own. Partly her rising up from the machine was her hypnotized obedience, not the strength of his arm. He turned her—her eyes were sleepy—smacked her cheek with his open hand. Why, she was already in her nightgown, probably snuck off to bed soon as he left the house.

"Don't, Ryder. I love you, Ryder," she pleaded. She was quiet about it so as not to upset him.

He threw her on her back onto the bed; her eyes were wide, her legs bent at the knees, feet on the floor. Her big eyes, silent, looked down her body at him, her mouth open just a little. He lifted the gown, pulled her panty leg wide. When he unzipped his jeans, he felt the bulge of the little stolen clock in the front pocket. Took less than two seconds to drop his trousers.

He liked to get her through the panty leg.

LEE

THE NEXT MORNING, LEE PUT HER MAKEUP ON EXTRA HEAVY so the bruise wouldn't show.

She had a new yellow spring dress to wear to church, and some panty hose, her first pair, which she lifted from the flat box with a simmer of anticipation. The hosiery seemed light as air in her hand. How could they survive the wearing?

Panty hose: two garments in one. Naked, she sat down on the dresser bench to pull on the hose. Up the fine mesh glided, past her ankles, calves, knees. Then she stood to stretch and tug the hose carefully to her waist. Now the panty hose covered her from toe to waist—she liked that. Compacting and constricting her flesh, their sheer power girdled her entire lower body. Across her thighs, the hose reflected the May morning sunlight with a fierce shine, in their effort to hold her.

Naked down to her waist, her breasts loose and soft, she bent her knees and took a few steps in her new panty hose. Almost like a pony, almost like prancing, first one, then the other, she lifted her knees, then placed her stockinged feet back on the floor. How clean and protected her feet felt against the uncarpeted boards. The panty hose covered her like another skin, protected her all the way up to the waistband.

Next came her brassiere. Cupping her breasts, the brassiere lifted her, held her breasts higher. Then her old slip, dingy, a disgrace. The box lid said they were *panty* hose, yet maybe she should take them off and put on some real panties underneath? But all that was hidden—who'd know? She lifted the new dress from the bed and let it slide down her body.

In that yellow dress—she fastened the narrow, matching belt on a tight notch—she looked like a canary bird and felt good enough to sing. She loved to sing at church. "Love lifted me. Love lifted even me." That phrase ("even me"), oh, she always put her singing soul into that. With more than her voice, she caressed the phrase, humbly and tenderly.

The sermon title would be "Be Ye Kind," and Ryder was going with her. Her mama was bringing her kids, who had spent the night over there. Be ye kind. Her mama had always been kind to her, even if Pa was something else. Her three would look so nice, and she wouldn't have had to get them ready. Bobby almost ten, getting big, his hair combed with water.

While she combed her own hair (she wished she *had* put on underpants first but she'd go ahead to church without them this time), Lee recited the rest of the verse, her favorite: "Be ye kind, one to another, tenderhearted, forgiving one another." That was her part, the forgiving—first Ryder, and way back, Pa. She could forgive just about anybody on a May morning with a new dress.

She did it wholeheartedly. She sat down at the dresser and put her little yellow hat on with the veil just coming over her forehead and eyes. At first she'd wished the veil was yellow, too, instead of black, but now her dark brown eyes appeared mysterious in the mirror as she looked out from the wide-spaced black netting of the veil.

The panty hose didn't like to bend for sitting. As she sat at the dresser she could feel the elastic at the waist dipping down in the back, slipping with the strain of encasing half her body. If they were going to do that at church, she might have to go in a bathroom stall and tug them up. The panty hose had come in the mail marked "Trial Sample" in a box so shallow it was hardly a box. And there had been a market survey sheet. They wanted her opinion!

She didn't like that little gaping at the small of her back—maybe she'd say that. But maybe then they would never send a sample again. She concentrated on positioning her yellow hat to just the right angle of tilt, toward the front.

Ryder stood behind her in the circle mirror and adjusted his tie. Like a big portrait picture: them in the mirror circle above the dresser. Could have been painted by Norman Rockwell on the cover of the *Saturday Evening Post*. Title:

"Almost Ready for Church." If Norman Rockwell did paint them, he wouldn't notice the bruise under the makeup. With her best smile, she looked up at her husband. He put his hand on her shoulder.

Ryder had fair hair, rather skimpy really, but his once-broken nose was always interesting to look at. His face was scrubbed pink, and he reminded Lee of a cowboy, with his nice high cheekbones. His eyes were a little narrow and slitty, though. And his teeth, yellow with smoke, were going, but they didn't show in the mirror picture.

"See," he said. "Done you good." And he turned and swaggered into the living room.

While she watched his back in the mirror, bitter bile rose from her stomach to her throat. He shouldn't of reminded her. Forget and forgive. You got to forget to forgive. He put a blight on a new day.

She made the ugly bile stop before it came into her mouth. Swallowed it down. The stomach fluid surprised her. Although it had never happened to her before, she recognized that vile fluid invading her throat.

This was her true feeling for her husband, and she knew it. When the mirror no longer held his image, she mouthed words. Not a sound:

"I hate you."

She liked to see her mouth working the words. How her lips and tongue shaped them. Her mouth started wide and got more narrow with each silent word: I hate you. She narrowed her eyes so they were slitty and mean.

She told herself more, just the shape of it, not even the quietest whisper: "I'll never hate *anybody* as much as I hate you." What a long, secret sentence he couldn't hear except for little pops of her lips. The pops were like code.

She reached for her compact, swiped the pressed powder with the puff, and gently applied more powder on her cheekbone.

LATER, IN CHURCH, when they were singing "Onward, Christian Soldiers," when she glanced at Ryder, she hated him again and added contempt to her hatred—the way he belted out the song like he owned it: "marching as to war."

Him? War? No. He just liked to ambush innocent niggers waiting for the bus and all his buddies with him. His rage at niggers controlled him. He didn't even run his own life.

Once he had said, *Only job a nigger's good for is wiping the street with his tongue, and then I wouldn't step on it.* And that was nothing but nasty talk. She knew it was nasty and there wasn't any need to be nasty that way.

Truth was, only person he dared to beat up by himself was his little wife— somebody *could* say that of him, and it would be true. Only person he dared to beat by himself was her.

" 'Rise up, O Men of God' "—she sang the new hymn just as loudly as he did. Pity was, that's what he believed about himself, that he was the right hand of God. " 'Have done with lesser things.' " He was just a lesser thing. She made her voice even louder than his, but still pretty, like she was singing to God himself.

What she wished for with all her might and knew could never never be: that she, Lee Jones, would have done with Ryder Jones. Someday.

Someday. Someday. Someday. Those words chimed like the bell of truth.

But that could never be. They belonged together.

Right in the middle of the song, she stopped singing. Her mouth was open, but no sound. A sigh slid right down the inside of her nose and out into the air.

MARTINI: CHRISTINE AND GLORIA

IN THEIR BOOTH AT THE ATHENS CAFE AND BAR, GLORIA said quietly to Christine, "Well, I missed out then, didn't I?"

"You might of missed out this spring. There'll be more."

Christine felt as though she would jump out of her skin if she didn't get some calming alcohol into her blood. Too much had happened. Too much done and too much not done. She wanted to storm into the streets, shout for people to turn out of their houses, march again. She'd even embrace the savage energy of the fire hose, let it spin her again.

Gloria sipped her 7UP. If she had anything with caffeine in it, then she couldn't get to sleep. She tilted her green eyes toward the ice in the glass and said in a low voice, "But Reverend King said it was a victory. Said it on national TV."

"You see any big change?" Christine's nerves jittered as though they wanted to play the bones. She could almost hear the sounds of bones clacking together in some artful hands.

"He said there was a committee—white store owners, A. G. Gaston—" Even to herself Gloria sounded pious and naive.

"While Shuttlesworth in the hospital, King just took over." Christine waved her hands over her drink, seemed to clear back the air. "King made a deal. Now he move on. Shuttlesworth try to tell him, 'Brother, don't just scald the hog on one side, you got to scald him on both sides.' "

Despite Christine's gestures and intense voice, Gloria was half listening to the jukebox playing Elvis: "Love me tender, love me true . . ." Gloria thought

Elvis was the *prettiest* white man she had ever seen a picture of. But why didn't anybody *say* he was pretty? The idea felt like her own secret observation, even though everybody had seen the same pictures.

"What I don't understand"—Gloria looked full in Christine's eyes. Yes, she could look somebody in the eyes if she started out about how *she didn't understand*. "Why King *want* to shut down?"

"He white-collar. Shuttlesworth blue-collar. That's the difference. Birmingham a stepping-stone for King. He fail in Georgia 'cause police play it smart and cool there. Wasn't nothing to put on national TV. Not no fire hoses and dogs. Not no Bull. King got to have his national coverage, and Bull Connor played right to him."

To Christine, Gloria's green-eyed stare meant she knew nothing at all about how the world worked. Gloria's innocence and ignorance mesmerized Christine. Just books, poetry—that was all good little Gloria understood.

Christine explained, "And King got to stop now 'cause Birmingham out of control and fighting back. Those guys on the sidelines? They ain't studying no nonviolence. Gandhi just some foreign nigger far as they care."

"King made everything work in Montgomery."

After Gloria uttered this undeniable fact, she waited to see how far it would take her. She felt that she'd dropped a stone down a well and was waiting for the splash.

"Let me tell you something," Christine began. "Montgomery ain't Birmingham. This steel town. Wasn't nothing here before the Civil War—Elyton Village, that's all. Birmingham grew up violent. Nothing plantation 'bout steel city. We more like Pittsburgh than Montgomery." Christine fished out her green olive and ate it. "And we so poor here. Black folks so desperate." But Christine knew that was inaccurate: very few were desperate for justice; most were afraid, worn down, cowed.

"Didn't we win something?" Gloria wondered how a martini would taste. "You want to come to Sixteenth Street with me some Sunday?"

"I might. Got to be at Bethel if Reverend Shuttlesworth preaching. You want to come with me?"

"Didn't we win something?" Gloria asked again.

"Yeah. Now educated, rich Negroes talking to rich white folks."

Gloria knew it was half true: they at Sixteenth Street weren't much involved with Shuttlesworth's organizing till King came to town. Sixteenth Street was the biggest and the richest of the black churches in Birmingham. Their class of colored wanted to negotiate. Here was the other half of what King had done: in the black community, he had smoothed over between those who wanted to wait and those who were already acting. Gloria's idea of victory contracted, became smaller, seemed more clear and hard-edged. Now well-off blacks were talking with working-class blacks.

In Gloria's wide-eyed silence, Christine heard the conclusion to her own thought. "Remember this," Christine added, the idea calming her better than gin as she articulated words: "This be about class—it not just about color." *And that class thing could scare Washington more than race,* she thought but did not say. *What if poor white was to realize they really in the same boat with poor black? They just fool themselves thinking they in the boat with rich white.*

Boldly, Gloria asked Christine, "How come you talk black when we in here?"

" 'Cause I'm home, and I mean what I say." Christine sipped her martini. Sometimes Christine thought she didn't half know what she was thinking till she heard herself saying it to Gloria. Nonetheless, mockery rose in Christine's throat. " 'Didn't we win?' you asking me." A mean energy surged in her arms and spine. "What you mean *we?* I didn't see any Gloria Miss Green Eyes marching, did I? I miss something?"

She wanted to hit Gloria, slap her hard, her and her cello, into reality.

AT FIELDING'S

"DO YOU KNOW HOW MANY PEOPLE WERE HURT, MISS SIL-ver, after these demonstrations?"

Mr. Fielding, the store owner, paused at Stella's switchboard desk. He spoke almost accusingly, as though she and the college students had caused the disruptions.

Actually, they'd done very little, and Stella felt ashamed. Only a few people, like Marti Turnipseed, had dared to align themselves with freedom. Tom somebody, too—very quiet, inoffensive-looking young man.

Many of the students thought Marti and Tom were freaks. Stella didn't. She made it a point to get close to them. To say hello. Pretty feeble on her part. But she was scared. She was doomed if she was kicked out of school. She had no future without school. Without a scholarship.

"Countless people beaten up." The store owner answered his own question. "Countless separate incidents of violence."

Stella wanted to please Mr. Fielding but she didn't know the right answer.

"They weren't directly in the demonstrations," he went on, alleviating her ignorance. "Four innocent colored people nearly beaten to death. People ought to be more upset. One was just a yard boy waiting for the bus. That's what came of demonstrations. Did you know that?"

"No, sir."

"Are people too upset out there to study? Classes going on smoothly?"

"Yes, sir."

They both stared down from the mezzanine at the customers on the first floor. The store wasn't crowded, but there was a smooth stream of people coming through the front doors. The women usually stopped at the lighted accessories counter, or at least glanced at it. The men went on. Stella liked to see young couples come in together. Mr. Fielding seemed like an eagle surveying his territory.

"This could be the beginning of revolution," Mr. Fielding went on with his musings. He needed somebody to listen. Why not the switchboard girl? "It could come to revolution," he told Stella again.

"It seems to be over. For now."

"People need to pray. People need to think about loving their fellow man."

"I agree," Stella said firmly. So that was where Mr. Fielding stood. It was hard to tell. He seemed angry. No, he was deeply worried. He cared about what was happening in his city. It wasn't just a business matter for him.

She cared, too. But what could she do besides smiling at Marti Turnipseed?

"You're going to graduate next year. Then what?"

Because his white hair swirled like cake frosting, Stella remembered her mother's words from long ago: *frost the sides of the cake first, then the top.* That was the sequence. Not advice she needed now; Aunt Krit made and allowed only plain cake in her house. No frosting. You could have a dish of canned peaches next to the cake.

Then what? Mr. Fielding had asked her.

Stella wished the switchboard would blink, the telephone would ring, and she'd have to answer it. That was her job, first and foremost.

"I don't know," she said. "Maybe go to graduate school. Get a master's degree." She thought, *He doesn't own me. He's been good to me, but he doesn't have a right to ask about my future. It's mine.*

"I see you're engaged."

"Yes, sir." A wave of nervousness swept over Stella. She could not think of her engagement without thinking of danger. *She your fiancée?*

"When's the wedding?"

"We don't know. We have another year of school."

From the balcony, she peered down through the glass top of the accessories counter on the main floor at a row of purses. Part of her job was to watch for shoplifters.

"That's right. You're smart to get your education. You've got a pretty little diamond there."

He surveyed his store. He didn't sell diamonds. The jewelry in accessories was set with rhinestones. He was glad not to be responsible for the quality of the diamond in Miss Silver's engagement ring.

In the shoe department Mr. Sole, a full head of gray hair, a gray mustache, was kneeling before another customer. Mr. Sole started at age twelve in the grocery department; he would have worked for the Fieldings for fifty years, come one more. Mr. Fielding intended to present him with a check for $1,000.

A thousand dollars, the phrase was hefty, had a certain thud to it. "To show appreciation," he would say, each word held tightly between his lips for fear that the phrase would burst at the seams. Mr. Fielding feared he might weep at the presentation banquet. How could he possibly convey the way Mr. Sole's devotion moved him: *$1,000. To show appreciation.*

Mr. Sole was Chinese. How in the world had he ever come to Birmingham? Mr. Fielding looked at the young woman sitting at the switchboard. Lucky. She had her whole future ahead of her. Who knew what she might become, might do? Would certainly feel.

"Where's it from?" he asked of her diamond. "Jobe Rose? Bromberg's?"

"Kay's," she answered.

He sighed. "Bromberg's is probably the oldest family business in Birmingham. Maybe Alabama. You get quality there."

Mr. Fielding watched Mr. Sole laboriously rise from his kneeling before the customer. *The soul of the shoe department,* new employees always joked. But it was true. Someday soon he would leave Fielding's, and all Mr. Fielding would be able to do would be to hand him the check, to say the words: "A token of our deep appreciation for fifty years of faithful service."

And then Mr. Sole would leave them. Mr. Fielding didn't know where Mr. Sole went to church, but he was sure he went someplace.

"Get your education," he said again to Stella. "That's something nobody can ever take away from you." He turned to go back to his office behind the switchboard. "Don't get mixed up in any demonstrations. You won't, will you, Miss Silver? Don't ruin your future."

"No, sir," she replied. *But I could,* she thought. *I can do whatever I want to.*

AFTER BUSINESS HOURS

"STEEL WILL DIE IN BIRMINGHAM," PHILIP FIELDING SAID to the inner circle. "It's dying now."

Twelve businessmen, in immaculate and stylish dark suits, silk ties hanging from their necks, stared at him, then nodded. Permission given to continue—and permission had to be given in this group for it to exist—Philip Fielding went on.

"We are the future in Birmingham—commerce and education. Particularly medical education."

Could he have continued if one face had darkened with disagreement? He must persuade them to change, but he could not dissent. No maverick—certainly not himself—could break away howling for integration. No, they had to move as a collective body, and yet the circle must be widened.

"Why do I say steel is dying? Why is that important to us?" All of them talked with the steel men, knew their attorneys as friends and neighbors, but the Inner Circle was a mixture of Christians and Jews who owned other businesses. "Foreign steel, cheap labor, no unions abroad. The unions are too strong now here in Birmingham. We all know that. But the economy of this city will rest more and more on us. To flourish—we *must* have one thing. What is it?" He saw anxiety rise on their faces like the mercury in so many thermometers in a heat wave. Quickly, he said, "Solidarity."

Everyone relaxed. The word was mumbled with approval. Now was the time to make the herd take a step. He spoke not from his heart—which was thoroughly conservative and loved most the South of his own childhood—but from shrewd necessity.

"With solidarity amongst us, we can afford to talk to *them*. I've already talked with A. G. Gaston. He's a reasonable colored man. A businessman. He's not pushy. He's as polite as any one of us. Most important he's a very successful businessman. He's respected in his community and we can offer him respect. I respect him. Bull Connor is an embarrassment to us.

"The idea, gentlemen, is to open negotiations. Then we can take time to plan our course. Then this rioting and demonstrating in the streets will end.

"A colored boy on his bicycle was badly beaten, nearly killed. He was nowhere near a demonstration. We don't want *that*, gentlemen. We're not for violence. Violence is the worst thing in the world for business. They call themselves nonviolent—and some of them are—devoutly so—but we have loved the peace and harmony of the races all our lives. We are the ones who really treasure and who really can create a nonviolent atmosphere.

"Couldn't you sit here just the same, if Mr. Gaston were sitting on my left, and maybe Mr. What's-his-name, who made a fortune in black beauty products, with him sitting between, say, Jerry and Mike? You could do that, couldn't you, Jerry?"

Jerry chuckled nervously. "I don't quite know what we'd talk about," he said.

"It doesn't matter," Fielding exclaimed. "It's the *tone* we're working with. We're accessible, in the right atmosphere. We'll work up to issues."

Mike said, "Everybody could talk about his church."

"Yes," Fielding said, "or temple. How is the atmosphere amongst people we're working with? We could talk about that. What do people fear and hope? Both sides. We can share that."

"Should we include pastors themselves?"

And so inch by inch, the unbroken circle moved away from the old intransigence toward being slightly more willing to negotiate with the other half of the citizens of Birmingham.

WHEN FIELDING GOT HOME, he collapsed into his La-Z-Boy and asked his wife to please bring him some orange juice.

"Are you all right?" she asked. Her little birdlike face was screwed up. At one temple Gertrude still had crossed bobby pins. She'd been too anxious to take down all her pin curls.

"Come sit with me," he said and drew her onto his lap. "I don't like it," he said. "I didn't want it. But Birmingham will change."

"Who was Mahatma Gandhi, Philip?"

"You remember him from the newsreels. Back in the 1940s. A tiny little brown man in a loincloth. He made the British give up India."

AT HER DESK

AIMING FOR 120 WORDS PER MINUTE, GLORIA TYPED AS fast as she could. While her fingers flew by touch alone, she kept her eyes on the Gregg manual; she loved to hear the ding of the typewriter bell at the end of the line, then her left hand flew up to the lever for the carriage return. Her ring finger felt the smooth metal curve, and—slam—the carriage rolled the paper down a line, and she was typing again, lickety-split.

It was a speed test. As soon as she got home from college, she gave herself two ten-minute speed tests every day. You had to deduct ten words from the word count for every error.

Still dressed in her pleated school skirt, she sat down at her desk as soon as she'd washed her hands. The typewriter was an old little Smith-Corona portable, Clipper model, but she felt lucky to have it. Very few of her acquaintances owned a typewriter—certainly not Christine. None had a car of her own. And what did it mean that she had these things? They made her shy, not normal. Because she was privileged, she must find a way to give back.

It was only three o'clock in the afternoon, and both her parents were at work. As tax accountants, her parents wore professional clothing, but few people saw them at their white-owned firm. They were kept out of sight, in a small special room, but they were crackerjack accountants, receiving regular raises and many expressions of appreciation from the owners. For Christmas, they were always given a frozen turkey and a plastic container of cranberry sauce, which embarrassed them, as they could easily afford their own.

They would leave work at 5:30 P.M., as would Gloria's four aunts, who would come quietly home in their gray dresses and white aprons, almost as crisp as when they left in the morning. The aunts would meet one another at bus stops along the route home till all four were together. They would come walking up the driveway quietly in their low-heeled shoes; sometimes two of them would be holding hands. *Domestics,* the sociology books referred to them that way. *Maids,* they called themselves, and each one, when in the world, would avert her eyes and seem as quiet and reserved as Gloria.

Wednesday night the aunts went to choir practice. During the week, from the garage apartment, Gloria could hear them singing in their barbershop quartet, a capella. Gloria imagined their four heads close together. From time to time one or the other would close her eyes in the bliss of making music— "Down by the Old Mill Stream," "Sail On, Harvest Moon, Sail On," "I'm Dreaming of a White Christmas," "Santa Claus Is Coming to Town." Now the house was quiet, except for the dozens of dings from the Clipper's carriage return.

Ten minutes of breakneck typing, then a few minutes to check the speed and accuracy, a walk around the room to loosen up, and the second speed test. Seventy words a minute. A second test: sixty-five words a minute. Gloria's pattern usually was to do better the first time—just seize the moment, all or nothing. Plunge in.

The typing was her insurance: in case she couldn't do what she hoped and prayed to do with the cello, then she could be a super secretary, one who could type accurately at phenomenal speed. Every month her average speed reliably increased by three words per minute, but she worried that she might be reaching the limits of her typing talent.

When she finished the second speed trial, Gloria fetched her cello from its special space between the head of her bed and the wall. The cello garage. The instrument stood vertically in a hard case—almost the size of a coffin; the lid opened like a door, which she would leave standing open ready to receive the instrument again two hours later. She removed the bow from its slot inside the lid. The music stand holding the unaccompanied Bach suites was already waiting.

She loved the moment after she sat down, when she fitted the curve of the cello's shoulder under her left breast. Now she was one with the instrument. Holding the cello between her knees, she tightened and then rosined the bow. Beginning on the open C string, she began her scales in four octaves. As always the thumb of the left hand complained when she went into thumb position for the higher two octaves, but she ignored it. She must earn the privilege of playing Bach, even in an empty house in an ambitious black neighborhood in Birmingham.

At the top of the scale, she remembered hearing rapid scales tumbling through the piano room window at Miles College. She'd never heard such assertive and fluid scale work, effortlessly running the eight octaves of the piano. It was thrilling. She'd gone to the window to peek in.

Red hair! A white man, obviously. Skinny forearms, the fingers of each hand a mere pale blur as they swept in unison up and down the keyboard. Stunned, a bit embarrassed for her spying, she turned quickly away after that snatch of a glance.

In the empty house, she paused at the top of her scale, recalling the pianist's oceanic competence. Then she raced down the scale, spiccato; with one note to a stroke, she bounced down, emanating perfect little spheres of sound, handfuls of tiny, bouncing balls of notes, showing off to herself.

AT THE GASLIGHT

WHEN PEOPLE WENT DOWN TO MORRIS AVENUE, THEY KNEW they'd gone back—not to the trappings of an earlier time, but back in a way you can never go back. Paved with brick, Morris Avenue didn't want any modern asphalt. It had warehouses, wholesalers, a black nightclub or two. It might have had a cathouse or two, who could say? When you came to Morris Avenue, dark in spite of the old-fashioned streetlamps, the whole street slung low, sort of under the viaduct that rumbled overhead with automobiles, you were getting past brick streets and gas streetlamps. Back to some destination. Back inside, to someplace in yourself you wanted.

THERE'S MAGIC HERE, Christine thought. Not the temporary relief of the Athens Cafe and Bar. Permanent magic—it was always there, if you just thought of the Gaslight nightclub. If you just thought of the throng of people, and you in the midst of it, a whole community ready for a good good time. And Gloria was beside Christine; Gloria trusted Christine to introduce her to the world of the nightclub.

Better than church, Christine thought. Better than preaching. Something wild here. Something that cost more money than Christine wanted to pay, but worth more than it cost. She knew the name of the magic. It was music, and her body was already singing, her feet wanting to tap, but they could only shuffle now 'cause the crowd was so large and moving slow to get in the door.

Everybody so well dressed and pleasant. Not like church. Not like Sunday clothes. Here you show a little cleavage, give out with the glitter. Wear bright and tight. Gloria's face—bright and eager. Christine loved the excitement on the women's faces. Giddy. And the proud glow of the men. Night out. Celebrating big.

But Christine didn't need any man. No, not her.

But wasn't that Lionel Parrish over there? Mr. Boss of the H.O.P.E. night school? And that woman in emerald green, rhinestone pin on the wide shawl collar. That wasn't his wife. Never see Jenny dressed up that stylish.

Lionel jumped when he saw Christine and Gloria. Rose up off his feet from the soles of his no-doubt well-polished shoes three inches straight up in the air. Him in the air, like hair levitates itself if you see a ghost.

He hurried to them, oh soooo friendly. Left his pretty lady standing, looking like nothing but cool and pretty in emerald green.

"Evening, girls." Big, overpuffed smile. "Didn't know my teachers was part of the nightclub set."

"It's my second time," Christine said. My, he did smell good.

"First time, here," Gloria said shyly. But then she looked up and her eyes darted round, reflecting the happy excitement. "I like it," she declared.

Lifting his eyebrows, Lionel Parrish said to Gloria, "Girl, I believe this place good for you." Pleased with her, pleased for Gloria.

"You come alone, Mr. Parrish?" Christine asked.

"Well." He shrugged his shoulders. Nice dark-striped suit. Touched the knot of his tie, smoothed down the length of the sapphire blue tie. "My cousin Matilda in town. She said she sure would like to hear the Man play the piano."

"He something," Christine answered.

"But she don't want Jenny to know we come. Jenny got no use for nightclubbing. You wouldn't mention this to Jenny, you happen to see her."

"I don't ever see Jenny often," Christine said. But she didn't like his request; it had the power to blight her good time—pollution in her blue sky.

"Gotta run," he said. "Thanks, girls."

He pecked Christine on the cheek, and oh my, she did stretch out her neck, did lean to meet that kiss, whiff in that good-smelling man. She embarrassed herself.

The crowd pressed toward the entrance.

"Must be several hundred us trying to get in," Gloria said.

"We'll get in," Christine reassured. "Just relax. Enjoy the crowd."

"You see anybody else we know?"

"Just Mr. Parrish." Christine watched him regain his lady, whisper in her ear, saw her face light up. She was extremely pretty, tall and thin, straightened hair, beautiful eyes and teeth. But mostly it was the glad expression, the flash of her.

EVEN DON FOUND IT hard to push his sister's wheelchair over the cobblestone brick of Morris Avenue. Stella would find it impossible to manage the chair, Cat had said, and he ought to come along, therefore, to help them. Besides, he'd enjoy it. Get to hear a truly famous man. An intimate nightclub. In Birmingham. "You won't have to go to St. Louis or New York City to hear him," Cat had told her brother.

Won't the audience be mostly colored? Don had asked.

That's the point, his sister had replied. *We're integrating.*

Don was surprised that Stella had jumped at the chance. Such a bookworm. But he liked her. She admired his paintings. Stella had asked for four and had hung one on each of the walls of her bedroom. He'd asked her, *What do your aunts think of them?* And she'd laughed to show herself risen above the opinions of others: *Aunt Krit says she likes pictures* of something, a scene. *And Aunt Pratt hollers from her room, "I think they're pretty," and Aunt Krit says, "You haven't even seen them," and Aunt Pratt lies and says, "Yes I have. I peeked when Stella brought them home."*

It was slow work and tough going to get the chair wheels over the humped bricks.

"Got any teeth left, Sister?"

"One or two," she answered.

"These heels are killing me," Stella answered. "But I thought everybody'd be dressed to kill." She grumbled about how all the weight of her body (which wasn't much) was funneled down on her toes and how her ankles were wobbling because of the stiletto hells.

"You look nice, Stella," Don said, in his self-conscious, semiembarrassed way. It was hard to look an overdressed woman in the eyes, even harmless Stella, and give her a compliment. Now he just glanced at her. So thin. She wore a white sheath dress with a very wide pink satin cummerbund. The dress had a few sparkly moments and some small pink, silk-covered buttons up on the left shoulder, with a companion decoration on her flank just below the cummerbund on the right side—diagonal interest. Her shoes were pink satin, dyed to match. Don hadn't imagined Stella owned such a getup. The pink silk buttons and the silver dashes on the shoulder were set right into the fabric, probably took a grommet setter to embed the decorations into the fabric that way.

"Your dress from Fielding's?" he asked.

"No. Pizitz."

Women thought Pizitz's line of clothes was more dashing than those of the other big stores, more New York, but Don thought Stella looked like the Gainsborough pink girl elongated, with accents on the diagonal, and set up in high heels.

"How do I look?" Cat asked her brother and the air in general.

"You both look awfully white," Don answered. He made it a point to tease Cat about her feminine vanity.

"Maybe I shouldn't have worn white," Stella said anxiously. "I didn't think."

"Nobody cares," Cat answered authoritatively.

Don saw they were ignored by the crowd for the most part. Despite the spectacle of a wheelchair bumping along a dark lamplit street in the warehouse district where it had no business trying to go, despite two young white women and a white man in a crowd of well-dressed Negroes, they were almost transparent. A few people glanced at them, inspected their faces.

Don noted one perfectly beautiful woman in emerald green had turned her head back as she and her beau passed by, had turned her head back to look Don in the eye and smile. Completely friendly and at ease. Probably visiting from the North. A rhinestone pin of a leaping fish with a ruby eye glittered on her half-turned shoulder. She moved over the bricks as though she were floating, though her shoes were just as ridiculous as the hobbling Stella's. She swung her high hips like a dancer, as though she were in an opera—*Carmen*.

Don thought he'd almost never seen a beautiful woman look so happy.

"I like being here," his sister said, glancing back at him behind her wheelchair.

Stella said nothing, and Don knew that she had come because his sister asked her to. Stella was too bookish to enjoy a club scene.

From time to time, Don took it on himself to caution Cat not to ask Stella to do too much for her. *"You don't want to drive her off,"* he'd said, and Cat had answered, *"But she's my friend. She wants to."*

Just in front of the entrance, they rolled onto some smooth pavement. People were polite, gave them room to maneuver through the doors, stood back while he tilted up the chair, lowered it, reared up, down five stairs. This was the part Stella really couldn't have managed. He wished the soles of his dress shoes weren't slick leather. He hardly ever took Sister anyplace that required being dressed up. When he dressed up, Don claimed the outing for himself, his own time.

By himself, he visited the artificial worlds: the Birmingham Civic Ballet, Town and Gown Theatre, the Birmingham Symphony Orchestra at the lovely Temple Theatre. He'd never met any of the orchestral musicians, but he'd learned the names of some of them from the program while he waited for the crowd to flow in. The faces in the crowd, like those in the orchestra—Herbert Levinson, concertmaster; Robert Montgomery, principal cello; handsome John Davis, principal French horn, who played the most exposed passages with perfect, piercing confidence—were becoming familiar. He wanted to know the people in this world, those up there on the stage, purified by bright light.

One time when Don had looked up from studying the concert program, there in the audience was Stella's dear friend Nancy and her friend Lallie, who was married. Nancy and Lallie had crossed the theater to come over to speak to him. Nancy was always at ease, and Lallie was like her and said, *I often have tickets to things and Bob doesn't want to go. I'll call you sometime,* and Nancy said, *She invited me this time; you'd enjoy it.*

After the precipice of steps, Don steered his sister's chair to a small round table nearby in the back of the Gaslight. Their table for three had a "reserved" sign that sat up like a little paper pup tent: RESERVED—CARTWRIGHT PARTY. Two folding chairs, nothing at all fancy, snugged up to the table, and a chair had been removed so that the wheelchair could fit. Except for the polished wooden dance floor, the floor inside the club was brick. The nightclub was a cellar with a low ceiling, probably a warehouse above, and many ceiling supports interrupted the view of the performance area. The piano was pulled up to one side of the dance floor. No stage. Spotlights were already focused on the piano, but it was just a big upright, like a vault.

The place was full and already buzzing with joy. Don looked to see if he could locate the woman in emerald green again, but instead his eyes locked for a moment with those of an older black man, whose face was wrinkled in a scowl. Immediately, Don started his eyes moving again, and he saw two other white people. Two young men—he might have seen them on the college campus, when he picked up Sister occasionally. The college boys each had a beer and were smoking cigarettes, trying to look suave. Not dressed up enough; short-sleeved cotton shirts, one plaid, one striped. Everyday clothes that didn't show enough respect. You respect celebration, celebrities. Don adjusted the collar of his tan sports jacket to make sure it was lying right; he touched the knot of his woven tie that almost matched the color of the coat but added a new texture.

This was a loud group at the Gaslight. Women's voices screeched high and penetrant. Men's voices suddenly boomed on recognizing a friend. Laughter bounced up and down the scale.

These people let go, Don thought. Not bohemian Paris, not the Village (he'd been there), but the South letting go, at its best. Unafraid. And the energy all flowed around their whiteness or went right through them, made them nonexistent.

TJ FELT HIS wife's gentle hand covering his, her kind lips right at his ear. "What you looking all scowled up and worried bout, TJ? Relax."

"That's why I'm here," he said. "And just look over there, at the steps."

"White girl in a wheelchair."

"Yeah, and over there. Two white boys. Smoking like they own this place. We don't want no trouble here."

"Do you see trouble?" she asked in her soothing, sugarcoated voice. "Once the lights down, you won't be able to tell black from white. They all right. Let it go."

"Not a month gone by, and four black folks beat bad. Who they think they are, coming here?"

The kid at the bus stop—he thought, but did not remind his wife—why *had* the white boys got him? He wasn't demonstrating. Just wrong place, wrong time. They didn't have nothing against that boy. And the newspaper! Hardly acted like anything happened. *Assault, murder!* That's what white folks did and got away with. The newspaper needed to scream.

Underneath his wife's warm hand, TJ's fingers twitched. At the demonstration, his fingers had picked up first a rock, then a chunk of brick. He remembered the thunk the brick made against the side of the policeman's helmet. The man had stumbled forward, but he hadn't fallen; he'd regained himself and kept running. Like a soldier, his buddy running beside him had reached out to steady him.

TJ had snatched the bottle from the wino next to him, thrown it dead at the back of the buddy, but the man hadn't flinched. And then a dog was at TJ's elbow, pulling off a patch of his denim jacket with his teeth, but TJ had jerked away from the snarling teeth, melted into the mob running at his left.

"Look at all these pretty clothes," Agnes said. "There's Matildy Jones with some handsome man. Look at his tie. I believe I'll get you a pale blue tie like that."

Agnes was always trying to get TJ into a long tie. He smiled at her, patted his bow tie. "I so used to wearing bow tie to work, I don't think I'd feel right something hanging down my chest."

"That's why you need one, man. So you know you off work. Would you please order me a 7UP?"

TJ turned to get the attention of the young waiter. Lord, he was skinny. Skinny as a girl, not a muscle on him, long curled eyelashes. He most made TJ sick to look at. He wished there was a sassy young girl waiter he could call to come get their order.

"I can't miss my music man," Agnes bubbled on, voice as pretty as a clear stream, "even if I have to come to a nightspot." She leaned toward him confidentially again. "Now you have that whiskey like you like."

JUST GLANCING THEIR WAY, Cat thought nobody would know Don was her brother. He might be her date. Or possibly Stella's date, but just as likely her date. Don was sitting closer to her than to Stella. Don was looking good. Cat could tell he was glad she'd made him come. They were integrating a public facility, and it was perfectly painless. Nobody gave a damn. People accepted them as though they were just like anybody else.

Everybody was sitting down at their tables, except the waiters, and unless you looked close you wouldn't even notice she was sitting in a wheelchair.

The lights pulsed again, and Cat's heart pulsed high in her throat, seemed to jump with little feet off the top of her stomach and hit the back of her throat. She hoped she wasn't going to get sick with excitement. This would be entertainment like they had in New York, first-class, famous entertainer, but here in Birmingham, here on Morris Avenue. And most white people were too stuck-up to notice who'd come to town. They were missing out. But not Cat, no, she was here with her group. She loved jazz, and she loved the blues.

When the electric lights of the Gaslight started to flick off and on, the voices rose in excitement, as though everything was transposed up a half step. Cat used to love that moment, when they lived in the country, when on the next-to-the-last hymn verse, the Baptist piano would crank up a half step in religious fervor. Now when the lights flickered, her heart transposed up a half step and she thought *I'm here, I'm really here. I'm sipping beer, I'm wearing a low-cut dress, I've got on a choker necklace, and I look like an adult.*

A thin waitress, no it was a waiter, came swivel-hipping through the chairs right to them. He had the most beautiful eyelashes Cat had ever seen.

The waiter looked at Don and said, "Last chance, you want anything extra?"

"I think we're fine," Don answered rather stiffly. He held his beer glass with both hands, barely glanced at him.

"Once the lights go down," the waiter said, looking sideways, "that's it."

The lights flickered again.

"See what I say," he said. "Y'all sure handsome." But he wasn't looking at them. "We glad you here."

"This is my sister," Don suddenly said.

"And who she, elegant lady with the pretty pink cummerbund?"

Cat heard Don snuff through his nose. He reached over and picked up Stella's left hand, displaying her little diamond. "She's my fiancée."

"Excuse me," the waiter said, and he turned around to leave, then looked back. "Y'all enjoy."

When Don let go of her hand, Stella thought, *Don't.*

Because he'd touched her, her hand felt atomic, like radium throwing off magic. Maybe her hand had turned green, like the painted numbers of a radium watch dial, maybe her hand resting on the table was glowing green. She couldn't move it. She didn't want to move it. But he had let go.

What would it hurt if she and Don held hands? Would Cat care? Would Cat feel left out? What about Darl? He'd never know. Cat wouldn't tell. It would be just for tonight, in the Gaslight. Why not?

Stella knew she was panting, her breath too quick. Don had only touched her. That was all. No, he had said "She's my fiancée." Those thrilling words. And Darl had said them in the cemetery. And then he'd gotten her a ring, a little diamond, the next day. They hadn't had time to think. She and Darl had looked at each other and were glad that the other was whole and untouched. Alive. Stella and Darl. Without a scratch. Out of danger. Darl had sold the Vespa and gotten her a ring. But she'd never liked little diamonds. She'd wanted an opal, a large opal full of mysterious blue and red. An opal like a window into the heart of things.

The club lights crashed into total blackness.

Quickly, Stella felt her left hand, inert on the table, with her right hand. Would it be extra warm? Not glowing green but somehow warmed to an abnormal temperature. No. Her left hand was like a lump of ice.

A spotlight jittered crazily across the dance floor. It swooped around, searching. The room held its breath. Suppose it was Don she was engaged to and not Darl? Darl seemed remote, as though he didn't exist anymore.

Don was an artist. Darl kissed her and kissed her, but he never said he loved her. He never touched her breasts, as though he was ashamed that they were small. Darl wouldn't be caught dead in a colored nightclub, but he'd taken her to a cemetery. What was there to love about Darl except his body? Plenty.

When Darl played the organ, his left foot reached down the foot pedals to unleash a sound that hooked the base of her being. That was where he was coming from—a glory so deep that it made Stella's body vibrate. But that sound was hard to remember here in the Gaslight.

The spotlight found a black man, wearing dark glasses, standing beside the piano. The room shrieked, erupted in applause as thunderous as a rock slide. Maybe the building was coming down on them. The spotlight widened and narrowed, widened and narrowed like a crazy eye pupil.

Darl might think he could read her mind. But he had no idea of who she was.

Stella let out a little yelp.

There was enough diffused light, so she could see Cat, grinning from ear to ear like a Cheshire cat, slowly clapping her feeble, noiseless hands. Making the gesture of normal. But Cat *was* enjoying herself; yes, Stella thought, she truly was. Her handicap might be visible to Stella, but Cat had forgotten it. At the Gaslight, you forgot who you had become; you reentered the old cave of the essential self; you knew your defining desires.

The musician held up just one hand, like a cop stopping traffic. A hush fell, total quiet.

He seated himself, and with what seemed a hundred hands, out tumbled a spiritual so raucous it was like the eruption of a volcano: Joshua fit the battle of Jericho. Jericho, Jericho—

And the crowd leapt to their feet, clapping, dancing in place.

Joshua fit the battle of Jericho, Jericho, Jericho.
Joshua fit the battle of Jericho,
AND THE WALLS COME TUMBLIN' DOWN!

They stamped, and clapped, threw back their heads, yelled it out, closed their eyes, sang with all their might, faster and faster, stretched hands held high shimmying down the air till suddenly it stopped—they all stopped. No more piano. They dropped breathless into their seats. They'd won. They'd done it. Fit the Battle.

Walls down, broken stone at their feet.

Then low and slow, quiet and heartbroken, the pianist played "Blueberry Hill" and sang. His raspy voice, so raspberry sweet, made love to the world.

Uh-huh, un-hum. That was all Stella heard, uttered so low. *Uh-huh.* So low so as not to interfere with anybody's hearing. The listeners each wrapped their arms around themselves, rocked themselves. Stella could see tears squeezing from some of the eyes, men and women.

Then they were safe. Their spirits had walked into the shade. Time to loll. Time to let go all the tension, just loll on back in the chair, sprawl. Relax and enjoy. Ecstasy, regret, pain, yes, they'd visit there again while he played and sang. Again and again, all through the night. Already they yearned for the yearning. How a body did *want.*

Aye, yi, yi, yi, yih: Stella remembered her mother singing unaccompanied to an ancient black woman at Helicon. *Blessed girl,* the old woman had said, her hand light as a wisp on Stella's head. But she had not been blessed.

The houselights gradually returned to low, so a person could see the drink on the table, maybe order something to eat. A light snack.

From the dim light the shapes of people emerged. There were two college boys—Freddie and Marshall—from Birmingham-Southern across the room. There was the handsome black couple: he with an opalescent blue tie, she in Irish green. Of course he was not Martin Luther King, but he resembled him, only taller. After studying the handsome man and the beautiful woman, Stella knew: that was what it looked like to be in love.

Maybe she wasn't in love with Darl, but she had promised. You do what you say you're going to do. Especially about a serious matter. About marriage. And when Darl reached with the toe of his left shoe for the low notes of the organ, he raked her soul; those notes harrowed hell and found the buried silver box where her soul was imprisoned.

She glanced at Don, but he was totally absorbed in the music, a faint flush across his skin. He had such nice hair, loose blond waves, fluffy hair. Cat's was straight as a stick and simple brown. Don had beautiful posture, even when he was relaxed. Don was *here,* but where was Darl—just a thought, a memory, a little ring like a manacle on her weakest finger.

People had started to dance. Some with a cushion of space between their bodies, hands and arms cocked high. Some plastered against each other; a man's hand practically on a woman's high ass. There was an older couple, dancing as close as anybody but with their hands above the waist, he in a bow tie, she in a flowered jersey skirt—purple—and matching overblouse. The woman could have worn the purple-flowered jersey to church, but now it was embellished by big drooping, glittery earrings. The couple moved in perfect synchrony, he steering. Stella thought she had never seen such sure, quick feet as those of this ordinary, aging black man. Ah, a fancy pivot, and his wife followed in purplish perfection, though her feet were already swelling out of the pumps, rising like bread where the smooth, black shoe left off across the front of her toe.

Cat leaned toward her brother. "Ask Stella to dance," Cat said in a stage whisper.

But Stella wasn't embarrassed. She was glad. Perhaps they would look as glamorous as the handsome man who looked like Martin Luther King and his beautiful partner in emerald green. Perhaps she and Don would seem as perfectly paired as they of the aging expert feet.

Don looked at her. "Would you like to dance, Miss Silver?" He spoke with just an edge of irony, as though to suggest he would now play the role of Ashley Wilkes, in *Gone with the Wind.* But there was always a twinkle of kindness behind Don's irony. His eyes invited her to play the roles with him.

"Sure," she answered, but she knew she was a poor dancer and felt afraid.

Since Don stood up, she stood, too. Suddenly the music slowed and the lights lowered again. The effeminate waiter was coming toward them.

"Let's dance," Don said to her, almost urgently, and held out both hands.

As soon as they were on the floor, it was as though he had walked onstage, as though he were acting a part and knew it perfectly. With his back held beautifully straight, he pivoted and took her as a partner, moved her, all in one gesture, so that she stepped back without a thought. They were dancing to perfection. She closed her eyes. How was he holding her? Appropriately. It couldn't have been better—she followed, and he made her graceful.

Blessed was how she felt. And she remembered Helicon again when the old black woman—*Aunt Charlotte!*—touched her head and blessed her. She had never imagined that all four members of her family would be taken, and soon. *When the ghost comes, Boo-hoo-hoo. Don't be frightened, Boo-hoo-hoo.* But of course she had been frightened, and for a very long time. In the woods at Helicon, she had fired a pistol. She had run through the woods with her arms stretched up, saying, *"Who, who, whooooooooo?"* Never imagining that death never stopped for only one.

But here they were, dancing on Morris Avenue, living, this moment alive, on a down-low street while the traffic rumbled above on the viaduct, dancing at the Gaslight, dancing among colored people. An inclusive world. Birmingham healing. Birmingham swaying into the future, tremulous as a soap bubble. Engaged.

Maybe she could heal, with her city, too.

THE LIGHTS WENT LOWER. Cat willed her brother to kiss Stella. Just on the cheek would be fine. Just a little brush of the cheek. But she felt sure he never would. As surely as she would never rise up from her wheelchair, he would never let his lips brush Stella's sweet cheek.

Maybe Stella could be her sister, closer than a friend. While she watched them dancing, Cat wished hard.

The table seemed desolate without them. Cat wanted there to be a candle on it. But candles would be a fire hazard. Once the Baptist church had had a banquet in the basement and there had been a big brouhaha over whether to have candles. Cat and Don had voted For. "A vote for romance," her brother had said to her, looking into her eyes with that mixture of irony and affection that she so much adored. As though choreographed, they had raised their hands to be counted: *yes,* for romance. And their side had won, but the minister had overruled the majority. "It would look like a honky-tonk," the minister pronounced. Just once. And the matter was settled.

Honky-tonk, a word heavy as a club and needed like a club to smash down onto the Baptist table just once: honky-tonk. No discussion. "No candles," the plump, clean-shaven minister had said, and part of Cat's religious life had grown dimmer. Naively, Cat had thought the argument had centered on whether candles would be *a fire hazard* before he blurted out: *honky-tonk*. The word had shocked her as much as if he had said *masturbation*. Or, *miscegenation*. She had seen her brother flinch.

Sitting in the Gaslight, Cat loved the sway in the music, so soothing. Her brother looked like a movie star. The perfect affect—slightly aloof—of a handsome star. Stella was a little clumsy, but the way Don looked at her! Like a star looking at the leading lady. The lights lowered again. Cat swayed her upper body with the music. It was "Blueberry Hill," again, slower, full of gravel, sung more seductively than ever. The pain of the world was in that man's throat, and the remedy for it, too.

WHEN LIONEL PARRISH HELD forbidden Matilda Jones, beautiful Matilda come south from Newark, New Jersey, to be with him, he asked *Is this sin?* Lionel Parrish prayed while he danced, her long body against him. His prayer was sincere, shimmering and deep as the color of his tie: *Thank you, Lord. Thank you, Most Holy One, for letting me live this moment.*

THEN A VOICE WAS in Cat's ear. Somebody was releasing her wheelchair brakes.

"Le's you and me dance," said a voice at her ear, and it was the thin waiter, his cheek beside hers. "Want to?" His face so close. She could see the mascara on his eyelashes, curled back in a perfect roll.

She nodded. She couldn't speak.

He bumped her over the bricks—she could tell it was hard for him—and then onto the smooth polished floor. She'd never rolled over such a surface, like gliding. Like a table knife gliding through a plate of warm fudge candy, she moved. He pushed her, riding in the chair, away from himself, out at arm's length, brought the two of them back close, moved the two of them together in perfect rhythm to the music. *It must be like ice-skating,* Cat thought. He arced the chair to the left, to the right, tried to put a curve in the movement. People gave them space. No pity, no scorn in their faces. He was finding out what the chair could do. Sometimes the waiter put a snazzy quick check in her gliding, when he reeled her out or pulled her in.

He left her still and danced his thin body around in front of her, reached out his skinny wrists, took her hands and pulled her to him, pushed her back. His face was impassive, masklike, impersonal.

But she sailed; she closed her eyes and sailed.

Don couldn't believe what he saw beyond Stella's shoulder, beyond the elderly black man, who had scowled to see him, now embracing his plump wife as though she were a cumulus cloud streaked with purple: transported beyond anger, the man was dancing with his wife. Beyond them, beyond everyone, Don saw Cat. His sister, seated, was gliding among the dancing couples. His sister out on the floor in her chair, moving, being moved to the music. Her eyes closed, her face, bliss. Suddenly, her partner twirled the chair, beautifully, in a slow circle, the spokes of the wheels throwing out spangles, the crowd giving room. Eyes closed, oblivious to spectacle, Cat was smiling. Dancing the impossible dance, on Blueberry Hill.

two

THE SLAUGHTER OF
THE INNOCENTS, September 1963

GLORIA

THAT FALL, THE FIRST SEPTEMBER SATURDAY, SHOPPING downtown, Christine pointed to a man entering a drugstore and asked Gloria if she knew who he was.

No, Gloria answered. She didn't know the man. She saw he wore an old brown hat, felt, even though the summer heat was still on them. Everything about his posture bespoke dejection. He slumped into his old clothes. The hat was too large and shielded much of his head.

Who wanted to look at that? Gloria lifted her eyes to the sky between the high buildings.

She intended to feel wonderful on this fine September day. The sky was a real blue; no gray haze from steel mills filtering out the color. A wind had come through, down between the office buildings and stores of Birmingham, and swept the air clean. Cleared the air all the way to the top of the sky.

Gloria was shopping with her friend—first time they'd gone out sauntering the sidewalk together, shopping. At least right now, that was all they were doing. Yes, over the summer, Christine, a grown-up with three kids, had taken her as a friend.

"That's Judge Aaron," Christine said. She grabbed Gloria's arm, pinched it hard.

Why did Christine sound stricken? "Naw. He can't be any *judge,*" Gloria replied. The man was dirty. Moreover, he was black.

"That's his name, I reckon. His mama gave him the first name Judge."

When Christine tightened the pressure on Gloria's arm, Gloria was annoyed. She didn't want any desperate clutching on a fine September day. She didn't want to stir up trouble. The time wasn't ripe.

Politics! Had to be something about the Movement, something about *Rights* for Christine to seize up like that. Gloria's father had said, "You want to get ahead, you work. *It's simple as that.* You get mixed up in demonstration trouble, you lose what you got."

Her mouth at Gloria's ear, Christine dropped her voice to a sad, confidential monotone: "His ma wanted her newborn, chocolate-cream baby boy to be addressed with respect, just like I want for my boys." While they walked in step, Christine's voice mused on, the voice of a hurt mother. "So his mother she gave her baby boy Judge for his name. 'Judge, what you ask for mowing the lawn? I give you a quarter,' some white man have to say, and her little boy hear that word *Judge* and he hearing respect."

Had her own mother named her Gloria, trying to put her forward? She doubted the naming tactic would work. "How come you didn't sign up for an economics course this fall?" her mother had asked. "How come you don't learn something about George Washington Carver instead of William Butler Yeats out at Miles College?" But her mother always supported her music.

Gloria raised her eyes again to the sky between the tall store buildings on Eighteenth Street. She loved for the clouds to puff up like that, so white against the blue.

"Well, how come you know that man?" Gloria asked Christine.

"I only saw him once before. I *think* it could be him. Somebody pointed him out. Just like I'm doing you."

"What for?"

"Klan did him." Christine's voice was flat and sad. "If that's Judge Aaron—they did him."

Gloria looked at Christine's face. All the energy was drained away; she'd never seen Christine quiet and drained. *Did him?*

"When Reverend Shuttlesworth tried to integrate Phillips High School," Christine went on, "that night, they just caught some black man at random." Christine's defeated voice began to recharge itself.

Gloria looked up and wished the heavenly blue would come right down between the buildings and envelop her. She wanted to stand swirled in soft blue. "Lavender's blue, dilly dilly . . ." Gloria wanted to live enrapt in a smooth song. Something more peaceful than "Blueberry Hill," something like Burl Ives sang when she was a little girl—"Lavender's blue, dilly dilly . . ." Just for today, just now, it would be fine to relax into lavender.

"Judge Aaron didn't have nothing to do with no Phillips High School!" Christine hissed. "Klan say Judge Aaron must tell Shuttlesworth what they will do to *him*."

Gloria gazed across the street at the slow-moving man. *Did him?* She couldn't see his face for the slouch of the hat.

"But they don't dare to touch Shuttlesworth," Christine added softly, malevolently. "No. He walk away from every assault. He say God with him; he a man afraid of nothing."

The soft blue stayed inaccessibly high above them. She had to listen to Christine. Couldn't turn a deaf ear.

The street looked more grimy. The people, colored like herself, more lost and lonely. Gloria felt her heart sinking because she knew to please Christine, to satisfy her own conscience, she would have to go with her to Woolworth's; she would have to sit up on a stool at the white lunch counter like any other human being.

Never mind the blue day; it didn't count anymore. Something that should never happen under any sky—she didn't know what—had happened to the defeated man across the street. This was the day of the brown felt hat.

There on the street, Gloria put her hand over her heart—like her grandmother—as though to calm its rapid beating. Grandma Susan, dead since Gloria was five. Grandma Susan, named for her grandma who had been a slave, always trying to soothe herself. *It just making a racket in there*, her grandma used to explain. Gloria felt her grandma within her own body, her grandmother's desire and her own for quiet and peace within herself. For her grandmother, for herself, Gloria pressed her palm between her breasts.

"You all right?" Christine asked sharply.

"I'll do it," Gloria answered.

"When?"

Gloria knew that Christine knew what she meant.

"Today," Gloria answered. "Before I lose my nerve."

The clothing of the shoppers grew vivid, swirled before Gloria like a hallucination. Bits of color here and there, like a flag undone. Gloria pressed her hand against her chest. Then she recognized her gesture as something new: hand on her heart, as though her body, without her consent or guidance, was already making a pledge of allegiance. *I pledge allegiance to this street, to my people, and to their need.* To the slouch of an old brown hat.

PIMENTO DREAM

"OH, NO," RYDER SAID, HIS HAND POINTING INVOLUNTARILY at someone or something beyond the car windshield.

When Lee saw her husband's pointing finger, she wanted to bite it, like it was a wiener.

Ryder was pointing to a black man coming out of a drugstore.

"What?" Lee asked. The word barked out of her. She knew she ought to sound more sweet. But he'd gone too far. For what Ryder done last night, she hated him. Would hate him forever.

She noticed that Ryder hesitated.

What? she thought impatiently. Staring at the closed glove compartment, she waited with her lips sealed. She wouldn't ask again.

Finally he said softly, "He's one we got good. Least I think it's him."

He stopped the car for a red light and streams of colored passed in front of them. They had to wait. She had nothing but contempt for Ryder mumbling about how he hadn't meant to come this way on the niggers' streets. Niggers doing their Saturday shopping.

But actually she felt safe enough. It was broad daylight. Sunny.

"Lock your door," he said.

He had insisted on taking her downtown so she could get some decent hose with a seam in the back, like the Lord intended. Ryder had claimed he just hated those panty hose things. *That was why he done what he done,* he had claimed afterward. He let her wear them all summer long, but they made her legs look naked. Like she wasn't dressed decent for the public.

Last night, he had taken his knife and cut out a diamond in the crotch. Yeah, he was a little drunk—it was Friday night—but he said he'd been wanting to do it over a month. He said he could taste how bad he wanted to.

He had held up the panty hose, laughed, and showed her the empty diamond, laughed. Lee burst into tears. She just sobbed. She blubbered out about how she had been specially selected by the company, selected *at random*, to test out panty hose. Through the mail. It meant she was special. Specially selected.

Finally he had said, "It's my Friday night and you don't stop that blubbering, I'll have to whup you."

"Just go ahead. Just go ahead," she had said, banging her hand on the kitchen tabletop. She was sure he wouldn't; he'd already gone too far.

So he had *had* to. He just grabbed up her rolling pin off the sink drain—the wood still looked a little damp from where she'd rinsed it off—and hit her on the shoulder with it. There was a crunch that must have scared him, so he turned her around to beat her butt where she was well padded.

Then she had gotten down on all fours and tried to crawl under the table. He grabbed the back of her hair and said, "Now you bark, Lee, you want to go on all fours."

"Wolf!" she said. She was crying. "Woolf, wooolf."

"I want you to say 'bow-wow,' " he sneered. "Like in Dick and Jane."

No real dog ever said bow-wow. He made her ridiculous.

"Bow-wow," she had sobbed. "Bow-wow."

But he was sorry afterward, he said. He'd meant it as a joke, cutting a hole in her panty hose. (But secretly she knew he thought it might be fun to do her through the diamond sometime. Yes, that was what he wanted.)

To prove he was sorry, he had gotten up this Saturday morning to take her to Loveman's. He loved her, he really did, and he wanted her to have nice things from the nicest store in town.

And there was that colored man coming out of the drugstore. *Oh no!* he'd exclaimed.

"What'd y'all do to the colored?" Lee finally asked. She knew he liked her to say *nigger*, but really that was pretty low-class talk when you could just as well say *colored*.

She wondered if she'd have had such hurt feelings about her panty hose if he'd just used her scissors instead of his knife. Trimmed it neat, instead of stabbing into the mesh.

"Well, we hurt him pretty bad," Ryder said soberly. "Him or somebody who looks like him." Not his usual tone at all.

And what could make Ryder sound like that? Almost she liked him a little better.

Lee clicked her Juicy Fruit gum in her teeth a few times. Its flavor was about worn out.

Juicy Fruit gum! Long ago a lady in a pretty house off Norwood Boulevard had introduced her to Juicy Fruit, when Lee was a little girl, maybe eleven or so. Such a sweet, soft-spoken woman, old, with her leg in a heavy brace. Lee saw it all again—sometimes her mind just left like that and stood on the edge of her pictures. Now she was seeing Norwood Boulevard and long ago. Her imagination just worked that way—just carried her on off.

Lee had approached a door with fifteen little glass windowpanes to sell some of their extra tomatoes from the garden, door to door. "I don't need any tomatoes," the lady with the leg brace had said, "but let Aunt Pratt give you a stick of gum." Juicy Fruit was the gum.

And then, after she said thank you so nicely, the old lady invited her in and had the maid fix Lee a pimento cheese sandwich, with the crust cut off the bread.

"What you daydreaming about, Lee?"

"Just a sweet old lady who gave me a sandwich when I was a kid. Off Norwood Boulevard. Aunt Pratt, she called herself."

"I know her," Ryder said. "We're kin."

Lee didn't believe him for a minute. She knew he'd make up anything that made him sound important.

After a silence Ryder mumbled, "I kind of hate to say it." He swallowed. "We took his balls off."

"Oh, no, Ryder." She made herself say it so sweet.

When you're afraid, be sweet: it was as though the woman behind the glass door were telling her how to act. Aunt Pratt was trying to help her. Lee replayed how she'd just spoken—so soft, as though she was pleading with Ryder to be good. *But that had already happened.* He couldn't change cutting that black man's balls no matter how sweet she said *Oh, no,* with her chin tucked down and her mysterious brown eyes looking up at him.

And besides, he would hit her no matter how she looked up at him, pleaded with her eyes. She never could be too sweet or too pretty not to hit.

"You can look back at him," Ryder said generously. (Whenever they drove downtown, he told her she must always look just at him, at the side of his face, that he would point out to her anything she ought to see on the street.)

Lee glanced back quickly at the colored man. All dressed in brown.

"I'd do it again," he said. "We should of done a dozen. Should of, last spring."

"Thing's quieted down now," she answered, her own voice quiet with fear.

"Don't you ever sit by no nigger on no bus. You get off and walk if you have to. I don't want Birmingham to end up like Montgomery. We can't have that."

She didn't say anything. She didn't have to. She knew he knew she wouldn't dare or want to do such a thing. Her thoughts speeded up as though they were running away. Sometimes when he was bad, she knew he really had meant to be funny. Maybe she ought to laugh when he seemed mad. Maybe he got madder if she didn't recognize his joking. He was sorry about the rolling pin; he had as good as said so. They were shopping now.

She heard his regretful voice again: *We took his balls off.* She saw him holding out the crotch of her panty hose, both his hands up in the panty hose, the ends of his fingers caught against the stretched film. The diamond shape was empty, the fabric cut away, jagged. She saw the palm of his hand through the clear space, saw his fingers stretching out the mesh away from the diamond space. His knife lay on the scratched metal top of the cook table.

"Didn't I ever tell you how we done it?" He hesitated. (Was he regretful? Did he want her to say it was all right?) "Thought I had."

"No, hon," she whispered. She kept her eyes on him. Saw him swallow and his Adam's apple go up and down. He licked his lips. Maybe he didn't want to describe it. Or maybe he was relishing it. His high cheekbones seemed to press his eyes into slits. He popped in a square of Chiclets gum; she could hear his teeth crunching through the candy coating. She watched his hands. She thought, *Unlock the car door—run!*

"I held his shoulders. Helped to hold anyways."

She could feel his hand on her own shoulders, last night, pushing her down, her crawling away fast, almost under the table.

"He was on his back, on the floor. Kicked like a jackrabbit."

If it was her, she'd want to bite. She shivered. Bite like a werewolf woman. There *were* some, but just in that one comic book (*quick, quick, she would picture them*). There had been one werewolf woman just as powerful as any of the pack loping over moonlit hills. If Ryder was to come at her with a knife in his hand, she'd spring to bite his neck on the jugular vein.

"Took two to hold each leg. Two others just jerked his pants down. We had took him to a deserted house."

He stopped again. Maybe he was sorry. But he glanced at her, made her ask.

"Then what?" she whispered obediently. She was almost too afraid for her voice to work, but he'd be mad if she didn't ask.

"One held up his pecker. Other stretched out his balls a little—" Something like a sob escaped from Ryder. *Suppose it was Ryder on his back,* Lee thought. Ryder went on quietly, "Then they just did it."

She sat silent, horrified. The silence was a ringing in her ears. The people on the street disappeared. She could feel the man's balls in her own fingers. His parts were soft and helpless. She could feel the soft marbles inside the sack, the skin of the sack corrugated like corduroy with fear. His body trying to suck in his balls to hide them.

Again, she heard the strange rattle, or hiccup that had come from Ryder's throat.

"Straight razor. Just a few swipes," Ryder said. "That's all it took."

She couldn't speak. It was like a hand was to her own throat. The stomach bile was wanting to rise, and she fought to keep it down.

Suddenly, Ryder slapped the top of the steering wheel with the flat of his hand as though he was slapping a horse. "Man," he said enthusiastically, "we poured turpentine on him. Still screaming like he'd gone crazy. Scalded him good with a quart can of turpentine so as he wouldn't forget. Gave him the warning. *Tell Shuttlesworth.*"

Ryder gripped the steering wheel, tucked his lips into his mouth, wagged his head from side to side. "Man!" Then he laughed. "That turpentine saved his life. We didn't mean to, but it stanched the blood flow. Saved him. We didn't kill him. That was him, walking around."

"I don't remember when you did it."

She didn't want to remember. What had he done to her about that time? She wanted to think of something else.

What might she do to him, if she couldn't stop herself and he was asleep on his back?

No: she wanted to think of something nice *for right now.*

Something for this moment driving to Loveman's Department Store, something that had nothing to do with blood and screaming in an empty house. She wanted him to step on the gas; she didn't want to look at colored Birmingham, all those colored folks looking at fall clothes in the windows. *Step on the gas.*

But those white robes she sewed—those robes, she saw them haunting, weaving around a black man. White-hooded men floating in robes she herself might of sewed, those men, one holding a straight razor, doing what they did. The colored man, pants gone, his naked brown legs kicking, and he would never be a man like them again. Bright blood on the hems of the starched white robes, robes they had given away on hangers, Christmas presents, with a big red bow at the base of the hanger hook.

But who'd *want* to be a man like them? Not her. She just hoped he'd had his children, that poor man. That man in the old brown hat, walking beside the Rexall drugstore.

Too much traffic to hurry, but Lee determined to put that stuff out of her mind. It was a fine, clear day. Actually, you couldn't see the face beyond the hat brim.

Now she'd picture something nice. Just project it right up on the blue sky between the tall buildings.

Maybe Ryder would take her up to Loveman's balcony to get a crustless pimento cheese sandwich. But she knew he wouldn't. He'd feel out of place up there with all the women and little girls eating a chocolate sundae. He'd call it a sissy place.

Pimento! So delicate and strange. Sometimes she even dreamed about eating a bread triangle, light as a cloud with filling of orangy pink. And about the genteel old lady behind a glass door grid.

"Reckon we could get some ice cream?" Lee asked quietly. "It's awful hot for September."

"Weather oughta turn after Labor Day," he agreed.

He saw a parking place and sped toward it, though there were no cars between him and it.

"After we get your new hose, tell you what I'll do. We'll go over to Woolworth's lunch counter or down at White Palace? Which one would you like, hon?"

He actually looked at her, turned his head all the way, smiled. Showed his yellow teeth.

She still hurt from the rolling pin, the kicks, but after he beat her, he was always sorry.

They had some good times then.

AT WOOLWORTH'S

"THEY DID IT FIRST IN GREENSBORO, NORTH CAROLINA,"
Christine told Gloria. "We're just gonna sit up on a stool."

Gloria looked at the circles of green leatherette on the seats of the stools at Woolworth's lunch counter. They reminded her of lily pads in her grandpa's pond in the country. She would just perch up there, like a frog on a lily pad. *Feet, move!* Gloria told herself.

She felt the rim of the stool against her hip. She put her foot on the dirty metal bar under the counter to step up.

Because she had already decided to do it, now it was just one step leading to another. She slid onto the leatherette. She didn't have to think; she'd already made a decision. Christine sat on the stool beside her. The countergirl looked down, scared of them; she didn't know what to do.

Gloria put her hand on her heart to still its beating. "I'd like to order, please."

"You can't," the girl said in a high birdlike voice.

Gloria could feel a strange calm rising inside her.

"I believe I'll have a hamburger with onions," Christine said into the air in front of her.

White customers at the counter were staring at them. A woman with blond hair clutched a slim tan-and-brown-striped Loveman's bag to her chest. "Oh no," the woman whispered, "not here," and she slid off her seat and stood there staring.

Other white people left their stools and melted away.

"Come on, Ryder!" the blond woman reached back for her husband, timidly touched his elbow. "Come on," she said urgently. She seemed terrified.

"I ain't leaving 'cause of two nigger bitches."

"Manager! Manager!" the countergirl shrieked.

Then the stubborn white man dismounted from the stool. His face was red and his slitty eyes were bugging out. He swaggered toward Gloria and Christine.

He stopped behind Christine, sniffing. "Stinking Communists!" he said.

He swung his head around to look at Christine, who sat like stone. Then he circled around to Gloria. He cleared his throat as loudly as he could. Then he spat on Gloria's cheek.

Christine suddenly clamped onto Gloria's wrist. "Let's go," she said.

The man retreated, put his arm around his wife.

"Don't y'all come back," his woman said vehemently. "Don't you ever come back sit down here no more!"

Gloria pulled a napkin from the napkin box to wipe her cheek. The man was still holding his Coke in a glass. Suddenly he tossed the contents toward Christine, but the ice cubes fell short, onto the floor. He slammed the glass on the counter, and it broke in a big jagged peak, but he didn't get cut. And he didn't pick it up, didn't aim it at her or Christine. Gloria placed her used napkin on the counter.

"I had a gun, I'd shoot you right now," the man said.

"He would," his wife said.

He stood there scowling with his hands on his hips. His wife put her hands on her hips, just like him.

Gloria took another napkin; then she let herself be led away. She let Christine pull her along gently. She felt sick. Wanted desperately to find a rest room she could use to wash her face with soap.

Christine whispered, "Next time, we'll come with a group. Plan ahead."

Gloria rubbed her cheek with the flat paper napkin.

SUSAN SPENSER OAKS

WHEN GLORIA GOT HOME, SHE WENT TO THE KITCHEN SINK
and scrubbed her cheek with dish detergent, then with raspy baking soda. She
hated that man! Hated him! Her skin was getting irritated. And his ridiculous
wife! Greasy blond hair. Her brown eyes—wide and pathetic. The way she had
held the Loveman's hosiery bag in front of her chest. When Gloria glanced
back, she had noticed how the woman held the slender paper bag with both
hands, delicate fingers, from its top, like a shield or breastplate.

Gloria hurried to the bathroom and washed with Cashmere Bouquet. She
wouldn't tell her mother. It would break her mother's heart.

Then she went to the family treasure chest. It was a sea chest, painted a
worn green. Nobody had any idea where it had come from, but it was large
enough to hold a small person. The women in the family had passed it down
and down to the oldest daughter.

Gloria knelt before the chest and opened it. She found the photo she
wanted. There she was, faint with age, but the cheek of Susan, her ancestor,
branded forever. Somehow Susan had learned to write and to read, though
before the Civil War the law had prohibited her learning. On the back of a
daguerreotype, her great-great-grandmother had written her name in her own
beautiful hand: Susan Spenser Oaks. She was an old woman in the picture, the
imprint of a wrinkled oak leaf on her wrinkled cheek.

The only other artifact they had of Susan was a book, but there were many
other treasures in the chest. Each mother had added one or two items, specified

before her death, to the heritage. Gloria wondered what her own mother would leave; what she herself would leave. Perhaps a worn cake of rosin.

To keep the binding together, an old navy blue strip of cloth and a faded green ribbon had been bound around the middle of Susan's book: *Nature*, by Ralph Waldo Emerson. Maybe the piece of cloth had belonged to Susan, too. The navy color had held in the cloth, but the grosgrain ribbon had faded to the color of sick grass. Gloria untied the cloth and the ribbon, like a double belly-band, and opened the cover. Inside the book, in a different hand than her ancestor's, Gloria read: *To my friend Susan, with love and joy on the occasion of our reunion, from Una, September 15, 1867, Nantucket.*

Her great-great-grandmother had had a loving, literate friend. With the book in her hand, Gloria sat down on the floor. How far back could she remember? How far back in her own life?

She remembered shopping when she was a little girl, with her mother, and streetcars still ran in Birmingham. They'd only been in the city a month or two, and lived in a little house, not this big one on Dynamite Hill. From the beginning, her mother had insisted on shopping at the best stores. At Loveman's and Pizitz, at Blach's and Burger-Phillips, with its electric eyes mounted on brass posts to open the door for you, regardless of color.

Back then, when Gloria was four or five, even little girls wore hats, secured with a cord, and white cloth gloves to town. Back in the streetcar days, when Gloria and Mama were shopping inside Loveman's, Gloria had taken the black elastic cord from under her chin. Her hat was a yellow straw, with a narrow brim; half a wreath of blue, red, and white cloth flowers decorated the front seam between the brim and crown of the hat. The hat's elastic always pinched the skin under Gloria's soft little chin. She forgot to put it back on when they walked outside, and a gust of wind blew the straw hat off her head and tumbled it into the street between the streetcar tracks.

"Stay here," her mother had ordered, and she ran on her high heels after the hat.

Down the street between the shining tracks she ran, glancing this way and that for safety. Then she bent from the waist and pounced on the crown. Gloria could see her fingertips dimpling the straw. And Gloria had obeyed perfectly—still and good on the sidewalk. Triumphantly her mother came back to her, fitted the hat onto Gloria's head, securing the elastic under her chin, where it promptly pinched. "Just like a cat," her mother said, "I pounced on it just like Purrfect catching a mouse." And she had. Never had Gloria been so proud of her sedate mother. Her short and buxom mother so quick and brave, saving her hat from the steel wheels of the streetcar. Her brave mother making a streetcar full of white people wait while she saved her daughter's hat.

HER MOTHER WOULD NEVER know a white man had spat in her daughter's face.

But then Gloria thought, *I'm going to have to do this again. Christine and I.*

KIND OF A GROWL

THE REST OF HER LIFE, LEE WOULD TELL PEOPLE THAT SHE had known when the bombing happened. She had been in Sunday school. Her class was still in session in the sanctuary that day. In the front near the altar, the twelve ladies had all stood up to sing. The hymn was "Fairest Lord Jesus," which Lee had always considered to be a beautiful, lady-type hymn. She had glanced up at the metallic vase of five white gladioli stalks, right in front of the pulpit. And she felt an explosion, very muffled, come up through her feet. It was quite some ways from Sixteenth Street Church to hers, but Lee always swore she had felt it, when it happened, September 15, 1963. And she *knew* something awful had happened. She just knew it as soon as she felt that vibration coming up through her shoe soles. And Lee was willing to tell anybody— then or now—the church bombing was shameful. That was really and truly wrong. *And it had to been white folks what done it.* BOOM. But muffled. Kind of like a growl.

It could have been her kids, those four girls.

Suppose they started bombing our churches?

In church, you have a right to be safe. Surely?

HUDDLED TOGETHER

SIX SUNDAYS OUT OF SEVEN, LIONEL PARRISH PREACHED
to his own little congregation, but on the seventh Sunday, he had explained to
them, he needed to be preached *to*. Needed some refreshment for his own soul.

He never had been to Sixteenth Street Baptist, and he wanted his family
with him. Two boys and two girls, a double double blessing from the Lord.
They'd missed Sunday school, taking so much time with their outfits, but he
was the one who, when they were all ready to go, made the delay. He told the
boys to shine their shoes with spit, and the girls to go back and daub a new
coat of white over the scuff marks.

"These shoes been wore all summer," Jenny said. "They can't look brand-
new." But she smiled at him.

Her dress was pale blue, with a white eyelet collar and wide, matching cuffs
on the short sleeves. Jenny hoped he noticed how sweetly she complied with
his wishes. She hoped he thought it was good to have such a wife. She turned
around on a dime to go help the children find the shoe polish, stowed under
the bathroom sink.

"I do like that color combination," Lionel called after his wife. "The blue
with the white." (He *had* noticed how nice she looked. It had taken him all
summer, but this morning he noticed.) He added, "Think I'll change to my
blue tie."

Glancing back, she smiled at him again. "That's the flashy tie," she said.

Lionel Parrish was a good-looking man, and they both knew it. Jenny didn't
mind if she just kind of quietly set him off. He *needed* to shine.

Crowding into the bathroom to work on their shoes, her daughters both took after him—so pretty, both Lizzie and Vicky—and the two boys looked like her—kind of homely, but that was okay. Resigned, the boys sat on the sofa to wait for everybody else. Put any man in a suit, and he looked good. George and Andy could just concentrate on their studies and be like their smart daddy in *that* way.

Jenny put down the toilet lid and used it to sit on. She lifted her foot; yes, there was a black streak, heavy, on the inside heel of her white pumps, where she accidentally kicked herself while she walked. She took the swab from Vicky and rubbed white over the streak, but it was too dark and still showed through. Still, the polish did veil the black mark to some extent; it was certainly less noticeable.

Lifting the pink terry cloth curtain (it matched a whole set of bath towels, hand towels, and washcloths), Jenny glanced out the window: *what a fine day.* Last day for summer shoes maybe. All four of the kids, ages six, seven, eight, and nine, were in school this September. A sparrow fluttered across the window. And today, as a family, an American family living right, her whole family would visit Sixteenth Street Baptist. She felt as though they had all been promoted.

But they were late. The children wouldn't get to meet the other children in Sunday school. Jenny rounded everybody up to leave the house again.

While they drove around the park, they saw quite a few others coming in just for church who hadn't been to Sunday school. Some girls were playing while they walked—tossing a purse like a football between them.

Lionel had to leave the car three blocks from the church, clear on the other side of Kelly Ingram Park.

"Y'all walk behind us," Lionel instructed the kids. "Two by two. Two girls, two boys."

Jenny knew he was proud. She felt just right. No need to hurry, get hot and sweaty. After a summer of wear, her white Sunday pumps were comfortable enough for a little walking. She tried not to let one foot kick the other. It was always the right one kicked the left.

"Jenny, I'm thinking I might apply for some grant money for the dropout kids," Lionel said as they walked toward the church. He took her hand—she was wearing white gloves—not a smudge on them. But the thick cloth muted the sense of his touch.

"Oh, yes," she answered. Surely he was proud of her, of her spotless white gloves, each finger enclosed in its own long little white box of cloth, the seams forming the edges. They were a family visiting an important church; two by two they walked on the sidewalk between the street and the park, the trees still green in September. They made their own little parade, like the animals marching to Noah's Ark.

"Use the grant to hire teachers," he said. Yes, he was proud of her, satisfied with her, she was sure of it. She was the mother of his four fine children: two boys, two girls. "Not just volunteers," her husband went on. "Try to give more kids, anybody, a second school chance who dropped by the wayside."

"There's way too many dropped out," she said because he wanted his echo. She noticed the magnolia tree leaves in the park were coated with a thick layer of dust and grime. They needed some rain to wash them off.

"With grant money, I could hire more teachers. Take more students. Maybe start something big." He purchased the word *big* up from his belly, rasped it in his throat.

"You already doing so much." Now he wanted her to plunge ahead; take the machete of her mind and make a swath through the jungle—"Pay *yourself* something," Jenny urged.

The air convulsed.

Shock waves grabbed their bones, collapsed their hearing. A terrific explosion.

There. Ahead.

At the church.

Jenny froze still, shrieked, and the girls started to cry.

Without turning around, Lionel held out his arms on both sides. "Children, come close," he said, but Jenny felt terrified by the timbre of his voice, which was surely not his own tone of speaking but the voice of God.

Huddled together, the family watched smoke and dust rising up above the greenery of the trees, yes, over in the direction of the church. They waited for another explosion. On both sides of his body, he hugged the children tight to him. Jenny stepped in front of the girls. *The atomic bomb,* she thought as the billow of smoke rose into the sky.

EVEN AS HIS OWN arms gathered his children, Lionel felt the arm of God across his own broad shoulders, God gathering him close, ready to protect the man who would be shepherd.

Lionel's four children imagined the sound again, though it had ceased, felt their souls rise up a little, try to leave their bodies, try to untether, then settle back into their unwounded flesh, burrow deep into the marrow of their bones. They felt their souls scurrying from danger. Each assured his soul in hiding, *Stay there, stay there. Don't come out. Not for years and years, you needn't come out.*

Their mother thought *What if we hadn't turned back to polish our shoes?* She remembered herself sitting on the closed toilet lid, her left shoe in one hand, the shoe sideways so she could paint white over the black streaks across the inside of the heel. She saw the polish applicator in her right hand, with the thick white polish impregnating the fabric of the swab; a wire stem connected the swab to its handle, which was also the screw-top lid for the bottle of polish. The lid was white to indicate the color of the contents of the bottle. Jenny pictured the applicator again and again. The shoe polish applicator had been the instrument of their salvation.

Beyond the trees was screaming and screaming.

RUBBLE

TJ KNEW HOW TO HUNT THROUGH RUBBLE. HIS HANDS found the bricks, checked their perimeters—what could be disturbed, what could cause a landslide if it were disturbed. He heard the sound of the explosion over and over: the cracking and falling, the destruction of walls, the spew of bricks, the shattering of plaster and glass, but he cocked his ear to the whimpering. There was life. Where there was whimpering, that small sound under the exploding screams, that was the sound of the trapped. He lifted a chunk of plaster, heavy, sharp edged. He couldn't see much. Already he was creating a pile in a bare spot, an accumulation of lifted objects. He could hear people digging frantically, perhaps covering up someone else as they tried to help. A cloud of dust scratched his eyes. Might as well close his eyes, dig by feel and sound. He believed the church had become a heap of rubble, but here was a broken table leg, a nice leg, turned and grooved, and the foot of it splintered off. Sometimes the dust would settle a moment, and he could see a great slide of debris, a child with blood on her face, yowling but attended by an adult biting his own lips.

He couldn't stand that—not a hurt child. His mind flew to Korea, the child like a crisp of toast down in the ditch. Not that—and his mind leapt back to now, to his wife, how he had embraced her the very split second after the blast, how he had taken her soft body, safe, yes, *safe*, pliant and soft, her large breasts, her soft abdomen, there were her swelling buttocks—Agnes, her body melded with him in that moment; closer to him then than in the most perfect synchrony of dancing or the merging of coupling.

Though the church burst, they found themselves yet alive! Only that. Standing, before the pew where they had been sitting. Together and alive, in the sanctuary, full of shrieks and smoke. Survivors! As after gunfire in Korea, he sensed the safety of the place where he stood. His soft wife, all loving in his arms. His wife, his precious dream of what life was.

And then, in the surety of her safety, TJ had felt his duty to release her. He must help. There would be no collapse of earth under her feet, and now it was for him, as a soldier, to give aid. Yes, he would scavenge for life in the broken wreckage. People had died; he could not doubt that. And people would have survived; from the perimeter he traveled through zones of disaster toward the wounded and the dead.

He saw the injured moving in a dust cloud, their faces frozen in the distort of howl. Inside his trouser pocket, his finger closed on his clean handkerchief, folded into quarters, ready to be a compress against the gashed forearm. He took the young person's hand and showed how to hold the press against the bleeding.

Through a gap in the roiling smoke he saw the out-of-doors. A wall had been blown away. This sliding debris under his moving feet was leading him downward.

Here was a deacon, his dark suit powdered white, thumping the back of a little girl doubled up in hysterical coughing. "Take her outside into the air," TJ said.

(So, he realized, he must already have left Agnes, turned from her, already preoccupied with his next mission. How could he have left her? Only instinctively; it could not have been a decision. He would have released her and turned not decisively but instinctively, using his preinstructed body without further thought, as surely as he made a turn in dancing, or lifted a suitcase, his body having precalculated its probable weight, in the hotel lobby.)

TJ's fingers were removing the paisley tie of the man standing beside him. At TJ's feet lay a man with his head resting on three bricks still mortared together; his pant leg was torn away and the femoral blood surging out. TJ applied the paisley tie as a tourniquet. Beyond the torn leg, to the left of his focusing, there was a worse horror.

TJ's gorge rose; skin had been charred, a small charred body. A child's shoe. A shoe.

Now TJ screamed. Now his voice joined the chorus of grief, horror, grief, outrage.

Was this what they had caused when they had answered the call in August, marched on Washington? He had been a part of the multitude gathered around the reflecting pools, the rectangles reflecting the sky, King's voice reflecting their hearts: "I have a dream, I have a dream, I have a dream when my four little children . . . not for the color of their skin but for the content of their character. . . ."

I live a nightmare, I live a nightmare. Now he was bending, lifting with his back, not his legs, forgetting his training, bending, his hands becoming paws, digging like a dog.

But he had held Agnes. His softly yielding Agnes. Raised Catholic ("Hail Mary, full of grace," that was what she said), and she had come to this Baptist place with him, after he went to Washington. Agnes had come to please him, because this church was a center for the struggle, because last May he had watched the children stream down the steps from this church speaking of nonviolence. Because he had to get into the heart of that idea before he killed somebody again. Killed somebody in his own country.

He knew what he could not face: the eyes of the parents of dead children. But he could dig. Dig with his bare hands. Dig for buried bone and blood-wet flesh.

THE FACE OF CHRIST

WHEN CHRISTINE LOOKED AROUND THE FINE CHURCH, SHE
had felt out of place and awed by the beautiful pews and carpets, the radiant
stained-glass pictures. At Gloria's suggestion, they'd come early to get settled.
They would watch the people congregate. In comparison, Christine's Bethel
Church seemed small and drab, but Christine told herself that the Holy Spirit
didn't care where he dwelt. Then she thought of Reverend Shuttlesworth and
how the spirit came into him at Bethel and through him to her. That was what
counted.

Gloria showed her the bulletin and whispered quietly about the worship
service.

"It has eight parts," Gloria explained, "including the musical prelude and
postlude." She put her finger on some boldface printing. "This is for the
responsive reading." Gloria had chosen a good spot for them, not too close to
the pulpit, not so far back you couldn't feel like a part. "He usually says something to make everybody smile about here," Gloria said, pointing her finger to
the page. "And—"

Christine and Gloria reeled from the blast. They sprang to their feet, bodies
shaking and trembling. The congregation erupted in screams. "Thank the
Lord, thank the Lord!" Christine screamed not because she was alive but
because her babies were safe. Little Honey, Diane, and Eddie; her children were
at their own humble Sunday school, not this rich place. Terrified, she and Gloria grabbed each other and sobbed and shrieked. Others rushed from the pews.

Bombed! Bombed in church! For nothing. For worshiping God. Christine howled for revenge. All the oppression of her life—her rage blew out the circuits of her mind. She seemed molten with hatred, but she clung to her friend and wept. Christine felt useless, immobile, devastated with hysteria. *Not safe in church.*

She sobbed with shame, boiled with hatred. No safe place. She wept with shame. *They* allowed no sanctity, no sacred place. And she? The force of hate left her mindless. Helpless. Bound to the shame of her own helplessness. Raped again, made helpless. She lost her mind with it. All she could do was cling to Gloria, hurting Gloria with the desperation of her clenching fingers. Christine could only clutch harder and harder until she felt the force of Gloria's own fingers squeezing back. But Gloria was not clinching out of terror.

As desperately as you need me, Gloria's hands meant, *so will I return your grasp.* Gloria's replying grasp was full of calm.

I AM NOT AFRAID, Gloria thought. *Here am I.*

Billows of dust came toward them, passed through them, passed on, and then Gloria saw, as she held Christine, that they yet stood in the place she had selected just before the explosion. Behind her, presiding high over the violated church, stood the full, stained-glass figure of Christ, faceless. Instead of Christ's face, a blank opened to the sky.

Christ's face, only his face, blown out. Gloria pressed Christine to her bosom, held her as tightly as she could. If they bombed again, she would save Christine, protect her with her own body.

No convulsion followed, except convulsions of screaming and fear.

Through the empty face of Christ, Gloria saw her world—a bit of treetop against blue.

What did it mean that God had let the face of his only begotten Son be destroyed? Where was the hand of God when it failed to protect his home and his worshipers from hate? Sunlight continued to pass, indifferently, through the stained glass still standing in the windows. Stained purple, the light caught the motes of dust that clogged the air, and purpled them.

"I'm going to be sick," Christine said, and her vomit splashed onto the polished wooden back of the pew. She sat down weakly. "I hate them so much, it's killing me." Christine put her arm on the back of the pew, leaned her face into the crook of her arm and sobbed.

Gloria let her be. Floured with plaster dust, Christine seemed shrouded. Over her navy blue suit, her skin, her hair, had been thrown a veil of powder. As Christine sobbed, dust rose from her shoulders. The wailing of the broader misery, police sirens, someone shouting orders washed over them, and every moment they breathed the dust and the odor of something broken open that should have been kept sealed.

SOMEONE SMALL

AFTER SHE FOUND HER WAY OUT OF THE CHURCH, AGNES stood on the street with hundreds of others. These were her neighbors, some of them. Many of them were strangers, but familiar in their Sunday-best dresses and heels, their suits and ties. Here were ambulances, police. A few white faces looking at what white had done.

Agnes saw her husband working in the debris. TJ was pointing out a spot to the white men. TJ was telling them what to do, working with them. He had forgotten his own black skin, their paleness.

When the woman next to her began to sob, Agnes reached out and drew the strange woman to her bosom.

A stretcher was carried into the rubble.

Agnes saw charred flesh. Unmoving flesh. Someone small. Poor naked body. Someone young.

Then Agnes saw a head. All alone. A child's head blasted from her body. And Agnes fainted.

She felt her knees hit the pavement, and she was gone.

HOMEWARD

"TAKE THE CHILDREN HOME," LIONEL PARRISH TOLD Jenny. "They're needing help over there. No need for the children to see."

"Y'all come with me," Jenny said. She took the hands of her daughters. "Andy, you and George hold their other hands."

As though they'd forgotten something at home, Jenny turned the children around on the sidewalk. The boys had to step on the grass because the walk wasn't wide enough to hold them all. Jenny glanced at the trees, saw their leaves were still coated with tired dust. Whatever had happened back there at Sixteenth Street Baptist, this world was the same here, a block or two away. Everybody else was running toward the church. They shrieked and the ambulance sirens and police cars screamed down the street.

"I want to help," George said.

"Your daddy say we all to go home. Can't no child help with this."

"I'm going to," George said, and he dropped Vicky's hand and ran.

"George!" Jenny shrieked, and her voice was like a bullet that stopped him dead in his tracks.

George turned and came back, but his cheeks were streaked with tears.

Jenny reached out her hand, and with the thumb of her white glove, she smeared away his tears.

"These just the first," Jenny said. "Gonna be many a tear before this day forgot. Come on now, baby, like your daddy said."

They walked on, Jenny thinking *I don't like turning my back on this*.

When they passed their parked car, George said, "Mama, ain't you gonna drive us?"

"You know I not ever learned to drive."

"Why not?" Vicky asked.

"We leave the car here for your daddy," Jenny said. "It be waiting when he ready to come home."

It would be a long walk in Sunday pumps. Buses hardly ran on Sunday. Already her right foot was kicking the left foot.

OLD AUNT CHARLOTTE

IN HELICON, ALABAMA, OLD AUNT CHARLOTTE TOLD HER aged children Christopher Columbus Jones and Queen Victoria Jones, "He'p me up to the Methodist church. I want to sit there."

"Let me get you a fresh head rag," Victoria said.

Chris pulled a quilt off his mother's bed to line the wheelbarrow.

The barrow lay upside down to keep out the rain, right beside the worn steps. With difficulty, Chris righted it, but he had to take his time.

"Let me walk," his mother was saying as she hesitated at the top of the three stairs. Her neck was bent down, but her body stood straight. She wore a clean, faded apron, and the clean head rag was a matching strip of fabric printed with now-faded red circles.

She over a hundred years old. She don't look it, Chris thought. Dressed up, matching clothes. *I look older than my own mama.*

"Church folks done be gone," Victoria said, "time we get there 'less you let Chris push you."

They already gone, Charlotte mumbled too low for even Victoria (standing right beside her on the threshold with her hand under Charlotte's elbow) to hear. Charlotte had felt their passing. Good children. Good girls. *We come to say good-bye,* one of the spirits had whispered. With utmost respect, *because you the oldest living.*

'Cause you seen so much, another girl-voice said. Words like distant cowbells.

We be waiting for you, when you come. The third girl had a low, patient voice, like creek-flow.

Grannie, would you tie my sash a little better?

They'd wakened her from her doze with their wispy young voices. Four spirits passing. They troubled the air over where she lay snoozing in bed. No more than breath, they wafted past, talking among themselves. Detouring. Little city girls, *leaving Birmingham.* They sang a hymn, so high up in the air, each with her own note but all together. They sang so high as they disappeared, grew small as four specks, into infinity.

They sang like they were already angels. Voices like chimes.

Doctor and Mrs. Doctor and their children, been several years now, not too long ago, had given her wind chimes when they visited. *Sweet as church bells,* Doctor had said. Maybe it was the chimes had woke her, four metal tubes stirring in the Sunday breeze.

Well, Charlotte would know when she saw the white folks leaving their church.

"You come ride in the barrow, Mama," Chris said. "I have you there in no time."

"I scared you spill me, Chris."

"Never have," he answered, looking sullen.

"No, I'll just walk. Not but a mile. They church not even started yet. Y'all come get on each side."

Chris felt his neck creak, his head bend a little lower—oh, just a tiny fraction of an inch closer to despair. When his chin touched his chest, he'd likely die. But not till then. Till then, his mama was the boss.

Slowly Charlotte crept down the steps. Victoria plucked the quilt from the barrow in case her mother needed to lie down beside the path and rest.

Tentatively, Charlotte sent one foot sliding forward through the raked red dust. Her shoe sole grated over the little stones under the dust. Then the other foot followed, sliding and scuffling.

"See," Charlotte said proudly. "That's how walking's done. One foot at a time."

"We'll get there," Victoria said. Her voice strong as the steel spring in a mousetrap.

"Reckon I'll stay home," Chris muttered.

His mother looked back at him and slowly smiled. "No, you come on, too, honey. Mama needs you to help her."

So the three of them slowly progressed to the edge of the yard. Then Charlotte stopped. She looked back.

" 'Little house, little house,' " she said. " 'Stay still as a mouse. Don't make a sound, and don't fall down,' " but she was living in another time. She was a young woman, and Doctor, just a boy ten years old, had stopped on this very spot, at the edge of the yard. It was white family's dwelling then, and Doctor had a long burlap cotton sack slung over his shoulder. He held the belly of the long bag bunched up so it wouldn't drag through the woods, get caught on little sticks and briars. Straight, smart little boy, with blue-gray eyes. He was off to the fields to pick a hundred pounds of cotton. Little sister—Miss Krit—was just born, that morning, in the house, and they told Doctor-that-was-to-be if'n he picked a hundred pounds, he could hold the baby. Standing on this spot, he had looked back at the house, and made up a charm: *Little house, little house, stay still as a mouse. Don't make a sound, and don't fall down.*

It had taken Charlotte a moment to rummage around in memory to find the words, but the charm had lasted all these years. The house still stood.

"Now we can speed up a little," she told her children, stepping beyond the yard onto the path through the woods. "I remember how this walking's done."

A small frail baby, Krit had been an easy birth for a woman who'd had five before. As soon as she came out, Charlotte had read her puckered face: this one would make trouble for somebody, later on in life. But so far, she hadn't. She'd never married, taken care of her mother in her old age, was taking care of Miss Pratt, stove up with the rheumatism. And Doctor's little orphan girl.

Today was a good day at Helicon in September, still warm enough for the pine trees to give out their piney smell. Their fallen needles, long and brown, were soft underfoot, but they could be slippery, and it was best to hold to somebody.

I wish you Birmingham gals could all just stay here with me, Charlotte thought. *Where had those specks gone? Enjoy this Alabama sunshine. These good smells. This soft path.* She breathed it all in, could feel her nostrils spread. *Reckon y'all's feet don't need no earthly path.* She had her faith, but it was a sad thought. *Y'all mighty sweet. Coming by my bed like that, tell old Grannie good-bye.*

Then Charlotte took such a mighty breath—life, life—it resounded like a snore, and Victoria said, "You all right, Mama?"

"Sure am," Charlotte answered and quickened her steps. *They've flown on.* Hardly stayed a second, just long enough for Charlotte to get her eyes open, see the place where they'd hovered in the empty air.

She glanced to her left, saw the pond below the spring all covered with green. She wished Victoria and Chris wouldn't let the water scum up that way. She swung her gaze to the right. Yes, there was her big rock. Even in the winter, when she sat down there, her boulder had stored-up sunshine to offer. She'd rather be buried under that rock than anywhere else on earth. Lie close to home. But that was a wish she'd never tell; she knew it was her duty to go into the church graveyard—colored side—when her time come.

Oh, she remembered now: she'd decided against dying. She was staying here. *Y'all come back to visit.* She sent the message out to all who had gone before. *Anytime.*

To her own children, she thought, *Now if you waiting for me to die fore you light out for the city, you barking up the wrong tree. You be here forever, you waiting for that event. I ain't making you leave, but I was you, I'd go while I still had some gumption.*

Here was the patch of oak trees to pass. Acorns still clung in clusters up among the green leaves. Charlotte thought an oak leaf was the prettiest shape in the world—the kind with lobes, not the red oak leaf. Too pointy. When she was just a girl, long long ago, she'd seen a woman with an oak leaf branded into her cheek.

And there was a dogwood with one red leaf on it already. Always the first sign of earliest fall when the dogwood started to turn red. Now they were onto the road leading to the church.

"One foot in front of the other," she encouraged her children. *Y'all ought to just keep walking. I want you to be free.*

She could hear a cardinal sing, and she sang back to it out loud, "Pretty bird, pretty bird." Birds always sang prettiest on a Sunday morning. "I love to hear the bird choir," Charlotte said.

"Yes, ma'am," Victoria said with a snap in that spring steel voice.

"I do too, Mama," Chris said, muted, and his mother pinched his arm a little so as he would know her thought: *You such a good boy.*

One foot in front of the other. Charlotte wished folks pent up in the cities could look down on them from one of their high buildings, see how peaceful and good things were here in the woods. Here everything just grew as it would, no matter who lived here or who didn't. They had the prettiest woods in the world. She saw goldenrod beside the road.

In the country, they didn't have much, but they didn't need much.

In the country, folks got along with one another. Acted right.

She wondered sadly about the four girls and why they'd passed on so young. Good girls. Dressed so nice. They needed to be here.

Ought to have been with her, in the country. They ought to have been four real girls come to visit their grannie in the country for the summer. Well, she guessed this *was* autumn coming on. She remembered the dark red leaf on the dogwood. School time.

The girls needed to be here, whenever it was, enjoying the birds and the green trees.

By the time Charlotte and Victoria and Chris reached the church, those inside were saying the benediction, in unison: "The Lord bless you and keep you; the Lord make his face to shine upon you. And give you peace. Amen." It was as though the building itself had a voice.

The sun glinted on the chrome of the cars parked all around the church. The cars were like a herd of little piglets snouting up to a sow.

"Quick, quick," Charlotte told her children. "Let me sit here on the stump. I got to see 'em come out. You all hurry on, then come back and get me. Hide now."

Charlotte settled herself on the stump. Yes, they were coming out now, first a few men—Charlotte eagerly looked at their faces, their arms—then the women—Charlotte held her breath, appalled—then couples emerged from the door under the steeple. Every white face, their hands and arms were marked.

Covered with blood, they were. Every one of them. Stained with guilt. She could see.

Smiling and pleasant, as though nothing had happened.

No, to them nothing bad had happened for the last hundred years.

AT THE CARTWRIGHTS'

"WE COULD GO TO THE FUNERAL," CAT SAID.

"We don't know them," Stella answered. "We didn't know the girls." Stella stroked the arm of the sofa. She could hardly bring herself to look at her friends.

"We don't know their families," Don said.

They sat in the Cartwrights' living room.

"Did this really happen?" Don asked. He jumped up and paced back and forth over the bare wooden floor, Goliath at his heels. "I find it so hard to believe." Don pressed the palms of his hands together, and they trembled with the force of his pressing. "That someone would do this."

Stella had no trouble believing in disaster. She remembered the rolling of the family car, how they had all tumbled, like clothes in a washing machine, the wash of blood. She stroked the sofa arm as though it were a cat. *But to bomb a church! Not a chance accident, but someone's plan. Someone who called himself human.*

"It's important for some white faces to be seen at the funeral," Cat said firmly. She looked at her brother, at her friend.

"There'll be an enormous press of people," Don replied, and Cat knew he was saying it would be too hard to get her chair through.

"There's quite a bank of steps," Stella added.

"We could just be in the crowd. Outside," Cat answered.

His toenails clicking, her little dog ran across the bare floor. He leapt into Cat's lap, and automatically, she smoothed his head, as soon as he had turned and settled himself. He was part Chihuahua, and he cocked his head, flared his big ears, and looked inquisitively from face to face.

"Goliath's puzzled," Don said, with dignified irony. "He's never heard us talk about this before."

"I don't want to stand outside," Stella said. "We'd be like spectators. It would be offensive to them."

"The one family wanted their privacy. A small gathering," Don said. "I'd certainly prefer that."

"The TV cameras will be there," Stella said. She imagined the coffins—three dead girls inside. No, the cameras could not look inside, see the little girls in their dark containers. She imagined their ruined bodies lying in their boxes. Stella felt herself there in the church, though the funeral had not yet happened.

No one else was there, just the empty sanctuary, gloomy, in twilight and silence. Tranced, Stella walked alone down the aisle. Three matching coffins were at the front, the fourth already in the ground. Stella pictured herself walking down the aisle of the church, hesitating beside a front pew, close to the coffins. Like three little boats at a dock, the coffins almost bumped the altar rail. Stella lay down on a pew, on her back. She closed her eyes. She folded one hand over the other, placed both over her heart.

"What do you think, Miss Silver?" Don asked her, and the spell was broken.

"I'd feel strange, pretentious going to the funeral of people I didn't know."

"The world knows them now," Cat answered. "At least their faces."

They heard the postman stuffing letters into the metal mailbox.

"Bombingham," Cat said, and they all were suffused with shame.

Goliath leapt from Cat's lap to run barking toward the closed front door.

"Goliath!" Cat called once, sharply, but she did not persist.

Except for the yapping of the dog, they listened in silence to the postman's steps resounding on the wooden wheelchair ramp, and he was gone.

After another volley of barks, Goliath turned, wagged his tail with satisfaction.

"It's too awful," Stella said. It was a stupid thing to say, but she wanted them to keep talking. She wanted somebody to find the right words. She stopped petting the sofa arm.

"Birmingham will never be the same," Cat said. Her sentence launched itself into the air above the bare boards of the living room and sank.

"King's coming back to speak," Don said hopefully.

Stella did not know how a person could be so brave as Martin Luther King.

So calm. She wished his words would inspire her. She always listened respectfully. She admired him. Yet he seemed masked to her. She didn't know him; his message remained impersonal for her.

"I want us to go," Cat repeated.

Stella thought of those households where parents must be dressing to attend their daughter's funeral. No matter what their pain, no matter how wrung with grief, now the families must put on their socks or their hose. They must cover their naked feet appropriately. They must slip their arms through the sleeves of a shirt or dress; they must tighten a belt, glance in a mirror. Other family members, friends would be there to help them, finding things, touching their shoulders, fighting their own tears. Glasses of water would be urged on the distraught. Sometimes lovingly, sometimes with a gruffness to hide inadequacy: "Here."

"I've brought you a glass of water," Aunt Krit had said to her, when she herself—only a child of five—had sat in the front row at the funeral parlor.

Aunt Pratt had sat in her wheelchair beside her. Stella remembered how small and young she'd been when her family was crushed. She was just a little girl, and at the funeral parlor Aunt Pratt, parked in the aisle, had reached over the rim of her wheel to hold Stella's hand.

Nancy sat on the other side, small as Stella, and held her other hand. Nancy's mother sat just beyond, with her arm around Nancy.

Stella studied Aunt Pratt's hand, which was sheathed in a flesh-colored nylon glove. Pratt wore such gloves to hide the ugly veins in the back of her hand and to conceal her thin fingers, twisted with arthritis.

Aunt Krit sat across the aisle, on the end of the row, so she could get in and out easily.

People were crying among the four closed coffins.

"Now he's dead," Stella had whispered to Nancy, but Stella felt even her lips were numb, almost too stiff to form words. "No," Stella managed to add. "Now they're all dead."

Nancy's beautiful eyes were full of sadness, but she kept her promise. She didn't cry. Stella had made Nancy promise they wouldn't cry.

"When they all go by," Aunt Krit had said, thrusting a glass of water at her, "we'll follow down the aisle. I'll hold your hand."

STELLA WONDERED WHERE Darl was this September morning, where was her betrothed, why had he not telephoned her nor she him? Why was she at the Cartwrights' with Cat and Don and not Darl?

Suddenly Don said, "How can anybody ever paint or dance or put on a play again in this city?" He jumped up and left the room.

"He's been crying all morning," Cat said.

"Have you?"

"Some."

"I can't. I feel numb."

From his seat in Cat's lap, Goliath cocked his head at Stella.

FOUR LAMBS

BECAUSE ONE OF THE DEAD GIRLS WAS HER COUSIN, CHRIS-
tine had a reserved space in the church. Across the crowded sanctuary, she saw
Charles Powers and his little brother Edmund. She set her lips hard against
each other to try to keep from crying.

She hadn't seen Charles or Edmund since May, drenched with water, in the
pandemonium of the demonstrations. Charles had stopped attending night
school after last May. Edmund had grown. Like herself, Charles and Edmund
were wearing the same clothes they had worn to the demonstration, not
because they wanted to say *that* and *this* are the same, but because these were
their Sunday clothes, their dress-up. She pressed her lips firmly against each
other.

She could not think about the dead children. She could not. She could look at the
coffins, at the flowers. She pictured the explosion, like the hoof of the devil,
splitting the church open; herself standing in the cloud of plaster dust, soul
blown out of her body. Like an empty vessel, she had filled, first with rage. Now
with despair. Things would never change. Things had to change now. Else this
would be in vain. God couldn't let this be in vain. Four lambs left on a bloody
altar. "Sow in sorrow; reap in joy"—wasn't that Scripture?

Christine determined to look at folks' clothes. She always took an interest
in clothes, loved stylish clothes. She herself looked fine in her navy blue suit;
because it was polyester, it had washed up in the kitchen sink, by hand, good
as new. Christine remembered the sludge of plaster dust in the bottom of the
sink, how she had swabbed it out with a used paper towel so the plaster

couldn't clog up the plumbing; then she rinsed what little bit was left down the drain. She had an impulse to catch and save a bit of the milky water, but she had just let it swirl down. She hung her outfit up over the sink to drip dry. And now the skirt and jacket were crisp, good as new.

Polyester was a blessing. She was grateful to those who invented, to George Washington Carver for inventing peanut butter, so cheap and so nutritious, to whoever invented polyester and No Iron.

Edmund's and Charles's clothes looked good, too. None the worse for hard wearing.

Lots of navy blue, black dotted around the church.

There was Lionel Parrish, her night school boss but now a part-time minister, a dancer at the Gaslight (with a woman, his cousin, not his wife), standing with another minister, now sitting down near the front, both in fine gray suits. She looked at the composure of Lionel's smooth, handsome face and thought of King, but then she saw his eye flash, and she thought of Shuttlesworth. She'd never seen Lionel Parrish flash out that way before now.

Lionel Parrish wasn't beaten—she could see that. He sat proudly in his expensive gray suit. He wasn't in despair, but then, it wasn't his kids dead. For that matter, wasn't hers. She tried to make herself glad. What was it Gloria said to try to cheer her? Gloria's grandmother's verse: "This is the day that the Lord hath made. Let us rejoice. Be glad in it."

But Christine imagined the electric chair. She imagined four electric chairs and four white men, one for each dead child, strapped into them. "And there shall be weeping and wailing and gnashing of teeth." That was Scripture, too.

She knew how she wanted the service to start: she wanted somebody to say, loud and ringing, "Vengeance is mine! I shall repay—thus saith the Lord!"

BECAUSE THE CHURCH WAS tightly packed, TJ was squeezed against Agnes. He was thankful for the pressure of her soft body against his. She hadn't wanted to go to the March on Washington, and he had felt alone without her. He had stood close to the Reflecting Pool. He'd faced the front, but that fine, sunny day, King was too far away for TJ to even tell which figure he was. But his voice was everywhere, amplified by the loudspeakers. It had surprised TJ to see the number of white people participating in the Washington march. White touching black in a friendly way. He couldn't help but be suspicious.

Couldn't stop himself from wondering who do they think they are? Almost he hadn't wanted them there. But what sense did that make? This was about integration. Equality and integration. He knew he wanted the equality part.

And where were the white faces? Where were the white people of Birmingham who were supposed to care and regret and detest violence?

He glanced around the church, people trying for dignified silence, but sobs breaking, some low, some spurting up loud, in spite of handkerchiefs and veils. But there was King. Here in Birmingham, TJ could see him fine. Here at home, he could see King.

In Washington, D.C., TJ'd looked in the Reflecting Pool, seen the wavering representation of the great pointed monument and the clouds, and King's amplified voice everywhere as though it emanated from the clouds.

Here to preach, King must be thinking of his own family. Was it safer over in Atlanta than it was in Birmingham? Over there they bombed Jewish churches. TJ had felt abandoned when King moved from Alabama back to Atlanta. King had four little children himself. TJ could see the sorrow in the man. He looked humble and beaten. What could he say? Four children blasted into eternity. What could any man say?

There was Fred Shuttlesworth embracing King like a brother, though some people said Shuttlesworth had had hard feelings last May about King. There was something fierce about Fred Shuttlesworth. The man was made out of energy and courage. He bristled with it.

When TJ looked at the coffins, he thought he was going to howl. He didn't want to do that. He made himself look at the leaders. He *had* to look at them now. They *had* to lead him through this. He heard Agnes crying beside him.

"Don't look at the families," he whispered to her. "Look. There's Dr. King. See there's Reverend Shuttlesworth." But she buried her eyes into his suit shoulder and sobbed. TJ knew that part of her grief was that they never could have their own children. And here were four gone to waste.

When Dr. Martin Luther King took his turn behind the pulpit, TJ thought, clear as day, *Somebody's gonna shoot him someday.*

TRIALS

THEY WERE OLDER THAN EDMUND, BUT HE'D NOTICED THEM. Carole was already buried. Once Addie had let him look through her eyeglasses. He knew them when they were alive. Before the service was over, Edmund decided he'd squeeze out of the sanctuary. He wanted to be standing on the church steps when they carried the coffins out. He had to be there to say good-bye.

He wished he could hug their mamas down near the front of the sanctuary, but they had family, women all around them. He'd just be a fly to them. A troublesome fly buzzing too close. Still, as he squeezed past all the knees, he kept his eyes on the parents. He knew that even though he was just a little boy, never again in his life would he be a witness to such pain.

But he had to be standing on the steps when the coffins were carried from the church, so he squeezed out.

Outside, Edmund saw a throng of grown people, everybody dressed up, crying and waiting. When he was grown, this would be something he'd do—go to funerals. But he was already here.

The steps were jam-packed. Grown people didn't want to make room for him, but he was little and they did.

He could hear the groaning and moaning swell inside the church. His mama had said God had to send trials and tribulations to test us. But why? Yes, the service must be ending. That must be the sound of hell, all that pain, all those tears and wailing inside the sanctuary. The crowd outside became silent. The TV folks got their cameras ready.

There was the end of the first coffin coming out the door, coming out like something being born, riding high up and unsteady on the shoulders of the men. Now the crowd groaned, and the pallbearers were trying to hold the box level, not let it fall, and the front tilted down to descend the steps. Here came the next coffin, and Edmund heard himself wailing. He stood stock-still, he didn't blink, but his mouth was open and spread, turned down like a sad clown's, and the sound was coming out.

He tried to get control of his tongue so he could say the right words. He had to speak. He had to say something out loud on this occasion. For himself, he had to speak, to make the words get round the stone in his throat. God would take his voice away if he didn't say the words.

Here came the last coffin. Everybody crying, all the faces glazed with tears. The crowd was swaying in grief with a sound that must be an ocean sound.

Edmund made himself swallow. He would swallow three times, he decided, then his tongue would be loosed and his lips would shape words. He was sick and weak, but he managed it. He could hear his high child's voice even if nobody else could: "Good-bye, Cynthia. Good-bye, Carole. Good-bye, Denise. Good-bye, Addie."

He watched the three coffins borne high passing over the crowd, coffins like boats on water, to the hearses. Hinged on the side, the big doors at the ends of the black hearses were swung wide open, waiting.

He had spoken in a little voice, but he'd done it. He'd said their names.

EDMUND'S MEMOIR: I BEGIN WORK AND STUDY

WHEN I CAME BACK TO BIRMINGHAM, ESTABLISHED AND grown-up, from Seattle, which is about as far away from Birmingham as you can go and still be in the United States, I came at the invitation of the Birmingham Public Library to speak as an author about my book *Religion: The Relief to Racism,* published at the turn of the millennium, A.D. 2000. It happened at the time of my return that one of the men who had likely bombed Sixteenth Street Baptist Church was on trial at the Jefferson County Courthouse, which is right next door to the Birmingham Public Library, host of the book festival.

At the trial, I saw the elderly parents of Denise McNair and the now middle-aged sister of Addie Mae Collins. No matter the outcome of this trial, I thought, no human justice can ever offer recompense for what they lost. There may have been other family members there in the courtroom; they were the only ones I recognized. Decades had passed, but still these people remembered and suffered. I had a book in my hand that I myself had penned, but seeing them made me want to write another sort of book, one that was less abstract and theoretical, one that was more personal, about what it was like to be a black child growing up in Birmingham.

I wanted it to be a happy story, at least in part, and not just dwell on the pain of that time. I looked around at the other people attending that trial as I pondered the idea of a memoir. There were a lot of sympathetic white people there. I felt sure Birmingham had changed. Maybe I could write about family life and community: how it was for us, emphasize the positive. How my friends and I sometimes played baseball with the white boys—Bubba and

John and all them. Pookie and George, the Greek boy. Whether I finish this memoir or not remains to be seen, but after I went back to my hotel room I began the words that follow.

By the way, my hotel, a completely integrated facility, was just across the street from the once-segregated library close to Richard Arrington Street, named for the first black mayor of Birmingham. Yes, the city did change. There was death, but there was rebirth. There was the seed of equality sown in pain, but there has been and continues to be the harvest. This hotel is named the Tutwiler, but it used to be the Ridgely apartments. The old Tutwiler was foolishly imploded—not a racist bombing, but destruction of the heritage of the city in the name of progress.

DESPITE THE PLEAS of our leaders after the deaths of the four girls, groups of angry people congregated, and more deaths followed. Black people, that is, were killed, one boy by the police, another by white Eagle Scouts. I myself got hurt, but it had nothing to do with those deaths. Still, when I look back at it, I see my little injury as a turning point.

One evening that September before the bombing, Mama called for me to come stand beside her. She was sitting beside the little coal fire in a straight-back chair. She wasn't doing anything, hadn't been doing anything, just sitting, staring into the fire with her knees spread apart, one hand on each knee. She sat straight and strong as a man, and I admired her. Suddenly she asked, though I'm sure she knew the answer, "Edmund-Skeet-baby, how old are you?"

It wasn't my place to question her question, so I just dutifully answered her. "I seven, Mama."

"Come here, baby." She put her big arm around me, and I put my skinny child's arm across her shoulders.

"Skeet, you can't be six or seven no more. You was old enough to demonstrate, wasn't you? You eight."

"Why, Mama?" I asked her in a soft voice. I wasn't surprised at all. It was nearly bedtime, and I was drowsy. It was like a dream, and of course you can be any age in a dream. In church sometimes I would enter just such a drowsy, hypnotic phase. I remember looking into Mama's scalp and at the skin of her forehead and the top of her ear. She was telling me I must say "Yes, sir" and "Yes, ma'am." I must not be *afraid*. But I had missed out on what she said was going to happen.

I was nearly hypnotized, standing close to my strong, low-spoken mother, staring into the little gully in her ear that ran down into a hole into her head. Inside that hole was Mama. If I could make myself small, I could just slide down that hole and live inside Mama's head. I hadn't thought of being afraid.

"Boss-man," she went on, "Mr. Stoner at the Stoner Grocery need a boy to work—straightening and picking up—in the grocery. Jus' down the street. He say he want a boy ten year old, but I say I got a boy—he ain't but eight. And he say for me to bring you up next Saturday."

I leaned close to Mama. My mind was quiet and blank. Unquestioning. Patient.

Mama murmured, "That right, Skeet."

Then she went on to explain the lies I was to tell: that I was in the second grade, that I had failed once because I couldn't read too good. Truth was, I'd never been to school at all, except Sunday school. She said Charles, my older brother, had just learned mischief at school, and she'd keep me sweet at home. Still, I'd demonstrated. Now she was telling me to look smart, but not to say anything at all that I could help. For three hours' work on Saturday afternoon, Mr. Stoner would give me fifty cents. Mama herself would come after me and collect the money.

WHEN SHE TOOK ME to the store, I remember staring down hard at the floor so I wouldn't have to look at Mr. Stoner, my first boss. Later, I would have my own enterprise by becoming a shoeshine boy. Mr. Stoner's pants legs had a sharp crease in them that scared me.

"He's not use to white folks close up," my mama said, but it was his sharp pants as much as his white face that frightened me.

"But, Marie, there are going to be white people all around him here."

Mr. Stoner's shoes were as shiny as plastic. Suddenly, right before my eyes, floated a green lollipop. In a white hand. A green lollipop wrapped up in cellophane. For me.

Mr. Stoner put his hand on my shoulder and guided me toward the produce. I held the lollipop in front of me like a traffic light: green, go.

The produce man said, "Why, he's no bigger than a tadpole. Come here, boy, and I'll introduce you to the artichokes."

I DIDN'T CONSIDER my work to be real work. Real work was at the blast furnaces where my paw worked stoking coal. Real work was on top of the church, roofing. Black men working. Sometimes today I wonder if being a minister or writing a book is real work because it isn't what my people meant by work—manual labor—when I was a boy.

Well, one evening shortly after the bombing, I'd been watching men roofing the little neighborhood church—not Bethel; that was too hard to get to except for special occasions when Reverend Shuttlesworth came down from Cincinnati—and I went outside again to play hide-and-seek around the lumber and the stacks of roofing, and I stepped on a long, rusty nail. My friends made a packsaddle for me and carried me to the house, the nail and wood block still dangling from my foot. I liked being carried like a king, but when Mama saw me, she grabbed me, ran to the rocking chair, held me close and shrieked, "Oh Lord, Oh Lord, Oh! Oh! Oh!"

The neighbor women came quickly, and Mrs. Little pulled the nail out in a slow, agonizing stretching motion. The blood dripped on the floor, and Mama and I bawled together as though I'd been crucified.

"You hush this cryin'," they said to Mama.

"I'm gonna call Mr. Stoner," Mama announced.

Mrs. Watson, gray-haired and skinny, presented a brown bottle. "I already got the peroxide," she said.

"*We* will take care of Edmund," Mrs. Little said, so prissy.

But Mama was already stepping over the spots of my blood on the linoleum, going out the door to borrow a telephone.

They put me on the bed. Mrs. Watson gave my sister, Margaret Rose, a cloth soaked in peroxide to press against my puncture. Then they left me with my siblings, and we four waited for our mother's return. I could see Margaret Rose was scared. She started taking off my other shoe.

"Not supposed to wear any shoes in bed," she said.

"I couldn't help it."

Margaret Rose and I tried to believe in the little household rules that would make home safe and orderly.

She hesitated, and then she said, "I know."

When Mama came back, heavy and fast, up the steps and in the door, she ordered Margaret Rose, "Get under the bed and fetch me out my good shoes."

Margaret Rose just stood there, waiting for Mama to explain.

But Mama wasn't about to explain to any eight-year-old: "Move, girl!"

Margaret Rose moved.

Then Mama told us that Mr. Stoner was going to drive up to the doorstep and take me and her to the Emergency. Margaret Rose was to sit with the younguns.

Mama put a jacket on me and went to stand on the porch. Big boy that I was, standing, she gathered me up in her arms as though I were light as laundry. It was good dark now, but finally we saw the lights from Mr. Stoner's car bobbing up and down as the car carefully dipped in and out of potholes.

When she put me in the backseat, Mr. Stoner said, "Well, Skeet, fella, so you stepped on a nail?"

"Yessir."

"Hurt much?"

"Nosir."

"What's the best way to get up the road, Marie?" She started explaining, but he interrupted her to add, "You did right to call me. Lockjaw's no joke."

And so I was taken to the Emergency Room and given a tetanus shot. I thought Mr. Stoner a kind man. When my foot healed, Mr. Stoner bought me a pair of beautiful brown lace-up oxfords.

One evening in early October, Mama and I sat on the porch steps where it was cooler than in the cabin. I was wearing just my socks, and she was polishing one of my brown oxfords. She was stroking that shoe with the polishing rag so gently, like it was a kitten. She had finished the hard rubbing, and gotten pleased, and started the gentleness. I watched her turning her head lopsided, smiling, loving that handsome shoe.

Finally she held both the shoes up together by their heels and asked, "How that, sugar man?" They glowed new brown and Mama's face was glowing, too. "Slip 'em on. Le's see how they look."

Wearing my clean socks, I slid my feet in. I scrunched my toes inside the shoes and the inner leather was slippery and smoother than mud. I took up the slack in the laces, and carefully tied the knots, which I had just learned to do.

"Stand up."

I stood up, and she surveyed me approvingly from top to toe.

"Skeet," Mama said, "nex' week you's gonna start in at the school."

I scarcely dared look her in the eye, but finally I did, and saw the shining there.

"I is!" I felt my whole body go glad.

"You sure is, doll-baby. First grade. You soon catch up."

Sadly, though my sister was almost nine, Mama told Margaret Rose she couldn't start to school just yet.

I LOVED SCHOOL from the get-go and still remember some of the lessons I learned. Only Mississippi paid its teachers less than Alabama did, but my teachers were wonderful people, and I remember their dedication with great gratitude.

I remember when my teacher, Miss Smith, put change in my hands and said, "Money is counted in pennies, nickels, dimes, quarters, and halves." And I shook them all together in my cupped hands, and they made a joyful noise. Now I could count my own pay.

Once Miss Smith wrote a word on the blackboard: *paste*. And she said, "It does not stick together. It is for mouths, or more exactly for teeth, but it cleans your breath, as well as your teeth—toothpaste."

I found it delicious as ice cream but not cold. It was to be spit out, which I thought a shame.

Probably using her own money to make the purchase, Miss Smith gave each of us a tube of toothpaste and a toothbrush. When I took them home, Mama said I must share my brush with my sister, and I gladly did.

And another day Miss Smith said: "There is a story about each one of you." And she printed my story on the blackboard. For everybody to read:

Skeet is seven years old. At home, Skeet has a mother and father, one sister, and two baby brothers. He has a grown brother named Charles, too. Skeet has pretty shoes. He works in a food store. His real name is not Skeet. It is Edmund Powers.

At lunchtime, I whispered to Miss Smith, "I was in the protest. I want to write about that someday."

"You can," she said. "Someday you can. And tell your grandchildren, too." Then her eyes filled with tears and she hugged me. Her voice changed. "I so proud of you."

"Don't cry, Miss Smith." I stopped eating my paper cup of chocolate ice cream. I stared at the little wooden paddle that came with the cup and felt something change inside myself. It was my spirit growing toward the future.

"I was too scared I'd lose my job to join in," she said. She took out the tissue she always kept tucked in the belt of her dress. I could feel her tears wanting to flow.

"I sure am glad you here to teach me," I said and smiled at her.

How did I know enough to say that? I think it was because she was kind to me, and her kindness elevated me to a new level of maturity. For a moment, she drew me up to her level of understanding, how we must all encourage one another. I wondered if she had been at the funeral after the church bombing. I hadn't seen her.

That day I viewed my first film clip in first grade. Miss Smith said, "You'll see the president of the United States and his family. Do not talk when I turn off the lights. Do not leave your seat. Do not laugh or cut up in the dark."

And there he came, projected onto the wall, walking and talking, with beautiful white teeth that were surely just brushed with toothpaste, and crisp thick hair, a little bit like mine. We saw him in special clothes called pajamas, smiling and playing with two little children. Tossing the little boy up into the air. A beautiful little white girl.

When the lights were on, Miss Smith said, "It is possible in this day and age, in your lifetime, Edmund Powers and all of you, for a Negro to become president of the United States!"

That was a hard time, the fall of 1963, but even while terrible things were happening and families were shattered, children were getting jobs, gifted with new shoes, sent to school, and getting inspiration and ambition from their teachers.

three

O SACRED HEAD,
NOW WOUNDED, November 1963

BOX OF MOONLIGHT

THE JIGGLING OF THE BED WAS WAKING STELLA.

The jiggling came into her consciousness from a distance, the way a horse rides toward the movie camera in a romantic western. The hoofbeats grew louder and louder till they were upon her, and she woke up.

But she was lying in her bed, and the room was full of moonlight. She glanced up over the headboard and there was a three-quarters moon gleaming like a shield. She had forgotten to pull the shade and close the curtains, the way her aunt always instructed.

The house and the night were absolutely still. No, an airplane was flying low over Norwood, headed for the airport.

During the summer, several times a week, she and Darl had walked over to the highest hill on Norwood Boulevard, only a couple of blocks away. They sat with their backs against the largest oak tree on the highest hill, and hugged and kissed for hours. Sometimes when a plane flew over large and low, it seemed just above their tree. Each window of the plane was clearly outlined, and Stella knew that on the other side of the line of portholes were rows of people in upholstered seats. Those travelers had no idea that she and Darl existed, that just below, for an instant, she and Darl were lying on the grass in a rapture of pleasure.

But the plane was passing over her bed now; it couldn't have awakened her.

She inspected the room—dresser with its bench and winged, three-way mirror, the highboy. How still the furniture seemed. The room had only three pieces of furniture in it. When Stella studied, she worked at the dining room table. Without moving, she glanced at the closet door, and it was closed and still, standing white and tall in the moonlight.

Then what had moved?

Stella became aware of her hand placed low between her thighs. She stirred against her hand. Yes, she had been rubbing herself. She had been masturbating. Stella smiled. She became a froth, a foam of amusement.

She had read that shocking word in one of her college psychology texts. Despite myths, the book said, masturbation did absolutely no damage of any kind, mentally or physically. Myths? No one had ever mentioned masturbation to her, let alone myths about it. Now she knew what it was. She giggled—she tried so hard to be *good;* in sleep her unconscious had tried to relieve her need. So much kissing and hugging, all summer. Then fall weather had set in, and they really didn't have a place to go.

Last night, with warm jackets on, she and Darl had walked to their giant oak on the boulevard, but the ground was too damp and chilly for sitting. All the leaves had fallen, and the bare branches stretched bleakly into the night sky.

They resolved to stay only till a plane had flown over. She stood with her back against the rough oak bark, and Darl pressed against her, kissing and kissing. When they heard the plane approaching, Darl flung himself flat on his back on the cold ground, spread his arms out in crucifix fashion, and said, "Raped by a jet plane!" All lit up, the plane roared over them.

Shocked at Darl's exclamation, Stella had just stood there staring down at him. Had she ever heard anyone say the word *rape* out loud? Then she thought of Professor Andrew Gainey, at the college, singing the rape song from *The Fantasticks* at the top of his lungs. It hadn't meant *rape* at all; it had meant *sex.* With his resonant, confident, gleeful voice, he was letting sex out of the bank vault and into the world. Beautiful.

Stella moved her hand from her crotch and touched her engagement ring. Such a sweet circle, topped with its little diamond. A diamond like a clear seed. Aunt Krit didn't accept Darl as her fiancé. "I don't believe you love *him,*" Krit had said. "When you set the wedding date, then I'll believe it."

Stella had asked, "Why don't you believe I'll marry Darl? I have a ring."

"I just know," her aunt said. "He's not right for you. I believe we might be distant kin to his family." But she never offered a shred of evidence.

From her bed, Aunt Pratt called, "No, we're not."

"He's no Prince Philip," Aunt Krit replied from the kitchen. That was it; she didn't think anybody but a prince might be good enough for *her* niece. "He's not Prince Rainier."

The aunts never disagreed face-to-face, but in their trans-room differences, Stella always rooted for Aunt Pratt.

Stella held up the ring to let the moonlight kiss it.

So, she'd been masturbating so hard, she'd jiggled the bed. She'd awakened herself. She laughed out loud, but quietly. *What kind of repressed southern lady coward are you?* Consciously, she placed the palm of her hand over her nightgown and rubbed. Nothing happened. That was fine. She smiled at herself again and made a vow to do just as she pleased with her body. But not to tell. Well, she could probably tell Nancy; they always confided in each other.

She hadn't told Darl but tomorrow after school and before work at Fielding's, she was going to the gynecologist. At the doctor's, she would get a prescription for birth control pills, and then she and Darl could do what they wanted. She wasn't as stupid as she looked standing against the oak tree on the boulevard: he had needs, and so, it turned out, did she. *Sexual* needs.

But Old Maid Aunt Krit was right that they hadn't set any wedding date yet.

Stella held her hand up in the moonlight and spread her fingers, as though she would seine the light. She looked at the opposite wall to see if the moonlight was strong enough to cast a shadow. It wasn't. The light was diffuse. The whole room was luminous; the dresser and the closet door, her hand, all were equally magical.

Quietly, she slid down from the high bed and sat on the bench before the three-way mirror. She wanted to see her face in moonlight. There she was. It was as though she were walking through the woods, came to a still pond, and looked down to see her own face. Here she was in a quiet room, a virgin fair in an enchanted world.

Tomorrow, November 22, would be an important day: she would get birth control pills, and a new world would open to her. But the store was open of course Friday night—a pre-Thanksgiving sale—and she'd have to go to work the switchboard, the same as every Friday night.

HOW THE NEWS CAME TO THE JONESES

"FIX MY COFFEE," RYDER JONES SAID TO HIS WIFE.

"All right, hon," Lee answered.

While she opened the door on the pantry cabinet, she glanced at her husband, who was working at the kitchen table. Ryder was as absorbed with his wires and clocks as son Bobby making a model airplane. Friday was Ryder's half-day off this month, and he was wasting the afternoon as usual. Up on the cabinet shelf beside the Maxwell Instant, she noticed the cylindrical cardboard box of Morton's salt.

Stealthily, Lee dumped the sugar out of the sugar bowl and into a cracked cup and hid the cup on a high shelf. She took the salt down, lifted up the metal spout in the lid. As the metal shunt came up, the cardboard creaked a little, but Ryder didn't glance her way.

Lee'd always admired how neatly made a salt box was—a sturdy cylinder completely closed, except for that one little snout of a spout, the box wrapped round with a nice navy blue label. Like it was dressed up to go out. The box never got out of working order either. She poured the salt into the sugar bowl.

Ryder was still absorbed in reading his bomb directions. She turned and flicked on the gas under the one-quart white enamel pot. She used that pot just to boil water, and it had tan mineral deposits on the inside. Lee had asked Ryder couldn't she have a little kettle for the stove, but he'd said there wasn't any need. Around the top of the white enamel pot ran a line of red trim, bright and nice, except where she'd banged it once and there was a black chipped place.

Ryder was reading the directions one of his Klan buddies had printed down for him. Handwriting like a second grader, Lee thought. It had occurred to her that since she had children of different ages, she could figure out at exactly what age each of his Klan buddies had stopped growing up. Ryder himself was about ten, same as Bobby, but Bobby was still growing. Some of the Klan were more like six or seven.

Suddenly she said to Ryder, "You know sometimes I wonder if the kids might be better off brought up Catholic."

"Catholic!" he yelled and banged the table with his fist. His soldering iron leapt onto the floor. "Now look what you made me do!"

She'd wanted to rile him, and she had. She was bored. He ought to pay more attention to her. Take her out to a movie. At least talk to her, not sit there playing like a child. "Well I was just thinking about it," she said, completely unruffled.

He responded to her ease with his own good humor. "Kennedy works for the pope."

She said nothing. Kennedy was the only politician who wasn't a complete bore, and that was just because he was good-looking. Ryder picked up his iron and inspected the tip for damage.

"That's one thought you'd better put out of your head, girl," Ryder said. "Catholics aren't real Americans."

She nodded at the mess of buckets and bobbers on the table. "I don't think they'll want any more bombs now for a long, long time," she said.

"You don't know nothing about it." The tide of scorn began to rise in his tone.

"How come you don't already know how to make it, if you done what you said you done?"

"There's different types."

"How'd you do the other?"

"It wasn't easy."

"I can smell Bobby's airplane glue all the way in here from the living room," she said.

"Yeah." He fell silent.

Lee wandered into the front room. The two little ones were playing Go Fish on the floor, proud that they knew their numbers well enough to compete. But it was Bobby she was proud of. He was 100 percent pure boy with a shock of hair on his forehead; she loved the way he was focused on making his model. Bobby was gluing the little gas tank onto the end of a fighter wing. He didn't even know she'd come into the room. She'd let him stay home with a cold.

Ryder ought to be proud of his kids, she thought. She imagined her children crossing themselves like Catholics did in the movies and thought how sweet and pious Bobby, Shirley, and Tommy would look. She'd known some Italian Catholics growing up. They were the same as anybody. Maybe happier, with their big families and huge dishes of spaghetti.

"Water's boiling," Ryder called.

"You know what, Ryder?" she said, reentering the kitchen. "I think it's nothing but ignorance to be down on Catholics."

"I don't want to ever hear you say that again." He sounded tense.

"Well what'd they do?" She selected a cracked cup for Ryder on purpose. "They didn't crucify Jesus."

"Hurry up, will you? You're slow as Christmas."

"Well, what'd they do?" She set the coffee and the sugar bowl and a spoon down in front of Ryder. "You fix the sugar to suit."

She watched him spoon the crystals into his cup, two teaspoonfuls. He stirred it to help it cool.

"Back in the 1920s, we had to shoot that Father Coyle."

She laughed. "You wasn't even alive back in the 1920s. How could you shoot anybody?"

"The Klan. It was a Methodist minister Klan member kilt him."

"I just don't believe that."

"That Father Coyle married the Methodist minister's daughter to a Mexican, and he was Catholic. He shot him on the porch of the priest house."

"I never read any Alabama history about that."

"It's not all in books, Lee. But people know, and we hand it down, from generation to generation." He sipped his coffee and yelled, "God-damn son of a bitch! What'd you put in my coffee?"

She smiled prettily, shrugged her shoulders, and said, "Same old coffee."

He licked his finger and stuck it in the sugar bowl, then in his mouth. "This here is salt!"

She licked her finger and tasted, mimicking him. "Why, I believe you're right." She was in a fine mood.

Springing out of his chair, Ryder dashed the contents of the coffee cup into the sink. He banged the cup on the drain board, and it broke in two, right along a crack line.

"Don't break up the dishes, hon," she said.

"Don't you stand there like an idiot with your finger stuck in your mouth. I asked you for some coffee."

"Well, I'll just have to start over." She turned her back to him, but she heard him fling open the cabinet doors.

"Where's the gol-durned sugar!" He was scanning the high shelves.

"I'll look, honey. You just sit down and figure on your bomb."

"Here it is!" he announced. "Somebody poured it out of the bowl and into this cup. You do that, Lee?"

"Now why'd I'd gone and did a silly thing like that, Mr. Ryder Jones?"

He sprang at her and slapped her finger out of her mouth.

"Mr. Tough Guy," she taunted.

He grabbed her hand and twisted her arm behind her back. "You better tell me the truth, woman, or I'm gonna teach you."

"Teach me what?" He wasn't hurting her much. "You're just making a tempest out of a teapot."

When Ryder jerked her hand up, hard, a switch flipped inside her. Something familiar and intense was beginning, though it was only afternoon.

"That hurts!" she said. "Stop it!" A current of fear like a thrill went through her. But suddenly there was Bobby standing in the doorway.

"Dad," he said, "whatcha doing to Mama?" He seemed scared but brave.

"Oh, Bobby," she said, "we were just playing." He looked small, just a little boy.

He brushed his forelock away from his eyes. "You said it hurts. Just now you said 'That hurts!'" All innocence, he was just asking a question. He had a cold in his nose.

Ryder said threateningly, "Go back in the living room, son."

Ryder was hurting her worse, but she wouldn't let on in front of Bobby. She just said to her son, "Please, Bobby, go on."

After the boy turned to go, the phone rang, and Ryder hurried to answer it. Then Ryder pivoted Lee around in front of him and slapped her hard across the face. "I got to go in to work," he said.

Then the doorbell rang, and everything sped up. While her head swiveled, she could see Bobby standing at the front door, talking to Bob Chambliss, then calling back to the kitchen, "Daddy, daddy, come quick. Mr. Chambliss says they shot the president."

Ryder ran through the house—"Hot dog!"—out the screen door—"No lie?"—and down the steps with his friend.

"I'm going, too," Bobby shouted back at her and ran after the men.

Unperturbed, Shirley slapped down a two of spades on the bare floor.

"What's happened?" her little brother asked.

"I dunno. Somebody got shot."

STELLA'S ODYSSEY

WHEN ELLIE SIGNALED THROUGH THE LIBRARY QUIET FOR Stella to wait, Stella had already gathered up her books and was about to leave the Birmingham-Southern College library to get a bus to town, then see the gynecologist, then maybe kill some time at Parisian's, then on to Fielding's and her Friday evening work on the switchboard. But Ellie said, "Wait." Stella stopped beside the railing around a large opening down to Circulation. Ellie leaned close to Stella's ear to whisper the news. Then Ellie drew back, her eyes locked on Stella, the corners of her mouth curiously turning slightly up.

Ellie was a friend, a talented actress, a liberal. Ellie certainly wasn't *amused*. Stella felt hysterical, as though she might lose her balance, pitch over the railing, and land down below, headfirst, onto the circulation desk. She saw her head breaking into two neat pieces. Her heart seemed to be caving in, and the book-lined world was filmed with tears.

But why this stupid twitching of the lips, as though I might smile? Stella asked herself.

Ellie added, still slightly smiling, "I can't believe it."

"Maybe it's a rumor," Stella whispered back. "Like 'The War of the Worlds'?"

"I don't think so. It was a real reporter. Dan Rather in Dallas, Texas."

They were taking turns leaning toward each other's ears in a strange, weaving choreography.

"But who's he?"

"The local reporter, in Dallas."

Now they controlled the curling of their lips; they assumed immobile expressions like stunned, fixed masks.

"I don't believe it," Stella said. "I have to go catch my bus." She didn't say *Today I take charge of my body, I get birth control pills.* "I have to go to work this evening."

As she pushed through the door, she heard a loud voice saying from the circulation desk: "May I have your attention. May I have your attention, please. We have terrible news. . . ." But now she was outside.

Stella ran as fast as she could on the grass around the library, then pell-mell like a child, down the steep hill toward Arkadelphia Road and the bus stop. *It can't be. Not after the bombing.* During that funeral, Stella had looked at herself in the mirror in her bedroom and said over and over "Coward!" Trees should burst into flame while she ran down the hill away from the college.

A new atrocity? Run! I won't believe it. It probably was true.

In 1956, she had wanted so badly for Kennedy to get the nomination for vice president. *Can't they see? Can't they see?* She was thirteen. How could they choose that plain Estes Kefauver? And the Democrats had lost (*Can my side really lose?*), though even her Aunt Krit had admired Adlai Stevenson, and voted for him. Aunt Krit said Stevenson was *actually intelligent.* Her voice had been choked with emotion, as though she, too, at last, had something in common with the life of the nation.

Then Krit had said, "You like Kennedy so much, read this." Aunt Krit's voice had to fight its way up from her throat. She wanted so ardently to instill her niece with values precious to herself that she scarcely dared represent them with words or deeds. "I bought it in the book department at Loveman's," Krit said proudly. "Kennedy wrote it. *Profiles in Courage.*"

Stella had made herself read each of the biographical sketches. *Aunt Krit doesn't want me to love somebody just because of his looks,* she had thought. Even then, Stella knew that Aunt Krit, in her gruff way, was trying to protect her from a dangerous susceptibility: *look-love.* But Kennedy was smart enough to write a history book. Aunt Krit revered that. "He wrote it while he had a broken back."

And now the man was cut down, in all his prime and glory.

Divorced from her body, Stella ran lickety-split down the wooded hillside from the college to the street. She leapt over rocks without noticing them.

When Kennedy had been elected president, Stella had thought smugly of her own ability to recognize his promise: yes, she herself had had some insight into politics and *intuition* about who was going to count. And his wife was beautiful and loved classical music and spoke French. Ellie, her friend, looked something like Jackie Kennedy.

Why had Ellie smiled? Was it the smile of embarrassment—that they lived in such an unbelievably cruel world?

After he had been safely elected president, people had said Kennedy never would have been allowed on the ticket for president if he'd been the vice presidential nominee running with Stevenson, who would have lost in any case. No Stevenson-Kennedy nor any other possible combination could have beaten Ike. That's what people said, and then Stella's smugness melted, and she knew how ignorant she was of the ways of the world and of politics. If, in 1956, she had gotten her wish, it would have doomed Kennedy.

But he was doomed. Shot or dead?

She'd reached the bus stop. It was a miracle she hadn't fallen down the hill. But she must have turned her foot. Her ankle was throbbing. Her body, too, was cramping. She felt as though her body was opening to bleed. It was supposed to be tomorrow, not today. The gynecologist didn't want her to schedule her appointment during her period. Maybe it wasn't much flow. But she could feel herself starting to bleed. He was bleeding in Texas. He might be dying.

Her books weighed so heavily that she felt too weak to hold them. They fell around her feet. She felt as though she might faint. This was the president. It was like saying God was dead, and that was what Nietzsche *had* said.

Stella gasped for air as she watched cars drive past the bus stop. Did they know? The president was shot. Her stomach roiled. When Stella's philosophy professor had enunciated Nietzsche's "God is dead" in his lecture, she had thought she was going to be sick. But the teacher said that for existentialists the death of the idea of God meant a certain kind of freedom. Exhilaration! But for others, that we were *doomed* to freedom.

She knelt to pick up her books. The professor had turned around and recreated on the blackboard a cartoon he'd seen. He'd written "God is dead" and attributed the quotation to Nietzsche. Then he'd crossed out the quote and written under it: "Nietzsche is dead" and under that line, he signed "God."

Half the class had laughed, relieved, and half the class had only looked thoughtful, including Ellie her new friend, who resembled Jackie Kennedy and was one of the few married students.

Kennedy couldn't die. What kind of world would this be, *essentially*, if the president was assassinated? But presidents had been assassinated before. Lincoln, the great Lincoln. What kind of country was this, that killed its great leaders?

Stella was starting to sob, and she knew this was hysteria. If her parents weren't gone, she wouldn't be crying like this. "I was too little," she whispered to the vacant bus stop. She'd study psychology, not graduate on time, but stay an extra year and be a psychology major instead of an English major. Just stay on at the college. She brushed dirt off her books. Maybe she wouldn't have sex, not yet. Maybe she wouldn't go to the gynecologist. Maybe she'd just go to work. She felt encased by drudgery, numb, and impenetrable.

But who was pulling up to the curb? Who was driving a strange car? An old two-toned Chevrolet Bel-Air? Who had come to release her?

Who but her fiancé, reaching across the seat to open the door for her, who but Darl?

She flung herself across the seat into his arms, closed her eyes, exploded into tears, pressed her cheek against his. Inside! She was safe inside. Her cheek was pressed tight against his freckles. She'd always loved his freckles. It made him pure in some strange way. Unique. Veiled. His face proclaimed for him that his essence was behind a curtain, as all of us were always doomed to be. She was trying to get past the veil with her pressing, to enter the safety of his mind, to merge. Not to be alone.

"Hey, hey," Darl said, laughing a little. "I know it's a cool car, but, hey, maybe I should have got a Cadillac."

All she could do was sob.

He took time to put the car in gear, then he reached his right arm around her. "Hey, Stella, baby. Is something wrong?"

She sobbed, moved her eyes down to his shoulder, and blubbered into his shirt. *Baby! How could he call her that? She hated it.*

"You like the car, don't you?"

She couldn't speak.

"Just try to calm down, darling—"

Darling. Darl called her darling and no one ever had before. She took a deep breath. It rattled all the way down into her lungs.

"That's right. Calm down now. Don't get unhinged. Try to calm yourself, Stella."

She opened her eyes. They were driving down Eighth Avenue. He was guiding the car among the sparse traffic.

"Oh, Darl. They've shot the president."

He kept his eyes on the road. "I know," he said. "I heard." He spoke quietly. He continued to steer the car.

"Is he all right?"

Darl needed his right hand to steer, to shift again.

"He died."

"Oh no!" The sobbing was stunned out of her. The car smelled of sulfur. Stella looked straight ahead at cars and delivery trucks flowing down a river. No, a road. "Oh no. Oh no." The two words flapped like a metal hinge winging through nothingness. She became that hinge becoming unhinged; the phrase broke into two parts, and dropped. Sometimes she moaned "Oh" and sometimes she ineffectually punched the word "No" into the air.

Darl remained quiet for a time. Finally he said, "It's a pity."

"Is he really gone?" Stella's voice quavered. "Are you sure?"

"They say so. On all the stations. I heard it in the cafeteria. The car doesn't have a radio."

She said nothing.

"But it's got a good engine." He sounded quietly happy. "And I like the colors. Cream and turquoise."

She said nothing.

"Did you notice the colors?"

"Darl, the president is dead."

"It's a pity. I don't believe in murder. I hate violence."

"His life is over. It's all over for him." The handsome president with the beautiful family was lying someplace on a cold slab. The fluids of his body were being drained away.

"I'm sorry he's dead," Darl said soberly. "But in some ways, I guess he deserved it."

"*What do you mean?*" She felt like a volcano erupting.

"If he hadn't backed King and Shuttlesworth and all the colored people, we wouldn't have had that mess."

"I'm *for* integration."

"Most people think Kennedy's ruined the South."

Stella sat up straight, away from him. Out the car window, she watched a large black bird with an ivory bill languidly rowing through the air. "Kennedy was trying to help *save* the South."

"I'm sorry he's dead. I wish he had just pulled back. Been patient." Darl sighed. "My dad said we'll never be the same, after Kennedy."

"But your dad's not glad?" She noticed her books spilled on the floor of the car. That was the way it was with books: you forgot they existed; you carried them around as though they were part of your own body. Then you looked down, and you were wading in them. She reached down to stack the spilled books onto her lap. *How Does a Poem Mean?* by John Ciardi. *Cry, the Beloved Country* by Alan Paton. Paul Tillich's *The Courage to Be.*

"I haven't talked to Dad yet," Darl said. "You need a satchel for your books."

The car seemed to be slowing down. The world seemed to be slowing, or was it time? *All the King's Men,* by Robert Penn Warren, still lay beside her foot.

"Darl, I think you might be glad."

"I'd say, more like relieved."

"Those four girls weren't doing anything. They were attending *their church.*"

"But he was doing something. He was backing up their leaders."

"Murder is murder." Stella made herself sit perfectly still. Without any movement of her eyes, she stared at the street flowing under the hood of the car. She breathed as shallowly as she could. She wanted to apply the brakes to the flow of time. *Pain is pain.*

Then she slowly asked Darl to do something she never regretted, not once. She asked him to stop the car. She told him, calmly, that she wanted to get out. She preferred to ride the bus, she said. Before Stella got out, she held out his ring toward him.

"I can't marry you," she said.

He gripped the steering wheel hard. Behind his brown freckles, his skin turned pink. His face was like a strange fabric: brown dots on a pink field.

"All right," he finally said. He shifted into neutral, then raised up the palm of his hand to receive the ring. "I won't be asking again, Stella. You better be sure." His eyes were full of hurt pride, or was it pain?

She pressed the ring deep against the skin of his palm and into the flesh. The ring made scarcely a dent in his skin but sat round and inviolate as eternity in the palm of his hand. The little diamond shattered light prismatically.

AND THEN SHE WAS standing in the gutter, a pile of four books held in the crook of her arm.

Stella watched the back of the turquoise and cream Chevy as he drove away. He seemed sealed up in the car. He became the departing car.

A yellow Volkswagen Beetle crept past her, and she thought *Yes, Darl is a peanut inside a one-hump shell*, though Darl was not in the Volkswagen. Her gaze shifted to Vulcan, lame-footed in the distance with his arm extended high against a cloudy horizon. Furious with herself for knowing Darl so little, she stamped her hurt foot. Her Aunt Krit was right: she wasn't going to marry Darl. Not ever.

She looked at the stack of books in her arm, hardcovers with stiff edges, countless pages held between. *All the King's Men.* Whatever the books might tell seemed unavailable, as though she had lost the ability to read. But she remembered—sitting beside her mother on the lime green sofa, her mother saying "All the king's horses and all the king's men / Couldn't put Humpty together again." Two fat tears ran down Stella's cheeks. Impatiently, she brushed the tears aside.

What did all that matter? Darl and her? A couple of college kids. Unhinged. John F. Kennedy was dead.

She watched the cream roof of Darl's car receding in the distance. Another car, an old red Buick, pulled into the lane behind Darl, and he was gone. She was not in any car; if it rolled and scrambled its passengers in a wash of blood, she would not be among them this time.

WITH DISBELIEF, SHE LOOKED at the sunshine. There were no trees to shade the ugly, concrete place where she waited. Here was a gas station, a metal sign proclaiming BUS STOP screwed to a creosote-soaked pole. She had to get to her doctor's appointment. She had to go to work. Why was everyone moving slowly?

It took an attendant many minutes—was it five? ten?—merely to walk around the front of a red Thunderbird convertible with its ragtop up. (How could a car be so fetching? So beautifully shaped and sexy?) The attendant's name was embroidered in chain stitch on his pocket: *Ryder.* He was wearing an old black cowboy hat. He stepped so slowly that she knew Ryder would rather be riding the plains of the West, being a cowboy, out in the open, not confined to this greasy apron of concrete, bending to get an order for gasoline, what octane, how many gallons?

Ryder hadn't reached the car window yet and already he was preparing a smile, showing his ruined mouth full of bad teeth and the black dead spaces between his teeth. He was still young, not more than thirty, Stella thought, giving his life over to being a grease monkey with filthy hands. He bent his body as though he were old, as though he had already entered his future.

He has grown old, wasted his life bending and smiling. This job has broken his body and spirit. Stella hated what life had dealt this nondescript man named Ryder, how life had cheated him, left him ignorant, fit only for this, a greasy black rag streaming from his hip pocket. Grease the color of midnight splotched his blue trousers. *Love his humanity,* she enjoined herself.

I can love him.

And after all why not him? Not just as neighbor, fellow human being. Why not accept the card that life dealt us? Call this man not Ryder but Romeo?

When she was twelve and had played with the boy next door, she had wondered *Why not marry him?* Aren't any two human beings basically suitable for each other? If they let each other be and also try to help each other? They had played together, shooting each other with rubber suction-cup darts. He was fat, something of an outcast, but she had understood: she was different, too. She liked playing with him. Wasn't everybody off the mark of normal, she had wondered naively then. So why pick and choose? Why say to anybody: *You are not suitable*.

Mama had once said to her, "Stella, try not to go to extremes in your thinking."

But why not? Why not follow logic to the end? Why wasn't logic as good as faith?

Only there didn't seem to be any life-logic unless it was all a matter of faith, of God's plan.

Certainly not her plan.

She watched the too-slender young attendant leaning toward the window that the driver was cranking down. Slender, not skinny, was the term she applied to herself. Poor Ryder. Poor nutrition probably. Bad diet, rotten teeth, yes, she'd seen the evidence in other such men. Ignorant, he didn't understand the importance of taking care of his teeth. What if she gave herself to one such as Ryder? Would he feel his life was blessed?

Ryder spoke to the driver. "Would you like a flag?" How strange—arrogant—his tone. Full of swagger. "We're giving them away free today."

He held out a windshield decal: the Stars and Bars. A Confederate flag.

"No thanks," the driver answered.

Today! Today, he's offering a free Confederate flag! Stella felt her pity for the dirty attendant draining away.

Ignorant and poor, he was from the underclass, who served the upper class. The underclass who turned much of their hatred and bitterness toward the blacks. He proudly imagined that it was possible for him to own the car he served, to sit in the driver's seat. After all, in a free country he could drive a Thunderbird into a filling station, same as anybody.

Ryder straightened up, slightly turned his head. He spat onto the greasy concrete. Was it contempt, this spitting? Maybe his lungs were bad, maybe his sinuses ruined with smoking cigarettes, and he simply had to clear himself.

The driver accepted the spitting as meaningless and told how many gallons to pump.

Stella listened to the soft swish of cars in the street, passing her at dirge speeds. She saw no sign of the bus. The cars crept forward. Darl had driven on without her, and surely there was relief in that. This was the real world, standing on concrete, isolated, struggling against fatigue to hold her books, her ankle throbbing. The world was not a male cheek curtained with freckles. Not that cheek she could wet with her own tears, kiss, playfully lick, if they lay under a giant oak on the grass of Norwood Boulevard.

Surely it was taking the grease monkey more than five minutes to fill the tank. Was he dawdling on purpose? (Darl had squirmed away, laughing, when, on that humid night so oppressive you had to create jokes to endure, she'd licked inside his ear, tasted the bitter wax from deep in the canal.) The driver showed no impatience. Ever so slowly the man in the driver's seat lit a cigarette. Stella wanted to run to him, to say *Stop! This is a gas station. Don't you realize the danger?* The man had frizzy red hair, a large nose, a small chin. He wore glasses with a clear rim. The way he dragged on the cigarettes was somewhat theatrical, too slow.

Stella moved her hand to scratch her nose. She saw her own hand had been slowed down, and it occurred to her that her perception might be distorted.

The motion had not *felt* slower; it had only looked slower. John F. Kennedy was dead. Time had woven itself into the air, and now they all lived unreal in a new matrix.

There were no authentic checks or tests to distinguish dream from reality, so said Descartes.

Standing in the doorway of the classroom with his cigarette hand out in the hall, Dr. Drummer had confided to the class that *he* had thought there *were* ways to tell the difference between dream and reality. And can you distinguish memory and imagination? she had wanted to ask. Which of them is real? Dizzy with memory, her body was lying in the cemetery on the towel near the giant magnolia tree. And Darl. He had been really there, too. The professor had leaned his body out into the hall to drag on the cigarette: he was obeying the rule for faculty not to smoke *in* the classroom.

Suddenly the dark men, like ghosts, had been standing on the grass very near her and Darl. It was as though they'd come out of the ground. Nothing had ever seemed so real.

Once, Dr. Drummer had confessed, he himself had had a mental illness, hallucinations. Stella had admired the matter-of-fact way he told the class something stigmatizing and private. Once Dr. Drummer had thought he had seen electric wires running everywhere, but he had tested the perception. He had approached the wall crawling with snakelike electric wires and tried to touch one: then the black cords had disappeared. As he finished his story, he pushed his glasses, black plastic frame, more securely up his nose. Dr. Drummer explained he had used one sense to test the other. You could test reality. Descartes's "Dream Problem"—solved. She doubted it.

Ryder spoke again. "Didn't notice the out-of-state plates. Staying down here long?"

"I think so," the man answered and fished dollar bills out of the slit of his wallet.

Ryder put his hands on his hips. "Fine day, ain't it?" he said.

She winced to think of Darl, smug behind his freckles, unaffected by murder. Probably it was someone just like this Ryder who had pulled the trigger.

The red-haired driver said nothing about the fineness of the day. "Would you mind to get the windshield?"

Maybe she was watching a contest. But usually the attendant did the windshield without any prompting. (Suppose she never married anybody.) The driver didn't have to be trying to dominate Ryder. ("Don't come unhinged," Darl had said to her.)

Ryder moved suddenly, like a spring uncoiling. "Sure thing."

How could you interpret motives, when observation itself was subjective? She had not believed Dr. Drummer's proof. Because she saw that he had taken comfort in it, she'd offered no challenge: Why can't more than one sense enter into the delusion? Why can't hallucinations just come and go randomly? Didn't life? (When she'd given back the ring to Darl, she had pressed the circle hard into his palm.)

In his "Third Meditation," Descartes had had the honesty to say there was no proof, only faith. His faith was that a universe bleared with illusion would be a cruel joke on humankind, and his faith was that God was no Jokester. But Descartes had not questioned the faith that other civilizations might have in other gods, and those gods not burdened with the attributes of omniscience, omnipotence, and kindness might have a different nature, some of them certainly pranksters to be appeased. (She was not going to marry Darl.)

"Now, would you check the air pressure," the driver said.

And Stella felt certain he was pushing Ryder.

"All the way from New York, huh?" Ryder said. And his voice purposely conveyed suspicion. "My line won't reach. You'll have to move back some." Menace in his tone, a warning: back up, back off.

"I think it'll reach," the driver said smoothly. "Would you mind trying?"

For a moment neither of them moved. The driver drew on his cigarette.

Suddenly Ryder spat again, but he walked around, pulled out the air hose and gauge, and checked the pressure.

Stella saw her bus in the distance, just the front of it. By faith, she assumed the unperceived body of the bus followed behind its face. About Darl, she had assumed too much. He had dropped the ring into the open slit of his madras plaid shirt pocket.

"Tires is normal," Ryder said to the driver. He sounded little and tired, the starch gone out of him.

Again Stella felt a rush of sympathy for Ryder. She wondered if he even owned his own car. What did the Thunderbird driver know about struggle? He looked nothing like a cowboy. *If he spins out,* Stella decided, *I'll hate him.*

The Thunderbird driver reached to his panel, flipped on the radio, and classical music poured out. He drove away carefully. She saw the Empire State on his car tag. Maybe he didn't know the southern language of contempt, how to lay down rubber at the feet of your opponent. Instead, Chopin's "Revolutionary" etude was billowing out.

That would be Rubinstein at the keyboard. *Rubinstein, Horowitz*—her mother seemed to love even their names.

Ryder took the rejected flag sticker out of his shirt pocket. He peeled off the backing and affixed the Stars and Bars of Dixie to the metal side of the gasoline pump.

Stella turned from him and watched the front of the bus gradually loom larger. It seemed enveloped in mystic vapors, as though it were a hot day, not November 22.

WHEN SHE BOARDED the bus, Stella saw Ellie sitting by herself, and she slid in beside her. Yes, this was a day for strange recurrences. *Maybe Darl will put the Chevy in reverse. Traffic will run backward, and he'll roll trunk-first back into my life.*

"I came after you," Ellie said, and she smiled her wide-eyed, open-faced half-smile. "You were flying down the hill. Then you got in a car."

"Did I?" How could she have been flying? Her ankle hurt. She imagined herself gliding, like a robin with outspread wings, at low altitude over the curve of the hill. Maybe time would roll backward, and the assassin's bullet would fly backward into the barrel of his gun. *Kennedy!* Her heart groaned.

"I always feel like an egg entering its place in the carton," Ellie said, "when I sit down on a bus."

Yes. Stella pictured the configuration inside a bus, the leather seats and chromelike holders for the fleshy vulnerability of passengers. The president was a broken shell, the yoke of him spilled out yellow and liquid. She muttered, "Humpty-Dumpty sat on a wall. . . ."

"Are you all right?" Ellie asked.

"I think so."

Outside the bus window, a preadolescent girl with her mother yelled to a friend who was with her mother, "The wicked witch is dead!" *Could she be referring to Kennedy?* The friends hurried together. They were all in stylish fall clothes. One mother said, "It's like the hand of God." Their faces glowed with excitement. Or was that glee?

"I saw you getting into a car," Ellie repeated. What did Ellie's face say to her? *You can tell me or not tell me, Stella.* The fabric of their skirts overlapped—Ellie's brown tweed flecked with orange, Stella's skirt a medium bright blue loose basket weave. For a moment Stella just stared out the bus window. Maybe the bus was stationary and someone was reeling the scenery past, like in an old movie. Beaming businessmen strutted on the sidewalk. Rejoicing. Making V for victory signs with their outstretched fingers.

"It was Darl in his new car." Then Stella held up her left hand, spread her ring-empty fingers so Ellie would understand.

"Oh, Stella," Ellie murmured. She reached up and took Stella's hand out of the air. She brought their clasped hands back to the leather bus seat between them, squeezing Stella's hand.

"My mother and I used to hold hands when we rode the bus downtown from Norwood," Stella said. "She never learned to drive."

(Out the window, a group of teenagers chanted, "One, two, three, four, who you gonna yell for? John-son, that's who.")

Ellie said, "I thought it was the president. I thought you were upset because of him."

"I was," Stella said. "I am."

"I still can't believe it," Ellie said, and she held on tighter to Stella's hand, pressing her knuckles against the seat leather. The skin of an animal no longer alive.

"We have to believe the truth," Stella said. "But some people don't care. Some people are glad." *I could never live in the same house with someone like that. How can I live in the same city with people who are glad about death?*

"I don't think so. I think they just don't know how to react." Ellie glanced apologetically at Stella. "I didn't," she confessed.

Couldn't Ellie see what was going on outside the bus window?

Stella glanced at the people on the bus, the variety of people. Housedresses; a pale gray business suit gazing out the window. No one was rejoicing. A man in blue jeans was staring unseeing at the black rubber runner covering the bus aisle; a neat cream sweater and a knife-pleated plaid skirt hung decorously over a knee and stopped three inches shy of the dirty floor.

Behind the WHITE ONLY sign, the colored people were mixed, just like the whites, as to cleanliness and fashion. They all stared at the floor, bodies slumped. They were utterly dejected, except for one young woman who sat upright, her chin tilted at an arrogant angle.

Everyone so many eggs, as Ellie had said, with their lives and potential hidden inside. Everywhere the framework of shining steel outlining the seats.

"We have to realize what it means to die," Stella said. "What it means for him. What it meant for them. The girls, younger than we are."

"Which girls, Stella?"

"All the dead ones. The four at church."

"Do you think you can imagine death?" Ellie said. Again there was that mild open look to her brown eyes, the encouraging half-smile on her face. The loving glow to her curiosity.

"Yes. I think so," Stella answered. Probably with no one but Ellie would she consider having such a conversation. Now she was scraping the words off her bones: to Ellie, who looked as receptive as Jackie Kennedy, she could present this pitiful pulp of words. "Because of what happened to my family. I had to imagine death. I had to grasp it for each of them. As individuals."

Ellie's half-smile remained. She said nothing. Nothing in her face tried to block out Stella's words. Ellie waited for the words to dissolve in the air. Then Ellie asked gently, "Where are you going?"

"To Five Points."

"I mean where are you going with that idea? That we should make ourselves imagine death." Ellie's voice was low and conspiratorial.

"I don't know," Stella answered. "For me, it was necessary to do, or I couldn't go forward with my own life."

Ellie's reply was a surprise: "I don't know if I can. Or if I want to."

"Maybe it's not necessary for you." Stella watched the knife-edge pleats of the woman's skirt swaying with the movement of the bus. "I mean to imagine death."

Ellie hesitated, then asked, "Why are you going to Five Points?"

"To the doctor."

Stella could see desire in her face. What did Ellie want to share?

"I'm going to see my therapist," Ellie said. "Most people don't know."

"Why, Ellie?" How could anyone so talented and warm need to see a therapist?

"I have depressions."

But Ellie was married. Once that was settled, wouldn't life be settled? At least partly? *Did I ever love Darl? Yes. When he played the organ I could feel my soul growl. Like a dog chained in a basement.*

"My mother had depressions," Ellie went on. "She was married four times. I'm not going to be like that." Ellie's voice dropped to a whisper. (How strange to whisper on a public bus full of strangers.) "I don't know if you know—she committed suicide. When I was thirteen."

Stella whispered back, "I'm going to the gynecologist. To get the new birth control pills."

Ellie's glance was conspiratorial. "But you're not engaged now?"

"I want them anyway," Stella said, surprised at her own answer.

"Do you think you and Darl might make up?" Ellie's face said she was ready to be hopeful, with her.

"No," Stella said.

Ellie just stared at her.

"I want the freedom," Stella said.

"We're all daft on freedom," Ellie mused.

Someone dressed like a giant chicken got on the bus and dropped the fare from orange, three-fingered mittens into the collection box, just like anybody else.

A young man in nice slacks, on the long side-facing seat, said with a grin, "Watch out. Chicken King'll get you."

The whole bus laughed, and the giant chicken settled on the sideways roost next to the wit.

Somebody in the back of the bus repeated, "What he say was 'Chicken King gonna get *you.*'" And a new chuckle of laughter rumbled, low and satisfied.

But Stella felt afraid because she and Ellie were laughing on the day the president was murdered. On the day she'd said what she wanted: *freedom,* whatever that meant. She pulled her hand from beneath Ellie's. The leather seats—the slaughtering of animals—offended her senses.

"What do you think of Sartre's idea," she asked Ellie, "that consciousness is nothingness?"

"I don't believe it," Ellie said. "I think consciousness is an energy. Energy is immaterial but it's not nothingness."

Suddenly a black woman, the one with the straight posture and tilted chin, spoke. She spoke from the back of the bus, right into the air, not looking at them, but as though she were making a general announcement. Not conversation.

"Energy is an exchange of subatomic particles. Under certain conditions, physics tells us energy and matter are interchangeable."

Stella wondered if she were hallucinating. Auditory hallucinations. No one seemed to acknowledge the event of that voice. It was as though everyone but her was deaf. But Stella had seen the Negro woman's lips move. One sense had corroborated the other. Her face was composed of interesting planes—sharp and angular, like a cubist study. The lips were fleshy and curved, contradicting the sharp planes of her face, making her beautiful in an irregular way. Her skin was an average brown, neither especially dark nor light. Her hair had been straightened and fell in a single, sculpted swoop to her chin.

No, Ellie was looking around. Her eyes were seeking contact with the speaker, the colored woman in the back, and Ellie was smiling warmly, but a little shy. "My name is Ellie," she said. Because Ellie was an actress, she could project her voice, yet it remained soft. Her low, sweet voice traveled the sunlight cave of the bus, all the way to the back. "What's yours?"

The dejected colored people glanced up, just their eyes, then fastened their eyes again, anxiously, on the floor. The bus driver was watching through his large, circular mirror.

"Christine," the woman spoke as she rose from her seat. One hand was curled around a chrome rail. With the other hand, she stretched and pulled the bell cord—*ding!*

The *ding* hovered in the portable air caged in the bus, canceling out the woman's name.

The obedient bus swerved to a stop.

Christine looked at no one; she descended the two steps and pushed through the split door onto the pavement. That sound—*ding!*—echoed again in Stella's mind. The rubber edges of the exit door bounced against each other.

To Ellie, Stella whispered, "It's not consciousness that's nothingness." She was glad to have Ellie back into a discussion with just herself. For the first time the idea came clear to Stella. "It's death that is nothingness. If you imagine death, you have to imagine nothingness. A total absence."

"But what do you think of Tillich?" Ellie asked, patting the cover of *The Courage to Be*. "The God beyond God? The God that appears when 'God' disappears?"

Yes. It was a place where Stella had sent her mind. Tillich's words had opened a door into an invisible wall, and beyond. She had struggled and struggled with the concept till she thought she knew what it meant. The God beyond God—the other side of nothingness.

"Tillich is the theologian who provides the best hope," Stella said. Her voice trembled: what was happening to her own belief? Old words played in her memory: "Jesus loves the little children / All the children of the world. . . ."

Maybe someplace there was an abiding love.

Maybe everyplace, a force as universal and natural as gravity. Goodness, or love. A natural force attracting people to one another.

"I have to get off for the clinic," Ellie said. She stood, and Stella noticed her clothes, a simple white blouse, a straight tweedy wool skirt. She was a bit heavier than Jackie Kennedy, more robust and normal. Less glamorous. Just a college girl. Loafers. Suddenly, Ellie reached down and touched Stella's shoulder. "Does it ever strike you," Ellie asked, "what a surreal place Birmingham is?"

But Stella couldn't consider the question quickly enough to reply.

Ellie added, "I'm sorry about Darl."

Stella didn't want her to leave. She needed more of Ellie, but she moved down the aisle and waited before the front door. Stella had wanted to ask about Buford: wasn't Ellie happy being married to Buford? A perfectly nice man, smart and kind; Stella liked him almost as much as Ellie.

Pulling his mechanical lever beside his high seat, the driver opened the bus door for Ellie. HOWARD STILES, Stella read the white lettering incised into his little black plastic nameplate above the large front window. Because the metal frame for the nameplate was open at one end, HOWARD STILES could slide out and another name be inserted. "Have a great day," he yelled after Ellie. "Nigger lover!"

Ellie was walking rapidly down the sidewalk. She didn't hear his taunt. Her round buttocks moving within the tube of the brown tweed skirt, Ellie swayed purposefully past a green trash can. *Pitch-in!* the can said.

Stella felt shocked and frightened. With Kennedy dead, did people think they could freely insult colored people?

Very slightly, Ellie nodded her head to acknowledge a Negro man, dressed in a royal blue business suit, coming toward her on the sidewalk. Stella had seen him before. The striking thing about him was that his trouser legs were cut off just below the torso. His legs had been amputated, and instead of shoes he had pegs. He seemed perfectly healthy. Not like Cat. In each hand he held a wooden mallet, like a potato masher, but more sturdy, of varnished oak. The base of the mallet was a rubber tread; the mallet handles were covered with leather. The man swung his body between his strong arms. Somehow Birmingham had allowed this: a black man dressed as well as any white man, a black man without legs who moved as confidently and swiftly as most people walked. He was a more successful human being than the bus driver.

Would his bed be a pallet conveniently close to the floor? Would his chairs sit legless on the floor? Nice chairs upholstered in white silk brocade. Would the walls reach only half as high before his ceiling capped them off? Suppose she and Darl lived in such an apartment. Would they crawl in the short door like dogs? Perhaps being half the size of normal, the sidewalk man in royal blue, swinging his body through his arms with utmost dignity, could have *two* stories in a single room, twice the space usually allotted.

Why hadn't the earth run out of space allotted for the dead? Some damp earthy space waited now to receive the president. Her heart groaned; where were the words for grief? "O Sacred Head, Now Wounded"—Bach's melody. That was what she longed for, but she needed Darl to play it. Her heart groaned. Perhaps it was an act of generosity to be cremated. But no, she, Stella, would want her own allotted space, underground, should she ever die.

Why not marry a black man? Even here in Birmingham? People did in the North. *Why not marry a legless, successful one?*

At the next stop, every Negro person on the bus got off. A great stream of them. Silently, she cheered: they were rejecting this driver who shouted "Nigger lover" and the transportation he provided. On the sidewalk some of them hugged and patted each other. In perfect dignity, they walked in separate directions. Stella felt she wanted to crawl somewhere on the pavement, like a penitent.

HOWARD STILES, she could report him to the authorities, the bus company. Useless. She had to be on time; she would free her body from its own female biology.

IN THE GYNECOLOGIST'S OFFICE, the woman doctor prepared to give Stella a premarital examination; had her lie on her back, feet in the stirrups, to inspect her virginity. *This is penitence enough,* Stella thought.

When she was dressed again, Stella took satisfaction in her clothes—a blue pleated skirt, full and loose at the hem, box-pleated neatly at the waist, a white turtleneck sweater, slightly angora—an outfit in Madonna colors, innocent blue and cloud white. But Dr. Bradstreet was not considering Stella's clothes; she was writing about Stella on her yellow legal pad, taking notes like a stenographer.

When Dr. Bradstreet looked up, she asked harshly, "What's the date for the wedding?"

The question entered Stella's heart like a stake. But she would not be slain. Why shouldn't any woman have a right to the Pill?

"Oh, we haven't decided yet," Stella lied.

Through round-lens glasses framed with clear pinkish plastic, Dr. Bradstreet, the wisest owl in Christendom, peered at Stella. Where had Stella seen such glasses before? Oh, on the frizzy red-haired driver of the Thunderbird, the emissary from the Empire State. Wise Dr. Bradstreet knew a miscreant when she saw her—never mind the masquerade of blue and white. Stella returned the gaze. Dr. Bradstreet believed she had a remedy named The Truth ready to pierce the defenses of any subversive Liar.

"When you know, telephone me. Then I'll prescribe the contraceptive a month before." She was grim and firm. Her graying hair was oily, dowdy. But she was a medical doctor. For women.

"Oh, it will be within the month."

"You can call me when you're sure of the exact date." Dr. Bradstreet wore her name on a plastic bar, blood red, pinned into a starched white jacket. LOUISE BRADSTREET, M.D., the name tag proclaimed. What did it mean to tell the world your name? That you yourself were surely something other? Not who you were pretending to be at all, but someone much darker, with hidden motives. Not a doctor *for* women, after all, perhaps. But there was the diploma on the wall: *Louise Bradstreet*. Beyond the veil of freckles, who was Darl?

"You don't seem comfortable."

"I was admiring your diploma." Stella felt found out. She blew out a smoke screen of words: "I'm going to graduate from Birmingham-Southern in May." Then she remembered her new decision about her studies. "At least I think I may."

"You may graduate in May?" The woman was cruel. She wanted to torture. "Why wouldn't you graduate in May? Are you in grade trouble?" She wanted to torture any woman who was not a doctor like herself.

"I might change my mind."

"Why would anyone change her mind about graduating?"

"I might change my major."

"Not at this late date. You can't."

But Dr. Bradstreet was noting the possibility on her legal pad. With her left hand, encrusted with diamond rings, she steadied the writing pad. Her right hand held a fountain pen, malachite green with a bright steel nib; PARKER was incised vertically, the letters stacked on top of one another down the clip on the cap. Stella couldn't read what words were being formed by the flow of blue ink from the green stick.

"Am I all right?" Stella asked her.

"What do you mean?" The woman was replacing the cap on her pen, laying the pen on the large replaceable blotter sheet. Four brown leather corners held the blotter board, like the black corners for replaceable pictures in a photograph album.

"Am I healthy?"

"You have a tipped uterus. You might have trouble getting pregnant."

"I can't have children?" Stella stared at the shaft of the green malachite pen displayed against the fuzzy, bland green blotter.

"I didn't say that. You *might* have difficulty."

"But I'm all right?" It was the uniformity of the color of the blotter and its repulsive texture that she disdained. Stella made herself look into the doctor's eyes.

"I saw nothing else of concern. More extensive tests could be run." The doctor's eyes bored into Stella. "Would you like more tests?"

"No." Stella stood up.

"I noticed you're not wearing an engagement ring," the doctor accused.

"It's at the jewelers. The diamond fell out. It's being repaired." But yes, she would call this doctor on Monday. She would give her a fictitious date. What could Dr. Bradstreet prove? She didn't have to see an engagement ring. Really poor people might not have a ring. But Stella was a student at the best college in Alabama.

"Now tell me what's really wrong with you," the doctor demanded.

"The president is dead," Stella blurted. Maybe that was the truth. Maybe she was a person who couldn't stand murder. Was that so bad?

"You're deeply upset." For the first time, the doctor sounded pleasant, surprised.

"I lost my family in a car wreck—"

"When?"

"Years ago—"

"Oh."

"My father had lung cancer—"

"Then he would have died anyway."

"I feel bad about the president and—"

"What else?"

"And the four little girls." Stella exploded in grief. She covered her face with both hands. She could feel the tears dripping through the cracks between her fingers. She leaned toward the blotter. The doctor would think she was crazy, but the words burst out of her like vomit: "I didn't—go—to their funeral."

Dr. Bradstreet came around from her desk. Was that her hand, very lightly placed on Stella's shoulder? Her hand was lighter than a bird coming to rest with tiny feet in the hairs of the partially angora sweater.

"No one really expected you to attend," Dr. Bradstreet said. Her voice was kind, now that she'd broken Stella open, seen inside with her hot little light. Yes, Stella had felt the warmth of the light trying to shine up into her body when her legs were spread. Then Stella felt the motherly bird-hand fly away, almost imperceptibly, a hand lighter than a dove, a bird small as a finch, white perhaps.

"Birmingham can be a very hard city," Dr. Bradstreet consoled. Yes, her voice was kind but not especially sympathetic to Stella. Still, there was something of mourning in Dr. Bradstreet's voice.

Stella stopped crying. She removed her hands from her face. Why, there was a box of tissues on the edge of the desk, all ready for the tragic patient. She took the proffered tissue and wiped her face. Took another and blew her nose. Yes, there was a trash basket beside the desk.

"I'll call you about the date," Stella said. She was going to win. She would have the contraceptive pill and she would do as she pleased. "Thank you," Stella added politely. She had created one hell of a smoke screen. Suppose she had just screamed, "I want to be ready for sex and not get pregnant!"

"If you haven't calmed down in a few days, I'll prescribe a mild sedative."

WHEN STELLA LEFT Dr. Bradstreet's office, she looked at her watch and saw it wasn't time yet to go to the switchboard. But why go anyway? The world was dead. She would take the bus down to the foot of Twentieth Street to the Church of the Advent. She was not a member—but Timmy Beaton, her high school boyfriend, had been a member. He had taken her there one Easter, shown her the enclosed garden ablaze with yellow daffodils, the largest daffies she'd ever seen. It had felt like Eden. Resurrection, rebirth by beauty. She would take the bus down Twentieth Street and sit in the garden by herself. She needed no one.

What's the matter with you? The doctor's harsh question buzzed her nerves. Of course there was plenty the matter with her. She had no parents. She had no president. She had no fiancé. She had school—at least until she graduated—and she had a job. When it was time tonight, she would go to work. Not the right work, only temporary till she graduated.

In the garden of the Church of the Advent, which was the most beautiful spot in Birmingham, she would meditate on the death of the murdered president. She would think about what it meant to be free, both personally and socially.

The bus rolled past Bromberg's jewelry store with its small discreet windows, past Russell Stover's candy, where you could buy a single piece for a quarter. A man who looked like Kennedy was pointing to his head, first the back, then the front. He pointed to his throat. His friend smiled while he listened.

A young black woman came out the door of Russell Stover's with a bag of candy in her hand. Yes, they could go there because there was no place to sit down. Everybody just purchased while standing at the counter. White and black stood at separate ends. White people were served first. Nobody had to rub shoulders for long. She saw the girl thrust her hand into the sack, bite into a piece of candy, and burst into tears. Like lone firecrackers, people were going off all over Birmingham.

Stella used to go into Russell Stover's with her friend Wanda, and Stella's favorite was a milk chocolate with a whipped chocolate creme interior. When you peeled the pleated paper cup away from the sides, you saw that its negative was indented in the flaring side of the candy. Usually a few delicate peaks actually rimmed the top of the chocolate on one side. When you bit into the candy, you could see that the whipped interior held a sprinkling of tiny air bubbles. And what had happened to Wanda, whose family moved away?

Be happy, Stella thought to Wanda. Wanda, the new girl in eighth grade, the outsider, had leapt in the broad jump as though she were catapulted across the air, and even seeing it from the rear, Stella knew something extraordinary had happened on the playground of Norwood School. She ran to Wanda, asking, "Did you fly? For just a second, were you flying?"

Be comforted, she thought to the girl with the candy sack. *Find a friend to share with.*

The bus was passing Lollar's Camera Shop, and on down the street, past Red Cross Shoes. Across the street was Blach's "Fair and Square." The emblem of the store was a carpenter's square, and within the elbow of that ruled right angle was a lily. Stella thought no other store had so sacred an emblem. It was what she wanted for herself in life: to be accorded the lily of beauty and a portion of *character,* represented by just calibration.

Martin Luther King Jr. wanted his children reckoned not by the color of their skin but by the content of their character. She wished that she had participated last August in the March on Washington.

The bus passed the YMCA; Stella had heard some cities had a YMHA, Hebrew, not Christian—Chicago, New York. Someday she would see those places. His voice floating over the Reflecting Pool before the Washington Monument, King had rated character above appearance. She had watched him on TV at the Cartwrights' as he addressed the demonstrators—everybody who would listen, really.

Even Aunt Krit wanted beauty, though, as well as an upright character. Among Krit's math papers waiting on the dining room table to be graded would be a copy of the latest *Vogue,* and once Stella had seen written beside a blue suit, one with a pencil skirt (the model's bonelike shafts of legs were crossed and ended in high-heeled shoes such as Krit never owned) topped by a short boxy jacket, the words "I want this, size 14." But surely Krit was only a size ten or twelve, and the fit would bag on her at size fourteen, and the point of the outfit would be squandered.

On the sidewalk, two well-dressed Negro men approached each other with hands outstretched. They shook hands warmly, then embraced each other. *They must be ministers, unafraid of Christian embrace. They need each other today.*

Down Twentieth Street, the people on the bus jiggled up and down, so many fragile eggs in a carton. On this bus, people were happy that the president was dead, adults with gleaming eyes like wicked children, like predatory animals, foxes. Probably the legless man could not mount the high steps of a city bus. The people on the bus chatted and licked their lips. In code, they spoke of Lyndon Johnson, "the hope of the South," as though the quiet colored people in the back of the bus didn't understand what they meant.

Why had Stella's heart beat hard when she rolled through the center of her city, down Twentieth Street, past Bromberg's (with diamond engagement rings in the small, strong windows)? Why did her heart roar when she passed all the dear stores? They constituted the context and thus testament to her own living. Why couldn't the city strive to be fair and square?

And on the right, the garden at the Church of the Advent was coming up, and now it was time to get off, to give the signal: *ding.*

She couldn't expect the church garden to boast flamboyant daffies—this was November—just a place to sit, to be away from the crowd (but she loved the people of her city). It was beauty she needed, the beauty of the garden no matter what its season. Beauty would save her.

General Omar Bradley, her mother had whispered long ago amid the patriotic people turned out for the parade. *Blessed boys* with *blessed guns* had saved the world from Hitler. How cold and stiff with standing Stella's body had been, a much colder November day than today. Blessed guns? *Mama meant the liberators of the death camps. But who or what could liberate Birmingham from its violence and racism?*

Stella wanted away from it all. If not Chicago, New York. No, she wanted to be alone in the garden with her essential self. She wanted to be without friends or strangers or family.

She walked rapidly, passed an acquaintance on the sidewalk, the liberal high school boy in her speech class, Blake, who had been a freshman when she was a senior. He had an undeveloped hand: that was what was wrong with him. He had a small pad of a hand that ended not in fingers but in little balls. The boy's eyes were coated with a glaze of unfallen tears, his lips swollen with grief. Oddly, she had been told at some party how Blake loved the president and idolized Jackie Kennedy. Bereft, Blake stalked Twentieth Street, toward downtown, grieving for his beloved president. He looked through Stella as though she were a window. No mirror for what *he* felt.

Stella reached out her hand to try to stop him. Blake could sit with her, in the garden. He pulled away and continued down the street.

Someone blared a trumpet. She looked back and saw a young man leaning out a window of the YMCA, the trumpet in his hand. He tongued the first measure, joyfully, of "Dixie."

Someone from the street shouted back, "The South will rise again!"

The trumpeter withdrew, and the window was lowered.

Blake sang loudly, in French, the opening of the French national anthem, the call to arms, as he stalked along. He sounded crazed with grief, but nobody accosted him.

Soon she would enter the garden. The golden sandstone church was just ahead. First a small building connected by a stone archway to the tower and sanctuary.

When Stella stepped through the arch, she saw the iron gate was closed. She put her hand on the knob above the keyhole, but the gate was locked. The black lacquered upright bars of the gate were too tall to go over. Her hope wilted. The church had let her down. What leadership had the white church provided in integrating Birmingham? Well, some *had* tried. What, for that matter, had Stella done for integration? She *thought* right. At least she had done that.

Through the grille, she saw the brick walk, gracefully curved, flanked with a short, clipped box hedge, still green.

Again, her hand grasped the black lacquered knob and tried again to turn it. Clearly locked. Timmy had taken her once to the Episcopal mass, on Christmas Eve, and she had been shocked at the censer and incense, at the ceremony of it all. Before the service, all the children had played together, not segregated by age, as in her own Methodist youth groups. Timmy had told her that a lot of these people were against racial segregation, were *working* against it, but when Stella was there, the air was full of Christmas.

"Make me fly," one of the little girls had said to Timmy, and his hands encircled her little waist, and he had lifted her above his head—he was a dancer in the Birmingham Civic Ballet. And then all the little girls had clamored, and stood in a line, and one by one, he made them beautiful as flying ballerinas. Some pedaled the air as they flew; some stretched out one arm, or both. One stood in the air with folded arms, stiff as a totem pole. Timmy had taken off his suit jacket, but his white shirt was sticking to his skin with sweat.

How he lived within his body, Timmy Beaton. Like Don, Cat's brother. Somehow proud to inhabit that particular body. Even if he walked across the room, his body said, *This is my life. I contain myself. I move myself from here to there. Proudly.*

She wished she could whisper to Timmy, *Make me fly*. But he was gone from her life. He was dancing with the New York City Ballet. He had braved his family and sought his *different* life, but he came back to visit, people said. He didn't call Stella.

In a corner of the November garden stood Saint Catherine—carved perhaps from cypress, she and the wheel that broke her, all carved from the same piece of wood, except perhaps for the outcropping spokes, which were stuck like removable pegs into the outer rim of the wheel. Saint Catherine rose from the ground like the curve of a calla lily. Deadwood, she was; the ghost of a tree that once grew, perhaps, in a Louisiana bayou, hung with Spanish moss. Stella remembered firing a pistol as a small child, in the woods at Helicon, shooting trees.

The carved whites of Saint Catherine's eyes had been painted silver, and Stella found the effect garish. The flow of the woman's body reminded her of Munch's *The Scream*. A thoroughly modern shape, a flame of anguish.

The silver of her eyes proclaimed *I am unnatural, the ghost of a tree. Return me to the swamp*. "Return me to my life, where scaly alligators brushed against my knees." Stella was shocked to find that she had spoken aloud for the statue of Saint Catherine. *Return me to Helicon.*

Stella shook the iron gate that barred her from the garden.

Before he left Birmingham, Timmy had kissed her.

Standing on the porch before her front door, she had hugged him. Sensing he did not want to kiss, she had chosen not to imply that he should. She had turned but found she turned within the circle of his arm, so that he brought her to face him again. Yes, he was kissing her, and the universe thrummed between their lips.

He had given her her wish, fulsomely without stint, and she had given back. Then quickly, she was inside her aunts' living room. She leaned against the wall, her legs weak, her body effervescent.

Oh, kissing, how she wanted it, forever! (With one finger, she caressed a vertical bar on the garden gate, felt under her fingertip how the black lacquer covered a roughness of chipped and pitted underlayers, for all its shiny bravado.)

Better than she'd ever hoped or imagined, though others had warned her, by dismissing their own first kiss. Nothing special, they had said. But not with Timmy. Not she and Timmy Beaton. No other kiss had ever equaled that—not all the dark, tantalizing night hours spent with Darl on the boulevard while the lighted planes flew low overhead. There was nothing wrong with her, she should have told Dr. Bradstreet: she loved kissing.

For warmth, Saint Catherine seemed to clutch the wheel to her in the November afternoon. Soon it would be dark. Stella moved her grip on the bars, and the square-edged metal was cold in her hands. The wheel was a part of Saint Catherine's body, embraced like a pregnancy.

(But she would have the Pill. She would!)

Gently Stella shook the gate again. It was right that she should be locked out. An airplane flew overhead. Would they be flying the president's body, his broken body, back to Washington? Or would his flag-draped body be moved by slow train through the country, as Lincoln's body had? Would the porch of the last car of the train display across its vertical grille a swag of red, white, and blue? Stella wondered if, at this moment, Jackie Kennedy was listening to the muffled roar of a jet engine, feeling the thrum through the soles of her shoes, wondering where her life had gone.

Stella released the black grille of the garden gate. She would walk on toward the public library, only a block beyond. It would be open, and she wanted inside. A white angora sweater, even with a close-fitting neck, was not enough for November.

She emptied her mind with the sound of her feet walking. She watched the toes of her green leather flats appear and disappear below the swinging hem of her blue wool skirt till she slipped through the library's revolving door into the hush of the reading room. *What does it mean, my feet are green?* What did anything mean?

THE REVOLVING DOOR turned as she pushed. The quiet library interior accepted her. She wanted a bare table before her. She folded her hands on the wood.

Her eyes lifted to the murals on the wall. What comfort did those painted myths of the world have to offer? Pegasus she had loved. And what was his average altitude, when flying? Cloud high, she thought. Those white wings would churn their way through cumulus, then higher even than stratospheric cirrus into the blank of blue and sunlight. Always, they moved her—the depiction of wings.

Among the figures on the enormous library mural was Brunhilde, the warrior maiden, her blond braids hanging beside her armored breasts, her horned helmet. Confucius spoke to those who would learn. Cleopatra sat on her throne, fanned by an Ethiope. She offered a wink to Stella and she made something stir the air—the sound of distant flutes?

Stella looked across the room into the bespectacled eyes of the conductor of the Birmingham Youth Orchestra, Herbert Levinson, who was also the concert-master of the Birmingham Symphony. Crossing the floor of the reading room, he returned her gaze. When she was in high school, she had played the cello under his baton. He remembered her. She should take up the cello again, change her life, honor her mother and the music her mother held dearer than God.

The conductor didn't speak. (His own instrument, like her mother's favorite, was the violin.) Reading misery in each other's eyes, he continued to move. It was enough. The blank oak library table had signaled like a flag. This glance. Yes, a slight shaking of their heads. Tears standing in their eyes. Not embrace. His lips moved without sound. (This was the library and one did not speak.) *I'm sorry,* he mouthed.

It was those transformed by pain that Herbert Levinson cared about. *Aye, yi, yi, yi, yih*—from her own bones came the lament, in a minor key. Darl had wanted her body and made himself wait, and now he would never have her.

Nor she him.

I'm sorry, she whispered to the air. Theirs had been a delicious intimacy, kissing.

Mr. Levinson had known Stella's sense of rhythm was unsteady, that it faltered (though her mother's never did), that Stella would never be reliable as a leader of her section, but he had seen her store of grief, was unendingly kind to her, and honored the way she had tried to steady her erratic heart.

Wait, she wanted to call after him. *You don't know about Darl! I was engaged, and now I'm not.*

Stella pushed her wooden chair back from the table, let the legs scrape on the floor. An ugly noise in the library. She glanced at the newspapers suspended by long bamboo canes, hanging in a rack. Here was the news from around the world: the London *Times* was there, *Le Figaro, Die Welt, El País,* and others, but none proclaimed Today from its headlines. None yet hurled the message with bold, three-inch letters of Right Now: **JFK ASSASSINATED.**

It's time. I will walk back up Twentieth Street to Third Avenue; I will turn the corner and walk three more blocks to work. I will feel cold, and I'll walk fast. "Hurry up, please, it's time"—a refrain from T. S. Eliot's *The Waste Land* echoed vaguely in her mind.

She lifted her books and purse from the floor and thought from "The Love Song of J. Alfred Prufrock": "I grow old . . . I grow old . . . / I shall wear the bottoms of my trousers rolled." She revolved through the brass door into the darkening outer world. "There will be time, there will be time / To prepare a face to meet the faces that you meet; / . . . And for a hundred visions and revisions."

Would she revise the scene with Darl, if she could? No, she told herself, she would not. Now she was free. She was cold but she was free. She walked more rapidly.

The dusk air of the city was festive, as though it were late December and approaching Christmas. Everyone walked briskly. They were exhilarated, these shoppers and commuters of Birmingham. No, there was a sad face. But was it some personal grief or the public grief that this was a country of assassins, of racists? *Aye, yi, yi, yi, yih* . . . She needed her mother's Yiddish to sing an ancient sorrow.

Stella passed a woman dressed in a winter coat, wearing a black cloche hat, an old-fashioned one. *Let it be my mother.* With one hand, she held the hand of her little daughter (also overly bundled against the cold). *Let me be her.* The woman's other hand held the handle of a blunt-nosed black violin case, gliding two feet above the pavement like a baby alligator. The texture of the case completed the masquerade of shape with a bumpy, reptilian skin.

Someday this city and all its inequity would sink back into being a swamp for amphibians, as it had been millions of years before, when the lush vegetation of ferns and palms laid itself down, and laid itself down again and again over the aeons, was sealed by the weight of water into a decay of dark ooze, till the patient mud compressed itself into the black seams of coal that lay everywhere in the hills, fueling the current steel industry. While Stella's green leather shoes hurried over the pavement, past the YMCA, she thought of the earth under the concrete, which would someday in the far future become broken and pitiful, useful for crushing her bones and those of all who now walked the street.

And now that Kennedy was dead, would the Soviet Union take advantage? Across from her at the Tutwiler, would Russian generals someday review their conquering troops? She knew not a word of Russian. Would Birmingham become a shell, bombed into rubble big-time, and not by the local racists? (But which was worse—to die at the hands of one's fellow citizens or of Communist strangers?)

Because of the steel industry, people always said (proudly) that Birmingham was high on the list as a Russian target. Number three, some claimed, after New York City and Washington, D.C. Or number five, after Pittsburgh and probably Atlanta, or Chicago. Perhaps Cuban missiles were aimed at Birmingham.

Seldom had the city seemed so triumphant, to Stella, as on this early evening in the wake of the president's death. This time someone else, far away in Texas, had done the dirty work. This time it wasn't a matter of a church and of children, who, by anybody's measure, were absolutely innocent. Or was the air charged not with triumph but excitement? She felt none of it.

She was a stranger in her city—*Aye, yi, yi, yi, yih*—though she had been born here, at old Jefferson-Hillman Hospital. Because of her people—her father not of the city but from the country; her mother not southern, but northern—had she ever belonged? Or was it something of her own sensibility, first her rigid faith, now her growing skepticism, that made her irrevocably odd? She was too thin, that was part of it.

She was cold. Even the fast walking failed to warm her. But up ahead—where was it coming from?—those voices humming. Three or four high, childish voices so ambiguous she could not interpret their mood. *Remember us,* perhaps they said. Spirit voices of those four little girls, sacrificed, like Kennedy, on the national altar. Had they come to guide him home? " 'And flights of angels' "—she thought of the mayhem at the end of *Hamlet*—" 'sing thee to thy rest.' "

If war comes to this country, Aunt Krit had always said before the car wreck, her voice choking itself, *we'll all gather at Helicon and hide in the woods.* Stella scanned the sky, but there was only the rosy sunset in the west, a lone passenger plane—Eastern Air Lines—circling the city before it headed for Norwood, and beyond, to the runway and the terminal. *But who was left to gather?* Her family already lay in the cemetery at Helicon. Now Aunt Krit couldn't bear to say the word *gather.*

Coming toward Stella on the sidewalk was a Negro woman in a stylish green coat, with a poodle pin glittering on the collar. Her hair was straightened to smoothness and turned under in a glamorous pageboy at the length of her shoulders. She walked confidently in high heels. Her face was sober, and she wore a black cloth around the upper sleeve of her coat. Stella wondered if it was safe for the colored woman—if one could mourn this way, safely? The woman's face was drained of expression. Stella wanted to catch her eye, but there was no contact. Stella touched her own upper arm, clasped it as though to say, My hand is forming a mourning band. I grieve.

The green-coated woman's high heels clacked past. A teenage boy with his hair swept back into a ducktail walked past; he had a transistor radio clamped against the side of his head. *Why should I disdain him?* Stella asked herself. These were just ordinary people. She'd known them, or people like them, always.

WHEN SHE TOOK HER seat at the switchboard and looked over the balcony into the store, she saw one of the women clerks take the arm of Mr. Hall, who was well dressed because he worked in men's suits, and swing herself into a little jig around him. Mr. Hall was too dignified for that; he let her go but gave her a quick nod and smile.

Mr. Fielding climbed up the steps from the first floor to her balcony. His eyes were fastened on her, and behind her chair, he paused to say, "You're not happy about it, are you, Miss Silver?"

"No," she answered.

He gave her a quick nod (agreeing?) and disappeared into his office, closed the door.

(*I mourn, too*—surely that was what he meant. *Yes.*)

Between the ringings of the phone, Stella talked with her friends. In a low voice, so that Mr. Fielding wouldn't hear her chatting, she asked Ellie how her therapy session had gone—"It helps," Ellie said. Stella reported that Dr. Bradstreet had delayed her birth control prescription. "She said she'd prescribe a tranquilizer though." (*What's wrong with you!*)

Down below, the store busied itself with the flow and ebb of Thanksgiving customers. The pillars were decorated with pictures of turkeys and overflowing cornucopias in colors of brown and orange. Stella called Nancy, who said that she thought people were mostly appalled by the assassination, that no true American could be happy, but Stella told her what she'd seen with her own eyes that day in Birmingham, how white children cheered and clerks danced in the aisles.

Because they always talked the longest, she last called Cat, who had been watching television and told Stella that Lyndon Johnson was already sworn in, on the flight from Dallas.

When Stella went to the bathroom, she found the cleaning maid in there, crying. She was wiping the mirror, her face washed in tears. "Sadie!" Stella exclaimed, and they opened their arms to each other and wept.

TOWARD CLOSING, SUDDENLY there was—*Oh!*—Darl, climbing up the steps. (Mr. Fielding, Stella told herself, was out of his office, making his good-night rounds.) Darl pitched himself into the seat; his face worn and conciliatory; he said he'd talked things over with his dad.

"We're going to drive to Washington," Darl said. "To pay our respects. He's taking time off. Dad said I could ask you if you wanted to come."

So Darl was sorry, Stella thought. So he, after all, was one of the true Americans (or his dad was) that Nancy had mentioned.

Stella asked if Darl's mother was going.

"She might. You could share the room with her, and Dad and I would bunk together. He said you could chip in on the gas money, if you wanted to."

She watched the customers come and go (Talking of? Michelangelo?— she'd always admired Eliot's rhyme in "The Love Song of J. Alfred Prufrock." Talking of the dead president?).

When she looked at Darl, Stella said bluntly, "I thought you were glad." (Her hand reached out to caress the buttons of the switchboard.)

"Not really," he said, eager to set things straight. "I just hate the violence. I wish people would be patient. Let things evolve naturally."

"Another hundred years?" She pictured prehistoric palm trees crashing in slow motion into a swamp. Her fingertips brushed the bland plastic buttons.

"It could be quicker than that," he said.

(But she had wept in Sadie's arms. Now she was strong for change.)

The phone rang and she pushed the button-line to connect; she answered in her usual cheerful voice. Before she finished, it rang again, and she said to Ellie, "I'm talking with Darl. He's here." She listened to the ambivalence of Ellie's silence. Stella added, "We're about to close. I'll call you from home." Then she hung up, took her time regarding Darl, his brown eyes the color of chestnuts.

"I could give you a ride home. I have the car now."

"No, thanks, Darl." She knew he wanted her to ride in his new car again.

"I'm sorry about the way I seemed. I wasn't glad. It's such a shock. I was glad about my car."

She could feel her hands beginning to tremble. She didn't want to give in. She wanted her freedom. She reached toward the plastic buttons, hoped for a phone ring. She knew now what was behind that mask of freckles—someone who adopted the position of his father. Someone who deferred to authority, the so-called wisdom of his parents. Someone willing to deceive himself.

"I can't—" she began to say.

"I'd like to give you another ring," he said.

"What happened to the old one? You don't have it?"

"I went up to Vulcan. Threw it off. I'm sorry."

Her diamond! She imagined it, like a meteorite, skating across a blackness, winking out. She felt his arm again, encircling her back and ribs, how it had been last May, on the balcony below Vulcan. In May, on the balcony she had stood beside him, her body a column of wanting. His arm crossed her back, and his fingers had lain among the spaces between her ribs. Probably he had thrown the ring as hard as he could, and it had sailed over the clearing and then arched into the trees on the long embankment sloping down toward the city. Had he listened to the sound of her ring falling through the bleak branches?

"Now that the trees are bare," she asked, "could you spot the demonstration?" She felt weak, spent. (He had thrown away their ring. Their chance.) The demonstrations were months ago.

"I didn't think about that."

Yes, she saw the pain in his face, too. He was numb with what he had done.

"I went to sit in the library, downtown," she told him. "I saw the conductor of the Birmingham Youth Orchestra." Did this information mean anything to him? "It was the only place I could think to go. The big reading room. For quiet." (Still he said nothing.) "To be alone."

"Won't you ride up to Washington with us? They say the president'll lie in state. Under the rotunda of the Capitol." He looked at the floor. "We'd be part of history."

"I need to stay here," she said. "I should have gone last August."

She could not imagine presenting herself passing the coffin of the president: she was too insignificant to go. And if she could see herself in the mourners' queue, she could not imagine joining Darl's people for the long car trip from Birmingham to Washington.

She would smother in the car with his family. All those miles. Their unwavering trust in the goodness of God. They would be trying to fold her in because their son perhaps wanted this strange girl. And, betraying herself, she would try to make all her attitudes and thoughts agreeable to them. She imagined the horror of it all: the polite, genteel reverence for the occasion (a few mild jokes as the car hurried along the highway) while each of her bodily organs turned into a screaming mouth, her heart, her lungs, even her silent liver. (That darkness she had seen emerging from her father's body; that had been his liver, his side opened by the auto accident like the pierced side of Christ.) Trapped inside Darl's family car, perhaps when they passed through the Great Smoky Mountains, even her liver would grow a mouth that opened its lips in agony to moan *My president is murdered.*

"I'm not comfortable with family car trips," Stella said and felt ashamed to dissemble.

"I understand," he said.

In the sincerity of his words, her father's car rolled on its back and over, and over again; her parents, her brothers, herself, tumbled together inside the car. The wash of blood.

"All right," he said. She saw by the hardening of his face that now he knew she was disconnecting him from her future, not reliving the past. (*But the past had come back. It had just come. And gone again.*) He stood up. "I needed to ask. I'm sorry."

Her gaze felt like a fumbling key trying to enter the pupil of his eye, to go inside.

"Yes," she answered. Maybe he'd felt trapped into being engaged, and now he was glad to be free. She remembered their stiff, quick walk over the dark slope of the cemetery. Perhaps being in such danger together had implied an intimacy even more insistently than if they had made love.

Down in the store, people were beginning to leave; she glanced at her watch. She drew the PA mike to her lips and switched it on. "Fielding's will be closing in five minutes. Thank you for shopping with Fielding's and have a pleasant evening." She felt dazed by the inappropriateness of her language.

"Good-bye," Darl said.

Now she had severed their connection twice.

She stared at his retreating back. No, she didn't want to marry him. But not to be engaged! Not to have some stake in the future! How could she even find her way home tonight?

AS THE EMPLOYEES WALKED out into the night, Mr. Fielding stood at the door, like a minister, and shook hands with each of his people. "Be safe," he said to each of them. They were surprised by his formal valediction. Stella thought, *He doesn't agree with them, but he loves them. He wants them to feel that he cares about them. A patriarch lives.*

Yes, that was what made a person be careful—knowing that somebody else cared deeply about her safety. She was Aunt Krit's responsibility; it was helpless Aunt Pratt who cared.

"Be safe, Miss Silver."

It was like shaking hands with her father. Mr. Fielding's cuff of white hair circled his head.

"I'm not engaged anymore," she blurted.

"Well," he said grimly, gathering his thoughts. "It will be all right, Miss Silver. You wait and see."

And she was out the door—the tail of her reply to him floating after her, *Thank you*—and she was walking rapidly past Brooks Furniture Store ("The working man's friend") toward Twentieth Street, where she would stand and wait for the bus. On big rubber tires, it would come toward her. Her feet hurried over the gray gloom of pavement toward the bus line. Like a long box of light, the bus would come, and she would ride to Norwood on big rubber tires. That was all. She knew how to get home. But what was there for her at home? An old white dog slowly wagging his tail.

Across the street at Cousin Joe's Pawn Shop, an outline of a diamond in pink neon, big as a wheelbarrow, blazed in the window. She thought of the big simulated diamond that sat on the arthritic finger of her Aunt Pratt; at home, Aunt Pratt would already be in bed—her leg brace with the attached shoe would be vacantly standing sentinel in the corner. So that she could breathe more easily, Aunt Pratt would be lying propped up on a stack of hard pillows, like someone in the eighteenth or nineteenth century.

Stella glanced across the street at the Lyric Theatre, where a lone girl sat behind glass in the lighted ticket booth a half-block ahead. Stella was glad it was not her job to be a girl behind glass. Over the lighted ticket booth, the movie marquee read *La Dolce Vita*. At home, Aunt Pratt would be tracing the outlines of large red roses in her wallpaper, trying to keep her eyes active and moving, but with the bedroom lights off, the roses are dark as old scabs.

Maybe Aunt Pratt would picture not Stella but her own childhood self playing with her siblings over fifty years ago in the sunny yard at Helicon. Stella pictured the small house and the dusty red clay around it raked into swirls and parallel lines. Aunt Pratt, young and able, ran across the yard. The sound of squirrel guns resounded through the pine-fragrant woods. Fifteen years later Aunt Krit would be born, and she, too, would play in the yard. Perhaps pour water on the ground and make mud pies from the red dust. Lift her head at the sound of a gun.

A city car horn blared, and Stella remembered the blast of a trumpet, a young man leaning out the window of the YMCA, but what had it meant? That these times were medieval, or would seem medieval in five hundred years; that a herald was needed?

It meant nothing. The sharp blast of the trumpet had been the descant to the continual sound of footfalls on the pavement in the late afternoon. *The trumpet shall sound*, Handel's *Messiah* proclaimed, and the dead shall be raised—*incorruptible!*

Stella saw three men come out of the theater; they passed the girl in the glass box.

Two came toward her; the third walked toward Twentieth Street. And who was that third man? She saw only his straight back, his longish wavy hair. She thought it might be Don Cartwright. A half-block ahead and on the other side of the street, Don might be walking to catch the bus on Twentieth Street. She picked up her pace; he walked swiftly.

He had such a beautiful straight back, such movie star hair. She seldom went to foreign films, but *La Dolce Vita*, yes; wanting a window on the sweet life, she had gone with Ellie. What had Don thought of it? It must have been poorly attended, or had the three men walked out in the middle? No one else stood now in front of the glass box waiting to buy tickets to the last show.

If she had been sure the man ahead of her was Don, Stella would have called to him. Sometimes she and Don sang greetings to each other, operatically. But not downtown at night, not across a city street, with a few cars passing between, and him half a block ahead. But she felt more and more certain that it must be Don—the short, quick steps. She lengthened her stride to cover the distance between them. She seldom talked to Don unless Cat was with her.

Perhaps when she was only twenty steps behind him, she would sing to him sotto voce, "Don-ny," starting high and then descending a ragged octave.

But she slowed her pace. She began to match her steps to his. She knew she would not catch up unless she walked faster, but this way, she seemed more connected to him. She would hypnotize herself with the measure of their walking.

A block traversed, and already it felt that the top of her head was lifted away like the lid off a coffin, and her essence was rising upward, dissipating into the night. Ah, yes, something of her spirit could move like breath, transcend the pavement and the street between him and her to curl around Don's shoulders like a cape. Comfort him.

And what comfort did Don need? That he could not make his sister free of her disease? That he was destined to watch Cat grow less and less capable over the years? Surely any brother would need to be comforted, when knowledge and caring became impotent.

At the Gaslight, after she and Don had returned to their table, when the elegant black waiter had swirled Cat on the dance floor and returned her to the table, the waiter batted his curled eyelashes and said, "Oh, I wish *everybody* could just dance together, don't you?"

Don walked on, back straight, across the gulf of the street. Sometimes the passing cars, gliding as quietly as ghosts, interposed themselves between her and him on the other side of the street. But hadn't something like her breath crossed over and settled like a scarf over his shoulders? And wasn't she with Don, then, though his back was to her? Again, she seemed to feel spirits in the air, a murmuring. Perhaps the Muses hovered around Don's shoulders when he painted.

Don stepped off the curb, crossed Twenty-first Street to the next block. Ah, Twentieth Street ahead; suppose, he caught the bus and she missed it? Then she'd have to stand waiting alone another full half hour; the buses ran infrequently at night. She began to hurry. Why should she go home alone?

Don turned the corner to Twentieth Street and was lost from view.

Now she did hurry. She imagined herself Eurydice following Orpheus out of hell. Wasn't there an opera based on the story? Gluck—and who was he, his name clucking from a crevasse in memory? If only she could sing a snatch of Eurydice's tunes to Don instead of her stupid slide on his name: *Don-ny*. But she must not lose sight of him, must not be left to find her way alone.

The black hand of the universe closed around her body. That hand wanted to squeeze. *Am I mad?* Perhaps she would talk to Ellie's therapist about her fear of being alone. But surely everyone wanted a shared life?

When she turned onto Twentieth Street, Don was nowhere to be seen.

AT THE BUS STOP stood a poor old woman vending newspapers, with her adult retarded daughter. Stella had seen them many times: two female lumps of human flesh, beside a skinny wire rack holding the *Birmingham News*.

Stella stared south, hoping to see the lighted bus moving down the canyon of tall buildings toward her. Had Don been nothing but an apparition?

Blake walked past her again, his face distraught. Had he been walking the streets all this time while she worked at the switchboard? Did he try to out-walk his grief? Two good feet, one good hand. But was that blood on his face?

Yes, and bruises. The sleeve of his jacket was partly torn away. He'd been in a fight. One of the pea-like nubbins on his stunted hand was almost torn away and dangled. He must have been *beaten*. But who would beat someone so vulnerable and why? Stella took a breath to speak to him, but he hurried on.

No one was trying to help him. It was too late at night to make such efforts. Everyone was isolated in night weariness. He was another obscure witness— still living—to the national violence.

Aimed south, a bus visited the empty spaces across the street from Stella and emitted two colored men. The Gaslight! They seemed not to know each other, went in opposite directions with no word of parting, but Stella thought she recognized them both from the Gaslight. One was a small black man; past middle age, he and his soft wife had danced like professionals, but unostenta-tiously with short sure steps. (But Donny had lengthened his step when he danced with her.) And the other Negro man, very handsome, in the prime of life, had worn a sapphire blue tie that flashed out like subtle neon. Yes, maybe she recognized Mr. Blue Tie. Maybe she had seen him dancing, in love, at the Gaslight.

Both men stopped, turned around as though they'd reached the limits of a giant rubber band, they shook hands warmly, and then parted again.

On the ridge of Red Mountain, Vulcan stood, thrusting a red torch into the murky night sky. Stella loved that tireless cast-iron arm. She imagined she could see the muscles between his straightened elbow and wrist.

Half an hour passed. Stella stood first on one foot, then the other. She felt her calves stiffening with cold. To ease her back, she shifted her books from one arm to the other. She idly admired how her purse matched her green shoes. Then she admired her shoes and how they matched the purse. Inside the purse was her Fielding's check, and she must not forget to take it to the bank.

When she was little, Mama took her to the Exchange Bank on South Side with its white marble counters. The marble glinted as though impregnated with sugar. After Mama and Stella did business at the high, sugary counters of the bank, they visited Mary Ball Candies next door. On the outside, a frieze of stylized dogwood blossoms crowned the building.

While she waited for the bus, Stella turned to see her reflection in the gleaming purple facade of Russell Stover's, closed for the night. Suppose the bus never came? But, no—here came the 15 Norwood. Its big lighted face swayed to a stop just one block away. Few people rode so late at night; it must be nearly ten.

At this distance, she saw the billed cap of a uniformed driver.

He is just as real as the president. Seated behind the big steering wheel, wrestling it right and left, the driver (an opaque nameless figure at this distance) has a life just as precious to him as John Kennedy's life was to him. Someday the driver now approaching only me will face death. Just as I will, or anyone will.

The newspaper-vendor mother reached out lovingly to push back a misplaced strand of hair from her retarded daughter's pale face.

The bus paused at the red light, then lumbered across the intersection. The driver saw Stella and arced toward the curb.

At that moment a quiet voice (tinged with irony) said, did not sing, "Miss Stella Silver, I believe."

"Don!" she exclaimed. "Where did you come from?"

"The cafe. I stopped for a glass of wine. I watched you as you waited."

Stella glanced at the cafe. She'd paid no attention to it. A thick film of dark amber plastic was drawn down behind the glass, and she'd never thought to try to peer beyond it. She never paid any attention to the cafe, not with purple-fronted Russell Stover's beside it. And he'd watched her, through the amber film. She didn't know what to say. He stood erect, his chest high, his stomach in (Donny's posture would never succumb to night fatigue), while she curved and slouched and shifted her weight with the weight of her books.

"Actually"—he went on past her uncomfortable silence—"I had *two* glasses of wine. I was drinking a toast to the film I just saw—"

"*La Dolce Vita!*"

"How did you guess?"

"I watched you come out."

The bus doors flared open to admit them.

"Really? So first you were watching me—how odd. Please, step on. After you."

"And also, it's the sort of movie you might watch," she added over her shoulder while mounting the steps. Stella had thought it bewildering, the depicted futility of innocence.

"Yes. Something to escape from the day's events." He spoke ruefully. Too lightly. Maybe he, too, had understood not wisely, but too well?

What could she say? They were walking down the aisle, on the grooved, black rubber runner.

"There's no escaping it," Stella said.

"Let's sit farther back." He chose a seat for two in the middle of the almost deserted bus. A colored mother and two children sat in the back. "Sister's watching it all on TV." When he said *Sister*—there was a swell of irony under the word, buoying it up.

No, Stella would not talk again about the tragedy. "I saw *Giant* a couple of weeks ago."

"Ah. The always beautiful Elizabeth Taylor. But *La Dolce Vita*. I wanted to be transported. To Italy. Land of opera. Don't you think that's necessary sometimes, Miss Silver?"

They sat down on the brown leather seat, side by side, facing forward.

"Land of Mussolini?" Stella added. (Once, a newsboy had sung out about the man, and her two brothers had picked up the refrain: "Mussolini kicked out of It-a-ly.")

Don turned his face away to look out the window.

"Yes, but that was long ago."

The bus softly lumbered past the Church of the Advent; Stella looked at the darkness of the grille and the black garden beyond, the garden now invisible in the darkness. Then the bus turned the corner and passed the Birmingham Public Library, its lights extinguished now. Her places—the places to visit and revisit endlessly. Her city.

Don tapped the cover of *The Courage to Be* on the top of Stella's stack of books and asked, "What's it about?" And she told him about the God beyond God, about the almost unnameable who might appear when the conventional figure dissolved into doubt. He listened noncommittally.

The bus slid down Eighth Avenue past the back side of Phillips High School, the shops for wood turning, drafting, metalwork—places she never went, places she was afraid of. These were the rooms frequented by boys who would be gas station attendants, work with their hands. She shuddered, then recriminated herself for her snobbishness. But suppose her destiny were to push plastic keys and to say *Hello, good evening, Fielding's* forever?

"Destiny can leap out of its den and drag you in to be its slave, forever," she said.

"What!"

"Destiny can get you, if you don't watch out."

"Worse," Don answered ruefully, "it can get you if you *do* watch out."

Now the bus was headed north on Twenty-fourth Street. It passed a strip of unpainted wooden houses. In the dim November light, Stella saw a lone fat woman sitting on her narrow porch. Her arms were bare, crossed on the porch banister. Her head lay on the arms, and she was sobbing. Her head was done up in a white bandanna, her arms were brown and lay across the weather-gray wood of the banister.

Stella felt a lump rising in her own throat, for the president, for Darl, for that woman whose bare arms must be cold in November. Yet the lighted bus, with Stella in it, was passing her by.

"You should try a glass of wine, sometimes," Don said.

"I will," Stella promised vaguely.

How abstractly her answer floated out. Who was this person beside her, chatting while the late bus carried them toward home?

"I broke up with Darl, my fiancé, today."

"Well." He glanced at her. "And how are you?" (He seemed afraid; would he have to comfort?)

"Okay, I guess."

"I hope you called Sister." Now he sounded like the country boy he was; no curl of urban irony lifted the word *Sister*. "No doubt she'd understand," and irony—or was it self-doubt?—reappeared.

He slid to the edge of his seat, turned, so he could look more fully into Stella's face. Pressing her spine against the back of her seat, she closed her eyes. She felt the tears ooze out. She felt his hand squeeze her shoulder.

"I thought it would be nice to be married," she murmured. She could feel the way her underlip was folding down and back on itself, the sob gathering in her chest.

Don gave something like a little laugh. "Most people do."

Stella had never seen a kinder face. It was as though he'd dropped the movie star mask. The beauty and sympathy of his character shone out at her.

"I'm sorry to burden you," she said. She felt like a crybaby.

"What can we do with our stories," he said, "but tell them?"

"I guess." But she was curious. What did he mean?

"When we tell them, then someone can comfort us." His beautiful blue eyes were looking at her. "When we tell, or sing, or paint, or make a film, it gives humanity another chance."

"A chance for what, Don?" There, under his high cheekbone, was a hollow where she could nest the curve of her face.

"To be. A chance to live a different life. A chance to sympathize."

"*Da*," she said. "That's what the thunder says in *The Waste Land*. One of the meanings is that we should sympathize."

"*Da?*"

"It's Sanskrit. I mean it's short for a longer word that's Sanskrit."

His eyelids lowered to half-mast. Would he disappear? Would he blink and be gone? When he raised his eyelids, would he also raise the mask? She closed her own eyes.

"Stella." He called her name. Summoned her. She looked at him. He sounded frightened. "You seemed to go away," he said. His tone was formal.

How much formality does it take to contain the spume of the heart? How much irony and rue?

"You'll marry someone else, Stella."

"And you?" she asked timidly.

He laughed. "Who knows?"

Then they stopped, frozen in their attitudes, he, on the edge of the seat, turned to look back at her. She pressed far back against the brown leather.

Past their reflections in the big bus windows was Norwood, the residential neighborhood that was truly theirs, more so than big Birmingham, though they claimed the city, too. The bus was passing the cluster of businesses on Twelfth Avenue—a photography studio, the Norwood bakery, the little sewing and notions shop, Murray's drugstore, with the teen hall in its basement. People loved the businesses of their community. How would she know who she was without them? They were as defining as the stack of books on her knee.

Don was reaching into his pocket. He drew out a large green plastic ring, the slightly adjustable kind that didn't quite complete its circle. On the top of it was a flat oval, and pasted there like a blank cartouche was a ruby-red piece of shiny paper. "I got it in a Cracker Jack box," he said. "Would you like to have it? In the meantime?" His face crinkled into a clown smile, as though he were trying to make her laugh. "Until something better comes along."

"Would we be engaged?" she asked, smiling a little.

"Why not? If you want to?"

"And if *you* want to," she said. "Until something better comes along."

Still he held it out to her. It reminded her of a large snail, but the red paper caught the light, reflected, like something burning. Perhaps the ring was a little window, and if she put it on, she would see inside her flesh where her blood was burning. But lying in the palm of Don's hand, the plastic ring was like a large snail.

"Did you and Cat ever race snails in the country?" Stella asked.

"We raced each other, Sister and I."

Still he held out the green ring, but his fingertips began to curl over it.

"My brothers and I, some of the kids, raced snails on our front porch. The house across from where I live now. We'd set the snails down in a line on the porch tiles, and they'd creep forward. We each had a snail. We crawled behind the snails on our hands and knees." Her knees had been bare and bony against the hard red tiles, and the black soot from McWanes Cast Iron Pipe Company—"fallout," her mother labeled it—pressed into her skin while she crawled behind the snails. "We could steer our snails in a straighter path by touching the tips of their antennae." (She remembered the tentative tenderness of their touch on the ends of those stalks. Some kids said snails carried their eyes there.) After the antennae slowly retracted, the snail would straighten its path. "They left silver trails behind that would last for days. My mother never minded."

"It must have taken patience to be a snail jockey." Still, he held out the ring, his fingers curling more and more inward like a mimosa leaf closing for the night.

"I'd take the ring," she said, "if you meant it."

"Really engaged? To be married?"

She nodded. One quick dip of the head.

He looked away. He looked worried. But he looked back and met her eyes. "Would you like to marry me, Miss Silver?"

She reached out and took the ring. Suddenly instead of putting it on her finger, she stuck out her tongue and put the tip of it through the ring. She drew it inside and closed her mouth and smiled for a second. She pretended she was a frog, green as the plastic ring.

He laughed out loud, and she stuck her tongue out again. He took off the wet ring and put it on her finger.

"There's a hitch or two," he said.

"What?"

"Well, I've signed up for the Peace Corps. I'm going to Tonga, in the South Pacific, for two years. I leave in a week."

"We can have an engagement party before you go."

"It's a long time to be separated."

"We'll write."

"We hardly know each other," he reminded her. Then he added with a laugh, "Maybe that's best. Like an arranged marriage."

"Only we arranged it ourselves. Approximately ten-twenty-five P.M., November 22. On the 15 Norwood bus."

"After a chance meeting." He stared at her. Seemed happy. "Thus," he said, "we embrace absurdity."

"Yes," she said. "No. We embrace each other."

They both sat still.

"You could sign up to come to Tonga, too."

"I think I'd rather stay here. Maybe take some more classes."

The two boys and their mother from the back of the bus stood up. The mother pulled the bell cord and led her children to stand at the back door.

The older little boy, about eight, Stella thought, with hair close cropped so she could see the beautiful egg of his skull, approached them. His eyes spread wide, he spoke to Don. "You really gonna marry this lady?"

"Really," Don answered.

"With that there Cracker Jack ring?"

"Edmund Powers!" his mother said sharply. "Get over here now and get off this bus with me!"

Stella smiled at him. "You're invited to come."

The mother pushed through the swinging door, and her children plopped out after her. "You just about got left behind, Edmund," she said loudly from outside, a public reprimand, really an apology for her son's intrusion.

This stop was the last one on Vanderbilt Road. Stella imagined the family walking down the side of Stoner's Grocery in the dark into the Quarters. The bus turned left, up Norwood Boulevard.

"This will be my stop, next," Stella said. She thought Don probably didn't know exactly where she lived. She would get home intact, after all. Engaged.

Don stood up. "The least I can do is walk my fiancée home."

Down the black rubber aisle Stella and Don progressed to the front of the bus. The driver pulled the door open for them—how mighty must be the muscles in his right arm, the one that worked the lever all day—and they were disgorged into Norwood.

The empty lighted box of the bus rambled on without them up the hill of the boulevard.

They walked down a little slope under the sweetgum tree, bare of leaves now, but they stepped on the decaying prickly balls, gone soft with a month of lying on the ground.

Don took her hand, his fingers lacing into hers. "You do mean it, Stella?"

Yes, yes. Let me attach my life to something, she thought. *Something that lasts forever and is real. Something random because there's nothing wrong with me.* She was glad, but she could not speak. She felt caught in a revolving door: it showed her the outer world, the inner world, but she was too unreal to step away from their whirling to enter either. She felt like a ghost trapped in the unreal.

"We can stop this anytime you want," he said.

Quick as that, she halted. She seemed to hear a sound like a phonograph winding down. Like disembodied voices dying of despair. She stood still—a mashed sweetgum ball under the instep of her foot—and something in her went dead.

How could he suggest they stop? They were engaged; they had taken every step together. They had mutually agreed. Her happiness died.

"Yes," she said. Maybe her words could overlay his. She resumed walking.

Her shoe toe scuffed through the dead sweetgum leaves, each one a brown star-shape. "Yes, I want us to marry," she said. But she felt dead and vacant inside.

It was useless. Why had he said they could stop? Didn't he care? Had he no desire of his own? Was he afraid she might sue him for entrapment? At every step, they had agreed.

But it was all right, she told herself, though he had ruined it: we can stop this anytime you like. Her soul had flared toward him, and now it struggled, shrank, and winked, as though it might sink and die.

She walked quickly forward, toward home. He was a human being and therefore someone she could marry. A man she admired and respected. This was the way it was done in many countries. The couple learned to love each other after the promise was made.

Her fingers were still laced into Don's fingers. She liked that. But because he had offered to retreat from the alliance, now her hand seemed detached, turned wooden at her wrist.

Stella glanced back quickly at the disappearing illuminated bus shouldering its way up the dark hill. Empty of passengers, it rose toward the crest of the first hill of the boulevard. Almost she could forget that it rolled on rubber tires. Almost she could imagine that it rose disconnected, immaterial, like a lighted box conveying invisible souls. She'd forgotten to read the nameplate of the driver. Her omission seemed horrible: she'd neglected to acknowledge who he was.

DEAR SELF,

—FOR SO I CALL MYSELF THIS DAY, NOVEMBER 22, 1963, for today I have become dearer to myself by becoming disengaged from one man and engaged to another. *Until something better comes along,* we both said. I felt a bit mad a good part of this historic day. I have mourned everywhere.

All day, I've wandered. Perhaps I'm better suited to live in a spirit world where the members of my lost family hold up its four corners—Mama, Daddy, Ruben, and little Timothy. He's too little to stand in the corner alone, just two years older than I was then. The four spirits of the little Negro girls visit them. My father was ever gracious, loved all children. Suffered them to come.

Taught us to shoot.

Even in the spirit world, I hover around the fringes, am not quite admitted.

No. Now I am cozy in my room, and the walls keep out the world that has purposefully slain a president, randomly murdered innocent children, spawned cyclones to demolish families, created illness and suffering of every imaginable and unimaginable kind. Made us to long for a wholeness we can lose but never possess. Yet I am cozy in my room.

On my four bedroom walls hang paintings, like shields, whose creator is none other than the man, the *artist,* to whom I am engaged to be married! Engaged on a well-lighted city bus plowing through the night.

Out of the frying pan and into the fire! But so what!? And why not, if it's what I myself choose? And if my choice hurts no one but myself.

Does it hurt Don?

No. For he has chosen, too. That is, if this step damages him in some way I am not guilty because the injury comes from his own willful decision making.

I feel so naked here. Shedding guilt. Writing in my own book. It has cleared my head of the madness. I hope never again to come so close to the abyss and shall fight hard to keep my curious feet (in their olive shoes) from—

But what of Don? And of the fact that I scarcely know him?

Do we know life?

No, but we marry it just the same, and whether we want to or not. It's folly to think one can choose wisely, and so why not choose spontaneously?

I died inside when he said *we* could stop whenever *I* liked. What did *I* have to do with it? I was under the illusion that *we* were acting on our mutual desires and inclinations. But he meant to be reassuring. Even I acknowledge his good intentions. *But the sentiment doesn't suit me.* Headlong. I *like* headlong and no regrets. *Je ne regrette rien.*

Perhaps I can't be pleased and should simply hate myself for my failure.

Perhaps this engagement—here's the ring on my thumb—is a joke. An act of spontaneous theater—merely amusing. No! I infuse it with meaning. We were not joking. Or, the joke has evolved, broken the back of its hard chrysalis to flutter forth, transformed. *Until. Unless.*

Don's paintings hang around me in the dim light of this bedroom. They have come unnamed, like children, but I name one, done only in shades of brown and tan, *The Nile River Sideways,* for it resembles a kind of crack in the earth, with tributary cracks. Sideways, because it divides its space horizontally, though I always think of the Nile as south-north, vertical, parting the desert. And another I name *Opulent Odalisque,* for it is touched with gilt, and while the forms are all abstract ovals, they seem to recline on one another rather like a woman might lounge back into unbelievable wealth. Well—

REALLY IT IS NOT the paintings but this dim light filtering into my chamber that swaddles me and asks for words.

My room is not all inwardness, for light from the streetlamp filters through the shades, and I remember how at night in the summer long ago I played under the streetlight with the neighborhood kids and my brothers. With Ruben (which means "firstborn" in Hebrew, doubtlessly named so by my mother) and Timothy (as in the books of the New Testament, no doubt read and loved by my Methodist father with his true-hawk nose and the red spider veins emanating at the juncture of nostril-flange and face). But I was writing of playing hide-and-seek outside at night, and something in me rejoins those shadow children.

I have fallen down, and so have taken time out to sit on the curb and press my elbow with my skirt. I am five, and I have not guessed that I am more than brushed by my encounter with the pavement. Yet when I look at my skirt, I have printed it with blood from my skinned elbow. I have printed three shapes, like hearts, on my skirt as I pressed my elbow against the cloth of my skirt.

My elbow was still covered—I remember—with a thick scab when the car rolled, and they were killed. But I don't want to think of that. A young doctor in the hospital asked me, "How are you today?" And I must have said fine because then he asked if I knew what had happened. I said I had played too rough and skinned my elbow. I showed my old scab to him.

I must have been a little out of it then, but I will *not* think about that. It was long ago.

I'm here in my room at my aunts. Aunt Krit, never married, the maiden schoolteacher, peculiar. (I could become her.) Aunt Pratt, older, widowed, a mother but her son lost, a deserter from war, half mad with anxiety about him and the arthritis that leaves her bedridden. (I will not become her, except for her brave love for whoever crosses her path. For me.) The same streetlight shines through the shades, and I can see the abstract paintings of my beloved looking in on me as though they hung on the walls of my mind. I have escaped the city, the world of accident and murder. I dwell not in the house of the Lord forever and ever, but in the room of my mind, here in the house of my aunts.

But what was it I wanted to say when I began to write in my book? That I am here and safe.

That's not enough. The people of my city—so many people feel . . . So many do not imagine him as a human like themselves. What I realize is that I still love these people. I am apart from them—*I feel so lonely!*—but this city is my home and they are my people.

Why am I more slain by assassination than by the murder of four Negro girls?

There is something wrong with my heart. I will change myself.

My heart convulses with sadness and terror.

Oh, I see a dark house! I know that desolate house. It is next door, the one

I grew up in. And the day before Aunt Krit sold it, she invited the neighbors to come and look around for anything they wanted to take. Then she sat in this house, with our lights out, and she called to me, "Come see, Stella. They've come with their torches."

Torches, she said, and I was alarmed because I thought they might be about to burn the house down, from the inside. I thought it ruthless of her to discard the furniture, ruthless to sell the house. These days she mumbles about the Negroes at Helicon, how they may be trying to establish squatters' rights on her property.

But what she meant by *torches* was flashlights, and I saw the beams of light shooting through the dark house at strange angles. It was as though the house was being skewered by light beams. I sat down beside her on the daybed that was against the windows. We looked out across the driveway, black as the river Styx, and she held my hand.

"Must you sell the house?" I asked in a small voice.

"I'll need the money, saved at compound interest, to send you to college."

She was the person who told me of the massacre of the Jews. Of the camps and the ovens. Sitting at the kitchen table, watching a faucet drip, I found her information too terrible to believe. Though I respected her, I reserved a corner of doubt. Of course she told the truth, in spite of my childish disbelief. Perhaps my incredulity was pride. How could she know so much more than I?

I'm tired and must sleep. I've had my day. I ventured from this bed and had a day of wandering and of planned commitments. A phantasmagoria of voices and visions and revisions. Of cruelty and kindness. A new engagement.

What do I love about Don? His posture—the way he walks in the world. That's almost enough. But his wit, too. His kindness to Cat and to me. That he paints.

But what was that I wanted to remember? That I must change my life. The deserted house and the shafts of light prying everywhere.

LIONEL PARRISH: LETTER TO THE FOUR FAMILIES, DECEMBER I

BECAUSE IT IS THE CHRISTMAS SEASON WHEN FAMILIES draw near to one another, I am thinking of you & of the missing member of your families. If I had the power to undo what has been done to your loved one, or to undo your own grieving & the vacancy in your heart, I would do so.

But my power is small. In my kitchen, my wife & our four children have gathered to make five loaf fruitcakes, which I am sending you with this letter, & one to Mrs. Kennedy. Do not be afraid to eat them. They are stuffed with goodness. We have folded both pecans & walnuts, citron & dates into the batter. Each one has done their part, even my youngest, little Andy. He has taken the paring knife & the cherries & held a candied cherry down on the cook-top & carefully sliced it in two, time after time.

May your hurt hearts be mended as you celebrate the child God sent at Christmastime to make us whole and free of sin through his sacrifice if we but believe and trust in him.

Please enjoy these good cakes we have baked. God is serving his own cakes in heaven where all the family eats at one table.

> With Christian Love and Hope,
> Lionel & Jenny Parrish. Children George, Lizzie, Vicky & Andy (his mark)

EDMUND'S MEMOIR:
A CHRISTMAS STORY IN RETROSPECT

CHRISTMAS EVE AND I REMEMBER WATCHING MY MAMA sit up in the bed; the light from the fireplace caught the oil on her high cheekbone. Papa's place was still empty. Mama was going to look round now. Yes, she did. I saw the whites of her eyes move round, and I closed my eyes loosely, not screwed up tight like I did when I was five.

Was brother Alfie asleep? And Sis Margaret Rose and little Willy? Their knees were pulled up and they lay rounded and natural. The quilts were up to their ears. Would my big brother Charles come visit for Christmas? Mama walked barefooted to the fireplace. Her white soles flickered under her feet like she was walking on light. She picked up a lump of big coal and laid it down into the glow. The embers shifted, breathed, and poo-pooed ashes. Mama looked round mean, scowling, right at me. But I didn't show any life.

She went back toward her bed and I thought, *Where's my Christmas roller skates? Gimme my skates. Mama! Mama!* She lifted back the quilts and got into her hollow. She was pulling the covers over her shoulder and then she was turning over, facing the wall and the space where my daddy should have been. I exhorted her to get up and find my skates. And Margaret Rose's white majorette boots. And Alfie—he's old enough to know. Never mind about Willy. *I didn't ask for no bicycle.* Nothing but roller skates. Bright and shining. When you hold a skate on its back and turn a wheel with your finger, click-click-click, it's got tiny little balls inside.

I dreamed that my mama was an angel that Christmas Eve long ago, an angel walking on light, her feet glittering, and then I saw it was because she was riding my skates. She skated all night; sometimes I said, *Watch out, Mama, watch out. White man's gonna get you.*

I was prescient in my dream, like a prophet of old.

Finally Mama fell, and her stumbling was like the little bells when you walk in the grocery store to buy a Moon Pie, like when you used to walk into Stoner's store on Vanderbilt Road and could walk into now, if the store were still there, after all this time.

EARLY MORNING, AND the small coal was rolling out of the scuttle like little bells and my mama was saying, "Ain't nobody in this house interested in Christmas?"

Then my pappie was climbing up the porch steps and he fell heavy against the door.

"Hey, woman, lemme in this house!"

In three mean steps Mama crossed the room. Alfie was sitting up, but Margaret Rose had sense enough just to hang her head over the side of the bed to watch. Because my big brother had already moved out, and my father didn't count, I was the man of the house. *Not him, me, I'm the man.* I anointed myself, and prayed, "The Lord is my Shepherd; / I shall not want."

"Whatcha mean come dragging in this house on Christmas morning?" Like a pan of dishwater, Mama's wrath flung out the door on him.

"Now, I done bought a little tree."

Mama cracked open the door.

"Why, sure enough." My mama's voice sung on open—wide and warm. And my sister whipped out of bed and ran calling, "Daddy's got us a tree!" and so did Alfie, and Willy babbled, and finally I thought it was safe, and I raised up in bed.

Then I saw packages! On the breakfast table, after all. *We shall not want.* I zipped over the linoleum floor like it was hot. I lifted my box and it was heavy with metal heaviness. Then I walked on over to the rest of the family. Against the tree, I measured myself taller than Daddy's little green tree.

THAT AFTERNOON ON CHRISTMAS Day, some of us skated backward and some danced and clapped. Some skated in a circle round the whole drove. For blocks and blocks and miles and miles. Our sound was big like airplanes.

I could keep up good even if I was little, and they wouldn't leave me up there alone on white folks' streets anyway. Not on Christmas. Then, all at once, I found a dime. Perfect, slender, weightless, it slid into my pocket.

And that's the happy part of a story that I hoped could start happy and end happy, but this world cannot be represented by the happiness of a poor boy finding a dime. I had much to learn of the ways of God and man before I found my calling, which was to follow Reverend Shuttlesworth, to become a minister as he was in the days of my boyhood and continues to this day. Not so long ago, I went to the trials in Birmingham (yes, Mama, there have been Trials as well as tribulations) of those who killed my little friends, and after the last aging white man was convicted, *there* was Reverend Shuttlesworth, age eighty himself, singing for all of us "Keep Your Eyes on the Prize." And his picture on the front page of the *Birmingham News,* triumphant.

BUT CHRISTMAS, 1963, WAS the next to the last day that I ever saw my physical father.

On December 26, Pappie got up cussing and puking. After he'd stirred up the air, our whole cabin smelled like Christmas gift whiskey, spoiled and rotted and puked up. At the steel mill Pappie was grabbed up by Big Man—that's what they called it then. I don't know what piece of equipment in the foundry killed him. I guess he was hungover, drugged with booze, careless for the first and last day in his life. They said to me "Can't nobody, not even the preacher, look in his box 'cause he don't look like hisself no more."

For a while, I didn't much miss my father—I hate to say that, but it's true. He was hardly ever in the cabin. That was Mama's domain. And besides, I still had my big brother, Charles, and Reverend Shuttlesworth was my spiritual father. But sometimes at night I could hear Margaret Rose snuffling for our father. Twice Alfie cried out "Daddy" in his sleep. Willy was too young to have any sense.

Sometimes I tried to think of my paw. "Paw, he dead," I would whisper to myself.

But I had a dream that spring, and it woke me up to reality.

It was starting to warm up and forsythia had already bloomed when I found my sister, Margaret Rose, talking to my school shoes on a crate beside my cot.

"You is a nigger and don't you forget it."

"Margaret Rose!" I said. "What you mean talking at them shoes like that for?"

She whirled around, very angry at me, and hissed that I was stuck-up. But I knew that wasn't true, and I took up for myself. "You're a lie."

Then Margaret Rose said something that I knew immediately to be wicked. She said, "If I want to, when I get big, I can sleep with any white man I wants to. But you ain't never gonna have a white woman, nigger boy." She began to cry but she went right on talking. "I is *glad* I'm gonna be a woman and not no worthless man."

"You're a lie," I repeated weakly.

"Ask Mama. If you know where she at. She gone off with Mr. Stoner."

I said that his wife was sick and that Mama was helping to care for the sick, like the Bible said she ought.

"It ain't in the Bible to take money. She takes his money."

"For working in the grocery store. We paid to work."

"For swelling?" she asked. "Ain't you looked at her?"

And I wondered, was Mama swelling? Like before Willy and Alfie? Speechless, my jaw dropped open and Margaret Rose walked out the door.

That night I dreamed President Kennedy, half his head missing, took my hand and led me up the mountain to look down an open hole in its peak. A long ladder led down there. At the bottom, a human-size metal Vulcan was making steel, and the cauldron was bubbling and spitting. I went down the ladder with the president, and there was my mutilated father tending the flames, his hands just raw flesh. Oh, he was dead! All at once the ladder was pulled up. Flames bubbled out of the melting pot and spilled on the floor and spread like water toward me, burned off my shoes and lapped up my legs. There wasn't any leaving that place.

Till the rooster crowed, my father, the president, and I burned in the furnace, and the veins inside our bodies ran with molten steel.

four

THE OVEN, Summer 1964

NEW WORK, NEW LIFE

WHEN SHE STOOD ON THE FRONT PORCH OF HER FIANCÉ'S sister's house—Boy Howdy! It was hot today—and rang the bell, Stella thought of gunfire—the sound was that penetrant. It was as though she, Stella, had pulled a trigger by poking the doorbell button with a fingertip. *No, Cat Cartwright actually *was* shooting. Cat was target practicing with her father's gun in the indoor shooting gallery that Mr. Cartwright had built. When Don left for the Peace Corps—some six months earlier—his sister had taken up shooting, aided and abetted by their father.

NOT A RICH MAN, a night watchman, Mr. Cartwright had brought home old sofa cushions from the junkyard, had straightened out quart tomato juice cans and quart grapefruit juice cans; he had cut thicker steel out of wrecked cars. With the old cushions and the metal he had lined the shooting gallery, a square tube, two foot by two foot. Cat sat in the pantry to shoot; the tube supported by stilts, jutted straight into the backyard for thirty feet.

She's a pretty good shot, Harvey Cartwright often told himself, *but even if her little hands was to tremble, the bullet likely couldn't get out of the tube.* In any case, by the time a stray bullet got through all his cushion-and-metal linings it would near 'bout be harmless.

From the time of his own hardscrabble boyhood, he had trained himself to accept and not to test out any idea that offered comfort. It gave Mr. Cartwright satisfaction to believe in the efficacy of his shooting contraption. Being a night watchman, he slept with earplugs so Cat could practice during the day when he had to get his rest. 'Course when he worked, he had to have the gun back in its black leather holster (he wished the holster were bigger; that might be safer if somebody ever tried to grab it away from him).

There wasn't no safety from germs. That's what Harvey Cartwright had told himself when his daughter, who used to run down the dirt road to meet him when they lived in the country, before they had to move to Birmingham, lay in her iron lung. *There was no way I could of protected her from germs.* The doctors had said it wasn't polio, and then it was polio, and then it wasn't polio and she could certainly come out of the iron lung for most of the rest of her life, till all systems would one by one shut down; it was degenerative what she had, somebody's *ataxia.* These days you could vaccinate against polio, if it had been that.

His daddy had given Harvey an air rifle when he was ten. Yes, Cartwright was comfortable with a gun: he'd grown up in the country after all. At his job interview in the city, they'd asked two questions—"Are you comfortable with a gun?" and "Can you walk all night?" Yes, he could walk all night.

With his next paycheck he would buy Cat her own weapon so she wouldn't be scared—he imagined his daughter's terror all too easily and had to imagine it, since she had never uttered a word of fear—her unprotected alone in the house at night, the world coming to what it had. His son gone, not to the army but to the Peace Corps.

His crippled daughter needed a gun. Especially since she was determined to do what she said she was going to do, starting tonight, and who could know what colored boy might track her home, break in, seeing how she was nearly helpless. Tomorrow, he'd visit the pawnshop, this time to buy, not to sell. At least she could still use her hands some. He had to take his gun to work, and Catherine needed one of her own.

The shriek of Stella's doorbell penetrated even new rubber earplugs, though gunfire did not, and Mr. Cartwright wished he'd hung out the sign *Just come on in, Stella.* He shambled toward the front door, zipping his pants; she'd seen him in his strap undershirt before.

And now Stella and Don were engaged. Mr. Cartwright shook his head—why would his son get engaged and then go off to an island in the Pacific Ocean? Maybe Don thought he needed some home tie to keep him off the native women. Well, being engaged or even married didn't stop most men—he could have told Don that. But Don never had seemed to be wild that way.

Harvey Cartwright had come to like Stella, at least to like that she visited. When Don was around, she'd been friendly, but Mr. Cartwright never noticed any spark between Don and Stella. She had been a faithful friend to Cat from high school on into college and all the way through college. Last May, she'd pushed Cat in her wheelchair up to get the bachelor of arts diploma. Mr. Cartwright would have liked to have done that part himself.

Now he rubbed sleep out of his eyes, looked through the sheer curtain over the front door at Stella's slender form. *Like a good ghost,* he thought and remembered he'd been dreaming of his dead wife. In the dream, she was scolding him when the doorbell drilled his mind. Yes, he believed in ghosts. His wife's ghost had visited him many times to give him good advice.

"Come on in, Stella."

"I'm sorry. I woke you up."

"That's all right." He turned away, padded barefoot back toward his bedroom. Then he remembered he ought to have confronted this able-bodied girl about where she was intending to take his handicapped daughter tonight, but he was too tired.

Climbing back into his bed, he thought, *Poor little thing, lost all her family in that car wreck, lives with those two old aunts, one of them crippled up 'bout bad as Catherine.* He liked to sleep under a sheet, even in the summer. *Him a doctor, first to die. One, two, three, four. Father, mother, two brothers, all four in her family—dead.*

Mr. Cartwright pictured the car rolling over: like a single dice. People tumbling like clothes in a dryer at the Laundromat. In bed, he rolled onto his shoulder, pulled the sheet with him. Five people rolled around inside, damaged to death. Only one lucky little girl climbed out the window, car lying on its side. She had told Cat and Cat had told him. Stella was covered with blood; her whole skin was red with it.

WHEN STELLA STEPPED INSIDE, she felt the blessed coolness of the room air conditioner. She walked through the house and stopped in the kitchen to cup her hands over her ears. In the pantry, Cat sat sideways, sighting down the jerry-built shooting gallery; she was going to squeeze off another shot. Goliath, sitting in Cat's lap, looked at Stella with large, long-suffering eyes. Cat fired the gun, and as soon as the noise was over, Goliath leapt down from Cat's lap and rushed Stella. The little dog's barking exploded in jealous rage.

"Goliath! Goliath," Cat said sternly, but the little dog barked till he was satisfied. Cat left the gun in its short stand (a reclaimed wig stand from the junkyard) and turned her wheelchair. As she repositioned, sunlight glanced from the spokes, threw a spoked wheel of light toward Stella.

"Baked apples in the oven," Cat said.

Stella's nose told her it was true.

"Dad said we could take his car. But he doesn't like it. Here are the car keys." Haltingly, Cat groped in her lap, held out the necessary key ring to Stella.

The keys were still warm, Stella noticed, from Cat's lap and from Goliath sitting on them. Cat's short hair was newly washed—she didn't wash it often enough and it tended to get greasy and stringy (funny, Stella thought, how dirty hair made a person look poor), but today it was a light brown haystack capping Cat's head.

"Your hair looks pretty," Stella said. "So we've got the car."

Although Stella's Aunt Krit owned a car, she took it to school with her every day. She'd taught Stella to drive, and she let her use the car once a week.

"Dad said to get to Miles we go out Eighth Avenue."

"So you told him where."

"Seemed best."

"I'm not going to tell the aunts." Stella knelt before the hot stove to take out the baked apples, something Cat couldn't manage. "At least not till we've got the jobs."

H.O.P.E.

WHAT LIONEL PARRISH THOUGHT WHILE HE WAITED FOR the white girls was: (1) they both had B.A.s and one was Phi Beta Kappa and (2) they were from here, and what did that mean? Not like white Judy Cohen from Berkeley, California, whose smile was . . . strained, should he say? Couldn't be *friendly*, since she didn't know anybody down here and there hadn't been time to make friends, but maybe *hopeful* of making friends, yes, call it hopeful. Hope was something he could relate to. It stood for what he was trying to do: **H**elp; **O**pportunity; **P**otential **E**nergy—the capital letters spelled out the word.

Lionel Parrish had talked it over with Mr. Bones, and when Mr. Bones sneered in derision, then Mr. Parrish knew it was the right name, just what the community needed: hope. Right on cue, yes, he could expect Mr. Bones often these days, and here he was!

With a skittering and a crash, a scrolled-up drawing of the human skeleton rolled down behind Lionel Parrish's desk. The bottom pole of the wall diagram dropped right into the chalk tray like the sharp rap of a ruler. When he was a boy, teacher had laid the ruler cross the palm of little Lionel's hands many a time like that.

Mr. Parrish sighed. "What you want to say this time, Mr. Bones?" he said, addressing the chart of the skeleton.

Trouble coming. That's all.

"Uh-uh. Future coming. Let the means reflect the ends. That's what I say. That's what Martin says Gandhi says. That's what Fred Shuttlesworth says. Now let's see what Joe Rumore says. You hush."

Mr. Parrish flicked on his small radio. *And now the weather, brought to you by Golden Eagle Table Syrup, Pride of Alabam. Temperatures soared to ninety-nine degrees today in Birmingham, and now at five o'clock in the evening, the thermometer reads ninety-eight degrees in the downtown area. Relative humidity ninety-eight percent. Zero chance of precipitation, and folks, it looks like it's going to be another scorcher tomorrow in Birmingham, your Magic City. Predicted high of a hundred degrees in our sizzling Magic City. . . .*

The sound of the phone pierced the radio patter. Well, he'd answer it. Maybe the white girls were canceling. He answered cheerfully, "*H-O-P-E, Help Opportunity Potential Energy here.*"

A stream of white-voice obscenities machine-gunned into his ear. Mr. Parrish gently set the receiver back in its cradle. He hummed a little church tune to himself. He picked up a pencil to be busy.

Push it out of your mind with a pencil. Might of been Mr. Bones; might of been his own good voice giving him good advice. But the gray pencil lead, sharp above the yellow pad of paper, did its own little nervous dance. He glanced over his shoulder at the grinning skeleton on the wall. *Now the Lord said to Lot's wife, Don't you look back.*

Okay. That was what he, Lionel Parrish, should have told himself about Matilda, what with Jenny and the children so good at home. But he had gone back to Matilda, and she had heated him up till blood boiled in his veins. Mr. Parrish rose from his chair and looked out the window across the city to see Vulcan standing on Red Mountain. *Help me, Iron Man!* He ought not pray to a pagan god, he knew that. You'd burn in hell for that.

Timid knock, timid white voice: "Mr. Parrish, Mr. Parrish."

And there was one: slender as a willow switch.

"There're too many steps."

What did that crazy white girl mean?

One in a wheelchair! Hey, come on! And she mad as a hornet, sitting in her chariot at the bottom of the steps.

"You said your office was street level," the crippled one said.

"Well, more or less. It is."

The standing one (hair straight and smooth, almost to her shoulders, then flip!) said her name, *Stella Silver,* and that she could get Catherine's chair up one step but not three, and he said that wouldn't be any problem for him, and when he reached out to pull her up, that Catherine commanded *Wait!* And then explained she had to release the brakes first (looked like her hands, too, were weak, kind of flipped back at the knuckles). She released the brake very slowly; he could have done that in half a second. Her hands moved like they *owned* the brakes, like they were little flesh clouds hovering over their own territory, but after she'd done it, she smiled up at him and wasn't any doubt: she liked him and wanted him to like her. Just as natural as could be.

It was heavy, chair and all, and he understood why that willow switch was smart not to try to pull wheelchair and passenger up three steps. He'd supposed all along they *were* smart, well educated, but turned out, after they got settled inside, and the phone rang and he ignored it, and the radio turned on by itself, and he laughed and said *Haints, I reckon* and they laughed, too, and they had got each other's names straight, turned out it was the crippled one who was the Phi Beta Kappa and she was also the one he'd talked to on the phone. Her voice was a little bit impaired, too, but that was faint.

"My name's Catherine," she said, "but everybody calls me Cat. 'Cause I'm so light on my feet." When she smiled, so slow, then he got it, her joke, and they all laughed together. Well, they'd swapped jokes, and right off the bat, too.

But they wanted to know what they'd be paid. He pussyfooted around a little, but he knew they could tell, and yes he had advertised in the *Birmingham News* like he was up and running, but . . . Truth was, H.O.P.E. was not yet funded.

"Matter of time," he added. "Washington knows about us."

"Federal funding?" Stella's voice near 'bout as full of doubt as Mr. Bones's.

"I *do* have a friend in Washington, D.C., and he has talked to a congressman, and there *was* reassurances. I assure you there were reassurances. See, we have a *better* chance we be actually operating. They look at deeds, not words. Not what we *planning* to do, what we *are* doing."

"Mr. Parrish," Cat said in her slow, thoughtful way, "is it the same for your other teachers. They're not being paid yet either?"

"They are volunteers. But see, they still college students at Miles. They still working on their B.A.s." He looked her square in the eyes. "I know it's different for you and Miss Silver." Suddenly the skeleton flew up, rolled itself up and shut. " 'Nother haint," he said, but this time nobody laughed.

"No." Cat spoke so slowly. "I reckon it's not different for us. We want to help." Then she quickly added, "Don't we, Stella?" like a burst of energy came down her nerve line.

Stella reached over on his desk and picked up the little Vulcan paperweight as though she owned it.

"Sure," Stella said, but she didn't look at him.

"There's something else I want." Cat waited before she went on. She swallowed like her tongue might be a little bit too big to manage.

"What's that?" he asked.

"When it's over, I want you to write a letter of recommendation to the Birmingham Board of Education saying I did a fine job and I managed my students by myself and never had a bit of trouble."

"Suppose you do have trouble?"

Now Stella had more to say: "They won't hire her. She's Phi Beta Kappa, but they won't take her. She did her practice teaching. The regular teacher was out sick two weeks, and Cat managed by herself entirely. She was fine. But the board said it didn't count because the teacher didn't *observe* Cat's teaching. And if somebody was in there observing, then Cat wouldn't be alone with the students, and they'd never know if she could do the job."

"They said it would make the insurance go up to have a teacher in a wheelchair," the crippled girl explained.

"Suppose you do have trouble, Cat?"

"I won't," she said.

(Boy Howdy! Like his Texas grandpa used to say. Her eyes bored at you like two pistol barrels.) "Yes, I'll write for you. Be glad to." The words just popped out. You didn't say no to pistols.

(No white Birmingham Board of Education cared what a black man said anyway.)

They were all sweating. He felt a great gush come out of his right armpit, and Stella had a little sweat-bead mustache. Cat's glasses having slid down the slick slant of her nose, she pushed them back to the bridge. (Her finger, like her hand, had a strange swayback appearance.)

"Mighty hot night," Mr. Parrish mumbled, "just like the radio say."

The white women looked at each other, settling it without speaking that they would volunteer, expect pay if it came down from Washington.

Mr. Parrish heard a mosquito at his ear.

"How safe is it for us to come out here?" Stella asked.

"What place *is* this?" he asked them. No evasion; his voice was hard, direct.

Cat chuckled. "Bombingham."

DRIVING HOME

WHILE STELLA DROVE MR. CARTWRIGHT'S LUMBERING OLD
car back toward Norwood, she thought about what Mr. Parrish had gone on to
say about safety. That his life was in the Lord's hands, and he supposed everybody else's was, too. That was all the insurance he needed. And Cat had asked
him if he ever did any preaching. Mr. Parrish had said sure he was a preacher,
sold funeral insurance, too, on weekends, since even those in the hands of the
Lord would need it sooner or later. (That was the way A. G. Gaston got to be a
millionaire, wasn't it?)

During the day Mr. Parrish taught math at Parker High School. Stella interrupted to say her Aunt Krit taught math at Phillips High. And Cat boldly asked
Mr. Parrish if Parker was still the largest all-black school in the world, and they had
all felt a kind of triumph over the whole continent of Africa, which, after all, could
have been expected to have the largest all-black high school. Cat had said the word
black, not *colored* or *Negro*, to a black man, and she had said it like it meant nothing
in the world except the word she needed to use to ask her question.

But Stella liked remembering the interview better than she had liked being
at Miles.

The car moved a lot like Mr. Cartwright, looked like him, too. Kind of a
wreck. Had seen better days. Don was too urbane to drive such a car; he preferred
the bus. In Tonga, he walked. He'd written that the king of Tonga—too heavy to
walk, his subjects were proud to say—was carried everywhere on a litter.

When they drove by the Municipal Auditorium, Stella's knees felt empty;
she remembered playing the cello there in the Christmas Festival, in the youth

orchestra with five hundred high school singers on the risers, pastel puffs of yellow, minty green, blue, cotton-candy pink amid the boys' dark suits. None of them were Negroes. She hoped they had had their own music festival at least. How would they have dressed?

She herself had worn a hoopskirt under her white net evening dress for the first time—she'd just entered high school—and the curve of the hoop had to be bashed in so she could get the cello between her knees. During the "Hallelujah Chorus," it had sprung out and zoomed the cello forward, but she had caught it by the scroll while it flew away and reeled it back in.

"Right when the basses come in," Stella told Cat, "in the ascending four-note scale." She sang it for Cat, pulsing the gas pedal with each word. "That's when the cello boinged out and skittered into the music stand."

Stella liked to tell Cat about ridiculous situations she'd gotten herself into. She thought it might console Cat a little, make her feel less bad that she couldn't walk. The large illuminated star was shining over Carraway Methodist Hospital, on the edge of Norwood.

(CAT IMAGINED THEY ILLUMINATED the star so ambulances could find their way to the hospital more easily.) But Cat was remembering how she'd met Stella at Phillips. It was a fire drill, and she'd still been able to get around on crutches then. The students all thought she'd had polio because her crutches were the metal type that didn't come all the way up under the armpit, the type you saw on posters. But she'd lost her balance and fallen in the crowded, rushing hall. She had been afraid of being trampled, but somebody (Stella) had stopped and stood in front of her, facing the stream of students. "Go round, go round," Stella had said over and over, quietly, but in the face of the oncoming students.

When the hall was empty, the fire drill an apparent success, Stella had sat down on the floor with Cat, and they had talked until the custodian happened by and said he'd just carry Cat out, though she hadn't wanted him to. Stella went out first to hold open one of the massive front doors of Phillips High School. When Mr. Wingard stepped out with Cat draped in his arms like a rescued princess, somebody saw them, and 1,700 students set up a mighty sentimental roar of approval. But the building hadn't been on fire.

Cat felt her own cheeks burn pink, but Cat saw that this new girl, Stella, could hardly keep back the tears that sprang to her eyes when they cheered. Stella was one of them and moved by their approval; she had had to wipe her runny nose with the back of her hand. For a moment Cat knew Stella was brimming with it: *We're all good people.*

It was the week after the Reverend Fred Shuttlesworth had been beaten with chains and brass knuckles in front of the school.

It turned out Stella was not exactly one of them: the *normals.* She was an orphan. Cat discovered Stella believed naively in being good and following the rules, as though that compliance would be a shield against the injustice of the universe. As the car moved toward home, Cat remembered her mother's laughter, a quiet cackle, almost delightfully out of control. Cat missed her mother, who was always amused by Stella.

After Stella's visits that first year to Cat's home, back in Phillips High School days, either Cat or her mother would laugh and say, "Well, she did it again." They meant Stella had eaten all of the baked apple, core and seeds, to be polite.

That was the past, when they first met in high school. Cat was tired now. Both she and Stella felt flat as pancakes, united in their fatigue. *Our essential sameness,* Cat thought comfortably. Together.

Good night.

Good night.

After Stella helped her out of the car, Cat insisted on wheeling herself up the ramp onto the porch. When she looked over her shoulder, Stella was already half a block away, walking into the night shadows toward home, some twelve blocks away. The door was unlocked—her father and his gun slept inside, waiting for the graveyard shift—and Cat entered the dark living room. His toenails clicking on the bare hardwood floor, Goliath came to greet her. He leapt into her lap before she had time to set the brakes. The chair rolled back a little.

AT MIDNIGHT, MR. CARTWRIGHT rose, listened to his daughter snoring in the next room, the dog snoring, too. At least the midget dog had a loud yapper. Mr. Cartwright strapped on his holster. Well, the timing worked out just like she'd said—getting the car back, he meant. Tomorrow when he went off to work, there'd still be some real protection in the house.

STELLA'S AUNTS

AS STELLA WALKED UP THE RED CLAY, STONE-STUDDED driveway to the back door of her aunts' home, Pal let out one deep bark from the shadows, recognized her, snuffed her leg, wagged his tail. Stella always spoke to nice dogs as if they were people—"How you?"—and ignored rude ones, like Goliath, as much as she could without seeming rude herself. When she went through the kitchen door, Pal slipped in with her.

Her aunt greeted the dog first. "I'm in here, Pal."

Aunt Krit sat grading math papers at the dining room table, but she laid down the pencil, red on one end and blue on the other, to claim Pal. She stroked his head with both hands, slender beautiful hands (Stella had inherited her hands from her Aunt Krit), saying over and over, "Poor Pal, poor Pal. You like to been brown, didn't you?" *Like to been?* She meant the dog only *lacked* a little bit of being brown. Actually Pal was pure white. He had an indistinct shading of pale tan over the top of his head.

To Stella, Krit said, "I don't like you out walking the street so late at night."

"It's summer. Lots of people are out late. It's only a mile."

"*They've* gone to bed." She nodded her head at the parallel house across the driveway.

The Gulf of Driveway! When Stella was little, it had been scary to cross the driveway at night; her father used to send her over with codeine tablets wrapped in a Kleenex to calm the nerves of Aunt Pratt. As soon as Stella entered the kitchen, Aunt Krit intercepted Aunt Pratt's medicine. A razor blade lay on the kitchen table. Aunt Krit sat down, unwrapped the tablets, and shaved off their sides. One whole tablet was confiscated. *She doesn't need all this.* It had never occurred to Stella to tell her father that Aunt Krit always reduced Pratt's dosage. Maybe he had guessed it. Maybe he sent too much *because* he knew Krit would interfere.

"Over there, they all went to bed an hour ago." *They* were the new owners who had bought Stella's home.

As though to contradict Aunt Krit, the kitchen light came on in the bedded-down house.

"It's a nice summer night," Stella said. "Except for the heat. I didn't feel a bit afraid."

"Boodle-worm."

Stella lifted out the chair at the end of the table—*You lift, don't drag, fine furniture*—and sat down companionably. Sometimes, truth told, Stella did feel afraid alone at night, but not after she'd acted righteously or done a good deed. Not after she'd been with Cat; after that, as she walked away, she stretched and luxuriated in her mobility. It felt so fine to walk that sometimes, when she was out of sight, she flew down the sidewalk. *How would it be to work at Miles?*

Pal sat down between Krit and Stella; he panted and stuck his penis out of its white furry sheath. The dog's penis fascinated Stella: bright pink, a distinct tip, tiny red blood vessels visible along its sides. Pal was bored. He nudged his chin onto her thigh, and she dutifully petted him. He wanted attention; affection was superfluous. Pal had short legs but a long back with a part down the middle and wiry white hair falling to either side. Stella ran her finger down the part to make his skin flicker and shudder.

"You want to help me grade a set?" Aunt Krit slid a rubber band off a stack of papers folded lengthwise; she stored the thin rubber band with two others on her wrist, like bangle bracelets. This was the first summer Aunt Krit had taught summer school. *I want to see what it's like,* she'd said, *for the money.*

She'd quickly decided she didn't like it.

They graded quietly. Aunt Krit's eyes could glance at a math paper and flag the slightest error; she didn't need to think about it; her eyes just lighted on the flaws: *I'm like a duck on a june bug,* she had said once to Stella, and Krit had smiled a wry, shy, crooked smile, her face shining with pride. Stella loved that rare smile: Aunt Krit pleased.

"'Nother goose egg!" Aunt Krit drew the red zero and sighed. "They're all nothing but failures and future criminals!"

If Aunt Krit liked a student, she marked his paper in blue; if she didn't, she used red; both colors were available at opposite ends of the pencil. For summer school students, she used only the red end of the pencil. After algebra, they began to grade geometry papers. "They're all headed for the penitentiary," Aunt Krit said indignantly.

Krit was thin and frail, always tired, never seemed strong or thoroughly happy. She disapproved of Aunt Pratt, blessedly asleep in her own bedroom, an invalid to arthritis and an accident that had ruined her knee. But Pratt had been derailed earlier; when Son—Pratt's grown boy—had been drafted into World War II and then had gone AWOL, Pratt lived with the constant fear he'd be caught and shot as a deserter. Her work was to worry, but she did it in solitude. Her deceased husband's pension supplied her few needs—for nail polish and perfume. When she had company, she sociably attended to her guest, offered gum or hard candy.

Krit couldn't stand Pratt's perfumes and powders and eyebrow pencils; her gaudy earrings, necklaces, and bracelets; her box of silly flowered scarfs, her endless packs of chewing gum (for Stella), her bright red belts and matching shoes. All day Pratt drew pictures, crocheted, and told stories to whoever came through the door. Didn't earn a dime.

Aunt Krit's favorite color was blue. She only wore skirts in shades of blue and beige, topped by a neat white blouse, sometimes with a little embroidery on the collar. The blouses hung straight from her shoulders to her waist. Even in her nightgown—sheer red nylon—Aunt Pratt, thin as Aunt Krit, sometimes wore her brassiere plumped up with thick sponge breasts.

Krit tossed down her grading pencil and declared, "Even if Don is Cat's brother, it would ruin the wedding to have her in it."

Stella said nothing.

"You don't *have* to have her."

"But Don wants her to stand up for us."

"Stand up!"

"Be *in* the wedding."

"At a wedding everything's got to be perfect. They delivered the rosebushes today. I'll have Old Uncle put them in tomorrow."

"They'll look great."

"I want it to be perfect. I'm inviting all the teachers."

Krit envisioned the whole backyard walled with white climbing roses in full bloom. The new rosebushes had two seasons to grow because Don had postponed everything and gone off to some dark island for the Peace Corps. "Boodle-worm," Aunt Krit muttered under her breath. She knew Don might never come back to marry her niece. Like that Darl. *Out of the picture.* Krit had never trusted Darl, his face hidden under all those specks. But Don was as fair and unblemished as somebody you could see on the screen. She liked him. He was like Alan Ladd crossed with Rock Hudson. Why did young people go off in the Peace Corps unless they were running away from something at home?

For a while, Krit and Stella returned to their grading. Finally Aunt Krit threw down her pencil again, took off her pale-rimmed glasses, and rubbed her eyes. "I don't believe I can grade another paper."

Stella looked at her and smiled. "Let's hit the hay."

Krit wished her niece wouldn't use slang. "Let me show you something."

Aunt Krit picked up a sheet of graph paper. With the straight edge and blue pencil, she divided it into quadrants. In two opposing quadrants, she drew opposing hyperboles till the widening flanges fell off the page. The blue-line hyperboles looked like two fish, nose to nose. "Now this one," Krit said, "is really the same as this one. It's gone through all time and space and come back." Her voice choked on the enormity of it. "While it travels, it gets closer and closer to the straight lines, but the hyperbola's lines will never become straight and never touch the asymptotes. The hyperbola draws infinitely closer." She sighed and touched the crosspoint of the coordinates with her blue pencil lead. "This spot, this place is God."

Then she set down the pencil, shot a meaningful glance at her niece, and went to bed. Aunt Pratt had been snoring from her bedroom all evening. *Not a care or a question in her head.*

After Krit climbed into the high bed, she always communed first with her dead mother, whose last illness with pneumonia and death had occurred in that same narrow hospital bed. To comfort herself and signal their union, Krit pressed her body into the mattress where Mama had lain. *If we stayed in Crenshaw County at Helicon, none of this would have happened.*

Krit let herself drift back to childhood, back to South Alabama, when they'd all been together and no one had seen an automobile. World War I was still in the future. Sometimes Krit had ridden with Jenny, her friend from down the road, in her pony cart. Jenny's hair, the color of taffy candy, was always caught up by a blue satin ribbon and hung in perfect long sausage curls down her back. Time to drift on back to when they'd all been happy. *Someday I'll have to tell the colored people to move out of my house.*

IN PRATT'S DREAMING HEAD, bombs exploded—World War II—and she feared her only son had been caught by the army, sent to the front lines, *might be hurt or dying!* Son! Son! And then his face under the helmet changed to Stella's when she was a little girl and had run over wearing her mama's cerise beret to entertain her crippled aunt. Stella brought her little friend Nancy with the big blue eyes and fringe eyelashes of a child movie star. "Let *me* be your nurse," they'd both clamored, struggling over a glass of water and spilling most of it. What was it: that speech Stella always recited, so perfectly with such confidence, with such expression? *Ladies and gentlemen, I stand before you to sit behind you, to tell you something I know nothing about. Admission is free; pay at the door; pull up a chair; and sit on the floor!*

Help! Pratt saw Son, bleeding, sitting on the floor, his body gushing from machine-gun fire in a hundred places. But now she was awake. And World War II had been over for years. Son was safe hidden somewhere. Maybe at Helicon. Maybe Chris slipped him food in the woods. Pratt hoped Krit wouldn't ever turn the colored folks out from the house. *Admission is free, pay at the door.* Stella said the words as though they meant something.

People all said Stella would probably be the first woman president of the United States. Someday everybody would forget the war. Pratt imagined the child president—*I stand before you to sit behind you*—who would grant her beloved Son a full pardon for desertion.

AND STELLA? HER DREAM was of a white rose, lying centered on a piece of graph paper, where blue coordinates crossed. The pure white flower represented God. Careful of thorns, she picked up the rose, unreal flower, with a hand you could see through, like clear plastic. Very lightly, she tapped her crotch with the white rose. Suddenly, in Stella's dream, a white dog, Pal, vomited a vile green substance. A bullet was fired along the trajectory of a hyperbola: it traveled past the slender tree trunks in the woods out through all space and time. Then it curved—because space, like a boomerang, is curved—and began rapidly to return.

IN CAT CARTWRIGHT'S DREAMS, every night, not just this night when she got her first job but day after day, week after week, year after year, she was running, gloriously running till morning came. Over a field, she ran this June night, 1964, in Alabama, holding the hand of her beloved brother, Don, who was going to marry her dear friend Stella.

LIONEL'S OFFICE

SECOND STRAIGHT NIGHT, FOLKS, OF ONE HUNDRED BURN-ing-hot degrees after sunset! Brought to you by Golden Eagle Table Syrup, Pride of Alabam, and by me, Joe Rumore, Alabama's only Eye-talian redneck. We sure wish we had a better forecast, but tomorrow looks just the same. No change anytime soon. . . .

Lionel Parrish snapped off the radio and said in his heartiest voice, "Come in, girls!" He appreciated that Arcola and Gloria, both fine students according to the dean, had come early. Oh, that Arcola, how she could smile! "Won't you have a seat." Arcola had a 1,000-kilowatt smile. Gloria had told him, shyly, she wanted to do something for her community.

"Your fan work, Mr. Parrish?" Arcola asked.

"No. Just look at it and *think* cool."

He wished he could get Gloria to look at anything other than her hands folded in her lap. How such a mole—she was a mole, Gloria, always hiding—thought she could teach high school dropouts was beyond his imagining. But somehow she had.

"What you want to see us about?" Arcola was not there to waste time, but she looked at him like she expected candy. She had a big braid (probably artificial) across the top of her head; made it look as if she had a crown above her pretty face.

What was that murmur? Why, Gloria had said something! (She had a good college record. Surely she talked sometime.) She said it again, a little louder. "Aren't we going to wait for Christine?"

He shrugged. "I 'spect Mrs. Taylor's going to be late." (Arcola smiled cheerfully. Her teeth were slightly outward spreading, but that just made it look like her smile was bursting right out.) Mr. Parrish went on. "What I want to know is, how things going?"

Arcola almost laughed. "Well, you know we not got any books, but things going 'bout as well as they can, considering."

"How 'bout the boys from Neighborhood Youth Corps?"

"Only reason they come to school is they're paid for it." (Did Arcola wink at him?)

"How they fitting in?" he asked.

"I smell a little cough syrup, don't you, Gloria?" (Gloria seemed deaf to all questions.) "Some of 'em nippin' codeine. No problem."

"They worn out time they come to class," Mr. Parrish said. He wished Arcola had higher expectations for her students than mere physical presence. "Most hasn't ever had a job before," he added.

"They okay," she answered. "I can't complain."

"Gloria, what do you think of them?"

"Yes, sir." Gloria spoke to her hands. (Like his wife, Jenny, Gloria hadn't learned the importance of looking a person in the eye.)

"Everything okay?"

"Yes, sir." (Matilda, his mistress, would look into the gizzard of anybody— boldly. He loved the bold overtures she made to him.)

"They aren't giving you any smart talk?"

"Well, Mr. Parrish." (Gloria had a pretty little voice, but she wouldn't look up.) "I'm a little bit afraid of them."

Arcola quickly said, "You scared? After you done sat in at Woolworth's?" She didn't wait for Gloria to answer. "Aw, these boys not any trouble. We got it under control, Mr. Parrish."

Like an arrow, the shriek of the telephone entered Mr. Parrish's heart. He didn't want obscenities coming in over the phone line when the girls were in his office. But they were looking at him. He had to answer. He could scarcely believe Gloria was somebody who would sit in. But she had been with Christine at the Gaslight. The sensation of dancing with Matilda passed through his body.

Turned out, the telephone questions were civil. He watched Arcola and Gloria listening to his side of the call; naturally, his volunteer teachers were curious to know how the head of H.O.P.E. would respond to inquiries.

Efficiently, with dignity. "Yes, we run the night school here. . . . It's open to anybody. . . . Yes, black or white. It's for people who want to pass the GED test. . . . You're welcome."

"Only we ain't never had," Arcola spoke sassily, "a single white student."

"I'm thinking about taking on a couple of white lady teachers, though." There, he'd said it.

"I be glad to work with 'em." (Blessed nonchalance. This was one well-balanced young woman.) "How come you want 'em?" she asked and picked up Vulcan to suck on his head. (Mr. Parrish wanted to tell her that wasn't a sanitary thing to do, but she sure did look cute, her tongue running over Vulcan's curls just like he was a lollipop.)

"Funding. Funding, for one thing."

"Suits me. Gloria, too."

He might as well tell them his concern: "I'm a little bit worried about Mrs. Taylor."

"She get along with Judy Cohen all right," Arcola reassured.

"Berkeley, California. These two new are from here."

"Well, what they like?"

"They both got brand fresh B.A. degrees."

"Guess that means they'll be over us."

The whole head of Vulcan had disappeared into her mouth. God! How did she expect him to ignore that.

"Do you have a B.A. degree?" he asked.

"I don't care," Arcola said. (Where did she get the ability to relax like that. Practically limp.) "I'm just stating facts, ain't I, Gloria? Christine's not going to like this." She smiled at him again. "You send 'em to me. I'll take care of 'em." (Yes, Arcola's fat braid across the top of her head was like a coronet.)

Gloria said quietly, "Reason Christine so bitter—one of those little girls at the church last September—she was Christine's cousin."

Mr. Parrish stared at Gloria as though she were some kind of bomb that had just detonated without exploding. Then he heard it again, the blast erupting through black children gathering after Sunday school. Burning through their bodies, through brick walls. He knew Arcola and Gloria were hearing the blast, too. The exact cadence of that sound, of what you had hoped it wasn't and knew it was. Sunday morning, September 15, 1963, in Birmingham. You knew where you were when the Sixteenth Street Baptist Church bomb exploded, you knew whose face you looked into next. Into Jenny's. Thank God they were late that day. With Jenny and his children, he had heard the thud of the bomb, then the first grief screaming over the rooftops.

That moment was like a place in his brain. He could visit it anytime. They all could.

"I didn't know she was related," Arcola said, her voice flat.

"Christine was there with me at Sixteenth Street," Gloria said. "That day."

Mr. Parrish reached for the ringing phone. When the small, cramped voice of obscenity probed his ear, he shouted, "Go to hell, you mother-fucking bastard!" He slammed down the receiver and held it down. He couldn't let loose. His hand trembled.

"Everybody gets crank calls sometime," Arcola said soberly. "We bound to get some. Sooner or later."

Mr. Parrish decided to sound official: "Thanks for stopping by." He lifted his hand from the receiver. It was hard to do, as though magnetism or electricity bonded his hand to the black phone. "Any problems—let me know. I want to keep those kids in school if we can. Keep the local white teachers, too."

IN THE OVEN

THERE THEY ARE, GLORIA THINKS, PALE BROWN HAIR IN the wheelchair. Thin woman pushing. Blond. How can Arcola just go up to people like that. Broken leg I reckon but no cast. Can't look anymore, but they right in front of me! Sound pleasant. I want to look again. I got to look. There! I must of said "Hello." Short boy-hair and blond shoulder-flip. We got your groups ready. Go there! Go there! You can't hear the crippled one move, her chair just roll so silent. She roll over to the science area. Arcola gonna help her. Yes, she does. Arcola pulls down the wall chart: human body, skin all gone; some muscles pulled back, heart showing, naked eyeball.

Gloria wishes she was home practicing the cello, or had it here to hide behind. She makes herself begin to teach the small group whose chair-desks encircle her.

"I want you to study these history dates. See how much you can remember. I wrote it out for you. Each got a page to study, but I want it back. Just start learning."

(Because I've got to listen and my heart thumping so bad: This is integration! Here it is in this room. This is what they all talking about!)

"I'M MISS STELLA SILVER—" (Gloria listens to her prissy white voice) "—and I'd like to know who you are. Would you sign this page, and also, please introduce yourselves."

"My name Charles Powers."

"I'm Mrs. Agnes LaFayt. It's spelled *F-A-Y-T,* but said *Fate,* like our Fate is in his hands." *So gentle and kind, Mrs. LaFayt, near 'bout fifty. Comes every night. Good influence on the young students.* Mrs. LaFayt reminds Gloria of her grandmother in the country.

"My name Samuel Powers."

Teacher says, "Oh, you're brothers then?" *But they're not and his name isn't Sam Powers.*

"Yes, ma'am," *they both say, and she don't know any better.*

"I'm Michael Powers."

"Really?" she says. *My group starting to listen in, too. Let 'em.*

"We all brothers."

Next boy, number four—*I ought to learn their names.* "I'm Charles Powers."

"I thought *he* was Charles Powers."

"We first cousins. Our mothers was identical twins."

"You sure do have a pretty name, Miss Silver." *That's Agnes LaFayt. She trying to help out.* "My niece's named Stella."

"How many nieces you got, Sam-Man?" *Don't you mock Mrs. Agnes, smarty boy.*

"Miss Silver, you want to know my nieces' names?" *Smarty, he's going nasty.* "They named Denise, Carole, Cynthia, Addie Mae. . . . You ever heard of my nieces?"

Agnes says, "That's not true, and you know it." She sounds so sad. "Don't do dishonor."

Miss Silver just says she'll get the names off the paper, but they won't stop.

"Truth is we all kin," one says *like he's doing her a favor to explain it.*

"Yeah, we one big family," another says, *but Miss Silver is through with all their nonsense.*

"My job is to help you to be able to pass the high school equivalency test in English."

"How can this be a school when they don't give us no books?"

She scoots her chair up closer to them. She's not going to let on scared. No. She move closer, her knee just about touching his.

"I wish there were books, but the program can't afford them. We just have to cope."

Mrs. LaFayt nods her head in agreement. "When Jesus taught the multitude, he didn't use any book. I don't think we need books, necessarily, to learn."

"That's right. Least I hope it's right." Miss Silver gives Mrs. LaFayt a little smile. Gloria thinks that Miss Silver isn't stupid; she knows who's on her side. "Would you all please move in closer so we don't disturb the other groups."

"It most too hot to sit close together," Charles says, but the others give their chair-desks a little scoot up. Charles rocks his desk, but it doesn't go anywhere. Charles demonstrated in May, got knocked down by the fire hose.

Mrs. LaFayt acknowledges Charles's point: "It sure *is* hot. Maybe I can bring us some fans one day before too long."

Charles glares at Miss Silver like everything's her fault.

"Bring yourself close. I don't bite." *Miss Silver wants them to like her, be in with her.* She takes one big breath, sits up straight and tall—maybe she's done this before—and she's going to just pitch in:

"A lot of people say, 'He *don't* do this or that' but that's not correct. You're supposed to say, 'He *doesn't* do this or that.' Let's each make up a sentence using 'he doesn't' properly. For example—I'll start—'He doesn't chew gum in class.' Now, Agnes—"

"He doesn't . . . understand the lesson."

Agnes is trying to tell her something more than grammar, but Miss Silver she's going to just go ahead, after a little nod to Agnes. Then she nods to Mr. Next-to-Agnes.

"He doesn't like . . . the heat."

And who would? My dress sticking to my back; sweat balls rolling down between my breasts. Windows jammed down 'cause there ain't no screens, and one billion mosquitoes waiting outside. You be outside in the dark, you looking in, you see us here, all our little groups, light on, working away.

"He doesn't like the fuzz."

Ulna, radius, humerus—the science group with the crippled girl, all in unison. Suddenly Gloria remembers where she's seen Cat before—at the funeral. Sitting outside the church in the crowd. In her wheelchair. Yes, Gloria remembers the girl in the wheelchair.

"He doesn't like to work on no Bessemer Highway."

"Good," Miss Stella says, like she's breathing out a balloon. "Good grammar is the highway to a better job."

"He *don't* like the teacher," Charles Powers says. *And the house of breath pops just like a pin pricks a balloon.*

But she says, "Doesn't. He doesn't like—"

"The teacher," Charles insists.

"Right. He doesn't like the teacher," she says, like it was any old sentence. "You say it."

"He doesn't like the teacher." But Mr. Smarty-Pants Charles mumbles because he's embarrassed.

"But we *do* like the teacher," Mrs. LaFayt says. So calm.

"Thanks. Now let's try the positive side: 'He does work hard.' "

Mrs. LaFayt catches the ball: "He does like school."

"He like to have a cigarette. You mind if we smoke?" Sam West trying to follow the leader.

If she lets hers, then mine sure tell me what to do. All my students want to leave off important dates in American history and go smoke.

"Not supposed to smoke in school," she says. "I'm sort of allergic to smoke. Now, if you were describing someone smoking a cigarette, what would you say? 'He smokes Winstons,' or 'He smoke Winstons'?"

"He smoke Winstons."

"No, that's not correct. It's 'He smokes Winstons. I smoke; you smoke; he, she, or it *smokes*.' "

"I burning *up* in here," Charles says, tugging at his shirt collar. His clothes look like he's slept in them a week.

"Miss, you mind if I be excused to get a drink of water?" Sam West asks.

" 'Course not. You don't have to ask about that sort of thing. You know. Just go get a drink when you want one."

Wrong answer, Miss Stella Silver. Give an inch they take a mile. There they go! One, two, three, four, five. Ain't but Mrs. LaFayt left. Oh-oh. Here's Christine steaming through the classroom door like a late battleship.

"Just where do you guys think you're going?" She so mad she could spit.

"Our new teacher say we can go get some water."

"You get back in your seats!" And they go back. *Sure wish I could boss like that.*

Miss Silver tells Christine, "They're right. I did say they could have a drink."

"They don't need no drink. You get back in your seat now."

"Ah, Mrs. Taylor, can I go to the bathroom," Sam whines. *Little-boy acting. He ain't got a prayer.*

"You just hold it. I said sit down!"

Miss Silver she's walking up to Christine with her hand held out, says, "I don't think we've met. I'm Stella Silver."

"Hi," Christine says, but she doesn't shake hands, and she's sure enough going to ignore her. Not much shorter you can say than *hi.* "You kids bring pencil and paper like I told you to?"

"I brought a half-sheet." Said respectfully, subdued. And another: "I got a pencil—if he lend me one."

"Shut your lip. Either you got your own pencil, or you not got one. How y'all expect to learn anything you don't come prepared? You want to spend the rest of your lives on the highway picking up white folks' litter? Huh? That's what's going to happen to you if you don't get a high school diploma."

"We were talking about subject-verb agreement," Miss Silver tells Christine, *but she don't pay no attention. Doesn't. I know better. When I'm scared, I think bad grammar.*

"I want you to learn some new words," Christine says like Miss Silver is just an insect. "But you didn't even bring any paper to write them down on. Your vocabulary is pitiful. You don't know the words for *nothing.*" Christine's face is all scowled up. "If you don't know words, how you going to express yourself? Tell me that."

"We all gots to work on our vocabulary," sweet Mrs. LaFayt says. "I know I do."

"Now you show Miss Silver what you remember." (Miss Silver looks interested. She keeps her mouth shut.) *"Perseverance,"* Christine calls out.

Guess I better let my group recite some.

"Turn your fact sheet over. What happened in 1776?"

Mrs. LaFayt is unclasping her black patent leather handbag. She gets out her word definition paper from last time so she can read. A voice in Gloria's history group startles her: "Declaration of Independence," her smart student answers.

"Perseverance," Mrs. LaFayt says. She checks her slip of paper again. "You got to *stick* to what you're doing. If you're going to accomplish it."

"You got that?" Christine asks them all. "What does *perseverance* mean?"

"Hangin' in there."

And Christine is pleased. She laughs a little. She wants to be nice. She's just got too much on her. She calls out another word.

"Vindicate!"

And Mrs. LaFayt is back in her purse, looking.

"Don't use your notes," Christine instructs. "You're supposed to know this. Your mind isn't inside your bag, Mrs. LaFayt."

But Mrs. LaFayt goes right on looking. "Well, I just need a little reminder. Let's see. *Vindicate* is to get revenge."

"Well, more like to clear yourself. 'He was accused of stealing, but when the truth comes out, he will be vindicated.'" Christine smiles more; she looks like a cannibal about to eat somebody up.

Christine goes on. "What you going to say, Charles, when somebody accuses you of a crime?"

"Not guilty."

Now he's in a good mood again. He's got his teach back. Charles probably wouldn't have demonstrated if Christine hadn't said she was going. Across the room, Arcola laughs (she's listening in, too) at clever Charles, who's tall as a basketball player and not really mean. Even Christine is amused.

"Mr. Parrish said for you to go help Arcola with her group," Christine says all of a sudden to Miss Silver.

"Really? I thought this was my group."

"This is my group."

I go, you go, he, she, or it goes; we go, you go, they go. That's Arcola's group.

"I don't think they need me," Miss Silver says, lightly.

I come, you come, he, she, or it comes; we come, you come, they come.

"Hey, Sam, do you come?" Charles punches his friend, real hard, on the arm.

"You shut your foul mouth," Christine tells him in words like knife blades. "I hear something like that out of you again, and you're going out. *O-U-T.*"

"I wish you would *both* be our teachers," Mrs. LaFayt says.

The break bell sears through the heat.

AFTERMATH: LIVING IT AGAIN

WHEN CAT LAY ON HER BED THAT NIGHT, HER FIRST NIGHT in the classroom, she couldn't sleep. She was too happy to even want sleep. They'd learned it; she coaxed them to learn the names of the bones in the legs and arms. They'd liked the Latin words. She'd told them about the humerus, the funny bone. She'd watched the glow of pride spread from face to face with the acquisition of a smattering of Latin and the knowledge of the invisible bone structure inside each human being. Lying flat on her back, Cat knew she smelled bad, but she'd been too tired to bathe. Her body soaked up the cool from the bedroom air conditioner like a sponge. So what if her armpits reeked. The classroom was a closed oven. Maybe tomorrow night, if the windows at school could be opened just a crack. . . .

AFTERMATH: "TRÄUMEREI"

WHEN STELLA WAS A LITTLE GIRL, THEY HAD GONE TO A swimming pool, and her mother, who couldn't swim, had walked in the water carrying Stella draped over her arms as though she were a princess or a bride. Stella had never felt such peace. The water was cool and her mother's body was warm and soft. Her brothers played with an inner tube; her father swam a slow sidestroke in the deep water.

After she left off Cat and the car, all the way walking home, Stella had felt like that: soft arms were cradling her; the universe loved and protected her. She was safe and happy. She deserved to be coddled. Of course the Negroes were resentful: she understood that. She had done her job.

At the swimming pool the PA system had played the Schumann "Träumerei," and later, though she was only five, she'd played it on her little cello, sliding effortlessly into fourth position for the soaring note that made the piece formidable. Her mother had accompanied her on the piano with slow chords.

As a very young child, she had seemed terrifically talented, a wunderkind. After her mother's death, she had seemed less talented each succeeding year. She hated to perform; she wanted to do only things that were personal and private. At the end of high school, she ceremoniously locked her cello in its hard case.

Lying in bed, Stella felt happy to be alone, out of the bright heat of the classroom. In the summer long ago before the accident, the sash beside the bed would be up and the bed nestled beside the window to catch the breeze.

The attic fan sucked in the cool of the night. Once her light was out, she spied on Mrs. Kolowski in her kitchen doing the supper dishes after her husband had gone to bed. It was magic, the way the dark of the bedroom concealed Stella. Utterly fascinated, she watched Mrs. Kolowski passing a dishrag over the stained plates. *That's her life,* little Stella had thought. *I'm getting to see her life.* Sometimes Mrs. Kolowski walked across the linoleum, a checkerboard pattern, red and black.

Stella thought of the Negro teachers she had met. Christine Taylor would be home now. At break time, Arcola had told Stella that Mrs. Taylor had three children, that she'd been married three times. Stella wanted to know their stories.

At her home, was the forceful Mrs. Taylor angry? Was she happy?

And what of Don on the other side of the world? He was just waking up as she was drifting off to sleep. *We can stop this anytime,* he had said the night of their engagement. *But why should she?* And why shouldn't she build something new in the meantime?

She felt tucked into multiple stories now. No longer the center of the universe. Sleepily, she stretched her bare toes against the clean sheets. She stretched herself the way "Träumerei" stretched toward sleep. The slide, with vibrato at the top. She felt happy.

She could drill new phrases into them—he *doesn't,* they don't—until the phrases sounded right; or she could go back to basics, so they *understood.* Not mere rote. She would do both. She would need to teach the concepts of subject and verb, of nouns and pronouns, of singular and plural. Tonight we learn to *conjugate,* to put together subject and verb in a certain *conventional* pattern. What is a *convention*? She would explain it all.

AFTERMATH: ARCOLA AT THE DRESSING TABLE

ARCOLA TOOK OFF HER BRAID AND PUT IT IN A DRAWER.
She checked her face for any sign of a pimple: none. She checked her nails,
painted plum, for any sign of a chip: none. *That Charles,* so tall and good-
looking. She wondered how long he'd been out of school; he might be just
about her age, even if he was a dropout student. He looked like he'd worked—
long flat arm muscles like a man. Somebody like that, a hard worker like her
father, if Charles could get some education—that wouldn't be bad. He'd have
to have an education though. Her daddy insisted on that. *I ain't been twenty years
at TCI saving for you, then you marry some bum. Pretty don't count. You learn, and you
marry somebody what wants to learn.*

Arcola thought she had the most wonderful parents in the world. One time
when they were doing the dishes together, her mother told her they weren't
ever going to have any more children. *Everything is for you,* her mother said. *We
wanted to provide right for you so we stopped when you came along.*

She, Arcola Anderson, had taught in the same room with white teachers. It
was easy. Arcola looked in the mirror and smiled at herself. She liked them.

She reached for the dark blue glass cologne bottle—Evening in Paris—and
dabbed a little fluid behind each ear. The spots of cologne felt cool. Now she
had some scent to dream on. She picked up her comb, held it close to her ear,
turned her head a bit to the side. Then quickly, she slid her thumb down the
teeth. The sound was magical, like fairy music. In the mirror, she watched her
eyes light up.

AFTERMATH: HOME FOR THE NIGHT

WHEN LIONEL PARRISH CAME HOME, HE HOPED TO GOD there wasn't any of Matilda's scent on him. He'd taken a bath before he'd dressed, and he'd taken care to buy Matilda Ivory, just like Jenny insisted on at home. He preferred the grit of Lava. Made a man feel clean. But his wife, Jenny, said he wasn't no laboring man; he didn't need Lava.

The children all liked to play with Ivory because it floated. But Jenny didn't let them melt off too much of the soap with floating it around in the tub. For the youngest, Jenny had made a little red paper sail on a toothpick and stuck it into the flat of the soap. She let Andy push up water walls with his hands to move his boat across the tub. Lionel liked to think of his littlest boy, naked and plump, sailing his cake of soap with its red flag around the bathtub, but that was several years ago when Andy was three. He himself had grown up washing in a galvanized tub in the kitchen, with the water heated on the stove.

"Hi, honey," Lionel said softly, and softly he closed the home door behind him.

His wife got up from the sofa, left her *Ebony* magazine there, softly put her arms around him; she breathed in a deep breath. And yes, he decided, he'd pleasure her, too.

"Honey," he said, "I hired two Birmingham white girls tonight, both with B.A. degrees."

JENNY THOUGHT *He's so fresh, so fresh, so fresh and sweet smelling* to the rhythm of his thrusting. How she loved to lie perfectly still—she was a good woman—and the bliss of it! She needed him so bad, all of him, and surely he knew that, her lying so still and good, how she needed this and would honor him with as many children as he saw fit to place within her. But this night, he pulled out and left his puddle outside on her stomach.

What was this sorrow, these two little tears like two orange seeds squeezing out of the corners of her eyes? Why did crying come as though something were sad? Why, indeed, when she loved him so and she could hear the breathing of their sleeping children?

CAHABA

THE BRIDGE OVER THE CAHABA RIVER WAS A NIGHT meeting place for Ryder's friends—all the bigs, the Exalted Cyclops, maybe the Imperial Wizard, Ryder's closer friends, Dynamite Bob Chambliss, Tommy Blanton, Bobby Cherry. When they sat together on the riverbank, sometimes their cupped cigarettes flared in the dark like little handheld campfires. When a flashlight cast a slat of light, the large shadows of the men loomed behind them. But this sunny afternoon, the riverbank was deserted where Highway 280 crossed the Cahaba.

Ryder had a ten-cent-store bamboo pole over his shoulder and a Maxwell House coffee can full of earthworms. Little Bobby had dug the worms for him from the backyard and begged to come along, but Ryder had said no. Ryder smiled to think of his older son's desperate whispering: "Tommy's too little." Bobby said they could slip off and leave Tommy in the sandbox. But Ryder wanted to be alone. He had wanted some peace and quiet, even from both his sons, carefully named for the men who were his friends.

The Cahaba was muddy and slow moving, but he'd heard you could get small catfish from it. He'd never been fishing as a boy. His father was too worthless to do anything with him. Once Ryder himself learned the tricks of fishing, he *would* take Bobby with him, and Tommy, too, when he was older. Maybe Lee and Shirley would pack a picnic, and they'd all come. She could bring the red-checked cloth they put on the kitchen table for Sunday dinner.

Since the riverbank looked muddy and a little slippery, Ryder moved back from the water and walked among the saplings edging the river. The rocks along the river edge were coated with slimy red-brown mud. No, there was a pretty flat one in the shade with moss on it. He'd heard you could catch fish on the quiet side of a big rock, that fish liked to rest there.

The whole woods were quiet down where he was. The car motors up on 280 sounded distant, as though they came from a world next door, not this one. Thick with their summer green leaves, the trees completely masked the road. There was a big sycamore close to the water, barkless and white from twenty feet on up toward the sky. He broke off one of the big, low-hanging flat leaves and laid it over the palm of his hand. The leaf was covered with a stiff fuzz. This green hand was bigger than his own hand, and he smiled a little, playing with it. The stem where it had detached from its twig had a clever little cup shape, very tiny.

Standing on the bank, Ryder tossed the leaf into the water and watched it float. It bumped along, getting caught occasionally on black, waterlogged sticks crusted with white scallops of decay. When the points of the sycamore leaf brushed a rock, they twirled the leaf back into the slow current, like fingertips pushing off from the wet stone. A film of water on one rock magnified a brush of gold otherwise indiscernible in the brown rock flank.

Ryder walked on and noticed the telltale three leaves of poison ivy climbing the tree trunks and springing through the sparse grass, but he had on long pants and work boots. No need to worry. As a boy, he'd never once caught poison ivy. The one time he went camping with the Scouts, they'd nearly all got poison ivy, but he was immune. The leader said Ryder must have a natural immunity, and everybody had looked at him respectfully. He had almost been embarrassed and had looked down at the wolf-head slide of his neckerchief. *Reckon we'll see any wolf?* he had asked shyly, and the leader explained in a kind way that the wolves were all out west. Who knew? Maybe the troop would raise money and go west someday, to Yellowstone. *All of us?* Ryder had asked.

Despite the shade of the tall trees, Ryder was hot, and he took off his black cowboy hat and used it to fan his face. As he walked, he was careful to carry his humped, metal lunch box on the level. The can of worms was at one end, with wax paper over it held tight with rubber bands, and his ham-and-cheese sandwich was in the other end. He had some peanut-butter cookies, too—with the crisscross on top—that Lee had baked for the kids. For just a moment, Ryder missed Bobby, his older son. Maybe Ryder would get Bobby a little black hat like his own. He could see Bobby beside him, his face tilted up catching the sun. But suppose they didn't catch any fish, this being the first time? Ryder hadn't wanted to face how disappointed Bobby would be. Bobby believed Ryder could do anything. Bobby loved his mom, too. *Devoted.* He was a devoted child to his parents. Wild blackberries glistened black and inviting off in a sun-drenched clearing.

Here in the woods, by the brown river, Ryder could think about all that, about what was good in his life. Sometimes he used his fishing pole to push aside the poison ivy or to hold back a briar. Out in the water, he saw a green glass Coke bottle floating along. In the hump of his lunch box, held up by the wire clasp, he had a thermos of milk. He could almost taste it, good and cold, washing down the bread and mayonnaise. He liked hearing the sound of his own feet moving quietly through the underbrush—just him and the woods.

A large brown rock, big as an elephant's back, lolled in the water, and Ryder decided he'd try standing there to fish. He took a giant step onto the rock and walked easily a few steps up its slope. Trash—milk cartons, brown sacks, even a muddy pair of navy pants—lodged against the far bank. From this height Ryder could see maybe an inch or two down into the brown water, and he saw a swarm of minnows, like big gnats, not too far out. The top layer of the water was a little more clear. He lifted the flap of his shirt pocket and took out the little brown envelope with three hooks of varying sizes in it.

Very carefully, he began to separate the hooks. It wouldn't be fun to have to work the barbed tip of a hook out of a finger. Wait! He should have brought wire cutters—just clip off the head of the hook if he should need to, instead of drawing it back through the flesh. He pictured the wire cutters among the other tools, dark with grease, in the toolbox at the service station.

Yesterday evening, a woman had driven up and bought thirty-five cents worth of gas. She had said, *Do you know why I buy gas at Texaco? It's because you support the Metropolitan Opera broadcasts on Saturdays.* Her friend beside her on the front seat, a girl with a short haystack haircut, had gulped with laughter. Crazy girls. The driver was so flat-chested she looked too young to drive. They hadn't meant any harm. He'd pumped the thirty-five cents, cleaned the windshield, and said, "Will that be all, ma'am?"

Carefully, Ryder replaced two of the hooks into the envelope and slid it back into his flapped pocket. From the other bank, a blue jay started to scold. His father had always hated blue jays, but Ryder never could figure out why. Maybe it was because they screamed "Thief! Thief!" Ryder's father could have left his last paycheck money on the table under the yellow sugar bowl—that was what Troy's father did when he deserted his family—but he hadn't. Not even spare change, not even any note. The jay jumped off a limb of a high oak and sailed above the water, his wings spread in two beautiful blue and white fans. A dragonfly, like a little helicopter, hovered over the water.

Ryder realized he was just standing on the brown elephant rock, remembering this and that, enjoying himself. But it was hot on the rock, and he put his hat back on. He needed to bait his hook. He set the metal box down, squatted beside it, and flipped up the shiny catches. He lay the cane pole on the rock and steadied it to make sure it didn't clatter off into the water.

Nothing had spilled inside the box. He removed the wax paper and took a worm out of the sandy dirt in the can. Bobby had added a little sand to the mixture, as though he were making a special dirt recipe to keep his father's worms happy. Ryder placed a worm on the rock and knelt to pierce one of the red segments with the barbed fishhook. Some men held the worm in their fingers, but he was wary of the hook, sharp as a needle glinting in the bright light. He noticed an old shirt swept against the near bank, and a wad of wet newspaper had caught there, too. Grains of dirt and sand clung to the body of the pierced earthworm as it roiled on the rock.

From his pants pocket Ryder took a nylon string and clumsily tied it to the upper loop in the hook. Then he tied the string to the pole. It had a groove to help hold the string. Standing on the lip of the rock, he dropped the string straight down toward the quiet place. The hook was hardly heavy enough to make it drop. Nonetheless, there was a still little pocket of water there, and the hook disappeared into it. Ryder jiggled the pole from time to time so a fish would think the worm was alive and wriggling. When he lifted the tip of the pole, he noticed the mud in the water was staining the white nylon line.

After a long time, Ryder's feet began to hurt, and he decided to sit down on the edge of the rock. There were all kinds of birds in the woods. One was a kingfisher, the same ugly color as the river, with a coarse beak and a crest like a crazy sort of crown. When Ryder had been in the eighth grade, full of piss and vinegar because his class and everybody in it was top dog and about to graduate, the teacher had brought in a freckle-faced little kid from first grade who knew all the birds and gave a talk on them. He had drawn a picture of a kingfisher with chalk on the blackboard, down low near the eraser trough because he was too short for an eighth-grade blackboard. When the teacher said, "Darl, tell everybody how you learned about birds," and the kid had answered "Cub Scouts," Ryder had felt his heart drop like a stone. When the kid left, the teacher didn't erase the row of birds outlined along the bottom of the blackboard. But who had taught him to draw like that?

It was too hot on the rock in the sun. Ryder was running sweat. This wasn't a good place. Ryder wound the line around the pole, collected his stuff, and walked on. He walked deeper into the woods, where it was cooler, and sat down with his back against a big oak. He decided to eat his sandwich and drink some of his milk. It was cold, but not quite as cold as he wished. Milk needed to be very cold to taste good. He watched ants and black beetles and centipedes walk over and under the fallen leaves.

Suppose I just never left this spot, he thought. *Suppose somebody found me years later, a skeleton, eaten by his own worms, him bony white, with his black hat still on his skull.*

"That's not going to happen," he said out loud.

He went back to the river. He tried a number of spots; he tried a new worm, and then two worms at a time on a larger hook. He saw a mangy black and white dog slinking along. It just glanced at him once and kept going. As Ryder moved along the river, he saw more and more trash clogging the banks. People had tumbled down old iceboxes and cardboard boxes full of junk. His mother had been proud to have her icebox when he was little, and the iceman had been nice to him. He remembered his great, sharp, iron tongs. Finally Ryder found a rusted-out car with no wheels at the end of a dirt road. All the glass was shattered, and the metal was dented where boys had shot the car. Honeysuckle grew over the hood and around the doors, but he decided to yank open a door. After carefully inspecting the car seat for glass, he sat. He just sat and listened, looked at the late sunlight glinting like stars in the tiny spaces between leaves. He admired a hickory with its big leaves like beaver tails. He'd never seen a beaver, but he knew they still had them out west. At sunset, sitting in the car, he ate his peanut-butter cookies and drank the rest of his milk, even though it was quite warm now.

Suddenly he took his pole and broke it twice over his knee. He placed the fishhook envelope on the grimy dashboard of the car. The car had been green, and it already blended with the woods. He stood up beside the car and dashed the sandy dirt inside the Maxwell House can and the remaining worms out on the ground. With his heel he crushed first one side of the coffee can and then the other till it was almost flat. Then he sailed the misshapen metal into the Cahaba.

As he followed the river backward—he'd come a far piece—night settled into the woods. It was easy to imagine his friends there on the bank, up ahead, close to 280 and the bridge—Tommy and Bob, all the others, talking and laughing. Maybe passing the consoling moonshine that entered your throat and gut like a stab of fire. "Where you been?" they'd say when they saw him coming down the path out of the dark. "Been fishing," he'd say.

It had been a good day, anyway.

AFTERNOON ROSES

I'LL TAKE THE AFTERNOON I NEED, STELLA THOUGHT, FOR *normality, for fun.* Even Aunt Krit used to tell her, "You can't *go* all the time. You have to have fun." All her life, Stella'd had fun with Nancy. Or comfort. At the funeral of her family, it was Nancy who held her hand. Stella couldn't remember time before Nancy was her friend.

Stella arranged to meet Nancy at the old red clay tennis courts on Norwood Boulevard at two in the afternoon. Nancy had to drive from across town—her family had moved over the mountain to Homewood—but her mother let Nancy drive the big black Cadillac. When they were little, Nancy's mother ferried them across Birmingham so that they could visit. And then Nancy's father had died, and the bond between the girls strengthened again. The car was old now, seemed a little hearselike; it was so long, not like the latest cars, but Stella loved that car.

Stella breathed deeply, filled her lungs with the air of roses. The high Cyclone fence around the court was bedecked—there was no other word for it—bedecked with climbing roses. Outside of a fairy-tale illustration, Stella had never seen such cascades of roses. Planted decades ago when Norwood Boulevard was a fashionable address, now the robust rose canes wove in and out of the fencing. The main stems topped the fence and then arched over like the curve of a wave, and underneath, inside the wave was a cool shady place where you could sit on the ground and wait. Bouquets of small clusters of roses, some white, some pink, some red, dangled through the fencing.

Because the tennis net itself was a piece of the Cyclone fencing, it had lasted more than twenty years. The net was rusty, but who cared? She thought of Stephen Dedalus in *Portrait of the Artist as a Young Man*, how he'd wanted to fly over the nets of language, religion, and culture of his homeland. This beautiful place existed because the city fathers had forgotten to destroy it when wealth moved over Red Mountain.

She could hear but not see birds chirping (were there four?), despite the mounting heat. She thought of Virginia Woolf, who, in her madness, heard birds speaking Greek. The tennis court birds were happy, but what were they trying to say?

Probably Nancy didn't even see her there, hidden among the roses. When Nancy jumped out of the Cadillac holding two tennis rackets and a can of balls, she looked like Doris Day, wearing only two colors—green shorts and a matching green-and-white-checked top. So fresh and fashionable! Her hair was up in a ponytail with an elastic band covered in white terry. Nancy's ponytail was a beautiful shape, like an S curve, an arabesque graceful as the cabriolet leg of a fine chair. Without looking at it, Nancy passed the stubby marble war memorial incised with the names of Norwood boys, dead now almost twenty years from World War II— *but what does it mean to be dead twenty years? A name incised in white stone.*

Aunt Krit was glad to have Nancy in the wedding; she would be a credit to the occasion. Aunt Pratt simply loved Nancy. Stella called to her friend (Nancy had outlasted Stella's parents, brothers), who waved the rackets in reply and then came to sit with Stella in the rose bower.

"We haven't done this in ages!" Nancy exclaimed. "I love coming back over here." Her face was bright, her big eyes the pale blue of forget-me-nots. She swung herself onto the ground inside the bower of roses.

When Stella told Nancy that she and Cat were teaching at Miles, at night, Nancy's face wrinkled in concern. "I'm not a bit prejudiced. You know that. But it's not safe."

Stella just shrugged and smiled.

"I know you won't listen," Nancy said. "What does Aunt Krit say?"

"She doesn't know. Not unless the birdies told her."

"Stella Silver!" But Nancy wouldn't scold.

NANCY LUXURIATED IN the beautiful summer day; her middle name was June, and she always loved this month, despite the ever-increasing fierceness of the heat. (Nancy didn't want to argue with Stella, she just added, "I'm Cat's friend, too, but I wouldn't go out there at night, even with Jesus. It's against the law, and, moreover, it's just not safe.") The sky was piled with clouds. Nancy knew they'd be hot after five seconds of play—the red clay court was baking in full sun—but she had brought a thermos of lemonade in the car. After they were tired of playing tennis, they'd talk, which was why Nancy came over anyway. They'd come back, sit under the roof of roses, sip lemonade, and talk.

Stella was wearing cutoff blue jeans, strings on the thighs, and a red T-shirt. Primary blocks of color. (Nancy was a student of color.)

The ball thunked and thunked between them (Nancy loved the sound of it), they called out the points *Love! Love!* (both of them were a little preoccupied), they swapped ends, they tolerated their sweating (they were girls again, not recent college graduates); they ignored the sunburning of noses, cheeks passing from pink to glowing red (huge puffs of white clouds crowned the summer day); and to Nancy's surprise, she won. Usually Stella, who was thinner and quicker, won. Then to Nancy's horror, she saw that Stella was going to run and leap over the heavy-gauge wire net to congratulate her.

Stella galloped like a colt, as hard as she could, but Nancy was afraid. She knew she herself could never clear the net. "Don't! Don't!" she yelled, but Stella, blocks of colors, red and blue, raced on. *You'll get hurt!*

Stella raised her front foot and arched over the net. She landed still running.

"You won! You won!" Stella shouted, happy, waving her tennis racket in the air like a pennant. Happy to affirm her friend. Happy to lose.

LATER THEY SAT again in the bower of pink roses.

"This is it," Stella said, "the heart of being alive. This beautiful flowery place."

"And the sky," Nancy added, nodding at the cloud puffs.

"I've never felt so strong or nice."

"Is it being engaged to Don?"

Stella wrinkled her forehead, hesitated. "No. It's *now*. It's friendship. Feeling and action."

NIGHT AGAIN: CARYATID

BITTERLY, CHRISTINE WATCHED CAT, PUSHED BY STELLA, cross the campus. It was only dusk. *Push, push, pushy white people. Had no business coming out here* to help. *Should of come out fifty years ago, when* help *was needed. And where were they seven years ago when Fred Shuttlesworth tried to enroll children in Phillips High School? Probably sitting inside, that's where.*

(Christine didn't suppose what she imagined was true. She would have been shocked to know that she had guessed the exact truth. Cat and Stella were safely inside Phillips High School, safely inside, when Reverend Shuttlesworth was beaten with chains in front of the school, his wife stabbed in the thigh.)

Christine supposed the white women had come early to chat with Arcola and Gloria. The white women wanted to be friends. Take charge. They'd be surprised to see she, Christine, was standing there, too, beside Arcola and Gloria. They couldn't see who she was, leaning against the building, a silhouette against the setting sun. But she could see them, bathed in red-gold. The metal of the wheelchair was like a chariot reflecting the dying sunlight.

Christine thought of Apollo, of Greek mythology, everything white marble. No reference to black people by the art teacher, but the Greek statues had full lips, curly hair sometimes. Christine loved the blankness of the eyes of the statues. That was the way she felt sometimes.

"Christine," Cat called. "You look like a caryatid standing there."

"Humph!" Christine turned away, but she knew what a caryatid was. She had learned it just today in art appreciation. Yes, her head felt like she was holding up a building on it. But how did Cat know that? Spooky girl, she'd recognized Christine immediately.

"They said they might come early," Arcola said to Christine. "Give us a chance to get acquainted." She sashayed across the little porch and down the one step. "What you got, Cat-girl?" Arcola called pleasantly.

Then Christine noticed: Cat's lap was full of little roses, all shades of pink.

"Didn't nobody tell me to come early," Christine grumbled.

"Hey." Arcola flashed her pretty smile back at Christine. Was that girl always relaxed? "You was out of here like a shot last night. We didn't have any chance to ask you." Then Arcola Miss Impudence winked at her. "You had to get to the Athens Bar."

"Stella picked them," Cat said to everybody. She held up her hand, signaling to Stella to stop pushing. "Let's just sit out here. Probably cooler than inside."

Awkwardly, Cat suddenly held out a chunk of the roses to Gloria. "For you," she said.

Slowly Gloria stepped forward and held out her hand. "Thank you," she said.

Stella reached down and picked up another bouquet from her lap. "These are for you, Arcola."

They were pairing up. Cat wanted to be friends with Gloria; Stella had chosen Arcola.

There was one bunch of pink left in Cat's lap.

"The stems are in damp tissue," Stella said. "They probably need some water."

Wordlessly, Cat held out the remaining bouquet to Christine.

As Christine accepted the rose bouquet, she muttered ungraciously that they'd put the flowers in paper cups so they wouldn't wilt in the heat.

"Where'd you get these little roses?" Arcola asked. She put her nose into her bunch.

"Norwood. They don't have much smell," Stella said apologetically. (She'd gotten some sunburn; her nose was brighter than the roses.) "They grow wild at the tennis court, all over the fences."

White girls playing tennis in a pink rose garden—the picture made Christine angry. Not at Cat, though, she wouldn't be playing any tennis. Christine imagined Cat sitting on the sidelines, probably holding a parasol up over her head. Cat wasn't sunburned.

Then Christine thought how pleased Diane, her little girl, would be when she brought home roses in a Dixie cup. She had some rose scent in her handbag she could pump on them.

Diane would sit and stare at those roses in the middle of the kitchen table as if they were TV.

HUMMING IN THE HEAT

CLAVICLE, STERNUM, RIBS, VERTEBRAE.

He does; they do. He sings; they sing. He has; they have. To conjugate—a pattern of three singulars, three plurals. What is a plural?

That Stella knows how to dig, Gloria thinks. She digs down and down, finding out what they don't know, what they need to know. *I want you to understand,* Stella has said over and over, *not just memorize.*

"Look, there's a dead bat outside on the windowsill." Always some distraction. Who said that?

GLORIA CAN FEEL the sweat drops starting to roll down her sides.

Christine accuses, "I thought I heard somebody in your group saying 'Tits.'"

Oh-oh. (*Was Christine smiling just a little bit?*)

Cat grins. "Yeah. Parts of the body. You know, we were learning parts of the body." Cat wasn't scared of Christine. (*What's wrong with Cat; not broken, kind of twisted, a little humped. Real weak seeming.*) "Somebody jumped the gun from naming bones to flesh," Cat says wryly.

"You can't let 'em say things like that," Christine snaps.

"Why?" Oh Lord, Cat asking like she just wants to know.

"Why!" *Christine can't believe it.* "Because they won't have any respect for you if you do. They don't have any respect anyway, but you got to make 'em *act* like they do."

"I don't want to come on too strong." Cat frowning up her face like she's really worried about coming on too strong. *Might as well be me worrying about coming on too strong, she can't even walk; I can't hardly open my mouth.*

"Hum! No chance of that." Christine spins around. "Arcola, didn't Mr. Parrish say Miss Silver supposed to help you?"

"No." Arcola shrugs. She looks down at the floor. "He said you was always late and so she better be with you. I don't care, though. You work with me if you want to, Stella."

"Late! What's he mean, *late?*" Christine talks like Stella's not even there. To Christine, Stella's just another mosquito.

"I reckon he means you not always on time, Christine," Arcola says.

"You see how easy it is to be on time, when you got three children at home and your sister always late coming to baby-sit."

Arcola answers quietly. "I'm not criticizing you."

"Sure 'nuff sounds like it. I think Miss Silver better work with Gloria now."

"Whatever y'all decide, fine with me." *Was that me, speaking up so quick? Wish the students would come on back from break time.*

"You *better* learn to speak up for yourself, girl, or this world gonna run right over you." *Christine speaks to me like I'm a child.* "Miss Green Eyes, you gonna be squashed flat as a beer can in the street."

"Yes, ma'am." *But I just did. I just did speak up. We've been getting along. Then, tonight, Boom! Christine comes down like a ton of bricks.*

"What you want to go picking on Gloria for?" Arcola asks, but she grins. "She's not hurting you."

"I thought last week things went pretty well, didn't they?" Stella asks. "Maybe we could work together, Christine."

"My name is Mrs. Taylor." She seals her lips up tight. *But I know Christine is my friend. When the church was bombed, it was me holding Christine. I wasn't nervous then.*

"I'm sorry. I'm just used to calling everybody by his first name." Stella speaks very politely, sounds sincere.

"So I noticed. You know, that's the trouble with you white people. You think you got a right to call anybody by their first name."

Now you shut us all up, Christine. Quiet enough now, Christine. Pin-drop time now. Ain't nobody gonna breathe now. How long this gonna last? Everybody holding her breath. Sure wish my voice box just open up—any old squawk be better than this. Silence. Silence. Silence.

"Mrs. Taylor?" That's Cat talking, so serious. "Have you ever made a mistake in your life?"

Arcola just *bust* out laughing.

"Yeah." Christine relaxes on down a little. "I made enough mistakes for everybody in this room."

"Ain't we all," Stella says quietly, regretfully.

"Not me," sassy Miss Arcola jokes. "I'm perfect."

Christine reaches over to whack Arcola's behind. "She think she gonna be Miss Negro America!" Christine's feeling high now. Feeling good.

"Why not be the first Negro Miss America?" Stella asks.

"Right on. Right on, there," Christine answers, but the bitterness still flavors her tone.

"Y'all gonna be sorry," Arcola teases. "I'm gonna be walkin' down the aisle, Bert Parks gonna be singin'—" She starts to sing, " 'There she is, beautiful Miss Black Amer-i-ca. *There* she is.' I have on my all-net evening dress, I be throwin' long-stem red roses out in the audience, and I won't give you all the time of day."

"Christine's cousin"—that's me talking—"she was killed in the church bombing." I think of Christine shaking in my arms, the face of Jesus blowed out of the stain glass. Me feeling strong. Feeling the bones in my body were strong and bright white.

"I'm sorry." Cat and Stella say it together, like a duet. Both say it. Both mean it.

"I wish more white people were sorry," Arcola says. I never hear her speak so sober and serious before. *Like me, Arcola's starting to want Freedom. She's ahead of me. She demonstrated in May of '63.*

Christine looks like she's going to cry. Arcola goes over and puts her arm around Christine's shoulder. Cat takes off her brakes and rolls over. She can't stand up to put her arm around, but she takes Christine's hand and presses it against her cheek. Just boldly picks up that drooping hand.

We all are quiet.

And then students are coming in.

Cat grins like a big Cheshire cat. "Think I could be the first wheelchair Miss America?"

"Naw, girl," Arcola answers. "They just want *normal* people. Like me."

And we're all comfortable. Miss Cat most of all.

Cat lets go of Christine's hand and rolls herself toward the science corner.

NIGHT AFTER NIGHT the students come, the room hums for an hour: review in every corner. Break time. Then new lessons for the second hour. June passes into July, and the temperature rises steadily.

AUNT PRATT ALONE

JUST BEFORE SUNSET, STELLA'S AUNT PRATT WANTED HER steel fingernail file, and she knew exactly where it was (she knew where all her things were) in the shallow drawer of her dresser hopelessly across the room. She'd have to wait till somebody who could walk well came into the room. She'd already taken off her leg brace. Then she'd ask, very courteously, if that able person would please look in the top, flat, handkerchief drawer and get her steel fingernail file.

She'd just picture something else instead of her steel file: the little wooden carved rose embalmed in a clear plastic bar. The tiny rose pin was in a box on the bedside cart; Pratt could reach her jewelry if she wanted to. Stella had liked to pin the red rose on the hem of her short skirt when she was a little girl, so she could see it better than if it was up on her shoulder. With her small thumb, Stella—poor little orphan—would rub the plastic over the rose again and again, but the delicate rose was safe inside the plastic.

These days, when Stella came into the room, she surprised Pratt— Why, who was this grown girl? Hair flipped up so even all around from shoulder to shoulder. Pratt often forgot now that time was passing. It had been the 1940s and now it was almost the mid-1960s, and what had happened to the 1950s? What was she herself doing all that time while Stella was getting bigger? And why was it that she was worried about Stella?

Stella had graduated, but she was always going to school, still. To teach, she said. She had decided to teach black children, like a missionary. Was that what integration was? Stella seemed strained and thin, but Krit never noticed.

Maybe Pratt imagined it. She spent her nights imagining now, and watching her stories on TV in the day.

The mirror over the old dresser was mottled and cast a darkness over anyone who looked in it. But a mirror could be resilvered, Pratt knew that. Someday, she'd have the big mirror brightened up and then it would flash, over there in the corner, like sunlight off the pond. Down at Helicon.

That day when Barney Chesser went mad from dog bite. The pond had flashed brightly that day. She'd noticed the brightness of the pond just before somebody—well, she knew who—had dashed in and said, *Barney's gone mad. He said for his sister to put down her iron—there in the front bedroom—to put down her iron and to pick up the twin babies and get out of there. Barney said he felt funny. He said Sis must lock the door.*

The doctor had his lariat, and he had been west once and knew how to throw a lasso. They broke out the window and lassoed Barney and threw loops around the bed and tied him to the bed, all the time his head slinging back and forth, trying to bite, the foam flying. If the foam landed on an open sore, you were as good as bitten, and no hope for you.

And what could they do for Barney Chesser, bit by a mad dog?

He'll bite off his tongue! one said. To prevent that, the doctor took his pearl-handled knife and stuck it between Barney's teeth. And Barney bit the pearl handle in two.

By nightfall, he was dead. And Pratt, in her house across the street, folded her hands on the windowsill and watched them douse the house with kerosene. Except for what was in the mad room, they carried out all the furniture. Pratt watched the men hold their torches to the corners of the house. She stood there, her arms folded across the windowsill, with little Son beside her till Gene, her husband, came back, and they all three stood together to watch the house burn.

Before she left this afternoon, Stella had stood in front of the mirror primping, but what was that place she had mentioned going to? *If y'all needed to find me, Cat Cartwright and I are working out at Miles College. I'd rather you not tell Aunt Krit, though.*

Pratt remembered Barney's sister Bernice, her only nineteen, snatching up her twin babies, hurrying, setting a baby on the floor once she was outside the front bedroom so she could lock the door. It would have been the big twin she sat down; she always carried him on the right, where she was stronger.

Sometimes Pratt felt the world was like Barney Chesser's bedroom. Somebody was going to go mad. Like Hitler did. Pratt wished, if she could, that she'd be able to pick up what was most precious and get out of there, if that happened in Alabama. Watch the whole South burn up, from a safe distance.

Stella ought not be out late after dark with colored people, but Pratt would bite off her tongue before she'd say anything to Stella, or Krit, about it. "Mind your own business," her mama had said, "if you want to get along with people." Men had been killed over in Mississippi: two Yankees and a darkie. "Civil rights workers," the TV had said.

Pratt ran her thumb over the top of the nail on her first finger. It had a split there; she could feel it. She wished she had her steel fingernail file.

LEE PLAYS BARBER

"AT THE KLAVERN," RYDER JONES TOLD HIS WIFE, "THEY say white teachers are going out to Miles College."

"Well, you can't believe everything you hear," Lee answered. "Now tuck your head down so I can shave your neck." She was proud of her new electric shaver. What with Bobby getting big and needing haircuts, and Ryder going to the barbershop every two weeks, and Tommy outgrowing his bowl cut, she figured they'd save in the long run if she invested in some barber tools. She'd stitched up a little white shoulder shawl with a turned-up pocket all round the hem to catch cut hair. She'd used some leftover Klan robe fabric.

"Bob said he saw an old Pontiac with two white girls in it turn in at Miles College."

"Maybe they was lost."

"Maybe it's time for some teachers and students out there to learn a lesson."

She lifted the shaver away from the back of his neck. "What kind of lesson, hon?" She let the shaver go on buzzing.

"Don't play dumb, Lee. You know I don't like that."

The shaver vibrated and buzzed in her hand like the most powerful bumblebee in the world. She thought how brave kids used to sneak up on bees massaging a clover head; the brave ones could grab a bee by its wings and hold it up buzzing between two clamped-together fingers.

Lee decided she'd better not say anything else to Ryder about his business. She put one hand on top of her husband's head and pointed his chin down. He let her, just like she was the real barber. Now the white skin rose up out of the cape, a little crescent of white skin below the sunburn.

"Ain't you 'bout finished?" Ryder asked impatiently. "I'm tired of this."

"I just wanted to finish up good so it would last."

"Kids at your mama's?"

"Yep." But why was he asking her that? It was Saturday night, first Saturday night of the month, Mama always kept them. "She'll bring 'em to Sunday school in the morning, hon."

"Lee, come round here to the front and kneel down and look me in the eye."

She obeyed at once, snapped off the shaver, and laid it on the kitchen table.

"Now," he said, looking down at her like he was a king on a throne instead of a fool on a stool. "Can I trust you, Lee?"

" 'Course, honey. I ain't done nothing." But she was feeling guilty and scared. "Not a thing."

"I'm talking 'bout the future."

Why did he look all nervous and eager? What did he want to do to her?

"Yes, you can, honey," she said. "Only—"

"Onlyest what?"

"Don't hurt me."

He smiled at her, and she felt the fear rise up her throat like the mercury column in a thermometer.

"I need to teach you something," he said.

"Oh no," she pleaded. "What I done done, Ryder?"

"I don't mean like that. I'm gonna share something with you. Something secret, and I got to know I can trust you not to tell."

"I won't ever tell anybody," she said. Her knees were hurting from pressing on the hard kitchen floor. Her eyes were just above the level of the tabletop. She looked at her barber tools lying on the kitchen table—the long skinny scissors with the extra loop for bracing. The little black plastic comb. The electric shaver, the dusting brush with the green plastic knob handle. The barber instruments resembled pieces from a doctor kit, special and expensive. "I could charge the neighborhood kids a quarter," she said. "Do their hair. Earn a little extra."

"Pay attention to what I'm trying to tell you."

She stared up into his eyes.

"I've got the directions, and the things we need"—he was almost panting—"to make bombs. I want you to help me practice it. Not to set anything off by ourselves, but just to practice. And I don't want you to tell a living soul."

"I won't, Ryder. I never would. But I don't know nothing about bombs."

"I do," he said. "Bob's been trying to teach me. You're good with your hands, Lee. I always been kind of clumsy, and my fingers is stiff from being out in the weather all the time."

"Want me to untie the cape now?"

"You can, but that's not the point. You got good fingers what with sewing and now barbering. You could help attach wires. That kind of thing."

She rose up from her knees. "Ryder, I'm not sure that's a woman kind of thing. I don't know if the other wives—"

"That's why it's got to be just our secret. I don't want you talking to any other wives about this. Not even if they're Klan. Especially if they're Klan."

Her gaze fell on the green plastic handle of the soft barber brush. Bombs? The handle reminded her of marble what with a few streaks of white running through it. She didn't want to bomb anybody. She could hear again the distant thud when the little colored Sunday school girls were exploded. She blurted, "I want another pair of panty hose."

"You what!" He was turning red in the face.

"Here, hon, let me dust you off with this soft brush," she hurriedly suggested. Lee knew that the soft dusting always soothed him. She made a stroke on his neck. He closed his eyes. She softly, softly brushed the little cut hairs from his neck and cheeks. Carefully, she brushed down his nose like she was painting his picture with the brush. The ugly color drained back down into his body.

"The panty hose could be my reward for helping," she said. "Just one pair. They're so modern. I just love them."

"I like you in a garter belt," he said, with his eyes closed.

She saw the lust tension gathering in him—just the words *garter belt*.

"Well, I could still wear a garter belt whenever you liked." She stopped brushing his face. "And I could wear the panty hose when I liked." He opened his eyes. She looked at him and smiled. "I got a garter belt on right now."

"And you'd study the directions and go over it with me?"

She carried the barber cape over to the garbage and carefully shook the hair out of the hem-pocket into the brown grocery sack. "Mama always said I could learn 'bout anything I studied on."

He slid off the kitchen stool and held out his hand to her. "Let's take advantage of the kids being gone."

He winked a nasty little wink, but suddenly she felt excited. They would just go to it, fast, before he hit her about something.

DAPPLED LIGHT

IN A SHADY GROVE, IN THE DAPPLED LIGHT OF LATE AFTER-noon, Fred Shuttlesworth took a little time just for himself in the wooded area behind Pilgrim Baptist Church. It was Monday, and he'd come down from Cincinnati to lead his regular Monday-night mass meeting. He sat on a large pitted rock because it helped him identify with the apostle Peter. "Upon this rock . . . ," Christ had said of Peter, "I will build my church."

And what was a church—any church—but a Movement? If the spirit inhabited a group of people, it didn't matter what church walls they were inside. They could be outdoors; they could be marching in the streets. Anybody in a demonstration was really in a church, a church on the move, because the spirit inhabited them and made their feet to move. The body was the temple of God and it was the Holy Spirit that came to live in the body and make it a temple.

This quiet place . . . with just him alone, quiet—it held a holy moment just like later, inside, when with all eyes turned upon him he would give his body, and his sweat, and his mind. The great flow of words would take form from his tongue and teeth and lips to tumble from his mouth like a mountain stream flowing from a cave in the high hills. . . .

But now for his quiet moment with nature, alone on a rock.

He liked the spotted light, not gloomy and depressed like the shade, not bright and overbearing, urgent and punishing like full sun. He looked up into the lacy leaves. They had special trees here. Landscaped trees they called river birch, with fine cut pale green leaves, and whitish bark, scaly, mottled with gray, unpredictable. *Where the Lord leads, I will follow.*

What was he without Scripture? More than the full armor of God, the Word was *inside* him. And the Word was *outside* him, suggested by the rippling of these little leaves and by the dancing shadows they cast on his skin. He thought of the four little girls who had passed, and his eyes filled with tears. He thought of his own children, their strength and their ready willingness to stand with him. And Ruby, his wife.

He placed his hand very gently, tenderly, on the rough, pocked surface of the rock, and his body remembered how he had lain, horizontal in his bed, and how he was lifted, lifted in his sleep, by the bomb placed under the floor of the house, directly under the position of his bed. It must have been a flash—all in a flash the bomb lifted the floor joists and scattered them, and lifted the floor planks and broke them, and lifted the legs of the bed and the bed frame, and the wire box springs up into the air, and the whole mattress and him on it in his pajamas. The sound roared around him, but he had been in the whirlwind of the Lord, kept safe in the eye of the storm. *Fear not, for I am with thee. . . .*

In the quiet, he pondered these things and loved the small still voice inside his bosom.

Two boys came walking toward him, nicely dressed, respectable. One was little Edmund Powers, the other was tall, looked like Edmund, his father? No, Edmund's father had died in the steel mills. No, it had to be his older brother.

"I seek you out, Reverend Shuttlesworth," Edmund chirped like a little bird.

"Come here, son."

He held out his arm and had the little boy sit beside him on the rock. He put his arm around him and drew him close. "Howdy-do," he said to the big boy.

"My li'l bro, he say I must meet you. My name Charles."

Fred Shuttlesworth took his time. This was the quiet place, later the frenzy and the shouting. He studied their faces, so much alike, smooth and quiet, but the boy's with a brightness and the young man's with a calm that meant love. He loved his little brother. He couldn't do much for him, but he loved him.

"Was there somethin' you wanted to ask?"

"Edmund, he say I must ask you what mus' I do to be saved."

"Saved?" Reverend Shuttlesworth asked shrewdly. "What do you mean by 'saved'?"

"Saved from sin," Edmund piped up.

Reverend Shuttlesworth squeezed Edmund's shoulder, but he said nothing. He continued to look at the big boy. Now the big boy couldn't meet his gaze. He looked down at his feet. He sighed. Charles threw his head back and stared at the sky, like a prisoner waiting for the verdict.

"Saved from this world, I reckon." Charles continued to gaze toward the canopy of leaves and the bits of pale blue that showed between them. "How mus' I be?"

"Come to the meetin'," Shuttlesworth answered. "Come see what the Spirit says to you. Let the Spirit tell you how you mus' behave."

Charles looked right into the minister's eyes. "Tha's what Edmund tell me." Charles smiled. "I mus' come to the mass meetin' and I mus' meet you."

Again the minister hugged the little boy. "How's your mama?"

"She fine," Edmund answered. "Baby, too. She name him Stoner."

Part of a chain of love, Edmund sounded happy. Shuttlesworth thought: Edmund's own big brother loved him; now he could love his little brother. Edmund smiled at his minister, and Shuttlesworth felt warmed. *Blessed boy, who could bring blessings to others.*

"But I don't work in the grocery no more," Edmund added. "I a shoeshine boy now."

FANS FOR AUGUST

AUGUST COMING, AGNES LAFAYT THOUGHT, AND I AM FINALLY prepared. Hurrying through the heat of early evening, she regretted that she was a little late to school—as though she wanted to make a grand entrance with her gift. Her shopping bag rustled noisily against her knee as she hurried. TJ had come, but he wanted to just stay with the car; he said he'd doze while he waited.

Agnes could see through the windows that the other students were already inside, and Mrs. Taylor, who was wearing her white jersey dress with the black and brown circles printed all over it, was standing up talking to the group. (Christine Taylor didn't need to wear such a middle-aged dress.) And there was the wheelchair and Miss Cat Cartwright, poor little soul so crippled up she could hardly write her own name. But they were just getting started.

"Now if you all would just pipe down," Mrs. Taylor was saying.

Agnes slipped in the door, held her shopping bag up high and pointed to it.

"What is it, Mrs. LaFayt?" Mrs. Taylor asked her.

"First off, I apologize for being late. I am so sorry."

"That's all right," Mrs. Taylor said, "for just this once."

"I thought everybody would be pleased, I brought us some hand fans." She reached in her shopping bag and brought out the one with her favorite picture: Jesus, the Good Shepherd. He was sitting on a rock, wearing blue and red, with a shepherd's crook leaning against the rock. Jesus held a little white lamb up in his arms, and all around scattered on the green grass were other sheep. Agnes had everyone's attention. She added, "Courtesy of Brooks Furniture Company in downtown Birmingham. They asked me to say that—"

Mrs. Taylor spoke sarcastically, "In case you can't *read* the advertisements on the back."

Agnes remembered how generously the fans had been piled into her shopping bag. The lady hadn't even stopped to count them; she'd just asked if that was enough, and Agnes had said, *Well, maybe just a few more, if you got 'em to spare, please.*

"The store lady asked me to say please come in and look at their complete line of air conditioners, if you in the market for air conditioners."

"You may hand them out," Mrs. Taylor said, "while I explain about the practice tests."

"I guess these will be our handheld air conditioners," Cat Cartwright said, and she chuckled at her own joke.

Agnes thought, *Suppose she can't flap no fan,* and the thought pierced Agnes that she might have pointed out the nice girl's disability. Agnes quickly sat down.

"Everybody say 'Thank you' to Mrs. LaFayt," Mrs. Taylor instructed.

A group of the young men said in obedient unison, "Thank you, Mrs. LaFayt," and smiled like good boys.

Mrs. Taylor began again. "How can I explain anything with y'all interrupting? 'How'd I do?' 'Answer my question?' Just please shut up and listen. If you can't answer a question and you can't eliminate one possibility as being wrong, then you *go on to the next question.* That's what I'm trying to get across. You don't just lay down and die. You keep going. Now there's not but one person in this room who did any good at all on that practice test. And you know why she did good? 'Cause she paid attention to what I been trying to teach you every week about *how to take a test.*"

"Was it me, Mrs. Taylor?" a quiet little guy asked.

Agnes thought, *Most of these boys paid by Neighborhood Youth Corps to come to school, but they trying.*

"No, it was not," Mrs. Taylor said. "It was Mrs. Agnes LaFayt."

Agnes felt faint with pride.

"Stand up, Agnes."

She got to her feet. Agnes tried not to grin. She looked humbly down at the floor. But her heart had speeded up. She felt her arms dangling at her side, limp and amazed. Jesus the Good Shepherd hung from one hand. Maybe she would be able to pass the real test when the time comes.

"Now, Mrs. LaFayt," Mrs. Taylor said, "you tell everybody how you went 'bout taking this test."

Oh, how her heart was racing. Did she dare to tell? Agnes always told the truth. She kept her gaze on the floor, but she turned her head a little on one side. Sort of aimed the top of her head toward Mrs. Taylor. All the students and teachers looked at her standing up among the wooden desks. The walls with blackboards, the banks of big windows on each side, were waiting. Waiting for Mrs. Agnes LaFayt to tell them.

"Well, first I read the question. And then I read the answers. And then I close my eyes and I says, 'Oh, Lord, is it A,B,C, or D?' and the Lord tells me, and I write it down."

The room erupted in laughter. Agnes was mildly surprised, but she had spoken the truth. "Not for every question," she tried to say, but they were laughing so loudly they didn't hear her. She wished Mrs. Taylor would tell her to be seated. "Just the hard ones when I don't know," she said. Even Mrs. Taylor was smiling big, like the joke's on her. Everybody was grinning—

Then a cherry bomb exploded on the porch of the building.

Every smile disappeared. Everyone was frozen at the desks.

Then the bullhorn voice: "Niggers . . . niggers."

Everyone became quiet.

"We see you all got some white women teachers in there with you. We think you better tell them teachers it's time to go back where they belong. We don't want to see no white teacher out here, come another night."

Everyone sat in stunned silence. Miss Cartwright and Miss Silver stared straight ahead.

The lights went out. No one moved. *Jesus, help us,* Agnes silently prayed.

Then Mrs. Taylor spoke calmly into the dark. Just her voice. "Charles, you and Joe go to the circuit box in the entry hall and turn the lights back on. Mike, you go round and tell Mr. Parrish to call the police and then to come here."

She's brave, Agnes thought. *She's a brave woman.* Agnes heard the three biggest boys get up, saw them moving toward the door. *What if the bullhorn was to shoot, soon as somebody goes out.* But Mike and Sam and Charles walked out safely.

"Anybody got a match or a cigarette lighter?"

Agnes recognized Arcola's voice, knew Arcola was talking to add to the calm.

"Wait!" That's Miss Silver. "They might shoot at a light."

But Christine—there she was, at the front, just where she was—flicked on her cigarette lighter. She tried once, twice, to turn the little wheel. Sparks fluttered and then it was on, like a little candle. The flame lit up Christine's face and neck. She looked pretty, like Jesus in the dark, in the fan illustration "Behold, I am the Way, the Truth, and the Light."

Christine smiled a sweet smile, her mother smile. Yes, Agnes had learned Christine had three little ones at home. Christine said, "They bluffing. You all just hold on now." Christine lit a cigarette. Absolutely against the rules. Christine was calmly defiant. She drew on the cigarette like a man, not touching it, and it glowed bravely in the dark, a little spot of red. Yes, Christine had to be daddy and mommy to her kids. She knew how to act like a man.

"We gonna learn," Mrs. Taylor said in her smooth strong voice, the red spot wagging. She took the cigarette from her lips, held it out in the narrow V of two rigid fingers. "And someday, sooner or later, everybody in this room gonna have his or her—that's right, you don't say 'their,' not 'everyone gonna have their diploma'—everybody in this room gonna have his or her high school diploma." Just like a preacher, she put in a silence, so they'd all look at her, let the words sink deep in. Nobody butted in. Mrs. Taylor held the room like a bowl of silence. "Now, Stella," she said, "let's conjugate one of your verbs."

And Miss Stella said, "I am at school."

And we all answered, "I am at school."

And she said, "You are at school."

And we repeated it: "You are at school."

And she said, "He, she, or *it* is at school. . . ."

There's always another verb to conjugate, and after "to be" Miss Stella start in on "to have" and we say it like we mean it: "I have friends, you have friends, he, she, or it has friends; we have friends, you have friends, they have friends."

Agnes heard herself say softly, "Now we 'bout like a family ready to sit down for Thanksgiving." She was glad to sit again in her desk.

Miraculously the lights came back on. Everyone looked at the faces around them as though they had just been born anew into life. Christine sat down in her chair.

JUST BEFORE THE August heat hit, the bullhorn man turned a classroom of codeine-nipping boys, young white and black women, and one woman about old enough to be a grandmother into a group of friends.

VIEW FROM OUTSIDE

ON HIS EVENING OFF, TJ SAT OUT IN THE CAR IN THE dark parking lot and watched the small brick building that held his precious Agnes. If he could have done so, he would have watched it every night. To let some air in, he unbuttoned his shirt a couple of buttons.

On top of a slope the building sat low to the ground. One step led up to a small porch held up by round white columns at each end, with two more columns flanking the step in the middle. Both sides of the one-room building had five big windows in a row. Despite the distance, TJ could see right in the lighted classroom—the young folks, the teachers (one white in a wheelchair), and his beloved wife.

As he sat in the car waiting, another car pulled into the lot. Three white men got out, but they didn't notice TJ. He was wearing dark clothing; he supposed he just blended right in. One of the men was carrying something horn-shaped in his hand, attached to a box. They moved like men on patrol—stealthy and purposeful. There was a stand of willows between the parking lot and Agnes's building, and TJ lost sight of them when they slipped among the long fronds of the trees. They were dressed in dark clothing, too.

TJ got out of his car and stood beside it. He saw the men emerge from the woods, but they headed toward the bigger buildings that sat up high on their foundations, not the little isolated one. It was cooler outside the car than inside.

TJ listened to the cicadas and the tree frogs screaming for rain. Agnes had taken fans to the school. When she hurried away from him, he had thought, *Slow down, Aggie. It don't matter, you one minute late.*

Suddenly the lights in the little low building went out. And the lights in the closest big building, too, just winked and were gone. TJ began to run. Before he got out of the lot, he determined he would kill them. If anything happened to Agnes, he would track them down and kill them. He stopped, went back. Read the license number on the back of the car. He had a hotel ballpoint in his pocket, and he wrote the tag number down in the palm of his hand. This way he could find them. He hated wasting time standing there, checking what he'd written against the Alabama tag, but he made himself do it.

Then he ran like a demon.

While he was in the grove of willows, his feet began to sink into the muck, up to his ankles. He heard a voice saying *Niggers . . . niggers,* and he began to think just how he would choke them one by one. His hands itched, and he remembered how, blind with dust, he had lifted the bricks and plaster in the bombed church. He saw the blood on brown arms and faces. He pictured again how people had moved like ghosts all covered in gray dust after the bombing. And that moment when he saw Agnes again, standing in the rubble, saw her knees buckle and her fall as though she were shot through the heart, and then he saw what she saw. The horror of it. Like John the Baptist, but a child, a young girl.

He charged the hill and was halfway up when the lights came back on. From this angle, he couldn't see as well, but the night class was all sitting down. He saw Agnes, from her neck up. Not even upset.

He'd been a fool. It was just the electricity had gone off. No, he had heard the voice: *Niggers . . . niggers.* But maybe he'd imagined that. Agnes was all right. He slowed down. His heart was beating hard, too hard. He ought not run uphill any more than Agnes should hurry. Her head looked so pretty, rising above the windowsill. She looked happy.

He saw three colored boys go in the door. Here came a man dressed up in a suit. Somebody in charge, probably. Mr. Parrish. TJ had seen this very man at the Gaslight with a beautiful high-style woman. Agnes had leaned over and said in TJ's ear: *I'm afraid it's not his wife.* Then Agnes had put her fingers to her lips—a secret—and he had nodded, agreeing. They didn't want to tear anybody down. That kind of carrying-on was too bad, but they had no intention of gossiping. Not about a fine-looking man like Mr. Lionel Parrish, director of the night school. And a preacher.

Mr. Parrish stepped up onto the little porch like he owned the place. Then he stopped in the doorway. He put one hand on the doorframe and stopped there. Real casual. TJ heard him say to everybody simply "Good evening," and TJ moved closer to listen.

"Sorry 'bout that, folks," Mr. Parrish said pleasantly. "I have people out looking on the campus for those guys. Everything all right?"

TJ heard a car motor starting down in the parking lot.

A wiry woman in a white dress printed with circles said, "Yeah, we cool." She had to be one of the teachers. Mrs. Taylor. Agnes had said Mrs. Taylor was the head teacher.

There were two white women, and the one with gleaming blond hair said, "Christine was magnificent." *Magnificent*—a word from a different world than TJ's world.

Mrs. Taylor's quick reply: "Hey, I thought that was Stella teaching this class, didn't you all?"

And then the voice of his Agnes, though somebody blocked his view of her: "Miss Stella sure do make it plain." Yes, that was Agnes. Never losing an opportunity to give a compliment, to raise somebody up: *she sure do make it plain.*

Then the blond white girl said, "Maybe it would be better if Cat and I didn't—"

Mrs. Taylor shot back, "Better for who? I thought I heard you conjugating verbs in the dark. I thought I hear you saying 'Who has friends?' You have friends, we *friends* on a first-name basis."

But the white girl was upset. Afraid. "Wait a minute," she said. "You know what I mean. You heard what they said at the window. It's Cat and me they don't want out here."

"Yes, and you know why?" Mrs. Taylor asked. She was getting mad. Yes, Agnes had talked about her. The Impatient One, Agnes had labeled her when she told TJ about school goings-on. "We already doing what they trying to stop," Mrs. Taylor declared. "We *integrated*. Yes, we are. Say the word, class."

And TJ heard his Agnes lead off, quietly, "Integrated."

"And that's not the end of it," Mrs. Taylor said, agitating herself. (TJ felt a chill. His feet were wet, his body soaked with sweat.) "They don't want anybody *learning*. In the slavery days, it was illegal for a colored person to learn to read and write. Learning is power."

The blond girl answered, "Y'all better face the fact—all of you—if Cat and I come back here, we'll be putting you in danger."

TJ moved so he could see better. See their faces. Who cared about integration? he wondered. This was about getting a diploma. Black teachers good as white ones for that.

But the crippled girl was talking again. Her hands were handicapped, as well as her legs, and she seemed to have something wrong with her throat. She said the bigots weren't worried about integration. Everybody sat still when she—Miss Cat—talked, gave her extra quiet and courtesy. She had trouble getting the words out, as though she had to squeeze them so they could fit through a constricted passage. "They're talking about keeping people as ignorant as they can," she said.

"That's the truth, Cat," Mrs. Taylor agreed.

"If I really thought that if Stella and I went away, your problems would be over, I'd go." It was hard for Miss Cat to get out a long sentence. "But I don't think so. They want to intimidate you in every way." She had to swallow and lick her lips, but she was determined to keep going. "They want to split us up." She said it like she was proud. "I'll bet you within one week (swallow, swallow), even if Stella and I left (swallow) and never set foot on the Miles College campus again (swallow), there'd be some redneck out there with a bullhorn (swallow) telling you that school was out for the summer. Permanently out. (Pause) We take a stand now, or there's not going to be anyplace left to stand."

"That's right," Mrs. Taylor said. But her face looked strange. Like she was going to cry. "I say it with Cat." Her voice was all quiet, like *she* could hardly get the words out. "Let's stand up for ourselves."

TJ looked at the class. They looked stunned. Then his Agnes does it. She stands up. A sob catches in TJ's throat. She's misunderstood—they were just *talking* the word—but she's standing there beside her school desk. Then Miss Arcola stands up and beams a lightbulb smile at everybody else. And Miss Gloria pops like a little short cork right out of her seat. Mrs. Taylor is up with her. One by one all the black folks are standing. In the doorframe, Mr. Parrish straightens up like a soldier. Stretches himself up on tiptoe, bounces on the balls of his feet. Last of all, white girl called Miss Stella gets up. She looks around at them. She wants to be brave, too.

Only person left seated is Miss Cat in her wheelchair. She suddenly shoots up her hand—reckon they know she *can't* stand up—and the whole room whoops with triumph.

FOUR SPIRITS

HER FOOT PRESSING THE GAS PEDAL, STELLA REMEMBERED
the imperative in the classroom thus: *stand up*—and it was Christine's voice
from inside Stella telling her what she must do. But also, and at the same time,
her mother's voice, as though time had no power at all to separate events.
Speaking not so much before Christine's injunction, but on top of it and
before it, finally simultaneously with it: *Stand up straight, Ruben, Timothy, Stella.
Blessed boys, blessed guns.* And again, the troops marched by, the waves of khaki
legs swept forward, row on row, down Twentieth Street, past the Tutwiler
Hotel, past the reviewing stand: *General Omar Bradley.*

Stella glanced across the car seat at Cat, lost in her own thoughts. Coura-
geous Cat. Stella felt alone with her fear. Though she spoke of marrying
Donny, already he was gone in the mists. Though her maiden aunt planted
scraggly rosebushes and expected them to become a garden wall for a wedding, the groom had become a ghost in the bright sunshine of the South
Pacific. Unreal.

Real was a sweltering classroom and the command to rise. To rise and
face fear.

Lines from T. S. Eliot, *The Waste Land*, came to her, of London, *Unreal City.
Unreal.* Had so many passed over London Bridge? Had Death undone so
many?

And then a quartet of voices swirled in her head, sang just above the metal
roof of the car, for her who seemed so normal:

How can you ever know us?
You will never know us.
We live like air
We are the air.

Like four stars, not voices, they seemed to wink out, tuck themselves back into blackness. Like four navels, they were round, shallow, and open, then they closed into a seam. Like four closed mouths with sealed lips. But they had sung to her. Would they sing again? Four silver voices, an ethereal descant.

And they sang again, immediately:

We are ever		*ta la.*		
	Ta la la		*la*	*la*
	Your living contains us			
	You will la-la,	*la-la*		

And already Stella learned: it is the *third* voice who loves me most. It is the third child who makes things clear: "We live like air," that voice had sung on top of and beneath and simultaneously with the others.

Come to haunt her: a quartet of spirits, as high as any random four stars, as inward as the four chambers of her heart. Voices like cloud-high birds. Too high to hear well. Specks hard to discern. Specks entering the ear. "Your living contains us."

Her ear could hear the uniqueness of each silvery edge. Their voices four wires on an ethereal lyre plucked simultaneously. But Stella liked the third voice best, the open one that didn't quite cease, and she would follow it, choose it to trust. "Your living contains us."

She had not gone, could not have gone to their funeral because she was not worthy. And Don was not worthy either. Only Cat had been worthy, and how she got there and how she got home again, she and Don would never know. "Perhaps as mundane as a taxi?" Don seemed to suggest in his dry, ironic voice, almost a monotone but a little lilt at the end: *taxi?* She cherished that particular tone of Don. She cherished it.

And wasn't the word *cherish* part of the marriage ceremony?

All four chambers of her heart contracted, signaled news too subtle to decipher. Perhaps the little twigs of rosebushes planted all along her aunts' wire fence *would* grow into a wall of white roses. Those spare green skeletal stems fanning out of the ground might become the backdrop for a white wedding, a garden wedding in two years. No, in only sixteen months, now. Eight months had passed since Donny left.

Donny, that was Cat's name for her brother, not Stella's. For Stella, that name registered less intimacy, not more. She squeezed her eyes tightly to envision the wedding.

Stella and Aunt Krit wanted large drooping white roses. Roses hanging like white silk handkerchiefs, heavy with virginity. On their silky petals would be a defiant touch of brown, or speckled red, here and there, marring and perfecting their pristine bloodlessness. Stella imagined the large, white roses gathered into a bridal bouquet and herself looking modestly down into their snowy petals. Brown spots for the nights she'd lain beside Darl kissing and kissing, her virginity intact.

"Good night, Kitty-Cat," Stella said. (She had taken the chair from the trunk, unfolded the smelly chair, helped Cat into it. Dear Cat.)

"Good night, Stella."

They had driven home in silence because their minds could not separate from the solidarity of the classroom.

Stella watched Cat muster the energy to propel her wheelchair up the ramp. She didn't want help. They had not discussed it: what of that terrifying promise to return tomorrow night to the death trap? Stella visualized the lighted building consisting of only one room, a small porch, Greek columns, and a single step at its front. What about that place? But Cat had wheeled away into her world, and now Stella must walk home, leaving the car for Mr. Cartwright to drive to work.

From the leafy summer trees, three voices, not four, sang together for Stella. She recognized them from the opera; she and Don had dressed up before he went to Tonga, attended, inhabited an impressionist painting that night. From *The Magic Flute*, in German, they sang. Three spirit voices teasing Papageno out of his aloneness, out of his desire to die for lack of a mate. So quick and silvery those Mozartian voices, high and nimble, singing in close harmony, singing a parallel melody. Singing from a time of powdered wigs and knee britches and a place far from Birmingham. But where was the voice she trusted, the voice of the lost child whom she loved most?

LIONS LOUNGING

IN THE GLOAMING, THE NEXT NIGHT, STELLA WALKED ACROSS the Miles campus toward her shadowy friends, three women and a man, sitting on the step of the portico. Though Cat was home sick, Stella, yes, she, had driven alone to the college. Before this night, Stella had willed herself to have courage—just enough to help Cat. When Cat's telephone voice had said *I can't come*, Stella had quivered with fear. So she would have to stand up for herself, or not stand up. But she knew she would go. *I have to go by myself to Courage College*, Stella told herself. She would not have the crutch of altruism for support.

Stella watched her new friends sitting on the step of the strangely classical portico. They stirred with uncertainty. Who was that approaching, in the gloaming?—they must be asking. She must seem disembodied without the wheelchair before her. No doubt they usually recognized her and Cat as a unit, a rolling sculpture: two female figures joined by her hands on the handles of the back of the wheelchair.

And what could she make of their shapes, lounging on the step? Three women. A fourth figure, a man who was a little apart. A man in a suit, handsome Lionel Parrish waiting with Christine, Arcola, and Gloria to see who would come back to school this night. He lounged like a lion on the banister slab beside the step, his back to the last streaks of sunset.

"You look like four shadows," Stella called to them, "haints risen from Hades."

Christine stood up, approached her.

"That you, Stella?"

"Who else? Without her better half."

"I sure thought Cat would of come." Arcola's voice floated musingly on the dusk.

"She would have. She's sick. She's flooding."

The three women shifted their positions uncomfortably, each in her own way. They hadn't expected this news in their conversation: menstrual blood. Mr. Parrish remained still as a stone lion. Somehow it was *necessary,* Stella thought, to say this in front of him.

Gloria spoke softly, in her high sweet voice. (She reminded Stella of the voice of the third spirit, the one she trusted. The one who wanted there to be meaning, as much as she longed for beauty. Who could look at the newspaper photographs of the four girls killed in the bombing and not feel her heart go out? Sometimes one countenance or another would stir the heart in a special way.) Gloria said, high and sweet, "I guess you're not a southern lady anymore, are you?"

"No," Stella said. "It's more important to be something else."

"Amen," Mr. Parrish said.

Stella felt the rareness of the moment. Could it only happen in the gloaming, in the gloaming? Did it happen every day when the seam between day and dark was smudged? Was this the moment to catch, the devotional moment: the last redness of the sun, the first starlight?

"Here's eternity," Stella said, and she gestured at them, the college campus, the sky.

"Come sit with us," Christine answered.

"Will the students come?" Arcola asked.

"They'll come." Mr. Parrish spoke without moving, as though stone were emanating sound.

"Where's your braid?" Stella asked Arcola.

"Home in a drawer."

"That's fine," Gloria murmured.

"My hair's short," Arcola said.

"And straight," Stella observed. The women, too, were like patient lionesses, sitting randomly on the steps in the dusk. And then she asked Arcola because she had to, or night would fall like a quick curtain: "Do you straighten it?"

"Yeah."

Then they became four women (because Stella joined the others) plus Lionel Parrish who were sitting in the comfortable twilight. Their quiet was a constituent of the moment; silence was essential to this distilled droplet of time. Mosquitoes began to gather, to visit their arms and legs and cheeks. When Mr. Parrish slapped at one on the back of his neck, the spell dissolved. The sun set.

"Not quite so hot tonight," he said.

"It was good of Agnes to bring fans," Gloria said.

Gloria was taking part; she was saying her sentences, the same as anybody. Such sweetness in her voice, Stella thought. *I love Gloria.* Until now, she had liked Arcola; she had struggled with Christine; she had neglected Gloria. And here Gloria was, a human being, carved out of space, as real sitting on the steps as any lioness or person.

Stella spread her hand on the cool stone. She felt its gritty texture, welcomed its solid and mute reality.

"I might write a short story someday," Stella said.

"What about?" Gloria asked, more promptly than anyone.

"About us." Stella pressed her hand into the stone. Of course she could leave no print. Maybe a fast-fading palm print of moisture on the stone. "Of course it wouldn't really be about us. I'd change everything."

"That would be all right," Mr. Parrish said. "We can't help but change things. No matter how good they are."

"Or how bad," Christine said.

Someone cleared her throat, but it was impossible to say who. The night whispered into Stella's ear:

Define us, O Lord!

Stella remembered the glow from the cigarette lighter the night before on Christine's face. How it had transformed her, made her beautiful. She remembered Darl, in the cemetery, the circle of young black men around them, how Darl and they had smoked cigarettes together. Suddenly she missed him. She heard indistinct words, high as a mosquito

Wistful . . . wishing . . .

Darl seemed like a kind of cousin—distant but someone to whom she would ever be connected. Someone she might see years later; she would say something and he would answer, "Only you would remember that, Stella." And if that happened, she would be exquisitely affirmed. But what hovered in the gloaming?

Eternity in a . . .

"Can you remember," Stella asked, "when you were first aware of racial prejudice?"

They were silent.

Finally, Mr. Parrish said, "It's in the air. Like breathing."

A frozen, jagged sea.

"Like particulate matter," Stella said. "From the steel mills."

But Stella was remembering Jack, a little boy she had played football with when she was very young. Jack's face had been freckled, too, like Darl's, and she had thought him indescribably cute. The essence of what a boy should be. After they were grown up, she'd turned around and there was Jack again, downtown, coming out of Thom McAn shoe store, tall now and lanky, not the compact little boy she had hurled her body against while she pressed the football into her ribs. When she saw him, all grown, she pressed a phantom football tight against her ribs; it became like a large heart, and she could feel it beating against her side.

In front of Thom McAn, looking thoughtfully at people jostling on the sidewalk, tall Jack had told her when he had first been aware of racial prejudice. Back then, when they were children, there were a few colored houses across the alley, behind his house. One day he had been sitting on a cinder block at the edge of the alley. He was just sitting there. Maybe he was staring. A Negro girl had come up to him and said, "What you looking at, you freckle-faced bastard?" His story had jolted Stella; she had thought prejudice was the burden of only white people.

Piano music trickled onto the Miles campus into the new night: Chopin. Stella sat up straight. "Is there a music department?" she asked.

It was an old piano, rattly. Still, it was Chopin. A nocturne her mother had played. Four mosquitoes sang at Stella's ear.

> *Zing zing zing zing*
> *zing zing zing*
> *Sometimes we just zing*
> *Zing zing   zing zing.*

"Christine?" Stella said.

"Uh-huh," Christine answered, relaxed.

"We've always been integrated. Our lives."

"What you mean, Stella?" The question sounded sharp. Then Christine modulated her tone, put her question in a sheath. "What you trying to say?"

"Our lives have always been layered together. We know each other. I don't think northern people always understand that."

"Separate and unequal," Christine said.

"That's right," Stella said. "But together. Inseparable, anyhow."

Stella saw that students were beginning to drift toward them from all parts of the campus. She couldn't see who. She wondered if somewhere the Klan was gathering like that. Converging toward some center, feeling their solidarity.

There was Agnes LaFayt. Walking slowly. She was carrying her shopping bag again.

"Time to get started," Mr. Parrish said. He stood up, became unglued from the slab where he had lounged casually on one elbow in his good clothes.

The four women stood up, shook out their skirts, dusted their hands against each other, leaned down to pick up their purses.

"Whatcha got this evening?" Christine asked Agnes.

Agnes smiled a tired little smile. She reached in her bag and brought out a handful of short white sticks. Six inches long, white, waxy.

"Candles," she said. "In case the 'lectricity go off again. I got us some candles."

AN OFFICE CALL

THE STUDENTS WERE CONGREGATING DESPITE THE THREAT.

When Lionel Parrish went back to his office, he flicked on the overhead light and opened his desk drawer. He got out a life insurance form. He tossed it onto the desk and twisted the scored stem on his desk light between his thumb and forefinger. More light. *Candles.* The woman made him ashamed. He would rather think of *ingenuity,* feel the details of invention between his thumb and forefinger. His face twitched with shame.

He was ashamed that he hadn't taken better care of his own mother. Ashamed about all the soft, middle-aged black women who were floating on through their lives toward some uncertain certain end with so little fulfill-ment. Maybe moments of pleasure in their marriage beds. At least at first, when it was all new to them. Transcendent moments in church when they were singing or praying. There should have been more for them. Not just crocheting their afghans and baking their pineapple upside-down cake. He and all the other black men should have seen to it for their sakes.

He turned out the overhead fluorescent light and sat again at his lamp-lit desk. He wanted to dwell in the circle of intimacy provided by the desk lamp. It was the way a scholar should look: cut off from the larger space, focused on what he was doing, on what he must do—his papers, his books. He would sit in a circle of light like a white man in a Rembrandt painting.

He looked at the new life insurance policy, the Old English script across the top, sharp pointed and black as a small wrought-iron fence. A fence to keep out bad fairies, and what were they but bad thoughts. Since he was a boy, he had imagined English fairies skittering at night across the surfaces of the worka-day world causing disarray with their tiny, shapely feet.

The black printing stretching across the top of the page was more like a bramble hedge than an iron fence. But it was an inadequate hedge, open on both ends, only out to the margins, not all the way across the top from edge to edge of the paper. As though any briar patch or even an iron lace fence could keep death at bay, no matter how curlicued and spiky. Still, it was a worthy page. The black ink representing the terms of the policy had been pressed and printed right into the fiber of the paper.

Lionel adjusted himself in the carved chair seat, which was carved to fit a human bottom, two parallel declivities, like shallow spoon rests, for his but-tocks. Yes, he could fit his behind right there. Oh, he knew the treachery of this chair: he wouldn't be sitting here long till smooth and polished became hard. Maybe he'd buy himself a cushion to sit on, a square cushion upholstered in green with corduroy strings tied to the backrest so the cushion wouldn't slip off.

Sighing, he opened the desk drawer again, just enough to get his fingers in. When he reached into the curve of his desk tray, he felt a fountain pen. It was a new kind that held an ink cartridge. He had a whole box of the cartridges, each a little sealed, translucent tube. He liked replacing them. He enjoyed piercing the end with the shunt of metal coming up from the nib.

In the past, he had thought marvelous the old type of ink pen, with a little lever on the side. You pumped the lever against a small rubber bladder inside the barrel of the pen to draw up ink from the inkwell. But those bladders wore out; the pens leaked. Still, he liked the squat glass jars of ink with the metal screw-top lids. The jars were cunningly made on the inside, with a shallow glass pocket, like a little chamber, inside. That was where you inserted the nib to draw up ink. Not down in the main jar, but in that special little in-swelling of glass that caught and held an appropriate amount. The dipping pocket hung inside the wider mouth of the bottle, like a window box hanging inside a room.

The accoutrements of status: a wooden desk, a proper (if uncomfortable) desk chair, a desk drawer with a tray for pens and pencils. A new cartridge fountain pen, and in the side drawer, obsolete but cunning, a squat glass bot-tle of royal blue ink.

The skeleton map unrolled itself on the wall. The wooden bar at the termi-nus of the chart clunked into the chalk tray. It was an announcement. Good as a fanfare. He refused to look; he had heard, and he knew what was next.

"How much you worth now, Mr. Parrish?" Mr. Bones asked softly.

"You've come back."

"Oh, I make office calls. Frequently."

Mr. Parrish refused to look at Mr. Bones. He just listened to him and then answered back to the mockery. Longing for distraction, Lionel read the heading across the policy, the black Gothic script. He kept his gaze within his circle of light. He knew who Mr. Bones was. A figment of his imagination. That didn't make him any less real. Bones was like Marley, a bit of undigested beef, a half-cooked potato lodged in old Scrooge's bowels.

"You feel pretty safe and snug in here, don't you?" Mr. Bones taunted.

"What you want me to do? Blow up city hall?"

"Listen to your bones, Lionel. What your bones say to you?"

"I'm here."

"Yeah, but I know how hard it was for you to get here. Started out, didn't you? Turned around and went back, didn't you? Had to start out again?"

"I'm here. I did it. I came back."

"You just about as brave as Miss Stella, I'd say."

"Just about."

But Lionel felt ashamed. He wondered if Martin Luther King Jr. ever started out of his hotel room, headed for trouble, and decided he needed to go back inside, get something, maybe, that he'd forgotten. And when he got back into safety, did he ever sit down in a hotel chair and rethink the whole thing? Wonder if he should just quit, just sit there till it was over. Maybe tune in the TV, hear the newscaster say, "We were expecting Dr. King to lead the group this afternoon, but assistants say he was unavoidably delayed. Dr. King sends greetings to the people here, reminds everyone that Love and Nonviolence are the path to Justice."

"So you think Education is the path to Power?" Mr. Bones said. "Just like Mrs. Christine Taylor said last night? You believe that, don't you?"

"Yes."

Lionel looked at the dictionary on his desk. He always kept it there. He wanted his teachers and any visitors to know he wasn't too proud to learn more, to look things up.

"You believe in Education, not Love?"

"Both help."

"Just thought you'd sell yourself a little more insurance, huh?"

"Why not?"

"But will you ever be worth as much as A. G. Gaston? Even in death?"

"For my family. So they be provided for."

"How we do provide! Let's see. What we got cooking? Grant proposal. Yes, grant proposal to the federal government. In case that comes through, we made ourselves one mighty high-pay H.O.P.E. administrator."

"I've got a chance. Especially with an integrated faculty."

"Bigwig administrator, he gots to have plenty of life insurance. In case Mr. Death, who I most decidedly do not represent, in case Mr. Death, if he was to show up in Bombingham—"

"It's for my family. If I was blown up."

"Expiation. Expiation. You can sing that to the tune of 'Alabama, Alabama, I will aye be true to thee.' And Death does know the way to Bombingham. He been here many a time. I guess he be singing in the choir when your funeral come round."

Lionel sat at his desk, his pen poised over the insurance form. How could he leave something to Matilda without Jenny finding out? How could he take care of the woman whose warm body was the flame of life?

"What was that she was saying about an hour ago?" Mr. Bones asked. Now he'd come off the wall. His voice was closer to Mr. Parrish's ear, and he supposed his visitor had even stepped into the circle of light. Mr. Parrish looked up. Okay, if Mr. Bones invaded the light circle, Mr. Parrish would look. There he was: a whole grinning skeleton, loose jointed, his jaw flapping up and down. No tongue. Because he stood within the golden glow of light, the white bones had taken on a faint golden sheen. Imagination could play tricks, Lionel Parrish knew. He had always had imagination. Yes, that was how his dear mother excused him when he was caught in a lie: *Lionel just has such imagination.*

"I guess you worrying about who's going to live and who's going to die among you demonstrating folks?" Mr. Bones's jaw had stopped wagging. He was just thinking loudly, with his immaterial brain. He was just thinking right into Lionel's mind. But then Mr. Bones's pelvis gave an obscene thrust. With his bony pelvis, he butted the air. And again.

And Lionel remembered Matilda, not more than two hours ago, making life so sweet that he didn't want to put his sorry flesh at risk ever again. *Put it in, honey.* That moment! *Oh, harder, honey.* Those moments. *O looooooover man.*

Mr. Bones began to fade into something shroudlike. Just a dark cloak. A cowl-shaded blackness where a face should have been. He was more terrifying.

With a voice that was distinct and nasty, he sounded like Police Commissioner Bull Connor talking on TV. Mr. Bones telling everybody: "We couldn't risk losing that woman, could we? That good ole ole-time *sex*. We too happy; we too content, to risk our sweet neck. You one nigger just got it too good. How many times, between your wife and your mistress, how many times a day you getting it, Lionel?"

"I have a right to my wife."

"She knows it. You can be sure that she knows *her* duty. When did she ever say no to you. Uh-uh. She lay there and say, I want to have as many babies as you want to put in me, darling. And she mean it. She sure 'nuff mean it. I ain't heard Miss Matilda say one word about having your babies. Have you?"

It keeps me pure, Lionel thought. It keeps me pure. This way, I don't touch Miss Arcola. She is ripe and ready to go. You know the way those boys look at her. Especially that one big fellow, Charles Powers. You see how he start wearing clean clothes, wanting to impress Miss Arcola. You see how now he even press his shirts, keep his hair trimmed close like a Sunday school boy.

"You want a little wheelchair stuff, Lionel?"

Mr. Bones's voice was fading, receding toward the wall. With one giant step, he would be hiking himself back up into the chalk tray, but Bones lingered a moment, just to prove he could. Just to prove Lionel Parrish had no power over the mocking voice, the ghastly presence. Mr. Bones hesitated quietly, just a minute, getting ready to move back into the chart.

Then Lionel could hear the heavy chart clattering reassuringly against the wall. Maybe it was the wind.

Wind? In this still-as-death oven? Lionel scraped his chair backward to get up. He'd open a window high, no matter what insects flew in. 'Nuff heat to have heatstroke, to hallucinate.

Faintly, Lionel heard the last thing Mr. Bones had to say for the night.

"Don't show it to Christine. She chop it off."

PICASSO'S BULL

THAT NIGHT, GLORIA AND THE OTHER TEACHERS SPOKE
while little white wax candles lay ready and waiting on the desk arms of their
wooden chairs. Gloria felt a balance in her soul; yes, each and every person had
a candle and a fan. When Sam West give Stella his red-sided cigarette lighter,
she had to ask, "Should I lay it down or stand it up on its base?" and Gloria
knew Stella was so old-fashioned she'd never held a cigarette lighter in her
hand till that moment. Neither had Gloria.

Jimmy Harlow held out a book of matches to Gloria, and she placed it beside
the dead little candle lying on her desk. The matchbook was black and had a
modern Picasso-like drawing of a bull on it and the words DALE'S HIDEAWAY.

"You been to Dale's Hideaway?" she asked Jimmy shyly.

"Naw, but my uncle he used to wait there. At Dale's Cellar, too."

Gloria decided she'd ask Stella to tell her about Dale's. That and the restaurant at Cobb Lane, with the she-crab soup. Suddenly she remembered Stella
saying of Cat, at sunset, with a man present: *She's flooding*. Yes, the interiors of
forbidden restaurants could certainly be discussed.

Gloria had had no interest in eating at the Woolworth's—that was just sym-
bolic, a step along the way. But she wanted to taste things so soft and flavorful
that she couldn't even imagine them now. She wanted to go inside the places
behind the intriguing names: Dale's Hideaway, Dale's Cellar, The Club, Cobb
Lane with the she-crab soup. She wanted to go there while she was still young.

"Jimmy," she said, "what was the name of the most important document
signed in 1776?"

"Declaration of Independence," he said, but now he was doodling, copying the drawing of the bull standing on its hind legs like a man.

"Way back in history, before history," Gloria said, "people used to draw animals on the walls of caves. In the south of France. Those bulls and horses have been there over ten thousand years."

Now Jimmy looked at her.

"I can draw," he said.

"But perhaps later?" she asked and made her voice as soft as the petal of a pansy. "The Declaration of Independence and the Constitution didn't include black people."

They knew that. That was one thing they weren't likely to miss on the multiple-choice test if it asked "What groups were implicitly excluded in the opening statement of the Constitution?"

"No women, either, white or black." Gloria liked her tone, so quiet, as though she were talking to herself. They had to lean forward to hear. "When they say 'men' they mean men, not everybody, like you might have thought they meant to say."

The six young men in her group bowed their heads and looked up strangely at her, as though she was embarrassing them. They didn't want to discuss a woman topic. "Does anybody know when women got the vote—black and white women?" And she had to tell them: 1920.

This was the way to teach when you didn't have any books. Fact by fact. You told them, you explained. You asked them to repeat it. One by one. That was the glory of her "classroom"; for a moment in time, everybody knew everything you asked of him. You didn't go on till they all knew it. Then everybody stepped forward together.

Gloria went to the window and threw up the sash. "Let freedom ring!" she said, and the big boys jumped up and helped her till all the windows were wide open.

AT BREAK TIME, Christine told Gloria and Stella, authoritatively, "You want to improve education, you not got to do but one thing and one thing only: reduce class size. We are cookin'."

"And put screens on the windows," Stella added.

Where was Arcola? Out on the porch hobnobbing with Charles Powers. Where was Jimmy Harlow? Suddenly Christine was inviting Gloria to go home with her after classes. "I want you to meet my kids."

"Thank you," Gloria said. Today was Aunt Carmine's birthday, but Christine's invitation was more important. Making friends was about the future. Every decision now was a chance to step boldly into the future. Christine would lead her forward.

"You say that 'Thank you,'" Christine replied pleasantly, "like I invited you to Buckingham Palace."

In the background, Gloria heard student voices tuning up like an orchestra. *I'm bored with these history facts,* Gloria thought. *My mind's wandering all over the place. When I finish school, I don't want to be any teacher.* The luscious cello section soli in Schubert's "Unfinished Symphony" sang in Gloria's mind. She wanted to go to New York.

"Now what was an indentured servant and how was that different from being a slave?" she asked her group.

Across the room, Arcola's group watched their teacher attentively. With her friendly ways and Colgate toothpaste smile, Arcola made people want to do right and enjoy themselves. She'd make these students *want to come to school.* They didn't care if she wore her glamour braid or not. She was just pretty, even if her skin tones were a little murky.

Gloria had always liked the even, dark blend of tones in her own skin, a strong darkness, more toward black than brown, but with brown and red in it. Mahogany, she thought. Like fine furniture. And she used to put her arm on the dining room table, when her mama had the protective pad off, to match up her skin tone with the polished tabletop.

One young man in the class was darker than Gloria, and she was fascinated by him. Every night she looked at him with satisfaction: just as dark as ever, across the room in Christine's group. Like somebody from Africa. He was married and wore a wide gold wedding band. The ring surprised Gloria, and she wondered how a shiftless Neighborhood Youth Corps boy had brought himself to get married and to have a gold ring. But it gleamed enticingly against his skin, which was dark as bittersweet chocolate.

How many mosquitoes, crickets, and moths flying around in this hot room?

And then the bell was ringing, lessons came to a bored halt, and school was out. All evening, the little white candles had lain unused. Agnes began to gather up the fans and the candles and to put them back into her shopping bag for safekeeping, till tomorrow night. Gloria hoped Cat would be back.

There was Mr. Parrish lounging against the doorframe; so casual but handsome in a lightweight suit and tie. Gloria loved the contradiction between his nice clothes and his relaxed body; he was sexy. She thought he was even better looking than Dr. King. Mr. Parrish had a wildness in his eye that made her think of Lord Byron and Mr. Rochester in *Jane Eyre*. Mr. Parrish made her think of her handsome daddy, too, and how she used to run and jump in his arms after Sunday school.

Arcola was asking Stella, "You want Charles and me to walk you to your car?"

Yes, Gloria thought, Stella might be scared without Cat for company. Not that Cat could protect a flea. Or hurt one.

"Thank you," Stella said to Arcola, and her smile showed tension leaving her face, an echo of the wide, relaxed smile Arcola always gave everybody. "Good night, everybody," Stella called out. But first she crossed the room to Gloria. *She's flooding*—had Stella really said that at sunset while they waited for students to show up? She walked across the room, reached out, and touched Gloria's forearm. The white girl didn't look at what her hand was doing; she just looked straight into Gloria's eyes. "See you tomorrow night."

Mr. Parrish asked Christine and Gloria to go with him to his office.

WHEN THE THREE of them stepped into the night air, it was like walking against a curtain of heat, pushing it forward with your nose, but never getting past it or through it. Christine asked Mr. Parrish if there had been any follow-up on the bullhorn man.

"Naw," Mr. Parrish said, and he snorted skeptically through his nose.

He sounded like a bull, full of power and glory, and Gloria thought again of the matchbook drawing of a bull standing on his hind legs like a man.

Once she had seen a real bull stand up and snort when her daddy had taken her out in the country, up to Winston County, where he had grown up. His people had lived there since the Civil War. When Alabama seceded from the Union, Winston County had seceded from Alabama, and Winston was called "The Free State." As a young man, her father had realized if he was going to make anything of himself, he'd have to leave farming and go to the city, to

Birmingham. Once established, he had gathered all his sisters into his garage apartment behind their new house in Birmingham.

During one visit to Winston County, Gloria had sat in the car to watch the men load a bull into the back of a truck with a stock rack added above the metal sides. Quickly, the beast turned around, then stood up, heaving his mighty chest onto the bars of the stock rack. It had melted under him like butter. For a moment, the bull just hung over the bent bars; then he commenced to kick and snort and struggle. Her father got out of the car to help, but he told Gloria and her mother to stay inside, that a bull was a dangerous animal.

Striding toward his office cutting across the sward, Mr. Parrish looked as though he could wrangle a whole herd even while he was wearing a suit. Like that standing bull, the matchbook drawing—Mr. Parrish was a kind of Minotaur, king of the labyrinth.

Her father had helped to put up the ramp again, to open the tailgate, to hold the rope on one side with three others, so the snorting bull could walk down to his kingdom.

When they entered the office, Gloria's eye fell on the little statue of Vulcan, and she couldn't help looking out the window to see what color light the real, true Vulcan was holding up, across the city, perched on the high ridge of the mountain. The Popsicle light was green. She recalled how Arcola had sucked on Vulcan that day at the beginning of the summer when Mr. Parrish had told them white women would be joining H.O.P.E. White women? Cat and Stella, they turned out to be.

When Gloria dialed up her mother, she was surprised to hear her mother's voice against her ear saying *You don't neglect your family for your friends*. Gloria didn't know how to reply. She took a breath. Then her mother added that Gloria could just *put in an appearance* at the birthday party and then visit her friend.

"I just wanted to congratulate you," Mr. Parrish was saying to Christine, "on the fine job you're doing." Then he looked at Gloria, as though he were beaming at a child. "You, too, Miss Gloria. I'm proud of you."

"Gloria's coming over with me to meet my children," Christine said.

"I have to go home first," Gloria explained. She felt depressed.

Ignoring Gloria, Mr. Parrish said to Christine, "You have three, don't you, and it's just you."

"My sister watches them a lot."

"I'd enjoy meeting your family, sometime, Christine. I have four children myself." He picked up some papers from his desk, as though he was bored and wanted them to leave.

As soon as Gloria and Christine closed the office door behind them, Christine said, "Oh, I forgot to tell him something. You run on to your aunt's party and come over to my place later." Then she told Gloria her address.

WHEN GLORIA GOT HOME, she went straight to the lit-up garage apartment. Chatter from the party clattered down the stairs. Her mother and father were already there, and Aunt Carmine's birthday teacup of flowers had already been presented.

"Girl, you ought to ask off early for your auntie's birthday," Carmine said reprovingly.

Her father winked at her. "You not missed nothing," he said.

Dressed like jewels—red, yellow, green, and blue—the aunts were resplendent. And the perfume on them!

On the occasion of each of his sisters' birthdays, Oliver Callahan gave them a small bouquet nestled in a teacup with a matching saucer. Each set was beautifully unique in its floral decoration; they never duplicated. "The cup garden," the sisters called the collection, and it was as colorful as they were. Tonight they'd displayed all the empty cups and saucers on a round table, then added the new one, filled with fresh flowers, to the group.

Gloria's mother still wore her staid professional clothes, but her father had changed to a Hawaiian shirt. Seated, he raised his glass for a 7UP toast to Aunt Carmine and her birthday. All the women hovered around him, ready to wait on him, or to touch him or to get his attention. Gloria saw her father, surrounded by his sisters, was as pleased as though it were *his* birthday. When he suddenly stood up to lead the toast, Gloria thought of Picasso's bull, erect in all his glory.

Once when she was very little, before they moved to Dynamite Hill, she had gotten up in the night to go to the bathroom. When she came out in the hall, there was her daddy coming out of the other bedroom. He was wearing only a T-shirt—maybe she dreamed it—and his member was standing up straight and tall as a little man the shape of a clothespin doll but much larger. With both hands, he had stretched down the white cloth till he'd covered himself. Unperturbed, he smiled at Gloria and said, "Go on back to sleep, sweetheart."

She had dreamed she was Snow White, pleasantly slumbering in the heart of a diamond, but Snow White's cheeks were the blissful color of a milk chocolate candy kiss, and her nose stuck up in an inviting little milk chocolate peak.

From over Aunt Carmine's birthday party array of cups and saucers, decorated with roses, cornflowers, violets, marigolds, snapdragons, lilies, clover, and hyacinth, her father smiled at her now, just as he always had.

"Daddy," Gloria said, "you remind me of Ferdinand."

"Ferdinand who, baby?"

"The gentle bull among the flowers, in the children's story."

Her fingertips rubbed her forearm, the place Stella had gently touched, and then she touched her cheek where the white man at the lunch counter had spat.

Were her aunts more like tropical birds or colorful jewels in their bright, tight clothes? In her quiet gray suit, Gloria's mother sat calmly among their flutter. Why should Gloria leave this? She was home. She'd telephone Christine, arrange to visit some later time.

CATHERINE'S STORY: A FRIEND OF THE BODY

CATHERINE HAD ALWAYS TRIED TO BE FRIENDS WITH HER body. When she was ten years old and suddenly started falling down, when she was eleven and it became difficult to put one foot in front of the other, when her daddy gave her a stick he had cut from the fence row to use as a walking stick, Catherine spoke lovingly to her legs, told them she knew they were doing their best, told them that they must *try*.

Every night after she went to bed she put Jergens lotion on her thighs, knees, shins, calves, feet, just slathered it on to stimulate the circulation. As she smoothed on the lotion, she said "good legs, good legs" to them, as though they were two long cats. Not wanting to worry her parents, she waited till they were asleep before she began the massage. She would whisper to her legs about long walks she had taken with Donny, and how she used to wade in the creeks and let the minnows nibble her toes. She reminded them that she wanted to have a bicycle someday, when her balance was better, and they could do the pedaling, if they were well and strong. What hills they would fly over, what blossoming trees—redbud, dogwood, and mimosa—they would skim under!

Once, when she was coming up the steps, the toe of her saddle oxfords caught the lip of the step and she fell. "Damn," she said, for the first time. She was twelve, and it was the first time she had ever said a swearword. The first time she had come close to cursing her failing body.

Her daddy was about to take Mommy to the doctor anyway, so he had taken Cat along, too. The doctor looked at the bruise close to her temple and said that it wasn't serious. "It's your mommy we got to worry about," he said to her, as though she'd been trying to get undue attention.

She tried, shyly, to tell him more. "Sometimes I can hardly walk," she whispered. "And I trip, like this time. Daddy gave me a walking stick." She didn't want her mother to hear.

"You're at the awkward age," he said. "Do you have your period yet?"

Catherine had said no; she didn't ask what was a period, but whatever it was, she was sure she didn't have it.

"Once you have the curse," he said, smiling, "you'll get more graceful."

She'd always liked Dr. Higgins. She felt reassured, but on the way home, in the car, she asked what a period was, and her mother had glanced at her father, and then told her that she would explain later, that they'd have a woman talk.

"Your mother needs to rest now," her father said.

When they got home, her mother went straight to bed. Catherine went to the kitchen and washed the dishes that had piled up in the sink. Standing up in front of the sink, she didn't have to move much. Her father came in and told her he appreciated her taking over the dish washing. She realized he meant she was to do it from now on.

From now on till when? she thought but didn't ask.

She stood at the sink carefully washing the dishes till she was stiff. Her pelvis felt like a chair into which the rest of her torso sagged, and her legs were as numb as the dumb legs of a straight-back kitchen chair. The dishes took a long time that night because Cat noticed her grip was becoming uncertain. Several times, a plate or cup would try to slip out of her grasp. She felt relieved when she got to the metal pots and pans. When one of them crashed down against the sink, she knew, even as it fell, that it could not break.

What her mother had was cancer. Cat herself was beginning to get breasts, and she wondered if they, too, would become cancerous. In the bathtub, she told them they were pretty, though one seemed slightly larger than the other. She told them to be good, and not to cause trouble. Getting out of the tub was a terror. She would turn around so that she was on her knees, grasp the side and push herself up. Once she slipped and her cheek smacked the porcelain and then skidded down the back slope of the tub; her nose went underwater. After that she drained all the water from the tub before she tried to get out, even though it meant soap scum would settle back onto her skin.

Finally she told Donny that he needed to be home when she took a bath, that he needed to come in when she called and help her out.

He smiled at her and said he would close his eyes; he promised. He wouldn't peek.

He didn't ask why she couldn't get out of the tub by herself, a thirteen-year-old girl. He knew. Together they conspired to try to keep their secret from their parents. Their mother hardly left the bed now. Usually their father was seeing about the fields or the fences when it was time for Cat to creep down the steps for school. They didn't walk anymore to the bus stop. Donny rode his bicycle all the way to school, with Cat sitting on the seat over the back wheel. The steps up the school bus were far too high, and she didn't want the other children to see that Donny had to help her. One day, when they stood at the top of the five steps from their porch going down to the yard, and they were late, Donny said, "Just let me carry you down."

"All right," she said, because she knew it took almost a minute for her to navigate each step.

He had swooped her up and whispered, "Just think of Rhett Butler carrying Scarlett up the steps to rape her."

The laughter had just burst out of her. Donny and she had never said the word *rape* before. But while he pedaled furiously along the highway, and she could barely hold on, she cursed her body. She cursed her hands, not her increasingly useless legs. She couldn't afford to offend the legs, but the hands ought to be reliable. She cursed her hands because they barely had enough strength to hold on safely, and she didn't want to tell Donny.

Sometimes, when she sat by the fire reading and struggled to turn a page, she saw him staring at her. He couldn't wipe the worry off his face fast enough.

Once in school, Mr. Whitlock, her science teacher, asked her if she would mind carrying a note down the hall to another teacher. She smiled reassuringly, but said, "I have a stomachache today. Maybe somebody else would be better." He looked at her peculiarly but said nothing in reply.

At the end of the period, he came and stood by her desk. He asked anxiously, "Are you feeling better now, Catherine?" She answered as brightly as anyone could, "Oh yes! Thank you." But he continued to stare at her. "You're one of our best students," he said. "Let me know if there's ever anything bothering you. We could talk. I know your mother's ill."

He was a washed-out-looking man, with clear plastic eyeglass frames and a girlish, Cupid's bow upper lip. His eyes were so kind that she thought she'd never seen anyone so handsome. Even in college, she sometimes dreamed about Mr. Whitlock. *We could talk,* he always said in her dreams. She had heard that he had gone back to school, gotten a Ph.D. in biology, taught at Florence State in northern Alabama, was the father of five children.

"Thank you," she had replied, back at the consolidated school. "Could you just give me a hand up?" And he had held out his hand to her, helped her stand, didn't say another word. She tried to walk straight, but just at the door, she lost her balance and swiped against the doorframe. But she didn't fall. She didn't fall.

On the bicycle ride home, a truck came too close to them, and she jerked away. She came off the back of the bicycle into a ditch, and then Donny and the bicycle careened off the road, too. She could see that he didn't have to fall. He'd wrecked to keep her company. The truck driver, a frightened farm woman, had stopped. The woman was crying. When she saw they weren't bleeding, she cried harder.

Donny told her just to let him put the bike in the back, the wheel was bent. To please drive them home. On the way home, she apologized, offered repeatedly to pay to have the bike fixed, thanked God that they weren't seriously hurt.

Then Cat had spoken up. "I may be hurt. Could you take us to the doctor instead? I'd like to talk to him, at least. Just for a precaution. I might be hurt internally."

Donny put his arm around her. He looked at her like the perfect big brother. "Really, Cat?" he asked.

"No," the woman said. "We're almost at your place now. We'll let your folks decide if you should go to the doctor." She turned off the two-lane onto the long driveway back to the house.

When they got to the house, Donny told Cat he would carry her inside.

"I'll leave the bike," he said to the woman, "so you can have it repaired."

Then he opened the truck door and slid to the ground. Cat scootched over to the edge of the seat and fell toward his outstretched arms. He turned around, hiked her up, once, higher into his arms, and carried her up the steps. As soon as they got inside, he set her on the sofa.

"I'm going to start lifting weights," he said ruefully.

"Do," she said. The glance of conspiracy passed between them. Almost she wished he would speak out. Almost she wished he would ask if they should tell somebody, and then they would talk about who to tell. But he didn't. He sat down beside her on the green sofa, and they both stared silently straight ahead. They both knew she was getting around with increasing difficulty, but they wouldn't admit it. Not out loud. On the bad mornings, she pretended to be too sick for one reason or another to appear at school. Donny would pick up her homework assignments. She never fell behind.

From the sofa they heard their mother snoring. Sometimes she groaned in her sleep.

"When I catch my breath," Donny said, "I'll carry you to your bedroom. When it's supper, I'll bring you a plate. I'll clean up the kitchen and fix something for supper. Try to rest."

"Thank you," she said.

That night, while she ate her baked beans with cut-up hot dogs, she heard her brother and father talking in the kitchen, over their supper. Although she was propped up in bed, with her dinner plate on her lap, she almost felt she was with them. She could hear Dad and Donny pull out their chairs. Soon, she imagined, Donny would ask in his stiff, polite way *How was your day?*

"There's something wrong with Sister," her brother said. Cat couldn't believe what she was hearing. "Her legs are weak."

"She spends too much time over them books," her father said. "Even when she's sick."

"That's not it," she heard Donny say. Staring at the tines of her fork piercing a segment of hot dog, she listened intently. She was terrified and grateful. There was a desperate, insistent note in Donny's voice, one she'd never heard before. "There's something making her weaker and weaker."

"She's not a sissy," their father answered. "She'll be all right."

No! She thought to Donny. *Don't believe it.*

"Like Mother?" Donny asked. His voice was shrill. "Like Mother, when you said the lump in her breast was too little to worry about?"

"You speak with respect," their father said. "Or I'll wear you out. You're not too big."

"Listen to me!" It sounded as though Donny might cry.

"You always was one to get worked up over nothing."

She heard Donny's chair scrape back. "All right," he said. "All right. I'll call the doctor about Sister and make an appointment. I'll ask the science teacher to drive us. He's worried about her, even if you're not. He asked me about her.

He said she couldn't write fast and he gave the class extra time to finish their last test so she could finish."

Catherine was mortified. Her cheeks flamed with blushing. She hadn't realized that Mr. Whitlock had extended the test time. Plenty of people beside her were still writing, even after he called time. *No!* she thought. Donny was just making that up to impress their father. *Mr. Whitlock hadn't noticed.*

"Don," their father said, and he sounded calm. "Y'all almost got runned over. It's natural to be upset. Just sit down, son. Let's finish our supper. Don't talk loud. You might wake your mother up."

"I'll *tell* Mother," Donny said, "if you don't agree to schedule a checkup for Cat." But his voice was calm.

Cat rested her fork in the baked beans. *Don't be harsh,* she thought. They knew how hard their father worked. Sometimes they talked about all the things he had to do while they were in school. They always ended by saying *He's doing the very best he can.* It was like saying amen at the end of a prayer. They both loved their father.

"I was planning to anyway," their father said. "But your mother hasn't got too much longer. She's too sick to let on now about Cat. I was trying to wait."

"How much longer?" Donny asked, and he sounded as though he was five years old.

It was just the question Cat had wanted to ask. *Mother? How long?* And she felt the tears gushing down her cheeks. She tried not to sob so she could hear the answer.

She couldn't hear, but she heard Donny sob and fight for his breath, get up from his chair, run through the living room and outside.

Then she heard the slow, heavy tread of her father coming to her room.

Then he was at the door.

"Catherine," he said softly. "Are you asleep?"

She closed her eyes and tried to pretend, but her chest was heavy, and the plate was tilting.

"Catherine," he said, alarmed. "Can't you get your breath?"

She opened her eyes and said, "How's Mother?"

He sat down on the bed, and it dipped deeply under his weight. He took her hand. "Catherine, don't pretend." He paused. "I tried to pretend your mother would have a miracle. That's what I prayed for. But I have to tell you and Donny. Dr. Higgins says it won't be long now. He says we ought to go to the hospital where they can keep her more comfortable."

Catherine cried till she thought she'd choke and vomit. Her father quietly moved the plate of beans and hot dogs and set it on the plank floor. Then he gathered her into his burly arms.

"For her sake," he said, "we got to bear up. If we can. That's about all you can do for your folks, Cat, when they're dying. Bear up."

Later her father helped her off with her school dress and into her pajamas. While he undressed and dressed her, he closed his eyes, and he averted his face, too. The slow way her father moved his arms—she could tell how sad he was. Tired to the bone.

THAT NIGHT WHEN the house was sleeping, Catherine slid out of her bed onto the floor. She puddled down onto her knees, slowly and softly. Donny had not come home, she was sure of that. But she knew where he was. He was in the barn, in the hayloft. He was covered with hay and warm and sleeping. Even in his dreams, he knew that she knew where he was. Catherine began to crawl toward the sound of her parents' tandem snoring.

Crawling was almost as difficult as walking. It was more unfamiliar and slower. But she couldn't fall when she crawled. She tried grasping the legs of heavy chairs, and she tried to hold on tight and to pull herself toward the chair, but her grip was too weak. In the end, she could do little more than undulate her torso, arch and heave her back forward, like an inchworm.

She heard the mantel clock strike once and knew it was half past some hour.

She was cold on the floor, and wondered, if she *could* regain her feet, if they might not suddenly work, the way they did sometimes, and if she might not walk like a mechanical doll across the room. But she could not hope to regain her feet. The balancing act of stacking bones on top of bones would be too difficult.

The mantel clock cleared its throat and then struck on and on. It must be the number twelve, she thought, clanging through the night. The clock threw out hoops of sound, widening and large as brass Hula-Hoops as they clattered down to the wooden floor. She stretched her hand out to feel the woolly edge of an area rug. She let her fingers stroke its nap as the last bong clattered down. Slowly she wormed her way forward till her whole body was resting on the rug.

Then she worked her way beyond the rug, first her hands and forearms, then her torso, then finally not even her bare toes were on the wool.

The clock struck twelve-thirty: a single bong.

Ahead was the large braided rug in front of the fireplace. *Another island,* she thought. And *I'm swimming over the boards.* Not an island, a continent, and *I will reach the shore.* The embers in the fire grate beckoned to her. A bonfire on the headland, she thought.

The clock struck once again, but she was fatigued and could not remember if it was one or one-thirty. But her fingers touched the scalloped edge of the braided rug. When she reached the middle of the rug, she lay flat and absorbed some of the heat from the fireplace. Perhaps she dozed a little, but when consciousness returned, the dark stillness of the house welcomed her. It was a welcome—her home at night, but still her home—a mysterious welcome of shades of gray and black.

When she reached the side of her mother's bed, she saw her mother's hand hanging limply over the edge. Once she scooted close enough, she reached up easily and took the hand. She could not squeeze but perhaps she could pull. No, her hand slid out of her mother's. Lifting her hand again, Cat fitted the palm of her hand against her mother's palm. She butted the relaxed hand, the way a calf might butt its mother's udder.

Finally, her mother spoke. "Catherine?" she said. Her voice had the texture of a china plate, its glaze crazed with innumerable spider cracks.

"Mama," she whispered. "I can't walk."

"You can't walk?" her mother asked feebly, incredulous, displeased.

"Only sometimes."

Her mother was silent. Catherine waited. She feared her mother might have gone back to sleep. "How are you?" Catherine asked.

Her mother took a long slow breath. It was a smooth breath, and it seemed to Catherine that her mother was pulling air up the slope of a long hill.

"Better," her mother said.

Catherine couldn't find her own words. She didn't know what to think. Finally she heard herself say, "That's good."

"Can you climb up here in the bed?" her mother asked.

"No. I don't think so."

"Then I'll push a pillow off for you. Let's not bother your father. He's so tired."

Her mother paused as though to gather her thoughts.

"I know," Catherine encouraged.

"Crawl under the bed," her mother said. "I'll work the pillow over the edge in a little bit." She breathed three quick breaths, as though she were panting. "You can sleep under the bed till morning. Then we'll see what can be done."

Catherine began a sideways inching toward the bed. When she was parallel to the bedframe, she slowly rolled onto her back. Needing to rest, she lay there beside the long plank of the bedframe and stared at the ceiling. Soon she would scootch sideways till she was under the bed. She wanted to sleep on her back. The soft pillow dropped down on her chest.

"I have it," she said.

Her mother didn't answer.

She was asleep, Catherine supposed. She removed the soft pillow from her chest and slid it under the bed. Already her hands told her how pleasant it would be to rest her head among the feathers. She cocked a leg so that one knee thrust up in the air, and the sole of her foot was flat against the floor. She pushed hard, and again. She visualized her head on the pillow, and all at once the back of her head *was* on the pillow. Cat felt safe under the bed, on her back. It was a house inside the house. A house with a very low ceiling. No one could sit up in such a house. It was for lying down, for resting.

IN THE MORNING, Cat saw her mother's bare legs hanging over the bed. Her nightgown must have hiked up.

"Harvey," her mother said, "come help me get up, please. I want to fix breakfast, and then we need to take Catherine to Dr. Higgins."

"Olivia!" her father said. "Olivia! Do you feel like getting up!" He was excited.

Cat heard his feet hit the floor, and he hurried around the foot of the bed. She saw his pajama legs standing beside her, and his bare feet. Long ago, his little toe had been dislocated and it was reared back in a fleshy curl.

"Just help me," she said. "I've not stood up so long, I'm 'fraid I might fall."

Catherine watched the tips of her mother's toes test the floor, and then the balls of her wan feet settled down, and she flattened the arch and her heels on the boards.

"Now pull," her mother said. "Gently. Not too fast now, Harvey."

Her mother's nightgown unwrinkled and fell down around her ankles, a cascade of white flannel with small blue roses printed all over. Flanking each rose were two tiny green leaves.

"Help me to the chair," her mother said. And she sank softly into it. "I'd like my robe, please." And he got it for her.

From under the bed, Catherine watched the hem of the robe swish by and the swaying tail of its dark green belt; the robe was the quilted maroon satin one that she and Donny had given Mother last Christmas, and the piping on the shawl collar and the deep cuffs was dark green to match the sash. The robe was very lightweight, as though the white batting of the lining was more made of air than of threads.

"Now," her mother said, "help Catherine up." Her father started for the door, but her mother said quickly with a chuckle, "Harvey, she's under the bed."

"What?"

"Look under the bed," and now her mother was laughing a little, as though they'd played a good joke on her father.

Suddenly, his face was upside down, looking at her.

"Well I'll be durned," he said. Then he got down on one knee and reached out both arms. "Just like sliding a drawer out of a chifforobe," he said.

It took two hours, but her mother cooked and they got dressed for town. As they approached the car, Donny came walking from the barn. He slid into the backseat next to Catherine. He patted the back of her hand. She always braced herself now, when she rode in the car: one hand on each side to help her keep her balance.

"I guess we're going to the doctor?" Donny said.

Cat nodded.

"Soon you'll be better."

But Dr. Higgins said he really couldn't tell what was wrong. "Neurological disorder," he said. "Or a different strand of polio."

He advised them to drive on to Carraway Methodist in Birmingham, and he would phone ahead.

"What do you make of Olivia?" her father asked. "Ought she check in, too?"

"See how she feels when you get there," Dr. Higgins answered. He surveyed her through his rimless spectacles held on with slender silver wires that ran from the lenses to curve around the backs of his ears. "Looks to me like Olivia's in a remission."

SO THE BIRMINGHAM DOCTORS began their tests to determine the cause of Catherine's debilitating weakness and lack of balance. The family sold the farm after a few months and moved to the city. Don was going on nineteen; he graduated from high school in the country and then started college in Birmingham. "I'll borrow the money," he quietly told his father. "They'll let me." He spoke with enough emphasis to cause his father suddenly to focus again on his son.

Cat was fourteen. They tried resting her in an iron lung. They tried hydrotherapy.

With her new silver crutches, she walked in the front door of Phillips High School, her brother and her father on either side of her, walking slowly. At home, Mother studied the house to make things more and more convenient for Catherine. "Why don't you saw the legs off the bed?" she asked Don, "and then Cat can get in by herself." And Don had said, "I'll hang a trapeze from the ceiling, too, for her to hold to." Their father worked all night at his night watchman job and slept most of the day. On Sundays, sometimes, they would drive back to the country and visit with family or friends they used to know.

A month before their first Birmingham Christmas, the Cartwright men left the females in the car to ask the board of their old church to help them buy a wheelchair for Catherine. Not that she would use it all the time, but just when they had a distance to cover. Cat could imagine what they had said almost as if she had been present and listening.

"So she can go shopping," her father would have said wistfully to the minister, just as if they had enough loose money for the daughter of the family to shop for fun.

The minister would want to know what was wrong with Catherine, and what they would do with the wheelchair when she got better.

Donny would speak up and say, "She's not going to get better. She'll get slowly worse." He would tell the truth.

"Why what's wrong with her?" the minister would ask.

Father would look helplessly at Donny, who would explain, "They don't understand it, but it has a name—Friedreich's ataxia."

"It's rare," their father would add.

(Later, Don told Catherine, with just a whiff of irony in his voice, that their father took strange comfort in that fact. "He told the minister," Don said, " 'She has a rare disease that's got a name and that's all. They don't have any cure yet.' ")

When Christmas was only a week away, Mother told Cat and Father that she didn't want to give Don but one thing for Christmas, and it would be in the toe of his stocking. She asked if they could guess what that gift might be. Catherine was shocked by the question, but she knew if she just sat in the wheelchair and waited a moment, from deep in her psyche the answer would come. "Wait," she said to her mother. "Let me think."

She thought about the essence of her mother, and the phrase "the bowels of compassion" came to her. She thought of Donny, and the term was "self-sacrificing."

Suddenly she reached down and released the brakes of her chair. In case she broke down and cried, *before* she cried, she wanted to be able to make a fast getaway.

"It's a key," she said. "A key for a little apartment all his own. Let's do it." And she wheeled away.

"He can't afford any apartment," their father was saying.

"Yes, he can," her mother said. "I've found one, and it's close by. It has a Murphy bed in the wall, so it's just one room and a kitchenette and a bath."

Catherine made it into the kitchen, where she took deep, long breaths to try to control her panic.

Faintly, she heard her mother's continuing explanation. "Don's going to get an after-school job, and he can use the money to pay the rent. After we get him started, help him just one month."

"I thought he wanted to save for a car," the father said.

"No," she answered. "He can ride the bus. He needs a place of his own. I won't have him sacrificing his life to us."

That night, Catherine lay in her bed and listened to the city noises. She liked it when a siren shrieked. Maybe it was for her. Maybe it was coming to save her. The tears rolled out of her eyes. That her brother needed to leave home, that he *had* to leave home! She felt ashamed. She felt the cup of herself filling with loneliness. Never for a minute did she want him not to have his own place. For the first time, she thought, *I hate my body, I hate it.* Then she told herself, *It's not me. It's not the real me. The real me is my mind and my spirit.*

She knew how it would be on Christmas morning. Don would go to his red-and-white peppermint-striped Christmas stocking. (Her own was winter-green and white.) He would see that it was mostly limp, but with a pointy weight in the toe. When he reached in, he would not believe what his fingers told him without seeing, but when he drew out the key, he would know, he would know immediately, and his face would ignite into the happiest smile she had ever seen.

There was a fire someplace in the city, and she heard the clanging of a bell added to the howl of a siren. *Keep them safe*, she prayed. Staring at the ceiling, she wondered where God was in her life. The ceiling promised nothing for them, for her. She felt that she needed an afterlife; that after this *thwarting*, she deserved to have something and not nothing. All her life she would be robbed, increasingly, of her power. Then she thought in biblical terms, not to God, but to her body, *I will contend with thee.*

When the real Christmas Day came, Cat saw a mysterious, loopy bulge in her own stocking. It seemed ridged like a skein of stiff rope or starched yarn. Mother unhooked the stocking from the mantel and handed it to her. She drew out an extension cord, looped like a figure eight, tying itself in the middle.

"It's the electric cord to your new typewriter," her mother said.

"Look, Sister," Don said, holding the brass door key in his hand. He gestured toward where their father was standing. Father whisked off a Christmas tablecloth, and there near the window was a low, handmade table. It had a stained and varnished plywood surface with a large cutout, so a person in a wheelchair could drive right into her desk. And on the table-top sat a big electric typewriter. Electric! How she had labored to form legible letters for her essays. On an electric keyboard, you barely had to push down.

"You can write your school papers on it," her mother said.

AFTER THEY WERE SETTLED in the city, after both Cat and Don had finished their freshman years in high school and in college, their mother suddenly and unexpectedly died in her bed.

Looking for comfort, his face bathed in tears, her father said, "She had her remission. She got that. She got her remission." Then he asked Cat to phone Donny. "You've got to tell him," he said. "I can't."

AFTER HER MOTHER'S DEATH, Catherine tried again to love her body—her mother had. She tried to believe that human beings were a holy trinity—body, mind, and soul. It was easy to believe in the last two, but was she really this person who spilled things and lost her balance, who bumped into things, who couldn't get up without a heroic effort, who dreaded the ordeal of getting on and off a toilet?

Murmuring compliments, she tried to bribe her body. Not only to appease it with lotions, but also to value and flatter her good points: her nice eyes, after all, were a part of her body. And her lips were nice—pleasantly full. Her hair could look shiny, if not curled in the latest flip style. She had tried the pink plastic cage curlers; she had tried the soft blue sponge ones with the white clip bar, but neither type was manageable. Her ears were small and delicate—"like seashells," her mother used to say. And she was a straight-A student—but with that consoling thought, she was slipping away from the body inventory into the realm of the mind. Well, she had a fine brain for thinking, if haywire in the motor control department.

In her bedroom, each morning, she sat before the long dime-store mirror hung low on the wall and started again: "You have nice eyes, bright blue, and the eyebrows are arched naturally in a pretty peak." She smiled at herself. "Keep your lips closed, so the slight gap between the front two teeth doesn't show." Rolling closer to the mirror, she inspected the mossiness on her teeth near the gum line and wished they made electric toothbrushes.

Even in college, she kept up the ritual of addressing herself in the morning, of saying something positive to her body to start the day. The day of graduation, she told herself, "You did it, you gorgeous woman! You earned a college degree." And Stella would come over to help her put on the black robe over her dress. When she and Stella got jobs teaching at the night school, she told the mirror, "You are a gainfully employed human being. You are an adult."

But the morning after the bullhorn man had threatened, she looked in the mirror and said, "You are a sniveling coward." It was morning, but she knew she could not go back. Not that night. Yes, she got her period, but she wasn't flooding, as she told Stella she was. She was afraid. "You talk big," she told her seated self. "But you are trembling, and it's only ten o'clock in the morning. You're afraid not that you'll be shot through the window but that you'll wet yourself."

She stared hard at herself and at the objects in her bedroom reflected in the narrow mirror. The room was very sparsely furnished, because she needed so much room to maneuver. Even if she had a comfortable, overstuffed chair in the room for reading, it would be too much trouble to get in and out of it. Though she never used them anymore, she looked at her crutches over in the corner. She decided to ask Stella to take them out, to replace them in the corner with a nice vase, and to put peacock feathers in the vase.

She missed her mother and thought of her grave near the little country church she had always loved. They had chosen a grave site near the cemetery driveway, so Catherine wouldn't have to get out of the car to visit it. Viewing the nearly vacant room, she missed her mother ferociously. Her mother wouldn't want her to risk her life to educate what she called "coloreds." For all her loving kindness, her mother had thought the races were different and should be separate, except where "necessity" dictated otherwise. "You can't hardly build two separate cities," her mother had said. "You've got to share electricity and water and things."

The room was full of sunshine, but it wasn't too hot yet. Donny had given her a new kind of blanket—a thermal blanket for fall—and it was very lightweight. In the mirror, Cat contemplated the bed. She used the loose-woven white cotton blanket as a spread, and she loved how modern it was. That it could be tossed into the washer and dryer and never needed to be ironed.

When she looked again into her own smart and mild blue eyes, she knew she saw fear. And it was not fear of wetting. She wanted to live. Suppose this was all there was to life? Sunshine and an almost empty room, a bed with a new-washed thermal blanket, smoothly made up. If that was all there could be to life—a certain domestic beauty and convenience—it was enough, and she would keep it as long as she could.

I will contend with thee, she promised the image of her seated self, the young woman in the wheelchair filling the lower third of the long mirror. *Neither disease nor danger will rob me of what's left.*

Then as clearly as though he were there, she heard Donny saying, "And what is life without honor?" In her mind's eye, she saw him walking the beach of his South Pacific island; he was wearing a sarong, his chest was bare, held high, covered with golden hair. So clear was the image, it seemed as though she were watching a movie. Donny had a walking staff in his hand, the kind you could cut in Alabama, one shaped by a twining vine into a baroque spiral, and she wondered where her old walking stick was, the one her father had brought to her when he had first noticed and yet denied the onset of her clumsy disease. With the beach sand in the background, Donny stopped walking, and skeptically said, "And what is life without honor?"

I'll go back tomorrow night, she promised herself. *Not tonight, but tomorrow night. A little compromise with death. I promise you,* she told her image, *I'll go back tomorrow night.*

And she would spend the day as an activist in her own cause and in the cause of people like herself. She rolled herself toward the living room and the typewriter. She would type a letter to the managers of each movie theater in town suggesting that they remove a few seats (perhaps in the back?) so that wheelchair patrons could sit in the row in their own chairs, so that two women could go to a movie together and not need a brother or father to lift one of them into a seat. She would write to the three city commissions (racists all, of one stripe or another) and suggest they not *discriminate* against wheelchair users of the public streets downtown, that at the busiest corners they make cuts in the curbs, little ramps, so that, unaided, people in wheelchairs might roll themselves from the corners of Pizitz or Loveman's to other stores across the street.

She would tell them that she was the president of a new group; she named it Access Available. As she laboriously rolled the typing paper into the platen, she thought that there really could be such a group. She would talk to handicapped people she'd met at Spain Rehab. Once the roller grasped the paper, she could press the Load button. She could go to the waiting rooms of hospitals and recruit other handicapped persons. *And I'll bet nobody would want to shoot us,* she thought. *And none of us would be packing switchblades or guns.*

With her hands suspended over the keyboard, she suddenly remembered her father had brought her a gun of her own. If she went back tomorrow night, she need not go defenseless. She could carry her gun.

five

SEED PEOPLE, September 1964

DEAR DONNY,

OUR KITTY-CAT WAS SICK THIS EVENING—NOTHING SERI-
ous, she'll be fine tomorrow—but I went out to Miles and taught anyway.
Without incident. But that is not what I want to write about. I'm sitting up in
my bed at my aunts' to write to you. Everything is quiet, and I have been looking forward to this moment. I have plumped up two pillows and have them at
my back. I write in a kind of still heat. I hope you are painting, at least small
watercolors. Lots of green. An ocean breeze.

What I want to write you about are my mother's flowers, when I was five.
Not her flower garden, for she didn't have one, but just the flowers that came
up perennially scattered around the yard in their designated spots.

I start with the yellow of the New Year. Beside the front steps, when I
lived next door, at the top, on either side were scraggly forsythia bushes.
They were never allowed to grow large, and I always felt sorry for them,
pruned into little square footstools. But on the side of the house was
another forsythia, growing on the bank that led down to the sunken, red-
clay driveway. And that bush grew in a lovely golden arch, close to the
ground. Once when I was mad at the family, I hid inside that golden cave,
and no one could find me. So strange to see their feet go by on the little dirt
path, not twelve inches from my eyes. I was both in the world and not in it,
for they had no consciousness of me. Is that like being dead?

I don't know, but it was thrilling.

In a way, I died when my family died. Sometimes the driveway is like the

Lethe River: having crossed over from one house to the other, I forget what it was to be alive.

Also, on our bank were irises, deep purple, lavender, and white. They came back strongly each spring (still do, from my vantage point now on the other side of the driveway). I loved their stalwart stems and the spearhead buds as much as the unfolded flowers. Yet surely the shape of the iris flower, with three upright standards and three falls is among the most satisfying of all flower shapes. The fleur-de-lis. Why is there such satisfaction in shapes? Perhaps you, as an artist, can tell me. And in the case of iris, the large *size* makes the beautiful structure more accessible.

You left Norwood for Tonga so quickly after our engagement that, of course, we scarcely know each other in terms of the deeper recesses of the mind. I treasure our one opera outing, though, and how we identified with the bird catcher. I imagine you now among orchids, their lavender petals lolling obscenely at your bare shoulder. I like our agreement *not* to know one another and to write only once a month. That thrills me! That we are committed and yet barely acquainted, except through Cat.

It is the *indulgence* of writing this letter that thrills me. That you are with me, listening, and yet of course that is illusion, since time must be bridged and transport accomplished before you read, and then I shall be in another place and time, not sitting propped up on pillows, on a loosely woven, lime green cotton spread. Yet we *seem* to be together in this moment. And I make you up. Yes, I know I do. I have imagined you. Now! You're not real! Boo! (That's just a playful taunt. If you, whoever you are, read this: then you are real.)

Such magic in language, as much as in painting!

From the flower kingdom of my childhood, I've given you forsythia in two locations and irises in three colors, dear friend. Almost Monet! Also imagine on the top of the slope between the house and red clay driveway, three weak pink rosebushes. They struggle for enough light, their soil is thin, and they're never given fertilizer. We are proud of them when they bloom each summer; Mother and I (age five) are pleased with the few puffy blooms that we do get, and they, with stems almost too weak to hold them upright, are lovingly snipped and brought inside for the dining room table.

These roses are not like the small, superabundant ones of the tennis court—the Norwood tennis court where I play, sometimes, with Nancy, my friend since age three. The tennis court roses are fantastically robust, multitudinous, the stems sprouting billions of stiff thorns. At home, our pink roses have spare thorns, big limp, loose blooms. We prop the chins of our roses on the rim of a tall, clear drinking glass.

In kindergarten, a teacher brought glasses with thick bottoms to class for us to decorate with sharp holly leaves and berries as Christmas gifts for our parents. How *thrilled* I was to get to create something beautiful and useful for my parents. I guess I thought they would share the one glass. It amazed me that the teacher brought in the glasses by the carton. We looked down into the open box and saw the cardboard partitions and the open rims of the glasses looking up at us, like so many fish waiting to be fed. Which to choose? They were without individuality. I chose the one from the middle of the grid—that was where I myself wanted to be: in the middle of things, surrounded by kindred spirits.

Anyway, one child pulled out a broken glass (from a corner position) and badly cut her hand. It was a terrible baptism of blood over all those pristine glasses. Not over my box, but another, and I saw the blood on the glasses.

What an awful image. Why do I write to you of the joy of forsythia, iris, and rose and then of blood?

Because I must display myself to you. We *must* be known to each other, and we have made a terrible mistake to think that mere acquaintance is enough. Because I must display my mind, like a bouquet of stalwart irises, emerging forsythia, and weak-stemmed roses, if you are to know me and thus care about my fate. Isn't that what we all ardently want? To be known? *And it is possible.*

I learned it at Miles. (Sometimes I call it *Courage College*.) There is no "other." We are all the same. Knowable. Last night at school we had a threat, but tonight everything went smoothly. No shattered glass, no bloody melee.

Don, I want to pray tonight for safety and wisdom. How far to go in working for change? When to stop? And I need to stop writing.

Dogwood! That was the tree my mother loved most. Ours was scrawny but glorious with white blossoms.

HE DOESN'T

WHILE AGNES DROVE HOME, SHE FEARED A CARLOAD OF white men might be following her. At one corner, she took an unexpected turn. When they went straight, she was relieved, but a few blocks later, they were behind her again. She tried not to think about it. *Just don't go down any dark alleys,* she told herself. *You be all right.* She knew sometimes a Negro was followed and nothing happened. It was their way of keeping people off balance.

It wasn't usual to see a car full of white men in the Miles neighborhood. Surely they didn't object to a harmless middle-aged woman trying to get a GED. Maybe they didn't see it that way. Maybe they were part of the bullhorn gang.

Well, her car was cooled off enough, she could roll up the window.

Wrong about that! Within two blocks, the car was an oven without any fresh air. At the next stop sign, she reached her hand down in her shopping bag to pull out a Jesus fan. It was the Good Shepherd, her favorite. She drove with one hand and fanned with the other. Occasionally she glanced in the rearview mirror.

Still there, but farther back. Or maybe that was a different car. It was dropping on back, *thank the Lord.*

She wished she could have books to take home to study on. She missed the science class, and she hoped Miss Cat was all right. Those words for the bones were hard to remember, except the upper arm bone, the humerus. The funny bone, Miss Cat had said. She was a good teacher. But it was Miss Stella who was the fanatic. She just went over and over the lesson. *Not, he "don't." Instead, he "doesn't."* Miss Stella said, "I know it doesn't sound right to you. But if we say it over and over, it will start to sound right. You've just got to memorize it for now, and trust me."

Just young girls but they were trying to help out. Agnes decided to step on the gas a little more. *I'll just widen the gap.* But she couldn't restrain her toe, how it wanted to press down, press down. The tree trunks on the sides of the street were zipping by in a blur.

Suddenly their brights were bouncing into the mirror and into her eyes. She heard them gun the engine, gather speed. They might try to make her run into a tree.

"Lord Jesus," she said aloud. "Into thy hands." And she gripped the steering wheel. She put on the brake, as though it could stop this from happening.

Noise big as a freight train, horn blaring they bore down on her.

And swerved safely around.

Her car shuddered to a dead halt. Their red taillights were disappearing down the dark street. They were putting on the gas. Speeding away. She hadn't been shot. No eggs or nothing thrown on the car. They were just gone.

"Thank you, Jesus."

But she was shaking. Both feet were on the brake pedal. She'd killed the motor. As fast as she could, she pressed in the clutch, turned the key, gave a little gas. Not to flood, Lord, not to flood. And she was slowly letting out the clutch, and she was moving forward. As she drove, she cautiously swept her head from side to side. *Sweep clean, sweep clean. They done gone. Swing low, sweet chariot.*

In ten minutes, she would be home. TJ would be at work, but she'd call her neighbor to come over and sit with her till her nerves quieted. Maggie would read the Bible and pray with her. Then they'd get to talking about church or sewing circle. They'd drink ice tea and stir it round with the long-handled teaspoons. Her hands were sweating so bad, the steering wheel was slippery. Maggie and she would have a nice evening till bedtime. She'd go right to sleep; she always did, and she'd wake up to TJ making a pot of coffee.

Honestly, she didn't care if the world changed or not. The white people she had always known were good enough. They spoke softly, cherished politeness. But now these strange, mean ones coming out of the woodwork. She just wanted to get her education and then a new job. She rolled her window down to get a breath of night air. God would make society change in his own good time. In the meantime, it was getting a good job that mattered. She would better herself. Let other folks better themselves, if they had the gumption. She rolled the window down six inches. Some kind of job for her to add to TJ's and they'd work and save maybe twenty more years, retire, and then they'd be done. She didn't want to cause trouble.

"You-all barking up the wrong tree," she said out loud to the empty street before her.

WHEN SHE GOT HOME, TJ opened the door before she could get out her key.

His face was troubled. Sad.

She put her arms around him. *But what was wrong?* Then he took her hand and led her to the sofa.

"Are you all right, darling?" he asked her.

"Just fine."

"Two things happened this afternoon," he said. He held up two fingers in a V, as though she couldn't count. She reached out and caught his hand in hers. She brought his two knuckles to her lips and kissed them.

"One was that I tried to register to vote this afternoon. I went down with the redheaded white man who spoke at church. Mr. Green."

"Did you make it?" She felt a rush of pride and hope.

"No. I failed to put a comma between the day and the year. I can try again in a month."

"That's not so bad," she said. And then it just blurted out of her, "Did you get to the part to put down our address?"

"Yes," he said. His voice was solid and polished. It reminded her of hickory wood—strong and smooth. Just what it was, nothing fancy. She loved him almost to idolatry.

"Let's go on to bed, then," she said. "I got mixed up and thought you'd be at work tonight. I'm tired out." She glanced at him to see if she might tell now. "I had a little scare," she added.

"Wait," he said. "There was two things I gots to tell you. Number two is this evening I lost my job."

"TJ!"

He didn't speak. While he just looked into her eyes, she found an answering awareness rising in her. He was the steadiest man in the world. It had never crossed her mind to worry that he might lose his job. And then the two pieces of news ticked like a clock in her brain: vote, job. Tried to vote; lost his job.

" 'Cause you tried to register?" she said.

"I believe so."

"That fast?"

"Let's sit on the sofa," he said. Still holding her hand, he took her to the couch. "They all connected, these white people. I put down where I worked. I had to."

"Bankhead Hotel—why'd they *say* you let go?" She was relieved to be off her feet.

"They say . . ." He paused to gather the story in his mind. He always took his time, Agnes thought. Got things straight, told it true. He licked his lips and spoke quietly, staring at the floor. "First, Mr. Armstrong say, 'We want a younger man.' And I say, 'I'm a veteran. I done fought two wars.' And then Mr. Armstrong say, 'That's what I told Mr. McCormick.' And I say, 'You question him?' 'Yes, I did,' he says. I just look at him and he look at me, and the whole thing start to dawn on me. Then I say, 'I'd like to speak to Mr. McCormick. He in?' And Mr. Armstrong say, 'I phone upstairs and tell him. I don't know, but I'll tell him.' Meanwhile I straighten my tie, shine my shoes just like I'm going on the job. Then Mr. McCormick himself come busting through the door, talking 'fore I can say anything. He say, 'I know you fought, TJ, and got honorable discharge, but I can't have any nigras what want to stir up trouble. Now if you want to take a week off to think, and then come back, you might get your job back.' "

Agnes squeezed his arm, "Well, it'll be all right then."

"What I said to him: 'Well, reckon this is good-bye then. After ten years and never a minute late and never a day sick.' And I walked out."

Agnes uncoiled like a jack-in-the-box. She threw herself on her husband and covered his face with kisses. "Oh, honey, oh, honey," she said over and over. "I just so proud of you." She commenced to sob. She put her head down on her knees and sobbed like the dam had broken. He rubbed her back, gently pressed into her muscles with his fingertips. Finally she looked up, her face running with tears, and said, "I married me a man. I didn't marry no nigger."

IN THE BASEMENT

WHEN GLORIA FINALLY DESCENDED THE FEW STEPS INTO
Christine's dim apartment, Gloria saw a woman sitting at the wooden kitchen
table, with four cans of beer in front of her. Her hair was combed up straight
and held erect by a tortoiseshell barrette. A little girl was perched on a stool at
the table, reading in the subdued golden light.

Christine said, "Dee, I want you to meet my friend Gloria."

"Howdy do," Gloria said quickly.

But Dee did not acknowledge her. "I think I'll just take me a little nap," Dee
said. She put an arm down on the table and plopped her head on her arm.

"And this is my daughter, Diane," Christine said to Gloria. Christine's voice
hurried from embarrassment for her sister's rudeness into pride in her daughter. "Diane's smart as a whip."

Diane turned her book facedown on the table and left her perch to
approach them. She led with her forehead, wide and clear of hair. The light
caught the curve of her forehead oddly and made it look like a single car light.
Unconscious of her shining forehead, Diane held out her hand. "Howdy do,
Miss Gloria," she said, and smiled brightly.

"I'll just check on the boys," Christine said.

Little Diane's lovely face made Gloria breathe carefully. Diane appeared as
Christine might have been as a child. Here was intelligence unsullied by bitterness; goodwill undistorted by hardship.

"What are you reading?" Gloria asked quietly, not to disturb Dee.

"About a horse."

Suddenly Gloria knelt, as though her knees had given way, and held out her arms to Christine's daughter. Diane walked straight into Gloria's embrace.

"Well, I see y'all done made friends," Christine said as she walked back into the kitchen.

Pressing Diane to her bosom, Gloria felt as though she'd entered the stable, as though she was beholding a sacred child, the future incarnate that must not be sullied. That must not suffer the degradation of segregation. She held Diane back at arm's length to look again at her face.

Diane accepted her gaze with perfect equanimity.

Gloria had never seen such beautiful skin, such glowing eyes. Diane's lips parted a little, as though she might speak, but she did not. The slightly scalloped tips of her new big-girl teeth showed.

"I used to read dog and horse stories," Gloria said. She got her feet under her and stood up. She spoke to Christine. "I learned more lessons from them than from the Bible."

"Girl!" Christine said and frowned slightly.

"I did," Gloria affirmed. "I learned to be loyal and brave. To suffer and endure. To have a steel will."

"Didn't know you had a steel will," Christine teased.

"But I do."

Gloria wondered if Christine had forgotten her own meltdown when the church was bombed, how it was Gloria who stood strong. But it was fine with Gloria if Christine had forgotten. As though standing between the pews again, Gloria felt herself a witness to fact: the face of Christ had disappeared, had been blasted out of the window. His glass-thick body was veiled in dust; his radiance muted.

Diane returned to the table, picked up her book again, and instantly lost herself in her story. Her eyes moved hungrily across the sentences on the page; Diane had absented herself from the conversation of the women. The ceiling light off, only a small lamp on the kitchen cook table illumined the pages of the open book.

"If I could paint," Gloria said quietly, indicating Diane, "I'd paint her picture. *Negro Girl with Her Book.* Or maybe, *Reading at the Kitchen Table.*"

"Dee," Christine said softly. "You asleep or playin' possum?"

Dee's face was turned from them, and Gloria couldn't tell.

"It's all right if she needs to sleep," Gloria said. She looked at the four cans of beer and wondered if *Passed Out* ought also to be included in the picture. *Passed Out Cold, with Niece Reading.* Social realism, a bit of squalor. Probably it was Dee who wanted soft lamplight to assist her slide into oblivion.

"I don't ever drink at home," Christine explained. "It's not good for kids to see."

Gloria marveled that Christine would reveal the idea while her daughter was in the room, even if she did seem absorbed in reading.

"Not what you say to kids," Christine went on. "It's what they see you doing."

For a moment, Gloria had no reply. She felt again that she was visiting a stable. There ought to be straw on the table or in a chair.

"I feel like Christmas," Gloria said. What should she call this place where she was? Apartment? Sounded belittling. House? It wasn't the whole house. She found the word and tipped it into the waiting sentence, without emphasis: "Your home makes me marvel."

"Christmas in this hot weather?"

Gloria smiled. "Now don't be a doubter."

"You like a sandwich, or a cookie? Glass of lemonade?"

"Lemonade, please. It's lots cooler in here than outside."

Christine took a package of lemonade-flavor Kool-Aid from a drawer. She got down a pudgy glass pitcher, tore back the top of the envelope, and dumped in the powder. While she ran tap water into the pitcher, Christine asked, "What you think of Mr. Parrish?"

It was on Gloria's lips to say *Oh, he's fine,* but she realized the question wasn't entirely casual. "Well," Gloria answered, "he said he wanted to talk, but then he didn't have much to say."

"I think he trusts us." Christine looked pleased and happy.

"Does Diane like school?" It was strange to speak of someone present as though she were absent, but the lamplight enfolded Gloria in its own kingdom. In the basement, space seemed partitioned by an invisible curtain; within each fold might reside a world with its story.

"She reads Dick and Jane at school. At home, she reads *Black Beauty* and *Mrs. Wiggs of the Cabbage Patch.*"

Diane looked up. "They both have horses in them," she said.

I could take her to visit the country, Gloria thought, but did she want Diane to see a bull dominate the bars of a stock rack? In her reading, Diane was claiming a world where animals were more honorable than people. "I used to want a horse so bad," Gloria said.

"Did you get one?" Diane asked. Her bright, calm face tilted up toward Gloria. Diane waited serenely to hear either yes or no, ready to build a world on either answer.

"Eventually, I did," Gloria said. "But it stays out in the country."

"How did you get it?" Diane asked. She closed her book.

Christine cracked an ice tray into the pitcher and stirred the lemonade with a wooden spoon.

"Aunt Dee," Diane asked softly, "would you like some lemonade?"

"I think she's resting," Gloria answered. "I got a horse by learning to play the cello."

"What is a cello?" Diane asked.

"It's like a big violin, but you hold it between your knees to play. My mother said it would be just like riding a horse to play a cello. Then she said if I learned to play the cello, they'd talk about getting me a horse."

"How old were you?"

"I was nine or ten."

"Am I six or seven?" Diane asked her mother.

"No, you're just one or the other," Christine answered. She smiled at her daughter, as though they were playing a game of secret logic.

"I mean," Gloria said, "I can't remember if I was nine or if I was ten."

"I was telling Diane about Schrödinger's cat," Christine said.

Gloria felt the room tilt strangely. "What do you mean?"

"You know. In physics."

"I know about angular momentum," Diane said proudly. *Angular momentum*, perfectly pronounced. Diane explained, "If your arms are stuck out, and the fire hose hits one shoulder, and you start to spin, you can spin faster if you bring your arms in. And then you can use your arms, too, to protect your breasts. Or chest."

Gloria sipped her lemonade. "Maybe you ought to teach science instead of English," she said to Christine. *Breasts?* Gloria had never heard a child of six or seven freely use the word *breasts*.

"I teach Diane everything I know," Christine said.

Dee snorted from the table and then began to snore.

"I'd like to learn how to ride a horse," Diane said.

"Who rode horseback across Europe during the Crusades?" Christine asked the child.

"Eleanor of Aquitaine."

"Maybe animals are disguises for angels," Gloria said. The room righted itself, and they stared silently at her.

Diane suddenly went to open a freestanding metal cabinet, a dish cupboard, but the bottom three shelves were messy with toys. The highest of the three shelves was Diane's, and she took out a white doll. "Her name is Eleanor," Diane said. Then she got out a small horse from one of her brother's shelves. Although the doll, dressed in a short, fur-trimmed ice-skating outfit and wearing boots with skates attached, was twelve inches high, and the horse no more than three, Diane placed the horse between the doll's feet to make Eleanor ride the horse. "She's riding across France," Diane said.

"Where is France?" Gloria asked skeptically.

"In Europe. Between Spain and Germany."

Propelled by Diane's hand, the big ice-skating doll rode the little horse across the kitchen table. Diane made clicking noises with her tongue and teeth to sound like hoofbeats. The horse trotted to the proximity of Dee's sleeping head, then whinnied and drew to a halt.

"Go on and lemme be," Dee muttered in her sleep.

"If something happened to me," Christine said, "I don't know what would become of my kids."

"Maybe—" Gloria said.

"No. You got your own growing and learning to do."

Suddenly Dee sat straight up. Her eyes were half closed and she only half opened her mouth when she spoke, but she was looking at and speaking to Christine. "You don't never teach me nothing, Queen o' Sheba."

NIGHT RIDERS

"I MARRIED ME A MAN, AND I DIDN'T MARRY NO NIGGER,"
Agnes said to TJ, and she felt joy, like a hearth fire in winter, springing to life in
her bosom.

Then she held out her hand and said for him to come on into the bedroom
with her.

"Let's shuck out of these hot clothes," she said, but really she didn't mind
the heat of the summer anymore.

"I believe you want to tango?" he said. "I believe you ready to *dance.*"

TJ was already in his bare feet. He unfastened his trousers and stepped out
of them.

"You wearing your young-man undershorts," she said. Her husband was
no taller than she, but she loved the well-molded brown legs against the white
Jockey shorts. She started unbuttoning the front of her dress, when she heard
a knock at the door. Her hand stopped. She looked at TJ. "Let's just not
answer," she said.

TJ picked his trousers up off the floor and stepped in one leg. "It won't take
but a minute," he said.

"I'm afraid," she said. "Let's not."

TJ said, "All right." And he picked up the blond baseball bat standing in the
corner. "I'll take the Louisville Slugger with me."

While he walked out of the room, Agnes buttoned up her shirtwaist dress
as fast as she could. She stepped back into her pumps. When TJ opened the
door a crack, four white men burst in.

Agnes charged into the room. "I done call the police," she shouted. "I done call them."

TJ had retreated to the corner. He had the bat cocked like he was about to hit a home run. "Y'all leave us alone now," he said.

But one of the men reached for the living room light switch and turned it off. She saw the rush of their dark bodies, heard the thud of the bat. "Aim for they head!" she shouted, and she took off each of her shoes. She attacked the mass of men, and a big hand pushed hard into her stomach. She staggered back but ran at the blob of them again and hammered at them with the heels of her pumps, one in each hand, till she heard the thud of a body hit the floor, and somebody white say *he's down.*

They turned the lights back on, and Agnes saw her husband with blood on his head, lying on his side on the floor. *Tom,* she crooned. He was little, like a little brown baby dressed like a man. *Tom!* She watched TJ draw his knees up, and two men kicked him around the hips and pelvis. TJ covered his head with his arms. One of the men was holding the bat by the big end, and he began to strike around TJ's head with the little end. Another man pushed his buddy aside and got out his own blackjack wrapped in leather.

Agnes sank to her knees and lifted her empty hands. "I pray, gentlemen, don't strike him no more. He's a good man. He never done nothing. Not to nobody."

"Who's with you," the blackjack man wanted to know. "Name names."

TJ groaned.

"You hear me!" And the blackjack cracked against his cheek, and blood spattered. TJ covered the place with his hand, and they beat the back of his hand, and the skin was gone.

"Lord help us; Lord help us," Agnes prayed, on her knees, pressing her hands together.

"Shut up," one of the men said and pushed her over.

"Jesus, save my Tom," Agnes prayed as she lay on the floor, but they continued to beat him.

"Speak up, speak up. We ain't got all night," one said to TJ.

"He can't talk," Agnes yelled. "He's unconscious. Oh, Lord, let him live. Let him live."

One man lunged against the wall and turned off the light again.

She heard the kicks and the blows, and she struggled to her knees. She heard a high keening, which was her own voice. She squeezed her eyes shut and entered the darkness where only God could dwell. Then her throat opened in hymn pitched heaven high, sung in her nightmare voice, " 'Father, I stretch my hand to thee,' " and she stretched out her hand into the blackness. " 'No other help I know,' " she sang through her sobs. " 'If thou withdraw thy help from me, where shall I go?' "

And suddenly, they stopped. She could hear them stopping, one by one. Just their hoarse breath. God was among them, staying their hand.

"Dead or alive?" one asked.

"Who has the power?" one of them asked, and she knew the question was for her.

"You do," she said. "You and the Lord."

"You speak for your husband?"

"I do."

Like the scream of the Holy Spirit, the sound of a siren tore the night. The four men ran for the back of the house. Police were running up the steps and flinging open the door. Beams from two big flashlights cut the darkness of the room as Agnes crawled toward TJ.

A white male voice filled the room: "We got a report a black man was raping a white woman in here." Their lights searched the floor, stopped on TJ's broken body.

"No, sir," Agnes said. "Four white mens done beat my husband." On hands and knees, she crawled toward him. She would shield him. They'd have to beat through her.

Somebody turned on the overhead light. The two policemen were holding drawn guns in one hand and the big flashlights in the other.

"Lord God," one of the men swore. He had seen TJ.

Suddenly Maggie from next door was pushing in. "Get some ice," she told Agnes. She felt TJ's skull and touched the wounds on his face. "I brought my first-aid kit," Maggie said, and she placed the little blue box in her lap and unsnapped the lid. Her gray hair was subdued into many horizontal sausage curls that covered her head.

The younger of the officers respectfully asked Agnes, "You gonna press any charges, ma'am?"

The other officer put his gun back in the holster. "Let's go," he said.

Agnes said, "We don't know who they were. They all looked alike."

"You who called?" the older officer impatiently asked Maggie.

"No, sir," she said. "I didn't call, but I heard the screaming."

Lord God, even they had exclaimed. The young one.

"You can be fined for a false alarm," the other officer went on in a cruel voice.

Agnes looked at them more closely. That one had straight gray hair; the other looked almost young as a boy, and he was little. Their badges flashed every time they moved their chests.

"You want me to call an ambulance?" the young one asked.

Maggie stood up. "We thank you kindly," she said. "But I'm a practical nurse. I believe he'll be all right."

Already Maggie was pressing a tea towel full of ice cubes against TJ's head. Agnes knew doors were opening across the street and throughout the neighborhood. People were watching and waiting. Outside, the police car light pulsed luridly.

"Jesus Christ, we don't have time for this," the older officer said, and they were gone.

"Hold that ice against his head," Maggie told Agnes.

"God was here," Agnes said. "I was at the bottom of the blackest pit and I called on the Lord."

"I called the police," Maggie said. "Claimed a white woman was dragged in kicking and screaming by four bucks. Gave your address."

Agnes scooted under TJ, held his precious head in her lap, and put the ice on his battered forehead.

The room was filling with neighbors.

" 'Open your eyes,' " Agnes crooned to TJ. " 'Open your eyes to Jesus. He loves you.' "

She watched TJ's eyelids flutter and open. But his face was a mask of pain. She tried to blot out the raw flesh image before her eyes with the memory of her husband, unhurt, holding the bat cocked over his shoulder, his face confident that he could hit a home run like Jackie Robinson.

THAT NIGHT, FAR BACK in the closet, Agnes hung up her dress with the bloody lap. In front of the bloody dress, she hung an older dress, like a drape, so she wouldn't see the stains. Though she never looked at the ruined dress again, many years later on the day of her death, her bed surrounded by three grown children she had raised to safety, Agnes knew the dress with TJ's blood still hung in the back of her closet. She felt again how it had been to insert the wire coat hanger into the shoulders of the dress, the act of hooking the hanger over the wooden pole.

WHEN MAGGIE BECKONED, their friends carried TJ to the bed. Maggie smeared his wounds with yellow Unguentine from a squat, square canister. She sent for her blue houndstooth ice bag, told Agnes to screw off the lid, which resembled the cap on a car gas tank, and to fill the rubber-lined bag with more ice. All Agnes could do was notice little things; she was afraid to look at TJ. She admired how the fabric was neatly swirled and gathered like a pinwheel into the metal rim around the opening to the ice bag's stomach.

She heard herself whispering, "Is he crushed?"

She whispered the sentence louder and louder till Maggie heard her and answered matter-of-factly, "Naw. He be all right."

The neighbor men left "to talk." Two women said they would sit up in the living room, for Agnes to go on to bed. Maggie needed to go to the hospital for the night shift, but she instructed three of the men to sit on the porch. *Yes, ma'am*, they said, eyes lowered respectfully. Maggie was the power who saved a man—that was acknowledged; she was short and squat, but she had used the power of quick wit and practical-nurse knowledge.

Alone in the bedroom with TJ, Agnes turned out the light and got into her sleeveless summer nightgown. Though it was her familiar thin cotton, printed with small green stars, she found it alien. Trying not to jiggle the bed, Agnes lay on her back beside TJ. He wasn't unconscious, just asleep. He, too, lay on his back, and she took his hand, the good one. The other one was encased in white gauze, already stained yellow where the Unguentine had soaked out. She knew his head was wrapped, too, like an Egyptian mummy, but she couldn't bring herself to look toward his face.

She feared to sleep, to wake, to find him—not wounded—but with his spirit defeated.

She felt so nervous that fire seemed to travel her veins. Usually, they cuddled together when they slept, though her friends told her they themselves never slept cuddled; it made men too horny. She had said, "I always make my man welcome." Many a night, he was gone to work. Every night he was home, after he'd gotten a bit of rest and sleep, he came to her. Sometimes twice or even three times in the night. Always, he was welcome and always she prayed after his pleasure that she might conceive, but she never did.

It was strange to sleep so straight—her lying there trembling—instead of cuddled with interlaced arms and legs. She felt that they were laid out like the dead, only she had the jerks. She could still hear the thud of the blackjack against TJ's head and shoulders. *He be mighty sore for a week,* Maggie had said. *But he ain't broke. He got a good hard head.*

Agnes heard again the moment when her lie "I done called the police already" became true, when the Holy Ghost screamed through the siren of the police, and the four brutal white men ran away. Now her hands were shaking like leaves on a cottonwood tree. She tried to picture the night riders individually, but she could not. One wore a white robe, belted at the waist by a stout white twisty rope; his hood was off, and his neck and head had looked naked. He had the blackjack. One had on a blue denim work shirt, with red thread writing on the pocket. But she had been too terrified to read, and she couldn't envision it clearly—just red writing on a blue shirt.

Now she remembered the one with the rope belt had had his hood on, when he came in. That he was the first through the door. And then he had pulled his hood off, and she had known even then that he removed it so he could see better to attack TJ. When the four men ran toward the back door, that one had held his hood by its point, and it had streamed behind him like an empty ghost head.

Agnes closed her eyes so she could be in the darkness with God again.

She began to move her lips, thanking God who could read soundless lips and hear her song even from beyond the stars. *Wonderful, Counselor, Almighty God, Lord is my Shepherd, Everlasting Father, Prince of Peace, Blessed are the meek, Jesus, I thank you for hearing my prayer. . . .*

She fell asleep praying and would awake with a prayer on her lips, but in the night, TJ opened an eye and spoke to her—"I love you, Agnes," he said—and she heard him, and heard the old surety in his voice. He still knew who he was.

An idea just cleft her mind like striking lightning: tomorrow night she would go back to her night school. She must. She wouldn't back down any more than TJ would.

She thought of the two women in the living room, one probably asleep on the sofa, the other probably dozing in the matching easy chair, two angels, old friends who were guarding her house for all their nodding off. The men on the front porch were like cherubim and seraphim.

. . . Sweet Jesus, Blessed Savior, with all my heart, I thank Thee.

IN THE MORNING, she finished her prayer, lying beside TJ, thanking God and muttering *Glory to God, Most High.* Then she got up, telephoned the Bankhead Hotel, and asked to speak to Mr. McCormick.

"Mr. McCormick," she said, "this is TJ's wife, Mrs. Agnes LaFayt, and last night four Klan men near 'bout beat TJ to death, so he not coming into work for a week. Then he be back to work, that all right with you."

She listened to his silence. Because she knew the man's mind, though she had never seen him, soon she would hear his inevitable reply. Like fingers in a sock puppet head, God would move his lips, start up his voice box.

Not the content but the tone of the man's voice surprised her: he felt shame. "Two weeks," he said. "With pay. Thank you for calling."

"Thank you," she said, and then she hung up the phone.

She saw TJ looking at her with his one good eye, the other covered with gauze.

"That was Mr. McCormick called, woke me up," she explained. "He say he sure need you to come back in a couple weeks, and I say 'Thank you.'"

RESURRECTION

"LISTEN," STELLA SAID TO CAT AS SHE PUSHED HER wheelchair across the campus at dusk. "Somebody good is playing the piano. Chopin." She stopped the chair. "My mother used to play that," she said excitedly.

"Why don't you go see who it is," Cat said. "I can wheel myself to class."

"It's a little Chopin prelude. I used to call it the 'Raindrop,' but my mother said it was another piece that had been nicknamed 'Raindrop.'"

"Go on, see."

Leaving Cat on the pavement, Stella cut across the grass to what she supposed was the music building. Suppose a budding André Watts were to be discovered at Miles College? Through the window, she saw the back of a pianist who was wearing a wild red wig. Now he was playing a Chopin Nocturne, and though she had not heard the piece for eighteen years, she anticipated and predicted every familiar note of it.

The window was open six inches or so, but Stella boldly grabbed it and sent it on up. At the sound of the rising window, the pianist did not turn around but broke off the Chopin and began to play and sing part of a Christmas carol: "Glo-o-o-o-o-o-o-o-o-o-o-o-o-o-oria in ex-cel-sis De-o!" Then he turned and saw Stella, with the upper part of her body thrust through the unscreened window, still standing outside.

"You're not Gloria."

"Oh!" Stella replied. "You're white."

"Come right in," he said. *Right* pronounced with the diphthong in the middle of it—*ie*. He was not from the South.

"I'll come through the door," Stella said, and she withdrew her upper body to walk around. Across the greensward, Cat was rolling steadily toward the portico. How brave Cat looked, making her own way. Just then Cat's purse tried to slide off her lap, and she moved one hand from the wheel to catch it. The chair curved out of line, but Cat caught the purse and straightened her course. Stella had noticed the purse was curiously heavy tonight.

The pianist had launched into the fanfare from Mendelssohn's "Wedding March" from the incidental music for *A Midsummer Night's Dream*. When Stella came into the door, he stopped.

"And you are?"

"Stella Silver."

He stood up abruptly with exaggerated politeness. "Miss Stella Silver, may I introduce myself? Jonathan Bernstein Green. No kin to the famous Leonard, though I wish."

"But do you prefer Bernstein's Beethoven's Ninth to Von Karajan's?" she asked.

"No," he said, soberly. "Though I fear the great Von Karajan may have had Nazi leanings."

He was walking toward her, with his hand stretched out.

"Ooooh," Stella said playfully, putting her hands behind her back. "I wouldn't want to injure a pianist's sacred hand."

"You're a musician."

"I used to play the cello. I gave it up."

They shook hands. His grasp was warm, the squeeze of it modulated to the exact pressure Stella liked best.

"And why did you quit?" He placed both hands on his hips, tilted his head to one side. Stella began to wonder if she had met him before.

She would tell the truth. Succinctly. He would understand. "I could have gotten a little better with a great deal of work, not a lot better. I had more talent in English. I might write stories someday. Or, I might go into psychology."

He still regarded her, with his hands on his hips. He was rather tall, thin, with crisp red hair, almost kinky. His ivory face was sprinkled with reddish freckles, and he had a large nose that tucked down at the tip, like an owl's. He wore pale glasses.

"Why are you here?" she asked.

"In Birmingham? Voter registration. At Miles? I met a teacher who said I could come out here and practice."

"I tutor in the evenings," Stella said. "My friend and I. For the GED."

"Then you might know Gloria Callahan."

It turned out that Gloria had invited him to practice a Beethoven cello-piano sonata. "I didn't know Gloria played the cello," Stella said.

"Well, there's two of you now." He looked puckish again. "I'll accompany both of you."

"No, I've really quit," Stella said. She felt sorry. "I always liked chamber music," she said. "Just the right amount of importance for each player."

"Let me see your fingers," he said.

She held out her left hand, and he inspected her fingertips for calluses. "Not a trace," he said.

"I know." She took her hand away. "Would you be from New York?" she asked.

"I am."

"I saw you buying gas at a station on Eighth Avenue. It was the day Kennedy was shot. A policeman walked around kicking your tires."

"I don't think so."

"I know that Chopin prelude. The nocturne, too."

He seated himself at the keyboard. "What would you like to hear, Stella?"

"The Ocean Etude." The conversation was like somersaulting down a hill on Norwood Boulevard, and she was going too fast. She was five years old; it was summer, and her brothers were tumbling down the grass beside her, and she couldn't stop.

Then his thunderous opening chord anchored the base of her being to the bottom of the sea. The music billowed out of the piano till she thought she would drown in it. She loved the excess of the piece, how it swept over the whole keyboard, starting with the deep notes in the base and running up to the high fringes of foam. *Incessant,* she thought, *the waves are always incessant.* And yes, a melody in all that roaring. She imagined her mother playing to her from the bottom of the ocean. Rivulets of salty tears stung her cheeks as they rolled down, and she thought how tears are distillants of blood.

"Don't turn around," she said, when he had finished. She fought to control her voice. "Now, play Debussy's 'The Engulfed Cathedral.' "

Only for a moment, his hands hesitated above the keyboard—"*La cathédrale engloutie,*" he announced, with a confident French accent—and then turbulence was replaced by solemn rising. She admired the back of his body, how his shoulders fetched the music up through the sea. The piano took on the resonance of an organ whose music was causing a whole cathedral to slowly ascend from oceanic depths. With the rich swelling of the music, massive stone arches shouldered their way through the water. Bells clanging, the top of the cathedral broke the surface of the sea.

Stella determined to remember only the triumph, not to anticipate the quiet sinking of the cathedral back into the depths.

After the murmuring waves at the end, he said, "Now, my little Christian. Whom did we resurrect?" He didn't turn around.

"My mother," she said. "I have to go."

WHAT'S THE MATTER?

CAT WATCHED STELLA, PALE AS A LILY, A THIN STALK BEAR-
ing radiant blond hair, glide into the classroom. *Not afraid, she walks in here like this is home.*

No. She's upset.

Cat backed her chair a few feet from the circle of mismatched chairs to meet Stella. Almost Cat didn't want to make the effort, but she willed her hands and arms to turn the big wheels. She was already beginning to sweat, and she knew she'd forgotten to put on any deodorant. She hated smelling uncivilized. And she'd worn sleeveless to try to promote air circulation.

Without any preliminary, Cat asked Stella, "What's the matter?" She was surprised to hear sternness in her own voice, as though Stella had no right to be upset.

"I've just fallen in love."

"What?" Cat thought that Stella was joking. Not a funny joke. Cat made herself smile, as though her own future and that of her brother were in no jeopardy at all. "With whom?" Only her careful grammar would have betrayed her to her friend, but Stella looked too harried to notice the clue.

"My mother's ghost."

"What do you mean?" Cat smiled broadly: Stella was joking. She had to be.

"With a redheaded, New York, hunchbacked genius pianist."

"Why?"

"Well, I guess he's not hunchbacked."

Cat was disgusted. She shoved her chair backward, hard. "Yes, and I'm going to buy myself a motorized chair with my summer wages," she said. "All three cents."

She watched Stella slip into the empty desk in her circle. *Not marry Donny!* Stella had no idea how cruel her joke was, a capricious thunderbolt hurled from the Olympus of the able-bodied.

Even before she sat down, Stella was already teaching. *What are the two main parts of a sentence?* she asked, and quick as a wink, Agnes LaFayt was saying "Subject and verb," and Stella was commanding *Everybody say it,* and they did. Cat felt fear rising from her stomach into her throat. And then Stella asked, *What does singular mean?* And they all said in unison, "One," and Stella asked, *What does plural mean?* And they all said, "More than one." *Three,* Cat thought, *Us three: Donny, Stella, and me.* And Stella was off again on the elusive agreement of the third-person singular pronoun and its verb: *Not "He don't" but instead, what, class?* And they said obediently but without conviction, "He doesn't."

Not marry Donny? What did she mean? She'd *promised.* And then Cat had to smile at herself. Since when did life keep its promises? But her hands jumped in her lap like fresh-killed chickens.

"What are the bones"—she had to swallow hard—"in the backbone called?" Cat asked, but it was hard to pronounce each word of the sentence, hard to articulate one word into the next. She and Stella had agreed: always start with review, whether the other teachers did or not.

"Yes," she said, "and the ones in the neck are (swallow) the cervical vertebrae." She had appointed Charles her amanuensis and taught him the meaning of the fancy word. She liked Charles; he was her favorite student. Big, strong, and kind. Over the summer, he'd come to accept her and Stella. Cat knew her hands were getting worse; it took forever to write anything by hand. Now she spelled c-e-r-v-i-c-a-l for Charles to print on a piece of notebook paper, to display for all to read. They all said it. Then he passed the ragged-edge paper to the person next to him, and each person copied, in turn, the new word. She waited.

"What is the largest organ of the body?" she asked. After review, she and Stella had resolved in their pedagogical discussions to pose an interesting question: step two. *Step,* Cat thought bitterly. The metaphor of the ambulatory.

Now the students guessed. They didn't know. They hadn't been taught. It had to be 105 degrees in the room. She was melting. She was afraid. Her future was melting, but she would keep going, keep up the teaching. She was determined. She had her gun in her purse.

It was good for them to guess; guessing excited the imagination, made the answer more memorable.

"It's the skin," Cat said. "The skin of an average person weighs sixteen pounds."

" 'Sixteen tons, and what'ya get,' " a student sang, " 'another day older and deeper in debt.' " His voice was high and reedy, not at all like Tennessee Ernie Ford's resonant bass.

"Sixteen pounds," Cat insisted, "not tons," but she smiled. Spontaneous expression, free association, were to be encouraged in a free school. Step three. Not suppressed, as Christine seemed to think.

"Skin ain't no *organ*," another young man said. And he killed a mosquito on his cheek, for emphasis. Blood lay splattered like a red seal on his dark skin.

"Yes, it is," Cat said. It wasn't *them* she was afraid of anymore. It was what was outside. The Klan, always ready to pull the trigger, to light the fuse. And the students and teachers were sitting ducks in the lighted room on the ground level. To keep from baking, they had to throw the sashes up, and still the schoolhouse was a brick oven. A white-skinned hand with a pistol in it would thrust over the windowsill, and the pistol would fire. *No!* She would fire first. She fingered the zipper on her purse.

"The skin serves the whole body. It protects us from germs," she explained. "It regulates temperature; without the sweat glands, which are part of the skin, we couldn't sweat and cool off. The skin has little holes in it, called pores, so the skin can breathe."

"I thought lungs was for breathing. That's what you said."

"They are. But the skin has to let in air, too. Through the pores. Now tell me three functions of the body's largest organ, the skin."

But they could only remember two. No one remembered that the skin kept out germs.

"If you have a cut," Cat explained, "then germs can enter the body through the skin. The tissue can become infected. You have to put disinfectant on a wound, if the skin is broached." Across the room, Agnes was looking at her, leaning toward her to learn.

"Don't ever give in to fear," Cat said.

They just stared at her.

Finally Charles said, "No, ma'am. We won't."

"If you do," she said, "it just makes it that much harder next time."

"It can be a *habit*," one said, as though he knew.

Cat took a deep breath. She had never been so afraid. She could feel the hair of her head trying to rise. *Stella crazy in love.* And yet it was just an ordinary night, sweltering hot. The mosquitoes were hungry. The moths were visiting. Out there, the tree frogs and cicadas were yelling for rain. Beyond the open windows, it was pitch-black.

"Would somebody mind fanning me hard, just for a minute?" Cat asked.

"I'll fan you, Miss Cartwright," Charles said gently. "We know you been sick." He took the Jesus fan out of her lap and flapped it vigorously.

She closed her eyes. "That feels so good." They all just sat there. *You ought to be a nurse,* she heard herself murmur to Charles Powers. And he murmured in reply, *Just womens is nurses.* Finally, she said, "I guess that was a minute."

Sam West said, "I fan you, too, if you want?"

"Thank you," she said. "But for now, back to human anatomy. Another thing about skin. Our hair follicles are located in the skin, and we also have oil glands in the skin. Two more things to remember about skin." She could feel her forehead breaking out in new sweat. "And skin has pigment in it. Different colors of pigment."

A moth flew against Cat's cheek, and she prayed, *Make me brave. Please, God, make me brave tonight.* But never had she wanted so much to be able to run. If only she could get up out of her chair, run to the car, wings on her feet, drive home fast, the cooling wind on her face.

Soon it would be break time, she told herself, and the night would be half over. And she would have to talk to Stella about Donny. Stella was firing machine-gun questions at the students; she was relentless. They would learn; every one of them. She pushed too much. Like Christine. Not like Christine. Stella was completely organized and confident about what she knew. Christine was less certain, had a leading edge of aggression instead of confidence. Stella's students were starting to squirm. At break time, Cat would remind her of step four: introduce humor. Break the tension.

In the distance, there was an explosion. Everyone in the room fell silent. The sound was muffled and far away. They couldn't be sure. How many times had bombs wrecked the homes, churches, businesses of Negro people in Birmingham? Around forty, and increasing. But, *thank God,* only four dead. Denise, Carole, Cynthia, Addie Mae—*how could one thank God for that?*

"Now I do believe," Agnes said, "that was just something letting down at the steel mill."

"Let's take a break now," Christine said.

The students scraped their wooden desk legs over the floor as they got up. It sounded like a great clearing of the throat. Cat rolled herself closer to an open window. Hoping for a breeze, she held her hands out the opening.

"Squeeze hard," Arcola said, behind Cat, "and I believe you wring water out of this air."

"I like your braid," Cat said.

"Yeah, I thought I'd better look like a queen, hot night like this."

But Arcola didn't look hot, and she smelled like Evening in Paris. Just the thought of the little dark blue bottle and the idea of eau de cologne made Cat feel cooler. Stella came over: and Cat noted critically that Stella was wearing faded red pedal pushers; they were old, and the fabric would be worn thin and cool. She'd had them when she was thirteen, an underage high school freshman, when she came to visit Cat on Saturdays. How easily Stella walked; how thoroughly she took movement for granted. Just below the knee the faded pedal pushers fastened modestly with metal D-rings.

"You feeling okay, Cat? You look flushed."

"I'm the one what's flushed," Christine said. "I'm just too dark-complected for you to see." She smiled at Stella. "You sure on 'em tonight. Like a duck on a line of june bugs." Exuberantly, Christine snatched a bug out of the air. She threw it on the floor and stepped on the shell. Cat heard it crunch, but she refused to look at the mess of fluid and broken shell on the floor. She might vomit.

"I'm inspired," Stella said. And then she commanded, "Listen!" She paused. "He's playing again."

"He been visiting the churches," Gloria said. "Talking 'bout voter registration. I told him, come over here and practice his music."

"It's Chopin," Stella said. " 'The Revolutionary Etude.' "

"Stella's smitten," Cat said.

"Naw!" Arcola said. "You tell us you gonna marry Cat's brother!"

That was Arcola going to the heart of the matter—quick and unafraid.

"But you don't have to," Gloria said softly. "I'd marry that music, I was you."

For a moment, Cat hated Gloria.

"Marry him yourself," Cat snapped.

"I don't find white men *attractive*," Gloria said, smiling. "I want to marry somebody like my daddy."

"Don't you marry a Yankee, Stella," Arcola teased. "We want you to stay down here with us."

Cat pictured Donny sitting under a palm tree on the sand, looking out at the ocean, and opening a disengagement letter from Stella. Maybe the piano guy was married. Stella couldn't be serious. And even if she was, she couldn't *make* it happen. But how would Donny feel?

Stillness welled up in Cat. How would he feel to be disengaged? Donny wouldn't much care.

He liked Stella. He respected her. But Donny didn't love her. (Cat imagined she was sitting with Donny in the sand.) He wouldn't much care if they never married. It was she, Cat, who cared. And if Donny did love Stella, she herself would be jealous. That was why it had seemed all right for Donny to marry her.

She pictured him alone reading the letter, then he looked up, looked out at sea. "Well," he said. He frowned slightly. A thousand times she'd seen that slight frown of disapproval about something that really mattered very little. He got up from the sand.

"What you thinking about?" Gloria asked.

But Cat said nothing. She looked anew at the people around her: pretty Arcola with her brilliant smile; Gloria with the lime green eyes, strange and startling; wiry Christine, all efficiency and ambition, softening every day. Over in her student seat, dear Mrs. Agnes LaFayt, who had come to them finished, soft and wise, always ready for lessons to begin again, slowly waving her fan. Now Agnes took out a dainty white handkerchief, edged with crocheted lace. These were Cat's new friends. They were chatting all around her, grabbing a few minutes to relax. People she more than liked; people she would protect. She touched her purse to feel the shape of her gun inside. She felt alone in her weakness and power.

"Stella," she said, "sometimes I think about what if we needed to move fast."

Stella uncocked her ear from the window. She reached over and pressed Cat's hand against her purse. "We'd run for our lives. You'd be going the same speed as I would. Only you'd be in front."

Cat felt tears glaze her eyes. "It's just so *damn* hot," she said.

"*Cat!*" all her friends chorused, except for Agnes, who hadn't heard, sitting at a remove.

Cat smiled, pleased to have shocked them. She took a deep breath, smelled the odor of the students' cigarettes from out on the portico. "What's he playing now?" Cat asked. Sometimes she feared that her hearing was duller than it used to be, and that her eyesight was a little worse.

"It's the movement called 'The Funeral March.'"

"Yeah," Arcola said. Her quick hand snatched a moth out of the air. "Movie music."

Christine walked to the door. "Intermission's over," she called to the students.

Cat felt something stiffening around her, as though her chair had become a giant metal fist. "But you know what?" Cat said to Stella. "I'm through with being afraid."

"I am, too," Stella said. "Almost." Then she smiled at Cat, and Cat basked in that loving smile, light without heat. Stella added, as though she could read Cat's mind, "May Vulcan hold you in the palm of his hand."

ANSWERS

YOU DON'T GET THROUGH WITH BEING AFRAID, GLORIA thought but did not say. They'd learn.

Did white people know anything about pity and terror? Could white women know anything beyond personal tragedy? *Who you,* she asked herself scornfully, *to dismiss personal tragedy? Pain is pain. Who you, Gloria Callahan, but somebody who never hurt for nothing in your life but a pony.* She looked at her friend Arcola, who deserved to be the queen of the world. *But now, I hurt. I hurt for my people.*

With her left thumb, Gloria surreptitiously caressed the hard calluses on the tips of the four fingers of her left hand. As she watched the students, refreshed now, come to their desks, Gloria wished she'd stepped outside, too, for the night air. She picked up her fan, which was Jesus at age twelve teaching in the temple. The skin of his face looked like porcelain, and he had been painted with a luminous brown eye. Vulnerable Jesus before his beard.

At least he had gotten to grow up.

When her church exploded, the terror came first in the sound, not just the heavy boom, but the quick snatch of plaster and bricks ripped from the lathes and studs of the building. The bones broken and thrown down so fast it was unimaginable. And then the rising pillars of dust dissipating into a dense cloud, the sanctuary suddenly a box of dust. Even before the dust settled, there was blue sky where the face of Christ should have been.

Gloria had saved a little of the pulverized wall, just scooped it up off the floor and put it in her pocket. Now the souvenir was at home in a little test tube she had stolen from the rack in the chemistry lab. The memento lay beneath her underwear. It was whitish, like the ashy residue from cremation, and she had stuck a cork in one end of the tube.

The classroom disappeared. She was home; with the brass pull, she opened the mahogany drawer of her highboy. She reached beneath the fine silky underwear to feel the glass tube and dry cork. She thought of the four young girls, killed. One decapitated. Others cooked to a crisp. Although the images were in her mind and could not be kept out, she closed her eyes. She felt as though she were welding her eyelids together.

"Miss Gloria," Mrs. LaFayt called her. "You feeling bad, honey?"

Gloria went and sat beside her, even though Mrs. LaFayt was in Stella's group. Stella wouldn't mind if Gloria took her seat for a few minutes.

"I was thinking about Sixteenth Street," Gloria said.

"I cry for them all the time. And for their parents."

"We don't talk about it as much as maybe we should," Gloria said.

"You got to move on." Mrs. LaFayt sighed as though she had the weight of the world on her. "Keep going." She paused, then leaned close. "Sometimes they sing to me."

"What do you mean?"

"Real high. All four together. High as angels, all four of them."

"Do they sing hymns?"

"No. I can't make out the words. I think they beyond any particular words now."

Gloria was intently curious. "But what do they sound like?" She realized she was holding Mrs. LaFayt's gaze with her own. She was looking right into her eyes. *This is the way I look at everybody now: straight on.*

"Kind of like little honeybees. Sort of humming a little golden song. All about honey and clovers and roses."

Suddenly Gloria felt brimful of tears. She got up. "We have to get started."

As she walked away, she heard Mrs. LaFayt humming her own little high, grating tune, as though she were trying to catch some remnant of their ethereal song, gasping for breath between phrases. Gloria glanced back at her, and saw Mrs. LaFayt gulp air, then close her ample lips firmly together, humming.

Gloria swallowed her tears, went back, and kissed Agnes on the forehead. Inside there, inside her mind, did Agnes really believe she heard spirits singing?

"Oh, honey," Mrs. LaFayt said, suddenly crying out. "The Klan near 'bout beat TJ to death last night."

"No!" Gloria said. "No." She knelt down in front of Mrs. LaFayt and pressed both Agnes's hands together inside her own.

Mrs. LaFayt straightened herself tall in her seat with a huge intake of air. She sniffed up her tears, collected herself. "But he'll be all right," she said. "Go on now. He's alive. He wants me to be here. Go on to your teaching. I'll talk with you later." And she pushed Gloria away.

Blindly, Gloria found her way back to her desk. *History,* she thought. *This is the real history. I ought to bring the newspaper to class for history lesson. Not that it tells. Not the* Birmingham News *anyway. And New York too far away to know.* She'd seen postcards of it at night: New York City, with its skyscrapers and all its lights shining. The whole city was like a gigantic lantern for the rest of the country.

And New York cared: Goodman and Schwerner, who died with Chaney in Mississippi, who worked for freedom, were from New York.

Someday she, Gloria Callahan, would play the cello in Carnegie Hall. Maybe Jonathan Bernstein Green would help her. As her left thumb caressed the row of calluses across the tips of her four fingers, she thought *just about hard enough, tough enough.* Callused enough to stand up to the days, months, years of practice.

In a long, jagged agony of breath, Mrs. LaFayt was snuffing up. Gloria's vision of New York shattered. Her little artistic toughness was nothing in the defense of what life could deal. She wondered what TJ had done.

Not just the four girls but Judge Aaron, in 1957, had done absolutely nothing. It was Fred Shuttlesworth who'd tried to integrate Phillips High School. And Judge Aaron, who had been castrated. Cause and effect didn't fit. That was the way it was with terror. There was no individual linking of cause and effect. Allegiance to justice was replaced by criminal rage. The world was broken, and you lived in fear. The four girls and Judge Aaron had just been black and available for slaughter. In the South, there wasn't any terrible thing that could happen that hadn't happened. Pandora's box had been wide open a long time.

When Jonathan spoke after church, Gloria had been shocked by his approach to change. He had said: "Never mind integrating education. Negro people have got to register to vote. Then come the jobs, the transportation, the education, the housing, the recreation, and the libraries." And she had spoken right up and said that she believed they had to work on all fronts at once. (That meeting was when she last saw TJ, small and natty in his Sunday suit. About the size of Sammy Davis Jr. Quick and vital.) And Jonathan had said *Maybe,* but he felt too many projects dissipated energy. Voting meant power.

Gloria slid into her seat; now she was supposed to try to make her students remember the basic steps in the creation of democracy.

At the Gaslight Club—she had seen TJ dancing that evening, dancing with his wife. She realized there had been a white girl at the nightclub, in a wheel-chair—that might have been Cat, but she couldn't remember the face, just the big wheels on each side of the chair, and her neighbor Eddie, the waiter, had taken the wheelchair person out on the dance floor and twirled her, chair and all. Eddie *swished*. She knew that Eddie had been in bed two weeks after other colored boys beat him in Oak Hill Cemetery, threatened to cut him.

Now to teach.

"Y'all ever heard of Nat Turner?" she asked.

No one had.

"Between the War for Independence and the Civil War, a slave rose up in Virginia against slavery—1830s maybe." But then she stopped. Nat Turner rose up *murderously*. She didn't want to hold that up as an example.

They all looked at the floor.

"Nat Turner hadn't learned the lesson, yet, of nonviolence. He didn't have any Martin Luther King Jr. to teach him. He didn't have any Mahatma Gandhi over in India showing the way. The things that history surely teaches us is that violence never solves anything. That's history's biggest lesson. If you don't remember anything else from this school, remember that."

"I don't know about that," Charles said politely. "We won the War for Inde-pendence, didn't we?"

Mr. Parrish was standing in the doorway.

"Could I have your attention, please," he said calmly.

Surprised by his presence, everybody looked up. They didn't quite believe he was standing there; they expected him to disappear in a moment, and then they'd all go on with their lessons.

"We've had a bomb threat telephone call in my office." Gloria felt the ripple of alarm run through the room. "The police have been called. Now we want to calmly evacuate this building. I want everybody to stand up, don't run, just walk quickly over to me and through the door." Already the students were on their feet and moving. "Keep moving, and move outside, and keep going." The students were converging on the exit. "Move over all the way to the side of the music building, and I'll join you when everybody's out." He added, "Just fol-low the music." Gloria guessed he was trying to sound light. Yes, Jonathan B.

Green was practicing the piano—Mozart. Gloria thought of Marie Antoinette, decapitated. Maybe only the Nazis were more bloodthirsty than the leaders of the French Revolution, or Stalin.

Stella was standing behind Cat's chair, already trying to push.

"Release the brakes," Stella said.

"No."

As though she didn't hear, Stella pushed harder, but the chair didn't budge.

"Stop, Stella," Cat ordered, though she hadn't raised her voice.

"What?"

Gloria saw Mrs. LaFayt was still sitting in her chair. Her hands were folded in front of her; her head was bowed, her lips moved in prayer. Gloria touched her shoulder.

"Let's go out now," Gloria said. "We'll pray when we get outside."

Obediently, Mrs. LaFayt rose to her feet. "Let me take my fan," she said. And she picked up the image of the Good Shepherd and held it to her bosom like a shield. " 'The Lord is my Shepherd, I *shall* not want,' " she quoted. She managed a smile.

Gloria saw that Stella was talking earnestly to Cat, whose feeble hands were covering the brake releases on her chair.

"Gloria," Stella called anxiously. "Cat doesn't want to leave."

Gloria saw that Mrs. LaFayt was headed for the door, rather slowly, but moving. Not looking back.

"What's wrong, Cat?" Gloria asked.

"I made a vow to myself," Cat said. "I'm not going to be intimidated anymore."

"It's a bomb threat!" Stella reiterated.

Gloria could feel hysteria just under the imperative tone of Stella's voice, and as she did, she felt the necessary strength in her own bones. The strength started in her shins and thighs; it was her legs reassuring her. *Stay or go,* her bones said. *We serve your will.*

" 'Course you could stay," Gloria said to Cat. She was careful not to move toward Cat. "But what's the point?"

Standing by the door, Mr. Parrish said impatiently, "Hurry up, everyone."

"Let's all go now," Gloria said.

But she stood still and calm. What was Cat thinking of, to want to stay?

Gloria felt that she was standing in between the pews in the church again; the same strength was in her now that she had offered to Christine.

"Your brakes stuck?" Christine called and bustled over.

Cat rotated her head to address Christine.

"I believe it's a bluff," Cat said. She spoke so determinedly, it felt like hate behind her voice. No, Gloria thought, it's power. Cat doesn't hate Christine. It's will against will, that's all. And Gloria knew Cat would win. No need to take sides. Hadn't she known when she lifted her eyes to the face of Jesus that it would be gone? Some things you knew in advance. Jesus himself couldn't stand to look at what hate had done on September 15.

"They just want to disrupt. Make people afraid to come," Cat explained with *murderous* intensity to Christine.

"We got to leave. Now!" Christine said. "Now!" Her voice spanked the air.

"Please listen, Cat," Stella implored. "They're right."

"No."

"You want to die?" The words burst out of Christine. "Maybe you don't care you live or die. I got children!"

"I won't go," Cat said, but the murder had gone out of her voice. Just flat fact was left.

"Mr. Parrish," Christine called. "This white girl gone crazy."

Stella tried to push the chair. She reached to remove Cat's hand hovering over the brake mechanism.

"Don't do that," Gloria said. "She got her rights."

And Stella obeyed Gloria. She lifted her hand away from Cat.

"I'm leaving!" Christine announced. Her glance seared Gloria.

Mr. Parrish approached. "Gloria, you go on now, too."

"Yessir," she said. "It probably is a bluff," Gloria said, but she followed Christine.

"Cat." Mr. Parrish sighed. "Black groups always getting bomb threats. Still we got to evacuate."

"I won't," she said. "They're watching. You know that." She smiled. "I'm going to hold down the fort."

"No, you're not, Cat," he said.

"Please, Cat," Stella begged.

Through the open door, Gloria called, "Come on, Stella. Let Mr. Parrish talk to Cat."

"You don't have to stay," Cat said to her friend.

"I promised you. I promised," Stella said.

"That was if we decided to run," Cat said. "I don't want to run."

"Stella, you leave now," Mr. Parrish said.

Over her shoulder Gloria watched Stella walk jerkily to the door and out. She passed Gloria, and then Stella began to run across the grass toward the others. Gloria moved only to the edge of the porch and stopped again to look back.

The open doorway framed Cat in her chair and Mr. Parrish leaning a little toward Cat, trying to reason with her. Around the campus, throughout the college, Gloria saw the lights were going out. First the science building, now the music building and the few lamps above the sidewalks. Somebody was at the switches. Gloria imagined him at the box. Somebody wearing a white robe and a white hood; a man's white-gloved hand was at the controls.

Students were huddling against the side of the music building. No, somebody was leading them around the corner to put the mass of the building between them and the H.O.P.E. classroom. No, Mrs. LaFayt was leaving the group and walking back to Gloria. Agnes LaFayt! Gloria started to call to her to retreat, but then Gloria stopped herself. *Who am I to say?* she asked.

When she looked back inside, what she saw sent her body rigid.

Cat's hand was coming slowly out of her purse. Cat's hand had a gun in it, and she was pointing it at Mr. Parrish.

"Now put that away," he said loudly, raising his hands.

"I won't," she said. "Back off."

"I could rush you, Cat."

"Better not."

"I could carry you out of here."

"My choice," she said. "Raise your hands higher."

Slowly Mr. Parrish raised his hands, his open palms toward Cat.

"I don't want to have to come get you," he said. But Gloria knew he was complying.

"Mr. Parrish, I like you a lot," Cat said. "I respect you and admire you. You rush me, and I'll fire. Don't doubt it. I know how to shoot."

"I'm your friend, Cat. We're in this together," he said. "We leave now, we come back tomorrow."

"You leave," she said. "I don't want to endanger you. Or anybody."

Gloria realized that Agnes LaFayt had come to stand beside her. Agnes reached down and took Gloria's hand.

"Mr. Parrish," Mrs. LaFayt called sweetly. Surely she was seeing the gun in Cat's hand, too. "Mr. Parrish, I want you to come on out here with the rest of us. Your family needs you, Mr. Parrish."

She sounds like she's his mother, Gloria thought.

Slowly Mr. Parrish lowered his hands. He turned toward the door. Already Cat was lowering the barrel of the gun.

"The Lord bless you, and keep you, Cat," he said.

Gloria held her breath. Now was the moment to turn and rush her, if he chose to. He walked out. He walked past Gloria and Mrs. LaFayt and kept walking. "Y'all come on," he said as he passed.

But Gloria and Mrs. LaFayt stood on the porch, looking in.

Just as Cat let the gun rest in her lap, the lights inside the classroom went dark.

"Maybe we hear police siren soon," Agnes said.

Gloria surveyed the campus. Not a light. At the outskirts, a little traffic passed. A few cars slowly pushed their headlights along, minding their own business.

From across the campus, Gloria heard sprightly piano music played in the dark: "The Marseillaise." There was something ironic in the way the man played the piece—*too* jaunty. *Why did that madman from New York choose to play the anthem of the French Revolution?* She shuddered to think of the French awash in blood, but their cause—one of class, not race—had been just.

Another song, the anthem of nonviolence, bloomed slowly in the dark:

We shall o-ver-co-o-ome
We shall o-ver-co-o-ome
We shall o-ver-come some-da-a-a-a-ay

Gloria felt as though she was on the moon. Through darkness from a great distance, she seemed to hear and watch the ways of human beings. But it was just over there, across the campus. *Le jour de gloire n'est pas arrivé.* The day of glory. *Gloire.* Another name for herself, a revolutionary name, a secret name of her own for her own inner strength: *Gloire.* An ugly word that stuck in the throat like swallowing a raw egg the way old country people did.

Agnes squeezed her hand. Inside the dark classroom, Cat was striking a match to light her candle. Gloria marveled that Cat's grip could manage striking a match. She saw Cat moving the candle away and trying to blow out the match. The aim of her breath was uncertain; her head bobbed. Gloria supposed Cat's gun was resting in her lap. The match blinked out, and the candle wavered and glowed.

Agnes LaFayt shuffled through the door. "Cat baby, I come to sit with you," she said as though she were speaking to a six-year-old.

"Is that you, Agnes?"

"Yes, it is," she said.

And Mrs. LaFayt was pulling a desk into Cat's circle of light.

"I was afraid," Cat said.

"I know," Agnes said. "Don't nobody like to sit by herself in the dark. But I sit with you."

"I knew if I gave in, I'd never come back," Cat said. She was pleading. To be understood, to understand herself. "I need my job. For my future."

"God willing, we all live to see the sun rise and the sun set, and we be back studying tomorrow night, thanking him."

"It's always a bluff," Cat said. "These bomb threats."

"Sometimes yes, sometimes no. It's in God's hands now." Agnes paused. "You want me to hold your hand?"

"Yes."

"Let me just get my own candle lit, then we hold hands. Then we feel brave."

Gloria watched Agnes dig into her purse, come up with the little wax cylinder. She touched her wick to Cat's flame. "This is what I bought these candles for," Mrs. LaFayt said. She reached out and held Cat's hand. "I used to be nursemaid to lots of white children," Agnes said.

"But not now?" Cat asked.

"I didn't have none of my own. That the only thing ever make me doubt God. TJ and I never had none. Too late now. But we try. We still try, remember Sarah and Abraham."

Gloria felt shocked. She could imagine Agnes and TJ dancing together but not trying to make babies. She felt the lean emptiness of her own youthful body and was grateful for her virginal intactness.

"But few years back," Agnes continued, "I couldn't work for white folks no more. TJ, he say he understand."

Gloria saw that Cat was growing more frightened, could hardly speak, while Mrs. LaFayt settled more and more calmly into her waiting. Gloria wanted both to leave and to stay to witness. In the wink of an eye, this quiet tableau could be transformed: blast and crashing down of walls, the room filling with dust, the building collapsing. The end of their lives.

Agnes went on speaking, keeping up both ends of the conversation. "And you know why I left taking care of white children? Well, it was one reason only. I loved 'em too much. Loved 'em too much."

"Sing," Cat said suddenly. "Please sing."

And Agnes's voice rose up like the wind rising in an organ, full and rich:

Trust and obey, for there's no other way
To be happy in Jesus, but to trust and obey
When we walk with the Lord
In the light of His Word. . . .

Gloria found herself walking into the room.

"I come to sit with you," Gloria said.

"Well, pull up a chair and sing," Mrs. LaFayt said.

With all her heart, Gloria joined the song. She wasn't sure she even believed in Jesus, but now she was inside the movement. This was protest and determination. Beside her, Cat was trying to belt it out, but with her speech problem, she only got a few tones.

"You got your candle?" Mrs. LaFayt asked Gloria between verses.

"Naw."

"Don't matter. We got two already."

Mrs. LaFayt began to pump her body at the waist, forward and backward.

Then a strong, male tenor voice—"To be hap-py in Jes-us"—entered the song, and Jonathan Green came into the room. "Hope you guys don't mind I join in."

He pulled a chair between Gloria and Agnes. Gloria felt that ten people had joined them instead of one. The room was almost crowded. He reached out his ivory hands on both sides. In the candlelight, his face was very pale, his hair a dark red. And then his voice took off, singing complicated running notes, weaving all around and in and out of the melody. He leaned back in his chair and sang as nonchalantly as though he were alone on the riverbank, fishing. Gloria and Agnes had to sing louder to hold their own.

Despite his being an ugly man, Gloria decided, he glowed. At the end, Agnes said quickly, "I believe your name must be Michael," and then she launched into singing "Michael, row the boat ashore, hal-le-lu-jah. . . ."

Gloria began her own riff, ornamenting the hallelujah so that it ran like a holy fire above all their heads.

LIONEL WATCHING

WHILE LIONEL WATCHED THE FLICKERING CANDLELIGHT from inside the H.O.P.E. classroom from a safe distance, he cursed himself. He had left the crippled girl in there, but she had pulled a gun on him. If the place blew up, he couldn't say that she pulled a gun. The school was pledged to non-violence. That was what the grant proposal to Washington had said: "In the tradition of Martin Luther King Jr. H.O.P.E. offers the opportunity to earn equality in the nonviolent quiet of the classroom."

Lionel Parrish couldn't believe somebody as helpless as Cat Cartwright would pack a gun. He'd seen how her hands wavered. She'd blow her own head off before she'd defend herself.

At his ear, Christine said, "It could go any second." She grasped his hand.

"Yes." He squeezed back. He didn't want Christine running off to die. Gloria, that mouse. And Mrs. LaFayt, the meekest of the meek!

They stared across the campus. The low one-room brick building hunkered close to the earth. The columned portico looked stately to Lionel, as though it were quietly proud of itself. The students had stopped singing; the dim light still flickered from inside their classroom. A profound silence settled on the gathered group. He began to count his sheep. All the students stared at the building.

Impulsively, Lionel held up his hand and closed his eyes. "Dear Heavenly Father," he said. "We pray for their lives. We pray for this campus and all the students, and for the buildings. We pray for peace and justice in Birmingham, and all of Alabama, and the world over, dear Lord. Give us courage. Give us wisdom. Help us to trust in Thee. Not our will, but Thine be done. In the name of Him who taught us to pray, 'Our Father, Who art in Heaven. . . .' " The group joined in the prayer. When Lionel opened his eyes the building was still there. He felt better.

At Lionel's ear, Charlie Powers spoke. "Who's that left inside? We ought to tell 'em to come on out." His tone was manly—one man speaking to another.

"I tried," Lionel said. "They insist on being where they are. They think the bomb call is a bluff."

"We ought to do something," Charlie insisted. "Tell 'em to come on out now."

"I tried," Lionel said again.

Stella said, "It's just five minutes till school will be out for the night. They'll come out then. That's their point. Nothing is going to cut out school." Every few moments, she flicked up her wrist to read her watch; the figures on it glowed a faint green.

Lionel wouldn't let himself ask *how much longer?* The group fell silent and waited. As the minutes ticked by, he became increasingly angry. The person who telephoned was a white, a redneck woman. He hated to admit it, but she had sounded concerned for them. He had believed they were really in danger. And now these women still in the building, one of them with a gun, of all things. All over the South, women were trying to take over the leadership roles. But he didn't want the school to close down in fear. Look what education was doing for Charlie Powers already.

Christine said, "Once they safe, everybody come over to my house. Let's talk about what we can do. In Birmingham."

"I can't do that," Lionel said. "As the director, I can't be involved in any sort of planning of protests." He dropped her hand.

"That's okay, Mr. Parrish," Christine said. "We understand." When she touched his bare arm, her fingertips almost burned his flesh.

"I think it's best just to continue what we're doing," he said. "Getting ready to take the GED."

"If you want to, you can come over later," Christine said.

Lionel reached over and lightly touched her. "Thank you. I'd like that. Cup of tea?"

Then Cat wheeled herself out onto the porch slab. The students clapped and hollered. Mrs. LaFayt emerged and stood beside her, clasping her purse to her stomach. All around Lionel, the students raised the volume of their approval. Gloria stood behind the chair, but nobody seemed to notice her. When Gloria tried to push Cat's chair toward the step, Cat looked back at her, made a circling motion—"turn me around"—with her hand. Lionel saw nothing of the gun.

After Cat's instructions to Gloria, Gloria turned the chair to take it down the one step backward, big wheels first.

"That's right," Stella murmured, as though she were there with them. "Backward."

Lionel said, "You did the right thing, Stella, to obey me when I said evacuate. Don't go making them into some kind of heroes."

"Look," Stella said, "that's Jonathan Green."

While the four figures moved off the porch, Lionel thought, *It could blow yet.* The white man was taking his sweet time. Cat's group had *no* sense of urgency. A monstrous fire could billow orange through the door and onto the porch and steps. Engulfed by a huge impatience, Lionel shouted, "Hurry up! Hurry up!"

"We're coming," Mrs. LaFayt's sweet voice called back to him through the hot night air. "We be there in a minute, Mr. Parrish."

He led the group out to meet the brave ones, but now his relief was bigger than his shame.

THE WHOLE SCHOOL walked with Cat and Stella to their car. After the women were seated inside, and the wheelchair had been folded and hoisted into the trunk, the white man leaned his head into the car and spoke to Stella. Lionel leaned his head in on the passenger side and said to Cat, "You bring that thing to school again and you're fired. No letter of recommendation, either."

Cat smiled at him. "I won't," she said. And he could see she was sincere, way too pleased with herself, but sincere.

Then Lionel looked across the seat and introduced himself to the white man.

"Jonathan Green, voter registration," he answered and thrust his arm past Stella to shake hands.

A New York Yankee, Lionel thought; he had a firm, warm hand. No sweat.

While they all watched the battered-up old car creep off the campus, Christine renewed her invitation to the students for a gathering at her place. Mrs. LaFayt said she needed to go home, and Lionel escorted her to her car.

When he stood alone at the circuit box with his hand on the big switch, he thought how just a half hour before, a white man had stood there. *Evil leaves a presence,* Lionel thought. He could almost smell the man—somebody stupid and poor. The tool of the rich white bosses. Somebody who didn't even know he had been created to fight their battles for them. Somebody stood here ignorant of the industrialists' fear of the unions, of their need for cheap bodies in dangerous places, of their need for replaceable black men in the steel mills. A man with no more mind than a robot had stood here and pulled switches. He had put his hand on the big switch not long before Lionel himself.

Lionel pulled the lever, but he wondered whose tool was he? A hum came over the campus, lights jumped on. Just a simple, functional metal handle made the change. *Let there be light.* Cool to the touch, the handle felt like a bony hand holding out a finger at him, pointing at him. Mr. Bones. *Let there be bright light,* the disembodied voice mocked sarcastically.

In the restored light, the hall stood barren. The cool handle of the lever still chilled Lionel's hand. He made himself let go.

Survived again? Now tell me, what do you want most out of this dark night?

"Christine."

CLOSE TO EARTH

"SQUAT DOWN IN FRONT OF ME," RYDER ORDERED LEE, "SO I can watch you. You try to slip off again, and I'll kill you."

Ryder wished he'd placed the bomb snug against the bricks of the building. Instead, he'd left the bomb half a foot away. Crouching in the deep shadow of a building, Ryder dug his fingernails into the top of Lee's shoulder and pushed down hard on her. He didn't just use his fingertips, he made his fingernails dig into the flesh where her sleeveless blouse left off.

"It's just a school," she whispered.

"Shut up! God damn it! They're coming out! Look at that!" *Why would they leave now?* he wondered. *Why?*

The bomb was against the back wall where there were no windows, and people were coming out the front.

"They're coming this way!" he said. He waited, ready to run, but the students went another way. Ryder hadn't realized that a college school, unlike high school, had a lot of different buildings.

The campus was mostly deserted, but he'd seen them—integrated—through the windows. They were walking rapidly away from the building. Ryder thought they looked scared.

"There's one of them *white* teachers." He said the word *white* like he was tearing it off with his teeth. "Bitch!"

"Honey, let's please go."

He paid no attention to Lee.

"We can hear the boom from the car," she said.

"I want to see it," he whispered. "I want to god damn see that shoe box blow sky high."

"You're hurting my shoulder," she sniveled.

He dug his nails in deeper, and he was glad they were dirty with car grease. Piano music drifted their way. "It's that redheaded fool," Ryder said.

"What's he singing?"

"Hell if I know. I'm gonna get him, too, someday. Look at that bitch over there. Her blond-headed and standing with all them niggers."

"It looks like nobody's left inside."

"Yes, there is. The wheelchair girl's still in there. They left her in there."

"They ought to take her out," Lee said anxiously. "It's just about time. They ought not have left her there. She can't even stand up."

"Tough luck. She's a nigger lover. How much longer?" He'd get one. At least one.

Lee balanced herself on her knees and the knuckles of one hand so she could hold up her wrist to see Bobby's Mickey Mouse watch.

"It's ten more minutes," Ryder said.

When he heard them starting up their protest song, he ground his teeth. Once again, he looked carefully for the wheelchair in the group, but it wasn't there. He'd get her. Then he saw that the older woman was walking back toward the night school building. Earlier, when he peeked through the window, he'd seen her. She'd been about the only middle-aged woman in there. Her hose were twisted into a knot to keep them up, just behind her fat knee. Talking to herself, she had been fanning like crazy. He'd never seen anybody look so stupid. And now she was walking straight into death when she could have been safe.

"She's too stupid to live," he muttered.

Then a young nigger bitch started after the old one: three. He'd get three, almost as many as Bob got at the church. To his great joy, the skinny Jew piano player walked toward the night school. He was going to die, too. *Hurry up, hurry up,* Ryder thought. *I sure don't want you to miss the party.* Ryder could hardly breathe he was so excited. *Four!* The hot night air slipped back and forth, shallowly, over his tongue. Ryder didn't feel anxious anymore. Just eager. He'd get four.

With his fingers locked into Lee's slimy shoulder, they waited. After a few minutes, when he didn't have anything else to think about, he realized his nails must have brought blood. In the comic book, Dracula's fingernails were pointed like a woman's so he could gouge. Ryder removed his hand and slowly took his fingertips to his lips. He didn't want her to notice he was tasting her blood.

He was getting away with it. He felt himself stiffen with pleasure.

"Lie down, honey," he whispered urgently.

"What?"

"Lie down so no flying brick'll hit you."

Obediently, she stretched out on the grass and dirt. He began to lift her skirt.

She giggled. "Honey, stop it," she said.

He hesitated. Stroking the hollow behind her knee, he thought how soft and smooth the skin was. Except the crease where it bent. The skin was hot and sweaty there. He thought about the black mammy's coffee-colored hose twisted into a knot behind her knee.

"I like that," Lee said. "That's so gentle."

He ventured up, exploring the back of her thigh. If she made a fuss, people might see them. They were in deep shadow, but her blouse was white and her skirt was a light tan.

"Honey," Lee said to her husband. "Lie down here beside me, so you won't get hit." Invitingly, she patted the ground beside her.

He knew they'd get dirty because there wasn't much grass to speak of, but he stretched out on his stomach. Several times, he secretly squeezed his pelvis as flat as he could against the flank of bare ground and released. It was strangely satisfying.

"How many minutes?" he asked, and she looked at the watch.

"We're almost there."

But the time came and went, and nothing happened.

The wheelchair girl came out onto the little porch, and the black girl twirled her around and backed her off the step. The mammy and the Jew followed them. They all joined the others beside the piano building, and they talked and jabbered like folks let out of church. His bomb sat abandoned against a brick wall.

Still, he begged the building to blow. Just to show them. Just to warn them.

"Maybe it's not going to," she said.

"Didn't you check them wires? Didn't you?"

"About ten times."

"Don't get smarty." *Blow, baby, blow.* He'd never been so tense, wanted something to happen so bad, except maybe for Lee to say yes, when he asked her to marry him.

"Oh well," she said.

"What do you mean *Oh well?* You don't care!"

Just then the whole group started to move away. He watched them drift across the campus. Sometimes one of them would laugh. They sounded happy. Not a care in the world. Off for a good-time Friday night.

"They're getting away," he said, full of wonder. "Scot free." He didn't know how God could let them off.

Then all his wonder turned to fury. It was Lee's fault. She'd done something wrong, he knew it. She was always thwarting him. Taking Bobby's side. *She didn't care*—that was the proof of it. He doubled up his fists and pounded the ground.

She giggled. "You look like a baby having a temper tantrum," she said lightly.

He leapt on her. He straddled her back and pinned her down and pounded her shoulders with his fists. She begged him to stop, but she kept her voice down. He stopped only briefly to unzip himself.

Lifting her skirt and throwing the tail of it up over her shoulders, he ripped down her panties, *yes*, there was her bare ass, *yes*, he was on her, fierce as a Comanche warrior riding his horse. With one hand, he shoved her face into the dirt because she was trying to buck him off. He was wild with his need, wilder than Dracula. He heaved and panted, explained, as he continued.

"I got to get some pleasure," he gasped. "I—got—to have—it."

AGNES'S HONEYBEES

WHEN AGNES REACHED HER CAR, SHE WAS SURPRISED TO see the packages on the backseat and the sack with three rolls of different Christmas wrapping paper sticking out of the top like candy canes.

In the evening's excitement, she'd completely forgotten her spree before she came to school. She felt ashamed of herself. All on a whim, she had given into the "Christmas Preview Sale" at the drugstore. She'd gone there just to get another ice pack for TJ. She had discovered a swollen place big as a goose egg on his shin.

But then the drugstore display showed all manner of nice toys for kids on sale. A big plush red bear, a little mirror and comb set made of pink plastic, a whole box of wooden paddles with rubber balls attached. She used to watch boys play with that toy when she was a girl. Big boys could dance on their roller skates and paddleball so fast the ball was just a blur. And next to the paddleballs were Slinkys, which could be worn on the arm like a bracelet.

And there the toys were, all in the backseat. Maybe she was just getting *too* impulsive.

This evening, she'd been outside, all safe, and she'd just had the impulse to walk right back in that building and sit down with Cat. What would TJ do without her? She'd known the girl had to be near 'bout scared to death, had to be, and if she wanted to sit with her—well, that was her choice to do. But going after Christmas now! Each toy had been like some child smiling at her.

Agnes settled into the driver's seat, and then she heard a voice clear as if he was sitting in the seat beside her. She knew that voice.

"That you again?" she said.

And then he shut up. Oh, he was a trickster, all right. She just waited patiently.

Then she heard him again; he had such a snide voice: "Second childhood, Agnes?"

As always, she spoke to him out loud. "Oh, I know you. I just ain't gonna pay you no attention. Can't get my goat."

"Now, Mrs. Agnes, you ought to be friendly. You privileged to have a friend like me. I'm your guardian angel, ain't I? You ought to look out for my welfare."

She started the motor.

He went on, "You look out for me—it just the same as looking out for you."

"Like looking out for a *part* of me, maybe. The worst part."

"Why, I'm just a little voice inside your own head."

"I got better voices than you to listen to." She took one hand off the steering wheel and pressed her bosom. "In here."

"You're getting too involved with impulsive people, Agnes. Hard telling what they want you to do next."

"You ain't nothing but mental illness."

"If you'd listened to me," he said, "you'd be a happy woman today."

"That right!?" she said. "I don't believe that and when I get home, I tell TJ you're bothering me again."

"Figure it up. Here you worried about a little impulsive spending! Consider that tithe promise. Instead of ten dollars on the hundred, suppose all these years you done just gave nine. Suppose that you had for yourself or your own loved ones one out of every ten dollars you gave the church, for—how long?"

"Thirty years," she said. And she thought how she'd stopped short of buying a little electric train at the pre-Christmas sale. "I been a faithful tither for thirty years." One dollar a week made fifty-two in a year. Take fifty-two thirty times and that was money worth having.

"And how's that good husband anyway?"

"He just like always. He good. He give me a brain pill when I get home, and you be knocked dead, you old haint." The doctor had explained it. Some people saw haints, others heard them. Once TJ told her the tithe was just too high a cut; they ought at least to take it out of what was left after expenses, not before. But when he saw the expression on her face, he never said that again.

"TJ good for sitting in the easy chair, yeah? He good on the dance floor and good at praying in the church pew. Oh, yeah. But where's all your fine children and grandchildren, woman?"

"They in my heart."

She heard laughter like bones rattling. Her hair tried to stand on end. She looked hard at the seat beside her. Just as she was about to see him, she had to look straight ahead. Something was passing in the road ahead, a kind of ghost cat, running hard from one side of the road to another. But she'd gotten a glimpse of him, Mr. Bones. As a child, she'd seen him in the old-timey minstrel shows, so she knew what he looked like.

In the car, sitting on the bench seat beside her, he'd been almost transparent. He'd had one skeletal foot cocked up on the other thigh. It was just the vaguest outline of bones, maybe something of the rib cage, that she'd discerned. He looked like an X ray.

"Li'l spirits," she called out as if she was calling the chickens to get their grain. "Little girls."

They came buzzing like honeybees.

> *We're here*
> *Don't be scared*
> *You be all right*
> *Once you get home*

HOW TO DREAM

TOO EARLY, AUNT DEE WANTED LITTLE DIANE TO CLOSE her book and go to bed.

"You try to read with a flashlight, and I skin you," Dee said.

Diane wondered if a person could be skinned like a deer, or a rabbit, but she didn't say anything to her auntie.

Mumbling, Dee explained she needed to put her head down quick and take her table nap. "I want this kitchen dark for my nap," Dee said. Even the lamp on low hurt Dee's eyes.

Diane wanted a biscuit and some molasses, but Dee would not hear of it.

"Gotta sleep, gotta sleep, gotta close these eyes right now," Dee said.

As she watched Diane lie down obediently on her pallet in the bedroom, Dee advised her just to drift on off to dreamland. Diane wished her bed wasn't so low.

When she heard Dee snoring in the kitchen, Diane knew her auntie had *drifted off*.

You need a boat to drift, Diane had thought, and she imagined herself a red canoe. What a lovely fresh-learned word: *canoe*. In the canoe, Diane had a paper sack with the top rolled shut, and the bag had a biscuit in it. The biscuit was wrapped in wax paper. In the top of the biscuit, somebody had jobbed a hole with her finger, and through the hole the innards of the biscuit had been saturated with molasses. Diane wanted the biscuit so bad she could taste it. And then she was tasting it, and another part of her mind knew the red canoe had taken her to dreamland.

But there were a lot of other people there too. Talking and talking. And her mother was in charge, of course. Diane dreamed she walked back into the kitchen, and she'd never seen so many people in the kitchen. Aunt Dee was sitting upright, alert. Her rooster hair stuck up straight and alert, too. Occasionally Dee said something. Dee was interested. Dee's voice was getting high-pitched and excited. *Woolworth's*, they were saying. *The Crystal, White Palace. Stools* and *counters. Hamburgers.*

Through a crack in the door, Diane saw the light of one candle burning. The electricity must have gone off, or maybe it was a secret meeting. Yes, it felt like a secret. "Pipe down," somebody said to Dee. But there was her mother's voice crooning to Dee, including Dee. The room was full of spirits all crowded together. Sprawled on the floor, perched on the counter. In a kitchen chair, a girl sat on a big boy's lap. "This is a business session," her mother said, but what was that in her mother's voice—something warm and bubbly, something sweet as candlelight.

And streets were mentioned and different times of day. *Nonviolence. Nonviolence.* The syllables clamored like Halloween noisemakers. Then feet were moving. *Non, nonviolence.* Spirits flew up right through the ceiling. They evaporated like a pan full of water neglected on the stove. Just a little more bubbling, then a hissing, and they were gone.

Somebody put a pot of coffee in the prow of the canoe, but Diane wasn't sure if she was in the kitchen with her mother or her mother was standing in the canoe with her. "They asleep," she heard her mother say.

Then the voice of one man, kind and quiet, such a pretty voice, like soft fudge.

The two of them, Mama and Pretty Voice, went back into the kitchen and turned into two trees, her mother was a pine with so soft needles, and the man was an oak. A squirrel scampered over his big branches. In clusters of two, acorns hung beneath his big leaves. Their voices were like the limbs of trees sometimes entwining and sometimes stroking the wind. Diane imagined herself sitting in that man's lap, like a big girl in a big boy's lap. "Best biscuit I ever ate," he said.

Then her mother was scooping her out of the canoe. *You just lie over here beside Honey on his bed,* she said. "Mama needs your pallet."

Mama and Pretty Voice must have spread her pallet on the kitchen floor. They wanted to rest in the forest by themselves, not in the bedroom with the babies. Occasionally, from the kitchen floor, they whispered or sighed.

"You're heaven," he said.

JONATHAN, THE PIANIST

BECAUSE STELLA WAS DRIVING THE OLD CAR SLOWLY AND carefully, it was easy for Jonathan to follow them. Because he didn't want to crowd them, Jonathan didn't follow closely. Leaning into the car window before Stella could turn the key, Jonathan had invited Stella to join him for a snack at Dale's Cellar, after she took Cat home. "Maybe" was all she had said. She had seemed very uptight. Grim, maybe depressed. Angry. When he reached his arm across her to shake hands with Lionel Parrish, Jonathan had thought she might bite his forearm.

People had told him that the girl in the wheelchair—Cat—had had a gun. That she'd pulled a gun on Mr. Parrish and Stella and made them leave her alone in the building. But Jonathan hadn't seen a gun. Just Agnes and Gloria and Cat sitting in the circle of candlelight singing hymns. Maybe he had been stupid to join them, but they had sounded small and alone. He had thought of Goodman and Schwerner, dead in Mississippi, and their courage. Which was more dangerous for outsiders like himself, the cities or the rural South?

When he saw Stella pull up to the curb in front of a house with a wheelchair ramp, he parked his car half a block back. *Maybe,* she'd said. Maybe she didn't want her friend to know she was going out without her. Did they live here together? Should he approach them? Cat had looked pleased when he and Mr. Parrish shook hands. She'd just beamed, as though she had arranged the meeting, a Cat swallowing two tasty mice. He'd be glad to take Cat out with him and Stella sometime, just not tonight, the first time. He remembered the emotion in Stella's voice when he had teased her: *Now, my little Christian. Whom did we resurrect?* The layers of feeling when she spoke: *My mother.*

At Juilliard, one of the teachers had asked the new student, Kabita Rana, who was half Indian, which of the late Beethoven sonatas she played. *All,* she answered, and Jonathan suddenly had straightened up like a prairie dog scouting for danger. *Play the 110,* the teacher had said, scowling. All the lines in the teacher's rugged face became deeper. The 110, a wicked curveball. Kabita bounced out of her chair as though it were a trampoline; she glided toward the piano noiselessly as a cheetah. *Aren't you afraid of this piece?* the professor asked. She glanced over her shoulder but continued moving. *Sure,* she said.

Ah, the layers she put into the one word!

Sure, the teacher repeated, trying to imitate her. *I like the way you say that,* he said; he smiled at her, a little puzzled. The other students were studiously unimpressed, but Jonathan knew they were idiots. Here was the real thing. He didn't know what kind of real thing, but the real thing. Only the battle-scarred teacher and he recognized it: the ability to communicate in some musical way many *contradictory* emotions at once, in a single word, perhaps a single note.

She had played the hell out of the Beethoven 110, from the simple heartbreaking opening melody to the fiendish fugue. She played fearlessly but without aggression. She loved the music too much to attack it. And she had stirred Jonathan's heart to its depths.

The way his own playing had stirred Stella.

What would it mean not to have a successful career as a concert musician? NYC seemed as full of teeth as the South, just filed down for different purposes. Despite the obvious dangers, Jonathan liked the pace of southern life; their soft drawl was oddly pleasant. Stella's was. The temple bombing in Atlanta back in the 1950s flashed before him. A warning. And other harassments: a gunman had attacked a synagogue in Gadsden, Alabama. Jonathan had no inclination to attend synagogue except on Yom Kippur.

After Stella parked—more than three feet from the curb—he watched her get out into the dim light and lift the trunk lid. The passenger door opened slowly; Cat must have given it a shove. The folded wheelchair seemed heavy, and Stella had to lean into the trunk at an awkward angle, but she grasped the chair confidently, set the wheels on the pavement, expanded the chair, put down the footrests, and wheeled the chair into the wedge space between the open door and the passenger seat. Ah, the distance from the curb had been intentional. Stella and Cat were a team, he could see, used to their routine.

When they went up the ramp, Stella pushed the chair from behind, and Cat worked the wheels to help her. Stella put keys in Cat's lap; Cat opened the door and then rolled inside. Quickly, Stella walked down the ramp. At the end of the ramp, she took off running down the sidewalk. She didn't seem scared; she just sped up, running in an easy, happy lope.

Jonathan started his car and followed her. Had she forgotten that she'd said "maybe"? Maybe she didn't understand that he meant now. She must live close by. But no, she ran a block and then another, taking time at the crossing to check for cars. He could easily overtake her, but he didn't want to. After four blocks, during a well-lighted stretch of sidewalk, she slowed down, and he brought the car up beside her. He tooted the car a gentle beep, she leaned down to check who was driving.

"There you are," she exclaimed. She crossed the easement of grass toward the car. "I thought I'd lost you back in traffic."

He leaned across and opened the door.

"Would Orpheus lose Eurydice?" he said.

She stopped. "You've got our roles mixed up." She sounded gay, happy to see him. Her thundercloud of anger had disappeared.

"You sound cheerful," he said.

"I'm free," she answered. "I feel free."

"Too free to go to Dale's with me?"

"Free *enough*," she answered. "But, hey, I'm engaged to Cat's brother."

"I don't care, if you don't," he said. "I've been out with married women."

She got in the car. "I've never been to Dale's."

"Probably too late for a full dinner. We'll just get a snack this time."

And the conversation began its happy weave. *Why were you running?* I like to make my heart pump. Especially after I take Cat home. *You said you used to play the cello.* Not anymore. That was my childhood path. Not now. *Maybe you just need fresh encouragement.* (But he didn't want to encourage her; maybe she knew what she was doing; maybe he trusted her judgment.) *When did your mother die?* When I was five. Let's not talk about it right now. I live with my aunts. *You seemed upset after the bomb scare.* I was mad at myself. For leaving Cat. For not being brave, like Gloria and Agnes. *But now you're not still mad.* I got over it. Cat and I talked about it. *And you're engaged to her brother?* We talked a little about that, too. To be honest, I'm not so sure. *Where is he?* On the island of Tonga, in the South Pacific.

Oh.

He added, "Actually, I haven't ever been out with a married woman."

"All the better," she said.

WHEN THEY PAUSED at the top of the steep steps leading down to Dale's Cellar, Jonathan offered the crook of his arm to her. *She's southern,* he thought. *Used to courtesy.* Then he remembered how she'd run, like a young gazelle. He glanced at her feet: socks and tennis shoes, but this was a fairly fancy place. Maybe she didn't know. But she was cultured, loved his playing. The phrase *genteel poverty* occurred to him. Stella took his arm and smiled at him.

At the bottom of the stairs, the restaurant was very dark.

"Stygian gloom," she said.

"You like Greek mythology?" he said.

A waiter approached them. He was wearing a gleaming starched white jacket. His skin was so dark that the coat almost seemed uninhabited. The restaurant began to come into focus for him, hazy clouds of low light here and there. Only a few couples. Three businessmen.

"Give us the most private table, please," Jonathan said. "The darkest table with the tiniest light."

"Yessir," the waiter said. "It's too late for dinner, sir."

"We'll have an appetizer," Stella said pleasantly.

"And dessert," Jonathan added.

After they got settled, Jonathan remarked, "This place feels like New York. Almost."

"Except all the waiters are black and all the customers are white," she said.

"I meant the ambiance. The darkness."

"I like it, too," she said.

She had chosen to sit with her back to the restaurant, facing only him and the wall. He liked that.

Then she was asking him if he had traveled, and because of the dark, he told her about traveling in Norway, and how dark the tunnels were there, how they

seemed to eat the light, and what you dreaded when you drove inside was seeing the red eyes of a cow or sheep glowing at you from the middle of the road.

She had never been out of Alabama. The fact amazed him—she seemed
well educated, spoke well, was obviously not conservative. *Genteel poverty?*

"Have you ever been engaged?" she suddenly asked him.

"Not exactly. Almost. I've had girlfriends." He thought of Kabita and felt
sad. His failure, not hers. "But you're engaged," he said. "Where's the de
rigueur ring?"

"I don't wear it."

"Why not?"

She seemed confused, and he wondered if she were a neurotic. His shrink
had told him to beware mirroring himself with neurotic women.

"Well, it's too big to stay on." Now she looked mischievous. "And it's too
cheap."

"Cheap?" A materialist. She had seemed ethereal, otherworldly. So thin.

Now she laughed. "Well, Don got it out of a Cracker Jack box."

He ordered chardonnay, shrimp cocktails for their appetizer, and a cherry
turnover with warm cheese sauce for dessert. She told him about her
engagement—which sounded like a freak or whimsical accident—to Don
Cartwright.

"But I meant it," she added. "Until recently."

"How recently?"

She shook her head and answered vaguely, "Somewhat gradually."

"Do you ever tell lies?" he asked her.

"I try not to. Why?"

"I just want to know what kind of footing we're on here," he said. He felt as
though he were sailing on Casco Bay, with a favorable wind. He'd liked Port-
land. Why hadn't he fled north from New York to Maine, instead of down here?
It could have gone either way till September 15. Suddenly he felt exhilarated.
He wanted to tell her about sailing in the harbor at Sydney, with his father,
when he was sixteen. Here in this underground hideaway in Birmingham,
things felt "down under"—as fresh and exciting as Australia.

"I've been engaged twice," she said, and he knew he'd intimidated her into
trying to tell the truth about herself. But she wouldn't be trying to be open if
she didn't trust him, if she didn't like him.

"What happened before?"

"He was incapable of radical thought."

He was startled. She sounded very judgmental. Globally judgmental. Yet she was speaking softly, smiling sweetly. She had almost drained her glass of wine.

"Are you a Communist?" he asked.

She just shook her head: no. Maybe she didn't trust him at all. Why did trust matter?

"You seem fairly conventional to me," he said. "In a good way, I mean."

"I'm not."

"I mean, like, you're not going to suddenly toss your glass down on the tile floor."

In an instant, the glass had shattered on the floor.

She remained perfectly calm, as though nothing at all had happened. The waiter came promptly with a whisk broom and a dustpan. "So sorry," Stella murmured in a genteel voice.

"Would you like another?" Jonathan asked, trying to match her imperturbable manners.

"I'd better not," she said. "That was the first glass of wine I've ever had in my life." Now she was smiling broadly.

"You're not telling the truth."

"I try not to lie," she repeated, impishly.

To hell with this, he thought. He cleared his throat. "Let's just cut to the chase and be frank with each other," he said. "Always."

"Well," she began gravely, "I was engaged to someone before Don. He was an organist, and I loved his playing. He used to drive a motor scooter, and I was terrified of it."

"Playing the organ must be like driving a tank," he said.

She made no reply, but he knew she disagreed. The shrimp cocktail, served in a collar of ice, was before them. The shrimp were large and plump. He heard himself saying, "They fly them in, from the Gulf." Then he heard himself adding stupidly, "I can't get enough of them," and she asked why, and he said, "Shellfish. In New York I never ate shellfish."

"I've never eaten shrimp before," she said.

"Christ!" he said. "This is a night of firsts for you." He felt good again, daring. "Ever been kissed?"

"Many, many times," she said. "Very, very beautifully." She looked happy to remember it, happy to be there with him talking about it. "We southern girls are very good kissers," and he knew why without her having to say so: *because we don't go much further.*

He ordered another glass of wine for himself.

He watched her watch him dip the flesh of his shrimp into the cocktail sauce. Then she did the same. She tentatively bit off the end of her shrimp. "It's delicious," she said. "So tangy. I like the texture." She ate another shrimp. "It's like eating my little finger," she said. She crooked her pinkie, dipped the knuckle in the sauce and sucked it clean, while she stared into his eyes. "Tastes just the same."

"Don't use so much sauce, so you can taste the fish."

What kind of life had she led? Unbelievably sheltered? Somehow *eccentric,* even for the South.

"My mother let me eat with my fingers and then suck on them. You can if you want to." She smiled, challenging him. "I'll let you."

"No, thanks," he said, and he could feel himself blushing. He stabbed a shrimp with his cocktail fork.

"The forks are too cute not to use," she said. "Three-pronged, like little tridents."

He drank his wine too fast to appear suave. The kitchen had closed; their turnovers were waiting under the heat lamp. Six shrimp were not enough for him. He coveted hers. Shrimp had never been so delicious. They had never tasted so firm and succulent, fresh like the Gulf. He almost didn't want the sauce, though he loved horseradish. "This is one of the best restaurants I've ever been in," he said, "ambiance-wise, company-wise, and food-wise."

"Methinks you have a whiff of the Underworld about you."

"Hades?" And the wine. More delicious with every sip.

"My favorite myth is that of Hades and Persephone," she said. "When I was engaged to the first boy, we had a dangerous experience. Then we got engaged."

"Isn't just living dangerous enough?"

Her blond hair was gleaming in the candlelight, with a beautiful up-scroll at the end, almost like a violin or an unfurling fern. She explained that Persephone got to live half the year with her mother, half with her lover: "the perfect balance."

"Do you have a nickname?" he asked. Shadows played across her pale face.

He loved how the darkness of the restaurant isolated them. He quickly said, "I'd call you Fern." He held out his hand to her across the table, but she didn't take it.

"Fern?" she repeated.

"Fern or Pheasant," he said.

"Pheasant," she said brightly. "I like that." And her eyes danced.

And the turnovers were there. She'd eaten all her shrimp. None left over for him.

"I'll never forget this," she said a little stiffly. "The night I first ate shrimp and drank wine."

Lord, he wondered, *where had those other boys been taking her?* Ed Salem's Drive-In? Across the front of Ed Salem's (always packed with cars), pink neon footballs blinked in series, simulating the arc of a pass. "Why is Vulcan's light sometimes green, sometimes red?" he asked.

"If it's red, somebody or some people have been killed in a wreck." She spoke as though the life were draining out of her.

He reached his hand to her again, and this time she took it. Neither spoke for a moment, then he said quietly, "Let's eat this before the cheese sauce gets cold."

He loved the sugary graininess of the sweet melted cheese, and the cherries were allowed to be authentically cherries, not mired in overly sweet goo. The pastry was flaky and flavorful—probably made with pure lard.

"My Jewish mother would be ashamed of the way I've eaten this evening," he said soberly.

"No, she wouldn't," Stella said. "She'd be glad you were having a good time. So would mine."

They'd eaten everything, with incredible relish. Drained their glasses. His best move would be to stand up, to take her home now.

"Pheasants are heavy and slow moving," she said, "when they rise." She spoke solemnly. "They have beautiful plumage. Fit for nature and for art. Hat decorations, anyway."

He nodded. She wasn't heavy. She was light as a wisp. With her fingertip, she swabbed up the last of the sugary cheese sauce sticking to her plate.

"My mother let me do this," she said.

"Do your aunts?"

"No." She smiled. "I wouldn't think of it." She licked her finger.

If this were New York, he'd be mortified, but it was only Birmingham. Actually, he was pleased with her. She was childishly, eccentrically, at ease. Maybe that's what she was demonstrating.

WHEN THEY WERE ABOUT to leave the restaurant, a young woman dressed in red stood up beside a table in the gloom.

"Stella?" she asked. And then, "I thought that was you."

Then she was embracing Stella, in her faded pedal pushers and checked shirt. This woman was dressed appropriately, in a seductive sheath dress with a soft cowl collar dipping toward her breasts. Her dark hair and eyes were somehow fiery.

"This is Ellie," Stella said, glancing at him out of the embrace. "We talk philosophy together."

"Really?" he said.

"Where's Buford?" Stella blurted.

"This is our friend Neil," Ellie said.

Neil stood up from his chair and shook hands. He, too, had a smoldering, fiery eye. *A good match,* Jonathan thought.

"Buford said for me to take her to see *Tom Jones,* while he was away. Great eating scene. Have you seen it?"

"It made us hungry," Ellie said and tossed her head.

"We've been out at Miles College," Stella said. "I teach there. Jonathan and I just met."

"Did you?" Ellie asked. She seemed troubled.

"He's a brilliant pianist," Stella explained. "Ellie's an actress, and she sings."

"Your aunts will be worried about you." Ellie smiled mysteriously. Jonathan thought he'd never met a more seductive woman.

When he offered Stella his arm to ascend the steps to Twentieth Street, she scampered up like a goat by herself.

In the Thunderbird, Stella said, "I guess I wasn't dressed appropriately for Dale's Cellar. I'm sorry. I should have changed."

Jonathan asked her about Ellie, and she said they'd ridden the bus to town together the day JFK was killed. Then she said, "Everybody falls in love with Ellie. It's her warmth. Me, too."

Jonathan replied thoughtfully, "But isn't she asking for trouble—going on a date when she's married?" He carefully kept condemnation out of his voice.

WHEN THEY APPROACHED the aunts' house, Stella asked him just to turn the nose of the car toward the driveway and let the headlights shine up it, that they always came and went by the back. It would alarm her aunts for her to come in the front.

"Thank you," she said. "I had a good time."

No physical contact whatsoever in her farewell. Skimpy words.

A short-legged white dog trotted down the driveway to meet her, and she stooped to pet his head. She petted the dog passionately, like a child, and he wondered why he was stirred by her. It was her oddness, maybe. It made him feel less odd. Jonathan wished he'd thought to call her Pheasant one more time. His hand stroked the mohair seat cover. The wool, though fine, could not be nearly so soft as the wing of a pheasant.

DEAR SELF,

TONIGHT, THIS ROOM AT MY AUNTS' SEEMS LIKE HOME.
I have found an anchor for my soul. It's in the music I love to hear, though I cannot perform it well.

Who makes the woeful heart to sing?—to use the phrase of an old Methodist hymn. It's not Jesus. Another Jew. I blaspheme. Jonathan. But the heart, my heart, must beat erratic, if it is to beat at all. I embrace my irreverence, my perversity, my failures, my lopsidedness, that I may be lukewarm, that I may blow first hot, then cold. My inconsistency and uncertainty. The depth of my sorrow and the height of my hope.

I can love. And I do love. Jonathan B. Green. Let me write his name again: J. B. Green. J. Bernstein Green. Jon Green. His name is verdant as the earth. His hair is like flame. I'm crazy as a jaybird.

And he?

I know nothing of what he feels. But how could he play the piano like that if he didn't know my heart? Subtle as my mother, but masculine. Perhaps he doesn't know he knows me. Even the pressure of his hand when we shook hands—perfect.

I am thirteen years old! Not the age of a college graduate at all. Emotionally, I am thirteen, throwing stem glasses on the floor on a dare! But emerging into the beginnings of my adult life in spite of that. What was I in college? Nothing but a giant child. So sheltered and innocent I was disembodied.

I think of the Negro waiters made visible by their white coats. I relish the image of the interior of the restaurant. Its darkness ignites me. I could lick my finger again to see if any of that grainy cheese sauce is left under the nail. I think of Manet's boudoir portrait of naked Olympia, lounging on a sofa, the dark servant behind her melding with the dark background. Flowers emerging. She staring boldly out of her frame. My eyes and ears are opened; my tongue has awakened—shrimp, horseradish, sweet, warm cheese and cherries. Ought to give me a bellyache! But it won't. I savor every mouthful again.

Before, I have been all mind. Smart enough, but so stupid.

I pause to read again what I've written.

AH, I SEE WARNING flags: I am enchanted by his music (as I was with Darl). I don't really know him, nor he me (as it was with Donny). Too much faith and trust on my part in the Don relationship, *that anyone could love anyone of goodwill.* Too encompassing! I have grown more cautious. Simply more sensible, perhaps?

But Don did/does speak to my soul in his own way: his kindness. Kindness made colorful with wit. I needed Don's kindness, his willingness to sacrifice almost everything—I saw it in his devotion to Cat. And Darl would have died to protect me. I wanted a *chevalier.*

Is it so easy to transfer love? As from Darl to Don?

It is if you're thirteen.

It is if love is only need.

But love is pleasure and delight, too. Wine and warm cheese sauce.

Make me fly!—that's what the little girls begged Timmy Beaton to do.

And I will require it of any husband: make me fly. And he may require the same of me.

Will I someday, an old woman of sixty, look back on these ruminations and muse, "How on fire I was then." Shall I ask, "And who was this Jon Bernstein—was that his name—Jon Green?" And "Did she (I) notice that Jon is a sort of variation on Don, and that *Don* starts with *D*, like *Darl*. And whatever became of *him*? Of them?"

But tonight I am not that forgetful creature of sixty. I am young and growing into my maturity, albeit belatedly. I shall have my life. My hand closes on it as surely as my fingers grip this pen. As surely I took up a cocktail fork this night, in a dark and seductive restaurant. (After I made the mistake of first using my digits and trying to cover up my lack of sophistication.)

How do I dismiss the warning flags? Darl and Don—who else were they, besides transcendently musical and supernaturally kind? Was there some lack in them as well as in myself? Darl was not weaned from his mother. His parents. And Don?

I don't know.

We reached out to each other on such a sad day, when Kennedy was killed.

I feel sad again. And Ellie? Is she troubled for herself or for me?

But I will not. I *will* not go sad.

I must note, briefly, that I was a coward today. I left the building when the bomb threat came. But is that being a coward? It's sensible. Probably Cat would not have stayed behind if I had not announced I was in love with Jonathan Green. She was refusing to abandon whatever was left of her ship. But why had she carried the gun to school in the first place? Her purse was heavy with it when we left the house.

I hope Cat will forgive me my fickle heart—or is it head?—my betrayal of Don. Ellie would.

Probably Cat will understand it all better than I do. I should never have told her Jonathan was hunchbacked and then dismissed such an attribute as a mere figment of my imagination. I cringe now at my cruelty.

SO SIMPLE, BLEAK EVEN—the interior of a practice room. Stark and bare. I go through a door. We are just a piano and two thin people in a bleached room. One male with red hair and skinny arms. One female, flat-chested, with blond hair. It is only the music itself that is glorious and complex. Encompassing and fulfilling.

Perhaps Jonathan is really only an emblem. Not the person himself but the promise that there may be such a person for me. One whose essence speaks to mine. He inspires in me a faith in life. Life has treasures. There are fine restaurants where adults sample new food, are curious about each other, *without compulsion.*

Independence, not engagement. Perhaps not even marriage. Just feeling. Nothing official. Ellie is my friend who understands the power of passion. She is not a college student settled in marriage. Not represented by a white blouse and a tweed skirt. She is a woman aflame with red.

What will come of my rush of joy? I feel incandescent, not red. And my flare of brightness has its dark streaks. I look at Don's paintings hanging around me in this room. They *interest* me. I feel sympathy for the soul that emanated them. But I am detached. Kind Don, prescient Don, who gave me permission in advance: *You can stop this anytime you want.*

Tomorrow I think the students and Christine are planning a sit-in. Gloria, my confidante, implied as much. I want to know Gloria, short and busty, I want to know all of them better. I have to work tomorrow. I can't possibly participate. I would stop them, if I could. Would I have the courage for protesting if I could go? I don't have to decide that. But I should quit this switchboard job. I've finished school and I should move on to find work that represents me. That promises the future.

Now I'm going to fold up this loosely woven summer blanket and put it away on the closet shelf. And, Don, forgive me, I must take down your paintings in this room. I will set them on the floor, turn their faces to the walls. The mind is a room. On my blank wall, I will imagine the bold stare of Olympia, engaging the world. Naked and unafraid.

For now, good night, dear old Self. I'll dream of pheasants, softly fluttering. Raising their heavy bodies into the air.

SATURDAY MORNING: EDMUND

ON TWENTIETH STREET, IN THE SKIMPY SHADE OF A LOAD-
ING ZONE sign, little Edmund Powers plunked his shoeshine kit down across
the street from the Tutwiler Hotel. It was Saturday morning. Might be some
businessman would want his shoes shined before lunch. Edmund knew they
could get their shoes shined inside the hotel, but might be they'd want their
shoes bright by the time they walked in the door. Not much business happening for a Saturday morning.

Edmund spied Mr. No-Legs swinging down the street, dressed in his good,
solid blue suit. *Can't shine his shoes,* Edmund thought. When the man passed,
Edmund said politely, "Howdy-do," and Mr. No-Legs answered him in kind,
not breaking the rhythmic placing of hand mallets before him on the sidewalk
and swinging his body through. Edmund had heard Mr. No-Legs had lost his
legs in Korea, shot off by a bazooka.

More white women out shopping than any white men doing business, but
sometimes men had Saturday meetings; sometimes a group would go laughing into Joy Young's. *Egg Foo Young,* Eddie read on the restaurant's window.
Well, he knew what eggs tasted like, anyway.

Oh, no, here came a madman. A sidewalk preacher. His mama had said,
"Now, you want to testify at revival, or in church—that's fine. But folks that
preach on the street corner—they got a screw loose, and I don't want you acting anything but normal when you out in public." She said it was dangerous to
be a standout.

But Edmund could feel the pull of it—just standing on the street corner, opening your mouth, and proclaiming the Lord. He might be able to save every soul in the city, he himself. Folks just needed to hear. It wasn't the people in church; it was the people out of church who needed to hear the Word. Over in Five Points, there was a statue of Brother Bryan, kneeling. He wasn't in Bible clothes. He had on an overcoat, and in one hand he held a hat with a crease in the crown. He was all white, even his clothes and his hat. The strangest thing about him was that he was praying looking up. Edmund had always been told to bow his head in prayer. It seemed disrespectful to look right up into the face of God.

If Edmund's mama would let him preach on the street corners, and he saved every soul in the city—who knew? Maybe right beside Brother Bryan, they'd make a statue of a little colored boy in all-white marble, kneeling, with his head respectfully bowed.

Here came the madman, wearing a sandwich board, written on with Scripture. The word *Blood* was printed extra big and in red. Full of curiosity, Edmund moved his shoe kit closer. Close by, another man with a sling sack of newspapers was getting ready to call out. Maybe some Mr. Big would buy a newspaper and read the headlines while Edmund shined his shoes. The man would hitch up his pant leg and then rest his shoe sole on the box handle, which doubled as a foot platform. Mr. Big would rest an elbow on his cocked knee and open the newspaper he'd just bought. When Edmund was finished with one foot, the man would step down with that foot, and change sides.

Edmund was proud of his little box kit. Years ago, his big brother Charles had made it in Manual Training class, sawed the boards to the pattern, nailed it together, sanded it, and varnished it with shellac. It had taken all semester. Edmund wanted to work with his hands, and that would be a hobby, when he was a preacher like his beloved Reverend Shuttlesworth. It was a good hobby for a minister; Jesus had been a carpenter.

To look busy, Edmund took out his strips of flannel; he had a black one and a brown one, and an oxblood one. He'd shake them out and fold them more neatly, be industrious. The sunshine was hot on his head and shoulders. If he pretended he'd just had a job and now he was straightening up his office, he might get just the right amount of attention.

In a loud voice, the preacher asked, not of anyone in particular: "Which are you? The wheat or the tares?" He stopped to let his question sink in. He spoke to the empty air, or maybe the blue sky above. He was a big man, poorly dressed in wrinkled tan clothes. "There's a grrrrrreat winnowing coming. The chaff will be blown away by the breeze." He pulled his unbuttoned shirt together across his T-shirt, as though he could feel a wind. "A breeze is coming to Birmingham. Watch out, brother! Watch out, sister! Are you washed in the *Blood* of the Lamb?"

The newspaper vendor—a small weasel man in comparison to the hulking evangelist—turned his back to the evangelist and called out just as loudly: "Extra, extra! Read all about it. King arrested in St. Augustine." The little vendor wore a flimsy cap with a bill, like a painter's cap.

"I say unto ye," the evangelist shouted, but there was nobody there but Edmund. "There will be weeping and wailing and gnashing of teeth." He pointed toward the sky. "There's a fiery furnace where God makes steel. He will cast down all pagan gods. Vulcan will tumble from the mountaintop, and Red Mountain will open and gush blood and rust."

Edmund couldn't help but look south to see if Vulcan was being uprooted, but Vulcan stood serene and shiny, holding up his arm, his head in the clouds.

The newspaper vendor yelled again in a high-pitched voice that demonstrators had been jailed in St. Augustine. He took off his paper cap to smooth his hair straight back from his forehead and temples, which were large and shiny. *Receding hairline,* Edmund thought. He felt knowledgeable.

A few people walked by on the other side of the street. Two men went inside the Tutwiler, and three white girls went in the Tutwiler Drugstore. A brown man in a matching suit with a felt hat shuffled by.

"King jailed in Florida," the weasel vendor screamed. Edmund had promised Reverend Shuttlesworth that he would go to jail, but he never did quite get the chance.

"Ten cents, only a dime. Read all about it."

Edmund had a dime, but he knew the vendor wouldn't like it if he bought a newspaper.

"Repent of your wickedness," the evangelist exhorted. Edmund thought, *But I ain't done nothing.* "Sin is a woman with jade in her navel! Sin is mixing of the races! Sin is eating blood and meat!"

The evangelist began to back up toward the vendor while the vendor backed up toward the evangelist. Edmund hoped there would be a collision.

"Good news! Good news!" the evangelist shouted. "Jesus is the *good* news!" A businessman in a suit walked right past all of them, the evangelist, the vendor, and Edmund, but the hulking evangelist said to Mr. Big in an ordinary voice, "Brother, can you spare a dime?" He actually held out his hand. Edmund knew what Brother Bryan would do. Once he'd given a beggar the overcoat off his back. "Brother, can you help?" When he wasn't fired up, the big old evangelist sounded old.

Mr. Big just kept walking. Edmund wondered if *he* should give the evangelist a dime, but before he could decide, the evangelist turned around and said to the vendor, "Brother, can *you* help?"

To Edmund's surprise, the vendor dug into his pocket. "I reckon so," he said. "What's the news from heaven?"

"It don't look good for this city." The evangelist shook his head sadly. "It's Sodom and Gomorrah. Can a hundred righteous be found? Can fifty righteous be found? Brother, can ten righteous be found?"

The vendor didn't answer.

"Well," the evangelist went on in an ordinary voice, "what's the news from earth?"

It was as though they were in church doing a responsive reading, or singing a duet. Edmund just crouched quietly beside his shoeshine box, listening.

The newspaper vendor said, "Seems like you got the bad news, and I got the good. They got that big nigger troublemaker in jail."

"That right?" the evangelist said.

"Wanna buy a paper?" the vendor asked. "Read about it?"

"Yeah," the evangelist said, and he gave the vendor back his dime.

Edmund wanted to laugh. Then both men turned their backs to each other and hollered out at the same time: "Extra, extra!" and "Repent! Repent ye today!" Edmund did laugh, but he tucked his head down, so nobody would see him laughing at two white men. They yelled their lungs out for a few minutes, and then they both stopped.

The vendor said, "People can't hear the headlines what with you shouting out."

The evangelist answered, "This is my corner."

Trouble, Edmund thought. He got ready to move quick, if he needed to. *Don't ever be caught in a cross fire*, his mama had taught him.

"Your corner?" the newsman asked. "Your corner is across the street."

But the evangelist stood his ground. "God changed it to over here. This morning. He said there was more business over here at the White Palace Grill."

"He's right," the vendor said. "That's why it's my corner."

They were both crazy. Edmund stood up slowly, not to attract their attention.

The evangelist slapped his sandwich board with his hand. "You eat meat?"

"Of course I eat meat. I eat right here at the White Palace Grill."

"That's not what they serve," the evangelist said.

"You gonna get yourself sued."

"I don't care. What they got is ground-up cardboard soaked in goat's blood."

The vendor took off his cap and smoothed his head again. "They have a place for people like you."

"In the Palace?"

"No. In the loony bin. Tuscaloosa."

"It's my work," the evangelist said. He sounded whiny. "You try to make a living peddling words."

"I do." The vendor held up a copy of the *Birmingham News*.

"Let's swap around. You stand over there across the street where I used to be, and I'll stay here. Gimme the papers. You can wear my sign." He began to struggle to pull the sandwich board up over his head.

"You gotta be crazy," the vendor said.

The evangelist got the boards off. He rolled his chest around as though it were good not to be confined, but his face contracted with meanness. Edmund could see it. The man was losing his mind in a new way.

"You're tired of your life, ain't you?" the evangelist said to the vendor.

He Klan, Edmund thought. *Not no preacher. He Klan. Watch out!*

The evangelist went on, "I can see it writ on your face."

The vendor wouldn't back down, but he spoke slowly and carefully, as though he'd considered the matter. "No, I'm not tired of my life." He took off his paper painter's cap, smoothed his hair, and put it back on. "I don't believe anybody's tired of their life. Unless you are."

"See," the evangelist said, and now his voice was all pleading, not a bit cruel. Suddenly Edmund knew what he was seeing—*multiple personalities.* He'd heard a sermon about it—how we have different people inside us, fighting one another. That was what was wrong with the evangelist. "See," the evangelist said, "I'm dying for a hamburger, but I can't go in, see. God's watching me. But if I took your place, then God would think it was you going in."

"God knows the difference between you and me." The vendor seemed shocked.

"He's taking a nap."

"What?" The newspaper vendor couldn't believe his ears, Edmund could tell. Neither could he.

"He's just dozed off," the evangelist explained. "God don't see good with his eyes closed."

"How do you know that?"

"It's the only way to account for the holy carnage that's about to happen here," the big evangelist said, and suddenly he spoke in the tongue of an educated man. "God's asleep. That's the only way it could happen. Undercover F.B.I., brother." He flashed his badge. "Give me your papers, and you get your ass across the street. You, too, sonny," he said to Edmund. "Take this goddamned sign."

SATURDAY MORNING: LEE

WHEN LEE WOKE UP SATURDAY MORNING, THE FIRST thing she did was to touch her poor mutilated shoulder. It hurt so bad she sleepily swung her legs over the side of the bed and shuffled her way to the good light in the bathroom to inspect her injury. When she saw in the mirror her whole shoulder was swollen and red, she woke up. Around each of the four curved lines, the flesh seemed infected. Then she glanced at her face. Her cheeks and forehead, even her neck, were red with fury. Her sleeveless night-gown was pink, but the flush on her face wasn't reflection. In wonder she stared at her face and saw she was still turning; she'd never seen herself so close to beet red. Then she realized her bottom was throbbing. It was shame that had really awakened her. Not the shoulder.

She hurt so badly she was afraid to go to the toilet.

She stalked back into the bedroom.

Yes, he was in bed. He had his elbow crooked back behind his head, and he was using it for a pillow. The real pillow was pushed aside. When he came in the night before, he had not wakened her. Though it was painful to walk, she hobbled over to the bed. No need to bend over to sniff him. Over his body hung the rank aroma of klavern beer, and Ryder had a smug little upturn to his lips.

Before she knew it, she had the broom in her hand. She had been to the kitchen and back. She wanted to bash him. She wanted to smack his nose into his head. While she tightened her grip on the broom handle, she realized she didn't have the right weapon. The straw end was too soft, and the handle end was too light. Quickly she used the broom to sweep away the cloud of beer vapors hovering over him. She felt witch-crazy—sweeping the air over him. If she bashed his upturned face with all her might, before she could come close to getting even, he'd just wake up. Leaning the broom against the wall, she glided noiselessly into the children's room.

Though she was aware of their three little shapes under the summer sheets, she didn't even glance at the children. She knew Bobby and Tommy were curled into the double bed; Shirley had her own little single bed. Her three little bears. Their beds almost filled the bedroom. Solemn as a judge, Bobby's baseball bat stood in the corner. His fielder's glove had slid halfway down the shaft. Lee bent over and started working the glove up the bat when Bobby said, "Mom?"

His voice was so pleased and fresh, she felt washed with guilt. She could feel all the blood draining out of her head while she stood up.

"Did I wake you up, son?"

"No, ma'am. I was already awake," he said softly, respectful of his sleeping brother and sister. "Just lying here thinking." He sat up.

He was wearing a Superman T-shirt to sleep in, and he was so adorable, she wanted to gather him in her arms and kiss him all over. She knew he was too old for that, and she blushed even to have thought of it.

"Mom," he said, concerned, "what happened to your shoulder."

She wanted terribly to tell him. She looked at him again, his brown hair down on his forehead. Really, she liked his hair better that way than when it was all combed with water for church. The dangling shock of hair made him look more like a little boy. No matter how much she wanted to complain about Ryder, she knew Bobby was too little to tell him about his father. Maybe when he was sixteen.

"Well," she answered slowly, "I don't know. Must of been mosquito bites I scratched in my sleep." But Bobby wasn't looking at her shoulder now; he was looking at her breasts, through the rayon nightgown. While she knew it was just childish curiosity, for just a second Bobby had looked like Ryder. "I got to go to the bathroom," she said.

By the time she stepped back up to the sink, she was wondering if she would go through with it—if she would ever get even with Ryder, and more. Though she dreaded it, she knew she had to sit on the toilet.

It hurt so bad to go, the tears came to her eyes and overflowed. She wished

Ryder could be locked up in jail for what he'd done to her. Well, at least she'd found the Miles College phone number in the telephone book—something he was too uneducated to do—and called in the warning. Even if the bomb had gone off, it would only have killed a few. Lee didn't want to kill those people, any of them. They hadn't done anything to her. She remembered her satisfaction when even the crippled girl had rolled out the door onto the porch and someone had turned her around and bumped the big wheels of her chair down the step.

Last September, Lee had felt the blast come up through the floor, just after the congregation had risen to sing. Again, nearly a year later, Lee shuddered with the vibrations of it. Her body had known something awful was happening. Right at that moment, something had happened that she'd always remember.

When she'd seen their photographs in the paper, she had thought, *They're nothing but innocent children,* and she knew the people who wanted to blow them up were crazy; they weren't just bad; they were so crazy with hate it was hard to imagine. And Ryder had almost made her blow up innocent people. It could have been somebody like Ryder or Dynamite Bob who did the first job. But not somebody like herself. After all, she hadn't done it. She hadn't killed anybody at Miles College, but if she had, it would have been Ryder's fault all the same.

Standing before the bathroom mirror, she gulped for breath. She knew when vampires looked in the mirror, they didn't see themselves. All the time she was thinking, she was staring at herself without seeing anything, but she wasn't a vampire. She hated blood. She was breathing hard. If you remembered somebody was as real as yourself, how could you kill anybody? As long as they didn't attack you. But they said the real nonviolent ones wouldn't fight back, no matter what you did to them. She could imagine herself, like the blond girl last night, standing around with them like they were just people. Like when you waited for the bus. Almost, Lee wished she could come to a college like that. It was outside agitators who stirred them up anyway. Coloreds weren't to blame any more than she would be to blame for things Ryder talked her into doing.

She focused in the mirror on her shoulder, on the four nail marks like crescent moons. It was Ryder she wanted to kill. And she knew how to do it. He'd taught her.

Quickly, she leaned over and flushed the toilet. Even though it wasn't her period, she'd have to wear a pad. But suppose she really did it? Killed him. She could make it look like an accident. Send the kids over to her mother's. His brother LeRoy was on the force; he'd want it covered up. LeRoy belonged to the same klavern as Ryder, but LeRoy wouldn't want his brother associated with bomb making. Not only smarter, LeRoy was a better man than Ryder. LeRoy was proud of himself and his police uniform.

Now why was that?

LeRoy was younger, and he'd grown up after their father had deserted the family. LeRoy had grown up better because he didn't have any bad example hanging around. And Bobby and Tommy would grow up better if Ryder wasn't there.

There was a gentle knocking on the door. "Mom, can I get in the bathroom now, please."

Bobby was a polite, good child. She asked him to tiptoe into the bedroom and please bring her robe and hand it to her through a crack in the door.

Without any protest, he did as he was told.

"Here, Mom," he said from the other side of the door. She reached her hand through, put on the robe, checked the toilet to be sure there was nothing shocking in it, and came out. Sweeping his hair aside, she couldn't resist planting a kiss on his forehead. "I'm going to send y'all over to Big Mama's," she said, "so your daddy can sleep late."

Didn't she sound like a good wife? Well, she was. But she was an even better mother.

"Want me to get them up?"

"Yes." She went to the phone and explained quietly to her mother: "Ryder wants the kids out of the house. He's making something. I don't know what. He said he wants to concentrate."

Concentrate—that was a word her mother used to use when Lee was a schoolgirl. "Never mind the radio or what all," her mother would say. "Just concentrate on your lessons."

Lee went to the cardboard canister of Quaker Oats; deep down in the oats was where they kept the directions for making a bomb. The folded paper was always coated with oatmeal dust when she drew it out. Well, she'd get dressed because once she made the bomb and started the clock, she'd need to get out herself. She'd just check to be sure he was sleeping soundly.

Once the kids were out of the house, she'd start on the wiring. She could use the dynamite sticks from last night, but she'd start all over with the mechanism. After he hurt her, Ryder had left her lying on her stomach, facedown, while he retrieved the dud bomb. She wasn't going to try the drip method again. She'd go over to the clock method. Not even on grass last night, but her face on the dark dirt, she had cried till her cheek was lying in a little mud puddle. If Ryder woke up while she was working on it at the kitchen table, she'd just smile sweet as pie and tell him she was practicing. If he didn't wake up, she'd put the bomb on the night table right beside his head. Whether he woke up or not would be a sign, whether to kill him or not.

She pictured the cloth on the bedside table. It had a ten-inch drop of crocheted lace that her mother's mother had made. She didn't want to blow that up. When Ryder saw the black mud on one side of her face, he had laughed and said, "Well, I guess you're half nigger." Before she set the bomb on the table, she'd take up the cloth.

She thought of the expression "Saturday night special" for the cheap guns that the coloreds bought. Well, this would be more special, and she couldn't wait till night. She needed to do it at least by early Saturday afternoon, before Big Mama would be sending the kids back to the house.

SATURDAY: AGNES

TRAFFIC ON TWENTIETH STREET HAD PICKED UP RIGHT
smart, Agnes noticed, with a lot of police cars circling the Tutwiler Hotel.
Where Twentieth Street T'ed into Woodrow Wilson Park, one of the police was
standing close to the bronze statue of a World War II soldier throwing a hand
grenade. Though it was a green statue, of course it depicted a white man, and
that was another white man inside the bright blue uniform standing beside
the metal statue.

What is love? She mouthed the question without making a sound, as her eye
fell on a little shoeshine boy industriously snapping his rag while he polished
a white man's foot. With complete confidence she answered, *God is Love.*

And it was right to tithe; it meant *I love.* She hadn't deprived TJ or herself of
anything *significant.* Her haint was kind of like Satan. TJ had given her her pill
when she'd come in last night. He had told her it was stress making her mind
act up—his getting beat up so bad. She hadn't added to TJ's load of worry by
mentioning the bomb scare. Now her mind was almost clear. *Get thee behind me,
Satan,* she mouthed, soundlessly.

Then an exclamation burst into the air—"Oh, no!"—for across Twentieth
over at the White Palace Grill, she saw Christine and pretty Arcola wearing her
braid. Agnes wasn't the only one looking. Just at that moment, a policeman
with a shepherd on a short leash stepped out of the Tutwiler Drugstore. *The
Lord is my shepherd.*

The police turned his head from side to side, looking all up and down
Twentieth Street. He waved down the street to Woodrow Wilson Park where

his blue buddy stood near the green hand grenade soldier, up on his pedestal. When TJ was a young man back from World War II, he had marched down this same street in a parade. Wasn't no statue to TJ.

Finished with his job, the shoeshine boy stood up and took his pay. The white man dropped the coins in the boy's palm, then he reached out and touched the little boy's nappy head! Agnes felt alarmed at so unusual a gesture; then she calmed herself and thought, *I guess that's progress.* Then she prayed with all her heart that that little boy would never have to go off to war.

She hurried up to the traffic light so she could cross over to speak to Christine and Arcola.

Them so glad to see her, Agnes hated that she must mention the cruising of the police cars, the flocking of the bluebirds, and the dog.

"Dogs!" Christine said, looking down the street.

The warning conveyed, Agnes let herself admire Christine, wiry and straight, in her navy blue polyester church suit. Arcola had on a neat pair of khaki slacks and a red-plaid blouse with short sleeves. Neat as a pin, like she'd stepped out of a Sears catalog.

"Just one," Agnes answered, but as she spoke, two more dogs and their uniformed handlers stepped out of the hotel lobby.

"Lady, I guess we better teach you to count," Christine said, trying to make a joke.

Arcola gripped Christine's arm. "If there's anything I'm scared of," Arcola said, "it's big dogs."

"They on leashes," Christine answered.

"Yes, they are," Agnes reassured. But the dogs were always kept on leashes till the moment of attack. "You know they can unsnap a leash so fast you can't hardly see what happened."

"Why shouldn't any black person, Arcola or me, sit at White Palace and order a hamburger?" Christine put her hands on her hips. "Don't talk scare talk, Mrs. LaFayt," she scolded. "The old laws being struck down every day."

"What you-all down here for?" Agnes scolded back. "You want to die with a half-eaten hamburger in your mouth?" She hadn't expected herself to talk back to Christine. The words were just in her mouth, and she let them pop out.

"I don't have dying in mind. I'm talking protest. Demonstration."

"Sit-in," Arcola added and flashed her sunshine smile. "Progress."

Agnes sighed. Wasn't any use to try to scold your teachers, she could tell that right off. Her impertinent words ringing in her mind, she could feel a headache trying to begin. She'd have to put a soothing tone on top of that. She spoke slowly, quietly, like the voice of history. "Back in the old days, you would hear 'So-and-so got a cross blazing in his yard.' And 'So-and-so she got rocks throwed at her walking from the bus stop.' And 'So-and-so, he dead.' "

Agnes remembered standing on her porch out in the country. Maggie was her neighbor then, too, and, long ago, Maggie had whispered words that still echoed in Agnes's mind. Well, she'd try to use the words for good, for warning these young women who had come up in a better time.

" 'Jim, he dead. He found hangin' on a peach tree down round Alabaster. His parts gone and they cut out his tongue.' "

"How change gonna happen," Christine asked impatiently, "we don't push a little? Who Jim anyway?"

"I'm thinking of your kids, Christine," Agnes softly continued. *His parts gone and they cut out his tongue.* "Who gonna take care of them—something happen to you?"

"I don't want to think about my kids right now."

"See what I mean?" But Agnes heard the resignation in her own voice. Wisdom was what you got from your own living; it couldn't be shared. Learning—that could be shared. Maybe. Not wisdom.

Christine put her hands on Agnes's shoulders. Softly, she looked into her eyes. "I don't want to think of my own kids, Agnes, 'cause I'm thinking of four little girls. My cousin and three others blowed up in church."

Agnes shook her head. "They don't want any violence done in their name. I know that. They gone to a better world."

Then Agnes recognized Charles Powers approaching them, from night school. He was smiling, looked so happy and pleasant.

"I knew I could count on you," Christine said to him.

"I've graduated from marching to sitting," Charles answered. "Howdy-do, Miss Arcola, Mrs. LaFayt." Suddenly, he crouched down as though he were sitting. He scooted fast, even though he was almost sitting down and made them all laugh.

"You don't have to 'Miss' me," Arcola said. "We not at school now."

"Your daddy know you down here?" Charles asked her. When he stood up straight, he towered over her. A big man. Agnes and TJ looked straight across into each other's eyes when they stood together. With hooded eyes, Charles looked down at Arcola affectionately.

Agnes was shocked that he reached out and touched Arcola's shoulder, but then, lots of schoolteachers ended up marrying their students. As Arcola said, they weren't at school now. And Charles was probably as old as Arcola. *People need to reach beyond their station in life*, Agnes told herself. *I'm not against that. He's a nice young man.*

"It's the dogs I'm scared of," Arcola answered. "I got bit once."

Fondly Charles said, "I ain't letting any dog bite you."

"May '63. I didn't know you then." She smiled a sweet smile.

"You go limp," Christine said aggressively. "We can't fight back. You know that."

Charles spoke right up to her. "I'm not so sure women ought to be involved."

"Don't give me that shit," Christine said. "Pardon my French, Mrs. Agnes."

But Agnes was reeling with shock.

Christine lowered her voice, but still Agnes marveled at the force in her voice.

"Martin Luther King got his start from Rosa Parks," Christine hissed. "She just one woman, and the South ain't never been the same since. And you think of those dead children at Sixteenth Street. Didn't nobody say, 'Now you send four little Negro boys down to prepare for Youth Service 'cause we don't want to blow up four little colored girls.' "

Why was Christine mad at Charles? Agnes wondered.

"You see some police dragging Arcola off by the hair of her head," she harangued on, "and you don't do *nothing*. When they grab you, Charles Powers, you go limp as a dead fish."

Her palms tingling, Agnes could feel how she'd grasped her pumps in both hands, how she had beat those men who were on TJ with the heels of her shoes as hard as she could. *You got to defend your own*, she thought, but she knew Martin Luther King would be ashamed of her. Still, he'd understand. Surely he would. Charles Powers was a fine young man, clean and straight, tall, hadn't filled out all the way yet. And his clothes were pressed and respectable. She remembered how he'd come the first time to night school, wrinkled and worn out, codeine cough syrup in his pocket.

"You and Arcola go walk around the block," Christine said to Charles and Arcola.

Christine just had to be bossy.

"We got an hour or more. We need to spread out," Christine went on. "Agnes, I need to talk to you."

Agnes thought that Christine wanted to apologize again: *I ain't taking none of that shit!* She sure ought to apologize, her a teacher, whether she was on school grounds or not. Agnes watched Charles and Arcola stop to talk to the shoeshine boy. Then she noticed the family resemblance between them. "Why, I believe that's Charles's little brother," Agnes said.

Christine said nothing. She fidgeted as though she wanted to talk, but she said nothing.

Agnes thought *Cat got your tongue for once?* but she said with dignity, "Mrs. Christine, can I do something for you?"

Christine sighed. Agnes waited. She knew Christine, shifting her feet on the pavement, would finally decide to get on with it. When she did speak, Christine's voice was tired and meek, as though it were coming from the lamppost nearby.

"I always kind of got the feeling that you and your husband done done all right?"

Now, Agnes was surprised, but she decided just to answer truthfully. She wouldn't be offended. "Yes, that's the truth," she said. "We both always been regular first at Eighth Avenue A.M.E., and now at Sixteenth Street. We save our money. We tithe, least I did when I was working, and we save. We gonna have a good retirement, I believe."

Still Christine looked worried, as though she hadn't gotten the answer she wanted.

"I know you ain't never gonna be no millionaire like A. G. Gaston, but you got some extra now, ain't you?"

"Yes, I do," Agnes said directly. "You need some money, Christine?"

"No." Then Christine hesitated again. She walked over to the lamppost and knocked on it, knuckles on metal. *Why she knocking on a lamppost like it some kind of door?* "But I kind of got one eye on the future," Christine said.

"What would you like for me to do?"

"I know you right about a lot, Agnes. And I do apologize for my language. I know life ain't no multiple-choice, machine-graded test. Once I go in that door to White Palace Grill, I don't know what might happen. You right. I might never come back out. Cat—she smart—she know that better than anybody. Cat called me up on the phone this morning at my house—"

"I'm scared these phones is tapped."

"They don't know me from any other nigger." Now Christine was impatient with Agnes for interrupting. "They ain't tapped my home phone. Cat didn't call at school. Anyway, she say in her little slow way, swallowing now and then, 'I been thinking about you, Christine. You and Agnes. You know Agnes is really a fine person, and she really brave—'"

"Oh, go on. She didn't say that." Agnes's heart was swelling with pleasure. Cat was the brave one, her holding her little white wax candle in both her hands, sitting waiting in the dark schoolroom for the bomb.

"Yes, she did, and she say a lot more good about you, too. She say that it take a lot of courage for a late-middle-aged woman like you to come back to school, try to get her GED. She say it take a lot of *determination* for you to come night after night." Christine went right on retelling, as though she were in a trance. "Every night sitting in that classroom with all the windows up and not a breath of air, and it just about a hundred degrees, and mosquitoes and moths and june bugs flying in, crawling on your clothes, in our hair—"

"She there, too." Agnes wished she'd taken care of Cat when Cat was a little girl. That was how much Agnes loved Cat, all of a sudden, with the cars going up and down Twentieth Street, and the police strolling along, king of the world. If she'd taken care of Cat, kept her clean and well fed, made her take naps, maybe she never would have gotten her disease.

"Let me get to what I'm trying my best to tell," Christine said. She shifted her weight from one foot to the other. "Cat say, 'But you know, Christine, there's a tragedy in Agnes's life. She never had no kids—'"

Agnes couldn't keep herself from gasping. *She never had any kids*—that was the way Cat would have said it.

" '—She never had no kids and she was made to take care of children. Made for it.' " Christine was speaking more and more rapidly. " 'And the sit-in coming on,' this is what Cat told me on the phone, 'it may be that there be a tragedy in your life, Christine. Or in my life.' And she say, 'You talk to Agnes, before time, you tell her anything happen to you, maybe she and her husband take care of your children.' And that's what I'm asking you, Agnes. Could you take 'em?"

Agnes threw her arms around Christine and burst into sobs of fear and gratitude. "Oh, honey, you don't have to ask me that. You know I'd take 'em. TJ and me, we ain't gonna leave your babies without no parents. Oh, honey—" Agnes grabbed Christine to her, tried to keep her safe with her own body. "Anything happen to you, they come right to our house, we got a three-bedroom house—we prepared for children, boys and girls—and they be just like our own flesh and blood."

While Agnes held her close to her body, Christine spoke in a gush, into Agnes's hair. "You know I could ask my sister. She used to 'em, but—"

"No, don't leave 'em with nobody but Tom and me. We done made our way. We ready."

"I got it writ on this piece of paper what I want. You take this, keep it safe. Dee wouldn't fight you, but I want everybody to know. I choose you."

Agnes began to kiss Christine right there on the street. It didn't matter who saw. But she listened to her thumping heart, how it wanted Christine to live and have her own life, even more than her whole being wanted the gift of children. Three children! She took Christine's typed-out paper, folded it, and kissed it, and pressed it next to her heart. She unbuttoned her dress right there on Twentieth Street and slid the paper insider her brassiere next to her flesh. They could snatch her purse, but they'd have to rape and kill her to get that paper.

"Now you go along," Christine said. "I don't want you anyplace 'round here 'cause that's my babies' future you got there." She gently helped Agnes rebutton. "And that's what this is all for." She nodded at the White Palace, a place no more segregated than any other diner, restaurant, or lunch counter in Birmingham. Someday her children would go inside the White Palace, same as anybody, and eat a hamburger.

Agnes kissed Christine again on her cheek. Half blind, Agnes made herself begin to move down the sidewalk, to the south. She could feel the hand grenade soldier and the police behind her, but with every step she put space between herself and them. TJ would never have to go as a soldier again. She tried to fix her eyes on the sky, to thank God for love.

But Christine must live to have her children. Still, she, Agnes, was loved, and chosen, and trusted. Her eye fell on the big Fair and Square sign of Blach's store, the square ruler and the lily, pretty as the cross of Jesus. *Thank you, Lord*

Jesus, she tried to just mouth it, but the words came out, and she knew she mustn't talk to herself out loud or people would think she was crazy.

"Wait," Christine called after her. Christine was standing where she was, but she called. *Softly and tenderly, Jesus is calling.* "You know their names, don't you?" *Calling for you and for me.* "Where the names come from. Diane, she oldest, and then I studied history, and the boys are named for kings of England." Christine in her Sunday suit stepped closer to Agnes, and the confidential words tumbled out. *Come home, come home, come home, come home.* "Eddie, Edward 'cause King Edward gave up all for the woman he loved, and I thought Eddie's father might love me like that, but he left for Detroit and didn't ever send for us." *All you children, come home, come home.* "And Henry, I call Honey, named after Shakespeare Henry the Fifth, who grew up wild but made a good man."

"I know their names," Agnes reassured. "Diane, Eddie, and Henry."

"I think Eddie might needs some glasses. I been intending to have him checked, but I never did do it."

"I get his glasses fit." *All you children, come home with me.*

Now they were holding hands, two women making one. Agnes stopped crying. She needed to listen and learn. She needed to know as much as she could. "Keep on," she said.

"That scar on Diane's shoulder. That just a chicken pox scar. I told her that was where she got her smallpox vaccination, but she ain't never been vaccinated really. I was scared of those vaccinations 'cause they say the germs ain't all the way dead. But I reckon I ought to go ahead and let her be vaccinated. And last Christmas wasn't so good, and I promised all of 'em, Santa Claus come double this year, if you can."

Agnes felt that a dagger had entered her heart. "Don't say that. Don't say that, Christine."

Christine shook her head. "You probably know better than me what younguns need. Don't pay any attention to this babble. Go on now."

But Agnes had to sound the warning. "My voices told me to shop, yesterday and again this morning. I got toys in this shopping bag. I been to the pre-sales, and me with no children that I buy for."

She saw horror pass over Christine's features. Her body was trembling inside her navy blue suit.

"You already got toys for my younguns' Christmas?"

"I been trying and trying to tell you. Don't do this sit-in. My voice say, 'Go look for Christine. Tell her go home this day.' "

"Well, you've told me." Christine was calming herself already. "I can't let myself be superstitious, Agnes." Her body ceased its trembling.

"You still got the choice, girl." Agnes's thoughts scrambled to make everything straight and fitting together. "Whether you live or die," she said, "these Christmas things going to your children. That's all *that* means. You live and keep your children for yourself."

SATURDAY: LEE

HER HOUSE WENT, NOT WITH A BOOM, BUT A LOW THUD and sudden collapse, as though a mallet from the sky had, with a single blow, pounded the structure earthward. The windows in the front bedroom blew out in a flash of light, and the entire corner of the house sank down. Immediately there were flames ready to consume the wreckage.

I can kill my enemies, Lee thought. *I know how. I know the long and short of it.* Why did that phrase please her so much? From her vantage point across the street, she puzzled over it an instant. *The long of it is deciding. The short of it is doing it.*

In the end, while he was snoring, she had snatched the beautiful crochet-lace-trimmed table drape, and she held it now, wadded up, pressed against her heart. Her treasure. She had taken her treasure away. In the end, she had cut away the clock and just lit the fuse. *Suppose I trip,* she had thought, but then she told herself the truth: *I won't.*

And then in her smugness, just after she positioned herself across the street, she remembered what she had seen. Just out of the side of her eye, running toward the lean-to back porch. She had seen Superman coming to save her worthless husband. Superman all shrunk little, and running like a little kid, not all-powerful and flying. Disappearing from her sight just at the moment of the boom, the exploding glass, the sinking down of the foundation, the refiner's fire.

That, she could not face. That, she would never ever face. She promised herself: she had not seen anything. That was impossible because Bobby had been sent to her mama's, and Bobby was a good child who obeyed. Run! She was the one who must run!

And she did. Nobody was looking. Not yet.

She ran like a wild woman. She made herself smile as she ran. When her neighbor a block away called out "Where you going?" Lee tossed back, "I won a prize. I won a prize. I'm going after it!" And she knew glee was all over her face because she had done it, and *that* was not imagined.

She was free. She had never been so terrified. Her bottom was healed now. She'd never been so scared and glad. She was strong as Wonder Woman, even panting like she was, and she held out one wrist to one side and the other to the other side to deflect whatever bullets or arrows might come. The sweat was pouring down her face, after she'd run half a mile or so. Lee made herself slow to a fast walk.

She saw a little colored boy pushing an ice cream cart, and she felt in her pocket. *Yes*, there was a dime. Just before she lit the fuse, she had picked up the loose change on the bedside table. She had done everything right. She'd sent the children, all the children, to her mother's, and Bobby was a good child, who always did exactly what she told him. Hadn't she said, *Y'all stay till I come to get you?*

The colored boy was barefooted, and the pavement was hot, but she knew their feet was tough and he was used to it by now, and he had ringworm on his neck, but she didn't care, the Popsicle would be wrapped up good. She folded the lace cloth into a triangle and draped it like a shawl over her shoulders. When she asked for orange, the boy lifted the thick square lid of his pushcart. Smoke from the dry ice came lofting out like he had the fires of hell in there. He reached down in it almost to the pit of his skinny brown arm, and out came her double-barrel Popsicle, with frost on its wrapper and its twin wooden handles sticking out.

Then she thought of Vulcan and his Popsicle.

"I've changed my mind," she said, and the boy looked scared, so she went ahead and gave him the dime, but she added, "I'd like cherry flavor instead of orange."

He peered down in the cold hole, returned the orange and brought up the cherry. Then he went on down the street, ringing his bell with new confidence and hope.

Red, old Vulcan, 'cause somebody died today.

She started to pull off the thin paper, but some of it wanted to stick to the frozen Popsicle. She breathed her warm breath on the stuck place to make it loosen, and it did—a science trick most kids hadn't known when she was growing up, but she'd taught all her kids.

Taught 'em every little trick she knew. And they'd taught others. When she was little, she'd kept the secret for herself. She could keep a secret. She licked the sweet colored ice. Cherry was more sticky than orange, she'd always thought.

She licked her Popsicle as she walked along. Not too fast, but fast enough. She was going someplace. Anyplace. Back when she was a child, she'd tested her theory about cherry and orange stickiness. Back when Popsicles were just a nickel each, she had bought two, and closed her eyes so she wouldn't see the color. It was her science experiment. A "blind" experiment to see which kind was stickier. She'd chosen cherry, but the teacher had said, though she couldn't see the colors, she could taste the difference in the flavors and knew in advance that way which was which, so it wasn't really what you could call a blind experiment for *stickiness*. Lee had been mortified.

When she was home, her mother had laughed at her, but then she had stopped, just all of a sudden, and said, "They can't expect a child to be a scientist. You done good, for the first time."

You can't expect any child to be perfect all the time. That was her mother's lesson.

Lee shook her head. She didn't believe that, and she didn't believe what you saw out of the side of your eye. Because that couldn't be true. Because she would never hurt one of her children. She had control about that. She bit off the end of one of the Popsicle columns, the left side first.

The lump of cold in her mouth cooled her tongue so hard it almost burned. For a moment she stopped walking to hold her Popsicle up in one outstretched arm, like Vulcan. Twice as powerful as Vulcan. If he could talk, Vulcan would say, *You did it! You had the nerve to kill, little girl,* because he was a *pagan* god. Her minister was agitating to have him pulled down. *Ryder deserved it*—seemed like Vulcan himself was rumbling approval from up on the mountain. She'd always liked Vulcan and felt proud of him. Birmingham was famous for Vulcan. Her minister was a weakling.

She licked and bit till half the Popsicle was gone, and there was the pretty jagged half, full of ice crystals on one edge like little needles. She heard the sound of a fire truck, its bell, and a siren. A police car drove right past her, lights flashing, red and blue.

She was just a lady with a white lace shawl who was enjoying a red Popsicle, walking along on the sidewalk.

People get what they deserve, she thought. Otherwise, God wasn't good, and he had to be good to be God. Justice was good. She'd done justice. Then she saw the pictures again—those four colored girls—the way they'd been in the newspaper. *They were just children.* And she didn't understand how God had let it happen in his own house. Maybe it was to make people think. Maybe it was to make people like her think. But that wasn't fair. God wouldn't make them die so a white woman would think. God was better than that. They had the same God as her; if that wasn't true, what was the point of sending missionaries to Africa?

Ryder hadn't suffered. That was the only problem. He hadn't suffered like he'd made her suffer. And he hadn't known she was the one who blew him to kingdom come.

But she felt fit. She felt absolutely fine. She loved her own sweat. The way she could walk and walk, and not get tired, at least not very tired. She glanced behind her and saw the bus marked 15 Norwood, felt her pocket—yep, there was her getaway money. She raised up her hand (just about like Vulcan) so the driver would stop.

She'd go back in time. She'd ride the bus to Norwood. She'd walk on Norwood Boulevard. She'd find the house where the kind old crippled woman lived. She'd chew Juicy Fruit again and take some home to her kids, especially Bobby.

What had she seen? She'd seen the deep lace, starched and white, of the cloth next to the bed, dangling not far from Ryder's face and the scar on his cheek. She never had asked him how he'd come by that scar. And now he probably didn't have any cheek or any head. *Stop! Or I'll blow your head off.* That was what they said in the movies. She imagined his head, still asleep, blowing out the window, but what had she seen? Just the roar of glass flying out, and the flames, like a refiner's fire. The quick purity of the flames. And a little Superman.

No, not that!

Here was the Boulevard, and she pulled the exit cord. She had to get out!

"Bobby!" she screamed as her foot hit the ground. "Bobby!" The bus pulled rapidly away. She was tearing her own hair out. "Bobby!" She began to run. She'd find the crippled lady. The crippled lady would let her in. She'd always been so kind. Whenever she'd remembered her all those years, she'd been kind. So fragile, like china, but just as kind as she could be. She remembered where the house was—up a little hill. And three children, just like hers, playing in the yard next door. The little girl had been blond, just like her Shirley. And right now, Big Mama was probably giving her own children little glasses of milk and taking the peanut butter cookies, with the crisscrossed fork marks on top, out of the oven. That's where her kids were, with her own mother, but *where* was that house?

Go up a little hill. It's close. Yes, if she turned right, she'd go up the hill, and she knew it was close to Vanderbilt Road. And then in her mind, she saw the house number, just like it was: 3621. She hadn't pictured that for many years. And there it was, in skinny metal letters: *3621*, and the two number had a little wiggle in it. All the thin numbers slanted decoratively. And she thanked God for letting her remember what she needed to remember and to forget what she needed to forget.

As she hurried up the porch steps, she could hear music from some TV show like *The Guiding Light;* yes, that was the sort of thing the old lady would listen to. Lee pushed the doorbell button and unleashed a terrible rasp of a sound. Did no one ever ring this bell? She heard movement inside, a slow thump, a sound like a dragging foot. Then the voice, "I'm coming," and *yes,* it was the same voice, with the same quaver, and from inside, the lady was running the clasp chain out of its metal slot and she was opening the door.

"Please," Lee said. "I came here when I was a little girl."

"Did you?" the woman asked slowly. She was cautious. Her face was more deeply lined than Lee had remembered it, but her hair was exactly the same shade of deep red, only now Lee knew it must be dyed. And then the woman's name, like the house number, came back to her.

"Aunt Pratt!" Lee exclaimed.

"Well, that's me," she quavered. "But you look all upset. Come on in, darling."

Lee had to restrain herself as Aunt Pratt moved slowly out of the way. How had she known Lee wouldn't come bursting in, knock her down accidentally? Or be a robber? Slowly, slowly, Aunt Pratt moved to one side and then gave the glass door a little shove.

"Come on in," Aunt Pratt repeated, as though she was speaking to a reluctant cat.

And Lee was inside. Yes, Aunt Pratt was dressed all in red, even her shoes were red. The same heavy metal brace with the leather knee pad encased one leg. The brace went right through the shoe heel.

"Lord, darling," Aunt Pratt said, "I don't really know who you are."

"I'm Lee Jones. I live over—over yonder."

"Oh, Lee. I remember. You're married to cousin Millie's nephew Ryder Jones."

"I never knew we was kin."

"Oh, yes. That's the connection." She spoke so carefully, her voice seemed all cracked. "Please sit down. I am so sorry. I saw it on the TV. Channel Six but not Channel Thirteen."

"I blowed up my husband," Lee blurted out.

"Oh no," Aunt Pratt said. "You must never say that again."

Lee was surprised, but she became silent.

"He blowed himself up," Aunt Pratt said. "That was on live TV. Sit down on that settee."

Slowly Aunt Pratt reached out with her good foot and dragged the brace leg after her. Thump and drag. Time was about to slow to a stop. Thump and drag till she reached the dining room armchair, built up with an extra thick cushion, that had been placed in the living room. "I don't get around so well anymore," Aunt Pratt said. "Did Ryder bring you to visit? I don't quite remember when you were here."

"I was trying to sell tomatoes and vegetables. I came to the front door, and you gave me some chewing gum." Lee let one hand wring the other. She couldn't help it. Over and over her hands tumbled like savage kittens.

"You need to calm down," Aunt Pratt said politely. "Go into the kitchen and open the icebox. Get out the juice and an egg and break the egg in it. That's what I always drink when I get upset about Son—"

At the very word, Lee bolted from the settee. She couldn't go outside. She hurried through the dining room into the kitchen. She did as she was told. It was on TV!

When Lee came back to the living room, Pratt told her to change the channel. "You must turn the sound down," Aunt Pratt instructed. "My niece Stella has a sick headache, and she's in that front bedroom lying down. I don't think she heard you though."

There was Lee's house! The firemen were hosing the house. *A tragic accident occurred today. . . .* Lee could hardly stand to listen. Then the camera panned over to her mother, and! Bobby! The sound came on and the lens moved close on his face, and in agony, he yelled, "Where's my mama?"

"Here," Lee yelled. "I'm right here safe with Aunt Pratt!" And she burst into ragged sobs.

"I was so scared," she told Aunt Pratt in jagged bursts. "That I might of killed my son, too, 'cause he might of gone back."

Aunt Pratt put her finger across her bright red lips. "Shhhh. You didn't kill anybody. Don't say that."

Then Lee knew she was looking into the face of goodness. She was a cracked-up old china doll, but Aunt Pratt was the goddess of goodness. Bobby was alive! Here was her second chance. Lee tried hard to calm herself. Realizing that she still had the tall glass in her hand, she gulped down the raw egg. The unbroken yolk was just a soft little ball traveling down to her stomach. Aunt Pratt was looking at her through her rose-tinted bifocals. "I believe I do remember you," she said.

"Are you my real aunt?"

"You can call me that if you want to. Just like Nancy. I've always been Aunt Pratt to Nancy, but I hardly get to see her since she moved over the mountain. Did you play with Stella when you were little?"

Lee just shook her head. The newscaster was saying *A neighbor saw Mrs. Jones hurrying down the street to collect a prize, but Mrs. Jones's mother fears that her daughter, Lee Jones, might still be in the house*—Lee began to sob again. Oh, how she hated to worry her mother like that.

"Well, turn it off," Aunt Pratt said. "It's all too upsetting. You need to call a cab and go home."

"I don't have the money," Lee said. She stood up to go.

"Wait, darling." Aunt Pratt reached past the starched handkerchief gathered up into a bow. It looked like a big butterfly sitting all across her chest. The thin handkerchief was printed with red roses.

"I always keep a little mad money tucked in my brassiere," Aunt Pratt said. And out came a five-dollar bill, caught between the two red pinchers of fingertips. "Go back to the telephone and call the Yellow Cab. It's in that little hall, off the kitchen. The number is stuck to the telephone stand with Scotch tape. You'll see it."

On her way to the kitchen this time, Lee was elated. She noticed the nice dining room furniture. The china cabinet had glass doors, and she could look right in at the stacks of dinner plates, fruit bowls, soup bowls, cups and saucers, all dainty and matching, decorated with a pale green border and a cluster of pink and blue flowers, and the clear, cut-glass goblets. But the kitchen furniture was old and beat up. The metal-top cook table was a lot like hers, covered with little scratches. People had tables like that all over Birmingham.

It was a pleasure to dial a taxi. Once more Ryder's sleeping face appeared like a picture in a frame in her mind. The picture even had glass over it. And then, strangely satisfying, Bobby framed in the TV screen, screaming for her, just for her. When she glanced around with the telephone receiver clamped to her ear, the whole world seemed to have glass between her and it. As though to touch the hard, clear barrier, she lifted her fingers. Lee said the house number right off to the dispatcher, as though she lived here. Good thing she knew 3621 by heart because the old auntie hadn't thought to tell it to her.

Lee wished she could come live here. She walked back toward Aunt Pratt, but she paused before the china cabinet. She saw her own reflection like a ghost hovering over the pretty plates. She admired the reflection of the deep lace on her shawl. Pratt had mentioned a Stella—probably a stuck-up snob—but surely somebody else lived here, too. Wasn't any man, Lee could tell that. This place seemed like old ladies, all hushed and dull.

She'd just have to rent a new place. But how would she pay for it with Ryder dead? Yes, he was really dead. Surely the TV was right about that. Lee glanced at the blank TV in the living room.

Waiting for Lee's return, Old Aunt Pratt was just sitting in the living room, with her brace leg sticking out, staring at the blank TV screen. When Aunt Pratt didn't know Lee was watching, her face was daydream still and vacant. Lee imagined Pratt did a lot of staring in space and waiting for people. For a moment, Lee felt depressed and sorry for Pratt—next to helpless, all fussed up in red. But Lee was excited. It was a strange and wonderful thing to see the house you lived in go up in flames in black and white on the TV. She imagined it again; the TV even had had the lapping sound and roar of the fire. She wondered if LeRoy had arrived yet.

LeRoy! Yes, he *ought* to take care of her and the children. That was the least he could do for his dead brother. She loved her mama, and that would be all right for a while for Lee and the children to live with her. Mama would bake her cherry pie for whenever LeRoy came over, and her apple one, too. He would come to call in his blue police uniform.

Lee wondered if LeRoy ever would get rough with her. She knew all men got a little rough from time to time. She'd just have to take it, if he did. That would be her job. As long as he didn't go too far. Suddenly there was a thrill in her body.

The image of Bobby and his voice crying out for her wrung her heart. But she knew she was safe, and she'd be home soon. Thanks to Aunt Pratt. Yes, she could have a nice home like this someday, with a china cabinet and chairs with silk burgundy seats. A policeman like LeRoy made lots more than a filling station attendant.

"You sure been good to me," Lee said to Aunt Pratt.

Lee took off her shawl, shook it out, and refolded it into a square with the layers of lace on top. It was like a square, shallow cake frosted with handmade lace. She placed it in Aunt Pratt's lap.

"Sweetheart," Pratt quavered, "you don't have to give me anything."

SATURDAY: LIONEL

AS SOON AS CHRISTINE RECOGNIZED HIM—HIS FORM reflected in the store window—Lionel Parrish saw a shy, proud smile spread over her face. But Christine looked concerned, too. Lionel loved that expression. It felt good to have a smart woman wrinkle up her face in all kinds of different ways because she cared more about you than herself. And it was all captured in the murky reflective glass—two ghosts, him moving toward her, then the way she turned toward him. The two of them almost making a wavering movie.

Pleased as punch, perhaps a little embarrassed about how she'd loved on him last night, she said, "What you doing down here?" She glanced around at the tall buildings.

"I came for the sit-in, naturally." He could hardly suppress the little swagger that ran across his shoulders.

Her face all frowned up, she said, "You ain't supposed to be studying no sit-in. How you know about this?"

"Stella called me. At school. Cat told Stella, Stella told me." He shrugged his shoulder. "Gloria's going to bring Cat down here for this. Did you know that?"

"I'm gonna get that Gloria." Did Christine disapprove or was she pleased? Lionel couldn't tell. With his mother, too, it had been hard to tell the difference. Christine queried, "Stella coming?"

"Just Cat. Stella said she was going to work at the switchboard."

"And what she mean calling you *at school*? How can she be so dumb? Agnes been saying it. That phone bugged. It bugged. Police know everything now."

Lionel refused to give up his relaxed state. It was just too becoming. "That's what I figured, too."

"You know Bull know and still you come?"

Lionel could tell she was touched. She'd let go of her peeve. "My best students and teachers are here." He leaned close to her ear and whispered, "My best woman is here." He drew back to watch her smile. "Might as well make myself useful," he said.

She reached out her hand for a quick squeeze. That was all right to do, Lionel thought. While the traffic moved past on Twentieth Street, they could have their little sidewalk drama. Christine had serious issues, social issues on her mind, and he respected that. Matilda just lived her own life, gloriously, happily, but Matilda wouldn't be putting her body on the line. And Jenny was a homebody; she was made to be a housewife. But this woman, with all her angles and abruptness, she was a mover and shaker. In more ways than one. Like she was starved.

"If you'd consulted me," Lionel said fondly, "I would have said there's only two things that move this community to change."

He watched Christine's face go soft again, pleased to be talking with him, confident suddenly that they were intimates. "What's that?" she asked.

"Prayer and money. Like May a year ago. It wasn't the marching, it was the boycotting brought Birmingham to its knees. Over in Mississippi, folks go and pray on the white folks' church steps Sunday mornings. We ought to do that. It shames them."

"You may be right." She shrugged. "But I got *this* going. What'd you say to Stella?"

"Oh, I tried to throw them off. I said Christine's way too smart to sit in at the *Tutwiler* Hotel Drugstore. She called it all off."

Christine looked troubled. "Agnes told me they do got dogs over at the Tutwiler."

"Was I right?"

"'Bout what?"

"You way too smart to go ahead with any sit-in today."

He saw her eyes narrow, knew that he had underestimated her.

"You don't have to be in this," she said. She spoke in a new key, one that was full of softness and hard as iron. "I didn't ask you to come down here and try to tell me what to think and do. You my love now, but I thought you believed in Martin Luther King. I thought you knew what nonviolent protest was all about." Then she licked her lips and added the barb, "Ain't you ever heard of Mahatma Gandhi or Martin Luther King Jr.?"

"Oh, is that who you are?" He returned the sting. "I hadn't noticed. You're not Martin Luther King, you're not him, Christine."

"Move aside. Out of my way, Mr. *H-O-P-E*. These ain't your buildings. You made me leave the classroom, and I was ashamed afterward. You stand in the White Palace door like George Wallace if you want to, but I'm walking right over you. Like we did him. I'm gonna order a big juicy hamburger."

Suddenly Lionel laughed. It was the only thing to do; his saving grace was humor. "Well, if you not Martin Luther King, I sure 'nuff ain't George Wallace."

SATURDAY: CAT

JUST GETTING INSIDE THE WHITE PALACE, CAT THOUGHT, would be a partial victory. "Hold the door open, please, Charles, so Gloria and I can get in," Cat said.

She wanted to be first. This time she wouldn't hang back. She'd lead the way. She and Gloria would get settled before the others came in.

Cat wondered if Gloria knew anything about maneuvering a wheelchair. Well, Gloria had gotten her down the steps at school, once Cat told her to revolve the chair.

"We be in there with you soon," Christine reassured. "You all get settled. Folks still gathering. We be there in five minutes."

Cat was in no rush. No rush at all. Stella's words still burned in her ear. *I won't do this, Cat. I'm going to work. Remember, Cat, I'm the survivor. I know what not to do. I'm begging you. Please don't go.* And Cat had simply replied that she'd call Gloria to come get her. She understood. She'd stalled, too, after the threat—the bullhorn voice in the dark.

So that her knuckles wouldn't scrape the sides of the doors, Cat drew her hands in and put them in her lap. There ought to be laws about the width of doors into public places, Cat thought, to make them more easily accessible to people propelling their own wheelchairs. It always made her feel helpless to fold her hands passively over each other, to look down and see them nested in her lap.

Gloria had trouble pushing the chair over the threshold, though it wasn't really any obstacle. The front wheels just tried to turn aside instead of bumping over. Gloria lacked confidence about managing the chair. Two bored countergirls watched them enter. At the end of the counter, a big man sat with a newspaper opened up wide. Usually men jumped up to help her with the slightest problem, but this man was absorbed in his reading. A gray satchel full of papers slumped on the floor beside the post for his counter stool.

Cat noticed the white hexagonals of the floor tile looked grimy. Judging the height of the counter stools, Cat knew she was going to have trouble getting up there. Even if she stood, the stool would be higher than her hip.

She could just see the headline: "Wheelchair Sit-In Sits in Wheelchair." But that was too long for anybody's headline. To Gloria, Cat remarked, "It's obvious this place wasn't set up for people in wheelchairs."

"Looks like they'd have a table or two, doesn't it?" Gloria replied. She sounded relaxed and friendly, almost like Arcola. Cat half listened for the crack of gum, but that really was Arcola's trademark.

The pretty countergirl blurted out, "Hey, don't I know you from somewheres?" Cat said she didn't know. "I don't think so."

The girl was unfamiliar, with brown hair done in a flip, like Stella's. She wore a little white cap that was crenellated across the top to suggest a castle wall. The other countergirl was tall and looked strong; she looked like a country girl come into the city to work. Cat spoke to her. "You're not from around Gadsden, are you?"

"Sylacauga," the girl answered. She smiled, and a little gap showed between her front teeth. Cat had one just like it. She smiled back, showing her front teeth.

The other girl, the one with the flip hairstyle, said, "I know you. I know you from school."

"Which school?" Cat asked. The girl seemed pushy. Cat really didn't want to get in a conversation with her.

"P-H-S. Phillips High School. Only you was on crutches then."

"I guess I stood out."

"We all thought you was the smartest thing alive," Miss Flip said.

Cat rolled up beside the high end-stool and set her brakes. "Gloria, would you come around to the front? Take my hands and pull?" Gloria tried, but she wasn't firm enough, and Cat sank back into her chair. Humiliated, she glanced at them. The countergirls were staring. The man with the newspaper had lowered it a little so that just his eyes were peeking over the top.

"I can help you," the bigger countergirl said. Her face was round and pleasant as a pie. "I used to help my old granny what was in a chair."

Before Cat could decide how to respond, the big girl had her hands up under Cat's armpits and lifted her up on the stool. "Steady now," the strong girl said. Then she pinched Cat's cheek. "Just want to be like everybody else sometimes, don't you, hon."

A wave of fury swept over Cat, but it was followed by a bigger wave of gratitude. She put her hands flat on the counter to help her with her balance.

"Gloria, you can fold up the chair and put it against the wall," she said. "Stand up the cushion, grab the seat sling, and pull up."

With her hands on her hips, the big girl watched Gloria struggle, then she said, "I know how." She brushed Gloria aside, released the slide on the cross braces, grabbed the seat in the middle, and jerked up. The big wheels moved closer together. She stood the cushion up on one end, between the wheels. "'Bout time for a change on that cushion cover," the girl said. While Cat felt her cheeks blush with shame, the girl dusted her hands together.

Her old classmate Miss Flip said, "I still remember your name—Kittycat Cartwright."

"It's just Cat, now. This is Gloria Callahan."

Because they assumed she was Cat's maid, neither of the girls acknowledged Gloria, nor did they offer their own names. Cat didn't think it was intentional rudeness. They each just assumed that Gloria knew enough: they were the white countergirls.

"Did you go to college?" Miss Flip asked.

"Yes. I work at Miles College now."

"That's the colored college." She looked puzzled.

"Yes, it is," Cat said, and she was pleased with herself. Just that simple, it was just that simple to let people know where you stood. But she could tell her heart was speeding up. She felt a little dizzy. Suppose she fell off the high stool? If she did, she hoped ruefully that it was just a leg that she broke.

Her classmate was shaking her head. "I wouldn't like that," she said. "Couldn't you get a job at a regular school?"

"No."

Cat wondered if Gloria had known that she was a reject, not simply an activist. She glanced at Gloria, but she was looking down, effacing herself in the familiar way of Negroes who felt out of place. *How many minutes? How many minutes had passed since they came in?* Both Cat and Gloria glanced out the window. Standing with her back to them, Christine was speaking to a small group. Cat felt disappointed that the group was so small. Turning her body had unbalanced her, and she grasped the metal rim of her stool.

"Could we have two Palace-patties?" she asked.

"Two to go," the girls sang out in unison.

"No, we'll have 'em here." Cat looked at Gloria. Cat hated to ask her to do it, but she said gently, "Don't you want to sit down, Gloria?"

Quick as a wink, Gloria was on the stool. She flashed her green eyes just once at Cat. Gloria was pleased that Cat had helped her to do it; her eyes said *thank you.*

"I can't serve her," Miss Flip said. "You smart enough to know that, Kittycat."

The country girl said, "We can make it, and she can take it outside to eat."

Cat said sternly, "White Palace Grill sells to black folks but won't seat them."

They both just stared at her.

"Suppose she sat in my chair and ate a burger-to-go."

"No," her classmate said. "They can't eat in here."

The big girl had hastily put two patties on a waxed sheet and was about to wrap them. Cat could tell the country girl was scared. This was the sort of thing people had warned her might happen if she were foolish enough to go to the city to work.

"Do you like onion?" Cat quickly asked Gloria.

"Yes, please," Gloria said, and she looked up.

Nervously, the country girl strewed diced onions over the meat and mashed the bread lids down. Her hands flew noisily over the waxed paper, folding it shut. She crammed the oval burgers into a white to-go bag and placed them on the counter in front of Cat.

"She can stand up in here," the pretty classmate said, "but she can't sit down anywhere." She was trying to be nice, matter-of-fact.

"Of course the wheelchair is my property," Cat said. "It doesn't belong to White Palace." She wished Christine would come in now.

The big girl babbled, "That chair is on White Palace floor."

Gloria mumbled, "My feet are tired. I want to sit down."

"What does she mean?" the country girl asked, almost hysterical. Her pleasant pie face was a mask of anxiety, and Cat felt guilty.

The newspaper reader had lowered his paper all the way to his chin. He was staring at her with avid interest. She felt like saying, *What's the matter, buster? Haven't you ever seen a handicapped person stand up for herself?*

Through the plate glass, Cat saw that Christine was moving toward the door. And there was Mr. Parrish. Now her heart began to race with joy.

"She means," Cat said as evenly as she could, "we're going on with our sit-in."

SATURDAY: GLORIA

GLORIA STIFFENED HER SPINE; SHE ROTATED ON THE counter stool just enough to see Christine lead Arcola and Charles Powers and a few others through the door. The white girl shrieked like a siren, "Sit-in!"

At Gloria, at Cat, at the whole establishment, Christine was grinning ear to ear. How she did love to be in the vanguard! Even Mr. Parrish was behind her. He was holding the door to let all the others in, but then he came in, too, the rear guard.

Christine sat right beside Gloria and reached over and gave her hand a squeeze.

"We'd all like Palace-patties, please, ma'am," Christine said pleasantly.

"I can't serve y'all." The pretty brown-headed girl, who looked sort of like Stella, tried to explain. "I don't know what you want to gain, but I lose my job if I fix you anything."

Mr. Parrish seated himself next to Christine. He didn't look at the defiant white girl, but he spoke affectionately to Christine. His chin down, his head cocked a little on one side, Mr. Parrish said, "I guess we'll have to eat a little salt and pepper." Then he looked down the row at the others.

Gloria looked, too. There they were in a row. Just a line of friends. Dark faces, her people, sitting peacefully, respectfully, at the counter of White Palace. After Mr. Parrish sat Arcola, then Charles, then the other three boys who had all claimed that day when Cat and Stella first came to teach that they, too, were named Powers.

Mr. Parrish was speaking with the back of his head turned to Gloria now.

She loved the back of Mr. Parrish's head, his crisp salt-and-pepper hair. "I don't know 'bout y'all, but this is the first time in my life I ever sat down inside a White Palace, and I'm just gonna eat a little something."

Christine poured a little sugar from the glass canister with the flip spout into the palm of her hand. Gloria thought, *It's like she's pouring the sands of time out of an hourglass. This is change. Like the song promises, "The times they are a-changing."*

Mr. Parrish turned back toward Gloria and Christine.

"Wait a moment," he said quietly to Christine. He put a restraining finger on her forearm. "Let's give thanks." He held up his other hand, closed his eyes, and prayed, but Gloria kept her eyes open. "I thank you, Lord, that we are here. Guard and guide us, Lord. Give us thy gentle spirit."

Everybody said Amen.

"Y'all are crazy!" the pretty girl said.

"This is spooky," the big girl said. She looked scared, as though she'd seen a haint.

They both unpinned their White Palace headpieces, set them on the counter, and fled. Gloria tried not to laugh. As the girl brushed past Cat, she said vehemently, "I don't know you!"

The man with the newspaper suddenly folded it up, lay it in his slouch bag, and picked the bag up by its wide cloth shoulder strap. He paused to put the strap over his head and position it on one shoulder. As he fled, Gloria thought he looked like somebody with a grain sack across his body, like she'd seen in paintings from the nineteenth century. Millet. Now the news of the day was the seeds of the future.

Every detail seemed of historic importance to Gloria, though she knew many Negroes had already held many lunch counter sit-ins all across the South. Still, it was historic for her, and time seemed to be slowing down. The white people were gone, except for Cat, and suddenly the place did seem spooky.

Christine said, "Looks like we got the joint to ourselves."

Charles Powers looked down the row at her. "How 'bout you cook us some Palace-patties, Christine?" he teased.

Then Gloria heard the warning for the first time. She heard danger because she was looking at Arcola, and the composure on Arcola's face collapsed like a bombed wall, all at once. A second before, Arcola had looked confident. Gloria listened hard till she heard it: the faint barking of dogs. She took a deep breath.

So this was what she'd missed, the terror of May, over a year ago, when Arcola was bitten by a German shepherd.

Christine heard nothing. She teased back at Charles. "You hungry, you cook 'em. I'm sitting here, man."

"You know," Mr. Parrish said, "Christ once addressed this same question. I believe it was at the Last Supper. 'Which is the greatest,' he asked. 'He who serves the meat, or he who eats it?'"

None of them but Gloria and Arcola had heard the barking. Arcola jumped off her stool, and Gloria feared she would run. She looked very nervous. But she didn't run; she was making herself be brave. She put her hand to the back of her head and prissed around the end of the counter. Gloria saw that Arcola's hand was trembling. She stood in front of the grill, where the french fries were still cooking.

Arcola lifted up the wire basket by its long handle and hung it over the empty pan to drain. Now Gloria noticed the faint sound of grease bubbling in the deep-fat fry pan. It too had a long handle.

Arcola said with nervous good cheer, "And Jesus said, it was he who served who was the greatest, didn't he, Mr. Parrish?" She shook her shoulders flirtatiously. "Being the greatest—me and Cassius Clay—I guess I better serve you all some french fries and burgers."

"I don't know if you should go back there, Arcola," Cat said.

Christine said sharply, "Let her have her day."

Then they all heard the dogs barking.

Quickly, Gloria took her burger out of the little white bag and unwrapped it. She bit into it ravenously. With her mouth full, she said, "Any of y'all want some of my and Cat's burgers?"

"Pass 'em on down," Mr. Parrish said grimly.

"Might as well eat 'fore we go to jail," one of the boys said.

Another said, "My mouth sho is dry."

"Pretty Miss Arcola," Charles said, trying to distract her, "would you mind to fix me a Coca-Cola?"

"Now y'all got to pay," Christine said, "if you gonna eat or drink anything."

Gloria could feel Christine trembling beside her.

"That's right," Cat said slowly. "No need to get booked for petty theft."

"Mr. Parrish," one of the boys said, "could you spare some Coke money?"

Slowly Mr. Parrish stood up. "Hush, everybody," he said. "They're coming."

Gloria heard the heavy sound of feet marching. Not marching like protest marching. Marching like soldiers marching. Fast and hard.

Without taking a bite, Christine stretched herself over Mr. Parrish's place and over Arcola's empty stool to hand a burger to Charles Powers. She said softly, "It sounds like a storm coming."

"Nonviolence," Mr. Parrish said. "Remember nonviolence. We don't want to make Fred Shuttlesworth and Martin Luther King ashamed of us."

"Malcolm X," one of the boys said. "I don't think he'd be shamed of us."

"Leave now, if you want to," Mr. Parrish said sternly. "You took the pledge. Leave if you can't keep it. I don't want to be ashamed of us."

Gloria thought about Gandhi, how when his people in India were violent to one another, he himself had gone on a fast. He had fasted nigh unto death, till all the rioting stopped. Maybe Mr. Parrish was just such a leader as Gandhi. And could she herself find a way to lead? Her heart hurt. With the gesture of her grandmother, she pressed her hand against her chest. "For Susan Spenser Oaks," Gloria whispered and then lay her palm tenderly against her own cheek.

"Make it cool," Mr. Parrish said. "Play it cool."

The thrumming of the marching feet and the barking dogs grew louder. Then it suddenly stopped. A bullhorn voice spoke in a snarl.

"This is Birmingham City Police Sergeant LeRoy Jones speaking. You are all trespassing on White Palace property. By authority vested in me by the people of this city, I order you to come out in one minute."

When he paused, no one moved. Gloria could see the big end of the megaphone, just on the other side of the glass door. He didn't need the megaphone. No one inside moved.

"This is your first warning," he said slowly and distinctly. "And it will be your last warning. Come out one by one with your hands clasped behind your heads."

"Don't nobody move," Christine said.

Frozen behind the counter, Arcola said, "Don't nobody even think 'bout moving." She looked at Charles and tried to flash her smile, but her face seemed to be cracking.

Gloria said, "Let's all hold hands."

When she reached out and took Cat's hand, she could feel how unsteady Cat was on the stool; on her other side, Gloria took Christine's. Cat's hand felt boneless; Christine's was long and hard. Mr. Parrish snapped his hand into Christine's, as though he was catching a fly. He had to tell Arcola to step forward, so she could be part of the chain. Gloria hoped maybe Arcola would be a little protected from the dogs behind the countertop.

Though she couldn't open her mouth, Gloria made her voice box hum. Christine heard her and began to sing off-key "We Shall Overcome."

Everybody joined in: "We shall overcome; we shall overcome someday. Oh, deep in my heart, I do believe, that we shall overcome someday."

Gloria saw the first megaphone man pass the horn to an older man.

"This is Captain Reese." He spoke rapidly. "Your time's up and we're gonna have to come in there and clear y'all out. If I was you, I wouldn't let that happen. I'd walk on out now at the end of your song while I was still walking."

On the other side of the plate glass, Gloria saw the newspaper-reading man take a radio telephone out of his satchel. He turned a crank fast and began to speak into it. He was standing on the edge of the street, looking first one way, then the other. A clump of blue-uniformed policemen were pushed up around the door. The dogs were standing stock-still, not straining, just barking over and over, like they were bored.

On Twentieth Street, somebody stopped his car, tried to back up. Horns were honking.

"I don't believe that was even a minute," Mr. Parrish said.

Gloria felt the sweat in Cat's hand, in Christine's.

A command was given, and the dogs were suddenly all lunge, fangs bared, and the door opened back and three policemen burst in at once. They entered with the noise of a tornado.

When a policeman grabbed Gloria by the shoulders, she let go of Cat's hand, and, quick as a wink, Gloria crashed against the floor.

"Go limp, go limp," Gloria heard Christine yelling through the noise of attack, but Gloria snugged into the quiet space between the stools and the counters, out of the way, so she wouldn't be stepped on. She was small enough. Blue legs hurried past her, and one of the boys down at the other end crashed to the floor.

Clubs whacked stools and the counter. The shouting clanged like metal voices. Somebody else squatted down beside his stool to hide. A policeman kicked the squatter in the chest till he unfolded and sprawled out on the floor. Everywhere shiny shoes were scuffling and kicking.

Christine was down on the floor, covering her head, but she was calling through the noise, "When they touch you, go down. Go limp."

But Mr. Parrish was holding to the edge of his stool with both hands, and they had skipped him, maybe because he was older, with gray in his hair. Everybody else was down now, and Gloria hoped Arcola was hidden behind the counter. Everybody else sprawled on the floor. They were like a carpet of bodies. Some were protecting their heads, and the police were kicking and kicking, and some were hitting shoulders, heads, ribs with their brown clubs.

"I like to see 'em like this," one policeman chortled. He was bent over, and she read his name on a bar: LEROY JONES.

He straightened up. "Tell 'em to pass those 'lectric cattle prods now."

"Y'all like joy juice," another said. People were bleeding, and Gloria closed her eyes, but still she heard the whacking of the billy clubs, and groaning.

"Nigger white girl!" somebody said. Somebody was talking at Cat. "Little princess on her throne." Was it LeRoy Jones? Gloria wasn't sure. Now they all sounded alike.

"Get in the floor with 'em or get yourself out of here."

Clear as a bell, Gloria heard Cat's voice. "No."

Then Cat was jerked off the stool, and Gloria saw her hit, headfirst, and her neck bend abruptly sideways.

"I'll shock your white ass same as theirs!" one of them yelled. And he rammed the prod into Cat's thigh. "Yankee bitch!" he yelled. "Tough girl, tough girl," he hollered. And he touched her in a new place.

Christine jumped to her feet. "Stop it!" she yelled. Christine was standing up, yelling in their faces. "She can't feel in her legs! She's crippled!"

"You next, nigger," and he tried to thrust the cattle prod at Christine.

Quick as a majorette, Christine grabbed the shaft of the prod, twirled it, and rammed the electric end into the policeman's stomach. Almost as fast, the sound of a gun went off, and Christine's blue dress was covered with blood, all over the front. The jacket and her white blouse, too, and she was sinking sideways.

Gloria couldn't help herself; from safe between the stools, she reached out toward his genitals, her hand was in the air. And then she stopped. She wouldn't.

Mr. Parrish was standing up, he was holding up his prayer hand. "Stop," he shouted. "In the name of Jesus, stop!" Gloria saw blood, like an exploding rose, bloom in the palm of his hand.

Then the dogs came in. One of the dogs crouched just in front of Gloria, and a rain of smoking grease showered down. *Arcola!* The dog yelped and then sprang over the counter. And another dog crouched and leapt fluidly over the counter. His long dog chest and stomach blurred past Gloria's eyes as he rose.

Out on the street, a white boy with nubbins for fingers pressed his hand and nose and agonized lips against the glass as though he wanted in. Gloria closed her eyes.

THE BULLHORN VOICE SAID, "All right. All right. Y'all done good. F.B.I.'s here. F.B.I.'s ready to look at these nonviolent colored people."

Gloria saw the gray satchel of the newspaper vendor swinging before her eyes. "Jesus Christ," he said. "Let's carry these people out of here."

JOSEPH COAT-OF-MANY-COLORS

HOLDING EDDIE AND HONEY BY THEIR LITTLE HANDS, TJ led the boys from the parked car toward Joseph Coat-of-Many-Colors Church. He registered the poverty of this church, an abandoned shoe box house, with a crude pyramid made of plywood mounted on the flat roof as a steeple. Not even a cross on top. When TJ and the children passed inside, he saw a cross on the altar table. The cross was two rusty concrete rebars wired together.

Because the aisle was narrow, Agnes and Diane walked behind TJ and the boys. This was Charles Powers's old church, and it was at his mother's request that the service would be here.

Of course the people would burst the seams of the building if they all tried to crowd in here, but it was way early now, and TJ knew people would not shove in but stand all around, in the churchyard and in the gravel streets. They would sort themselves out in the slots between the houses, all of them mere cabins or a few shotgun houses as poor as this one converted into a church. This early, only a few people sat inside scattered on the backless, gray-painted benches.

Joseph Coat-of-Many-Colors. Here the windows were not the color-infused glass shattered at Sixteenth Street. Here the glass was simple windowpane, painted thinly with house paint, a checkerboard of many rectangular colors. TJ appraised the workmanship. The paint on the glass—red, yellow, blue, frank colors—had been applied with care. Nothing slapdash. The bristles of the brush had left their straight, vertical marks, and through these narrow streaks in the colors came the sunshine.

The coffins had already arrived. Four of them. Closed, thank God. Against his will, TJ saw again the little Korean girl, coffined only by the steep sides of a ditch, naked with most of her body burned black and crisp by a flamethrower. Her straight black hair, her forehead and open eyes were untouched. She wore her hair in bangs. TJ closed his eyes, but eyes open or closed, he could not bring down the shade on that memory. From behind, Agnes was touching him. Maybe she'd seen him flinch his eyes closed, tight as a fist closing. Maybe she thought he flinched at the sight of the four coffins. Agnes had known all four of them from night school—Christine Taylor, Arcola Anderson, and their friend, the crippled white girl, and her fellow student Charles Powers.

The coffins matched, each upholstered in gray cloth, and TJ wondered which was which. He saw a boy holding to the end of one coffin. He had his arms around it, as well as he could get them around it. His cheek rested on the gray cloth, and he was crying sideways onto the upholstering. His mother stood there sniffling, one light-toned baby up in her arms and three others, a girl about nine and two little dark fellows whose hands were held by their big sister. Somebody had given the little boys, younger than Honey, tiny green bow ties to clip under their chins. TJ touched his own bow tie. The mother was fighting back her tears, but the boy, maybe seven or eight, who embraced the coffin wore his pain on his face. His tears flowed unabated, and TJ's tears began to flow in sympathy.

"I believe that must be Charles's family," Agnes whispered and nodded. "Here's Gloria."

TJ was startled: Gloria had green eyes like a white person. She said the coffin next to the Powers family was Christine's. TJ didn't sob, but his eyes wept steady streams of tears.

Gloria stood beside TJ and Agnes and the children. All of them looked at the coffins, the pulpit, and the altar table where four red roses stood in a brass vase in front of the pulpit. No other flowers. On the table, a white cardboard sign folded like a tent read: "Memorial donations accepted for Freedom Groups."

Sitting off to the side were four white people. Two young ladies, and a man who looked like a movie star, all tan, with wavy light hair. A broken-down, work-weary white man, not too old, old before his time, took a wrinkled handkerchief from the side pocket of his shabby suit and blew his nose.

"After you've gone up," Gloria said, "I'll introduce you to Cat's brother. He came back home from the Peace Corps for the funeral, and her father." She spoke sympathetically but businesslike. "And that's Stella. She was a teacher, with us." Yes, TJ had seen her through the classroom window that hot night before he was beaten.

Somebody began to play the piano softly. TJ was surprised the church had a piano. When he looked over at it, Agnes explained that Mr. Parrish had had the piano trucked over from the college. A white man with red hair was playing softly. Five white people.

TJ thought he'd never heard a white man play so sweetly. He wondered if there were going to be a lot of white people there, but he knew better. Not down here in the Quarters where the street wasn't even paved, and it having rained last night. Hell, rain or no rain—none of the power would come, he knew that. TJ wished the city would send a representative. Just one official white man.

"Let's go on up," Agnes said quietly, and they led the children to the coffin.

"This is your mama's last bed," Agnes explained to the children. TJ couldn't say a word. He squeezed the hands of the little boys. Diane began to cry first, and then Eddie and Honey. "She wants you to kiss her box," Agnes said, sobbing, "and tell her good-bye."

TJ let go of the boys' hands, even though he hated to, even for a second. Though Agnes set Diane free to be with her mama, she kept on talking to the children. Standing behind the younguns, Agnes told them about how in heaven Christine was loving them and would always love them. How they could always find her in their hearts. After a while, Agnes moved closer and touched their shoulders, and told them that their mama had planned ahead for them, planned should anything ever happen to herself, TJ and Agnes LaFayt would take care of them and love them. "And we do," Agnes said. "Now let's go sit down, and just think about your mama, and hold her in our hearts."

TJ could hardly bear it. He thought he'd rather been beat to death than have this happen. *Suffer the little children*—what had Jesus meant saying something like that? Then Gloria asked him how was he feeling, and he got his voice again. Her eyes were pretty and kind, even if they were green, and she looked right into him, like she knew how bad he was hurting, and she was hurting too. To TJ, the young woman seemed remarkably calm. Not uncaring. No, she cared.

TJ knew he looked a sight with the lump still on his forehead, but it didn't show up as bad as it would have if he'd had gauze on it. His pant leg covered up the swelling on his leg.

Here came three white people in wheelchairs, and a blind man with a white cane with a red tip. The movie star man, the brother, got up to greet them. He led the blind man up the two steps to the coffin on the far right, and the blind man's eyes rolled up as he touched the gray cloth and moved his lips. So that was the coffin that held the crippled white girl. One after the other, the brother was picking up the handicapped people out of their chairs, marching up the altar steps holding them in his arms, and letting them stretch their hands down to touch the coffin. Then he carried them back to their wheelchairs.

The movie star was a compact man, but TJ knew he must be awful strong to tote them so easily. One woman and one man were just thin little people, but one of the handicapped women was plump and wore a tight black dress and a black hat with a few black feathers—she was a fashion plate. After the wavy-headed man got her out of the chair, he had to hitch her up higher, the way you did with something heavy, though it was hard on the back. Dangling in the air, her plump feet looked swollen where the black patent leather high-heeled shoe cut into her hose. Long ago, TJ had watched how feet dangled, when he gave up his white buddy. When somebody pulled him away from TJ's chest, hitched Stonewall up in his arms, and carried him away to put in a bag.

Suddenly TJ sobbed convulsively. And there was Agnes's arm around his shoulders, and he made himself stop for the children's sake. He wished he'd worn his army uniform though. Even if it was a bit tight now. He looked again for the feet of the plump, crippled white woman. There she was, in black, sitting in her shiny wheelchair. Her feet were pale and clean, rising like biscuit dough around the curve of her black pumps.

The fourth coffin had to hold the young woman, Arcola Anderson, but her folks weren't here yet. Still the pews were starting to fill up with the early birds. The piano man kept playing, softly and well. It was comforting to know who was inside which coffin. TJ's gaze traveled up the two steps, and for a moment he dwelt with each of them: the young man, Charles Powers, on his far left, with the wet spot where the little brother had cried; then Christine; then came the pulpit surrounded by three chairs covered in threadbare red velvet, and on the other side, it was Arcola Anderson, and then the white girl, Cat, inside the coffin on the far end.

Starting to get hot, TJ thought, and he knew what with the rain last night, it would soon be awful humid, too. Hot as August. Somebody else was thinking the same, because men all around were lifting up the windows. Raising the painted windows was like taking off a mask. Now anybody could clearly see how run-down this neighborhood was, and TJ felt ashamed that it was such a poor place. He and Agnes had a good house in a former white section, not a Quarters house. Still, he glimpsed some zinnias or marigolds here and there around somebody's doorstep. Nothing like Agnes's expensive dahlias, all shapes and sizes, looking like fireworks and sparklers in front of their porch.

Straight through an open window, a honeybee flew in. It buzzed directly to one of the roses on the altar and disappeared for a moment into the heart of the red flower. TJ nudged Agnes. "Lookie," he said.

They were sitting close together now, what with the crowd congregating, and he could feel Agnes's side expand, almost like a chuckle.

"I know," she said. "Here they come." She did chuckle, just once. Three more bees flew in, straight to the altar. Each bee had its own half-opened rose. All through the service, TJ would watch them, how they crawled around the petals, ducked inside, fretted the golden centers with their feet.

"They say your heart got four chambers," TJ whispered to Agnes.

She just smiled and nodded, clasped his hand.

Now he took out his handkerchief and carefully wiped his forehead of the sweat and his cheeks of his tears. Over the wound on his forehead, he just patted tenderly. Every child there, even the tot in Charles Powers's mother's arms, was well behaved and nicely dressed, but they seemed sealed in grief and pain. Heat and humidity and the smell of dying leaves had already invaded the church.

To help the time pass till the service, TJ made himself think the words to the melodies the piano played.

When he started feeling faint, he took out the individually wrapped peppermint pinwheels from his pocket and gave one each to Agnes, Diane, Eddie, and Honey. Agnes had Honey stand up and sit between them. Now each child sat next to an adult. From inside all their mouths, TJ heard the peppermints clacking softly against their teeth and small slurping sounds.

The church was full before Arcola's parents came in. Her father burst in like a steam locomotive. He ran down the aisle and threw himself sobbing on his daughter's coffin. His wife tried to lead him away, and Gloria went up to help, too, pulling gently at his shoulders. Finally Gloria leaned her face down next to his ear and whispered something long. Then he straightened up, and Gloria calmly led the parents to a reserved space close to their daughter's coffin; TJ watched them settle across from him and his. The man had lost his only child, and God had given three to TJ, all in the same hour.

I, GLORIA

I WATCH THE REVEREND MR. LIONEL PARRISH, MY BOSS,
come in behind the altar, through a little door I never noticed existed. Appropriately, it is a "Christian" door, one with a raised cross in the upper portion,
and below it, two sections suggest an open Bible. From the outside, the minister enters dramatically, with a flash of the ordinary world behind him. I
remember that day when the face of Christ was blown away and the ordinary
sky presented itself. Mr. Parrish's right hand is done up in a big white bandage,
which all can see, and Mr. Parrish uses it to wipe his forehead. All can see the
sign of recent violence, but I see the splatter of blood blooming out of the bare
palm when, at the White Palace, he raised his hand in prayer. From my safe
place between the stems of the stools, I saw the bullet enter his raised palm.
Now the gauze bandage is pristine white, and I must focus on this place and
this time.

I turn to see if Mr. Parrish's wife and children are here. And there they are,
nearly halfway back. His wife, Jenny, has the saddest face I have ever seen. Not
torn with pain, like Arcola's father or little Edmund Powers. Just sad. The resignation I have seen so often on the faces of my people, here intensified. Her
face looks carved. Jenny Parrish sits with their four children, two on each side
of her. The youngest are close to her sides.

It is a long way between me and where Jenny is. This was a four-room shotgun house, but all the walls have been removed, a few supports left standing. I
look back the length of the house, with the dividing walls removed. From the
platform, Mr. Parrish is signaling at me. He wants me to sit in one of the three

chairs with him, close to Christine, who was my friend. But they were all my friends. He wanted Stella to sit up there, too, but she has said she can't, that she doesn't deserve to, so one chair will remain empty.

Stella sits close to her living friend, Nancy.

There is Sam West from school walking toward the front. He's wearing a sports jacket and nice pants. He approaches Stella and kneels in front of her. "You doin' all right?" he asks her, but he looks over her head and not into her eyes. Still, it's remarkable that he's gone down to greet her. I can't hear what she says because she's facing the front. He shows her a fan he has in his hand. "You get too hot"— he's looking sideways—"give me the sign. I come fan you, Miss Silver."

She holds out her hand to him. At first he doesn't see it, then he jumps a little and shakes hands.

For the first time, he looks in her eyes. "We thank you for coming," he says. "I don't know what to say." He shakes his head back and forth and looks down. "I so sad about all this. Charles was my bes' friend."

She nods, but he is looking at the floor. Then he straightens up and walks back to his seat.

One by one, Cat's brother carries her friends to her coffin to say good-bye. Once, Cat told me, he carried her all the way up Vulcan to see the view.

I walk up the two steps and take my place on the platform.

Now I look out at a sea of faces, all black. Way in the back, I see Dee, Christine's sister. I will her to come forward, but she doesn't budge. I go down from the platform to fetch her. My mama and my four aunts, dressed in dark clothes, watch me, but my father's hand covers his whole face. When Dee sees me coming, she shakes her head *no*. I stop. I glance at my mama, and with two motions of her head, she tells me to let Dee be and that after the service she will take care of Dee. I return to the platform.

The only white people here are the ones I know, clustered close to the front, and Cat's white handicapped friends. No, here comes a white man I don't know. He is extremely well dressed, in a light gray suit. It even has a matching vest and a fine gray silk tie. His hair is white, but it looks a little creamy, like butter frosting set off by the gray suit. He wears shiny glasses, and he has his mouth tucked tight and grim, as though he's afraid of crying.

Everybody is looking at him as he makes his way down the aisle. But he doesn't walk importantlike. He walks quickly, rather bravely, just to say "I'm here."

Stella looks back, sees him, and is surprised. She scoots sideways, crowding the others, to make room, so he can sit next to her.

Later I find out that this is Mr. Fielding, who owns the big department store where Stella works at the switchboard. Later I learn what he is whispering into Stella's ear: "I'm here to be with you, young lady. Like your father would be, if he could."

Now Mr. Parrish rises to begin the service. He will speak, and we will answer, as in a responsive reading. He speaks quietly.

STELLA LISTENING

Brothers and sisters. On the rock of God we stand. All other ground is sinking sand.

All other ground is sinking sand, the congregation intones. Stella is numb and silent.

And we come here today as sinners. Sinners. Believing in the Redeeming Blood of our Lord Jesus Christ, which was shed for us. There is a fountain filled with blood, drawn from Immanuel's veins. And sinners

Sinners, the congregation repeats after him.

Sinners plunged beneath that flood—lose all the guilty stains. And we believe

Stella hears the first quaver of emotion; he quavers on the second syllable of be*lieve.*

in the resurrection of the body, and that these dead will rise again at the latter day. The corruptible will be made incorruptible

Here, Stella notices, is emphasis and vibrato on the first syllable of *incorruptible,* but immediately he drops the quaver. She will pay attention—to everything. If there's any solace in his message for her, she wants it. Cat! Christine! Arcola! And Charles!

and the crooked straight, and

With falling emphasis.

the lame shall leap for joy.

And Stella can't bear it. Oh, he cannot help but glance, just the quickest movement of his eyes, she knows she would, at Cat's coffin, *because she was the lame among us.* The congregation audibly breathes together. In spite of herself, Stella thinks, *We bond and become one in understanding.* Mr. Fielding puts his arm across her shoulders.

I've seen you before, haven't I, brothers and sisters? We saw each other when four little girls attending church on Sunday were killed by a bomb hidden in the church, here in Birmingham. And I seen you in Jackson, along the highway, didn't I? When somebody started shooting from ambush— you were there, weren't you? And I was there. We were there in Detroit, Michigan, and we were there in a place named of all things Liberty, Missis- sippi, when Herbert Lee was murdered for helping voter registration. We been here *before,* haven't we, brothers and sisters. We know this place. Yes, we know it. This is the place of the skull.

Stella sees Gloria is out of her chair. She's standing up, short and proud, and she's singing in her own pure voice like a stab that pierces Stella's heart and comes out the other side: "Were you there?" *Was she? Was she?* Stella's heart accuses. *I should have been.* Guilt comes to knot itself with grief, and the two constrict and contend with each other, and the pain in Stella's heart is excruci- ating. Gloria sings out and through and above and beneath the entire congre- gation, "Were you there when they crucified my Lord?" Gloria cannot stop herself till the room is full of her beautiful voice.

Were you there?

Lionel Parrish repeats.

He takes up her words and now his speaking voice has surrendered to the full grip of inspiration, soft, low, and trembling.

Yes, I think you was. But I'm here before you today for a very special rea- son. I'm here because one of these dead, dying in my *arms* at the White Palace, said to me, "I liked you from the beginning, Mr. Parrish. Preach it for me." That's what she, or he, asked: "Preach it for me." No, it doesn't matter which one. I'm not going to say which one asked it. That's not the important thing.

We been together in grief before. Us here. We don't have enough of *any- thing* else,

So quietly, he speaks.

but grief. *That, we are well acquainted with. But brothers and sisters, it's hard*

His voice rises and will rise; Stella waits for it to lift her above the coffins of her family, of the four girls, of Kennedy's bier, of these heart-dear friends coffined before her. *Lift me!*

it's hard, it's hard to see you again.

The congregation all stir in their seats; they are uncomfortable; they know what's coming; the introduction is over. Even Mr. Fielding and the white people shift their weight. All try to prepare to face the facts here at the front of this church. He starts low and gentle, again. He must climb the hill again. Stella wonders *How many times must we climb it?* But she is thinking of the myth of Sisyphus, not Golgotha. Gloria seats herself.

Dearly beloved (his eyes circle the tabernacle: all are included; the walls disappear), **we are gathered here at Joseph Coat-of-Many-Colors A.M.E. Church to mourn the passing of four young people—and I name them in alphabetical order by last names—Miss Arcola Anderson, Miss Catherine Cartwright, Mr. Charles Powers, Mrs. Christine Taylor. Bless them.**

Bless them, everyone says.

We standing at the skull. Crying.

Crying.

And as they say the word, people sob and thrash, and weep afresh.

Wishing we could have them back.

They groan with mourning.

And yet if we believe in Jesus, if we believe in Jesus, if we believe—

And the cadence falls, as Stella knows it must. One cannot build and build, one must fall back, then build again, lest somebody's heart be left by the wayside. This is the rhythm that catches all in its net and none will be left behind alone. But does Stella believe? How can she?

He whispers his inevitable question, like a hiss.

—then how can we want 'em back?

How *can* we want them back? If we believe.

We want them back for *their* lives, for the living they ain't done.

Yes, Stella agrees. She joins the church in its mourning. *Cat, my precious Cat!* Stella joins everyone present, in grief, if not in belief. *Arcola! Charles! Christine!* And with that last name the rafters of her mind ring. Four angels from four corners blast those names against her head, their trumpets pressed against her skull, and she is afraid of fainting and falling.

That's why we mourn. (His quiet voice stills the ringing of her head.) **That's why our hearts is heavy. In spite of belief in Jesus, we got to mourn**

these four young people for the *living* that passed on. For Arcola Anderson—if you knew her, you loved her. Always having a joke, Arcola, always making things smooth and friendly. Also working hard at her studies, getting ready to go out in life well educated. That's lost. That's gone now. Her daddy and her mama—Jesus will comfort you. Jesus *is* with you. Christine Taylor, mother of these three young children here. She trusted those children, trusted 'em over, to Sister Agnes and Brother TJ that day. But Christine won't get to play with 'em again or see them grow to be fine adults. But Christine did *this!* She made her statement. So that *all* children could grow up in a world that would be more fair. More equal. So white and black could sit down together. Like we are now.

And I mourn, I mourn for Catherine Cartwright. With all my heart. She was a natural teacher. She was dedicated to teaching. And she got to teach a little bit. But what a waste, what a waste, brothers and sisters, that we won't have Cat. She had a great friend, Miss Stella Silver, who came out to Miles College to teach with her, and Miss Silver and her friend is here with us to mourn, and Cat's brother and her father. And I know you'll all want to extend the right hand of fellowship to them.

I mourn Charlie Powers. Mr. Charles Powers. A young man, making his way in the world. It was my privilege to see how he was changing, how he was becoming a steady man. And he didn't forget his mother or his little sister or three little brothers, after he left home. He visited them, shared what he could, showed what it was to be a man. He was with Christine, in May 1963, when Bull Connor turned on the fire hoses and let loose the dogs. But Charles Powers valued education, just like these three young women, and he went on from protest to be a pupil in the night school.

But that's over. That's all over. For *all* of these. Black and white.

We'll miss 'em.

We'll miss 'em.

We miss 'em *today;* we miss 'em *tomorrow;* we miss 'em *forever.*

Stella catches his fearless allusion to George Wallace, who vowed, just so, that segregation would be unending. The congregation breaks up into separate utterances, shocked out of unity.

That's right. Tell it. Lord. Lord, help us. Preach it. Preach it right.

George Wallace, he try to tell us 'bout yesterday, today, and tomorrow. Let him wave the flag of Old Dixie and the flag of segregation, but I tell you,

I tell you, I tell you. Together today; together tomorrow; together forever. One world! God didn't make but one world. And he didn't send but one Son.

They are stirred, and he lets everyone settle. Stella knows: *he wants us to settle again.* He wants his people to settle once again. And again he drops back into his quiet voice; he is not a preacher who shouts all the time, instead he makes music of a sweet and low and startling trumpet blast. Lionel Parrish's bandaged hand waves out wounded and white, but it is not the badge of surrender. Not now, not ever.

Let me explain about Time. There be *eternity.* God's time. There be *change.* Our time.

I think I miss loved ones most at change of season. Then I think, if only they could see this. See the coming on of autumn, the way the leaves from the mighty oak trees fall down and curl on the ground. And then when we lift our faces, how blue the sky is through the bare branches. I don't think white people realize sometimes what a comfort the mere blue of heaven is to poor folks. And then when the colors of spring come on. The many colors, bright and various as the colors in Joseph's coat, the coat his brothers made him before they sold him into bondage—

When the colors of spring arrive and the dogwood blooms, I wish the dead could open their eyes, could open their eyes and see Nature, see what he's gave us here on earth, to enjoy. Yes, I'm sad when the seasons change. Change. I think change is the essence of our lives here on earth.

I don't want to stagnate. I want to develop myself, and I know they wanted to develop themselves—Charles and Catherine and Christine and Arcola. And it makes me sad to see any change in the season that those whom we love and who have passed on would have enjoyed.

But now summer is a-goin' on. Without these dead. The robins still here; bluejays still screaming "Thief! Thief." Up in the trees, the seed pods from wisteria hanging like grapes. Remember how we breathed in that wisteria aroma last spring? We'll try to smell it in the air when we go out of here. Because we remember springtime and *resurrection.* If the fall comes, so, surely, will the spring. And let's appreciate the beauty of the earth, and take comfort in it. Dahlias—so bright and cheerful—dahlias blooming in everybody's yard, and zinnias so round and perfect you want to take 'em to the fair. Jesus loves us.

He lifts his arms and opens wide his hands, as though to embrace the four coffins and the dead within.

And where are they? Them? They lying in the coffin, you say?

And his preacher question comes to Stella, burrows into her secret mind, *What can I believe?* But it's Gloria standing up and speaking out: "They with us. They in us," and the question is irrelevant. Gloria opens her mouth wider, and her voice opens up, and she's singing "Abide with Me." And the piano so soft—Jonathan—knows her key, the piano comes to help her, and all sing, but Gloria's voice leads clearest, and she becomes the leader she was born to be, and Stella sings, too, following the voice of her friend:

> *Abide with me: fast falls the eventide;*
> *The darkness deepens; Lord, with me abide!*
> *When other helpers fail, and comforts flee,*
> *Help of the helpless, O abide with me.*

> *Swift to its close ebbs out life's little day;*
> *Earth's joys grow dim, its glories pass away;*
> *Change and decay in all around I see;*
> *O Thou who changest not, abide with me.*

> *I fear no foe, with Thee at hand to bless;*
> *Ills have no weight, and tears no bitterness.*
> *Where is death's sting? Where, grave, the victory?*
> *I triumph still, if Thou abide with me.*

> *Hold Thou Thy cross before my closing eyes;*
> *Shine through the gloom and point me to the skies;*
> *Heaven's morning breaks, and earth's vain shadows flee;*
> *In life, in death, O Lord, abide with me.*

For a moment, Stella believes. She believes in love, the blessed community. In life, in death, there is love. Yes. That simple. And her heart overflows. She puts her hand and then her head on Nancy's shoulder, and cries with complete abandon, cries down the years for those dear and lost. Nancy sobs with her.

I tell *you*. Birmingham can't hold them. They left *this* city. They walking in the heavenly city, and I can see them there.

I see them, the congregation intones.

They walking on the streets of gold. They're holding hands, all of 'em, like us, healthy and happy, walking, walking, walking to the throne of God.

Cat's brother bursts into tears.

Throne of God.

And heavenly hosts—

Heavenly hosts—

Agnes screams, and TJ buries his face in both hands. Christine's children yelp in terror.

But there's Gloria, standing, shouting it out: "Freedom walking!"

And Mr. Parrish tells her, "Sing it out!"

Gloria shouts, "Freedom gonna come. Freedom gonna come. Lift up your soul, brothers and sisters. Lift up your voices"—her voice is loud and angry; she can't help it. Stella imagines flames darting from Gloria's eyes and ears. But the piano is starting to play while Gloria ignites. She flashes the mahogany of her skin, the green of her eyes, the bone of her teeth. And what is that tune Stella hears? Jonathan is playing the whole orchestra on the piano for the "Hallelujah Chorus" from Handel. Stella leaps to her feet. She rises to shout "Hallelujah," with no notion of the content of belief, and the congregation becomes a cacophony of cries, each heart opening. Jonathan is beating the music out of the piano, and people are not singing but shouting in anger, singing in anguish.

But piano doesn't want this to continue too long. Piano looks for peace. Gloria's singing voice comes back, but she has to stamp her feet for a while to finish the frenzy. Then Gloria opens from her deepest heart. Stella sees Gloria's shining face open and change and her being empty itself of hate. Gloria rises up from that dragon darkness that reached up from hell to grab her, and she will not be swallowed by hate.

Jonathan is playing beautifully now, big and ringing, triumphant, not angry, all over the keyboard. *Hallelujah! Hallelujah!*

Mr. Parrish shouts *Praise the Lord* over the music, and everyone shouts *Praise, praise the Lord,* and all stamp their feet to let out the last of what needs to go. The retreating rumble of their feet is like dying thunder, and Stella recognizes the establishment of vacancy, and the calm approaching to fill it.

Finally Mr. Parrish raises his bandaged hand and speaks again in a voice that signals it is finishing. His voice goes ordinary. He soothes and seals then for the closing words.

From the platform, Gloria looks down for a moment into Stella's eyes. What Stella sees in Gloria's green eyes is peace. And more. The glitter of strength. Mr. Parrish has done his work. Something passes between Stella and Gloria. They sip the common cup.

"And so," Mr. Parrish continues in his ordinary voice, "we go from the place of the skull, we go from the foot of the mountain, we go up from the fiery furnace, we leave the steel mills *burn*ing in the valley, we climbing *up* Red Mountain, we going to the top of the mountain. Flesh and blood, bone and skin of humanity take the place of the Iron Man." He sounds again like a normal man, speaking in sensible tones. "We lift up our hand in compassion for all. All Birmingham. Black and white." He takes a breath.

"We look down at sorrow—we left sorrow behind—we look down at injustice—we left injustice behind—and we look up at Love. Yes, my people, we look up at love and justice and mercy. Beyond Vulcan's iron arm, beyond the high-sailing clouds, and even beyond the starry firmament."

Amen, amen.

"Lift your hand and bow your heads," Mr. Parrish exhorts. "O Lord," he begs, "be merciful to me, a sinner." His knee thumps down on the floor. Never has Stella heard such an anguished cry as that of Mr. Parrish opening his heart. And she loves him, naked in his repentance, for whatever guilt and need he here acknowledges. "Forgive those who have murdered," he prays fervently. "Take those to your kindly bosom who have suffered and died, and whom here we mourn. You are the resurrection and the life. And whosoever believeth in you shall not perish but have everlasting life.

"And those dearly departed, they shall live in our hearts—not just these, Lord, but the others—those four others, those hundreds others, those thousands others who be lost to our memory but not to our imagination, all those who died or suffered for the cause of human dignity."

AT THE END OF the service, young Edmund Powers crosses in front of Stella to go to Gloria.

Still a young boy, but he moves slowly, gravely, as though he were an old man. He's all done with crying. Without the preaching and praying, Stella becomes heavy. The words buoyed her up, but now she slips under the tide of grief. She wonders if she can move at all. No, she can only sink. In spite of the heat, she becomes cold and numb. Helplessly, she can only see and hear.

As Stella watches, Edmund looks up at Gloria and says, "I feel sent to tell you." He speaks solemnly.

Gloria is all crisp vivacity. She swiftly hugs the little boy and says, "What's that?" His head tucks just under her bosom. The top of his head curves like the shoulder of a cello against Gloria's breast. Stella remembers her own cello, how it sang in the throaty timbre of Yiddish.

Pressed against Gloria's body, Edmund murmurs, "God say we must keep music in our soul. 'Make a joyful noise, all ye lands.'"

In amazement, Gloria releases him, as though she realizes that in this child, there is a preacher, an evangelist, a burning coal, and she must treat him more circumspectly.

Released, Edmund approaches Stella. He is shy, but he looks up in her eyes and utters his prophetic message. Stella sees his lips move, but she feels that she is looking at him from the bottom of the sea, through a lid of ice.

"Ma'am, God say we to take love to our hearts. That's all he say."

six

SPIRITS IN THE SNOW, January 1965

JONATHAN

"I CAN'T DO THAT ANYMORE," STELLA SAID TO JONATHAN after the funeral. By *that,* she meant teach at the H.O.P.E. night school. "I can do something else."

She looked at him as though she couldn't see him. The hand he held was icy, but her face had a *hectic* to it (the Shakespearian term came sadly to his mind), the flush of red hysteria Jonathan had seen on the faces of pale female students at Juilliard before they broke. But Stella surprised him by not crumbling, by going on to say, "Instead, I'll help people practice for voter registration."

Later he heard that the whole stifling week in early September after the funeral, she'd stayed in her bedroom. She'd told everyone *I have to grieve my way. I have to grieve it out.*

He had thought of Bach's cantata *Christ lag in Todesbanden*—Christ lay in the bonds of death. Though he didn't know her well, he pictured her on an austere bed, dressed in Sunday clothes, her hands clasped, waiting for the agony to pass. He imagined the bed to be neatly made, spread with a white candlewick coverlet. The bed like a bier with Stella decorously centered on it almost filled the room he had never seen where temperature did not exist. It was unlikely, but he hoped sometimes she thought of him, found minor comfort in the idea that beyond her walls were friends.

She would see only her aunts, people said, her old friend Nancy, her college friend Ellie, and Cat's brother. Later Jonathan had heard that Stella and Don had broken off their engagement. "We're like brother and sister now," they had told everyone.

Jonathan felt a small flame kindle in his heart.

IN OCTOBER, STELLA did begin to work with voter registration. She remarked to Jonathan, "It's easier to deal with older people. One at a time."

BY NOVEMBER, JONATHAN and Stella were going together to concerts, movies, organizational meetings, lectures, dances (she was a poor dancer); she asked to listen to him practice, and she invited him home to meet her old aunts, both of whom he adored. Eventually he took her back to Dale's Cellar for a full dinner. They had lobster, and she said that she'd never eaten lobster before.

After the Veterans Day parade, at Twentieth Street and First Avenue in downtown Birmingham, she introduced him to a short, freckle-faced man named Darl.

Rather awkwardly, she asked Darl if he'd enjoyed the parade. He responded that there ought to be at least one float honoring those who'd died in the struggle for civil rights. "They've served their country and given their lives. Just as much as any soldier," he said. Suddenly Stella reached up and hugged him, then she turned, took Jonathan's hand, and guided them through the dispersing crowd.

As they walked away, Jonathan remarked, "You certainly were glad to see *him*," and she told Jonathan that Darl was the man to whom she was first engaged.

"He's changed," she said. "I'm glad."

Wordless, Jonathan put his arm across her shoulders.

"I used to love to hear him play," she said. "Especially Bach."

He watched as the streets cleared of people who had witnessed the parade. "I remember," Jonathan said. "Drove a motor scooter."

She told Jonathan that she had broken up with Darl, "about this same season, late November last year, when Kennedy was assassinated." She seemed distracted, as though her mind had moved away from Darl and their engagement.

Jonathan felt jealousy flare from the pit of his stomach. He knew he didn't want her to ever say of himself, casually, *I used to go out with him.*

He felt surrounded by strangers, noticed the day was gray and dreary. These people moved slowly; none of the quick, businesslike movement of a New York street. He thought of Kabita and the last date they'd had, a visit to the Metropolitan Museum to see fashions based on cubist art.

"You're a survivor, aren't you?" Jonathan said to Stella. "Twice engaged."

She said gravely, "That's nothing to feel guilty about." Then she pointed to the emblem of the department store beside them. "Fair and square," she said. "I used to think justice and beauty could save the world."

He asked her what she thought could save it now.

"Nothing," she answered. "Personal strength and luck."

CHRISTMAS EVE, THEY parked in front of the aunts' house under the dim illumination of the streetlamp. The Thunderbird was cold because the heater was broken, and the ragtop provided no insulation. Suddenly she turned to him and he to her, kissing and kissing, and touching each other till they were panting and enveloped in a mist of their own breath. Their teeth were chattering so much that they began to laugh.

"We could go to my apartment," he said. "I'm sorry the heater's on the f-f-fritz."

"I want to," she said. "Not yet though."

"When you're ready."

He walked her to the front door, where they kissed tenderly.

"Soon," she said.

He knew she meant it. He knew after several months she would go home with him. That was what a southerner meant by *soon,* said in that eager, promising, reassuring tone, the ultimate flirtation.

NEW YEAR'S PARTY, 1965

SO MUCH HAS BEEN WON, JENNY PARRISH THOUGHT AS SHE handed up a twist of crepe paper—black and white twirled together—to her husband on the stepladder. Lionel had bought six bottles of champagne and had them on ice in the big washtub. Pregnant again, Jenny put her hand on her belly. *And you be the very best part of it,* she thought. Lyndon Johnson had signed the Civil Rights Act on July 2, 1964. On that night Shuttlesworth had tested the waters, gone to the dining room of the Parliament House Hotel. He was seated. But violence and killing were still going on all over the South. Lionel wanted to go down to Selma, work with King, who was planning to come back to Alabama in January for mass meetings. It was still difficult to register to vote. Jenny knew that lives would be lost in Selma.

"Heard on the radio," Lionel said, "it just might snow." He stretched to fasten the streamer to the light fixture.

"Don't tell the children," Jenny said. "They wild enough already."

At that moment, she saw Agnes and TJ and their three standing on the porch. Agnes was older than Jenny had thought she would be—kind of old to be herding three children. When Jenny opened the front door, Diane burst in, all a-jangle. She had a jingle bell sewn in the crown of her stocking cap. "It's gonna snow," Diane announced. "I caught a snowflake on my tongue."

Jenny's four came piling into the room. George walked right up to Diane, held out his hand like a grown person, and said, "Howdy-do, I'm George Parrish."

"And I'm Miss Diane Taylor."

"Whew!" both Agnes and Jenny exclaimed together.

"This must be Buckingham Palace," Jenny said.

Lionel climbed down from the stepladder and held out his hand to TJ.

"Help me move all this furniture against the wall, Brother TJ," he said. "We might want to dance tonight."

"Agnes said some white folks due to come."

"Said they was. Stella and Jonathan, from the night school. And they're bringing a friend, Miss Ellie."

"I saw the police cruising," TJ answered.

"Let 'em cruise. This here a private party."

"Lookie there at the window!" Agnes said.

They all looked. Thick as feathers from a ripped pillow, snow was drifting down.

THROUGH THE WINDOW of the Thunderbird, Stella watched the snow pelt the red hood and melt. "The only question is—will it stick?" Stella said.

"Stick?"

She was wearing a red scarf Jonathan had given her for Christmas. She looked like one of those delicate, hand-tinted postcards from the 1940s—with her blond hair curling up from the red wool.

"Accumulate," she explained. "That's what southern children always ask. Is it cold enough for snow to stick?"

"In about ten minutes the sky will open full scale and we'll be ankle deep in snow."

"How do you know?"

"I've only seen it snow about two hundred times in New York," he said.

Once, she had told him that she loved him best while he was playing the piano, and he had said that every day he loved her more than the day before. She had laughed and said that he must be thinking about writing a country-western song. For a while, he'd tried to get her to take up the cello again, but she'd said for him to accompany Gloria on the cello. She enjoyed listening, she had said, and he accepted that.

"What's your favorite piano piece now?" he asked.

" 'Jingle Bells,' " she said and laughed. "No, the Mussorgsky, *Pictures at an Exhibition*. Especially 'The Great Gate of Kiev.' All that grand clanging."

He reached across and stroked her cheek with his knuckle. "Maybe someday we'll go there. To Russia. To Kiev."

"If the world doesn't blow up," she answered.

"Stella," he said lightly. "Do you want to talk about getting married?"

She glanced back through the rear window. "Maybe you should slow down. Ellie's almost a block behind."

"Not used to driving in the snow. She should have ridden with us."

"She's fine. And, Jonathan, *dear heart*, I'm happy the way we are."

Nothing she said ever made him doubt their connection. She had said they had *the trust beyond trust*.

"What way?" he asked. He recalled that Ellie was wearing the sexy red sheath dress.

"Less naive."

He reached over and pressed her knee. "I've never been naive."

"I have," she answered. "Stubbornly so." Snow was beginning to pile up in people's yards, in the sprays of pine needles and also on the broad, flat leaves of the magnolias. "Has it already snowed in New York this winter?"

"My mother said it snowed for Thanksgiving."

She tucked her feet up under her and asked, "Will they like me?"

"Your mother was Jewish, so as far as they're concerned, you're Jewish. And college educated. That's all that matters." But he knew they would adore Stella. "You're presentable," he teased. They'd be surprised by her careful tact and extreme politeness. To them, she would seem ever so slightly exotic, as she did to him. Suddenly he lusted after her. There was no other term for it.

"Let's do get married," he said.

She smiled. "May we listen to the forecast?"

He flipped on the radio.

"Folks, it is snowing in Birmingham! Look out your window, and y'all'll see, snow is coming down, believe you me! Joe Rumore, here, Alabama's only Eye-talian redneck. Predictions are for an inch accumulation in the next half hour! Up to six inches tonight, New Year's Eve, 1965! You ought to head for home early, folks. Be careful after those late-night parties. We don't want to see Vulcan's light turning red tonight, folks."

IN HER OWN CAR, Ellie turned up the heater. She'd forgotten her coat. Buford had called from out of town just when Stella and Jonathan drove up and honked in front of the apartment. *I have to go*, she'd said. *I'm going to a party.* He was irate that she would party on New Year's without him. She started to tell him she was going with another couple, but she changed her mind. She had the right to make her own choices. He ought to trust her. When he protested, she had slammed down the phone and run outside, clutching her car keys.

She moved her head so she could see her eyes in the rearview mirror. Mascara and eye shadow were perfect, slightly theatrical. She looked wonderful. She smiled. Though she couldn't see her mouth, the light in her eyes intensified. She'd not been to an integrated party before, but she'd always loved dark skin. Aesthetically, it was her favorite color for skin.

If there was a piano, maybe she'd sing and Jonathan would play.

AGNES PUT HER COAT back on and stationed herself on the porch to watch the children play in the yard. She had gained weight since the children came. "Happy weight," TJ called it. The children were mostly running around with their tongues stuck out catching snowflakes, or trying to gather up enough snow to make miniature snowballs. They were talking about building a snowman and a snow fort. She loved seeing their three play with the Parrish four.

When she stepped inside every fifteen minutes or so to get warm, Agnes watched the children through the glass door. Sometimes TJ or Jenny Parrish came to chat while she watched. Jenny had told her that Lionel wanted to name the new baby Charles if it was a boy and Christine or Matilda if it was a girl. "It's not my business," Agnes said, "but I'd love to see you give this baby your name, Jenny." Jenny had hugged her. Agnes loved the way Jenny's round belly pushed up against her, held her close to life.

WHEN A MEAN WIND gusted hard and mythic snow flew horizontally, every child stopped playing.

Diane saw that the wind was strong enough to stick snow against the window screens, and TJ's face behind the window, helping Agnes watch them, became a white cloud.

Eddie knew that he must be strong and stand against it. He closed his eyes and thrust his face into the wind.

Little Henry-Honey looked for Agnes and saw her standing on the porch, drawing her coat collar close against her throat. He remembered the soft warmth of her body and decided to go to her.

George thought of the moment when the church blew up, when his soul had tried to leave his body, when it had hidden in the marrow of his bones. When his mother's voice had tethered him and kept him from seeing the rubble, from helping his father.

Lizzie and Vicky Parrish worried about their mother. Suppose the baby in her tummy got cold? But their mother was inside; they could see the golden light, where surely it was warm. They would go inside now and help their mother. With the points of the scissors, they would pierce cellophane and take it off the paper plates. They would shake salty nuts into glass dishes.

Andy Parrish wondered at the color of the snow, more white even than Ivory soap. He remembered his bathtub soap-cake boat and how he blew on its red sail to make it move. If he held up a red sail—maybe a kite—would the wind blow him out of the yard? Would it blow him up into the clouds? He held his arms out at his sides, hoping to catch the wind.

The wind blew two cars down the street: a red convertible with a white top and then a blue car. After the cars parked, two white people—Jonathan and Stella—got out of the lead car, and one white woman in a red dress, by herself, got out of the second car.

And then a third car passed, pale green, with two white men in it. The wind blew that car speedily down the street, past the house and the bundled-up children.

SEEING THE CHILDREN IN the yard, Jonathan said to Stella, "Spirits in the snow."

Agnes and TJ's children ran forward for hugs, as they always did.

Diane cocked her arm on one hip and asked, "Is this the best snow you ever seen?"

"Absolutely," Jonathan said, and he squeezed her hard and flicked the big sleigh bell sewn in the top of her chartreuse stocking cap. He turned to see that Ellie was picking her way through the snow in her high heels. He glanced at Stella's warm coat and scarf, her feet in her sensible rubber-soled green flats, and went to help Ellie. Her arms were incongruously bare, and she looked very glamorous with her dark hair and glittering long earrings blowing back. Vulnerable.

"Ellie's going to freeze," Stella remarked, but already Jonathan was putting his arm around her bare shoulders; Ellie's skin was strikingly warm to the touch.

Diane danced at his elbow, fearlessly introducing herself to the strange white woman.

"What was your next best ever snowfall," Diane demanded of Jonathan, "after this?"

Somehow the question pierced him, and he remembered when he and Kabita had come out of the Metropolitan Museum into a snow shower at dusk. He remembered how the snowflakes had caught in Kabita's long dark hair. He pulled Ellie against his side; she was slightly plump, no, voluptuous, like a dark-haired Marilyn Monroe.

He steered Ellie toward the lighted house, behind Stella.

"Y'all come on in now," Agnes called from the porch to the children.

All the children, a little herd of them, gathered at their elbows and moved toward the house. From the street, a car honked its horn, but Jonathan didn't bother to turn. Somebody celebrating early.

Kabita had been as slender as Stella. When he and Kabita had admired the heavy stone sarcophagi in the Egyptian wing, he'd discovered that she'd read all of Shakespeare. Kabita had remarked that you could really tell the difference between genius and talent when you compared *Antony and Cleopatra* with Dryden's *All for Love*. Her innocent remark had made his blood run cold; he had wondered if someday someone would say that about his playing of Chopin in comparison to Rubinstein's. He had told her so, and Kabita had refused to console him. *We'd all better keep practicing,* she had teased and winked at him. He had loved her, among the sarcophagi, for her honesty.

Agnes looked into his eyes. Her gaze startled him, as though he had been found out.

"You don't have to be homesick for no snow," Agnes said. "We gets snow."

STELLA WAS DELIGHTED to see Gloria at the party, but she was surprised when Ellie said to Gloria, right off, "You have beautiful skin."

Yes, Stella admired more fully the mahogany red of Gloria's complexion.

"Thank you," Gloria said. She was not fazed a bit. "I'm letting my hair go natural."

Gloria's hair surrounded her head like a dark nimbus.

When Stella introduced Ellie to Lionel Parrish, he said, "You're most welcome, pretty lady." Lionel put his arm proudly around Jenny. "We already got two of each. This one's the *bonus.*" How at ease Lionel was among all his guests, black and white. In his ease, Stella, too, felt easy and welcome. Usually shy at parties, she suddenly knew she would chatter, perhaps say amazing things. But then she always felt free when she was with Ellie.

"Y'all come sit in these kitchen chairs and talk to me," Gloria said to Stella and Ellie.

Gloria led the way, tooting on a noisemaker, blowing it obnoxiously into people's faces. *Arcola!* Stella thought. *She's taken on Arcola's ways,* and she felt a pang of sadness. *Cat!*

"Girl, you still got your cello?" Gloria asked Stella.

JONATHAN LISTENED TO GLORIA explain that she needed instruments. She wanted to start an orchestra. "Not just teach kids to toot horns." And then Gloria blew her party horn exuberantly.

Jonathan turned to look out the window.

It was dusk and the snow was still falling. The Parrish home was filling with happy people, but he felt sad and told himself that sometimes this was the way it felt when you were away from home on New Year's, and it was snowing. He remembered the city lights and the lamps in Central Park, how he had put his arm around Kabita. Together they enjoyed the yellow lights against the gray sky, and the white snow still coming down. Here in Birmingham he suddenly felt bereft. It pleased him that snow was covering everything. He wondered how far south the snow would reach? Montgomery, Mobile?

Then he felt Stella's arm around him.

"I love the snow in the evergreens," she said. "When I was a little girl, Aunt Krit gave me a candle of a little green pine tree, with snow on its boughs. It was my first Christmas without my family. It pleased me that she had picked out just a natural tree for me, not a decorated one. I never said so to her, but it made me feel understood, and I was grateful to her."

He hugged her against his side.

"What did Aunt Pratt give you?"

"A huge rag doll. She'd made her just my size. She had very pink polished cotton skin and yellow yarn hair."

Jonathan put his lips in Stella's hair and kissed her head. She didn't doubt that she was his and he was hers—just the way she leaned against him said that.

"Gloria's going down to Selma to help with voter registration," she said. "Ellie's interested, too."

Yes, he loved Stella. She understood him, and he needed her.

Suddenly, they saw Agnes, all bundled up, out in the yard scooping up snow in a big saucepan. She moved fast, bending and scooping in her gray coat with a gray scarf tied over her head. When Agnes came inside, snow frosting her shoulders and dusting the gray, fringed scarf, she said, "I'm gonna make this Yankee boy some snow ice cream!"

STELLA GLANCED OVER at Gloria and Ellie, gabbing in the straight chairs like two old country women on a front porch. Ellie reached over and familiarly fingered the miniature harmonica hanging on a ball chain around Gloria's neck.

Immediately Gloria took the little thing to her lips and, impromptu, played a rousing rendition of "O, Susanna!" The jaunty, confident tune penetrated the party hubbub. "Play it again," Stella called, and so did others. There were Gloria's aunts, colorful as tropical birds, egging her on. And over in the corner, that quiet couple must be Gloria's parents; Stella had met them at Joseph Coat-of-Many-Colors. Gloria looked like her mother, but she was dressed as flamboyantly as the aunts.

Everybody sang with gusto, especially Jonathan, right in Stella's ear: "I come to Alabama with a banjo on my knee. . . ." The room resounded with it. "O, Susanna, O, don't you cry for me. . . ." Stella looked at the faces, mostly dark, a few light. Some stoic as stone, some singing with twinkling jauntiness, some with patient determination making a promise to the future that there *would be* no more reason, someday in the South, to cry for me or my children or my people.

How could Gloria possibly get so much music out of an instrument only an inch long? So much volume and sprightly, saucy hope.

And there was Ellie, rising above her personal angst, radiant for freedom in some form that combined the personal and the private.

Gloria was even able to smile as she played; her shoulders danced as she blew herself into an instrument half the length of her little finger. Stella remembered how Gloria had stepped forward not in joy but in anguish to speak and to sing at the funeral, her soul projected by her voice. *No matter who dies,* Stella thought, *the South will always have more Glorias to step forward, to lead.* But then Stella thought of how few they were, gathered in this house, a snow-storm swirling about them.

When the singing stopped, Jonathan murmured of Gloria, "She's really very talented."

Stella spoke from her heart: "I'm glad she can play the cello, and I don't have to." She peeked out the window again. Brigades of bundled-up children were bringing Agnes snow for her ice cream. Yes, Stella remembered, it seemed to take bushels of snow to make snow ice cream. She could smell something hot and savory, too, emanating from the kitchen. They were baking hot breads—banana bread, and something with cinnamon and dates, and there was the spe-cial aroma of walnuts baking in batter, a smell that made even your teeth water.

JONATHAN EXCUSED HIMSELF to go to the bathroom. He wanted to be closeted, alone for a while. In the bathroom, he thought again of how Kabita and he had stood on the steps looking at the city in the snowfall. He flushed the toilet. And then he remembered another picture, a photograph of the mothers of Chaney, Goodman, and Schwerner. They too were standing at the top of a flight of stairs in New York, leaving the funeral service for Andrew Goodman. Their black purses dangled from their wrists in front of their linked bodies. They had all lost their sons to the Klan: Schwerner and Goodman, white boys from New York. Goodman killed his first day in Mississippi. Chaney a local worker, Negro, from Mississippi.

Jonathan looked at himself in the bathroom mirror and wondered if he had a fraction of their strength. He wished someone would compose a trio for three male singers with an amazing piano part, a trio for young male voices, preferably aged twenty-one, twenty-one, and twenty-five, preferably two white and one Negro. And a complementary one for their middle-aged mothers, something that would let them shriek their grief. He thought of the weight of Mississippi earth—an earthen dam constructed with bulldozers—under which Goodman, Schwerner, and Chaney were found.

Maybe Jonathan had been in Alabama too long. Maybe his luck was running out and it was time to leave. Stella seemed ready to go to Selma, but how did he feel? Heavy. Depressed. It was New Year's and he should feel hopeful, be looking forward to change. He thought of Lionel's sermon at the funeral. He needed something to help him spill his sorrow. He was ashamed of himself for longing for Kabita, for times back then in New York, for wanting now to hold Ellie in her fiery dress and warm body.

He left the bathroom and wandered the party. Stella was sitting happily between Ellie and Gloria, and he knew that another friendship circle was forming. Ellie might betray her husband but not her friends.

EVENTUALLY, LIONEL HURRIED among the champagne glasses to get ready for the countdown.

Ellie stood up quickly, breathlessly happy. When Stella and Gloria stood up, Gloria ecstatically threw her arms around Stella, without reserve, and Stella returned the embrace with the same joyful freedom. Jonathan envied Stella, wanted to ask her for help.

At Jonathan's elbow, Jenny said, "This is our first champagne," but Lionel was popping corks as though he were an old hand at it.

On the other side of Jonathan, someone quietly raised his glass and said, "Here's to my friend Medgar Evers, a great leader, assassinated June 12, 1963. Jackson, Mississippi."

So others were remembering, too. The big man was standing alone, toasting the air.

Jonathan lifted his glass. He didn't want to intrude. He said quietly, "To all the martyrs." He thought of a thirteen-year-old boy in Birmingham, on a bicycle, murdered the same day as the four girls. Shot by young Eagle Scouts. The boy's name was Virgil Lamar Ware. Jonathan had still been in New York then, practicing his fool fingers off. But he spent hours rummaging in drawers till he found his old Eagle Scout certificate, which he burned in the kitchen sink, and resolved to prepare himself to try to count for something in the South.

"To Virgil Lamar Ware," Jonathan added softly.

To his surprise, the man next to him glanced at him, and raised his glass.

"To Johnny Robinson."

"Who was he?" Jonathan asked.

"Killed same day as Virgil. As the girls. Shot in the back by police breaking up a crowd."

Jonathan opened his arm to the man, who stepped forward. A big man, full of grief. When the man stepped away, his eyes and nostrils were running tears.

"Johnny was in with a crowd of kids throwing rocks. I knowed his folks." He wiped his nose on a square of white handkerchief, then turned away to face the party and the countdown. Lionel hastened to fill their glasses with the sparkling champagne.

Moments before midnight, Lionel solemnly raised his hand for silence. They all looked at the scar like a star in his palm.

"We're here to have a good time," Lionel said. "To celebrate that we are alive. That we can carry the torch. But we don't none of us forget. Not September 15, 1963." He paused to gather his composure. "Not our recent losses—Joseph Coat. Not the losses before or after September 15 due to racism. Not Medgar Evers; not young men from the North this last June in Mississippi and James Chaney; southern children, our own young. Tonight we also honor those young and old, white and black, who may yet lay down their lives for equality and freedom. Martin Luther King's coming back to Alabama, working in Selma and the rural parts for voter registration.

"I can't do better as we greet the New Year, 1965, I can't *do* better than to remind you of the words of Dr. Martin Luther King Jr. He said that 'the innocent blood of these little girls may serve as the redemptive force that will bring new light to this dark city.' Remember, friends, Birmingham and the United States got to feel the redemptive force, not just sorrow. We got to bear up that light, each and every one. In my mind, old Vulcan up there watching for the New Year come in—he holding up the light of love in this pure and blessed snow."

Lionel lowered his arm and put it around his wife's shoulders.

"Now, sisters and brothers," he said energetically, "count on down."

At midnight, the guests all toasted one another and yelled "Happy New Year!" Gloria continuously blew her horn obnoxiously onto noses.

Stella came to Jonathan and said, "I think we should go now."

Ellie said that she wanted to stay longer.

"We'll look after her," Gloria answered.

At the door, Stella said to Lionel, "I hope 1965 is good to you and Jenny. It's going to be good to Jonathan and me."

Jonathan was shocked at her public forthrightness, her confidence in them.

"That's right," he echoed. Yes, he would let his disappointments and frustration go. Yes, he would embrace this odd and wonderful woman who loved him.

Lionel announced, "Before they go—a toast to a happy couple!"

And everyone yelled, "Happy New Year!"

AS THEY WALKED TOWARD THEIR CAR, ANOTHER CAR SPED by, blasting its horn.

"Wild night," Jonathan remarked.

"I love the snow," Stella said. "I had a wonderful time." She glanced at him, knew he had seemed troubled during parts of the party. Inside the Thunderbird she leaned over and rubbed her cheek against his prickly whiskers.

"Would you like to grow a curly red beard?"

He turned on the motor and pulled away from the curb. The tires crunched in the snow.

"Anything for you," he said.

She believed him. She believed every word his lips and his body uttered.

He glanced in the rearview mirror, and Stella turned to see a car, iceberg green, hurtle past. There were four men in the car.

"It's starting to get slippery," Jonathan said as he drove on.

At the next traffic light, the same pale green car rushed up, behind them again, blowing its horn. In this light, it looked too pale, almost white, but definitely the same one.

A great dread clenched Stella's heart.

Irritated, Jonathan glanced in the rearview mirror again. "What's their problem?" he said. "The light's red."

"Maybe they were afraid they couldn't stop in time," Stella said. "That they'd rear-end."

"I hope not," he said. "Does anybody ever ski or ice-skate around here?"

"There's an indoor skating rink in Eastlake," she said. "But the rental skates are worn out, and the ice barely covers the refrigeration pipes." She remembered how she had begged and begged Aunt Krit to take her ice-skating till finally she'd gotten to go. Her sneaky plan had been to learn to skate and then show off to Nancy. But at the rink, Stella had had to cling to the railing to get around; her ankles were too weak. One patch of ice was a rusty brown smear from the decay of the pipes underneath, and it was harrowing to bump along over the almost exposed pipes. Suppose her blades sliced into the pipes; suppose the pipes had poisonous gas inside? She would never take Nancy to such a dangerous place.

"I'll teach you to ski," Jonathan said. "We'll go to Maine or Vermont. If we got married tomorrow that could be our honeymoon."

"We could," she said. She glanced over her shoulder. She could see the ice green car. "I'm afraid of that car behind us," she blurted.

"I'll just slow down and let them pass," he said. "They can make the next light, if they hurry."

But the car—two white men in the front seat, two in the back—sped straight toward them. The driver threw on his brakes, and then veered out of control into the oncoming lane. The car coming toward them pulled aside and onto the curb, honking its own horn. Careening past, the men on the passenger sides rolled down their windows and yelled.

"Yankee, go home! Nigger lovers!"

"What the hell!" Jonathan said.

"Speed up," Stella said.

"What?"

"We need to get away from them. Turn down the next side street."

ALL THE STREETS WERE choked with snow. A few adults were out in the wee hours on their lawns, building snowmen. *Now, we're safe,* she thought. But they were tense. They drove for blocks, clenching themselves, not talking.

"I'm not a believer anymore," she said suddenly. "Not the way I was." She remembered Darl's defiant angel in Oak Hill Cemetery.

"And you're okay with that?"

"I've evolved. It's been as natural as that."

"You know I don't care. Evolve again, if you want to."

"What's happening here in the South. King's courage. Shuttlesworth's. This rising of the South, it's a Christian movement. Oh, I know, plenty of Eastern intellectuals down here. You guys. Maybe some Buddhists, for all I know. Gandhi was a Hindu, and he's the fountainhead of all of it; he's immensely important to King. But the rise of the Negro in the South is really a Christian story. It has to be told that way."

"Oh, no," he said.

"What?"

"That car, it's with us again."

"Kiss!" she said. "Kiss and step on the gas."

Quickly she leaned to him, brushed his lips with hers, and the Thunderbird shot forward. They raced toward Norwood, straight out raced down Eighth Avenue.

"Maybe the police will follow," she said. "Faster." The speedometer rose, forty, fifty, sixty. "Can you see them?" A wake of snow spewed out behind them.

"No."

So they were safe again, not far from home. She wanted not to go home, though, but to sit in a private place and talk and talk. It was only just past midnight. Aunt Krit wouldn't be expecting her so soon. She wondered about Jonathan's sadness at the party.

"Turn," she said. "Then turn into the cemetery. It'll be beautiful."

This evening no chain stretched across the columns marking the entrance.

" 'Abandon hope,' " Jonathan murmured, " 'all ye who enter here.' " But he smiled, mocking his former mood. "I can barely see where the road is," he added as they rolled between the stone pillars.

"Keep moving. I want to go deep in."

He killed the headlights. "It's so bright," he said, "with just the snow reflection."

"Go deeper," she said, and he did till they were almost hidden among the snow-shaggy evergreens, the magnolias and snow-bent cedars. The bare limbs of the oaks and elms were shelves for snow. The car crept slowly through acres of monuments and trees.

Finally she felt concealed in the deep folds of the cemetery. Because of the hills, they could see nothing of the streets. He slowed the car, and they could hear the solitary slush and creak of the tires through the snow.

"Turn off the engine," she said, and he did.

They coasted to a quiet stop, like a boat coming to a dock. Falling snow curtained the landscape.

"Listen," he said. He rolled down his window a little, and she did, too. "We could be in another country." Bits of snow drifted through the open space at the top of the window.

"What lovely silence," she said. "So much peace here."

He waited, listening, and then he said, "Yes."

"I wish Cat were buried here." Cat's grave was in the country near a sunny meadow. "No, I don't," she amended. Don had said when they were kids, he and Cat used to run in the meadow behind the church, before Cat got sick.

"Just listen," Jonathan said, "and look."

So she did, wondering at the hush and beauty of the snow as it shrouded shrubs, monuments, and trees. Gradually, the racing of her heart was slowing down. Again, she remembered the little wax tree Aunt Krit had given her, bedecked with snow, and when she'd won a grade school contest reciting poetry, a pearly bracelet with a large charm—a basket full of jewels. Those lovely gifts had been comforting.

"Do you mind Christmas carols?" she asked. She watched the snow melt as it hit the warm red hood of the car.

He laughed. "No, of course not, but I thought you were skeptical."

"I love Christmas carols anyway." Then she sang to him:

> *In the bleak midwinter, frosty wind made moan.*
> *Earth stood hard as i-ron, water like a stone.*
> *Snow had fallen, snow on snow. Snow on snow,*
> *In the bleak midwinter, long ago.*

"That was lovely, Stella," he said.

She smiled; yes, to create loveliness—that *was* the only answer. Not her singing but the beautiful words to the carol. "Careful, or I'll convert you," she said. The cold air nipped her nose.

"Look," he said. "There's a rabbit."

And there was a little brown rabbit creeping across the crust of snow. He turned and showed them just his cottontail, almost indistinguishable against the white. Snow fell steadily.

"It's a Christina Rossetti poem," she said.

"Whose tune?" He rubbed his hands together briskly to warm them.

"I don't know."

"Such a measured, mournful melody," he mused. "Very beautiful. Do you want to get out? Walk around."

"No. I feel safer in here. Warmer, too." She rolled her window back up. "It's snowing harder now. Feel my nose," she said, and he did. Then she felt his. Her fingertips loved the fine cartilage of his nose. "Mine's colder," she said. The snow was starting to accumulate and hide the red of the hood. "*The crimson and the white.*" She thought of the alma mater of Phillips High School, how those closing words always moved her; she missed Cat again and other classmates, and wondered where they were and what they were doing.

"Sing the rest of the carol," he asked quietly, and she did, what she could remember:

> *An-gels and arch-angels may have gather-ed there,*
> *Cher-u-bim and ser-a-phim throng-ed the air;*
> *But His moth-er on-ly, in her maid-en bliss,*
> *Wor-shiped the Be-lov-ed with a kiss.*

Looking across the car seat, hearing how the song had bent its meaning when she sang it to him, she wanted to lean through the frigid air and kiss him. Behind his face, fern-shaped frost patterned the window. Surely she knew now what it was to adore another person. This man. This brilliant musician, who didn't mind her singing. Who had made a pilgrimage south. For no one in particular. For everyone. Because Eagle Scouts had shot a boy off his bicycle.

Not just the frost but the driving snow was erasing the world. Downward pelting snow, thicker than angel wings thronged the air. But she wouldn't kiss yet; she would sing the next part to him. What, after all, did she have to give him? Maybe then.

> *What can I give Him, poor as I am?*
> *If I were a shepherd, I would bring a lamb;*
> *If I were a wise man, I would do my part;*
> *Yet what I can I give Him—give Him my heart.*

Then they heard the sound of a car motor.

"Rub the frost off," he said. With the palms of their hands, they circled the frost off the glass. Through the peepholes, they both saw the shape of the green car, blurred to whiteness now, preceded by twin cones of light from its headlamps.

"This was a mistake," she said.

"Don't say that," he answered with a quick glance at her. "It wasn't a mistake"—his voice as gentle as though they had seen nothing. With the softness of his tone and gaze, he seemed to offer her a gentle animal, something softly alive and vulnerable—a rabbit, a lamb.

"I'm sorry," she said. "I'm really sorry."

The green car wasn't racing anymore. It was coming slowly into the cemetery, pale lime green again, humped, on the one-lane road. Its headlights tunneled through the falling snow.

"They haven't seen us," she said. "They'd be coming faster if they had. We're camouflaged by the snow."

"Can you run?" His question was sharply urgent, full of energy.

"Like a deer."

They swung open the doors, closed them quietly, clasped hands, and ran cross-country. Dodging around the monuments, she slipped, and he held her hand tighter, to the point of pain. Just before they rounded a shielding spruce, Stella glanced back. Down through their headlights cascaded showers of snow.

From the other side of the spruce, they heard a shot split the air, and the sound of glass breaking.

"They're shooting your car," she whispered.

"Our car," he said, and she felt married to him. "Just run!"

"This way," she told him.

Glancing back, she saw the snowfall was quickly filling their footprints, and she began to hope.

"You go left, I'll go right," she said. "Meet you beyond the thicket of obelisks. See where the angel is?" *Darl's defiant angel.*

"Yes," Jonathan said.

They parted and ran. Stella heard many guns fired at the car. Tires exploded—one, two, three, four—with each explosion, she increased her speed. The men would cautiously approach the car; they would hope to find two bodies slumped onto the floorboards. She made herself run harder; she leapt the low tombstones in her path. The men would crane their necks to look through the shattered windshield. When they saw the car was empty, they would howl and curse, but she loved and would love the strength in her legs and her own running, alone, at top speed over the snow. The cold air refreshed her cheeks. She was weightless and indefatigable. *I will live!*

The men would stand around and talk. Somebody would notice the footprints.

Snow! Snow harder! she implored the heavens. *Faster,* she implored her legs. As she ran, she lifted her arms in a V above her head. *Here the ghost comes, boo-hoo-hoo*—her blood zinged in her body. Maybe snow already had filled the footprints. *Don't be frightened, boo-hoo-hoo!* Jonathan was almost a speck, a dark, vertical dash, running parallel to her in the distance. She ran almost as fast. *The past comes to help us.*

Behind the angel they ran into each other's arms; Jonathan seemed startlingly large and human. She, too, panting, seemed large and fleshy, full of breath and heaving.

Snow fell thickly between their flushed faces. "Quick," she said. "I know where we can hide." She remembered the perfect magnolia where the lone Negro hid, and the rocky draw that lead to it. Surely the rapidly falling snow would cover their tracks. Almost. She surveyed the vague landscape till she saw a rounded dome, like the top of a giant gumdrop.

"Dry creek bed," she gasped. "No footprints."

She could see fear in his eyes, but he nodded assent.

"I've been here before," she assured.

They skittered down the draw. Bits of snow were caught in the grooves where water had scored the rock, but not enough snow for feet to imprint. Soon the steep dry course leveled out, and they passed through the colonnade of sycamores. She glanced up at the branches against the pale sky. But there, where the ground began to slope away to the open meadow, was the magnolia cloaked in white. Beyond the tree, unbroken snow covered the grass, but here, with one long step directly from the rocks underfoot into the tree branches, they entered obscurity.

She passed into the tree as though going through a door into a hut. She entered the tree as though entering a story, a crevice in a fairy-tale book. He followed.

She recalled that summer night when a dark figure had tucked himself under the low-hanging branches and disappeared. Snowcapped now, the leaves seemed to hide them with scoops of Agnes's snow ice cream. What had that summer fugitive thought of Darl and her, as surprising as ghosts? *White folks, lying on the ground!* They'd kept his secret; he'd taught her how to hide.

Within the tree, she and Jonathan wove their bodies between the thick branches so that they could stand upright. Their cold feet moved among old leaves, brown and brittle, and they stepped on rotting magnolia cones like honeycombs. Perhaps a few bright red seeds were still hidden in the spongy folds of the cones. The musty odor of magnolia rose from the debris.

"We can climb up," she whispered.

He glanced up. "It's made for climbing." He almost smiled at her.

"Yes, but it's weak wood. Brittle. We can't both be on the same limb, even a big one."

The magnolia *was* easy to climb, but they ascended as slowly as sloths. Their bare, cold fingers hooked over each limb so carefully that no snow shattered from the outer leaves. Inside the canopy of leaves, the air was still, but occasionally a view opened to the outside. When they climbed into the dome of the tree, higher than the road, they could peep out and see the vast snow-field studded with monuments.

In the distance the four male figures stood with the two cars. Their car was parked twenty or thirty yards from the mutilated Thunderbird. Because the men now concealed their bodies in white robes, only their movement distinguished them from the landscape. Stella thought how the Finnish army, on skis and dressed in white, had surprised the Germans. One of the Klan members lifted his arm repeatedly, driving a knife into the canvas top of the car.

"Insane," Jonathan said. "They look like demented witches."

"Haints," she corrected, but the pointed hoods *were* witchlike. She marveled at how the forms of the men blended with the fallen snow.

One pointed hood circled the Thunderbird. He stopped beside the driver's door as though to study the ground. *"Hunters in the Snow,"* Stella said, more to herself than Jonathan, but he answered with the painter's name in a whisper, "Brueghel." She took off her red woolen scarf, wadded it up, and concealed it like a nest in a crotch of the tree. The tracker moved to the front of the car, put his hands on his hips, paused to gaze down the road and around the car. The snow was falling less furiously, and the view began to clear. Still Stella felt safe within the snowcapped dome of the tree.

Another man stood behind the Thunderbird, aiming his rifle at the license plate. He shouted—the cry was thin—and motioned with one hand for his buddies to stand back. The tracker obeyed. As soon as the shot was fired, a whoosh of flame enveloped the Thunderbird.

"Better it than us," Jonathan murmured.

The four men retreated from the blaze. A pillar of black smoke rose up. They backed toward their own car, disrobing, ready to leave.

When they grasped the tapered hoods and pulled, they revealed ordinary heads. One was almost bald. A heavy, short man. A tall one with a sloping head. Ordinary enough men. Their robes were rosy in the reflected light of the burning car. Each of the men walked backward, as though mesmerized by the majesty of destruction. Suddenly Stella realized the car might explode. *"Watch out,"* she heard herself say, in a normal voice. Jonathan reached past the tree trunk to touch her lips. He gently pressed them together.

The four Klansmen took off their robes and carefully folded them, glancing from time to time at the fiery car. It burned like a chariot from hell. The men opened the trunk of their car and placed the folded cloth inside. They seemed naked in their jeans and long-sleeved shirts. They hadn't worn coats under their robes. One of them held his rifle at arm's length and shot into the sky. He continued to hold out his rifle as the shot echoed through the cemetery.

Finally, he pitched the rifle into the trunk and closed the lid. In unison, the men opened the four doors and disappeared into the humped car.

Jonathan put his cold hand on top of hers. She shuddered. They were like two cold buzzards sitting in the tree.

The Klan's car engine sputtered but started, began to back down the one-lane road. Then the driver swung the rear of the car off the road, trying to turn around. Spinning helplessly, the tires became stuck in the snow, and three of the men got out in their shirtsleeves to push. Among the snowy leaves, Jonathan and Stella sat perfectly still, perfectly patient. At last, the car was turned around; again the three men disappeared inside it, and the car crept back toward the gate, retracing its faint tire marks. For a while, Stella and Jonathan could see the glow of the car headlights moving through the snow. Then they vanished.

"Let's go," Jonathan said.

Slowly, stiff with cold, they climbed down.

"We were lucky," Stella said when they stood on the ground beside the tree.

"They didn't even try to track us," he replied.

She thought otherwise but said nothing. Stella felt great blocks of sadness inside her shifting and settling. "We're alive," she almost whispered. Her throat was sore, numb with tension. The snowfall was subsiding.

They seemed afraid to touch each other.

"Follow the rocks?" he asked.

"No. It's quicker to cut across." She led the way across the grass. It didn't matter if they left footprints. "We're headed toward the wall," she said.

She must put one foot in front of the other. She remembered how: numb, you walk away from fear. And why had she come back to this land of monuments and giant trees? *Turn into the cemetery.* She should apologize again. *I'm sorry,* she had said. *Don't say that,* he had replied in his gentle voice. She watched her shoes and his sinking into snow, now deep enough to chill their ankle bones through thin socks. She thought of her scarf left behind, high in the crotch of the gumdrop magnolia, a bright red nest.

They walked soberly and separately past the dead. Then one or the other of them, she would never remember which one, tentatively reached out to the other. With the exchange of a glance, they walked faster, as though they had someplace to go and the will to get there. The snow surrounded them in crystalline brilliance and the trees with snow-shagged mystery. They began to run. Suddenly exuberant, they gave all their bodies to running. Then she let go of his hand and by herself, in sheer joy, leapt a snow-decked monument.

When she rejoined him, they ran together, stride by stride, till they gained the perimeter. They pushed through the prickly holly-tree hedge and scrambled over the snowcapped stonewall. Holding hands, they walked soberly, casually, on the sidewalk between the wall and the street with its ordinary cars moving cautiously over the hard-packed snow.

DEEP IN THE NIGHT ("Aunt Krit, I'm spending the night with Ellie whose husband is out of town"), she dreams it differently:

A dozen Klansmen pursue her through the snow-choked graves; they grab her wrists and she sinks on her knees into the snow. Like white wolves, they encircle her in their robes and one comes forward and speaks in a voice gray as gravel: "I'm gonna whup her." In her nightmare, Jonathan lies behind her on his side in the snow, a slow red worm emerging from his nostril. She watches their hands hanging out of the white robes—ordinary hands? One wears a wedding ring; one has a small Band-Aid tenting his knuckle. She feels the cold metal of a pistol placed on the bulge behind her ear, and another cold barrel shoves against her breastbone. Aye, yi, yi, yi, yih.

With both hands she pushes aside the guns, breaks through their circle, leaps monuments as though they are tennis nets, and runs again through the snow for her life, her life, her life.

When she awakes, her tensed legs trembling with joy, her body cradled in her lover's arms, she fears only that what is real—her life, her love—might be imagined.

postlude

BRINGING IN THE SHEAVES

HELICON HOMECOMING

IN THE WOODS, A VERY OLD MAN IS TALKING TO HIS
mother, whom white people have called, for long years, Old Aunt Charlotte.

They stand at the edge of a clearing where their ancient shanty leans into a mean wind.

"Mama, I gots to go," he says. "They say there's a march coming to Montgomery. Black folks marching for freedom."

"Look at the sky," she says. To the south, the sky is blue, but from the north gray fluffs, shoulder to shoulder, are coming in. "There's snow in them clouds," she adds. "I seen it before."

"Been so long—"

"I can remember. You could, too, if you tried. Forty, fifty years ago. It snowed. Way down here. You remember. Snowed from Birmingham all the way down here and to Mobile and the Gulf."

"Mama, I was just a boy then."

"No, you wasn't. Not any more than you's a boy now." Not quarreling. Banter. Entertainment. Making the time pass with a few sparkles in it.

"I had white hair, then?"

"Sure 'nuff."

They stand together in front of the small dun house with boards soft as worn denim and look at the sky. Each can see that a few specks of white are striking the face of the other, skittering off their cheeks.

"Mama, I gots to go. I got to take my own steps. I come home again."

But if he raises up like that, Charlotte knows what could happen, what *has* happened to the uppity.

She holds out her hands and snowflakes float into her palms. The sky has become a uniform gray except for a few bays and inlets of blue far to the south.

"I'm leaving," Chris says. "Gots to freedom walk."

"We'll send for you," Charlotte says to her son, "when the roof's back on."

He looks at her strangely. "I loves you, Mama. You done the best you could, by everybody. White and dark." He starts to walk the path through the woods.

CHARLOTTE SPITS HER snuff onto the ground. "I can make snow, too," she says. "Brown snow." She chuckles, looks wickedly at her daughter. But Victoria has her blunt nose tilted up, studying the clouds. Charlotte looks with her. What a multitude of snowflakes!

"It's cold," Victoria says. "We need to move inside."

"You can go, baby. Hurry and you'll catch Chris on the path."

In a few patches around the yard, the snow is beginning to stick. It looks like white scabs.

Victoria turns toward the house. She slowly crosses the yard and climbs up the step.

"I'm going to enjoy this snowfall," Charlotte says to no one.

It's good to be alone. Just herself and the house and yard. The sky. She settles herself on one of the two steps to the dogtrot. Soon all the rake marks in the red dust will be covered. She'll see a pure field of snow, whiter than the best field of cotton. "Y'all should of left long, long ago," Charlotte says quietly to the vacancy. "This ain't no place for y'all younguns."

Now there is enough snow on the yard to resemble a threadbare quilt. In the woods, snow is nesting in bright white clumps in the pine needles. "Come on, snow," she says. "Let's cover this."

She holds out her hand. On her palm, she catches a clump of snowflakes. She can see a few sparkling spines sticking out from the glob. After the snow melts in her palm, she tastes the moisture that came down as snow. Her tongue is a warm dove on a cold nest. She wipes her wet hand on her dress.

From behind her, Victoria silently leans down to place a folded quilt over her shoulders. Charlotte looks down at the pad of quilt to see which one it might be. A thick, nice one, pieced curvy to suggest an inlay of blue and yellow ribbons on a white background.

She relaxes under the thick warmth. Then she says, "This be so pretty. All this." The house faces east, and she looks at the land from north to south. "I'm thankful I'm here to see it."

She sits for half an hour, and all the cold red dust is blanketed with snow. Charlotte smiles broader and broader at the falling snow. "Tha's right," she says from time to time. "Come on."

Birds are flying around like they've gone crazy. A blue jay cuts across the yard screaming. Some smart sparrows are perching on a limb, fluffing out their feathers. "Y'all better eat," she advises them. "Ain't night yet."

She sits on the steps till she begins to turn to stone. The gray sky is darker now with the approach of night, and still the snow is falling. The woods and the yard are beautiful. The quilt slides from her narrow shoulders, but Charlotte no longer feels the cold. She tries pinching her cheek, but the flesh is too stiff and hard with cold to pinch up. She can feel her fingernails scratching at her skin.

"Time to come in," Victoria says behind her.

Charlotte prepares to enter her home. Her daughter's hand is under her elbow, helping her. It takes a while to unfold her body, but once standing, Charlotte looks up once more. From on high, the snow comes right down into her eyes. She blinks and looks and blinks again. She can scarcely get her fill of it, thick as it falls. All that long drifting down of snowflakes, just to fall on her! But she goes inside.

A FEW EMBERS glow in the fireplace.

Victoria takes a newspaper from the top of the knee-high stack and crumples it fiercely into a loose ball, which she throws onto the embers. While the paper ball flares up, she lays fat pine kindling in the flame, and then with her bare hands she lifts a big lump of coal from the scuttle and throws it into the grate. The kindling catches right up and begins to snap and pop. Charlotte smells the burning turpentine in the pine sticks and draws the aroma deep into her lungs. For a moment she feels she is a pine tree, a young one, ready to grow tall and strong.

Crawl in bed.

Charlotte looks up and sees the ceiling. She has forgotten the ceiling. She wishes it was gone and the roof, too, so she could look right up through the rafters and see the sky, have the snow fall on her face while she lies down.

Plenty of covers. Charlotte has always kept her winter bed with three quilts. A soft, old-friend quilt closest to her. Old on bottom, newer, newest. Newest, hardest, and prettiest on top. Still, she wishes she'd not left the freshest quilt outdoors, the white one with the wavy blue and yellow ribbon design.

Fend for yourself, she says to it. She means to sound encouraging, but the pretty young quilt is too far away to hear; she feels sorry for such a pretty quilt out there, alone in the cold.

"Live forever," she says out loud. She remembers them all in the room: Doctor and Mrs., the three children. "I will," she promises the little girl. *Blessed girl.*

"Victoria," she calls. She hears her voice like a dry leaf, full of veins and fissures, spreading and crackling itself across the room. "See you in the morning."

Victoria backs up to the fire, lifts her skirts high in back to roast her legs and fanny.

Now close, eyes, so I can see.

THERE ARE HER FOUR schoolgirls, hovering.

Sing me, she says to the Birmingham girls, the bombed Sunday school girls. *Sing high,* sweet cherubims, *and not a hint of hate.*

With a wish, the ceiling is gone, and the roof.

Lying straight and comfortable under her quilts, she begins to rise. She tilts slightly to pass between the open, snowcapped rafters. From the top of a rafter, she pinches a little snow and puts it like snuff between her lower lip and gum. Rising higher, she passes into swirls of snow. Her mattress comes right along under her, the quilts flapping at the sides while she ascends.

Jesus is raising the dead, like he'd promised he'd do and did do, when he walked the earth.

Black is the night. She reaches out her hand through the snow to try to catch a sparkling star, tiny as a wedding diamond. But oh, the groaning below, mouths distorted in pain. Still, she can ask it of them, and she does. *Sing me!*

From all around her, through veils of falling snow, the spirits are gathering.

AUTHOR'S NOTE

WHEN I WAS A COLLEGE STUDENT IN THE EARLY SIXTIES in Birmingham, Alabama, I promised myself, if I ever did become a novelist, that I would write about the acts of courage and tragedy taking place in my city. I would try to re-create through words what it was like to be alive then: how ordinary life went on, how people fell in and out of love, how family members got sick, how people worked ordinary jobs, tried to get an education, worshiped, looked for entertainment, grew up, died, participated in the great changes of the civil rights struggle or stood aside and watched the world change.

There were many horrors and haunting events but none more powerful than the murder of the four young girls to whom this book is dedicated. In my imagination they stand in a sacred circle, a ring of fire around them. I do not step into that circle. That is to say, I do not try to re-create them. Their families and friends are holding them dear the way they really were.

I have created fictive characters for the reader to know and mourn. The event at the White Palace is meant to stand not for any particular historic event but to suggest some of the many atrocities that occurred between May 17, 1954, when the United States Supreme Court outlawed school segregation in *Brown v. Board of Education* and the assassination of Dr. Martin Luther King Jr. on April 4, 1968, in Memphis, Tennessee, a death preceded by the deaths of many less well known people, including, on February 8, 1968, those of Samuel Hammond Jr., Delano Middleton, and Henry Smith, students in Orangeburg, South Carolina, killed when highway patrolmen fired on protestors.

For the sake of readers too young to remember, some of the historical events alluded to or presented in a fictive framework in *Four Spirits* include the beating of the Reverend Fred Shuttlesworth in front of Phillips High School (where I was a student) in 1957, and the repeated bombings of his home and church; the castration of Judge Aaron; the appearance and speech making of Birmingham Public Safety Commissioner Eugene "Bull" Connor at Ku Klux Klan rallies; the peaceful and unnoted occasional integration of the Gaslight nightclub on Morris Avenue in Birmingham; the demonstrations of May 1963 led by Reverend Shuttlesworth and Dr. Martin Luther King, among others; the assault on those demonstrators by fire hoses and police dogs, as ordered by Bull Connor; the jailing of thousands of schoolchildren protestors, as well as Dr. King and other leaders; the joining of mass meetings by a few white college students, such as Marti Turnipseed; the bombing of Sixteenth Street Baptist Church and the deaths of four schoolgirls; the 1963 and 1964 Mississippi murders of Medgar Evers, of James Chaney, and of New York activists Michael Schwerner and Andrew Goodman; the assassination of President John F. Kennedy; the educational effort made on the Miles College campus by a number of white people, including myself and my friend Carol Countryman, who, like Catherine Cartwright in this story, came to the campus in her wheelchair. Carol lived to become a pioneer for rights for the handicapped, eventually making a trip to Washington, D.C., assisted by our mutual friend Nancy Brooks Moore, to speak out in that cause.

ACKNOWLEDGMENTS

TO MY LITERARY AGENT, JOY HARRIS, AND TO MY EDITOR, Marjorie Braman, I owe a joyful debt of gratitude for their belief in me and this book and their indefatigable work on our behalf. They have become dear friends.

My thanks must also begin with my gratitude to my husband, John C. Morrison, for his constant support in the writing of this book and for his considered comments that helped to shape it. I also offer a special thanks, within my family, to my brother John Sims Jeter, who encouraged me and corrected many of my mistakes, while working on his own first novel, and to his wife Derelene Brooks Jeter, for her heartfelt praise and astute suggestions. My daughter Flora Naslund and her partner, Marty Kelley, always cheer me on in my efforts to write, as do Sara and Michael McQuilling; Debora, Paul, David, and Ryan Morrison, my stepchildren; and David Rizzolo, Debora's husband. I also thank my brother and sister-in-law, Marvin Jeter and Charlotte Copeland, for their support.

For reading every draft of the novel and freely giving of their time and insights, while completing their own novels, I thank especially Lucinda Dixon Sullivan and Karen Mann. Other writer friends whose critiques I have cherished include Julie Brickman, Marcia Woodruff Dalton, Greg Ellis, Robin Lippincott, Eleanor Morse, Jeanie Thompson, Neela Vaswani, Mary Welp, and the actor/director Sheila O'Neill Ellis. I can never thank each of you enough for your generous advice.

A very special thanks to Nancy Brooks Moore, my lifelong friend, and Ron

Countryman for their careful reading and much-needed encouragement. I also thank Richard M. Sullivan and Elizabeth Chadwick for their advice about the opening sequence. I thank Callie Hausman and Thelma Wyland for directing me to essential reading in my research and for their faith in me.

Many other friends—including Lynn Greenberg, Maura Stanton, Richard Cecil, Alan Naslund, Paul Bresnick, Leslie Daniels, Deborah and David Stewart, Ralph Raby, Maureen Morehead, Nana Lampton, Charles and Patricia Gaines, Jake Reiss, Frank and Diana Richmond, Elizabeth Sulzby, Luke Wallin, Daly Walker, Bill Pearce, Denzil Strickland, Katy Yocom, Jim Rooney, and Susan Soper—have encouraged me in ways for which I am profoundly grateful.

I thank all my colleagues and friends at the University of Louisville, especially Tom Byers, Suzette Henke, and Karen Chandler, and all my colleagues and students of the Spalding University M.F.A. in Writing Program. I thank the University of Louisville for granting me a sabbatical leave, during which I worked on research and the writing of this novel, English Department Chairperson Debra Journet, and Dean of the College of Arts and Sciences Jim Brennan. Over the years, grants from the Kentucky Foundation for Women have been particularly sustaining, as well as from the National Endowment for the Arts and the Kentucky Arts Council. The Birmingham Civil Rights Institute, the Sixteenth Street Baptist Church, Kelly Ingram Park and the Birmingham Public Library, the Rosa Parks Museum and the Southern Poverty Law Center in Montgomery, and the Martin Luther King Jr. Museum in Atlanta have provided places of inspiration and reflection for me, as has the King memorial of rushing waters in San Francisco.

A special thanks to the University of Montevallo, Alabama, where my husband and I shared the Pascal P. Vacca Chair of Liberal Arts during the spring of 2003, and to Elaine and Bobby Hughes, and Bill and Loretta Cobb, among many other new Montevallo friends.

And to my newest friend, Chris McNair—how can I ever thank you enough for letting me into your life and for taking the author photograph for *Four Spirits*?

Sena Jeter Naslund
MONTEVALLO AND BIRMINGHAM,
MARCH 2003